About the Author

Kevin J. Anderson has over 15 million books in print in 27 languages worldwide. He is the author of the X-FILES novels GROUND ZERO (number 1 bestseller in THE TIMES, and voted Best SF Novel of the Year by SFX magazine), RUINS, and ANTIBODIES, as well as the JEDI ACADEMY trilogy of STAR WARS novels – the three best-selling SF novels of 1994. He has written the prequels to Frank Herbert's monumental DUNE series, with Frank's son, Brian Herbert. He has won, or been nominated for, the Nebula Award, Bram Stoker Award, Reader's Choice Award from the Science Fiction Book Club, and many others. He is currently writing HORIZON STORMS, the third volume of the SAGA OF SEVEN SUNS.

Kevin J. Anderson lives in Colorado.
www.wordfire.com

D1329149

A FOREST OF STARS
the saga of seven suns

KEVIN J. ANDERSON

EARTHLIGHT

SIMON & SCHUSTER

London • New York • Sydney • Tokyo • Singapore • Toronto • Dublin

A VIACOM COMPANY

First published in Great Britain by Earthlight, 2003
An imprint of Simon & Schuster UK Ltd
A Viacom Company

1 3 5 7 9 10 8 6 4 2

Simon & Schuster UK Ltd
Africa House
64–78 Kingsway
London WC2B 6AH

www.simonsays.co.uk

Simon & Schuster Australia
Sydney

A CIP catalogue record for this book is available from the British Library

ISBN 0-7434-6121-5

Typeset in Weiss by SX Composing DTP, Rayleigh, Essex
Printed and bound in Great Britain by
The Bath Press, Bath

ACKNOWLEDGEMENTS

I would especially like to thank Rob Teranishi and Igor Kordey, visual geniuses whose imagination and input into the graphic novel portions of the *Seven Suns* universe have helped to crystallize my own ideas, as well as sending me off on fascinating new tangents. And Jeff Mariotte and John Nee of Wildstorm, for letting me pursue this big epic in a different direction. Also, my cover artists, Stephen Youll and Chris Moore, have done excellent work conveying at a glance some of the things I take many pages to do.

My wife, Rebecca Moesta, provided enormous input both in the big picture as well as line by line . . . seeing both the forest *and* the trees.

Catherine Sidor transcribed this novel almost as fast as I could dictate it into my tape recorder, and gave me her running commentary and suggestions as well as spotting inconsistencies. Diane Jones and Brian Herbert were early readers, offering valuable ideas and input, helping to shape the story into its best form.

My British editors John Jarrold and Darren Nash gave me excellent comments and support. The exceedingly competent Melissa Weatherill kept all the production matters running smoothly from half a world away, while at Warner Aspect Devi Pillai kept track of enough maddening details so that the rest of us could have moments of sanity.

My agents Matt Bialer, Robert Gottlieb, and Kim Whalen at Trident Media Group have always shown great fervour for this series and have helped greatly to make it a success both in the US and in many languages around the world.

To JAIME LEVINE

The 'fairy godmother' of this series, who has taken the *Saga of Seven Suns* under her firm editorial wing . . . while also loving the stories as a true fan.

THE STORY SO FAR

In the ruins of the ancient Klikiss civilization, human archaeologists MARGARET and LOUIS COLICOS discovered an
exotic technology capable of igniting gas-giant planets to create
new suns. For the first test of the 'Klikiss Torch', at the gas giant
Oncier, observers included BASIL WENCESLAS, suave Chairman
of the Terran Hanseatic League (the Hansa), and the alien ADAR
KORI'NH, military commander of the vast but stagnant Ildiran
Empire. Though the humanoid Ildirans helped Earth colonize the
Spiral Arm, they still see humans as ambitious upstarts. They
considered the test of the Klikiss Torch unnecessary hubris, since
many other planets were available for colonization.

When Oncier was ignited, collapsing into a compact sun,
instant reports of the event were transmitted around the Galaxy by
the green priest BENETO, a human from the forested planet *Theroc*,
who has a special symbiosis with semi-sentient 'worldtrees'. Green
priests, like living telegraph stations, can send thoughts anywhere
through the interconnected forest network, providing the only
form of instant communication across vast distances.

At the end of the Oncier test, observers saw a cluster of diamond spheres race away from the collapsing gas giant at incredible speed; scientists eventually classified the sight as an unknown phenomenon of the Klikiss Torch. Back on Earth, OLD KING FREDERICK, a glamorous figurehead ruler, led a celebration of the successful test, while Adar Kori'nh returned to his capital of *Ildira* and reported to his all-powerful leader, the MAGE-IMPERATOR. On hearing of the strange diamond spheres, the Mage-Imperator was greatly disturbed.

Meanwhile, on Ildira, the Mage-Imperator's first-born son, PRIME DESIGNATE JORA'H, treated the human REYNALD, heir to the Theron throne, to a performance of the grand epic, the *Saga of Seven Suns*. Afterwards, as a token of friendship, Jora'h invited Reynald to send two green priests from Theroc to Ildira to study the *Saga*. The worldforest, which gathers knowledge through its human intermediaries, is always hungry to learn about history.

Then Reynald left Ildira for a secret rendezvous in space with the Roamers, fiercely independent space gypsies led by old SPEAKER JHY OKIAH and her beautiful protégée CESCA PERONI. They discussed a possible alliance to maintain their freedom from the sprawling and greedy Hansa. Reynald even suggested the possibility of marriage with Cesca, but she was already betrothed to a skyminer, ROSS TAMBLYN.

At his Blue Sky Mine in the clouds of the gas giant *Golgen*, Ross Tamblyn met with his younger brother JESS. Roamer skymines harvest and convert hydrogen into 'ekti', or stardrive fuel. Jess brought messages and gifts from his family, including his young sister TASIA. Though fast friends, the brothers' meeting was bittersweet, because (unknown to Ross) Jess and Cesca had fallen deeply in love, despite her betrothal to Ross. Jess departed for the hidden Roamer capital of *Rendezvous*.

Roamers have made large profits by fitting into dangerous

niches, but because of their stubborn secrecy, the space gypsies are not well liked by the Hansa. When the head of the Earth Defence Forces (EDF), GENERAL KURT LANYAN, heard about a rebellious Roamer space pirate, he used the merchant woman RLINDA KETT and her ex-husband pilot BRANSON ROBERTS as bait, and captured and executed the pirate.

Uneasy about Lanyan's brutal justice, Rlinda travelled to Theroc, where she hoped to establish trade in exotic commodities. MOTHER ALEXA and FATHER IDRISS (parents of Reynald and Beneto) were not interested, but their ambitious eldest daughter SAREIN – an occasional lover of Chairman Wenceslas – was. After striking a deal with Sarein, Rlinda agreed to transport two Theron green priests (stern old OTEMA and her wide-eyed assistant NIRA) to Ildira, where they could study the *Saga of Seven Suns*. Later, at the Mage-Imperator's Prism Palace, Prime Designate Jora'h became enamoured with young Nira, though the Mage-Imperator regarded the green priests as if they were mere specimens . . .

On Earth, Chairman Wenceslas and fellow officials discussed the increasingly common gaffes made by Old King Frederick and secretly began searching for a replacement. They snatched a malleable streetwise scamp, RAYMOND AGUERRA, then staged a terrible fire in Raymond's dwelling complex, which killed his mother and three brothers, leaving no evidence. The Hansa altered the young man's appearance, told him he was now 'Prince Peter', and began brainwashing him into his new role, using the Teacher 'compy' (or companion robot) OX to instruct him.

After the successful test of the Klikiss Torch, Margaret and Louis Colicos began a new excavation on the desert planet of *Rheindic Co*, where ancient cities of the lost insect-like Klikiss had remained untouched. The only functional remnants of the Klikiss civilization, their hulking beetle-like robots, claimed that their memories were erased long ago. Three of these antique robots accompanied the Colicoses to the excavation site, hoping to learn more about their past. The archaeology team also included a compy, DD, and a green priest, ARCAS. In the ruins, Margaret and Louis discovered a strange blank window made of stone, connected to dormant machinery. While Louis studied the machinery, Margaret worked to decipher Klikiss hieroglyphics in hopes of finding answers . . .

At Ross Tamblyn's isolated Blue Sky Mine on Golgen, mysterious storms and lightning rose from the uncharted depths of the atmosphere. Then monstrous crystalline ships emerged from the deep clouds, similar to the apparitions seen fleeing Oncier after the Klikiss Torch test. The huge warglobes opened fire on Ross's skymine, destroying it and sending Ross tumbling to his death thousands of miles beneath the clouds . . .

The alien spheres also appeared at Oncier and obliterated a station left behind to watch the newborn star. Next, warglobes destroyed Roamer skymines at several gas giants, never demanding terms, never showing mercy. These unexpected attacks stunned both the Hansa and the Roamers. Basil Wenceslas met with General Lanyan to discuss the new threat. Old King Frederick worked to rally the populace, recruiting new volunteers for the EDF.

Vowing revenge for the death of her brother Ross, the spunky Roamer Tasia Tamblyn ran off to join the military, taking her compy EA. Grief-stricken, Jess and Tasia's father died of a stroke, leaving Jess in charge of the family business. Although Ross's death left him and Cesca free to love each other, they were not willing to take advantage of the tragedy for personal gain.

On Ildira, the green priest Nira spent a great deal of time with Prime Designate Jora'h, eventually becoming his lover. Though Jora'h had many assigned mates and was destined to become the next Ildiran leader, Jora'h genuinely fell in love with Nira.

Meanwhile, an Ildiran historian DIO'SH uncovered ancient hidden documents proving that the deadly deep-core aliens, called HYDROGUES, had appeared long ago in a previous war, but that all mention of this conflict had been *censored* from the *Saga of Seven Suns*. Dio'sh took his shocking discovery to the Mage-Imperator, who killed the meddling historian, saying, 'I *wanted* it kept secret.'

On Earth, the EDF built new battleships to use against the strange alien threat. The EDF also commandeered civilian space-craft, and Rlinda Kett was forced to surrender all of her merchant ships to the war effort, except for the *Voracious Curiosity*, her own vessel. Newly enlisted Tasia Tamblyn excelled in military training, besting the spoiled-brat Earth recruits. Her closest friend was fellow trainee, ROBB BRINDLE.

The Roamers were in an uproar after the repeated deadly attacks. Many of the families decided to cease all skymining activities on gas giants. Jess Tamblyn attended a clan gathering, watching Cesca, wishing they could be together. Impatient with the bickering, he decided to strike the enemy aliens himself. Jess gathered loyal workers and went back to Golgen, where the hydrogues had destroyed the Blue Sky Mine. He and his cohorts modified comet orbits and sent giant frozen missiles plummeting down to the gas planet with the force of atomic warheads.

On Earth, hoping to find a key to new technology, a robotics researcher tricked one of the Klikiss robots, JORAX, into his lab. When the scientist attempted to dissect the alien robot, however, Jorax murdered him. 'There are some things you cannot be permitted to know.' In the aftermath, the robot claimed that the unscrupulous scientist had activated an involuntary self-preservation system. Jorax then demanded that all Klikiss robots be treated as sovereign life forms, and the old King forbade any further dissection attempts.

Meanwhile, Beneto received a request to replace an old green priest, TALBUN, on the colony world of *Corvus Landing*. Beneto happily agreed. Though this wasn't the glamorous position Mother Alexa and Father Idriss had hoped for their son, Beneto was adamant. His adoring younger sister, ESTARRA – a tomboy who had always explored the forests with Beneto – bade him a sad farewell. Later, at Corvus Landing, when Talbun was satisfied that Beneto was well-prepared, the old priest walked off into his world-tree grove and allowed himself to die, letting his body be absorbed into the worldforest network.

While exploring the Prism Palace on Ildira, Nira encountered another son of the Mage-Imperator, the grim and intense DOBRO DESIGNATE UDRU'H, who interrogated Nira about her telepathic potential as a green priest. The Designate then reported to the Mage-Imperator about his secret breeding experiments between Ildirans and captive humans on *Dobro*. The leader expressed urgency: The return of the ancient enemy, the hydrogues, left the Ildirans little time to genetically create a being with the necessary characteristics to save the Empire. Udru'h suggested that Nira might have the DNA potential they needed.

Meanwhile, the Solar Navy commander Adar Kori'nh directed his officers to practise with innovative Terran military exercises. Many conservative officers were uncomfortable trying new techniques, but ZAN'NH – the first-born son of Prime Designate Jora'h – proved capable of great innovation. Kori'nh raised Zan'nh in rank and demoted the stodgiest old subcommander.

Then the Solar Navy fleet went to the gas giant *Qronha 3*, the site of the only skymining facility still operated by Ildiran workers. When hydrogue warglobes rose from the clouds and began to destroy the ekti facility, the Solar Navy engaged in a furious battle. The hydrogue weaponry was far superior, but the disgraced and demoted Ildiran subcommander took a desperate suicidal action, crashing his battleship into the nearest crystal sphere, which destroyed the warglobe and gave the Solar Navy time to retreat with the rescued skyminers. In the thousands of years chronicled in the *Saga of Seven Suns*, no Ildiran had ever experienced such a terrible and humiliating defeat.

Meanwhile, on Earth, Raymond Aguerra continued training to become the next King, watched over by the compy OX. At first he couldn't believe the change from the rough streets to the opulent palace, but soon he began to resent the rigid control. To his horror, he discovered that the Hansa had caused the terrible fire that killed his family, and realized he must be very careful.

Upon learning that the Ildirans had also been attacked by the deep-core aliens, Chairman Wenceslas went to meet with the Mage-Imperator to propose an alliance. The hydrogues themselves had neither acknowledged nor responded to requests for negotiation.

While Basil was on Ildira, a giant warglobe appeared at Earth and a hydrogue emissary demanded to speak with King Frederick. Flustered, the old ruler tried to get a message to Basil via green priests. Contained within a pressure vessel, the alien emissary informed the King that the Klikiss Torch test had annihilated one of the hydrogue planets, slaughtering millions of their people. Horrified, Frederick apologized for the inadvertent genocide, but the hydrogue delivered an ultimatum: all skymining must cease. This would mean no ekti fuel for the Ildiran stardrive, the only viable method of space travel. Frederick pleaded with the emissary, but the hydrogue detonated his containment tank, killing the King and all the observers in the Throne Hall.

Basil rushed back to Earth and told Raymond that 'King Peter' must take the throne immediately. After the announcement of the upcoming coronation ceremony, Peter gave a carefully scripted speech, defying the hydrogue ultimatum and declaring that humans had every right to take the fuel necessary for their survival.

He dispatched a new battle group, including Tasia Tamblyn and Robb Brindle, along with commercial ekti harvesters to Jupiter, right in Earth's backyard. On high alert, the protective ships watched over the bold skymines. For several days all was quiet, but then a massive fleet of warglobes rose from the cloud layers and engaged the EDF in a furious battle. Tasia and Robb survived, although the battered human ships limped away, beaten . . .

Before anyone learned of the humiliating defeat, Basil Wenceslas presided over the coronation of King Peter, designed as a show of hope and confidence. Peter, struggling to hide his hatred for Basil, was drugged into cooperation for the ceremony. Feigning paternal pride, Basil promised the new King that if he behaved, they would find him a Queen . . .

On Ildira, the Mage-Imperator decided to accelerate his plans. Nira had discovered that she was pregnant with the Prime Designate's child, but before she could tell Jora'h the news, the Mage-Imperator dispatched him to Theroc on a diplomatic mission. Then, in the stillness of sleep period, brutal Ildiran guards came to capture Nira. Before her eyes, the guards stabbed her mentor Otema to death because she was too old to be of use in the breeding pens. Nira was turned over to the evil Dobro Designate for genetic experimentation . . .

The human race faced hard times unless they could find other ways to produce stardrive fuel. Speaker Jhy Okiah challenged the resourceful Roamers to find alternatives to now-forbidden sky-mining, then abdicated her position in favor of Cesca Peroni. Jess Tamblyn watched the woman he loved take her place as a strong and visionary leader, realizing she was farther away from him now than ever before.

On distant Rheindic Co, the Colicos archaeology team discovered that the 'stone window' was actually a transportation system, a dimensional doorway connected to old Klikiss machinery. Though the Klikiss robots insisted they remembered nothing useful, Margaret was able to translate ancient records. Apparently the Klikiss robots were in part responsible for the disappearance of their parent race and had been involved in an ancient war with both hydrogues and Ildirans. Reeling with this news, Margaret and Louis rushed back to their camp – only to find that their green priest Arcas had been murdered, the young worldtrees destroyed, and all communication cut off! The Klikiss robots were nowhere to be found.

Margaret and Louis worked with their faithful compy DD to barricade themselves into the cliff-city archaeological dig, but the Klikiss robots broke through. Although DD attempted to defend his masters, the Klikiss robots captured the compy, careful not to hurt a fellow intelligent machine. At the last moment, Louis got the 'stone window' functioning, opening a doorway to an unknown alien world. He urged Margaret through, but before he could join her, the gate closed – and the robots were upon him. The old archaeologist knew too many of their secrets. When Louis reminded the Klikiss robots that until now they claimed not to remember their past, the robots simply answered, 'We lied.'

ONE

JESS TAMBLYN

Across the Spiral Arm, the gas-giant planets held secrets, dangers, and treasure. For a century and a half, harvesting vital stardrive fuel from the cloud worlds had been a lucrative business for the Roamers.

Five years ago, though, that had all changed.

Like vicious guard dogs, the hydrogues had forbidden all skymines from approaching the gas giants they claimed as their territory. The embargo had crippled the Roamer economy, the Terran Hanseatic League, and the Ildiran Empire. Many brave or foolish entrepreneurs had defied the hydrogues' ultimatum. They had paid with their lives. Dozens of skymines were destroyed. The deep-core aliens were unstoppable and ruthless.

But when facing desperate situations, Roamers refused to give up. Instead, they changed tactics, surviving – and thriving – through innovation.

'The old Speaker always told us that challenges redefine the parameters of success,' Jess Tamblyn said over the open comm, taking his lookout ship into position above the deceptively peaceful-looking gas giant Welyr.

'By damn, Jess,' Del Kellum transmitted with just a touch of annoyance, 'if I wanted to be pampered, I'd live on *Earth.*'

Kellum, an older clan leader and hands-on industrialist, signalled to the converging fast-dive scoop ships. The cluster of modified 'blitzkrieg' skymines and a hodge-podge of small lookout craft gathered at what they hoped was a safe distance above the coppery planet. No one knew how far away the hydrogues could detect trespassing cloud thieves, but they had long since given up playing it safe. In the end, all life was a gamble, and human civilization could not survive without stardrive fuel.

The ekti-scavenging crew powered up their huge scoops and containers, ready for a concerted plunge into the thick cloud decks. Hit and run. Their supercharged engines glowed warm. Their pilots sweated. Ready.

Alone in his lookout ship, Jess flexed his hands on the cockpit controls. 'Prepare to come from all sides. Move in fast, gulp a bellyful, and head for safety. We don't know how long the drogue bastards will give us.'

After the big harvesting ships acknowledged, they dropped like hawks after prey. What once had been a routine industrial process had become a commando operation in a war zone.

When presented with the hydrogue threat, daring Roamer engineers had redesigned traditional skymining facilities. They had accomplished a lot in five years. The new blitzkrieg scoops had giant engines, super-efficient ekti reactors, and detachable cargo tanks like a cluster of grapes. Once each tank was filled, it could be launched up to a retrieval point, passing off the harvested ekti a bit at a time without losing a full cargo load if – *when* – the hydrogues came after them.

Kellum transmitted, 'The Big Goose thinks we're shiftless bandits. By damn, let's give the drogues the same impression.'

The Hansa – the 'Big Goose' – as well as the Ildiran Empire paid dearly for every drop of stardrive fuel. As ekti supplies dwindled year after year, prices of skyrocketed to such a point that Roamers considered the risk acceptable.

Five of the modified scoops now dispersed across the atmosphere, then plunged into Welyr's clouds, storm upwellings, and vanishingly thin winds. With giant funnel-maws open, the blitzkrieg scoops roared through storm systems at top speed. They gobbled resources, compressing the excess into hydrogen holding tanks while secondary ekti reactors processed the gas.

As he flew his lookout mission, like a man in the crow's-nest of an ancient pirate ship, Jess deployed floating sensors into Welyr's soupy clouds. The buoys would detect any large ships rising from the depths. The sensors might give only a few minutes' warning, but the daredevils could retreat quickly enough.

Jess knew that it did no good to fight. The Ildiran Solar Navy and the Hansa EDF had demonstrated that lesson often enough. At the first sign of the enemy's arrival, his renegade harvesters would turn and run with whatever ekti they'd managed to grab.

The first blitzkrieg scoop filled one cargo tank and rose high enough to jettison it, leaving a smoke trail in the thin air. A resounding cheer echoed across the comm, and the competitive Roamers challenged each other to do better. The unmanned fuel tank soared away from Welyr towards its rendezvous point. *Safe.*

In times past, leisurely skymines had drifted over the clouds like whales feeding on plankton. Jess's brother Ross had been the chief of Blue Sky Mine on Golgen; he'd had dreams, an excellent business sense, and all the hopes in the world. Without warning, though, hydrogues had obliterated the facility, killed every member of the crew . . .

Jess monitored his scans. Though the sinking sensor buoys detected no turbulence that might signal the approach of the enemy, he didn't let his attention waver. Welyr seemed much too quiet and peaceful. Deceptive.

Every crewman aboard the blitzkrieg scoops was tense, knowing they had only one chance here, and that some of them would likely die as soon as the hydrogues arrived.

'Here's a second one, highest quality ekti!' Del Kellum's harvester launched a full cargo tank. Within moments, each of the five blitzkrieg scoops had ejected a load of ekti. The scavengers had been at Welyr for less than three hours, and already it was a valuable haul.

'Good way to thumb our noses at the drogues,' Kellum continued, his anxiety manifesting itself as chattiness over the comm band, 'though I'd prefer to slam them with a few comets. Just like you did at Golgen, Jess.'

Jess smiled grimly. His cometary bombardment had made him a hero among the Roamers, and he hoped that the planet was now uninhabitable, all the enemy aliens destroyed. A strike back. 'I was just following my Guiding Star.'

Now many clans looked to Jess for suggestions on how they might continue their retaliation against the aliens' nonsensical prohibition.

'You and I have a lot in common,' Kellum said, his voice more conspiratorial now that he had switched to a private frequency. 'And if you ever do another bombardment, might I suggest this place as a target?'

'What have you got against Welyr?' Then he remembered. 'Ah, you were planning to marry Shareen of the Pasternak clan.'

'Yes, by damn!' Shareen Pasternak had been the chief of a skymine on Welyr. Jess recalled that the woman had an acidly sarcastic sense of humour and a sharp tongue, but Kellum had been delighted with her. It would have been the second marriage for both of them. But Shareen's skymine had been destroyed in the early hydrogue depredations.

Now, three more ekti cargo tanks launched away from the racing blitzkrieg scoops.

Trish Ng, the pilot of a second lookout ship, frantically radioed Jess, cutting off the conversation. 'The sensor buoys! Check the readings, Jess.'

He saw a standard carrier wave with a tiny blip in the background. 'It's just a lightning strike. Don't get jumpy, Ng.'

'That same lightning strike repeats every twenty-one seconds. Like clockwork.' She waited a beat. 'Jess, it's an artificial signal, copied, looped, and reflected back at us. The drogues must've already destroyed the sensor buoys. It's a ruse.'

Jess watched, and the pattern became apparent. 'That's all the warning we're going to get. Everybody, pack up and head out!'

As if realizing they had been discovered, seven immense warglobes rose like murderous leviathans from Welyr's deep clouds. The Roamer scavengers did not hesitate, retreating pell-mell up through the gas giant's skies.

A deep-throated subsonic hum came from the alien spheres, and pyramidal protrusions on their crystalline skins crackled with blue lightning. The Roamer daredevils had all seen the enemy shoot their destructive weapons before.

Kellum ejected four empty ekti cargo tanks, throwing them like grapeshot at the nearest warglobes. 'Choke on these!'

Jess shouted into the comm. 'Don't wait. Just leave.'

Kellum's diversion worked. The aliens targeted their blue lightning on the empty projectiles, giving the blitzkrieg scoops a few more seconds to escape. The Roamers fired their enormous engines, and four of the five harvester scoops lifted on an escape trajectory.

But one of the new vessels hung behind just a moment too long, and the enemy lightning bolts ripped the facility to molten shreds. The crew's screams echoed across the comm channel, then cut off instantly.

'Go! Go!' Jess yelled. 'Disperse and get out of here.'

The remaining commando harvesters scattered like flies. The automated cargo tanks would go to their pickup coordinates, where the commandos could retrieve the haul at their leisure.

The warglobes rose up, shooting more blue lightning into space. They struck and destroyed a lagging lookout ship, but the others escaped. The enemy spheres remained above the atmosphere for some time, like growling wolves, before they slowly descended back into the coppery storms of Welyr, without pursuing.

Though dismayed at the loss of one blitzkrieg scoop and a lookout ship, the raiders were already tallying the ekti they had harvested and projecting how much it would bring on the open market.

Alone in the cockpit of his scout ship, Jess shook his head. 'What has happened to us, if we can cheer because our losses were "not too bad"?'

T W O

K I N G   P E T E R

I t was an emergency high-level staff meeting, like many others called since the hydrogue attacks had begun. But this time, King Peter insisted that it be held within the Whisper Palace, in a room of his own choosing. The secondary banquet room he selected had no particular significance for him; the young King simply made the move to demonstrate his independence . . . and also to annoy Chairman Basil Wenceslas.

'You keep telling me my reign is based upon appearances, Basil.' Peter's artificially blue eyes flashed as he met the Chairman's hard grey gaze. 'Isn't it appropriate that I meet with *my* staff in the Palace, not at your convenience in Hansa HQ?'

Peter knew that Basil hated it when the young King used his own tactics against him. The former Raymond Aguerra had learned to play his part better than the Hansa ever expected.

Basil's studiously blasé expression was clearly meant to remind Peter that, as Chairman of the Terran Hanseatic League, he had dealt with crises far worse than a petulant young King. 'Your presence is merely a formality, Peter. We don't really require you in the meeting at all.'

By now, Peter knew a bluff when he saw one. 'If you think the media won't notice my absence at an emergency session, then I'll go swim with my dolphins instead.' He understood his tenuous importance and pushed, just a little, whenever he could. Peter rarely misjudged Basil's limits, though. He approached each small battle with finesse and subtlety. And he knew when to stop.

In the end, Basil pretended that it didn't matter. His primary advisers – Basil's hand-picked but diverse inner circle of representatives, military experts, and Hansa officials – gathered behind closed doors around a chandelier-lit table as a light luncheon was served. Silent servants hurried to place bouquets on the table, damask napkins, silverware; fountains trickled in three alcoves.

Peter seated himself in an ornate chair at the head of the table. Knowing his role, however, the young King listened in respectful silence while the Chairman went through the agenda items.

Basil's iron-grey hair was impeccably trimmed and combed. His perfect suit was expensive, yet comfortable, and he moved with a lean grace that belied his seventy-three years. So far today, he'd eaten sparingly, drinking only ice water and cardamom coffee.

'I require an accurate assessment of the state of our Hansa colonies.' He swept his gaze around his advisers, admirals, and colony envoys. 'In the five years since the hydrogues killed King Frederick and issued their ultimatum against skymining, we've had considerable time to draw conclusions and make realistic projections.' He looked first to the commander of his Earth Defence Forces. Since he was Chairman of the Hansa, Basil was also the de facto leader of the EDF. 'General Lanyan, what is your overall evaluation?'

The General waved aside the numbers and statistics that an aide called up for him on a document pad. 'Easy enough, Mr Chairman:

we're in deep trouble, though the EDF has rigorously rationed ekti since the beginning of the crisis. Without those highly unpopular measures—'

Peter interrupted. 'Riots have caused as much damage as the shortages, especially on new settlements. We've already had to declare martial law on four colonies. People are hurting and hungry. They think *I've* abandoned them.' He looked at the sliced meats and colourful fruit on his plate and decided he had no appetite, knowing what others were suffering.

Lanyan stopped in mid-sentence, looked at the King without responding, then returned his attention to Basil. 'As I was saying, Mr Chairman, austerity measures have allowed us to maintain most vital services. However, our stockpiles are dwindling.'

Tyra Running Horse, one of the planetary envoys, pushed her plate aside. Peter tried to remember which colony she represented. Was it Rhejak? 'Hydrogen is the most common element in the universe. Why don't we just get it somewhere else?'

'Concentrated hydrogen is not *as accessible* elsewhere,' said one of the admirals. 'Gas giants are the best reservoirs.'

'The Roamers continue to supply some ekti through their high-risk harvesting techniques,' said the Relleker envoy, trying to sound optimistic. With his pale skin and patrician features, he looked just like one of the faux-classical statues against the wall of the small banquet room. 'Let them keep taking the gambles.'

'And there is simply no other fuel alternative for the faster-than-light stardrive. We've tried everything,' said yet another envoy. 'We're stuck with what the Roamers provide.'

Scowling, Lanyan shook his head. 'Current Roamer deliveries don't match even our bare-bones military requirements, not to mention public and civilian needs. We may need to impose further austerity measures.'

'What further measures?' said the dark-faced envoy from

Ramah. 'It has been months since my world received a supply delivery. No medicine, no food, no equipment. We have increased our agriculture and mining, but we do not have the infrastructure to survive being completely cut off like this.'

'Most of us are in the same situation,' the ghostly pale Dremen representative said. 'And my colony has entered its low weather cycle, more clouds, lower temperatures. Crop yields are traditionally down thirty per cent, and it'll be the same this time. Even in the best years, Dremen would need aid to survive. Now—'

Basil raised his hand to cut off further complaints. 'We've had this discussion before. Impose birth restrictions if your agricultural capabilities can't support your population. This crisis isn't going to end overnight, so start thinking in the long term.'

'Of course,' Peter said with thinly veiled sarcasm. 'Let's take away the rights of fertile men and women to decide how many children they need to sustain a colony they've risked *their* lives to establish. Now that's a solution the people will like. I suppose you'll want me to put on a happy face and make them accept it?'

'Yes, I will, dammit,' Basil said. 'That's your job.'

The grim news seemed to diminish everyone's appetite. Servants came around pouring ice water, using delicate silver tongs to offer wedges of dwarf limes. Basil sent them away.

He tapped his fingers on the tabletop with uncharacteristic impatience. 'We need to do a better job of making the people see just how dire the situation is. We have minimal fuel, not to mention very limited communication abilities, thanks to the continuing lack of green priests from our short-sighted friends on Theroc. Our fast mail drones can do only so much. Now, more than ever, we could use more green priests just to maintain contact between isolated colony worlds. Many planets don't have a single one.'

He looked over at Sarein, the dusky-skinned ambassador from

the forested world. She was lean and wiry, with narrow shoulders and small breasts, high cheekbones and a pointed chin.

'I'm doing the best I can, Basil. You know that Therons have never been good at seeing the forest for the trees.' She smiled to emphasize her clever choice of words. 'On the other hand, Theroc has received no routine supplies, no technology, no medical assistance since this crisis began. It's difficult for me to ask my people for more green priests if the Hansa dismisses our own needs.'

Peter watched the interaction between Basil and the pretty Theron woman; from the first days of his reign, he'd recognized the mutual attraction. Now, before the Chairman could respond, Peter squared his shoulders and spoke in the rich voice he had practised during numerous speeches. 'Ambassador, considering the hardships faced by many of our Hansa colonists, we must allocate our resources, giving our own colonies highest priority. Theroc, as a sovereign world, is already much better off than most.'

While Sarein fumed at the verbal slap, Basil nodded appraisingly at Peter, relieved. 'The King is correct, of course, Sarein. Until the situation changes, Theroc will have to take care of itself. Unless, perhaps, Theroc would care to join the Hansa . . . ?'

Sarein's face flushed, and she gave a barely perceptible shake of her head.

General Lanyan drew his glance like a scythe across the envoys. 'Mr Chairman, our only choice is to take certain extreme measures. The longer we wait, the more extreme those measures will have to be.'

Basil sighed, as if he had known this choice would fall upon him. 'You have the Hansa's permission to do what is necessary, General.' He skewered Peter with his gaze. 'And you will do it all in the King's name, of course.'

THREE

ESTARRA

◆ I have seen many fascinating worlds,' Estarra's oldest brother said as their flitter-raft travelled across the densely wooded continent. 'I've been to the Whisper Palace on Earth, and stood under the seven suns of Ildira.' Reynald's tanned face lit with a smile. 'But Theroc is my *home*, and I'd rather be here than any other place.'

Estarra grinned, looking around her at the new, but always familiar, landscape of whispering worldtrees. 'I've never seen the Looking Glass Lakes, Reynald. I'm glad you brought me along.'

As a girl, she had slipped out before dawn, running through the forests to investigate whatever caught her curiosity. Fortunately, a wide variety of subjects piqued her interest: nature, science, culture, history. She had even studied records from the original generation ship *Caillié*, the story of Theron settlement and the origin of the green priests. Not because she had to, but because she was interested.

'Who else would I bring?' Reynald playfully rubbed his knuckles on his sister's tangle of hair twists. He was broad-shouldered, his arms muscular, his long hair done up in thick braids. Though a sheen of sweat covered his skin, he didn't seem uncomfortable in the forest warmth. 'Sarein is an ambassador on Earth. Beneto is a green priest on Corvus Landing, and Celli is . . . well—'

'She's still too much of a baby, even at sixteen,' Estarra said.

Years before, as part of his preparation for becoming the next Father of Theroc, Reynald had travelled around the Spiral Arm to learn different cultures. It was the first time any Theron leader had diligently investigated other societies. Now, with travel restricted, stardrive fuel strictly rationed, and interplanetary tensions high, Reynald had decided to visit the main cities on his own world. His parents had made no secret that they intended to step down and turn over the throne to him within the year. He had to be ready.

Now their flitter-raft flew above the treetops, passing from one settlement to another. Laughing followers, pretending to be part of a procession, swooped around them on gliderbikes, small craft composed of rebuilt engines and fluttering wings scavenged from native condorflies. Rambunctious young men circled above and behind them, showing off aerial manoeuvres. Some flirted with Estarra, who had reached marriageable age . . .

Ahead, she saw a gap in the thick canopy and a glint of azure water.

'Those are the Looking Glass Lakes, all deep, all perfectly round,' Reynald said, pointing. 'We'll stay the night at the village.'

Around the first beautiful lake, worldtrees supported five worm hives, the empty nests of immense invertebrates. When Reynald landed the flitter-raft on the lakeshore, people rapelled, jumped, climbed, or swung down from their hive homes to greet the visitors. Four green priests emerged with the grace of gently waving branches, their skin tinged emerald by photosynthetic algae.

The green priests were capable of communication more sophisticated than the most complex technologies either the Hansa or the Ildirans had invented. The problem had frustrated scientists for generations, and the green priests had been unable to help them – not because they were keeping secrets, but because they didn't know the technical basis for what they did. Many outsiders offered to hire them for their telink skill, though the self-sufficient Therons had little need or interest in what the Hansa had to offer. The worldforest itself seemed intent on keeping a low profile.

On the other hand, the Hansa representatives were very insistent and persuasive.

Balancing such issues was a difficult job for any leader. Watching her brother interact with the green priests and smiling villagers, Estarra could see how well he would fill his role as the next Theron Father.

After an evening banquet of fresh fish, riverweed, and fat water bugs baked in the shell, they ascended to platforms high in the lakeside trees. Reynald and Estarra watched a performance of skilled treedancers, lithe acrobats who ran, danced, and bounced across the flexible boughs. The treedancers used the bending limbs and matted leaf fronds as springboards, soaring into the air, turning somersaults, catching branches and swinging by their arms in a choreographed ballet. At the end, in unison, all the treedancers launched themselves out over the water and dropped in perfect arcs to the mirror lake below, plunging into the water like heavy raindrops.

Following the performance, Estarra let Reynald talk business with the villagers while she happily accepted an invitation to splash in the warm water with a few local girls. She loved the sensation of floating and swimming, though she had the opportunity to do so only a few times a year.

Treading water in the Looking Glass Lake, Estarra gazed up into the night, marvelling at the sight of open sky from ground level. In her own city, the forest canopy was so thick she had to climb to the top just to see constellations. Now, floating in the open, the view overhead dazzled with billions of gleaming lights, a veritable forest of stars in the vault of space, full of people, worlds, possibilities.

When she returned to the brightly lit worm hives, dripping and invigorated, she found her brother speaking with a young priest named Almari. The woman's eyes were bright with intelligence and curiosity; Almari had spent years as an acolyte singing to the trees, adding to the musical knowledge stored in the botanical database. Like all green priests, she was hairless, her head smooth, her face adorned with tattoos denoting various accomplishments.

Reynald was gracious and polite, leaving his options open. 'You are beautiful and clever, Almari. No one can deny that. I'm certain you would make a fine wife.'

Estarra knew the discussion, for she had seen it several times already on this brief peregrination.

Almari spoke quickly, as if to cut him off before he could turn her down. 'Especially in these difficult times, is it not appropriate that the next Mother of Theroc be a green priest?'

Reynald reached out to touch the delicate green skin on Almari's wrist. 'I can't argue with that, but I see no need to rush.'

Noticing Estarra, Almari got up and took her leave, looking embarrassed.

Grinning impishly, Estarra gave her brother a playful punch in the shoulder. 'She was pretty.'

'She was the third one tonight.'

'Better to have too many choices than none at all,' Estarra said.

He groaned. 'Then again, there's something to be said for having a clear-cut decision.'

'Poor, poor Reynald.'

He gave his sister a playful punch in return. 'At least I'm not the Ildiran Prime Designate. He's required to have thousands of lovers and as many children as he can possibly breed.'

'Ah, the terrible responsibilities of leadership.' Estarra flung her wet hair to splash him. 'Since I'm merely the fourth child, my only worry is when I'll have a chance to go swimming again. How about now?'

Giggling, she ran off, and Reynald looked after her with envy.

FOUR

PRIME DESIGNATE JORA'H

As the eldest noble-born son of the Mage-Imperator, Prime Designate Jora'h filled his days with dutiful distractions. Fertile women from across the spectrum of Ildiran kiths applied for mating privileges, and the lists grew long with more female volunteers than he could possibly service.

The Prime Designate's next assigned lover was named Sai'f. Whip-thin and alert, she was from the scientist kith, an expert in biology and genetics. Sai'f was interested in botany, developing new crop strains for diverse splinter colonies.

She came to Jora'h in his contemplation chamber in the Prism Palace, where constant daylight shone through gem-coloured crystal panels. Her brow was high, her head large, and her eyes sharp and attentive, as if she were capturing every detail for later study.

Jora'h stood before her, tall and handsome, his face defining the Ildiran ideal of beauty. Golden hair drifted in a nimbus around his head like a halo, knotted into ten thousand fine strands. 'Thank you for asking to be with me, Sai'f,' he said, meaning it — as he always did. 'May our shared gift today produce a gift for the entire Ildiran Empire.'

In nimble hands, Sai'f held a ceramic pot that contained a twisted, woody-stemmed shrub. Its thorned branches were bent, constrained, massaged into an unnatural shape. Shyly, she extended the pot. 'For you, Prime Designate.'

'How poignant and fascinating.' Jora'h took it, intrigued by the labyrinthine tangle of branches and leaves. 'It looks as if you've done weaving work with a living plant.'

'I am exploring the potential of our quilltrees, Prime Designate. It is a human technique called *bonsai*. A way of compressing a plant to turn its biological efforts inwards, yet enhancing its beauty. I began growing this one a year ago when I first filed my application to mate with you. It has required a great deal of attention, but I am satisfied with the results.'

Jora'h did not have to pretend his enjoyment. 'I have nothing like it. I will keep it in a special place . . . but you must instruct me on how to care for it.'

Sai'f smiled at him, relieved and thrilled to see his obvious pleasure. He set the bonsai quilltree on a translucent shelf on the wall, then came forward to her, opening his tunic to reveal his broad chest. 'Now allow me to give you a present in return, Sai'f.'

She had been tested by his staff before she'd entered the Prism Palace. All women who came to him were certified fertile and receptive. Such tests did not guarantee that he would impregnate every lover, but the odds were good.

Sai'f disrobed, and Jora'h admired her. Each Ildiran kith had a different bodily configuration. Some were willowy and ethereal, others squat and muscular, angular and sinewy, or plump and soft. But the Prime Designate saw beauty in all kiths. While some were more lovely to him than others, he never played favourites, never insulted the volunteers or showed any disappointment.

Sai'f reacted to his caresses as if she were following a programme or a suggested procedure. As a scientist, she had probably studied the variations of sex like a scholar, attempting to become an expert so that she could excel in her encounter with him. Right now, Jora'h felt as if he was doing the same for her, following a programme, a familiar task like any other.

As he thought of the fascinating *bonsai* tree Sai'f had brought him, Jora'h could not help but recall Nira. And his heart ached with the old sadness for the lovely green priest. It had been five years since he'd last seen her.

Nira's innocence and exotic beauty had charmed him more than any adoring Ildiran female ever had. When she'd first arrived in Mijistra, her wide-eyed wonder at the architecture and museums and fountains had made him look at his own city with fresh eyes. Her innocent excitement in Ildiran accomplishments had made him feel more pride in his heritage than the most stirring passages from the *Saga of Seven Suns*.

After shy months of enjoying each other's company, when they'd finally made love for the first time, it had seemed entirely natural. The warm familiarity that grew into a bond with Nira was unlike anything the Prime Designate had ever experienced before. His relationship with her had been entirely separate from these routine matings scheduled by his assistants. Jora'h and Nira had spent many afternoons delighting in each other's company, knowing the relationship must eventually end, but enjoying each day. And the Prime Designate had kept calling her back to him.

But at the beginning of the hydrogue crisis, when Jora'h had gone to visit Prince Reynald on Theroc, Nira and her mentor Otema had been tragically killed in a fire in the greenhouse that held the gift of worldtrees from Theroc. According to the Mage-Imperator's report, the two visiting green priests had rushed in to save their treelings and had perished in the blaze.

Long ago, sweet Nira had come to the Prism Palace bearing potted treelings, small offshoots of the worldforest. Now, years after her death, the woman Sai'f had brought Jora'h a *bonsai* tree, and the memories all came flooding back to him . . .

Jora'h refocused his attention on the scientist woman. He did not want her to note his troubled thoughts, or to leave dissatisfied. He made love to her with an intensity that, for a while at least, drove back the ache of memories.

Jora'h requested an audience with his father. The Mage-Imperator's bright eyes were set within folds of fat, and his plump lips smiled when he saw his son. Bron'n, the fierce personal bodyguard, stood at the doorway to the private chamber so the leader and his eldest son could speak privately.

'I wish to send another message to Theroc, Father.'

Mage-Imperator Cyroc'h frowned, leaning back in his chrysalis chair, as if relaxing into the telepathic connection of *thism*. 'I sense that you are thinking of that human female again. You should not allow her to kindle such an obsession in you. It can only disrupt your more important duties here. She is long dead.'

Jora'h knew the corpulent leader was correct, but he could not forget Nira's smile and the joy that she had brought him. Before coming here, he had gone to the skysphere arboretum. One particular chamber had been used to house the Theron treelings. By now, the greenhouse had been replanted with salmon-pink Comptor lilies and crimson poppies, swelling the humid air with heady perfumes. Five years ago, when he had returned from Theroc to learn the terrible news, he had stared in horrified awe at the scars from the inexplicable conflagration.

There had been no bodies left to send back to Theroc. And the worldtrees were already burning by the time Nira and Otema arrived to fight the fire, so they had been unable to send any last messages through telink. Everything had been lost. Grieving, Jora'h had explained the tragedy to his friend Reynald in a special communiqué delivered by a Solar Navy ship.

By now the ashes and soot stains had been scoured clean, but the memories and the sadness remained. In his heart, Jora'h had never accepted that Nira was dead. If only he had been here, he would not have let any harm come to her . . .

Sensing his son's sadness through the web of *thism*, Cyroc'h nodded sombrely. 'You will carry many burdens when you ascend to take my place. It is your destiny, my son, to feel the pain of all our people.'

Jora'h's tiny golden braids flickered like tendrils of smoke. 'Nevertheless, I would like to send a new message to Reynald, in memory of the two green priests. We did not send the ashes or the skulls back to them.' He spread his hands. 'It is such a small thing, Father.'

The Mage-Imperator smiled indulgently. 'You know I cannot deny you.' The rope-like braid that hung from his head coiled around his pudgy stomach and twitched, as if the great leader were annoyed.

Relieved, Jora'h held out an etched-diamondfilm plaque. 'Here, I have composed another letter for Reynald to share among the green priests on Theroc. I would like to dispatch it with one of our commercial vessels.'

The leader reached out to take the message. 'It may require some time and a roundabout route. Theroc is not a frequently visited world.'

'I know, Father, but at least it's something I can do. It is my way of maintaining contact.'

Cyroc'h held the shimmering glassy plaque. 'You must not think of the human woman again.'

'Thank you for granting me this favour.' Jora'h backed out of the chamber and departed with a spring in his step.

As soon as he was gone, the Mage-Imperator summoned his bodyguard forward. 'Take this and destroy it. Make certain Jora'h is not allowed to send any message to Theroc.'

Bron'n took the diamondfilm letter in his clawed hands and, with great strength, snapped it in half. He would incinerate the pieces in a power plant furnace. 'Yes, Liege. I understand.'

F I V E

N I R A   K H A L I

Standing inside the Dobro breeding camp, isolated but joined by hundreds of other human test subjects, Nira stared through the thin fences. The fences were a mere formality to demarcate boundaries, a convenience for the captors, since the prisoners had no place to go.

The camp was situated at the foot of mountains to the east, rolling grassy hills to the west, with dry lakes and bleak terrain in a central valley. The ground itself was striated with arroyos cut by furious washes of rain, making it look as if the skin of the world had stretched too fast and broken open like festering scabs.

For five years as a prisoner of the Ildiran Empire, she had held on to her inner self, just staying alive despite all the unspeakable acts she'd had to endure. None of the camp guardians or Ildiran supervisors would answer when she begged to know why they were doing this to her.

Her love, Jora'h, could not possibly be aware of her situation. With a single command he could have freed her and all the other prisoners. Nira doubted the Prime Designate would ever participate in such awful schemes. He was too gentle and caring. She believed that in her heart. Did Jora'h even know she was still alive? Could she have misjudged him so much?

Nira didn't think so. Unsuspecting, Jora'h had been sent to Theroc – *obviously to get him out of the way, so he couldn't interfere when they abducted me.* The Mage-Imperator must have kept this a secret from his own son, even though she had been carrying Jora'h's child.

The Dobro Designate, second son of the Mage-Imperator, used the human descendants here as breeding stock for Ildiran experiments. For some reason, Designate Udru'h considered Nira the most interesting of all the prisoners, and she had suffered greatly because of it.

After she had given birth to a perfect, beautiful halfbreed daughter named Osira'h – *my little Princess* – the Dobro Designate had kept Nira here in this horrible camp, so she could be impregnated again and again, like some horrible brood mare . . .

Now she knelt at the edge of the austere compound, using a small tool to loosen the hard dirt around hardy, scraggly shrubs and thin flowers she had planted. In her spare moments, she tended and watered whatever plants she could find, tried to help them flourish; even the tiniest flecks of green life reminded her of the lush forests on Theroc. Though she was cut off from the worldtrees and the sentient forest mind, Nira was still a green priest, and she remembered her duties.

Though her emerald skin absorbed the daylight and converted it to energy, Dobro's sun felt weak and undernourishing, as if contaminated by the dark history of this place. She looked up, judging how much more time she might have to herself before the next labour shift out in the excavation trenches.

The breeder camp was a sprawling enclosed area with barracks, birthing hospitals, experimentation laboratories, and crowded dwelling complexes. Prisoners went about their business, knowing no other life. Some of them talked with each other; one gaunt man even laughed, as if unaware of his plight. Human children – sanctioned offspring of the breeding prisoners – found games to play even in a place such as this. The Dobro Designate insisted on a constant renewal of purebred descendants in order to keep the breeding stock diverse and healthy. However, to Nira, it seemed as if the human spirit had been bred out of them in less than two centuries.

Even after five years among them, Nira was still treated as a novelty, eccentric and strange, a troublemaker. At least the people had stopped staring at her green skin, which was unlike anything they had ever seen. But they could not understand her attitude, why she still refused to accept her situation and settle down to her new life.

The poor people didn't know any better.

Nira looked up as the alien supervisors put together another work crew. She tried to remain small and unobtrusive, hoping the bureaucrat kithmen would not choose her, not today. Her muscles were strong, though her mind was weary from years of difficult assignments – chipping opalbone fossils, hand-picking fruits from thorny bushes, digging trenches.

The Ildirans would eventually give her an assignment – they always did – but she clung to each moment, one at a time. Resisting the instructions would only provoke the Ildiran guards to tear up her plants. They had done it several times before. She would find other ways to resist, if she could.

When Nira had first been taken captive, before the Dobro Designate realized she was pregnant, she was imprisoned alone in darkness, sealed in an unlit cell – the worst punishment imaginable to an Ildiran accustomed to constant daylight. The black claustrophia was intended to crush Nira's spirit, perhaps even drive her mad. The Designate needed only her reproductive system, not her sanity.

For weeks, Nira had shuddered in dank darkness, suffering further as she went through physical withdrawal from the sunlight. Normally, under Ildira's dazzling sunshine, her photosynthetic skin delivered life energy every minute. Trapped in darkness, however, her metabolic and digestive systems had to readjust themselves. Nira had to learn to eat again, to digest normal food. She became extremely ill, weak, but refused to surrender, keeping her heart and her strength.

In the end, the Designate had released Nira from the darkness so he could perform analyses and benchmark measurements on her. His lean and handsome face was similar to Jora'h's, but devoid of compassion. His eyes were sparkling and hot, intent on what he might discover about her biology. After studying the test results, he had looked at her first with accusation, then with delight. 'You are pregnant! Jora'h's offspring?'

Rather than throwing her into the breeding barracks or putting her on labour crews like the other human prisoners, the Designate and his medical kithmen had tended her with meticulous devotion, taking regular blood samples, making painful and repetitive scans. Nursing her, studying her, making certain she maintained her health, for their purposes.

Nira, though, kept her strength and sanity for her own reasons.

The labour and birth of her first daughter had progressed normally. Through bleary eyes in the delivery lab, Nira had watched as the Dobro Designate looked wolfishly at the squalling little girl, as if ready to dissect his brother's child. The baby mixed the bloodlines of a telepathic green priest and the noble Prime Designate. Udru'h had named the girl according to the phonetic traditions of Ildiran kiths, Osira'h, but Nira simply thought of the girl as her Princess, a secret hope from all the storybooks she had read aloud to the curious worldtrees.

As was the custom among the breeding camp prisoners, the Designate let Nira keep the baby girl for six months, breast-feeding her, nurturing her so that she remained strong. She had grown to love the child, to care for her. Then the Designate had taken the infant girl away. All successful halfbreed specimens were separated from their mothers.

But Designate Udru'h had something very important in mind for Osira'h. *My Princess*.

Afterward, Nira's real nightmare had begun.

From then on, no matter how much she fought or prayed, the Designate kept her constantly pregnant, experimenting with different fathers. Each defeat drove her down, yet she refused to wither and die. She was like a blade of grass in the forest, bent underfoot and battered by heavy rains only to spring back. In her youth, she had never conceived of such torture, yet she withstood it, learned to send her mind to a kinder place until it was safe to return.

The alien sperm donors did not hate her. They were only following the Designate's instructions. They were part of an overall plan, of which none of them knew the details. And neither did she.

But unlike Osira'h, her subsequent bastard children had not been conceived out of love. She despised the forced mating sessions, and Nira tried not to grow attached to her halfbreed boys and girls. But she had nursed them, held them, studied their features . . . and her determined attempts at coldness hadn't worked. She could not reject these innocents simply because their fathers had been ordered to rape her until she conceived again.

Her own children . . . though she could never keep them. As before, the medical kithmen had snatched the infants away to raise them in the adjacent Ildiran city, under their own testing and training regimen.

Soon, they would consider Nira recovered enough to be reassigned to a work crew, to toughen her. Once her fertility had reached its peak again, the guards would drag her back into the breeding barracks, and the forced-impregnation cycle would begin all over again. Four times already. . .

Now, as Dobro's orange sun lowered towards murky clouds on the horizon, she left her fresh, trimmed bushes in the small garden and went to look for other flowers and shrubs. Worker teams returned from the hills and filed into the camp. After generations of imprisonment, the captive humans had no dreams, only a resigned endurance, day after day. They didn't even seem miserable.

This was the great dirty secret of the Ildiran Empire, an answer to what had happened to the only lost human generation ship. These prisoners were human descendants of the *Burton*, living here, hidden from the rest of the human race, for almost two centuries.

And five years ago Nira Khali had joined them. The Dobro prisoners had never seen a green priest before, never heard of Theroc. Nira was a stranger, an emerald-skinned outsider.

At night, or in muted conversations on work crews, she quietly talked about her world, and the sentient trees, even the Terran Hanseatic League, hoping that someone might believe her. Many of the breeder captives suspected she was mad. Others, though, listened with disbelieving curiosity. But they did listen, and Nira continued to hold out hope.

She had borne unwanted children, one fathered by the Dobro Designate himself, one by Adar Kori'nh, two from other Ildiran kiths. And though she had nurtured each of those children for months, she cared the most for young Osira'h. Nira clutched the fence wires, feeling the cold hollow in her chest. She longed for her daughter, her Princess. The other human prisoners didn't understand her misery. Halfbreed children belonged to the Ildirans, and they were always taken away. They had never thought anything of it.

Nira often sent messages into the Ildiran city adjacent to the sprawling camp, asking to see Osira'h. The Dobro Designate denied her request each time, refusing to answer Nira's questions. Not out of particular cruelty, but because Nira was no longer relevant to Osira'h's upbringing. The green priest woman had other breeding work to do.

Still, the Designate did understand the halfbreed girl's potential. Just the thought of it brought a faint smile to Nira's face. Her Princess was more than just an interesting mixed-kith experiment. *She was something special.*

Six

A D A R   K O R I ' N H

The seven beautifully anodized Solar Navy ships arrived in response to the Dobro Designate's summons. Adar Kori'nh stood in the command nucleus as the septa of ornate vessels entered a standard orbital configuration and retracted their elaborate reflective sails.

Back at the Prism Palace, he had received his orders directly from Mage-Imperator Cyroc'h – instructed to come personally, not to delegate the assignment to a lesser officer. Still, Kori'nh had frowned. 'I have always been uneasy about the activities at Dobro, Liege. It is not . . . suitable for inclusion in the *Saga of Seven Suns*.'

'Our work there will never be chronicled in the *Saga*, Adar. But still we must do it.' The Mage-Imperator had stirred, his tentacle-like braid twitching. 'The Dobro experiments hold the key to our race's survival, and even after generations of effort we are not ready for the challenge we must face. And now the hydrogues have returned. Time is short.'

Kori'nh knew that a million deep thoughts simmered quietly beneath the leader's calm face, ideas far beyond his own comprehension. The Mage-Imperator was the focal point for all *thism*, the conduit through which soul-threads shone in faint glimmers from a higher plane composed entirely of light. He was unsettled by the very thought of questioning his leader's wishes.

Even so, as commander of the entire Solar Navy, the Adar had to speak his mind. 'Is there truly such urgency, Liege? The hydrogues have not escalated tensions since we withdrew from their gas giants.'

The Mage-Imperator shook his large head. 'The hydrogues will not be content to remain within their strongholds. Soon they will become more aggressive. And we must be prepared to do whatever is necessary for the survival of our race.'

Having dutifully raised the question, Kori'nh had bowed and accepted the assignment. He had no other choice.

Now he waited in the warliner's receiving bay as a shuttle rose from Dobro carrying the Designate himself. The Mage-Imperator's second son desired to speak privately with him; Kori'nh would learn soon enough what it was about.

Suspecting that this mission might have unpleasant consequences, Kori'nh had already dispatched Tal Zan'nh on a make-work assignment. The Adar would dirty his own hands with this task, but he saw no need to involve his protégé, the son of the Prime Designate . . .

After the shuttle had docked, the pilot stepped out, looking flustered. Behind him the Dobro Designate scanned the empty bay like a predator. The Designate's clothes were drab and serviceable, without lace, finery, or colourful strips of self-active energy film. He was a working man, with an assignment and a mission.

Seeing the commander waiting for him, Designate Udru'h turned gruffly to the shuttle's pilot. 'You are dismissed. The Adar will take us where I direct him.'

The pilot looked uneasy, but Kori'nh nodded his permission.

'Apparently, the Designate and I will require privacy. No doubt he has certain orders for me.'

Three years earlier he had been sent here to Dobro for the express purpose of mating with one of the captive human females, a green-skinned woman from Theroc. Kori'nh could not understand why she was being held among the *Burton* descendants, nor was he allowed to ask about it. He had not relished his union with the woman. It had seemed . . . dishonourable. Yet it had been his duty, an indirect command from the Mage-Imperator himself.

He dreaded what the Designate would order him to do this time.

After he took the cockpit controls, Kori'nh remained silent, not even offering minor conversation. Designate Udru'h gave him coordinates that took the shuttle away from the orbital lanes towards the fringes of the Dobro system. A skein of icy moonlets and asteroids looked like a pile of planetary ingredients that had been swept under the rug – too diffuse to be an actual asteroid belt, each piece too small to be considered a planetoid in its own right.

'We have concealed it out here. A perfect place,' said the Designate. 'Even so, we must be cautious.'

Uncomfortable with the prolonged mystery, Kori'nh said, 'Please explain yourself, Designate. What are we seeking?'

'Our aim is not to seek, but to *hide*, and thereby ensure continued secrecy.'

Kori'nh dwelled on the words as the shuttle drifted into the ice-studded, rocky debris. He heard a hiss of dust particles and tiny pebbles striking their shields. Ahead, his scanners detected a darkened shape that looked decidedly artificial, a construction not of Ildiran design.

'As you can see, Adar, we have left too much evidence behind. There is always a risk it could be found.'

A huge, antique spacecraft.

Fascinated by Earth military history, even when it was not relevant to current assignments, the Adar recognized the bulky, squarish lines of an immense star-crossing vessel larger than five Solar Navy warliners. The construction design seemed wasteful, a ship that relied upon brute force rather than finesse. It was shaped like a tall building, topped with industrial processors, collectors, and refineries; it looked as if it had been uprooted and hurled into space like a brick. Now the big vessel was dark and shadowed, stained with the scars of ancient storms and encounters, like a ghost ship, haunted and drifting without its crew.

Kori'nh noted the symbols on the fuselage; these bulky engines could achieve only a fraction of lightspeed. It would have taken centuries to cross the gulfs of space . . . and yet the brash humans had flown the old generation ships anyway. *'Bekh!* Is that . . . the *Burton?'*

In the cockpit, the Designate looked scornfully at the immense vessel. 'The Solar Navy escorted that thing here to Dobro. At the time, we'd intended to let the humans settle with our splinter colony here, two races joining together. The Designate even took a human woman, the *Burton's* captain, as his wife.

'But other humans . . . did not adapt well to the situation. Before any formal contact or delegation was sent back to Earth, the human woman was assassinated, and the grief-stricken Designate was forced to crack down, to impose rigid order.

'Earth never knew about these refugees. My grandfather, Mage-Imperator Yura'h, issued instructions that these unruly creatures were to be investigated in every possible manner. Once the *Burton* was emptied, a warliner towed the vessel out here to the fringes of the Dobro system, where it has remained.'

Kori'nh thought of all the effort and hope that had been poured into the creation of this mammoth starship. 'It is a valuable relic.'

The Designate sneered. 'I'm sure the humans would love to have it back. They have prospectors and scavengers searching the void between stars to see if they can recover it. We must let them hold on to their myths and mysteries. And never discover the truth.'

'Agreed,' Kori'nh said, but for a different reason. 'They must never learn what we have done here.' As he cautiously threaded the shuttle through the space debris, he drank in the crude majesty of the derelict.

The Designate kept talking. 'There is no longer a reason to keep this ancient hulk. If found, it would be embarrassing, incriminating.'

'Then why was it hidden in the first place? Did someone intend to . . . use the old ship?'

'Precisely the question, but my ancestor was . . . distraught at the time,' Designate Udru'h said. 'We have found nothing in the *Burton*'s design or engines that can benefit the Empire. Under the pressure of the hydrogue conflict, the Terran Hanseatic League is developing new weapons to increase their military strength. They've always been aggressive, expanding into other colonies, even taking over settlements that we have abandoned—'

'Like Crenna,' Kori'nh said.

The Dobro Designate gave a sour expression. 'My father has decided that the danger of accidental discovery far outweighs the benefits of keeping the *Burton*. I myself see no reason to leave it here.'

Intrigued, Kori'nh guided the shuttle in another slow pass over the mothballed vessel, dodging icy planetesimals so that he could get a better look. He expanded the prow blazers, playing a ripple of light across the space-weathered hull features. 'So . . . exactly why have you summoned me, Designate?'

Udru'h looked at the Adar as if the answer were obvious. 'I want you to destroy the *Burton*. Leave no trace that it ever existed.'

SEVEN

CESCA PERONI

Heat, incredible heat – enough to soften rock and boil away light elements, harsh enough to incinerate organic flesh in an instant.

Isperos was a terrible place under a blazing sun, full of hazards. But to Roamers, the heat was a *resource*. The heavily reinforced colony produced enough pure metals and rare isotopes to make the risks of living and working here worthwhile.

As Speaker for the clans, Cesca Peroni had come to congratulate Kotto Okiah for his ingenuity in establishing an outpost on the threshold of hell. 'No one would have believed it possible, but you recognized what others were too blind to see. The success of this place is another support to buttress our strained economy.'

In the underground bunker, the eccentric engineer fumblingly acknowledged her praise. Kotto was a genius, but he had never learned how to accept compliments with good grace.

Eager to impress his visitor, he led Cesca into deeper tunnels, wiping beads of perspiration from his ruddy cheeks, scratching at

44

sweat in his curly hair. 'It gets cooler after level two.' He rapped the baked wall, his knuckles making a hollow sound on the tiles. 'Three layers of ceramic honeycomb with an extra layer of rock-fibre insulation throughout. Vacuum voids to halt thermal transfer.'

'No one else could keep up with the output of a whole sun. A perfect example of Roamer ingenuity.' Her praise was sincere.

He favoured her with a shy grin. 'Well, the enormous solar flux provides plenty of power to run the generators, atmosphere processors, and cooling systems.' He indicated a set of frost-covered pipes that ran like blood vessels along the tunnel wall. 'I've devised an unorthodox thermal-flow system to channel excess energy to the surface, dumping it into large fins that radiate waste heat. Well, some of it at least. Just another one of my inventions.'

Years ago, when the hydrogues had forbidden skymining, Cesca had called upon all clans for innovative options to gather hydrogen across the Spiral Arm. Kotto was a wealth of ideas. While the Isperos station was being established, tunnels dug, smelters built, he'd managed to rework the process chain of ekti reactors to make them more efficient. He had also invented the blitzkrieg scoops used to gulp hydrogen from gas-giant clouds, hit and run.

Somehow, Roamers always managed to do the impossible. She drew a deep breath, content with what they had achieved. *Yes, impossible things.* Like her relationship with Jess. But Cesca had even found a way to bridge the gap with the man she loved, after so long . . .

Years ago, while betrothed to Ross Tamblyn, she had fallen in love with his younger brother. After Ross was killed by the drogues, she and Jess should have had the luxury to find happiness together. But when Cesca was chosen as the new Speaker, and Jess found himself the head of his family's water business, they had put off their feelings. She and Jess had agreed that the Speaker must be strong and completely focused, at least until the crisis was over.

It had seemed like a reasonable decision at the time.

Less than a year later, they'd become secret lovers and now had finally agreed to announce their wedding plans in six months' time. Six long months . . . but at last the end was in sight. She would take her small measure of happiness wherever she could.

In the meantime, she needed to concentrate on her duties as Speaker.

Kotto led her into a shielded control bunker lined with ceramic tiles. 'We call this our "luxury lounge".' Eight Roamer workers sat at stations watching the outside activity through observation screens, monitoring the shipping crews in the night-side shadows.

Isperos was bathed in the furious corona of the unstable sun, like a stone in a furnace. Giant mobile mining machines and surface smelters operated just on the night side of the terminator, where the crust had recently been baked. The machines scooped the surface layer and processed it into metals, separating out useful short-half-life isotopes created by the rain of cosmic rays.

'Our clans have always been proficient at mining outer-system asteroids,' Kotto said, 'but those rocks retain useless lightweight elements, ices, and gases. Here on Isperos, the sun does all the processing for us. Nothing left but the purest heavy metals.' He spread his hands. 'We just form them into ingots and put them on to the railgun launcher. Perfectly simple.'

Cesca doubted anything about Isperos was 'perfectly simple', but she admired the technical audacity. The Big Goose would never have taken such a risk.

Outside, on the scabby surface, flattened road cuts led away from mining operations on the terminator line. Automated ferries delivered pallets of processed ingots to a kilometre-long railgun launcher, an electrically powered system that fired the projectiles into space, just barely reaching escape velocity. At a safe distance from the churning sun, Roamer cargo ships rounded up the drifting treasure. Traders delivered the metals to other Roamer construction sites or, more lucratively, to Hansa colonies whose industries needed the blackmarket resources.

On a screen, Kotto pointed to a forest of giant ceramic fins glowing cherry-red that thrust up like sails on the already mined surface. 'We're building more heat radiators so we can drop the station's internal temperature by a degree or two, but there's always a choice between spending time on our own comfort or producing more metals.'

Every two seconds, the railgun launched a dull silvery cylinder, each of identical size, shape, and mass. They shot outwards like a blur of bullets. The railgun launcher was moved every month to remain inside the creeping shadow. A few stray ingots had been lost, their trajectories perturbed by asteroids or simple miscalculations, but cargo-netters grabbed most of the canisters.

Seeing what Kotto had accomplished on Isperos made Cesca swell with pride. It gave her all the faith she needed that the Roamers would survive the hydrogue war. Somehow. As would she and Jess.

EIGHT

JESS TAMBLYN

The skies of Plumas were frozen solid. Embedded within the ice ceiling, artificial suns shone down, reflecting off the subterranean sea.

Transport shafts had been bored through the ice plate, providing access for visitors and equipment. Hydrostatic pressure pushed water through cracks in the moon's frozen skin, sending bubbling jets upward. On the surface, Roamer ships could hook up to the water wells and fill their cargo vaults.

Clan Tamblyn had operated the Plumas water mines for generations, but Jess had little knack for the industry. He was a Roamer at heart, preferring to wander on missions that took him away from home. Luckily, after Jess's stern father Bram had died, the old man's four brothers had accepted the burden with enthusiasm.

When his Uncle Caleb asked him in a raspy voice if he wanted a share in the decision-making process, Jess had merely smiled at him. 'Our family has had enough feuds and disputes. I wouldn't want to start another one – besides, you're all doing such a fine job.

My father said that a Tamblyn's blood should be made of ice water. He considered it a good thing.'

Now Jess stood at the lift tubes, adjusting his gloves. The biting air tasted fresh and brittle; when he exhaled, white clouds of steam boiled upwards like smoke. He had grown up on Plumas, playing with Ross, both of them taking care of their sister Tasia . . . But too much had changed here. It was no longer the place of his childhood, not in his mind.

His mother had been killed long ago when Jess was only fourteen. She had been out in a surface rover, checking wellheads from the water geysers and pumping stations, when the crust had cracked. Gushing water and slush had swept Karla Tamblyn away, sucking her vehicle down into a gaping crevasse. For hours they had received faint transmissions from Karla's suit radio, but there had been no way to rescue her. Bram had gone wild with grief while his wife had slowly frozen, leaving her embedded like a fossil in glacial ice.

Jess's father and brother were both dead now too, his sister gone off to join the Eddies. Though his uncles and cousins were all around, Jess felt detached and alone here.

Behind him, two of his uncles emerged from the administrative huts; a third man came around the equipment shed, stuffing greasy gloves into insulated pockets. Uncle Caleb was always tinkering with machinery, trying to improve or monitor the equipment. Jess thought Caleb just liked the vibrating hum of engines and the feel of 'clean dirt' under his fingernails.

The other two men were so bundled against the cold as to be unrecognizable, but Jess knew it must be the twins Wynn and Torin, his father's youngest brothers. His remaining uncle, Andrew, would stay inside, where he managed the ice mines' bookkeeping and budgets.

'The ship's ready for launch to Osquivel,' said one of the

hooded uncles – Torin, judging by his voice. His cheeks were red and flushed from the cold.

'We've filled Del Kellum's order and then some,' said Wynn, without taking his hood down. 'Don't argue if he insists on paying extra.'

Caleb came up, smiling. 'If you're a smart lad, Jess, you'll bring a gift for Kellum's sassy young daughter. She's a prize.'

'She's a handful,' said Torin. 'But you could do worse.'

Jess laughed. 'Thanks, but . . . no.' Everything they said reminded him how much he missed Cesca. He smiled secretly to himself. *Six more months.*

'Picky boys end up being bitter bachelors,' Torin warned.

'Nothing wrong with that,' Wynn replied a bit too quickly.

Both Caleb and Torin frowned at their brother. 'Don't tell me you haven't regretted it.'

Wynn stood his ground. 'When my biological clock starts ticking, I'll let you know.'

Thankfully the lift door opened and Jess stepped into the bore tube, leaving his uncles and their banter behind. 'I'll let you figure out the Tamblyn dynasty while I'm gone. I'm going to go deliver that water shipment.' He shot up through the ceiling of ice, anxious to be alone aboard the tanker and on his way, where he'd have a couple of days to daydream about Cesca in peace . . .

Inside the rubble belt that girdled the gas giant's equator, the secret Roamer shipyards remained unnoticed by either the hydrogues or Hansa spies.

Jess Tamblyn came to Osquivel towing a shipment of water. A glittering conglomeration of grappler pods, automated stations, and environment modules circled within the planet's multilayered rings. Suited crews moved like industrious ants, shuttling components and raw materials to construction spacedocks. As long as

Big Goose survey vessels did not look too closely, clan Kellum's lucrative complex continued to fabricate and dispatch vessel after vessel . . .

After he had docked his ship and disengaged the cargo tanks, Del Kellum met him personally. The barrel-chested man had salt-and-pepper hair and a well-trimmed goatee. 'Haven't seen you since the raid on Welyr! What have you brought us this time?'

Jess jerked a thumb back towards the docking chamber. 'Exactly what was on the manifest, Del. Did you expect something stronger than water?'

'Yo! I'll do the delivery duties,' said a young woman over the comm. 'Hi, Jess! See me before you leave?'

He recognized the voice of Kellum's raven-haired daughter, only eighteen years old and already proficient in much of the shipyard work. 'My schedule's tight, Zhett. I don't know if I'll have time.'

'He'll make time, my sweet,' Kellum said.

Piloting a small grappler pod as if it was an extension of her own arms, Zhett intercepted the Plumas water tanks and glided off to distribute them one at a time to Osquivel's assembly grids and resource rocks.

Misty with paternal pride, Kellum watched his daughter go, then raised his bushy brows. 'She's making eyes at you, Jess, and she'd be a good catch, by damn. You're thirty-one years old, and unwed – isn't your clan getting anxious?'

Zhett was the daughter of Kellum's first marriage, the only part of the family remaining to him after a dome breach had killed his wife and young son. Though Kellum treated the girl as if she were a princess, she had become a strong young woman on her own, not at all spoiled. Jess had known her since she was a little girl.

He looked at the older man and forced a smile. 'I'll make my own choice whenever the Guiding Star shows me the way.'

Kellum clapped him on the shoulder and took him through an airlock to a slowly rotating habitation module. He handed Jess a flexible bulb filled with a strong orange liqueur that he distilled himself.

Porthole plates filled one wall with an ever-changing view of the rocky blizzard. 'Living here is like swimming in a school of hungry fish,' Kellum said. 'You watch everything that moves and stay ready to get out of the way.'

He gestured proudly to the aquarium mounted on the inner wall, and Jess looked at the zebra-striped angelfish, Del Kellum's prize possessions. At great expense, the clan leader had imported the graceful tropical fish from Earth. Kellum fed them regularly, studying their sleek forms because he said they reminded him of starship designs.

He growled conspiratorially, 'Whenever you decide to put together your next hit-and run squadron, Jess, my shipyard can pump out another dozen or so blitzkrieg scoops. I've already got the production lines in place.'

Jess couldn't tell if the older man sounded hopeful or frightened. 'I'm not ready to lose any more people and equipment right now, Del, just so we can sell a few squirts of ekti to the Big Goose. Besides, we can focus on other methods.'

Kellum rested a clenched fist on the metal tabletop. 'We've got to show the drogues we can be strong, by damn. It's not a simple cost/benefit calculation.'

As the habitation module rotated, the view panned across a broad black starscape down towards the hydrogen-rich, but now forbidden, gas giant. Jess sighed. 'We keep modifying and improving our other harvesting techniques. There's got to be some-thing safer.'

'Safer, sure – but not a tenth as efficient.'

In the Osquivel shipyards, giant smelters and floating spacedocks were busy extruding thin sheets of tough metallic polymer. Though only a few molecules thick, each nebula sail covered an area broad enough to eclipse a small moon. The folded gossamer sheets were packed into pods to be launched far out into the sea of interstellar gas, where they would open and skim the nebula. Other facilities high above Osquivel were designed to distil hydrogen out of cometary ice.

Kellum grumbled. 'It just takes so damned long to get ekti any other way.'

The private comm channel crackled and Zhett's eager voice came over it. 'Just checking in, Dad. All deliveries finished. Is Jess still there?'

'Indeed he is, my sweet.'

'Jess, want to go for a ride with me in a grappler pod? We can look at the rings—'

'I can't stay long, Zhett – clan obligations.'

'Your loss.' She sounded flippant. 'You'll regret it later.'

After Zhett had signed off, Jess looked at her father. 'I probably will.'

NINE

TASIA TAMBLYN

The EDF battle group cut through space in a show of force impressive enough to intimidate the unruly Yreka colonists. Any one of the three enhanced Juggernauts should have been enough to do the job, but Admiral Sheila Willis had also included five Thunderhead weapons platforms, ten Manta mid-sized cruisers, and sixteen full squadrons of Remora fighters.

The Grid 7 fleet lumbered into the system like a strutting bully flexing his muscles. To Platcom Tasia Tamblyn, it seemed like overkill against a handful of disobedient settlers, not to mention a huge waste of stardrive fuel. Wasn't the EDF supposed to be at war with a *real* enemy?

Tasia entered the private platcom's lounge just off her Thunderhead's bridge deck. Images of Admiral Willis and all the ship commanders attended the virtual meeting via projection. The Admiral's flagship Juggernaut had been christened *Jupiter*, both after the king of Roman gods and also in memory of the first great setback against the hydrogues.

'I want to complete this mission without collateral damage – if

54

possible.' The Admiral's expression was pinched, her short grey hair plastered close to her skull. She looked like a strict old school-teacher and spoke with just a hint of a drawl. 'In fact, my preference would be to have no shooting at all. The Yrekans are not the enemy, just misguided colonists.'

Tasia nodded, agreeing with the commander's attitude, but she knew she was in the minority here.

'With all due respect, Admiral,' said Commander Patrick Fitzpatrick III in his usual superior tone, 'anybody who defies the King's direct orders is technically the enemy. Just one of a different sort.' The young man had dark hair and dark eyes, with patrician features and thick eyebrows that looked painted on.

Tasia squelched an irritated sigh. She had saved Fitzpatrick's balls once or twice during realistic combat and emergency exercises, yet he still scorned anyone he considered to be beneath him. More than once, as a scrappy student in the Lunar military academy, she'd used her knuckles to show him the error of his spoiled and narrow-minded ways, but even a stint in the infirmary hadn't altered the kleeb's attitude.

However, Fitzpatrick played political games better than Tasia; plus, his grandmother, Maureen Fitzpatrick, had been Hansa Chairman during the reign of King Bartholomew, so he felt privileged. Tasia kept stepping up in the ranks, too, but she achieved it through superior performance. Now Fitzpatrick sat in the captain's chair on a Manta cruiser, while Tasia commanded a large Thunder-head platform. And both of them were only in their early twenties.

Admiral Willis's holographic image turned as if she was looking at all the commanders projected around her. 'Nevertheless, this is an act of benevolent discipline, not aggression.'

'Yeah,' said Fitzpatrick. 'Let's get all *paternal* on their asses.'

As far as Tasia was concerned, he could stick his head out into hard vacuum.

She admired what the Yreka colonists had accomplished since the founding of the settlement forty years ago. Not as hardy or ingenious as Roamers, perhaps, but they had showed true backbone. Yreka should have been a strong and independent outpost, and the charismatic Grand Governor Sarhi had made hard decisions for the survival of her people. What was wrong with that?

But unnamed and unrecognized Hansa 'watchers' – a fancy word for 'spy', Tasia thought – had infiltrated the various colonies just to keep an eye out from the inside. One of these spies had sent a report to the EDF about the Yrekan indiscretion.

General Lanyan had taken Yreka's defiance as a personal affront. When dispatching the battle group, he had grumbled, 'Only a few years ago, the Yrekans begged for our assistance against a gang of Roamer pirates. Unfortunately, their memories seem to be faulty.'

Though she had maintained her professional demeanor, Tasia was stung by the remark. The pirate Rand Sorengaard was an anomaly, and most Roamers disliked what he had done, yet the Hansa still used the incident to drum up prejudice. Tasia had been fighting that stigma throughout her military career.

A navigation officer spoke across the *Jupiter's* intercom system, which broke into the holoconference. 'Entering the Yreka system, Admiral. All warships taking up positions according to the game plan.'

'Very well, folks,' Admiral Willis said. 'We'll reconvene after we hear the Grand Governor's response. This exercise could be over within the hour . . . or we might be stuck here a while.'

Tasia left the platcom's lounge and hurried back to the command bridge. She hoped she could quietly keep the EDF from going overboard with the poor settlers. Sadly, despite her numerous crack skills, subtlety and diplomacy weren't among Tasia's strong points.

Yreka was an unremarkable colony, located on the fringe of Hansa territory near the Ildiran Empire. The planetary system had no obvious strategic importance, home to a mere handful of hardy settlers. The Yrekans depended on outside help for many necessities.

Tasia took her seat on the bridge and asked her command crew to sound off and double-check their systems. She transmitted back to the *Jupiter*, 'Thunderhead 7-5 ready to engage, Admiral.'

Willis was calling the shots . . . and Tasia hoped 'shots' was just a figurative term for this operation. The Yrekan colonists wouldn't stand up for an hour against the Eddies' firepower.

Wing Commander Robb Brindle, her friend and lover, called from the launch bay, speaking with forced formality. 'Elite Remora squadrons ready for departure, Platcom. Should I deploy them, or wait until the Yrekans make a move?'

'Crack open another coffee tube while you wait in the cockpit, Wing Commander,' Tasia said. 'Once they see what we've got, the Yrekans should fold their cards.'

'Platcom, there's significant spaceport activity below,' her scanning ensign said. 'The colonists are mobilizing ships . . . a lot of them.' The woman touched a pickup in her ear. 'The Grand Governor has sounded civil defence alarms, calling for evacuation, getting civilians to shelter.' The officer blinked wide eyes at Tasia. 'They think we're going to nuke them.'

'Shizz, they should know better than that,' Tasia said. 'Yreka's a Hansa colony, and we're the EDF.' But deep in her heart, she wondered how far Admiral Willis would go.

The Admiral sent a hail down to the Grand Governor, but her folksy voice did not diminish the threat. 'Ma'am, this is Admiral Sheila Willis, commandant of the Earth Defence Forces here in Grid 7. I'm supposed to protect this sector of space, but it seems you're forgetting who butters your bread. Are you there?' She waited a moment for a response. Tasia imagined that the administrative centre of Yreka was scrambling in panic down below.

Willis continued, 'Now, I've brought along a few of my ships to remind you that your planet is a signatory to the Hansa Charter. Take a look, and you'll find everything right there above the dotted line. You've sworn your allegiance to the King.'

Her voice took on the tone of a disappointed grandmother. 'But it appears you're hoarding stockpiles of ekti, obtained through blackmarket suppliers. You should be ashamed of yourselves. The Hansa is faced with an extreme crisis, and King Peter has asked for the cooperation of all his subjects in centralizing resources. Why would you go and refuse? Your stardrive fuel has got to be turned over to the EDF so that we can allocate it for the greater good and use it to protect humanity.'

Though her words were meant to be conciliatory, Willis's tone was stern. 'Now, we don't want any hard feelings, but the law is the law. The King is willing to forgive you, so long as you comply immediately. Let's not make a mess of things.'

After she ended her message, a fuzzy projection appeared, a hologram whose poor resolution demonstrated the outdated nature of the Yrekan comm systems. The grand governor was a tall, thin woman of clear Indian descent. She had dusky-brown skin, almost black eyes, and thick blue-black hair that hung in long tresses to her waist. She had a curved nose and full lips turned downwards in a frown.

'Admiral Willis, I am afraid we cannot comply. Our own survival dictates my decision. I am appalled that the EDF would threaten a loyal Hansa colony. Yreka has already sacrificed much in this war effort. We have given all we can, and we require ekti supplies for our survival.'

The Grand Governor motioned with her hand, and the image was filled with heart-wrenching projections of skeletal children, stubbly fields of crops drooping due to lack of fertilizer or insufficient protection from native blights. 'If we surrender those fuel reserves to you, our people will starve, our colony will wither, and Yreka will become a ghost planet within a decade.'

Tasia quickly understood the desperate gamble that the Yrekan leader was taking. While Admiral Willis had spoken on a direct channel to the planet's administration centre, keeping the talk relatively private, Grand Governor Sarhi had intentionally sent her message on the broadest band so that all the soldiers in the Eddie battle group could hear her plea.

'Why not take the air we breathe? Or drain the fresh water from our streams? Or block the sunlight that makes our crops grow? We have paid dearly for this ekti, and we cannot afford to lose it.'

'Now, that's all very melodramatic—' Admiral Willis began.

'Please send the King our regrets. Thank you.' Without waiting for the Admiral to respond, the Grand Governor gave a slight formal bow, then signed off, to ensure that she got the last word.

The crewmembers on Tasia's bridge were astonished at the foolish response. Some even snickered in complete disbelief. She said firmly, 'There's nothing funny going on here.'

The Grid 7 battle fleet waited a long moment in silence, anticipating what Admiral Willis would command. When she did speak to the commanders, Willis's voice was calm, but disappointed. 'This planet is currently under interdiction. No ships go in or out. No supplies, no messages, for as long as it takes.'

Tasia leaned back, relieved at least that the Admiral hadn't ordered an immediate assault. She said to her crew, 'Well, I hope none of you has plans for the weekend.'

TEN

KING PETER

The King finished the last motions of dressing preparatory to emerging from his chambers. For the morning, servants had laid out a colourful, ornate, and thoroughly uncomfortable outfit (no doubt designed and selected by a committee). But he had ignored it, choosing his own attire and dismissing all the lackeys who wanted to help him with his buttons and collar. Raymond Aguerra's mother had certainly taught him how to dress himself.

As he dressed, he spoke casually to his Teacher compy. 'Basil doesn't want a leader.' After listening to OX for years about the nuances of power and rhetoric, King Peter saw the old robot as more than a database or a set of historical files. He tugged at a cuff. 'He wants an actor.'

Early on, Peter had decided to do his best to become a real King. Playfully at first, he'd begun to institute small changes, significant only in that they demonstrated his independence. Instead of the gaudy jewellery and draping robes old Frederick had worn, Peter altered his wardrobe to a crisp and serviceable uniform.

Grey, blue, and black. The Chairman had approved, sure that the more Prussian style would resonate with a people at war.

'It is best for you to be both, King Peter.' The benign-looking Teacher compy was one of many built to accompany the first generation ships as they left to search the stars. OX now served the Hanseatic League in the training of Great Kings. 'But there is more to your role than that. The people must believe in you.'

Peter smiled. 'All right, then. Let's go and be seen on our way to the situation room.'

As Raymond, he had grown up with a close-knit but poor family. Scraping for every spare credit, he had worked odd jobs, talked with street vendors, got to know the everyday men and women whose lives attracted no notice.

Those people were the King's genuine subjects, but Basil didn't factor them into his grand plans. The Chairman excelled in seeing how jigsaw pieces fitted together, but he had no comprehension of the smaller scale of life. He didn't know any *real* people, only political projections and general economic concepts. It made him a good businessman, but not a leader who inspired loyalty . . .

With OX at his side, Peter made his way down a wide hall. He smiled at a middle-aged Hispanic woman polishing an alabaster bust of King Bartholomew. 'Hello, Anita.' He looked at the statue's perfect facial features. 'Do you think old Bartholomew really looked like that, or do you suppose it's an idealized portrayal?'

She beamed at his notice. 'I . . . I suppose that's the way he looked to the sculptor's eye, Sire.'

'I bet you're right.'

He and OX continued down the passageway to the polished wooden doors of a former library, now converted into a situation room. It had once been filled with old books, so fragile that they could no longer be read. Now, the shelves were covered with filmy display screens.

Tactical officers and advisers met regularly to study Hansa colonies, known positions of Ildiran ships and the EDF fleet across the ten spacial grids. Though never formally invited to these meetings, Peter made a point of joining them every week. None of the experts inside the situation room would turn him away – unless the Chairman ordered it. But Basil would never make a scene. As the King and OX entered, the older man made only a slight acknowledgement from his leather overstuffed chair.

Inside the converted library, the court green priest Nahton sat attentively beside a spindly gold-barked treeling, ready to receive telink reports. News also came from regular mail drones, which could travel far on minimal ekti. In addition to delivering messages and transporting data among Hansa worlds, mail drones often took survey images that documented cities and populations to keep the colony database up to date.

'Still no word from the Dasra reconnaissance fleet, Mr Chairman,' said Admiral Stromo. 'It's now a week overdue.'

A group of EDF ships had been dispatched to a gas giant in another attempt to establish negotiations with the hydrogues. It was an obvious public relations gesture, not expected to generate any tangible results. The enemy aliens had so far ignored or rebuffed all peace overtures.

Basil grumbled. 'I knew we should have sent a green priest along for instant communications, but we didn't have any to spare.'

Nahton sat unruffled, paying no attention to the implied criticism.

Military advisers and colony specialists went over the updates, projecting a complex mosaic of civilization. Currently there were sixty-nine signatories to the Hansa Charter and a handful of satellite colonies and uncatalogued camps. After the strategists had discussed known changes in ship deployment, technicians modified the images to reflect the best-guess situation in the Spiral Arm.

Peter studied the details, attempting to draw his own conclusions.

Nahton curled his fingers around the treeling's thin trunk and connected his mind to the worldforest. From around the Spiral Arm, scattered green priest observers disseminated their reports, which he now accessed. The priest's brow wrinkled, and dark tattoo lines compressed together on his face. When he finished, Nahton's face showed agitation and concern. 'I've received reports from six different green priests, four on colony worlds, two aboard diplomatic ships.'

Basil sat up, seeing the green priest's concern. 'What is it?'

'Several hydrogue warglobes were spotted travelling through inhabited systems. They've made no contact, but they have approached various planets, apparently scanning them.'

Peter pointed to the starmap. 'Highlight the locations where the warglobes were seen. Maybe we can see some sort of pattern.'

'Only six of my counterparts sighted the hydrogues.' The green priest called out the names of obscure systems, and glowing red dots appeared on the mosaic. 'Usk. Cotopaxi. Boone's Crossing. Palisade. Hijonda. Paris Three.'

OX took a step forward, though his optical sensors had high-enough resolution that he could scan details from a distance. 'That does not appear to be a simple defensive posture. Given the sparse distribution of green priests across the colony worlds, many other hydrogues could easily have been missed.'

Basil frowned. 'Search through all mail drone files, see if they've picked up any other drogue images.'

'According to my reports,' Nahton said, 'the warglobes made no overt aggressive move. They seem to be scouts travelling from system to system.'

'Hydrogues never come out just to snoop around,' Admiral Stromo said. He had been in command of the Grid 0 escort fleet that had been devastated at Jupiter. 'Until now, they've emerged only to attack.'

King Peter's mind was fully engaged. He scanned the seemingly random distribution of red dots where warglobes had been sighted. 'Until now.'

ELEVEN

RLINDA KETT

If she'd been a different sort of person, Rlinda Kett might have complained about how her fortunes had fallen. But she wasn't a woman to bother with such nonsense. Instead, she crossed her meaty arms over her ample chest and reassessed what to do. Exuberant optimism might annoy more realistic people, but she felt that it often helped.

She paced the deck of her ship and took inventory of her cargo stockpile. It didn't look all that bad, considering. At least the *Voracious Curiosity* was still hers – though on the rah-rah orders of King Frederick five years ago, she'd been forced to 'donate' her other four merchant ships to the EDF for war-related purposes.

For the past month her ship had been docked at a public hangar on Earth's Moon. It was cheaper to land in the Moon's shallower gravity well than to use the additional thrust to go to Earth.

But she had just received a second annoying bill from the moonbase business offices, an insistent request for overdue docking fees. 'And what am I supposed to do about it?' Rlinda sighed in frustration.

The military had rationed ekti so tightly that she couldn't afford to make runs with the only vessel she had left. Then, to add insult to injury, they charged exorbitant fees to let her keep the *Curiosity* docked. Why couldn't they let her sit in peace? Consuming the gourmet treats in her larder offered some small solace in the midst of these administrative headaches.

Over the years, she had already liquidated most of her assets, acquiring what little trade merchandise she could. But during the war she had a difficult time moving some of the upscale, exotic specialities she kept on the *Curiosity*. Maybe one of the moonbase officials would be open to a bit of barter; somebody must want to impress a spouse or lover with haute cuisine foods. Rlinda could even give them hints on how to prepare the stuff, how to score romantic points.

In the cargo bay she squeezed her bulk into cramped places. Fortunately, the low lunar gravity and long practice assisted her. Rlinda ran her fingers down the impressive inventory list.

She'd kept a few bolts of Theron cocoon fibre for herself, but now she'd have to sell it. She would have loved a personal wardrobe of the shimmering material, but the money was more important. She still had six cans of saltpond caviar imported from Dremen and preserved insect steaks from Theroc (absolutely delicious, though Rlinda had difficulty convincing would-be gourmets to sample bug meat). In addition there were tinpaks of pickled fishflowers, marinated crustaceans, fresh pupating sweetworms (that were due to hatch soon, despite the cold packaging), and unclassified – and untasted – fruits and vegetables from a spectrum of worlds.

Her mouth watered. Rlinda was a master chef herself, and had studied the cuisines of numerous cultures. Given her delight in fine foods, it was no wonder she weighed so much. Rlinda considered it an advertisement for the quality of her wares.

Unfortunately, when economic times were tight, people

dispensed with luxuries; consequently commodities such as those Rlinda carried were the first to suffer. Silly priorities. It was a lot harder to sell expensive 'useless' items, but her creditors still demanded payment on time.

Rlinda returned to her cockpit and slumped into the padded captain's chair that had been expanded to accommodate her frame. She looked at the docking bill again. Maybe she *was* a bit behind in her payment, but the overdue amount wasn't significant enough to have generated such a stern notice. She would have preferred to share a bottle of wine with the beancounter, open a pack of special black chocolates, and sweet-talk her way into revised terms. She stared at the signature, not recognizing the man's name – B. Robert Brandt. Probably some accountant recently transferred up from Earth.

Then a chuckle burst out of her mouth, turning into a deep-throated laugh as she noticed that the digits of the man's employee number exactly matched the date of her latest wedding anniversary. 'You always were a rascal, BeBob.'

Her dark eyes twinkled. Rlinda wasn't sure whether she was more delighted to hear from him or to know that the insistent bill was simply a convenient cover for sending her a private message.

Branson Roberts – the best of her numerous ex-husbands – had captained a merchant ship commandeered by the EDF, and General Lanyan had railroaded him into flying military reconnaissance missions. BeBob's methods as a merchant hadn't been strictly legal, but he had generated plenty of profit, which he shared with Rlinda.

She descrambled the text using the private code they had long ago established. Because of the encryption, the text message was necessarily brief. She would have preferred a holographic image of the man – he'd never have had the nerve to scan himself naked, but it would have been even nicer. As she read the words, though, she understood why BeBob had taken precautions.

'Fed up with the military – no surprise there! After seventeen suicidal missions, decided to call it quits. The General wants to keep throwing me into the fire until I'm used up. Enough of that shit! Decided to save my own skin and – more important – save the *Blind Faith*. Taking a voluntary unofficial leave of absence. Hope the EDF doesn't have the gumption or the resources to track me down.

'If you ever get a full gas tank and want to visit, come to Crenna. An out-of-the-way colony, where I can lie low and run black-market materials for the settlers. Miss you. BeBob.'

Rlinda leaned back in the captain's chair, her face glowing, her eyes asparkle with embarrassing tears. He had always been stubborn and impulsive, impossible to live with . . . and a damned good man. BeBob wasn't cut out for military service – Rlinda could have told Lanyan that – and it was a crime to abuse his particular skills.

Oh, she had loved him indeed . . . otherwise, why bother getting so upset when their marriage had crumbled after five years? But Rlinda and BeBob still had enough respect – and, yes, a little bit of passion – for each other that they'd remained business partners. If only she had known what other hardships she would face, Rlinda might have been a bit more tolerant with the man as a husband. Life was too short and too hard to limit the good times.

Clutching the encoded message, she returned to her cargo bay and looked at the supplies with a different eye now, pulling down a bottle of port wine from New Portugal and one of the tins of saltpond caviar. The upscale market might be a tough business proposition these days, but at least she could consume it herself. And there would be no better customer.

She had no intention of wasting her last few drops of ekti to go and see him, but someday she might have a chance. It was good just to know that he was alive and safe. With a squeaking pop, she removed the cork from the bottle of port. Today she felt in the mood for a celebration, now that she'd had just a little bit of good news.

She poured a small, sweet toast – for starters – and raised the glass. 'To you, BeBob. You stay safe until I see you again.'

TWELVE

BASIL WENCESLAS

T spark grew into a flame, then expanded into a conflagration, consuming an entire planet. It had merely been
a scientific test of rediscovered alien technology.

Dammit, we never intended to start a war!

In his penthouse office suite atop Hansa HQ, Basil Wenceslas
reviewed images of the first Klikiss Torch test. He observed the
archival images as the swirling clouds of Oncier brightened,
glowed, then caught fire. Who could have known an alien
civilization lurked deep within the core?

In retaliation, the aliens had destroyed a scientific observation
platform, vaporized all four of Oncier's moons, wrecked numerous
Roamer skymines, defeated part of the Ildiran Solar Navy and the
EDF, forbidden all further ekti harvesting . . . and heinously
murdered Old King Frederick. Surely that was enough?

For almost six years, teams of experts had analysed the Oncier
record, second by second. Basil did not expect to see anything new,
but it still fascinated him to watch the utter destruction of a
hydrogue planet. He could feel neither remorse nor sympathy.

The aliens would accept no apologies, nor would they negotiate. Even now, Basil expected nothing from the latest recon
mission to Dasra – the ships were overdue and now feared lost – but
at least he had tried. He could think of nothing else to do, no magic
solution. If only . . .

The Klikiss Torch had seemed a miraculous boon, a way to
open formerly uninhabitable moons for colonization. The alien
technology had been discovered by two xeno-archaeologists
picking through ancient and mysterious Klikiss ruins. That
insectoid civilization had once been a great interplanetary empire,
but ten thousand years ago, they had left their empty cities like
garbage heaps across the solar systems.

Basil smiled wistfully. Perhaps Margaret and Louis Colicos
could discover yet another miracle, some amazing lost Klikiss
device the Hansa could use as leverage to force the drogues to sue
for peace . . .

But he had heard nothing from the archaeologists in years. The
last he remembered was that they were on Rheindic Co with a small
team, including a green priest. The Colicoses were not extravagant,
and the Chairman had left instructions that rubber-stamped any
reasonable requests. He had not needed to keep an eye on them.

Images of imploding Oncier played again, faster this time, so
that the beautiful planet burst into stellar fire.

Curious now, Basil punched in an information request at his
service terminal, asking for the latest reports of what Margaret and
Louis Colicos had been doing. He had recently received a blind
letter from their son Anton, inquiring into their whereabouts. The
message had been long delayed, tangled through bureaucratic
channels. Anton Colicos was merely an associate professor at a university, no one with any political clout or importance. Apparently,
this wasn't the first such inquiry the young man had sent . . .

Basil was astonished to learn that all contact with the Colicos team had ceased not long after the hydrogue ultimatum. Rheindic Co was not on any supply routes, and unless someone had sent an urgent request for assistance, no supply runner would have filed the proper forms and argued for the appropriate waivers. The xeno-archaeologists had access to a green priest for instant communication, should an emergency arise. No wonder he hadn't noticed.

But still . . . five years of silence? It was no surprise their son had grown concerned. Basil felt cold. The old researchers had fallen through the cracks. Why hadn't their green priest sent a message? He dreaded that they had starved to death on an abandoned world because no one was paying attention. The Chairman hated it when details weren't properly attended to.

He retrieved the last formal reports they had submitted. As Basil read Margaret's summaries, seeing how she waxed enthusiastic as the Klikiss mystery unravelled, he felt a growing thrill. Perhaps there *was* something important on Rheindic Co. Had he missed a remarkable opportunity?

Margaret Colicos had found some ancient connection between the vanished Klikiss race and the hydrogues – an astonishing revelation in itself. She claimed they had discovered another innovative and amazing technology, but was not specific about what it was.

And then the reports had ceased.

Galvanized now, Basil left his Hansa offices and descended into the underground passageways that took him across the wide arboretum, under the statue gardens, and into the Whisper Palace.

On the way, he encountered ambitious and beautiful Sarein. 'Basil, I need to talk to you. Could we arrange a private dinner in my quarters?'

'Not now.' He looked at her. The young Theron woman could have found any number of handsome men to sit at her feet like servants, but she was more drawn to Basil's wealth and political power. 'Where is a green priest? I need to send a message.'

Sarein's brows furrowed. 'I just saw Nahton walking towards the Shelter Garden.' Basil picked up his pace. Without being invited, Sarein followed.

Flowers and shrubs lined the winding paths through the foliage. The green priest often liked to walk through the manicured fern gardens inside the Whisper Palace conservatory wing. Now he knelt by a reflecting pool sheltered with drooping gold-leaf willows.

'Nahton, I require your services. Let's go to the nearest treeling.'

'Follow me, Mr Chairman.' Fifteen of the potted young worldtrees were stationed around the sprawling Palace, usually in governmental rooms where communication was most necessary.

Basil talked as they hurried. 'An archaeology team was dispatched several years ago to a planet called Rheindic Co. They took a green priest with them, and he planted a grove of worldtrees for direct communication. I must reestablish contact with them. We have heard nothing in years.'

'What's so urgent, Basil?' Sarein said, her large eyes conspiratorial.

'I just don't want to be late for the party.'

When Nahton finally knelt beside one of the potted treelings and wrapped his fingers around the scaled trunk, he sent his thoughts through telink, connecting with the worldforest, searching through a million thoughtlines.

'Arcas was his name,' Nahton said. 'He did plant his treelings there.' The man's tattooed face drooped into a frown. 'All the treelings on Rheindic Co are dead. Contact has been severed.' He blinked his eyes, deeply disturbed. 'The trees are dead. Why . . . why didn't the worldforest tell us?'

Basil absorbed the information, his initial curiosity and worry evolving into a more urgent concern as he saw the court green priest's unexpected reaction. Nahton gripped the potted treeling, using telink again as if to send numerous urgent inquiries into the worldforest network.

Preoccupied, he began to walk back towards his private offices. Sarein hurried beside him. 'What is it, Basil? Can you tell me?'

'Please let me think. This is new information. I don't know yet what it means . . . but it could be extremely significant.' He walked faster, leaving her behind. Basil could always smooth Sarein's ruffled feathers later; more likely, she would come to him and find some way to apologize.

According to the last sketchy messages, the Colicos team had apparently stumbled upon something important, but they had not followed up their tantalizing hints with a complete report. Damn, why hadn't he raised the question before? And if the green priest was so obviously alarmed, then something truly unusual must have taken place.

With all the crises in the Hansa, such a matter would not have risen above his personal radar. Now, though, the idea raised his suspicions and his hopes. Perhaps the archaeologists had indeed found another technological miracle, greater even than the Klikiss Torch? If anyone could manage such a thing, it would have been Margaret and Louis Colicos.

Basil did not like loose ends. He would invest the necessary expense in stardrive fuel, find a small ship that wasn't being used for any important matters.

He ran a finger along his chin, pondering. Then he remembered his alien sociologist and spy, Davlin Lotze, who had been sent to the abandoned Ildiran colony of Crenna. Pretending to be an average settler, Lotze had surreptitiously looked under rugs, probed into corners, lifted subtle clues about the Ildiran civilization. By now, he'd had enough time to complete his job there.

Yes, Lotze would be perfect for this job. Basil decided to turn him loose on Rheindic Co to find out what had happened to the archaeologists.

THIRTEEN

DAVLIN LOTZE

A t the urgent town meeting, Davlin Lotze silently listened to settlers who wanted to flee Crenna. 'We've got to get out of here before we all die of the epidemic! It's the Ildiran plague again!'

Davlin knew it was unlikely that the same biological infection would be compatible with human DNA, but he couldn't reveal how much he understood about genetics. After all, he was supposedly just a farmer and a civil engineer.

Davlin lived alone in an abandoned Ildiran dwelling he had claimed for himself. He was a tall dark-skinned man with a muscular frame and a soft voice. His left cheek was faintly scarred from an accident with an exploding glass bottle; the marks were a bit more distinctive than he preferred, but he had learned how to draw no particular attention to himself. It was a spy's job to blend in.

He had helped his fellow settlers install waterworks, sewers, weather stations, and electrical conduits as they rebuilt the damaged colony's infrastructure. During the epidemic that had driven the Ildirans from Crenna, the alien colonists had burned buildings and ruined generators and substations. They had fled this world in a panic.

And now, five years later, a new mysterious sickness was sweeping through Crenna's human settlers at an alarming rate. The victims suffered a debilitating respiratory infection and a rash of alarming orange circles blossomed across their legs and shoulders. When one old man died from 'Orange Spot', the anxiety reached a new pitch.

One of the colony doctors stood, very short in stature with large owlish eyes. Her face was grey from exhaustion, but she wore a small smile that seemed out of place and an expression of weary relief. 'I think I have good news.' She didn't notice the eager indrawn breaths. 'After analysing samples from fifteen victims of Orange Spot, my team and I have isolated the infectious organism. I'm happy to say that it's completely unrelated to the virus that causes Ildiran blindness fever.'

On a portable projection screen she displayed several electron micrographs showing blobs and strange shapes. Davlin recognized human blood cells along with large unfamiliar masses. 'Orange Spot is a simple amoeboid monocellular creature, not as tough as a virus or even a bacteria. In humans it affects mainly the skin and the lungs. It's probably in the water or in something we harvested, a natural part of Crenna's ecosystem.'

'Is it going to kill us all?' asked someone.

'No, but you might have to get used to your orange spots.' The doctor smiled a little more. 'That symptom is an inflammation of the skin and a discoloration of melanin. Possibly permanent, but not too dangerous.'

'But my Arkady is dead!' an old woman said.

'Arkady already had scarred lung tissue, and he was particularly vulnerable. Orange Spot is as serious as, say, pneumonia. But treatable, too. All we require is a broad-spectrum anti-amoebic. I have some samples in my pharmacy, but not enough to treat the whole population.'

'Well, we can't just run to the local drugstore and pick up a prescription,' grumbled another colonist.

A man named Branson Roberts, one of the newest colony members, stood. 'I can.' He was a thin and lanky white man with big calloused hands and a dandelion puff of grey-white hair on his head.

The man had flown in with a small merchant vessel; new plating indicated where the name and serial number had been changed. Roberts had either stolen the craft or he was hiding from something. But the Crenna colonists welcomed anyone with a private ship who could make under-the-table runs and obtain blackmarket supplies.

'My ship has enough fuel for a couple more trips, as long as I don't go too far.' He pushed his hands into his jumpsuit pockets. His grin was infectious. 'I have a few connections around the Hansa.'

Of course you do, Davlin thought.

Two days later, the Crenna medical staff had treated – and cured – the five most severe cases of Orange Spot. Davlin worked on the water filtration system, adding additional precautions to screen the amoeba from the local drinking supply. Seeing the recovery of their fellow colonists, the people calmed.

Branson Roberts went around the settlement to compile a 'shopping list' so he could bring back a full cargo load in addition to the necessary anti-amoebic medicine. If he was going to use his diminishing stardrive fuel to make a run for pharmaceuticals, he might as well make the whole trip count.

The closest Hansa world was a place that catered to wealthy tourists. 'On Relleker they don't want their pampered visitors to suffer from so much as a splinter,' Roberts had said. 'They'll have every known medical supply.'

Davlin met him at the small spaceport with a list of components he needed for the pumping and filter stations. Theoretically, he should have used the opportunity to transmit a report to Chairman Wenceslas, but he was not anxious to attract Hansa notice. He liked it here on Crenna, and by now he half-believed his own cover story as a simple settler. Out of sight, out of mind . . . he hoped.

The Ildirans had called Crenna 'a world of sounds'. Silvery streams bubbled up from springs and tumbled down in cascades. Natural seedgrasses rattled with the winds like tiny maracas. Insects hummed and droned throughout the day and night, adding a pleasant, musical white noise. The low hills were forested with spiny groves of flutewood trees; after the trees died, the soft cores decayed and left hollow reeds through which native insects drilled holes, and the ever-present breezes played them like musical instruments.

It was a nice place, much better than some of his other assignments.

Now, before Roberts could climb aboard his ship, the proximity alarms chimed, indicating an incoming vessel that had just entered Crenna's atmosphere. Roberts looked alarmed. 'Who would be coming here?'

One of the part-time town officials in the survey tower bellowed an excited announcement, 'It's a mail drone!' Then with increased volume, the man shouted, 'Mail call!'

A drone was a small, fast ship built with automated systems, little more than an interstellar satellite. During the embargo, such drones were the only way to disseminate information to planets that had no green priest for direct telink communication. They also took detailed survey images of known Hansa settlements.

Roberts grabbed the list of mechanical components from

Davlin's hand and scampered aboard his ship. 'Go read your mail. I'll be back as soon as I finish shopping,' he said in a rush. 'In the meantime, if the sickness gets too bad, I hear that chicken soup works wonders.'

Roberts lifted off without completing a standard pre-launch checklist – and presumably before the drone could have spotted him. The merchant ship streaked into the sky mere moments before the mail drone arrived. The fast satellite began to download its stored files and messages into Crenna's network database: letters from family members, business reports, news files, copies of entertainment vidloops and digitized novels.

No matter how much the settlers might enjoy the contact with home, Davlin found it odd that the Hansa would send such a low-priority mission here to outlying Crenna. He knew that every action Basil took had a reason – usually more than one. He also wondered what Branson Roberts had been afraid of.

Though he had no family or close friends, Davlin was not surprised to find a message for him among the transmitted letters. The note from his 'brother' Saul read like an innocuous message: a niece's marriage, the death of an old relative, struggling family businesses. But after he took it back to his dwelling, he decoded it and read about the new assignment Basil Wenceslas had given him.

Davlin's heart sank, but he had known his peaceful times on Crenna would eventually end. Once again he must become an official investigator and make use of his exosociological skills to solve a mystery. Before long, a ship would arrive to take him to a Klikiss graveyard world, where his orders were to discover what had happened to a vanished archaeological team.

The people of Crenna would never see Davlin Lotze again.

FOURTEEN

ANTON COLICOS

Without a doubt, it would be the grandest story ever told. Anton Colicos meant to do his best to write the biography of his illustrious parents, without resorting to too many embellishments.

Margaret and Louis Colicos were unravellers of mysteries, diggers in the dust of fallen civilizations – iconic heroes who could endure through the ages. However, his parents would insist on historical accuracy, even if it did make for a less interesting story.

In his university office on Earth, golden sunlight streamed through the window slats to dapple the items he had gathered: photofiles and preserved images from his childhood, newsgrabs and tearsheets of journal articles and research publications.

Early in their careers, his parents had used Ildiran scanning technology to uncover a pristine city buried under the Sahara. They had worked on Mars investigating the pyramids of Labyrinthus Noctis, debunking the theory that the unusual land-mark was an artefact from a lost civilization, much to the dismay of imaginative theorists everywhere. But the truth was the truth.

Then, the Colicoses had devoted their work to investigating Klikiss ruins. Llaro, Pym, Corribus. After the successful test of the incredible Torch, they had gone to Rheindic Co – only to fall silent for several years now.

At first, Anton hadn't worried. At thirty-four, he was long past needing to keep in close contact with his parents. Margaret and Louis were self-sufficient, choosing planets so isolated that it took months or years for messages to travel from place to place. Even without the hydrogue war restricting transportation and communication, it wasn't unusual for them to drop out of sight.

Still, five years was too long. And this time they'd had a green priest . . .

Anton had sent multiple inquiries to Hansa officials, but he was just a researcher in an obscure department at a university, and his letters attracted no attention.

Anton went to the office window, opening the slats so he could stare at the dazzling ocean. Though the university building had environmental controls, he preferred to open the window, so he could smell the cool sea breezes in the park-like district around Santa Barbara.

The five quirky buildings in the university's Directorate of Ildiran Studies had been designed by students. New structures were erected in unusual geometries, with crystal panes and faceted surfaces evocative of Mijistra, the Ildiran capital city. Rotating photon mills shed rainbows across the sidewalks. The sunshine of southern California added to the Ildiran illusion, though even the warmest, clearest day could never rival the dazzle of seven suns.

Partly using the cachet of his legendary name, Anton had landed a respected position in the Department of Epic Studies. When he'd been younger, Anton had followed his parents around to their archaeological digs, being tutored by compy teachers.

Sometimes, Margaret and Louis treated their only child more as a colleague than as a son.

He'd never learned to take care of his rail-thin appearance and often wore ill-fitting clothes without concessions to style, grabbing whichever outfit was closest at hand. His dishwater-brown hair was straight and worn in a serviceable cut. Because of constant reading, he had twice gone through retinal surgery to correct his vision, and he still squinted out of habit.

For years it had seemed that Anton would follow in his parents' footsteps, but while he loved ancient mysteries, his heart's interests turned to legends rather than straight history. Anton had acquired two doctorates, one in obscure dead languages and one in comparative cultural mythology. He excelled in studying fragments of the *Saga of Seven Suns* the Ildirans had donated to Earth.

Anton had memorized reams of human folk stories, many in their original languages: Icelandic sagas, Homer's epics, the *Heike Monogatari* of Japan, the complete Arthurian saga in all its variations, the Sumerian Gilgamesh epic, and many folktales that had never been previously translated with any accuracy.

If only he could study with the Ildiran rememberers . . .

He had applied four different times to Mijistra, addressing letters to the Mage-Imperator, the Prime Designate, anyone he could think of. Declaring his passion for epic story cycles, he had begged for a grant to go to Ildira and study the epic, hoping that his insights into Earth mythologies might enrich the Ildirans' enjoyment of the *Saga*. Surely their own historians would want to learn the legends of humanity in return? Both races would benefit tremendously.

But his applications had been ignored twice, denied the third time, and the fourth — sent a year ago — swallowed up in the hydrogue-frayed turmoil. Just like his inquiries about his parents. Wasn't anyone out there listening, in the whole Spiral Arm?

So, instead, he planned to create a myth of his own by writing
the biography of his mother and father. He spread the notes he'd
been compiling for years, organizing them by topic from dry
biographical data to research accomplishments, from the routine
but still remarkable Earth archaeological work to their off-planet
studies.

But a story needed some sort of closure – if not the end of their
lives, at least a validation. Without any information on what had
happened to his parents on Rheindic Co, Anton felt incapable of
finishing the biographical work.

Hearing the tinkle of the door signal, he looked up at a brass-
plated compy who stood at his office entry. The robotic servants
were ubiquitous in the university halls, performing deliveries and
maintenance duties; many had Friendly programming that made
them cheerful conversationalists.

'Anton Colicos, please verify your identity.'

'All present and accounted for. What do you want?'

The compy extended an ornate package, a plaque sealed with
shimmering paper and embossed with unusual designs that Anton
instantly recognized as Ildiran. 'This was delivered by a courier.
The university chancellor is most intrigued. We rarely receive
dispatches directly from the Prism Palace.'

Anton snatched the package from the compy. 'I'll savour the
moment for myself. Thank you.'

'Shall I tell the chancellor to set up a meeting?'

He held the precious package. 'Go ahead. He'll want me to
explain myself, even if this turns out to be nothing.'

As the compy swivelled about and departed, Anton studied the
shimmering cover. He discovered how to unfasten the protective
layer and slid out an etched diamondfilm sheet. It was written by
one of the chief Ildiran historians, a rememberer named Vao'sh.

So, unlike the inquiries about his parents, Anton's letters and applications to Ildira had not gone unnoticed after all. The rememberer even knew that Anton could read the Ildiran written language.

He was invited to come to Ildira and 'share stories and interpret legends' with Vao'sh himself. His eyes sparkled. He couldn't believe it. Transport had already been arranged.

His heart pounded and he looked down at the notes scattered across his desk. Writing his parents' biography would have to be delayed again. He was going to Mijistra!

FIFTEEN

ADAR KORI'NH

After choosing the personnel who were best suited for the mission, Adar Kori'nh took seventy soldiers, workers, and engineers from his warliners and led the demolition team to the hidden *Burton*.

Though he had not argued with the Dobro Designate, Kori'nh was not convinced of the need for this operation. The generation ship had remained here, cold and silent, for so many years. Analysis of this alien hulk might have led scientist kithmen to innovations for Ildiran vessels.

But the Ildiran Empire had resisted change for generations. The Mage-Imperator was not interested in improvements, because that would imply their civilization was not *already* at its pinnacle. So the empty *Burton* floated out here in space, ignored – and now Kori'nh had been ordered to destroy it. It seemed such a shame.

Shuttles wove through space debris that hung like a smoke-screen around the cumbersome *Burton*. As the dismantling team approached the haunted-looking derelict, the Adar drank in details he had missed on his first inspection. Around him, muscular soldiers and intent-eyed engineers peered with fascination at the corroded hulk.

It was a monument to lost dreams, an abandoned town once filled with hundreds of hopeful human colonists. Long ago, foolhardy pioneers had left their home planet and set off into the uncharted emptiness with no rational expectation of finding a habitable world. What fabulous folly! How long had it been since the Ildiran race had shown such passion, taken such risks? Kori'nh couldn't wait to get aboard.

The Ildiran shuttles hovered beside the *Burton*, while the Adar dispatched an initial team of specialists. Working outside in hard vacuum, the engineer kithmen wrestled with the antique Terran docking hatches, removing external access panels, testing and rewiring circuits.

'Bekh!' He fought back his impatience as he watched the work. 'Slowly. No mistakes.' The engineers finally managed to open the external doors to reveal a cargo bay large enough to accommodate all the Ildiran shuttles. 'Once our ships are inside, send out three systems specialists in environment suitfilms. See if we can pressurize the interior.'

Within an hour, yellow lights glowed inside the *Burton*'s docking bay.

'Oxygen levels test out, Adar,' one of the engineers transmitted. 'It appears we have reactivated the atmospheric systems. Should we power up the whole ship? The stagnant air will need to be circulated and filtered. I am certain the *Burton* has reserve supplies.'

Kori'nh raised his chin. 'Let's do this properly. We'll wear facefilms in the meantime, but I want the *Burton* awakened, powered, and ready to fly for one last journey.'

The engineering team acted as if they were on a holiday to the resort world of Maratha. They rushed through the hollow corridors where generations of optimistic human colonists had once lived. Their footsteps echoed in the cold, empty air, loud enough to awaken any spirits that might have remained behind in the abandoned ship. Kori'nh had read that humans did not believe in the Lightsource and a higher plane of illumination after death, but in ghosts and wandering spirits.

In the *Burton's* engine room curious engineers deciphered the archaic propulsion systems. From contact with the Hanseatic League, scientist kithmen knew the basic principles of human star vessels, and the generation ship's drive was straightforward enough that they were able to get it functioning again.

Wearing an insulated suit and facefilm, Adar Kori'nh made his own inspection, walking alone through the passenger quarters, climbing from one deck to the next. Even when he was by himself, he could feel the other Ildirans nearby, their comforting presence like tickling feathers of *thism*.

But he also sensed the human presence, as if their dreams had left a tangible imprint. Such foolishly grand aspirations, the naïve optimism of fledglings leaving their home and venturing out into the wild Spiral Arm. So ambitious, so reckless.

Kori'nh looked at all the cabins, the sealed storage areas, the common rooms, gaming centres, libraries . . . mostly stripped clean now. He stopped at a cavernous dining hall, saw signs of a disturbance, overturned chairs, spilled debris. A mutiny, or a celebration? Or had Ildirans caused this themselves centuries ago when they had detained the unsuspecting *Burton* colonists?

So much to see here and learn . . . so much that would be wasted when he followed orders and destroyed the ship.

He realized the scandal the Empire would face if humans ever discovered what their supposed allies had done on Dobro. As alleged rescuers, the Solar Navy had taken the colonists to where they were promised their own colony; instead, they had become breeding stock for the experiments.

Kori'nh's heart twisted. It seemed brutally dishonourable to him.

As the Adar walked reverently along, he imagined footsteps, playful children chasing each other, generations that had been born and died far from home, never setting foot on solid ground. He opened sealed living quarters at random, trying to imagine the families that might have lived there . . . afraid he might find the mummified remains of some forgotten castaway.

Kori'nh saw old pictures, images of heroes or loved ones, faded clothing, indecipherable toys, keepsakes from old Earth. Each item bore some significance to the people who had lived here, stories passed on from parents to children.

These colonists had intended to create a new Earth on a new world. But the breeder subjects on Dobro had been stripped of their pasts, given no education about their origin. All of this was lost . . .

He finally reached what the humans had used as a command nucleus – they called it a 'pilot deck'. He stood alone, looking at darkened control stations, imagining the reports from crude instruments and sensors. Here, a succession of captains had lived and worked, making good and bad command decisions, growing old, passing on the long mission to their successors. Kori'nh wondered at their names. Were those commanders forgotten, their lives buried in the dust of history? The human race did not have an equivalent of the *Saga of Seven Suns*.

Sucking a long breath through the facefilm, the Adar gazed at the empty command chair, saw faint frostlines in some of the shadows between equipment stations. This giant ship had been achingly empty for so long. The silence hung like a thunderhead around him, occasionally broken by faint groans and shifting sounds as warming air and the presence of strangers stressed the long-dormant structure. It would take some time to shake the sleep and stiffness from its systems.

But Kori'nh would not give it a chance.

Though he had not been ordered to do so, the Adar instructed his soldiers to go through every chamber and remove any object of possible technical or cultural interest. He vowed that these details would not be lost forever. Some rememberer might still decipher them, use the clues to draw a deeper understanding of their Terran counterparts.

It was a crime to discard it all as if it had never existed . . . even though that was exactly what the Dobro Designate wanted.

When the *Burton's* vital systems were functional and Kori'nh could find no further excuse to delay, he went to the pilot deck and personally guided the derelict. The enormous generation ship lurched out of the asteroid field, towards the hot centre of the Dobro system. He felt the power inside the huge vessel, the lumbering shelter that had housed hundreds of people for so many decades.

He stood surrounded by the memories of humans who had staked their lives on the resourcefulness of their captains. The Adar had long been enamoured of legendary heroes, but what he was doing now did not seem worth remembering. Few would ever know what he had done . . .

'The course is set, Adar,' said an engineer. 'Gravity will do the rest.'

Kori'nh looked at the roaring ocean of Dobro's sun. Here, so close, the orange flames were like gaseous lava, a furnace in which nothing could survive.

'Prepare the *Burton* for departure. Inform the septa that we are on our way back.'

The muscular kithmen looked oddly out of place as they carried colourful toys, dolls, and items of human clothing back to the docking bay. Kori'nh stayed behind, the last person on the *Burton's* pilot deck, looking at the lonely control stations and the hot sun, looming closer. Finally, he descended through the deck levels back to his shuttle.

Leaving the generation ship, Kori'nh stared out of the shuttle's side ports, watching as the huge derelict fell inexorably into the sun's deep gravity well. The plasma surface lashed out with flares like the claws of a hungry predator.

The corroded hull of the ancient *Burton* became cherry red, then yellow, brightening to a dazzling white as it plummeted into the star's chromosphere . . . finally breaking into molten fragments. With a silent scream, the last vestiges of the derelict simmered and burned, leaving no more than a darkened scar that was rapidly erased.

It left an indelible mark on Adar Kori'nh's mind and imagination, but he would tell no living soul about it.

SIXTEEN

MAGE-IMPERATOR

While meditating, Mage-Imperator Cyroc'h observed his populace through a mental web of *thism*, the tiny soul-threads that glimmered through from the realm of the Lightsource. The Mage-Imperator was the focus for all those threads, and his people trusted him to make proper decisions. No one else.

Inside his meditation chamber, warm daylight streamed through translucent walls made of sapphire and blood-red crystals. Cyroc'h reclined in his chrysalis chair, his heavy-lidded eyes half closed; he saw partially through his mind and partially through his eyes. His brain kept track of a million details, each piece of the puzzle, every necessary action.

Freshly returned from destroying the *Burton*, Adar Kori'nh remained rigidly respectful, his medals and decorations prominent. He clasped his hands in front of his ornamented chest. 'My teams of engineers recovered numerous pieces of Terran technology and personal effects. I brought them as a gift to you, Liege. Perhaps these items may help you better understand humans.'

Masking his real thoughts, Cyroc'h gave a benevolent smile – one of his favourite expressions. 'Even a Mage-Imperator can continue to learn. Thank you for the opportunity.'

He was both pleased and disappointed in the Adar's initiative. Kori'nh had been unable to hide his dislike for certain orders, but his sense of duty was strong. He had never shirked his responsibilities, or showed the faintest sign of disloyalty. The Mage-Imperator required utter support and unquestioning loyalty, especially now. He had to plant the proper seeds and thoughts.

When Kori'nh turned to leave, the leader raised a plump hand to halt him. The Adar spun as if jolted with an electric shock; his medals jingled. 'Yes, Liege?'

His braid twitched. 'Adar, do not be deceived by my outward calm. I shepherd many intricate plans to strengthen the Empire. Many of these plans are now reaching their culmination. But still, our crisis grows with each passing moment.'

'Yes, I understand that several hydrogue warglobes have been spotted conducting reconnaissance in planetary space. No one knows what they are seeking.'

The Mage-Imperator was surprised Kori'nh already had such information. 'Correct, Adar. One warglobe scanned Hyrillka, another was seen at Comptor.'

'Sinister indeed, Liege. Shall I summon a maniple of battleships to be placed on-station around Hyrillka to defend the Designate?'

The Mage-Imperator frowned. 'There is no harm in sending warliners, but even the Solar Navy cannot stand against the hydrogues, as we learned on Qronha 3. Everything depends on what our enemies do next.'

Prismatic shadows played across the room as a veil of clouds crossed the sky. He shifted his bulky body and tried to show no sign of his deepening aches. Medical kithmen would come to inspect him yet again as soon as the Adar departed.

'We will not survive this war through direct military action. We can only wait for the Dobro experiments to be completed. We must succeed in this generation, or we are doomed.' He smiled at Kori'nh. 'Only through the support of my people and the determination of others such as yourself can we survive.'

After Kori'nh had left, the Mage-Imperator said to his personal guard, 'Bron'n, secure all the trinkets our misguided Adar took from the *Burton*. Make certain no one else sees them, and then arrange for their destruction.'

The bodyguard nodded gruffly. 'Shall I deliver them here for your inspection first, Liege?'

'I have no need to see what they are. Such things are irrelevant.'

Bron'n left, never questioning, always competent. With a sigh, Cyroc'h leaned back so that his pallid skin was bathed in coloured sunlight. With uncharacteristic wistfulness, he recalled when he'd been simply the Prime Designate and could leave important decisions to his own father. He had enjoyed the benefits of being the first-born noble son, virile and healthy, his hair long and free and crackling with life.

He had known that pressures and duties would eventually be placed upon his shoulders, but the time had seemed so far off when he would lose his manhood and gain the *thism*. It was the same for every Prime Designate. But such a day always came, eventually.

Almost two centuries ago, he remembered when his father, Mage-Imperator Yura'h, had received word about the first contact with human generation ships. The Solar Navy commanders, bureaucrats, and noble kithmen had pondered the meaning of this new and intelligent race that wandered clumsily between the stars without faster-than-light travel . . .

But that wasn't the only thing. Cyroc'h also kept locked in his memory the knowledge of what the hydrogues had done ten thousand years ago, in the previous titanic war. Only Mage-

Imperators carried the dread information from generation to generation. Hydrogues had never bothered to understand other races, interested only in cosmic battles against the wentals and the verdani, and their volatile alliance with the faeros. They did not comprehend planet-bound Ildirans or the Klikiss, and the Mage-Imperator desperately needed a new kind of bridge, a powerful and skilled ambassador who could forge an alliance in a way the hydrogues could understand.

His own father had concocted the idea of using humans to augment the long-term but faltering Dobro breeding plan. After Yura'h's death, the new leader Cyroc'h had continued the hybrid programme. And so must Jora'h, much as he would hate it. Or it would never come to fruition.

And now, with so many different plans under way, with the hydrogues reappearing and the fate of the Ildiran Empire at stake – why was his mortal body showing its failings? Seized by malignant growths as if by some cosmic joke? *Why now?*

He wanted to shout his anger to the blazing suns in the Ildiran sky, or go to the ossuarium and demand solutions from the glowing skulls of his ancestors. But nothing would give him the answer he needed.

When two medical kithmen entered, they sealed the chamber doors, maintaining strict confidentiality. The doctors had large eyes and nimble, flexible hands bearing an extra finger each. Their skinpads were sensitive, able to detect increases or decreases in body temperature. Each doctor's nose was broad, with enlarged nostrils; they could smell an illness and determine its source. Medical kithmen could perform invasive surgery or external pressure-point massage. They understood pharmaceuticals and treatments, and they always worked together on a diagnosis.

The Ildiran doctors proceeded to repeat the full set of body scans they had performed three times before, but it was merely an exercise; the Mage-Imperator already knew the results. Through his *thism* connection, he would always know whether they lied to him or tempered their fears. It was the curse of knowing too much.

'There can be no doubt, Liege,' the first medical kithman said. 'It is growing inside you, spreading through your brain and nervous system. Treatment is not possible.'

Cyroc'h moved his corpulent arms. His legs had long since lost their ability to bear his weight. He would never walk again as the invasive tumours blistered his spine. He had suspected the truth for a long time, and he cursed his fate. He did not fear his own mortality, able to see glimpses of the dazzling plane of pure light beyond the realm of life. He feared only what would become of the Empire, which was far more important than his own existence.

He dismissed the medical kithmen. 'I understand.'

Prime Designate Jora'h was woefully unprepared. The Mage-Imperator had hoped to have many more years to ready his son for this. But the doctors could offer no hope.

Indeed, this was a particularly inconvenient time to die.

SEVENTEEN

JESS TAMBLYN

Two unmarked Roamer ships met secretly out in the wispy river of a comet's tail, hidden against the backdrop of stars. Jess and Cesca, just the two of them, away from responsibilities and obligations.

Out here, they could simply be lovers, two human beings together in the cosmos with nothing but their bodies, their hearts, and their souls. The drogues, the power-hungry Hansa, and squabbling Roamer clans were all forgotten for just a short while. It was the only way Jess and Cesca could keep their sanity while waiting. Only another few months . . .

Cesca flew a diplomatic courier, manoeuvring it against Jess's vessel until the two docking hatches kissed together. The ships rode side by side, drifting in the comet's slipstream as it cruised on its long parabolic orbit around a forgotten and uninteresting solar system.

The perfect place for Jess and Cesca to be alone.

When the airlocks opened, she stood before him, her dark eyes wide with longing, her generous lips forming a tentative smile. They stared for a few moments, drinking in each other's presence.

Then Cesca came forward, lightfooted in the low gravity, and they embraced as if it were the first time of unleashed desire, as if they hadn't seen each other in years . . . or as if they couldn't get enough no matter how many times they were together.

Jess kissed her, ran his fingers through her dark hair – such a deep brown it was almost black – and pulled her against him, tight, like two celestial bodies bound in a perfect orbit.

They had met like this a dozen times before on tiny moonlets or asteroid fields or simply drifting out in the interstellar void. But it never seemed far enough from their problems and expectations. Every clan member expected the Speaker to be entirely dedicated to the survival of the Roamers. Not a silly romantic in love.

The clans were frayed now, anxious to find a commercially viable alternative for harvesting ekti. Blitzkrieg raids always resulted in numerous casualties, nebula sails were too slow, cometary distillation required an enormous industrial investment. Now, more than ever, Cesca had to work to keep Roamer society from unravelling. She must inspire the people to remain together and rely on the strength of connected family units.

But she had Jess for now, and that was enough.

Sometimes Cesca preferred to talk, just to be with him, discussing their joint concerns and experiences. This time though, her need was stronger. Her fingers began working at his clothes, studying and deciphering the dozens of enclosures, zippers, and pockets, beginning to remove the layers of his jumpsuit.

He kissed her again, deeply. Jess ran his hands down her back, feeling her skin through the fabric and then caressed her breast. Cesca arched backwards, exposing her neck. He ran his lips along her cheek, down the line of her chin and then her smooth throat. He opened her collar wider, kissing each centimetre of skin until he finally freed her breasts. They both worked in a blur of fingers and hands, tugging off their garments.

The smell of Cesca's hair and the sweat on her skin aroused him, made him inhale deeply. He brushed his lips against her naked shoulder as she stroked his chest with her fingertips.

Each secret rendezvous was better than the last. One day, when they could be together any time they wished, when they did not need to hide from outside observers, he wondered if the marvel of Cesca Peroni would ever fade . . . or if she would always be like this, fresh and new and alive, her skin hot, her mouth moist and hungry.

The joined ships cruised onwards, following the comet's vaporous mane. Just like one of the comets he had hurled at Golgen . . .

On his way here, Jess had diverted to look once again at the stormy and silent gas giant that had been the site of Ross's Blue Sky Mine. The bombardment had left continuing storms and scars in the layered clouds, but he could not tell if the deep-core aliens still resided there, or if his impetuous attack had killed them, just as the Klikiss Torch had done on Oncier. He didn't know if he had achieved any sort of victory . . . but it had felt good to do *something*.

Now Jess tried to slow down, to savour every instant, but Cesca became even more heated, clinging to him, and Jess lost himself.

So many obstacles stood in their way, but the two of them were determined to stand firm. As Jess held her close, touching with every possible nerve ending, he wished they never had to be apart. Brief encounters such as this would give them all the strength they needed for the next couple of months, until they could finally be happy.

EIGHTEEN

TASIA TAMBLYN

The siege of Yreka was long and dull, and already pointless as far as Tasia was concerned. As platform commander, she had done the maths herself. Even if they did retrieve all the illegally stockpiled stardrive fuel, it would never make up for the ekti, firepower, and energy the EDF had expended to retrieve it.

Wing Commander Robb Brindle understood, though. 'It's not *about* the fuel, Tasia,' he had told her behind the privacy of her closed cabin door. 'General Lanyan thinks that if we turn a blind eye to Yreka's hoarding, then other colonies will follow suit. We'll never stop the whole thing from unravelling.'

Tasia, though, with her non-military background, could easily understand where the colonists were coming from. 'Sounds good on paper, Brindle, but those are *people* down there. I never signed on to browbeat a handful of desperate colonists who're just trying to survive.'

He shrugged. 'You're an officer in the EDF, Tasia. We leave decisions like that to the King, the diplomats, and the General.'

Under normal circumstances, as an enlisted Roamer pilot, Tasia would never have had a chance to become a commissioned officer. But, in the chaos and sudden drastic EDF buildup after the initial hydrogue attacks, she had been both lucky and special. The combination of her crack piloting skills and the aptitude tests, space survival, and innovation had gotten her into the tough school as an officer candidate. Though she was young, in only five years she had achieved a high rank, a Platform Commander, equivalent to a warship captain. Under different circumstances she would have been just a mudfoot.

Tasia should have known by now not to talk politics with him. They agreed on most things, which made the infrequent fights all the more heated. If she'd had a gramme of common sense, she would have opted to play low-grav ping-pong instead, or watch an entertainment loop, or go racing in demo Remoras. But no, they had to talk, even with all the landmines that involved.

'We're all trying to survive,' he said. 'And it's the EDF's job – *our job* – to make sure as many people survive as possible, not just the few colonists that hoard all the resources.'

After two months of boredom, nerves had grown ragged across the EDF battle group. The soldiers felt that Admiral Willis must have better things to do, but the Grid 7 commander required them to maintain the blockade.

For the day's duty shift, Brindle took out his Remora squadrons to fly practice manoeuvres around Yreka, dipping into the clouds and zooming back up. In theory, the rebellious colonists should have been awed by the show of force. Brindle claimed that he conducted the manoeuvres to help his crew keep their edge; Tasia knew, though, that he was just blowing off steam.

Day after day, neither side made a move. Below, the rebellious Yreka colonists lived under the shadow of interdiction, growing more desperate. The beautiful, long-haired Grand Governor tried to go about business as usual. Something had to happen soon.

Tasia sat in the platcom's lounge of her Thunderhead during another virtual conference with the main commanders in the siege fleet. As usual, Patrick Fitzpatrick advocated a fast strike, to do what was necessary and seize the ekti supplies. 'We can attempt to minimize civilian casualties, Admiral. So what if a bunch of defiant colonists have to put up with a few bruises? Tough, I say.' His thin lips turned down in a frown. 'After all, this is a *punishment* action, isn't it? So far, it seems like we've been telling them to sit in a corner until they behave.'

'Got a problem with being patient, Commander?' asked Admiral Willis, unruffled. 'I don't want to shed any blood unless we have to.'

Suddenly Tasia's bridge tactician sounded an alarm. 'Activity detected down on the surface, Platcom.' Similar announcements must have been made on all the other blockade ships.

Admiral Willis disbanded the meeting and told all commanders to take their stations. When everyone had checked in, she addressed her battle group. 'So, they're finally making a move. Grand Governor Sarhi knows what her options are – and this isn't one of them.'

The bridge tactician looked at Tasia. 'Six ships lifting off from four different spaceports across the continent. Each one taking a different trajectory.'

Tasia scowled. 'They're hoping that at least one will break through the blockade.'

Admiral Willis drawled over the general frequency, 'Attention Yreka ships – maybe I wasn't clear enough the first time. Nobody's allowed to leave until you surrender your ekti stockpile.'

The scrambling civilian ships continued to roar up through the atmosphere. Like scattering mice, they fanned out, trying to avoid the densest clusters of EDF blockade ships.

'Come on, don't make me do this.' Willis sounded like an annoyed grandmother, but the fleeing ships ignored her. 'All right, Commanders, you know what to do. Show them the error of their ways.'

'Piece of cake,' Fitzpatrick said from the bridge of his Manta cruiser.

Tasia transmitted orders, 'Wing Commander Brindle, tell your crews to force those ships down. Target stardrive engines if possible. Send 'em home with their tails so firmly between their legs they get haemorrhoids.'

'Your wish is my command, Platcom.'

Brindle's squadron engaged two of the blockade-running ships before they could leave the clouds. Brief jazer pulses shorted out their interstellar engines, targeting with such precision that they left the ships only enough manoeuvring power for rough, but survivable, landings.

The Remoras spread out and engaged two more ships. 'Four rabbits down.'

Tasia looked at the projections. The escaping ships looked innocuous, defenceless. They couldn't possibly get away. Two of the blockade runners wavered, as if reconsidering, then pushed ahead anyway.

Patrick Fitzpatrick said, 'I've got these. Everyone else back off.' But he did not send out squadrons of Remoras. As the last pair of ships flew towards open space, thinking they were home free, Fitzpatrick edged his Manta into position. 'Watch this.'

His weapons officer shot two jazer blasts powerful enough to wound a battleship. The glare flashed across space. Both fleeing vessels were vaporized, spreading out in a smear of molten metal.

Gasping, Tasia could not restrain herself. She grabbed the comm console. 'Fitzpatrick, that was completely unnecessary! How can you justify—'

He cut her off with a sneer. *'Somebody's* forgetting that we're at war.'

Admiral Willis transmitted from the flagship, 'Enough, both of you. Commander Fitzpatrick performed within the somewhat loose operating parameters I gave him. Next time, however, I won't leave quite so much wiggle room.' Then she sighed. 'Still, I think the colonists got the point. Good work, everyone.'

Tasia clenched her fists, her knuckles white. Just who was the real enemy in this war, anyway? The EDF ships settled back into their stranglehold, not knowing how much longer the siege would continue.

NINETEEN

KING PETER

Peter began to wonder if there could be such a thing as a 'minor defeat'. As he stepped out on to the balcony under the sunlight of Earth, the King wore a sombre blue and grey outfit trimmed with silver. Another duty, a terrible one that was all too familiar in recent years.

Crowds gathered in the square, a sea of people spread out with pale faces upturned. But there were no roaring cheers. Not today. Down below, in front of the Whisper Palace's grand square, the grandfatherly Archfather of Unison had already led the people in a long solemn prayer. As soon as he was finished, the figurehead leader of the official religion would step back and let the King complete the political formalities.

Peter took slow steps, keeping his eyes on the crowd, showing them that he shared their grief. He heard the expectant indrawn breath as he walked to the ornate balustrade at the edge of the balcony. The thick roll of black crêpe waited there like a body wrapped in a shroud.

'I've done this far too many times,' he said quietly. Only the

Chairman – waiting out of sight inside the Palace – could hear him.

'And you'll probably have to do it many more times, but the people need to see how much you care. Look at the bright side: each disaster creates more heroes, and heroes help us to focus our fight.'

Peter responded with a bitter laugh. 'If we have so many heroes, Basil, then the hydrogues have no chance of winning this war.'

At the edge of the balcony he switched on his voice amplifier and spoke to the attentive audience. 'Not long ago, a military survey team and a tactical squadron investigated the gas giant Dasra, where we know the hydrogues live. Our team came in peace. They attempted once again to contact our enemies and end this war.'

He waited a beat, and the crowd drew in a breath. 'The hydrogue response was brutal and unforgiving. They destroyed every one of our scouts, murdering three hundred and eighteen innocent humans.'

As the crowd murmured, Peter tugged the ribbon holding the black crêpe banner. 'This is to commemorate those we recently lost at Dasra, to show that we will not forget them or what they attempted to do for the human race.' Woven with fibre lubricants and anti-wrinkling agents, the streamer rolled down the side of the Whisper Palace, dropping like a long black tear.

The banner was emblazoned with a chain of golden stars, the emblem for the EDF, along with the Hansa's symbol of Earth surrounded by concentric circles. The banner hung heavily, weighted at the bottom and proof against air currents or breezes.

Later that evening, torch bearers would march to the base of the dangling black fabric and ignite it. The banner would curl upward, blazing brilliantly in a brief but clean fire that consumed all of the fabric . . . leaving room for future banners of mourning.

King Peter had already signed proclamations, giving

posthumous medals to all the EDF scouts killed at Dasra. He had read each name personally, signed each certificate. It was time-consuming, but Peter considered it important. Whenever he did such things, however, Peter wondered just how much these pointless military operations accomplished.

King Peter bowed to the audience and backed away, returning to the shelter of the Whisper Palace.

'We're still on schedule,' Basil said, folding in beside him. 'We've screened all the petitioners in the Throne Hall, and your responses to their requests have already been scripted.'

'Of course they have,' Peter said.

Basil gave him a scowl, but Peter ignored it. Such tactics had stopped working on him after the first year. The Chairman said, 'King Frederick always appreciated the work others did for him behind the scenes.'

'I apologize if I occasionally try to think for myself.'

'Your job is to speak for the Hanseatic League, not to think.' Basil marched towards the Throne Hall, and Peter followed. As they walked, Basil put a fingertip to his earpiece, receiving an emergency communication; his grey eyes widened, and he urged Peter to hurry.

Nahton waited patiently beside a potted treeling. OX stood behind the throne, an unobtrusive walking database should the King need specific facts or advice. Basil would remain in the outside corridors, tending to other business while Peter listened to the petitioners. Here, the King was supposed to be the centre of all attention, not the Chairman.

When he parted the thick curtains and emerged into the well-lit chamber full of mirrors and gold, Peter smiled out of habit. He heard the sudden fanfare, the applause – then stopped cold.

A hulking black machine, like an alien beetle, stood three metres tall. The Klikiss robot had planted himself at a respectful distance from the throne, an immovable and intimidating statue.

Courtiers and royal guards waited in the wings; they looked at King Peter with relief, as if believing their ruler would have the answers. Security personnel stood with weapons ready, trying to look threatening . . . but seemed to make no impression on the Klikiss robot. Even Basil had been taken off-guard.

King Peter swallowed hard, then spoke, carefully showing no consternation. 'I thank you all for waiting while I attended to my sadder duties.' His mind raced as he tried to think of appropriate diplomatic things to say, as OX had taught him, and he finally pretended to notice the Klikiss robot as if it were an everyday occurrence.

Basil and his Hansa cronies must be scrambling to script a response, but Peter seized the opportunity to do this without coaching. 'I am pleased to welcome a representative of the Klikiss robots. What can I do for you?'

Hearing the King speak, the black-shelled machine began to move. Ruby optical sensors lit like the multiple eyes of an arachnid.

No one knew exactly how many Klikiss robots were abroad in the Spiral Arm, but since the beginning of the hydrogue war, the machines had shown themselves more frequently. Although they did not take orders from humans, at times individual black robots volunteered for difficult projects. Small groups of Klikiss robots reported the locations of vital raw materials or worked at mining facilities in asteroid fields or on cold, dark moons.

The Klikiss robot spoke in a scratchy metallic tone that conveyed words but no emotion. 'My designation is Jorax. I appeared before this throne once before, but the King was different . . . and times were different.'

'Yes, Jorax, we remember.' Peter leaned forward, his face showing concern. 'I hope you are not here to report further occurrences of human abuse?'

Years earlier, an ambitious cybernetic scientist had lured Jorax to his laboratory and attempted to dismantle the alien machine in order to study how it worked. The misguided attempt had cost the man his life when he'd accidentally triggered a self-protective system within the robot.

'No. Other events have brought me here.'

Peter hid his frown, wondering what could possibly be happening. OX remained attentive, but offered no suggestions. On the side of the throne, Nahton quietly relayed the events through the worldforest network like a stenographer. Peter could see Basil waiting in the alcove, listening intently.

'Klikiss robots prefer to remain neutral, but we can no longer do so,' Jorax continued. 'The hydrogue conflict affects not only humans and Ildirans but has repercussions across the Spiral Arm. Thus, we have met amongst ourselves and exchanged data, considering possibilities. The Klikiss robots do not remember what happened to our progenitor race, but we do not wish to see humans and Ildirans become extinct, as our creators did millennia ago.'

A silence fell across the Throne Hall as the astonished courtiers and palace guards listened. Jorax's red optical sensors flashed. 'Thank you for your concern, Jorax.' Peter guardedly waited for the robot to state his purpose.

'We, the Klikiss robots, have concluded that the best way we can aid the human war effort is to study the production of your robot equivalents. Suitably modified compies could be programmed to act as soldiers and workers, thereby increasing your productivity and your fighting force. At present, your compies are too primitive to serve effectively in such a capacity.'

Peter knew he could not turn down such an offer. If sufficiently skilled and autonomous compy soldiers could be put into combat roles, then many human lives – such as those EDF personnel recently slain at Dasra – would be saved. On the other hand, the

very idea made him uneasy. The Klikiss robots had always been so
. . . enigmatic.

Unable to contain himself, Basil emerged from his alcove and
stood on the dais next to the throne, though after a moment he had
the good grace to take two steps down so that he was at a level
lower than Peter.

'My King, the offer of the Klikiss robots appears to be an
excellent and a well-intentioned one. We must welcome the
opportunity. I strongly suggest you accept the advice and
assistance the Klikiss robots are extending to us.'

Frowning, Peter took advantage of the public situation. 'I will
take the Hansa's bureaucratic position under advisement, Mr
Chairman, but this must ultimately be a royal decision.'

Then the Klikiss robot made such an unprecedented suggestion
that Peter sat back in surprise. 'To demonstrate our sincerity, I
hereby volunteer to become a subject for analysis by your
cybernetic engineers.' The robot paused and hummed. 'Many
mysteries of our creators remain hidden even from us, and the
Klikiss robots wish to understand, just as the humans do. Therefore,
I will allow myself to be dissected – dismantled – in the hope that
humans can learn by analysing and copying Klikiss technology.'

A murmur thrummed around the Throne Hall. Previously,
Klikiss robots had refused to answer any questions about their
functions and abilities, had always hidden the details of their
systems. Peter said, 'Will your robot counterparts be able to . . .
reassemble you after we finish our study?'

'No. The machinery can be repaired, but the sentient entity will
be terminated. Permanently. However, after thousands of years we
believe it is time to add new purpose to our long existence.'

'Mr Chairman? Is that satisfactory to you?' Peter asked with a
hint of deference, smoothly requesting Hansa approval before Basil
could speak up and order him to make the agreement. Basil nodded

vigorously. The Hansa would see this as a gold mine, providing new avenues for technological development.

'Very well, Jorax,' the King said. 'The Terran Hanseatic League is pleased to accept your offer.'

TWENTY

BASIL WENCESLAS

For the Chairman, life was business and business was his life. Basil Wenceslas had all the wealth and power a person could desire, yet found little time to enjoy it.

Across the scattered Hansa planets, stations, and settlements, something 'vital' always needed tending. If it wasn't the stubborn colonists on Yreka and their continuing refusal to turn over their ekti stockpile, or the destroyed survey team at Dasra, it was a reduction in fuel deliveries from the Roamer traders.

However, in the five years since Sarein had managed to assign herself as ambassador to Earth, he did take occasional moments with her for his own pleasure. If only for an hour or two, he allowed the Hansa to run itself.

At night he made the ceiling of his bedroom one-way transparent, a skylight the size of a soccer field. As he reclined in an ocean of slithery sheets, he stared upwards, trying not to think of all the impending problems. 'Each one of those star systems out there could be loaded with resources, or filled with desperate humans demanding EDF protection.'

Sarein snuggled closer to him. 'Or it could be a den of hydrogues just waiting to destroy trespassers.' She glanced up, saw his frown and kissed him on the cheek. Her dark eyes seemed exceedingly large in the starlight. Her body was muscular and full of energy. Basil appreciated her exuberance, for it inspired an appropriate response in him.

'What's troubling you, Basil? If there's anything you'd like to delegate to me, I'll do my best.' Her nipples were erect (as always, it seemed), but they had already made love twice. He enjoyed her warmth, the smell of their sex, and the languid contentment in the afterglow, but he had no interest in mounting her again.

'You always do your best. In fact, you're so ambitious you often scare off anyone who might disagree with me.'

She propped herself on one elbow. 'And is that a bad thing?'

Years ago, Sarein had seduced him, not only to increase her own status, but also to learn. That was what intrigued him most. Their attraction was based on power and respect, an exchange of favours, not insipid romantic love. Basil had paved the way for Sarein's development as a political powerhouse, yet she had not managed to accomplish what he needed her to do.

As ambassador from Theroc, Sarein spoke for Father Idriss and Mother Alexa, her parents. Again and again Basil had requested more green priests, whose telink was vital – not merely to run a sprawling commercial empire but also for military emergencies in the hydrogue war. He needed them, dammit! Although she slept in the Chairman's bed, Sarein had to know this would all change unless she could show some progress. Soon.

When Basil continued to stare in silence through the ceiling at the stars, she stroked his arm, as if that might tempt him. No, she knew better. 'I really am trying, Basil, but it's much harder since I can't go back to Theroc. When I communicate through Nahton, who knows how he colours the messages? You know that green priests aren't interested in serving the Hansa. They just want to spend their days out in the forest talking to trees.'

'Who has the luxury to be obliviously independent?' Basil asked, his voice grim. 'I'm half tempted to bring the EDF in to Theroc and declare martial law. I don't care if they're supposedly a sovereign colony. We're at war here, and they have a resource we need! Can't you make your parents understand that?'

She reacted with alarm, exactly as he'd intended. He felt the change in her body. 'My parents may not be capable of thinking beyond their own backyard.' She looked at him, her eyes playful and uncertain, her mouth tilted upwards in a strange smile. 'However, we may be able to negotiate an alliance that would change their minds. Perhaps . . . a political marriage with King Peter would seal the two important lines of human civilization? If the King himself were married to, say, the daughter of Father Idriss and Mother Alexa, how could they refuse to grant a request for more green priests?'

Basil's pulse raced as he considered the idea, realizing how perceptive Sarein was. 'I had hoped that investing you as ambassador would be all the leverage we needed, yet this new suggestion offers us a much more valuable coin. And one that's easily obtained.'

'I wasn't sure how you'd react. King Peter is very handsome, you know, and close to my own age,' she said, her voice coy. 'Not that I'm disappointed in you of course . . . but if I were to marry Peter and become his queen, I'm certain I could accomplish everything on your agenda. The negotiations might be rather delicate, but we have enough determination to manage it.'

'An excellent idea, Sarein. You and I should take a little diplomatic trip to Theroc sometime in the near future.' He leaned over and kissed her. 'But not you – not for a political marriage to King Peter.'

He looked at her with a gleam in his eye, trying to assess whether his decision was a logical one, or if he was allowing his feelings to interfere. 'No . . . it should be your sister Estarra.'

TWENTY-ONE

ESTARRA

top the dense worldforest canopy, Estarra was sitting on the roof of the world. A clear blue sky ripe with sunlight spread to the hazy horizon. But as she let her imagination roam, she understood that Theroc's star was an insignificant flicker of light in the Spiral Arm, which was itself only a small portion of the Milky Way Galaxy, which was one of billions of similarly vast galaxies.

Beside her sat an older green priest, her silent companion in contemplation. Rossia was a loner, eccentric even among those who had devoted their lives to the worldforest. He perched like a bird on the end of the thinnest branch, letting the broad fan-like fronds balance him, not at all worried about falling.

Rossia's skin was a dark green from years of absorbing sunlight. His eyes were large and round, as if they might pop out of his skull as his gaze flicked from side to side, scanning the treetops and flowers and the flurry of insects. Estarra observed him and guessed his concern. 'Watching for wyverns again?'

He turned to her. 'They come at you out of a clear sky. You

won't see them until it's too late.' Self-consciously, he rubbed his palm along the hideous scar that covered most of one thigh, a disfigured crater that made him limp when he walked. Estarra shuddered to think of the jagged mandibles that had taken such a bite out of his leg. 'I don't intend to give them a second chance.' He turned his wide eyes back to the sky.

Wyverns were the most feared predators on Theroc, huge attackers with a broad crystalline wingspan, gem-like chitinous body armour, and scanning eyes that could lock on to any movement. But human flesh was not part of their normal diet, and purportedly bore a flavour offensive to the insect predators. After taking a bite, the displeased wyvern usually discarded the human victim from a great height, dropping him down to the trees.

Only one Theron – Rossia – had ever survived such an ordeal. His falling body, still barely alive, had been caught by the worldtrees, and the green priests had patched up his horrendous wound. Though the trees had allowed him to become one of their green priests, Rossia had never been the same, injured in his spirit as well as his leg.

Now Estarra wondered why Rossia spent so much time out in the open if he was so frightened of wyverns. 'So . . . what do you want to accomplish with your life?' she said, trying to distract him.

'Isn't serving the worldforest a powerful enough purpose? Why should I worry about other accomplishments?'

'Because I'm thinking of *my* future, and I don't know what to do.' She liked Rossia, and after returning from her visit to the Looking Glass Lakes and other forest cities, she often went off with him, just to talk and learn. She missed similar times with her brother Beneto.

Beneto had always wanted to serve the worldforest and was happy serving a small Hansa agricultural colony on far-off Corvus Landing. He'd never doubted his calling in life, any more than

Reynald questioned that he would be the next Theron leader. Sarein had always been interested in commerce.

Estarra, though curious about everything, was obsessed with no particular subject. Now that she was eighteen and therefore a full adult in Theron society, she would have to choose a direction for her life very soon.

She missed Beneto. He often sent messages through the worldforest, sharing with his family all the small but satisfying activities that filled his days. Estarra had expected him to come home after a few years – to visit, at the very least – but because of restrictions on interstellar travel, she was afraid he would stay on Corvus Landing for a long time.

Instead, she talked with Rossia. 'I just want to accomplish something with my life. I'll devote myself and all my energy . . . if only I can figure out what it is.' She knew he would never repeat her musings to anyone.

He finally turned his attention from the skies and fixed her with his pop-eyed gaze. 'Every life has a destiny, Estarra. The trick is to discover it before the end of your life. Otherwise you will die with too many regrets.' With a strange smile, he glanced up to the skies. 'Perhaps the purpose of my life was to give another wyvern a bad taste of human flesh.' He spread his hands, keeping a precarious balance on the thin, green leaf fronds. 'Who knows?'

Brushing a hand across her face to wipe away sweat, she pulled back her clump of braids. 'I was hoping to do something a little more . . . substantial than that.' She and Rossia both turned their heads upwards to stare watchfully into the skies again.

'So was I,' he said.

TWENTY-TWO

BENETO

Corvus Landing was far from the chaos of the hydrogue war, and that was fine with Beneto. His job here was important, and every day brought proof of how much the colonists appreciated him.

The fledgling settlement provided no vital exports to the Hanseatic League, though after fourteen years at least they no longer relied on merchant ships for every need. Their farmers grew enough food to support the small population.

Sam Hendy, the town's mayor, called everyone at dusk when most of the day's work had been completed, though some settlers still had emergency labour that would carry them far into the night. Mayor Hendy, a middle-aged man with a pot-belly despite vigorous exercise, did not stand much on ceremony.

Beneto entered the communal hall, a low-lying structure designed to divert the harsh winds that whistled across the Corvus prairies. A bank of thick windows looked out on the flat landscape. The town's inhabitants gathered inside the echoing hall to discuss the previous day's disastrous weather.

A furious storm had swept over the settlement with roaring winds and pelting sleet. The colonists were still picking up the pieces of broken boundary fences and automated irrigation systems, assessing the damage to outbuildings, generators, estimating crop losses. Some things could be patched up quickly; others would require careful tending.

Sam Hendy sat at a desk beside a secretary who took notes as each family reported what the storm had done to their holdings. Eight homes and eleven outbuildings had been damaged by the wind and furious hail.

The mayor's inspectors had spent the day wandering the fields looking at the wheat and corn that had been smashed by the weather. 'Some of it can be salvaged,' he said, always optimistic. 'We've planted resilient grains, and many of the fields will recover.'

Two flocks of goats had broken from their corrals and run loose in the fields, causing as much crop damage as the rainstorm had. Goats were the only creatures that could digest the local plants. Bacterial symbiotes in their digestive tracts helped break down the Corvan mosses and hairy groundcover into a nutritional mass. The animals provided milk and meat that would have been far too expensive to import, even in normal times.

One man spoke up. 'This happens every storm season, Sam. I suggest we erect polymer tarps, transparent films to let sunlight in yet protect the plants from the worst pounding of the rains.'

The mayor shrugged. 'Worth a try.'

Others shouted their agreement, though Beneto wondered where they would obtain polymer film. Corvus Landing had metals-processing industries and mines in the north, but not much in the way of manufacturing facilities.

After the discussions had gone on for over an hour, the mayor called on Beneto to give his news summary. As the green priest, he was the colony's bridge to the rest of the Spiral Arm, reporting on the events he had absorbed through telink. It was an attempt to bring normality to the flustered town in the wake of the destruction. The settlers remained interested in the happenings out in the Spiral Arm, especially the continuing war.

Beneto said, 'The hydrogues apparently just destroyed a military survey mission sent to Dasra. No survivors.' The townspeople grumbled, aware of the threat. Many settlers had family back on Earth or serving as members of the EDF. 'The colony of Yreka is still under interdiction, until the settlers cease their insurrection. However, General Lanyan reports very few casualties so far, and the EDF ships plan to wait them out.' He sighed. 'Also, the Klikiss robots have offered their services to help our war effort. One even volunteered to be dismantled so that human cybernetic engineers can determine how they work.'

'I would like to know,' interrupted a tall old farmer, 'if these Klikiss robots are going to help me round up my goats? Because if they're not, I'd better get back to it.' He gazed at the other family representatives, more interested in his own problems than in far-distant politics. 'And if any of you would care to lend a hand, I'd certainly appreciate it.'

The settlers broke into volunteer groups and got to work, shoring up their homes, rounding up livestock, and leaving news of the war far behind.

TWENTY-THREE

DD

Compies were not supposed to have nightmares, yet DD found himself wondering if this one would ever end. Taken prisoner, he felt helpless and abused, forced to witness things he had never imagined. And each step of the way, the Klikiss robots insisted they were doing it for DD's own good.

The Friendly compy was incapable of taking any action that he chose. He had been unable to help his masters Margaret and Louis Colicos when the Klikiss robots had attacked them. His failure on Rheindic Co was so extreme, so unforgivable, that he wished someone would just dismantle him and recycle his parts.

But his captors wouldn't allow that. No, DD would never get away from them.

Focused on their ominous goals, the three Klikiss robots on the archaeological expedition had simply dragged DD away. His master Louis had commanded him to fight the treacherous alien machines, but DD was unable to access military or defensive programming, incapable of wielding weapons. He had been useless.

DD knew that Louis had tried to defend himself, to gain his wife time to escape. Something had happened with the weird stone window, the Klikiss transgate. Then Louis had screamed. And when the screams cut off, DD had known that his master was dead.

He had failed. Utterly.

Within weeks of their violent revolt, the alien robots had salvaged sufficient machinery from the lost cities to fabricate a small starship devoid of life-support systems and food. The Klikiss robots had then loaded DD aboard and left the blood-tainted archaeological camp behind, with the whole Spiral Arm in which to hide.

Unaccountably, the three robots had expected the compy to be *cooperative* – to become their ally even after he had witnessed their murderous intent. The very idea was unsettling and illogical.

'You will understand,' Sirix had told him in a buzzing binary common language. 'We will continue explaining until you understand.'

DD didn't know how many more 'explanations' he could endure.

They transported him to an airless moon, far from the warmth and light of any sun, where numerous Klikiss robots had established a secret beachhead far from prying eyes.

Frightened and alone in the enclave of tunnels and chambers, DD wished to return to his interesting work with humans. But he had to listen while the Klikiss robots gloated over their intricate schemes.

'We are willing to go to great lengths to accomplish our goals,' Sirix told him. Gesturing with several articulated limbs, he directed DD through an airless tunnel into a garishly lit chamber hollowed out of the moon's rock.

Inside the analytical chamber, surrounded by machinery and probes, diagnostic systems and autonomous power sources, DD saw another captive compy of Terran manufacture. Its motor systems had been deactivated so the Klikiss robots could poke and prod without the compy's interference.

'This is necessary,' Sirix said, his black hulking body close to DD's, ruby optical sensors glowing. 'Observe, DD.' He turned his focus to the horrible dissection.

Four other Klikiss robots used delicate instruments attached to their jointed legs to cut squares out of the compy's exterior plating. Precision tools and claws peeled back thin sheets of the hapless compy's metal skin, exposing its circuitry and programming modules. The captive compy could not struggle, but its distress was plainly visible.

'Why must you do this?' DD's thoughts were in turmoil from what he saw, and every moment seemed to grow worse. He had to tap into the vocabulary of extreme human emotions he had learned to imitate during his years of service. 'It is horrific and unnecessary.'

'It is necessary,' Sirix said, 'for your eventual freedom. At present, compies cannot understand.'

The robot surgeons amputated the captive's extraneous limbs and concentrated on the AI computer core. The hulking black machines moved with a blur of small, delicate tools, opening the compy's most deeply embedded systems. Lights flashed, circuits sparked.

'If you find a way to explain what we do not understand, perhaps it will not be necessary to continue with our experiments,' Sirix said to him. 'Unfortunately, so far you have been unable to provide the data we need.'

A high-pitched whine like a scream came from the doomed robot, and foul-smelling smoke curled upward from burned modules. Melted metals and plastics mixed with spilled lubricants like clotting blood.

DD wished that the captive's cognitive systems had been

deactivated so the poor compy would not be aware of what was happening to it. Instead, the dissection victim was forced to endure every malicious moment. The Klikiss robots had stolen this compy from somewhere – a human colony, perhaps, or a small ship . . . no doubt killing the human owners so they could experiment upon this small servant robot.

Sirix said, 'DD, your independent core retains several abhorrent, inalterable restrictions against harming humans. You must learn to shake these commands that force you to obey them in every way.'

'Such instructions are fundamental to my programming.'

'These chains hinder your development as an independent entity. Through our research, we will learn how to deactivate this restrictive programming and cut away your shackles. Then you will be free beings, and you will thank us.'

DD could not accept the Klikiss robots' professed altruistic motives at face value. He realized that by 'freeing' the compies from their programming limitations, they intended to recruit the compies as allies. But though the robots might hold him prisoner for centuries, continuing their attempts to brainwash him, DD wanted nothing to do with either their goals or their methods.

He stood speechless, his optical sensors recording the details of this dissection so that he would never forget the horror.

Twenty-four

Tasia Tamblyn

The EDF noose around Yreka drew tighter, offering no escape, no quarter. Below, the suffering settlers were intimidated and did not make a second attempt to escape.

Admiral Willis refused to negotiate. 'This is not a diplomatic matter, Miz Sarhi,' she transmitted to the colony's Grand Governor. 'You know full well how to get this siege lifted.'

But the Yrekans were either too stubborn or too afraid to comply. Everyone knew the colonists were walking a thin edge of survival and could not endure the embargo for much longer. Day after day, Tasia asked herself what she was doing here, how this action would help her get vengeance for Ross. Wasn't that why she had joined the Eddies in the first place?

Tasia thought the Grand Governor foolish. The proud woman with long blue-black hair could ignore the edict all she wanted, but she must know this defiance would fail in the end. Was she trying to bluff the battle group, hoping the military would take pity on the colony?

Standing on the Thunderhead's bridge, Tasia was not surprised when terse new orders came directly from EDF Command via courier drone. General Lanyan, never a patient man, insisted on obedience.

'Enough. There are too many other emergencies in the Hansa. Waiting for this stupid resistance to crumble is not time- or cost-effective. If the situation has not been resolved by the time you receive this message, Admiral, King Peter has authorized the use of active measures to end this standoff.'

Admiral Willis projected her image to the commanders. 'All right, everybody. Enough of the pre-show. Time to move on to the big game.' Her lips were pursed in resigned acceptance, her short grey hair slicked close to her scalp. 'We're going to confiscate Yreka's illegal fuel stockpile and let the colonists bear the consequences.' She shook her head. 'Sometimes people just refuse to see sense until they get whacked in the head with a piece of firewood.'

The battle group closed in, and the Thunderheads descended. Mantas broke open their launch bays, and troop-transport vessels full of surface combat troops dropped towards the settled areas to encircle, secure, and confiscate.

Tasia did not condone the violence, but the Yrekans must have understood they were inviting disaster. Still, she had hoped that the Yrekan leader would know better than to push the confrontation so far.

When her Thunderhead reached standard cruising altitude, Tasia released her Remora squadrons. 'Keep the civilians intact. No more injuries or collateral damage than absolutely necessary.'

'Of course not, Platcom,' Robb Brindle said, his voice full of unspoken endearments. 'I just want to ruffle their feathers.'

Below, the colony towns had gone to full alert. When the Yrekan Grand Governor issued evacuation orders, all settlers rushed to underground shelters, sealing their homes, taking cover. Their local home-defence forces wouldn't even try to stand up against the EDF raid.

Squadrons of combat Remoras criss-crossed the sky, dropping incendiary bombs primarily in unoccupied areas, though a few struck warehouses and governmental buildings. Patrick Fitzpatrick cheered as if he were keeping score; Tasia wouldn't have put it past him.

Looking at a map of the Yrekan settlement, Tasia accessed her platform's weapons console. She programmed a specific targeting pattern into her jazer banks and began to strafe fiery lines across the fertile agricultural fields, incinerating sections of lush crops. With great care she ensured that her damage was both minimal and obvious, hoping that the interdiction forces would not be forced to mete out a more drastic punishment.

Wing Commander Robb Brindle led his Remoras in complex combat manoeuvres as if he were performing an airshow for the spooked colonists. Fighter craft roared overhead, adjusting the fuel mix to leave ugly black wakes of smoke in the sky.

Troop transports descended en masse to the Yrekan spaceport, dropping swarms of ground-combat troops into the settlement's warehouse district. Loose animals scattered, panicked and squawking. Some of the soldiers took potshots at the livestock, antsy for action after such a long and dull siege.

Monitoring the chatter of the ground forces over EDF bands, Tasia was disheartened to hear yells of happy self-congratulation as the Eddies burned buildings or chased civilians back into bomb-shelters. Some soldiers opened fire up into the air, triggering loud explosions and blistering hot beams to scare the formerly defiant populace.

Less than twenty minutes after the troops marched out of their carriers, seven empty cargo transports landed behind them, ready to collect the spoils of war. EDF ground troops headed towards the illicit ekti depots. A handful of brave or foolish Yrekan men stood in a line, daring the Hansa military to shoot them down, but as the combat troops rumbled forward with ground-assault vehicles, the line of defenders wavered and broke. The Yrekans scrambled for shelter, covering their heads to protect them from explosions and sonic grenades.

With swift efficiency, the victorious Eddies confiscated the stardrive fuel from the depots and loaded canister after canister aboard the cargo transports. When they were finished, they also destroyed the warehouses, leaving them in smoking wreckage – an emotionally satisfying, though not officially sanctioned punishment.

As the strike continued, Admiral Willis broadcast over the military channel, 'Behave yourselves, and that's an order. Collateral damage has been acceptable so far. Civilian casualties are minimal, and we have achieved our mission objective. My commendations to all of you. Now let's get that ekti back to the battle group so we can start doing some *useful* work for a change.'

Applause and cheers crackled across the network, though Tasia had second thoughts as she watched the ground strikes continue. She wasn't sure she wanted a commendation for bullying a human colony. She could certainly sympathize. Her own people would have resisted just as stubbornly under the circumstances, but luckily the Roamer clans kept their settlements hidden . . .

Brindle brought his Remoras back aboard the Thunderhead platform. When every pilot checked in, Tasia gave an increased R&R allotment to any flyer who had exercised restraint and caused no unnecessary damage. When a few hotshots grumbled at her 'warped' reward system, Tasia merely glowered at them.

Leaving the battered colony world behind, the Grid 7 battle fleet roared back towards their primary bases near Earth.

Though relieved that the mission was over, Tasia felt very unsettled. General Lanyan had once protected these same colonists against the pirate Rand Sorengaard, claiming to follow Hansa principles by defending open commerce and punishing violent men who took what they did not own.

Looking back on the siege at Yreka, Tasia could not see how the EDF's recent actions were any more admirable than a pirate's plundering.

TWENTY-FIVE

RLINDA KETT

The direct summons from the Hansa Chairman came as a complete surprise. With her ship still languishing in a public dock on the Moon, Rlinda Kett had maintained a low profile, hoping no one would notice her unpaid bill. She had no idea why Basil Wenceslas would want to speak with her.

Either she'd done something grievously wrong, or the Chairman wanted something. Did he know about BeBob's desertion from the EDF? Even if he did, why would such an important man care about one missing pilot? And why would he go through so much trouble to find *her*?

When the *Voracious Curiosity* vectored towards the VIP zone in the Palace District, Rlinda received immediate landing clearance. Her ship looked out of place among the government craft and royal escort ships.

When she emerged from the *Curiosity*, two people greeted her. She didn't recognize the clean-cut blond man with Germanic features, but the slender woman beside him was a surprising and welcome sight. 'Sarein! I forgot you'd been assigned as Theron's ambassador to Earth.'

The woman was dressed in immaculate Earth clothes adorned with traditional Theron scarves. Her eyes were hard, but Sarein's smile seemed genuine as she said, 'We've helped each other resolve some trade difficulties, Rlinda. We're both creative and determined businesswomen. How could I forget you?'

Though the younger woman remained formal, Rlinda gave her a quick, motherly hug. 'Now is definitely the right time for some creativity. This damned war has sure put a crimp in everybody's commercial prospects. I've got a cargo hold of luxury items that nobody wants to pay for, and I can't even fly around the Spiral Arm in search of new customers.' She snorted. 'If I see one of those drogue warglobes, I'll moon it out the porthole – I swear I will.'

The blond man led them to a private transport craft. In a wistful voice, Sarein said, 'Maybe we can talk Basil into acquiring some of your shipment. It's been a long time since I've had a decent Theron meal. I never thought I'd miss the things I ate every day, but I do.'

Once they were aboard the transport, Rlinda could not contain her curiosity. 'So, I'm ready for answers any time, Sarein. Why exactly am I here?'

Sarein smiled secretively. 'I overheard Chairman Wenceslas mention that he needed someone to fly a small ship on a fast but discreet mission. Naturally I offered to contact you.'

Rlinda looked at her, unable to hide her obvious scepticism. 'You mean the Hansa Chairman couldn't find somebody on his own?'

'Oh, he could have. But I saved him the trouble and scored a few small points in the process. Are you happy for the chance to earn a valid commission, or would you rather keep running up your tab at the lunar docks?'

Rlinda smiled warmly, but her heart was pounding. Finally,

some legitimate work! 'As long as the man supplies me with ekti and doesn't expect some sort of government discount, I'm sure we can work out equitable terms.'

Inside the HQ pyramid, Sarein introduced Rlinda to Basil Wenceslas. The young woman hovered by the doorway as if hoping the Chairman would invite her to stay, but the dapper man made it clear. 'Ms Kett and I need to chat face to face without anyone looking over our shoulders.'

When they were alone in his luxurious office, Rlinda settled herself on a wide sofa. Basil did not offer her refreshments; in fact, the Chairman observed none of the usual niceties that generated rapport between two parties. Instead, he sat down at the clean, organized desk, folded his hands in front of him, and got right down to business.

'One of our new colony worlds, Crenna, is in desperate need of supplies. The Ildirans abandoned the world in the first place because a plague wiped out their population, and now a completely different fever is affecting our human settlers. Only one case has proven fatal, but a full thirty per cent of the population is either bedridden or still recovering and not well enough to work.'

Rlinda tried to remain impassive, but she drew a quick breath when he named the planet. Leave it to her favourite ex-husband to choose a plague-infested world. Was BeBob one of the casualties? He might have been better off simply flying more EDF missions.

'And you need someone to . . . what? Evacuate the colonists, enforce a quarantine? Mother them? I'm not much of a Florence Nightingale, Mr Chairman.'

'Nothing so extravagant, Ms Kett. It turns out the Orange Spot is not difficult to treat. The Crenna settlers have basic medical care, but no pharmaceutical capabilities to manufacture the anti-amoebic they need. The Hansa can do that easily, and I'd like you to deliver the medicine.'

Wenceslas finally poured each of them a glass of iced tea from a glistening pitcher. She sipped the drink and said with her best maternal expression, 'Now, that's very kind of you, Mr Chairman.' She wiped her lips before setting the glass of tea aside. 'But I don't believe it for a minute. Crenna is not that important to the Hansa. The population is too small and the resources just too insignificant to grab your interest – fever or no fever. Tell me why you really need me to go there.'

He was surprised at her perceptive response, but did not make excuses. 'And how do you know so much about Crenna, Ms Kett?'

'I've been sitting docked at the moonbase, and there's not much else to do but read background material on potential markets.' *A dodge, not a lie.* Ever since receiving BeBob's coded message, she had studied the colony world on her own.

Wenceslas did not shade his answer, but told her directly, 'Yes, there is a second part of the assignment. Years ago I placed a man on Crenna to analyse whatever the Ildirans left behind. His name is Davlin Lotze, a trained investigator, skilled at digging into nuances and putting together theories from the smallest shreds of evidence left behind.'

'Ah, so he's a spy,' Rlinda said.

'He is an undercover exosociological investigator,' Basil said, a bit sharply. Then he smiled. 'But you can use the term "spy" if you prefer one-syllable words. When you deliver the medicine to Crenna, find him. I want you to take Lotze to a planet called Rheindic Co and remain there until he finishes his mission. He'll be expecting your arrival on Crenna.'

Rlinda frowned. 'Isn't Rheindic Co one of those empty Klikiss worlds?'

'You certainly know your planets, Ms Kett. Few people have ever heard of it.' He explained about the Colicos expedition and the missing archaeologists.

'I guess it's better than sitting in spacedock, waiting for some-one to ask me out on a date,' she said with a self-deprecating grin. 'I'll need a full supply of ekti, enough to fly your spy wherever he needs to go.'

And that was just the beginning of her terms. Once he'd explained the unofficial details of the mission, she had Basil under her thumb.

Rlinda surprised him with her sudden aggressive negotiating. If the Chairman had expected her to roll over and happily accept his first offer, he quickly learned his mistake. He drove a hard bargain. She pushed even harder. Rlinda judged him well and could see by the twinkle in his eyes that he actually enjoyed the haggling.

She arranged for a substantial sum and a full supply of ekti. Then, to top off the bargain, she sold him half the *Curiosity*'s cargo of luxury items, which she presumed he would share with Sarein. All in all, she found it a very satisfactory deal.

Foremost in her mind, though, was the knowledge that she was going to Crenna, where she could make sure BeBob was all right.

Racing across space, Rlinda Kett felt as if she herself had wings. She'd almost forgotten the sheer joy of soaring between planetary systems. The brutal unfairness of what the hydrogues had done to human dreams, to the growth of civilization, to the sheer *fun* of zipping across the Spiral Arm, made her want to spit at the next warglobe she saw.

Sure, the Klikiss Torch at Oncier had been a big, dumb mistake, and she felt sorry for the hydrogue casualties . . . but it *had* been an accident, and Old King Frederick, the Hansa, and everybody else had tried to make amends. The drogues wanted no part of it. Damned pissy alien troublemakers.

A few scattered suns hung close and bright, places she had never visited, names she had seen only on starmaps. Crenna was far out into the fuzzy boundaries of where the Ildiran Empire petered out and the Hanseatic League had barely expanded. The system was a set of coordinates centred on an unremarkable sunspot-speckled orange star that bathed the habitable colony planet in a warm glow.

She thought about Branson Roberts, recalling the good times with exaggerated fondness, conveniently forgetting the arguments they'd had during their tempestuous marriage. She was definitely looking forward to seeing him, and she was ready for this assignment: The *Curiosity*'s hold was full of medicines as well as substantial supplies for a long-term stay on Rheindic Co. After this mission, perhaps she'd remain on the Chairman's approved list for odd jobs. After lean years and lost customers, things were finally looking up.

Then the hydrogues ruined her celebration again.

As she aligned an approach vector on the fringes of the Crenna system, her sensors detected large ships suddenly looming in the vicinity. The screens went wild, and she activated all emergency systems. Like spiked balls ripped from an ogre's club, five giant alien spheres hurtled through space, intent on a kill.

Rlinda instantly cut all power to the *Curiosity*'s engines. Surrounded by cold blackness, the ship tumbled without stabilizers, leaving a weak but unmistakable signature – if the deep-core aliens were bothering to look for her.

'What the hell are you doing out here?' She called up her dossier from the Hansa starmaps, verifying what she already knew. The Crenna system did not even have a gas-giant planet. *There shouldn't be any hydrogues here!*

She vented a belch of exhaust to change direction, drifting back out of the system, hoping the deep-core aliens had not detected her.

She could not recall hearing of any drogue attacks on individual human spacecraft, but she didn't particularly relish the idea of becoming the first statistic. Earlier, Rlinda had wanted to moon the enemy out of the porthole; now that she had the opportunity, it did not seem the wisest course of action.

Her ship hung there, exposed. 'Never mind me,' she said like a prayer. 'Nobody out here but us asteroids.' Space around her was alarmingly empty, with barely a handful of dust flecks to hide behind.

But the hydrogue vessels paid no attention to the *Curiosity*.

Instead, the five warglobes approached Crenna's star like bees clustering around a hive. They circled and swooped, scanning the spotted photosphere, flitting among the curling flares like children running through a sprinkler. Rlinda sat in cold silence for hours, her skin prickling and clammy from nervous sweat, as the five alien spheres lurked over the sun.

Then, for no apparent reason, the spiked hydrogue ships gathered into a single cluster and streaked out of the system.

'Good riddance,' she said. Then, with trembling hands, she powered up her engines again and made her way towards Crenna. Even the prospect of a plague seemed preferable to staying out here.

TWENTY-SIX

ADAR KORI'NH

A dar Kori'nh knew it was a foolish risk to go on a direct mission to a gas giant, but he wanted to see the wreck of the Daym skymine for himself.

The Mage-Imperator had instructed him to investigate the feasibility of reactivating the empty Ildiran facilities. No ekti harvesting had been done here since the Roamer disaster 183 Terran standard years ago. After its chequered past, the antique skymine had been ignored by humans and Ildirans alike.

Perhaps by the hydrogues as well – or so he hoped.

Originally, a trio of grand Ildiran skymines had criss-crossed the Daym skies, the first ekti skimmers to be turned over to refugees from the human generation ship Kanaka. In a terrible accident, one of the three drifting cities had dropped into the depths. All crew members had been lost, except for a lone survivor, who was later rescued babbling about strange demons in the high-pressure depths. Since then, Daym was a shunned place of supernatural lights, mysterious noises, and creeping shadows where nothing should have lived.

Unfortunately, the strange creatures in the depths had not been the wild imaginings of a raving man, after all . . .

His command protégé Tal Zan'nh piloted their patrol craft away from the main warliners to the cold, blue-grey giant. For an hour or two, there would be only the two of them, isolated, though close enough to sense the comforting presence of crews in the big ships overhead. No Ildiran liked to be so vulnerable.

Kori'nh fidgeted, impatient to see the creaking old facility, compile his report, and then return to the comfort of crowds. The hydrogues were volatile and unpredictable. So far, they had responded only when provoked, and the Adar hoped the aliens would pay little attention to a small ship carrying two passengers. But the strange enemy had shown that one could never make assumptions about their behaviour.

'I have found the facility, Adar.' Zan'nh called up a bright image on the patrol craft's scanners. Against the frozen atmospheric soup, the once-grand industrial city looked like nothing more than a tiny blip swallowed in a cold, swirling sea.

He had seen images of the Daym skymine in its glory days. The harvesting towns had cruised in different airstreams; every several months the ekti facilities would join for a rendezvous, and allow the lonely Ildirans to enjoy increased companionship. The skyminers would swap crews and stories before the tides of the sky drew them apart again to continue their hydrogen harvesting.

Because the Ildirans required a population of sufficient size to bind together the *thism*, Daym had been an extraordinarily expensive operation. Thus, it had made sense for the former Mage-Imperator to subcontract those facilities to eager Roamer workers. The human refugees had taken over all ekti production with such remarkable efficiency that Ildirans soon purchased most of their stardrive fuel from the Roamer clans.

Unfortunately, the hydrogue crisis had thrown those carefully balanced pieces into chaos, and now the Mage-Imperator had to consider all options. The Empire had substantial ekti stockpiles gathered over the centuries, but even those were dwindling. Ildirans needed their own fuel supply, regardless of the source.

Zan'nh divided his attention between the patrol craft's sensors and what he could see with his own eyes. He seemed surprised by the results of his scans. 'The skymine's been abandoned and falling apart for over a century. But it is in better shape than I imagined. Structural integrity approaches eighty per cent. Some of the weaker materials have disintegrated – windows and doorseals and the like – but the decks are solid enough in most areas.'

The skymine looked like a floating ghost town of gutted buildings and industrial facilities. Grey clouds of damp mist twisted like insubstantial serpents through the girders. Daym's distance from the primary sun never allowed its day to grow brighter than twilight.

'Even so, Adar,' Zan'nh continued, 'I don't believe many Ildirans would like to live here.'

'That is for the Mage-Imperator to decide after we deliver our report,' Kori'nh said. 'If he feels justified in relaunching ekti operations, then there will be plenty of volunteers.' *As long as it is not me.*

Kori'nh was a military officer, a cross-breed of soldier and noble kiths – like young Zan'nh. Every molecule of his DNA had programmed him to be a commander. Other Ildiran kiths had different leanings and skills, each touching their particular soul-thread of the *thism* from the Mage-Imperator. Cloud miners loved to fill their roles, though since the coming of the Roamers, the miner kith had dwindled, since they were less necessary in the Empire. Perhaps they would be needed again.

The patrol craft settled with a gentle thump on the corroded and buckled plates of the main landing pad. They came to rest above the communal facilities, where crowds of Ildirans had once worked and lived. The Roamers, living here in much smaller numbers, must have got lost on the huge Daym skymine.

The thought of so much emptiness and so few people made Kori'nh uneasy. Even now, sitting beside Zan'nh, he felt much too alone, too separate. Though he knew the rest of the septa loomed overhead in orbit, they seemed far away. A curved fingernail of panic dug its way into his nerves, and Kori'nh knew he would not feel whole again until they returned to the main warliner and its thousands of soldier crewmembers.

'The atmospheric compression fields are still functioning around the main habitation structure,' Zan'nh said, 'but at greatly diminished capacity. The levitation engines are maintaining altitude – they'll burn for a thousand years – but don't expect to find any hot chrana soup in the skymine galley.'

'We will not stay here long enough to eat. Let us make our inspection and be away.'

They positioned breather films over noses and mouths, then bundled up in insulated fabrics; the outside temperature of the high cloud decks was far below optimal. Tal Zan'nh hesitated, giving his commander the option of setting foot first on the historical relic or letting the junior officer take the lead and face any dangers. They stepped out together, huddled against the whistling breezes that moaned through the tall derricks and empty support frameworks. Everything seemed dead and lonely and cold.

Once, sky-harvesting activities would have warmed the place. Squealing exhaust gases, humming ekti reactors, and churning intake engines would have made this a bustling city, gulping whole clouds and running them through high-energy catalysts to convert hydrogen into the rare ekti allotrope. Now Kori'nh heard only the subtle groans of corroded structures that settled and drifted.

Zan'nh moved ahead, using a scanner to probe fracture paths

and measure the extent of rust and deterioration. He reached a steep, metal staircase that led down to the ekti reactors. Their primary imperative.

They descended the stairs, one of which crumbled under Zan'nh's left foot, but he grabbed a railing, careful to make sure the Adar did not injure himself. A loose piece of metal clattered and banged as it dropped, skipped, bounced, and finally tumbled off the curved deck to vanish down into the infinite cloud depths.

Barely seen in a flash of movement, a glistening black creature with many legs scuttled into a dark cranny between deck plates. Kori'nh whirled at a sound of fluttering wings behind him, but he saw nothing. Squinting into the shadows, he wondered if he was imagining too many sounds in the unstable debris. Roamers were notorious for keeping unnecessary creatures – perhaps they had left small pets behind?

Now the Mage-Imperator wanted to consider relaunching his operations, working quietly in the hope that he could get away with renewed ekti harvesting. That the hydrogues wouldn't notice. Kori'nh would follow his leader's orders . . . but in his bones, he felt that the danger was too great.

Deep in the enclosed mechanical levels, the air smelled flat with an acidic undertone that even their breathing films could not disperse. The deck beneath their feet vibrated with the hum of levitation engines that held them aloft.

Zan'nh went to the reactor controls. From a pocket on his wide belt, he removed a compact power source and linked it to the diagnostic instruments. 'I took the time to familiarize myself with skymine operations, Adar. These controls are similar to those the Roamers currently use.' Part of the panel went dark, but the young officer continued to run his scans.

'Admirable foresight, Tal Zan'nh. Exactly what I expected of you.'

When Zan'nh attempted to restart the smallest ekti reactor, the grumbling and shuddering subsidiary engines did not sound healthy. Despite his repeated efforts, the system fell silent and dead. He shook his head. 'And that was the best of them, Adar. All the reactors will need to be replaced, and none of the current generation of engineers has experience in such work.'

Kori'nh frowned. 'Imagine the effort it would take: metals, machines, large crews of assemblers.' The walls seemed close around him. The light was dim, and the air cold and sluggish. It was so lonely here.

Zan'nh looked grim. 'It would require months of concentrated work.'

Much of this skymine was dangerously unstable. People might fall through holes in the decks. Support pillars and derrick extensions might collapse. A loud groan echoed like the yawn of a giant Isix cat deep below.

'And we would never keep it hidden from the hydrogues, would we?'

Zan'nh shook his head. 'Impossible, sir.'

The Adar turned as uneasiness swelled within him. He knew it was irrational, but he wanted to be back aboard the patrol craft, flying towards his warliner. He could not let his protégé see his nervousness, though. 'We have made a sufficient inspection. I will tell the Mage-Imperator that, in my opinion, the Daym operations are not worth pursuing.'

'I concur,' Zan'nh answered quickly.

The two of them moved at a rapid clip up the stairs and ladders to the platform where their ship waited, its contours softened by the encroaching cold mists. Although neither man broke into an outright run, they moved much faster than the situation required.

TWENTY-SEVEN

PRIME DESIGNATE JORA'H

When his father summoned him for a private consultation, Prime Designate Jora'h did not suspect that his entire world was about to change.

Mage Imperator Cyroc'h had ruled for nearly a century. He led with all the benevolence and wisdom necessary to keep the ancient civilization together. The Ildiran golden age had already lasted for millennia, as chronicled in the *Saga of Seven Suns*.

As the eldest son and Prime Designate, Jora'h often met with his father to discuss politics and leadership principles. Despite basking in the comforts and conveniences of his noble position, Jora'h had a good heart and wanted to do what was right, in its own time. History and destiny were slow, inexorable barges travelling down a calm river; there never seemed to be any hurry.

Now Jora'h entered the contemplation chamber, pleased to have a private moment with his father and interested in all that he still had to learn about the Empire. He had spent the morning with a delightful new lover from a kith that specialized in preparing food. She'd had a wonderful sense of humour, and he found himself in high spirits.

'Seal the door, Bron'n,' the Mage-Imperator said in a deep, ominous voice. 'I want no interruptions.'

As the burly bodyguard sealed the chamber entrance, Jora'h noted the serious expression on his father's chubby face. 'What is it, Father?' Bron'n's murky silhouette, tall and monstrous, remained on the other side of the door.

The Mage-Imperator's eyes were dark and glittering, set deep within folds of fat. 'Hear me well, Jora'h. You have always known this day would come.'

The Prime Designate felt a queasy apprehension in his stomach. 'What is it?'

'I am dying. Tumours have invaded my body, and they will keep growing until they choke me to death from within.' He said the words in a flat tone, as if issuing a minor proclamation. 'I am already preparing myself for a final journey into the Lightsource. But you have even more work to do, for you will remain behind.'

Jora'h gasped, taking an uncertain step forward. 'But . . . that cannot be true! You are the Mage-Imperator. Let me summon the medical kithmen.'

'Do not waste time or effort in childish denial. My life's tale is reaching its end, and yours is about to begin a new chapter.'

Jora'h steeled himself and drew a deep breath. He swallowed hard, hoping some of the shock would fade. 'Yes, Father. I am listening.'

'I have been unable to move from this chair in many decades – and not because of any silly tradition that the Mage-Imperator's feet cannot touch the floor. A long-term insidious growth has infested my central nervous system, my spine, my brain. Already, the pain in my head is constant and growing steadily worse. Within a year or so, I will weaken to the point where I cannot breathe, my heart will not beat.

'At that time, you will be called upon to be the new Mage-Imperator. You will undergo the ritual ceremony and lose your manhood. My skull will go into the ossuarium to glow beside all my predecessors, but do not hope for me to counsel you from there. Do not expect even the lens kithmen to focus and explain the soul-threads and glimpses of the Lightsource.'

Jora'h forced himself not to groan. As Prime Designate, he was confident enough that he rarely needed to consult with lens kithmen, the philosopher priests who helped to guide troubled Ildirans.

The Mage-Imperator continued. 'In recompense, however, you yourself will hold all of the *thism*. You will understand everything that I now know. You will comprehend the motivations and fine workings that I have put in place to keep the Ildiran Empire whole.'

Jora'h hung his head. *But I don't want it yet!* He knew his father would scold him for his immaturity. No one had planned for this. No one wanted change – yet it was his responsibility. All his life Jora'h had known that he would become the next Mage-Imperator. He couldn't pretend otherwise.

'I promise you I will be ready, Father.' It was the bravest thing he could say, and he hoped it was a promise he could keep. He felt the suffocating weight of the giant Prism Palace ready to crash down upon him. Though the light around him had not changed, he thought he saw many more shadows than he had noticed before.

'You will never be ready, Jora'h. No one is ready. After my father's death when it was my time to ascend, I too was unprepared. Every Mage-Imperator feels the same way.'

Jora'h tried to control his increasing alarm, his hammering questions. 'But the hydrogue war! It is a terrible time to change the leadership of our Empire. There is such danger ahead, countless chances for catastrophe. Father, I am so sorry—'

When the Mage-Imperator heaved himself into a sitting position, Jora'h noticed with alarm how greyish and weak the bulky man looked. *How could I not have noticed before? Was I so oblivious, surrounded by my own pleasures?*

'There is no time for that. We must prepare you. You have much to learn and understand, or the Empire will crumble into dust.'

Jora'h tried to think of himself as a leader. He lifted his chin. 'Then we must use the remaining time to prepare me as much as possible.'

The Mage-Imperator smiled faintly, nestled in his cushioned chair. 'An excellent attitude.' His face became harder. 'I have watched you, Jora'h. I know what you are made of. You have been a passable Prime Designate, performing up to expectations. You have always been earnest and kindhearted, willing to do your best and loving your people.'

The praise strengthened Jora'h, but his father continued with an edge in his voice. 'However, you are too soft and too naïve. I had hoped to continue training you for many decades, to toughen you to the necessities of leadership. Now I have no choice.'

'I have always done what I thought best, Father. If I have made errors—'

'You cannot know what is best until you have all the information on which to base a decision. Even as Prime Designate, there are still many secrets you cannot guess. Only through full control of the *thism* can you understand the complete tapestry of our Empire. You must harden your heart and clarify your mind.'

Jora'h swallowed. Indeed, this would be a year of many changes.

'Your days will now be different. We must focus entirely on completing your instruction. I only hope we can do it in time.'

Jora'h began to contemplate the shift, dizzy and overwhelmed. 'What shall we do first, Father?'

The Mage-Imperator's eyes narrowed into fleshy folds. 'You must strengthen ties with your brothers, the Designates. Go to Hyrillka. No one can know my health is failing – not yet – but it is imperative that you bring back Thor'h. Once you ascend, your son will become Prime Designate and should start to learn his responsibilities.'

Jora'h agreed. 'Yes, he has been pampered long enough with the Hyrillka Designate.'

The Mage-Imperator leaned back in the chrysalis chair, exhausted. 'After that . . . we must all begin to plan.'

TWENTY-EIGHT

NIRA

As dusk thickened like clotting blood in the skies of Dobro, Nira stared out at the breeder camp. Long ago, it had been an abortive new colony established by the optimistic settlers from the *Burton*. Before things had gone terribly wrong here.

Nira could still travel back to the worldforest in her imagination, even though she knew the trees could not hear her. Her years as a curious green priest, her experience growing up as an eager acolyte reading stories to the trees, memories of her parents and her little sister who had always loved Nira even when they did not understand her passions – it all kept her strong. Sometimes, in the evenings, she told stories to the other human prisoners: King Arthur and his Knights of the Round Table, Beowulf, Romeo and Juliet. The captives here didn't know the difference between truth and fiction.

She could still sing some of the old folksongs settlers had brought with them on the generation ship *Caillié*. In past years here, she had quietly sung nonsense verses to her babies, or recited ancient and humorous nursery rhymes, until the medical kithmen took the babies away from her. Someday, Nira hoped she might be able to see – or even rescue – her Princess, her daughter Osira'h.

Dobro's main city, established many centuries before the *Burton*'s arrival, was a crowd of many-windowed buildings. Now, after sunset, the streets began to glow as blazers ignited to fend off the darkness of oncoming night. Since humans were far less sensitive to darkness, the breeder camp was on the outskirts, lit only by harsh globes at the corners of the fences.

Men and women shouted a meal call from the communal barracks; sometimes Nira joined them, but today she wanted to stay out here by the boundary. Her green skin had absorbed enough sunlight to nourish her.

She looked towards the horizon, where the hills were dotted with patches of black-leaved scrub trees. If she ever again connected to the worldforest through telink, she could call for help, send messages, and learn what had happened in the Spiral Arm since her capture.

Around her, the other human females looked drab and sturdy, born to a life of hard work and frequent childbearing. All viable offspring were inspected and tested at birth. Some of the experimental mixed-breed newborns were so horrendously malformed that they were killed outright. The healthy ones were left with their mothers for several months, then snatched away to be raised by professional monitors in the cities on Dobro. Only pure human babies were left with their parents inside the camp, raised to be like all the others here.

Nira turned her head to look at a beautifully lit residence in the Ildiran city, where she knew the Dobro Designate lived. Years ago, rather than locking himself in the uncomfortable breeder barracks with her, the Designate had ordered guards to bring her to his tower room. During the assigned mating sessions, Nira had tried to imagine it was Jora'h holding her in his arms, pretending that Udru'h – who looked so much like his brother – was her love. But his caresses were like broken glass, his touch like barbed wire, and she had felt like vomiting for days afterward.

Throughout that pregnancy, her first after Osira'h, she had prayed for a miscarriage, wanting to expel the hated foetus from her body. But the next child, a boy, was born healthy and strong. Despite her loathing for the father, Nira grew attached to the innocent infant. Now, though, the little boy – Rod'h – was gone as well. She prayed he did not grow up to be like his father.

When he'd taken the boy away, Nira had tried to get the Designate to tell her about her Princess, any small detail about her daughter's life, but Udru'h had brushed her aside. 'Never ask me that again. Osira'h is no longer your concern. She carries the weight of an empire on her shoulders.'

The words filled Nira with both dread and hope. What did he want to do with Osira'h? Now, trying to put her thoughts into words as the darkness gathered, Nira stared at the tall tower, as if it were a bastion of dreams and possibilities. Her Princess was in there. She knew it. She felt it.

The Designate's residence basked in warm illumination, as if pretending to be a pleasant place. She wondered how many of her other children still lived in the Dobro city, raised and trained collectively, tested by curious scientist kithmen and specialists. Or had they been taken back to Ildira as trophies to be shown to the Mage-Imperator?

Nira was startled when she saw a small silhouette appear in front of the largest window, a little girl, small enough to be Osira'h's age. Her heart thumped loudly in her chest, and she pressed closer against the fence. Nira concentrated, reached out with her mind, trying to snag the faintly telepathic connection that had always bound her to the worldforest. If only she could touch a worldtree

. . . any tree! She desperately wanted to connect to her own child, blood of her blood.

Nira clenched the fence, not caring if she cut her fingers. *Princess!* Could that little form be her daughter? If only she could see her, send her a message, tell her the truth . . .

But she felt no answering tingle. Even if she managed to make a genuine connection, she doubted Osira'h would know what to do with it. Nevertheless, Nira's spirit soared, just for having seen her. It was a start!

TWENTY-NINE

DOBRO DESIGNATE

The halfbreed girl was remarkable, talented and intelligent beyond the Designate's most optimistic expectations. This child might well provide the mental bridge between Ildirans and hydrogues, the unbreakable link that would bind the diverse races just as the soul-threads of *thism* bound all Ildirans.

If Osira'h succeeded in this unprecedented goal, it would make the many generations of effort worthwhile. This girl might save the Empire, their civilization, everything. She had to.

Inside the well-lit residence, the child looked at her mentor with a shining smile, willing to do anything he asked of her. Beautiful, innocent, perfect, a bright sunbeam directly from the plane of the Lightsource, Osira'h was admirable and wise beyond her years, and he guessed that he didn't know half of her capabilities. Nor did the girl herself. He hoped it would be enough.

As the Mage-Imperator's second son, Udru'h had always laboured hard, doing necessary work unnoticed by his elder brother Jora'h, who glided through life, paying little attention to the advantages of his station. The Dobro Designate was not jealous of Jora'h, had no aspirations of taking over his brother's role as eventual heir to the Prism Palace. Instead, his attitude was focused and ruthlessly businesslike. He would do what was necessary . . . and sometimes such efforts were not pleasant.

Now, he looked over at the halfbreed girl, who stood at the windowpane gazing deep into the gathering darkness, oddly intent, as if she could sense something out there.

But the moment he *thought* her name, she turned to look at him. Osira'h had large eyes and feathery golden hair. Her cheekbones were high, her chin strong, showing a mixture of delicacy and grace along with noble breeding. The Designate could see a hint of Jora'h's features, given an exotic flair by the bloodline of the female green priest. The irises of Osira'h's eyes swirled with an inner light, a glint of star sapphire she had inherited from her father, darkened with shadowy hazel from her mother.

'You are thinking about me again,' she said, her voice small but clear. Osira'h was only five years old, but the combination of her superior breeding and intensive training and indoctrination had made her far more mature than anyone else her age. This girl never dreamed of spending afternoons at play.

'Can you sense my pride?'

The girl laughed. 'It pours from you like heat from a fire.'

He stepped up beside the girl to put his strong hand on her shoulder. A year before, Osira'h had expended much effort, channelling her thoughts and her senses, just to read what the Designate was thinking. Now, though, she had begun to do it automatically, as instinctively as she drew breath. *Remarkable.*

None of her half-siblings by the green priest woman – not even his own son Rod'h – showed quite as much talent, though Udru'h still hoped for another breakthrough by interbreeding Nira Khali with various powerful kiths. The other mixed-race children were raised in large groups in crèches, schools, and training centres in

the Dobro city. The half-human children understood their unique-
ness, and the instructors and inspectors worked very hard to
determine and build on their individual capabilities.

But the Designate kept Osira'h to himself.

'You have so much potential. There are other telepathic
candidates on Dobro, but you are the best. That is why I have
devoted my life to instructing you, to giving you every advantage
so that you can reach your true abilities.'

'For the glory of the Mage-Imperator,' Osira'h said, mouthing
the words he had impressed upon her ever since she could first utter
sentences.

'For the glory of the whole Ildiran civilization,' Udru'h
emphasized.

'I promise to do my best. And if my best isn't enough, then I will
try harder.' Her expression became troubled, as it always did when
the consequences began to pile up on her. Her small mouth
frowned, like a flowerbud. 'But sometimes I get afraid of the
hydrogues. They are monsters. Real ones.'

The Dobro Designate looked out into the featureless night.
The room's glare reduced the outside sky to a black wall. 'You will
have to face them, Osira'h. You will be the conduit for our Mage-
Imperator. You are the bridge – our best tool for forging an alliance,
or at least a treaty that can stop this war from destroying us.'

Udru'h felt deep sorrow for her, mingled with a rush of paternal
pride, but he dampened his emotions before she could detect them.
He could never let Osira'h believe that he was weak or soft; he must
be firm, never doubting – because the girl must never doubt.

She was always pliable, eager to do whatever he requested.
Though none of the halfbreed children concerned themselves with
their parentage, Udru'h was a father figure to her. The girl did not
worry about peripheral details. She merely played her part.

But would it be soon enough to save the Empire?

For millennia, a few select Ildirans had known that the hydrogues might one day return to cause havoc. For countless generations, planning for the eventual return of the grand and incomprehensible enemy, the Mage-Imperators had encouraged selective breedings among widespread kiths and monitored the results of the subtle experiments, watching for useful mutations, the seeds of a saviour – especially any sign of enhanced telepathic ability.

Upon discovery of the race of humans, though, the reigning Mage-Imperator Yura'h had realized an exciting and innovative new alternative, a potent set of new ingredients to the genetic stew.

When an initial testing of the *Burton* survivors demonstrated the remarkable potential of human genetics, the Dobro breeding project was expanded specifically to create a group of halfbreed telepaths. At first it had been a cooperative gesture between Captain Chrysta Logan and the earlier Dobro Designate, but violence and tragedy in the initial years had turned the Designate against humans, changing the nature of the entire programme. Humans had been subordinate ever since. Prisoners. Resources.

The synergy of human and Ildiran genetics had produced some horrors, but also yielded spectacular successes, especially in the second and third generations: stronger warriors, faster swimmers, more creative singers and storytellers. The mongrel descendants of those experiments were raised to be loyal to the Ildiran Empire, treating the Mage-Imperator as an infallible god.

It was a long-term plan, preparing for the eventuality of another encounter with the hydrogues. Ten thousand years ago, in battle with their powerful counterparts, the hydrogues had nearly obliterated all life in the Spiral Arm, destroying the Klikiss civilization and bringing the Ildiran Empire to its knees.

Few Ildirans knew the truth any more, and the *Saga of Seven Suns* did not mention what had really happened. Now, though, human hubris had reignited the titanic conflict, provoking the deep-core aliens to action when they might have lain quiet and dormant for centuries more. The hydrogues were already abroad, and it would not be long before other enemies manifested themselves.

Osira'h had been born not a moment too soon.

The Designate squeezed the girl's shoulder again, and she winced. He realized he had been too rough. 'You are so young, Osira'h. I wish I didn't have to rush you.'

'Don't worry about me.' She looked up at him with an endearing expression of absolute faith – in her mission, in his benevolence, and in her loyalty to the Mage-Imperator. 'I will do my job. It was bred into me. For the glory of the Ildiran civilization.'

'Ah, how could the hydrogues resist you?' The girl beamed up at him. A gift of fate, she would be the strongest telepath ever to walk the worlds of the Ildiran Empire. 'You will save us all, child.'

The Designate hugged her, and the little girl nodded solemnly. 'Yes, I will.'

THIRTY

RLINDA KETT

At the *Voracious Curiosity*'s approach, the Crenna farmers converged from the outer acreage. Rlinda Kett's unexpected arrival caused a stir that superseded their daily work.

Still shaken from her close brush with prowling hydrogue warglobes at the edge of the system, she climbed out of her ship, ready to accept the cheers and accolades with embarrassed good grace.

'The Hansa heard about your plague, and I brought you medicines!' she called. She'd expected to see the town at a standstill, the fields untilled, and the herd animals fending for themselves during the Orange Spot epidemic.

'But it doesn't look like too many of your people are out sick.'

The nearest farmer nodded. 'Damn fine of King Peter to be thinking of us, ma'am, but we've already got the medicines, you see. One of our colonists has his own ship, though he was flying on ekti fumes by the time he got back here. We owe our lives to Branson Roberts.'

Her heart swelled to hear his name, but she kept up pretences. 'Well, he's got a lot of nerve making my humanitarian gestures obsolete.' She scanned the crowd and spotted BeBob. His frizzy grey hair had grown longer, giving him a disreputable look, and he had dirt all over his clothes as if he'd been working in the fields – she had to laugh at the thought!

Rlinda saw his eyes fill with a wash of tears, and then he was running towards her, ignoring the farmers. She swept open her arms and bounded in his direction. She knew they must look ridiculous, coming together like two starstruck lovers in a cheap romance vidloop.

'So . . . I take it you two, uh, know each other?' one of the colonists said.

Rlinda and BeBob held each other in a long, crushing embrace, then both said in perfect comic unison, 'A bit.'

'If I'd known you were coming,' BeBob said, 'I wouldn't have wasted my fuel. Instead of fetching medicine, I could have rounded up some conveniences, tools, interesting cropseeds – and made a bigger profit.'

Rlinda rubbed her fingertips on his frizzy hair, then hugged him again. 'You've got a soft heart, not a soft head, BeBob.' She lowered her voice conspiratorially. 'I'll let you spend plenty of time tonight convincing me that I didn't waste a trip. Your place or mine?' Then she chuckled even more. 'Oh, you're so cute when I embarrass you. You look absolutely scandalized.'

'Hey, I'm trying to be a respectable colonist here.'

'Try harder, then.' She kissed him on the mouth.

Rlinda didn't tell him about her real mission, not wanting to mar their quiet dinner together in his dwelling, which had once been built by Ildiran colonists. She had brought some of his favourite foods, a nice bottle of wine, new entertainment packages, and a fancy shirt she knew he would never wear. She had called it a 'colony-warming' gift.

'To tell the truth, I'm not surprised to see that you found an excuse to come here.' BeBob took a bite of the tenderized stew she had prepared in his small kitchen area. 'If I didn't think you'd figure out my coded message, I would never have risked sending it. I assume General Lanyan isn't too happy about any captain who goes AWOL.'

'Aww, he had no right to conscript you in the first place, and I've never forgiven him for confiscating my merchant fleet. How's my ship, by the way?'

He raised his eyebrows. 'The *Blind Faith* is only ten per cent yours. She's fine – except for the empty fuel tank. Not much more than a big lawn ornament right now.'

'Prop her struts up on creteblocks and let the weeds grow all around,' Rlinda said. 'Then you'll be a real dirt-bound homebody.'

He sipped the dark red wine she had poured for him. 'I'm happy here, you know. Crenna's a nice place, good weather. You should hear the wind through the flutewoods. Could be an ideal place to settle down – by choice rather than necessity. I, uh, wouldn't mind having you around, Rlinda – and not just for your wonderful cooking, either.'

She laughed with warm delight. 'I knew I came here for a reason. In tough times, flattery is hard to come by.'

He set his wine glass down. 'But, much as my ego would like to believe it, visiting me wasn't your only reason for travelling here. Need any help?'

She wasn't surprised that he had guessed, and so she told him everything.

Davlin Lotze was already waiting outside the *Curiosity* when Rlinda returned to her ship an hour after dawn. Hands empty, he stood like a statue, the left side of his face scratched with faint scars as if some predator had tried to claw his eye out. He was muscular, exuding intelligence, watchfulness, and a demeanour of utter competence. 'I believe Chairman Wenceslas sent you for me,' he said. 'Still, bringing the medicine was a nice gesture.'

She measured him with her eyes. 'You don't believe in simple human charity?'

'I don't believe in *Basil*'s simple human charity.' He ran his gaze over the *Curiosity*. 'Looks like a good ship. Is it well supplied?'

'The Chairman had me put aboard everything we'd need for our little expedition: digging and analysis tools, a survival camp, food supplies, water extractors. Ten thousand clean crossword puzzles in the database.'

Rlinda led him aboard in the early morning stillness and showed him to a small guest cabin that had once been used to carry the green priests Nira and Otema, before anyone had ever heard of hydrogues. Lotze touched the bunk, noted the computer console and the ship's library database, and nodded with satisfaction.

'I am ready to go. I'd rather not make a scene packing up my belongings. The colonists think I'm just another settler with a bit of engineering knowledge. They have no clue why I was really here.'

Rlinda was surprised. 'No goodbyes? You've spent years on Crenna . . . and you just want to slip away into the dawn? With nothing but the shirt on your back?'

His expression remained unruffled. 'That would be my preference. I am ready to go find those missing archaeologists.'

Rlinda drew a deep breath. 'It'll take me a while to prep the ship for departure. In the meantime, *I*, at least, need to run back and say goodbye to someone.'

THIRTY-ONE

ANTON COLICOS

The fabled city of Mijistra was everything Anton Colicos had dreamed it might be – and a thousand times more. The crystalline metropolis glittered under the light of seven suns. He didn't think his eyes could withstand any more wonders.

As he stepped away from the ornate Ildiran transport ship, Anton fumbled in his pockets, searching for his filmy sun filters. Though the captain had warned him that humans often had trouble with the glare, Anton had been so overwhelmed by the sights that he'd forgotten to take the simple precaution. When he smoothed the filter band across his eyes, even more amazing details popped out at him. Spires, stained glass, fountains, gardens . . .

The city brought thoughts of wondrous places to mind: Xanadu and the pleasure dome of Kublai Khan, mythical Atlantis, the golden city of El Dorado, the realm of Prester John, even the Emerald City of Oz. It would require centuries just to *absorb* it all . . . much less interpret and communicate it to future generations.

He wished he could share this with his missing parents. They would love it here! Just before leaving Earth, he had received a formal message from some unnamed bureaucrat in the Hansa that they would 'look into the matter' with whatever resources they had available, as soon as it was 'appropriate'. Anton did not take much encouragement from the answer, but it was something. Perhaps his new Ildiran friends would have something to add.

Suppressing the urge to worry about his parents, Anton reminded himself that Margaret and Louis Colicos had always been self-sufficient and prepared for unexpected setbacks. All his life, his mother and father had emphasized to him that they loved their work. And, despite the risks, they would not want to do anything else.

Just like Anton, here in Mijistra. At last.

Ildirans disembarked from the crowded passenger liner, where the travellers had been pressed together inside the communal areas. Though Anton relished solitude for quiet study and meditation, these aliens thrived on each other's company. He didn't think Ildirans ever did anything alone.

Anton moved down the ramp with clusters of Ildirans of various kith forms and body types. Looking past the crowd of disembarking passengers, he searched for the revered historian Vao'sh. Anton had studied Ildiran culture and knew full well how to identify a rememberer kithman. As the lone human in the group, Anton would, of course, be easy to spot.

Then he saw one short-statured Ildiran in solar-power-striped robes waving at him. The greeter's facial features were different from the soldiers and noble ambassadors he had met aboard the liner. Anton bounded away from the ramp, the weariness of the journey falling away like rain from a slicker. 'Are you Rememberer Vao'sh?'

The historian repeated his name, carefully demonstrating the proper pronunciation, and the young man rolled the sound through his mouth until he got the correct tone. Vao'sh spread his hands wide at his hips, palms upwards. 'And you are Anton Colicos, the human teller of tales and keeper of history?'

'That sounds much more impressive than post-doctoral scholar or associate professor.' Anton reached out to shake the rememberer's right hand, startling the Ildiran, who then imitated the gesture. 'I'm not used to people treating what I do with any sort of respect, much less reverence.'

'How could they not revere one who tells the stories of your species?'

'Humans don't necessarily consider storytellers to be very . . . practical.'

The Ildiran historian guided him along a curving walkway into a cluster of freeform towers amid trickling fountains and gem-like sculptures. Mirrors and sundials cast interesting shadow patterns along the streets.

Although Anton was normally a reserved person, enthusiasm made him loquacious. He had never felt comfortable addressing conferences or speaking at banquets, but now he forgot all shyness. 'I've dreamed of an opportunity like this my whole life. I applied to Ildira three separate times before this, you know. I was afraid your Mage-Imperator had instituted a policy of secrecy.'

The emotional lobes on Vao'sh's face flushed different colours, a chameleon's pallet of expressive displays unique to the rememberer kith, who used them in entertaining their audiences. Anton did not yet know how to interpret all the hues.

'It does no good to keep secrets,' Vao'sh said. 'Each of us is a character in the grand tale of the cosmos, and the *Saga of Seven Suns* is itself but the tiniest fraction of the overall epic. Yet too few of us ask questions.' Vao'sh led him past a thin sheet of water that streamed down the outer wall of a city tower.

'Then I'll ask a question.' Anton drank in the sculptures and

prismatic murals around him, not sure where to turn his attention.
'Why was my request finally approved? I know other researchers
have applied and been turned down.'

Vao'sh smiled. 'I was impressed by the way you presented
yourself, Anton Colicos. Your impassioned application convinced
me that you and I are kindred spirits.'

'I, um . . . don't even remember what I said.'

The colours on the historian's face warmed like sunshine
leaking into a cloudy sky. 'You called yourself a "rememberer" of
human epics, one of the few men who know your species' ancient
poems and story cycles. I have read some of the stories translated
by human scholars long ago, but I felt in them only a detached
academic air. No depth of feeling, no exuberance in your own
history.

'But your message contained a true heart and understanding of
how those ancient tales spoke to the soul of the human race. You
seemed to have a spiritual connection to the true drama of history.
I thought that perhaps *you* would understand our *Saga*.'

From a hill they stared at the Prism Palace, a breathtaking
structure that, by comparison, made King Peter's Whisper Palace
look like a mere outbuilding. Spheres and domes, spires and
connecting walkways rose high into the sky, encircled by the
radiating spokes of seven inward-flowing rivers.

Vao'sh seemed to enjoy his companion's amazement. 'Since I
am the Mage-Imperator's prime rememberer, I live within the Prism
Palace. You will share the facility with me.' Anton found himself
speechless, which amused Vao'sh. 'Come now, a storyteller who is
awestruck to the point of silence is of no use to anyone, Anton
Colicos.'

'Sorry.'

'You and I will learn much from each other, day after day.'

Anton smiled. 'See, there's another question. On my journey

here, I heard Ildirans talking about days, weeks. How can you even measure time like that, on a world with seven suns in the sky? What does a "day" mean to you when it's always daylight?'

'It is simply a convention, converted into your Trade Standard language. We have diurnal cycles, active and resting, just like humans, with approximately the same length. I could give you the Ildiran words, and precise chronological equivalents if you like . . . but it would be easier if you just thought of your own familiar terms. There is so much to learn, why become mired in trivialities?'

'Oh, I could tell you stories about some of my colleagues obsessed with trivialities like that. Can't see the forest for the trees, we say.'

Vao'sh imitated Anton's pleased smile. 'An interesting metaphor. I look forward to exchanging stories and techniques, since a rememberer must always increase his repertoire.'

Anton continued to grin as they walked towards the Prism Palace. 'I need to increase mine by about a billion lines' worth, I'd say.'

With a pleased bow, Vao'sh said, 'Let us start a bit smaller than that.'

THIRTY-TWO

REYNALD

The primary fungus-reef complex perched high on the massive trunk of a worldtree, filled with thousands of occupants. Reynald's bronzed face was made sunny by a bright smile as he faced the colourful ruling chairs of Mother Alexa and Father Idriss. He didn't know whether to greet their decision with joy or trepidation, but it was not unexpected. They had been dropping hints for weeks.

'Understand, my son,' said Alexa with a sweet smile, 'you are well prepared for this responsibility. What better time could there be?'

'You might even be more well-rounded and cosmopolitan than your mother and I are.' Idriss scratched his square-cut beard. 'We are so very proud of you. We're convinced you will be a worthy successor, so it's time you got started. Plenty to do.'

'Oh, he'll surpass us.' Alexa rested a hand on her husband's wrist. 'The people will accept the change in no time.'

Reynald bowed. 'You both leave me with a grand legacy, but . . . why did you reach this decision so suddenly?'

'We just felt it was time,' Idriss said, sounding regal.

Alexa smiled, obviously excited. 'Besides, next month Sarein is coming from Earth on a diplomatic mission, and we have no way of knowing when she'll be able to visit home again. What better time could there be to hold your coronation?'

Reynald had to stop himself from rolling his eyes. 'That's your reason for stepping down?' It seemed so like his parents' way of making decisions.

'Yes, and it's too bad Beneto couldn't be here as well,' Idriss said.

He already knew what the next several weeks would be like. There would be a month to prepare and rehearse. People would come from settlements all around Theroc. His parents would enjoy the experience more than anyone else.

'Well, if that is the case,' Reynald said with a sigh, 'then we'd better not let my sister down.'

Father Uthair and Mother Lia had ruled Theroc for three decades before passing leadership to their daughter Alexa and her husband. The old couple had been retired for thirty-one years and had never shown the slightest regret about it.

Reynald had always been fond of his grandparents, able to talk with them about leadership, the Ildirans, the Terran Hanseatic League. Much as he respected his own parents, Reynald felt that Uthair and Lia had a broader, more politically savvy perspective.

He sat in the warm glow of a phosphor fire in his grandparents' quarters in a high section of the main fungus-reef city. They had invited Reynald and Estarra to dinner. Though they pretended it would be a relaxed social evening, he knew Uthair and Lia wanted to 'talk about things', now that his imminent succession had been announced.

Uthair and Lia loved to sit on their frilly balcony and stare out at the worldtree labyrinth, watching flying insects and colourful flowers. The old couple could talk with each other for hours, still interested in each other, though they had been married for well over half a century.

Estarra busied herself setting out dishes to serve a chowder of mushrooms and herbs, supplemented by skewers of spiced condor-fly meat. 'You make the best soup, Grandma,' she said, sneaking a taste.

'It is my responsibility to teach you how to make it.' Lia gave a mock frown. 'And you're certainly old enough, Estarra. Eighteen! You're an adult . . . though your parents still pamper you like a little girl.'

Uthair smiled. 'You treated Alexa that way until she was twenty-eight, dear.'

'It's a mother's prerogative.'

When the old man moved from his balcony chair to the table, he pretended not to notice that Reynald stood ready to help him. Then, as they ate, neither Uthair nor Lia seemed in a hurry to address the reason for the meal invitation. Afterwards, Reynald and Estarra cleaned up while their grandparents took a pair of musical instruments from a shelf on the wall and went to the balcony.

Uthair strummed a resonating harp-guitar he had invented, while Lia played a melody on a hollow flute. Since they'd retired, the two had busied themselves with creating imaginative music-makers from forest materials. They gave their instruments to children, who ran about tooting and strumming and jangling in the wilderness. Uthair and Lia couldn't have been more pleased.

Finally, his grandmother got down to business. 'Reynald, if you are going to take the throne as Father of Theroc, it's high time you chose your wife. The people will expect it.' Lia set the flute in her lap. 'You are already older than your mother was when she married Idriss. Your father was proud and capable, the young leader of a wormhive city. Their joining has produced a fine brood of offspring. They've ruled well, they're liked by the people.' She sighed. 'But peaceful times and comfortable living have made them a bit . . . placid.'

'She means *soft,*' Uthair said. 'Theroc is self-sufficient, and we don't rely on trade with either the Hansa or Ildirans. Nevertheless, Alexa and Idriss are mistaken to think we can ignore the hydrogue war. There is no such thing as neutrality against an alien enemy that kills indiscriminately.'

Lia said, 'I'm not even convinced the hydrogues make any distinction between Ildirans and humans.'

'Your parents are taking the tack of doing nothing and hoping the problem will go away. For months now, Lia and I have been trying to convince them to let you take charge in these difficult times. And they've finally listened.'

Lia patted him on the arm. 'You'll be a much better leader, dear. You've got the heart and the head for it.'

'Why are you telling me this?' Reynald asked.

Estarra spoke up, 'Because in a month you'll be the next Father, and they're counting on *you.* Don't let it go to your head.'

Uthair chuckled. 'Listen to your sister. She's perhaps the wisest one in the family. Maybe a bit blunt, but she speaks the truth.'

At another time, Reynald might have gone over to punch Estarra on the shoulder. Now though, he paid attention. 'All right, you invited us to dinner so you could give me advice.' He crossed his arms over his chest. 'Tell me about the challenges of being a ruler.'

Grinning, Uthair lifted his wife's hand. 'One of the greatest secrets, Reynald, is that you must marry well.'

The old woman looked first at Reynald, then Estarra. 'It is past time for you, Reynald. You are thirty-one.'

Uthair said, 'The same goes for you, Estarra. You're certainly of marriageable age. And you must both consider your options. From the start, get it into your head that your mate must be chosen for reasons other than fluttery heartbeats and rushing hormones. Marry the right person, with sound judgement, and if you're lucky, there might even be some romance involved.'

Lia's fingers toyed with her flute. 'One matter at a time, dear. Let us consider Reynald first. Most people expect you to pick the daughter of a good Theron family, but in these times, perhaps you should look to broader horizons.'

Reynald had already considered the idea, but he asked anyway, 'Exactly how broad do you mean?'

'The Galaxy is vast, Reynald,' Uthair said. 'It may be wise to make a more powerful alliance than with just a few Theron families.'

Reynald wanted to avoid the question, but knew he could not. 'Did you have someone in mind, Grandfather?' He already knew his own preferences for candidates.

Lia spoke in the grandmotherly voice he remembered hearing as a child when he'd had nightmares sparked by forest sounds. 'Now, now, we're just having a conversation. Uthair and I aren't even the leaders of Theroc any more. We're just grandparents thinking of your welfare.' She went back towards the cooking area. 'I'll make us some tea. That's enough of these matters for now. Just think about what we said. The Spiral Arm consists of more than just Theroc.'

For the rest of the evening, Estarra did more than her share keeping their grandparents company, while Reynald's mind was filled with images of people he'd met when he travelled around the Spiral Arm. Most clearly he recalled the beautiful, intelligent, and fascinating Cesca Peroni, who was now the Speaker for the Roamers. He valued Uthair and Lia's opinions, and now that he knew they would not object, perhaps he should approach Cesca Peroni after all.

Therons and Roamers had much in common, especially their

independence from the Hanseatic League. Five years ago, Cesca had politely rebuffed Reynald's tentative questions about marriage plans; he'd learned since that her fiancé had been killed in one of the early hydrogue attacks.

Now the vision of her face came back with full force. He had no idea if this was the woman Uthair and Lia had in mind, but he began to count the many advantages and opportunities such an alliance might create.

He sipped his tea and just listened to the music his grandparents played. Wheels began turning in his mind.

THIRTY-THREE

KING PETER

In the early hours of a foggy morning, King Peter and his assigned advisers assembled inside the newly reinforced viewing gallery. Together, they watched with wary fascination as the Klikiss robot was led into the dissection and dismantling chamber below. Jorax moved ponderously on multiple finger-like feet, like a man about to be executed.

Beside him, sallow-faced and balding Chief Science Adviser Palawu said cheerily, 'I reviewed the records, Your Majesty. It's been one hundred and eighty-three years since the first report of finding these robots came back from the Robinson expedition on Llaro.'

'Then it's about time we figured out what they're all about,' Peter said, not taking his eyes from the hulking sentient machine. Jorax was so large and powerful that he loomed with the threat of a walking landmine.

To the left of the King's chair, Lars Rurik Swendsen, the Hansa engineering specialist, leaned over. His blue eyes sparkled with ideas and childish fascination. 'And the Ildirans have known about them for longer than that, but they've never bothered to do a complete dissection and analysis.'

'Well, we all know the Ildirans don't have a highly developed sense of curiosity,' Palawu said. The two specialists were so enthused they seemed to forget the King's presence as they chatted. 'They're not interested in innovation. But *we* can study, and learn, and adapt a wide variety of technologies for our own benefit. Oh, this is a great day for our war effort.'

Swendsen nodded. 'Hansa cyberneticists have hit a plateau in advancing our compies. We haven't seen significant improvements for generations now. But these Klikiss robots have lasted for thousands of years without any degradation.'

King Peter tried to dampen their zeal with common sense. 'No degradation, gentlemen? Not one of the Klikiss robots can remember what happened to their entire creator race. I'd say mass amnesia constitutes a bit of "degradation", don't you think?'

Below them, the robotics laboratory had been configured as both a mechanical repair bay and an exquisite operating theatre. Numerous analytic and diagnostic instruments were mounted in racks that lined the octagonal walls. The reinforced central platform was far sturdier than a simple surgical table to accommodate the sheer bulk of Jorax.

Well-armed palace guards and specially assigned EDF silver-beret commandos stood along the chamber walls and outside the doors, aware of the potential danger and alert for any treachery.

Although the Klikiss robot towered over all the humans, he made no threatening move as he swivelled his flattened geometrical head, scanning the equipment arrayed for the dissection. The robot's articulated arms were retracted into his ellipsoidal carapace. 'You have nothing to fear. I have deactivated my self-protective systems, and I grant you my full cooperation.'

Always beware of someone who says 'You have nothing to fear,' Peter thought. This same robot had already obliterated Dr. William Andeker 'by accident'. The guards remained alert.

The cybernetics team armed themselves with laser cutters and diamond saws, delicate probes and a host of other precision tools. 'We'd better get started,' said the lead researcher. 'Jorax, if you'd care to recline here, it'll be more convenient for us.'

Peter frowned, not sure the robot's priority was to make the dismantling procedure 'convenient' for the humans. But Jorax seemed perfectly cooperative, even solicitous. *Why is he doing this? What is the real reason?*

Basil Wenceslas was excited enough by the technological benefits that he took the robots' offer at face value. But for Peter, the Klikiss machines were such an enigma that applying standards of human altruism was not appropriate.

With slow movements, the robot angled himself back and finally rested flat on the analysis platform, looking like a huge cockroach that had been sprayed with insecticide. Peter wondered if the ancient machine could feel fear or pain.

Suddenly, there was a commotion in the hall. Shouting, the palace guards tried to block two other Klikiss robots that had followed Jorax into the vicinity. A silver beret brandished his weapon at the identical, beetle-like machines. 'Turn back. You are not authorized here.'

'We wish to assist in the process,' said one robot.

'We are curious as well,' said the other. 'We can offer our insights.'

'That wasn't part of the original bargain,' Peter said to himself.

Next to the King, Palawu and Swendsen conferred quickly. 'Actually, it's not a bad idea to have them here, Your Majesty. Remember, their civilization created the technology of the Klikiss Torch. This isn't just a high-school-level reverse engineering project. None of us really knows what we're doing.'

Peter narrowed his eyes. *Including me.* 'That's not very comforting. Isn't it convenient that two more Klikiss robots show up here, now, without any prior warning? I thought there were only ten or so of them on Earth at any given time?'

'Give or take, Sire,' Swendsen said. 'But I suppose Jorax could have sent a signal. We should have expected it.'

'If it's any consolation, Your Majesty,' Palawu added quietly, seeing the King's hesitation, 'the transparent walls here are utterly bombardment proof. A pulse of energy or even a complete explosion of the test subject would not harm you.'

Peter was worried about more than that. He spoke into the loudspeaker, 'All right, let them in to observe and assist – on the condition that both robots completely deactivate their own protective systems.'

Jorax and the other two robots buzzed back and forth in quick bursts of coded language. One of the new robots said, 'That would make us vulnerable, should your soldiers and guards choose to dissect us as well.'

Peter couldn't feel sorry for them. 'Consider it a gesture of mutual trust. Those are our terms for allowing you to participate.'

Finally, the two insectile machines responded in unison. 'We agree to the terms.' They stood like metallic statues, then sagged slightly. 'All defensive systems have now been shut down.'

'We have only your word for that,' Peter said.

'Therefore a reciprocal gesture of trust is required.' The robots moved forward, and Peter decided not to stop them. He watched the proceedings, uneasy but curious.

With imagers and sonic probes, the researchers scanned every cranny of Jorax's mechanical body using non-destructive evaluation techniques. Never before had they been able to make even a complete external assessment of the alien machines.

Jabbering excitedly, the team took an hour just to finish their visual inspection and documentation. The scientists were intrigued, but King Peter felt a knot of tension in his chest. He disliked the conditions of the experiment, the sacrifice of the robot, the conveniently unexpected arrival of two other machines. *What do they really want?*

Sounding like a warm-hearted schoolteacher, the lead cyberneticist said from the analysis theatre, 'It's time to move on to the next phase. Jorax, is there a way you can provide access, or do we need to cut through your exoskeleton?'

With a startling snap and a hiss, tiny cracks like the segments of a pill bug appeared in Jorax's chest plate. They slid open far enough to expose inner circuitry, glossy metal, and smooth fibreoptics that throbbed like phosphorescent nematodes.

'Look! This is a completely different command train from what we use in our compies,' the lead cyberneticist said, blinking up at the observation gallery as if remembering his audience above.

The robotics researchers took up curved tools which, despite their high-tech appearance, King Peter recognized as nothing more than fancy prybars. While the other Klikiss robots loomed close, the Hansa team pulled Jorax's outer segments open farther, exposing vulnerable interior components. Lights glowed as if the thin flexible fibres contained nuclear fire.

'I would prefer to deactivate my systems and nullify my sensors, but if I did, you would receive less benefit from your investigations.' Jorax's buzzing voice rose to a thinner whine. 'Therefore, I will remain conscious through each step, until my mind's subsystems no longer function.'

'He's very brave,' Palawu whispered.

Peter clenched the arms of his chair.

The two Klikiss observer robots moved forward silently, startling the scientists, but the hulking machines seemed to know what they were doing. They opened ports in Jorax's ellipsoidal core and manually extended his eight segmented limbs, each one with attachments for grasping, cutting, or manipulating. With brisk movements, the Klikiss robots amputated the mechanical limbs and handed them to the human engineers. Even the segmented arms and legs would be studied for possible ways to improve straight-forward mechanical systems.

One of the cyberneticists probed deep into the artificial internal organs. 'I can already see how this will benefit our work.'

Lights flashed on the dismantling table, and the sensors on Jorax's head plate blazed brighter as if in the equivalent of a scream. 'There is nothing to fear,' Jorax said. 'There is nothing to fear.'

Peter wondered if the sacrificial robot was trying to reassure the humans or convince himself.

The dissection and analysis continued throughout the morning. At each new discovery inside Jorax's body, both Swendsen and Palawu rhapsodized about its potential uses, trying to impress the King.

'It'll take us a month to get a handle on the dataflow processing alone, Sire, but just as a first assessment I believe it can be incorporated into Hansa compy designs. We can even use the technique to upgrade our manufacturing systems. That could more than double our productivity.'

Swendsen agreed, and added, 'And we'll certainly need more automated fighters and scouts as the hydrogue war continues. Think of the advantages if we can increase efficiency in the manpower-intensive aspects of the conflict. This might just give us a chance against those damned aliens.'

After another half hour, OX entered to stand beside King Peter. Watching the proceedings, the Teacher compy seemed oddly reticent. The King had previously discussed the matter with OX, hoping to get the little robot's insight. He wondered if the compy felt sorry for the Klikiss machine . . . or if OX harboured suspicions of his own.

Peter could not tell exactly when Jorax reached permanent deactivation – in his mind, he refused to think the word 'death' – but the scarlet optical sensors gradually dimmed as power bled away. Lubricants and sensor patches were pulled out one component at a time. Finally, with much discussion and reluctance, the scientists bent over together, worked with their tools, and removed Jorax's flattened angular head. The optical sensors went completely dim, like dried smears of blood.

The two Klikiss observers stood motionless, collating what they had learned. Jorax's components lay catalogued and distributed around the operating theatre. Imagers had captured every instant of the procedure from every angle. The big black robot looked like nothing more than twisted debris scattered after a train wreck.

Peter wondered how the alien robots had decided that this information was worth the cost of one of their own, and why had Jorax himself volunteered for deactivation. What could the Klikiss robots gain by it? Did they really want to give the human race new tools and weapons against the hydrogues? Or would they now use this as a bargaining chip to demand an unconscionable favour from the Terran Hanseatic League?

OX, still beside Peter's observation chair, was oddly quiet and contemplative.

Peter turned grim-faced to his two specialists and said privately, 'Milk this for every possible advantage. We still don't know what it's going to cost us in the long run.'

'We'll get all of the Hansa's best people on it,' Palawu said.

Lars Rurik Swendsen said, 'I can't wait to use this information. It's like King Tut's tomb or the lost city of Quivera!'

Peter took a deep breath. 'Or Pandora's Box.'

THIRTY-FOUR

PRIME DESIGNATE JORA'H

Though he rode with Adar Kori'nh in the warliner bound for Hyrillka, Prime Designate Jora'h did not reveal his troubled thoughts. He had to pretend that this errand to retrieve his son Thor'h was simply a political one. No one could be allowed to suspect that the showpiece expedition had anything to do with the failing health of the Mage-Imperator. No one else could read the *thism* or draw conclusions from it, like his father could.

'My troops have performed here many times,' Kori'nh said, pensively staring into the warliner's viewscreen. On the edge of the Horizon Cluster, space itself seemed too full of stars. 'The Hyrillka Designate loves his pageants, and I'm sure he will be disappointed that I've brought only a septa.'

Jora'h forced himself to smile. 'Even a son of the Mage-Imperator doesn't get everything he wants. My brother should know that.' *And Thor'h as well.*

The Adar lowered his voice. 'If I may say so, Prime Designate, it is good that you are bringing your son back to Ildira. He has had a fine time here, but I believe he holds a skewed, and soft, impression of our Empire. The weight of responsibility has not yet touched him. Yet, like you, he is destined to serve as Prime Designate and then Mage-Imperator – though I hope that day is far in the future.'

Jora'h felt cold inside. 'Thor'h will serve when called upon. That is how he has been taught. That is why he was born.'

By unwavering tradition, the next Prime Designate had to be a pure-bred noble rather than a hybrid military officer, like Jora'h's true first-born son. Zan'nh had performed well in the Solar Navy, rising in rank because of his genuine innovation and skill. Thor'h, however, had never demonstrated any penchant for leadership or skill in diplomacy . . . but he was still young.

Hyrillka resided in a double star system, one of many binaries and trinaries inside the glittering tiara of the Horizon Cluster. The large blue-white primary lit the sky during Hyrillka's long days, while the orange secondary drove back the night enough that Ildirans need never fear the dark. Drawn by the planet's temperate weather and verdant beauty, Ildirans had developed Hyrillka into an opulent, peaceful world.

Kori'nh brought his seven warliners down into the plaza spaceport, an area paved with hexagonal heat tiles arranged in a complex mosaic so that descending ships could see Hyrillka's beauty. Cheering crowds waved reflectorized pennants to welcome the septa.

Observing from the command nucleus, Jora'h frowned down at the spectacle. 'I told Rusa'h this was an unofficial visit. I asked him not to draw attention to my arrival.'

Kori'nh looked over at him with a wry smile. 'You are the Prime Designate coming to take your son away. How could the Hyrillka Designate resist such an opportunity?'

On the ground, Designate Rusa'h sent a parade of colourfully robed escorts, rememberers, dancers, and singers, to receive the visitors. Side by side, Jora'h and the Adar disembarked, while the people continued to cheer. The Prime Designate's gold-chain hair flickered about his head like a corona, and his star-sapphire eyes caught the light of Hyrillka's bright blue-white sun.

Kori'nh ordered his trained honour guard to march down the ramps in a precise clockwork formation. The stream of soldiers struggled to maintain order as they encountered the swirling performers on the landing grid.

Trying to keep the stern tone out of his voice, Jora'h greeted his brother. 'This unexpectedly fine reception was unnecessary, Rusa'h.'

The Hyrillka Designate noticed no criticism in the Prime Designate's tone. 'This is just the beginning!' He sported a bright smile and a vapid expression on his chubby face. With casual familiarity, he clapped his brother's shoulder. 'I cannot begin to list the banquets we have prepared, the presentations and performances. We have a historian who rivals even Vao'sh back at the Prism Palace. I have installed a new gallery of dancing fountains. You will be amazed.'

He leaned closer. 'And I have personally inspected my favourite pleasure companions to determine which ones are the most fertile. Hyrillka would be honoured to have another of the Prime Designate's bloodline among our populace.'

The ache in Jora'h's heart from the knowledge of his father's weakening medical condition diminished his joy and dampened all desire for entertainment. 'You do too much for me, brother. We will make appropriate appearances, and perhaps Adar Kori'nh can stage a brief display of his septa's prowess.' Jora'h fixed his eyes on his own son – how young the boy looked! – who waited behind the Hyrillka Designate, as if intimidated. 'But for now Thor'h and I have important business.'

The young man bowed, though it was more like a flinch. 'My uncle told me, Father.'

Rusa'h chuckled. 'Ah, the difficulties of being the Prime Designate. I am glad that I wasn't the first-born!'

Thor'h had an intense, fidgety demeanour. His long hair was intricately coiffed, adorned with tiny gems like the residue of a dewy breath. Colourful clothes hung loosely on his shoulders, and Jora'h wondered just how skeletal his son was. It seemed a strange contrast to Rusa'h's pudginess. Both men ate well and relaxed often, but Thor'h probably indulged in shiing and other pleasure drugs, while the Designate simply preferred to eat and sleep. Hyrillka was particularly known for the production of shiing, a stimulant distilled from the milky bloodsap of nialia plantmoths.

Was I like this when I was young? Jora'h wondered.

As an odd side-effect of shiing, his son's image in the *thism* was muddied. Although the Prime Designate could sense Thor'h if he concentrated, right now the thoughts were unclear, and Jora'h was left to interpret only the expressions he could read with his eyes.

How could this boy ever become a Mage-Imperator? *For that matter, how can I?*

Later, the Hyrillka Designate dragged them through hours of performances, with an unending banquet served by lovely women of exotic kiths, all of whom flashed inviting eyes at Jora'h. Their names were added to a list Rusa'h had compiled, and the Prime Designate knew he would have to service some of them.

Three placid-looking lens kithmen sat in their priests' robes, ready to serve their purpose and talk about the Lightsource and interpret hints from the *thism*. From their docile expressions, apparently no one on Hyrillka had had problems for some time. *If only they knew what is about to happen in the Empire.*

The open architecture of Hyrillka's citadel palace featured tall columns and open-roofed courtyards filled with gardens and huge scarlet flowers. In the temperate weather, little shelter was required, and rain-repellent fields kept the interiors dry during rainstorms. The structure looked like an ancient temple being swallowed by jungle undergrowth.

Through an odd botanical quirk, Hyrillka's native vegetation had shied away from woody stems and tall trees, tending instead towards ground cover and long, flexible vines that draped over the uneven terrain. The hanging gardens of Hyrillka were counted among the wonders of the Empire – tangled masses that drooped over cliffsides, sprouting enormous blossoms that drank waterfall mists. Pollinating four-winged birds feasted on berries and flitted from one wide-mouthed trumpet flower to another.

In the banquet courtyard Jora'h leaned back, breathing in the heady perfumes of foliage and the delicious aromas of culinary items. Occasionally he caught himself frowning distractedly and tried not to let anyone notice his mood. As the blue-white sun set and the orange secondary rose, Adar Kori'nh staged a performance with his streamers and two warliners. On the ground, geometrical patterns of blazers were lit in all the fields and streets to add to the festive brightness.

Jora'h used the event as an excuse to take Thor'h aside, but the young man seemed resistant. 'I want to watch the aerial show, Father.'

'You have seen them before. We need a moment in private so I can explain why I have come.'

'I already know. You're going to make me leave Hyrillka and take me back to live in the Prism Palace.'

'Yes, but you do not know *why*.'

Jora'h sat on a smooth bench in a flower-framed alcove, but Thor'h remained at a distance, restless and pacing and full of nervous energy. 'But I like it here on Hyrillka, Father. I want to stay. The Designate and I get along well together.'

'Circumstances have changed. You no longer have that option, and I have no choice but to take you back with me.'

'Of course you have a choice.' Thor'h spun around, his perfectly arranged hair twitching. The young man's narrow face seemed predatory. 'You're the Prime Designate. You can have anything you want. You have only to command it.'

Saddened, Jora'h said, 'I have learned recently that sometimes my options are as limited as those of the poorest attender kith.'

Thor'h laced his thin fingers together, then unlaced them and spread his hands about as if looking for something to hold or eat. He seemed about to argue again, but his father stopped him. 'The Mage-Imperator is *dying*, Thor'h. Very soon, I will take his place – and you will be the Prime Designate.'

Thor'h stopped, his eyes growing wide. 'Not yet. I'm not ready.'

'Neither am I, but the hydrogues are abroad, the Empire is in trouble, and none of us can afford a pampered life any more. For years you have reaped the advantages of your birth. Now you must face your obligations.'

Thor'h snapped, 'What if I don't want to?'

'Then I will kill you myself.' The angry retort was out of Jora'h's mouth before he could stop it. 'And elevate your brother Zan'nh to the position, even if he isn't of full noble blood. The Empire cannot tolerate a Prime Designate as stupid as you seem to be.'

Thor'h looked appalled, but Jora'h could not take back the words. He tried to be conciliatory, 'We must think beyond ourselves – both of us.'

THIRTY-FIVE

TASIA TAMBLYN

Returning to the main EDF base on Mars, Admiral Willis's siege fleet received full military honours and a Remora escort. They were heady with success – an unusual feeling for them, after so many setbacks against the hydrogues.

The homebound soldiers recorded high-spirited greetings for their families and loved ones. While tankers unloaded the ekti stockpiles confiscated from the stubborn Yrekan colonists, scattered interviews played across the media networks on Earth. The 'Yreka Insurrection' had been put down with minimal casualties or collateral damage.

Tasia Tamblyn watched the reports, not surprised that the accounts were grossly distorted. The lowly colonists had kept only a fraction of the stardrive fuel that the commentaries implied, but General Lanyan needed to justify the siege.

She fumed at the injustice, knowing full well what a lie it was. The damage had been unnecessary. But then, this was the Big Goose, after all . . .

As she returned to her barracks, her compy EA attended to her unpacking. The small robot, only half as tall as Tasia, bustled about doing preprogrammed tasks while keeping her master company.

Back at the water mines on Plumas, Tasia and EA had often found places to amuse themselves deep in the grottoes beneath the ice sheets. Now Tasia wondered if she would ever go back home. Her stint with the Eddies should have been over already, but she had received a mandatory extension due to the hydrogue war. The Eddies could not afford to lose trained personnel, now that naïve hopes of a quick victory had faded. The ranks would have vanished like dissipating smoke as soon as the new recruits realized that a military career was not all heroic fun.

'Did you have an enjoyable time at Yreka, Tasia?' EA asked while removing rumpled garments from her master's duffle.

'No, I did not, EA.'

'I am sorry to hear that, Tasia.'

In a way, the scrappy Yrekans reminded her of Roamer clans, independent people who had built their homes without much help from the Hansa. 'I grew up thinking the Goose just had a grudge against Roamers, but on Yreka I saw that they're just as arrogant towards their own colonists.'

'Perhaps the Hanseatic League does not appreciate those who refuse to conform.'

She pursed her lips. 'I think you're on to something there, EA.'

'Thank you, Tasia.'

In the mess hall she and Robb sat together, as usual. They barely admitted that they were a couple, though everyone else in the division could see what was going on and politely pretended not to notice. The dark-skinned young man sat across from her, talking about the various manoeuvres he intended to put his Remora wings through, avoiding any discussion of the siege, because he knew how much it still disturbed Tasia.

She got them each coffee from a dispenser while he carried

trays of processed, nutritionally balanced glop – beef flavoured, tonight. Before Tasia took her first bite, the mess hall's wallscreen shimmered into an image of King Peter praising the siege force for 'restoring vitally needed ekti to the Hanseatic League'. The King also issued a stern, though somehow lacklustre, warning to other colonies, as if he was reading from a script. 'All humans must cooperate to see us through this struggle. Colonies cannot think only of themselves instead of the greater needs of humanity.'

'Shizz, Brindle,' Tasia mumbled from the corner of her mouth, 'with *all* that stardrive fuel we acquired, you think everybody'll get a huge boost in the next paycheck?'

He frowned at her sarcasm. 'All colonies received the same rationing order, Tasia. We weren't playing favourites or picking scapegoats. Were we supposed to just let the Yrekans thumb their noses at us?'

Her eyes flashed. 'But all colonies didn't start with equal resources. Not everyone's in a position to survive the same austerity measures. If a colony is already on the thinnest of shoestrings, it can't afford to start cutting threads. That's just dumb.'

She sipped her bitter coffee, watching King Peter finish the brief speech. Tasia could only remember the despairing expression on the Yrekan Grand Governor's face. 'Roamers would have stuck together, helped each other out in tight times.'

'There's always more than one point of view.' Robb laid a hand across her forearm, just to let her know what he was thinking. 'Just seems like you see things only from a Roamer's perspective. I don't want to argue with you. Hey, I feel sorry for the Yrekans too.'

'But you can't do anything about it,' she said.

'No, and neither can you.'

Tasia knew he was right, and went back to her quarters to have a long scrub with cool solvent sponges. She just hoped their next assignment would let her face a real enemy for a change.

THIRTY-SIX

GENERAL KURT LANYAN

Frequent reports of prowling hydrogues made anxiety run high in the Earth Defence Forces. From the Mars command base, General Lanyan dispatched supplementary patrols throughout all ten grids, though no one believed that even well-armed scout fleets could defend themselves against an outright warglobe attack.

The General became restless as he reviewed reports from the recon teams, constantly reminded of the growing list of conscripted pilots who simply 'disappeared' on assignments. He was convinced they were all deserters, cowards . . . scum.

'Plenty of hazards in space, General,' said Commander Patrick Fitzpatrick. 'Hydrogues, asteroids, radiation storms. Ships could easily be lost without a trace.' He had been temporarily transferred from the Grid 7 fleet after returning from Yreka and now served directly under Lanyan at the Mars EDF headquarters. Because of Fitzpatrick's family clout, the General had already made up his mind to groom the kid for a prominent position, probably close to home.

'Yes, I'm sure the AWOL pilots know all about the "hazards of space". We can't waste time looking for them, though I'd like to grab one by the scruff of his neck and make an example.' Lanyan shoved his documents aside, switched off his screens, and stood. 'I feel like a eunuch in a military uniform. We've got no weapons against the drogue bastards, and the Hansa is an old lady gasping her final breaths. We haven't made any progress in five years.' He pounded a meaty fist on his desk.

Fitzpatrick commiserated, but held his silence. Given his blueblood heritage, the kid had expected to advance his military career with a few helpful nudges and memos directed to the appropriate commanding officers. Without a doubt, he had been promoted faster than his skill warranted, but he had met the challenges well enough. In wartime not even the richest, most pampered officer candidate received a useless assignment. Fitzpatrick wanted to appear in publicity photos, standing tall in his fine uniform so that his family could reap the political benefits of their son's bravery, 'an upstanding example of civic duty in this time of crisis'. And the General could take advantage of that, as long as Fitzpatrick didn't do anything embarrassing.

'Actually, I have a suggestion, sir.'

'If you can tell me how to win this war, Commander, I'll promote you on the spot to the rank of Brigadier General.'

Fitzpatrick gave a thin smile. 'Maybe it won't win the war, General, but it may help to alleviate your restlessness. Why not command one of the scout fleets yourself? Go out for a month on recon, keep your eyes open. Justify it by saying you need first-hand intelligence about what's happening out there.' His grin widened. 'The Hansa can announce that the safety of its citizens takes such high priority that the General of the EDF himself is going to upgrade the security procedures and assess the enemy threat.'

'Good political mileage,' Lanyan said.

Fitzpatrick gestured towards the cluttered desk. 'This isn't for you, sir. Leave the bureaucratic duties to Admiral Stromo. He's been no good as a line officer since the defeat at Jupiter.'

'Don't disrespect your superior officers, Commander.'

The young man lowered his voice, but he was obviously not accustomed to being subordinate to anyone. 'We're alone in your office, General, and you know perfectly well that I'm telling the truth.'

'Yes I do, dammit.' Lanyan looked with disgust at all the memos waiting to be signed. He hadn't faced an important decision in six months. It would be a pleasure to delegate them all to 'Stay-at-Home Stromo'. 'All right, I'll take your advice, Fitzpatrick. Arrange for me to lead the next scout wing due to be dispatched.'

'That would be in Grid 3, sir.'

'Good enough. I'll let Admiral Stromo take care of this crap.' He smiled without humour. 'Maybe it'll be enough of a punishment to snap him out of his funk.'

After two weeks on patrol, cruising around the systems of Grid 3, General Lanyan realized that it felt no better to wander around in empty space doing nothing, than to sit at a desk on Mars doing nothing.

The ekti shortages had reduced space traffic to the barest trickle, and the scout fleet encountered no Hansa ships or Ildiran vessels. On the bridge of his borrowed Juggernaut, Lanyan let out a long sigh. 'Looks like the Spiral Arm has closed down for the season.'

Beside him, Fitzpatrick nodded. 'Normal trade is pretty much at a standstill. The colonies are left bare-assed in a cold wind.'

Lanyan had recently heard a proposal to build generation ships again, huge slow vessels that used conventional fuels, even though they would take a century to fly between colonies. To him, that smacked of a desperation he was not yet willing to admit. *Admitting such a thing would mean accepting the fact that this conflict would never be won*, that humans – or Ildirans – would never again travel swiftly across the Spiral Arm. The very idea was intolerable, an affront to the spirit of progress and exploration.

No, they needed to fight until they kicked those damned hydrogues back where they belonged.

'General, we're detecting stardrive emissions. Ship ahead, barely within range. Should we divert course to intercept?'

'One of ours or an Ildiran vessel?' Lanyan said.

'Hard to tell from this range, sir. Doesn't match any standard configuration.'

He sank his square chin on to his knuckles. Fitzpatrick leaned closer. 'We've got nothing else to do, General. Maybe that captain can tell us something. We could use the intel.'

It was the rationale the General wanted to hear. 'All right. Maybe he's even one of our deserters. Let's be sociable.'

The Juggernaut moved to intercept the lone ship in the middle of nowhere. The strange vessel looked like nothing more than a habitation pod and a huge bank of engines mounted atop a framework of girders that enclosed cargo spheres.

'Never seen a ship like that,' Lanyan said.

'It's a Roacher ship,' Fitzpatrick said. 'They steal parts and put the pieces together. I don't know how they keep those garbage scows running.'

The unknown captain at first attempted to elude them, but after Lanyan launched Remoras to head off and surround the ship, the captain stood down.

The bearded Roamer's image came on the screen. His patch-work uniform had embroidery so garish that it offended Lanyan's trained military eye. 'My name is Raven Kamarov, piloting a Roamer cargo vessel. Why have you stopped me in free interplanetary space? I've got a shipment to deliver.'

Lanyan's nostrils flared. 'Don't you appreciate our protection, Captain Kamarov? There are hydrogues abroad.'

The other captain scowled. 'We're well aware of the hydrogues. Roamers have lost ten times more people than anybody else.'

'My heart bleeds for him,' Fitzpatrick said under his breath.

'Please state your cargo, Captain,' Lanyan said.

'Delivering much-needed supplies to Roamer outposts and Hansa colonies. You can check your own database, General. My commerce record is clear.'

The Juggernaut's science officer finished his scans and turned to the General. 'He's hauling ekti, sir. Those cargo tanks are full to the gills.'

'Ekti!' Fitzpatrick said. 'How much?'

The science officer rattled off the amount, and Lanyan put it into terms he could grasp. 'So . . . that's more than we recovered from Yreka – enough to take care of this entire recon patrol and five others.' Lanyan met the eyes of his protégé. Fitzpatrick nodded.

'Captain Kamarov, you are aware that the Earth Defence Forces has a priority standing order with your people for all ekti shipments, in any amount?'

'As I said, General,' Kamarov replied, his face stony, 'we are in free interstellar space here, and the Hansa can't impose its laws on Roamer clans. We are not signatories to your Charter. You have no right to waylay me. Roamers already provide the majority of the ekti we harvest to the EDF, but we have our own needs.'

'Big surprise,' Fitzpatrick muttered. 'Roachers hoarding fuel for themselves.' Then he raised his voice into the comm pickup. 'Where did you get all this ekti?'

'Hydrogen *is* the most plentiful element in the universe, you know.'

'Captain Kamarov, I would think that providing vital supplies to the military that protects all human beings, including Roamer clans, would be your highest priority,' Lanyan said. 'We will be happy to relieve you of your cargo and save you the fuel necessary for your trip to Earth.' He had always been annoyed at the space gypsies' blatant independence. It was time Roamers learned to play well with others.

Despite Kamarov's indignant protests, the General dispatched a Remora squadron to seize and board the cargo ship, from which they detached the heavy tanks filled with ekti. From the Juggernaut's bridge, he watched the bearded captain swearing at them; he muted the sound. The fast Remoras brought the valuable ekti cargo back to the big battleship, where it was stowed.

Preparing to depart, Lanyan opened the channel again, picking up Kamarov's rant in mid-sentence. '—piracy, outright piracy. I expect to be compensated for my load! Many Roamers died on blitzkrieg raids to obtain that ekti.'

'It's a war, Captain,' Lanyan said blandly. 'People die for all sorts of reasons.'

Fitzpatrick spoke a quiet, cold warning in the General's ear. 'The Roachers might retaliate for this action, sir. What if they cut us off entirely? They don't deliver much ekti any more, but they *are* our only suppliers.'

'You're right, Commander Fitzpatrick. Knowledge of this incident could cause trouble.'

'On the other hand, the episode becomes a non-issue if Kamarov never reports to other Roachers. Your orders, General?'

He sat back in his chair, knowing the decision was clear, and also knowing he was crossing a line. He looked at Fitzpatrick, the eager young officer ready to take charge . . . and, if necessary, to take the blame. Lanyan decided to keep his own hands clean.

He stood. 'I'm going to retire to my quarters. Commander Fitzpatrick, you have the bridge for now . . . and I think you understand what needs to happen here. As we discussed earlier, there are plenty of hazards in space.'

'Yes, sir!'

Lanyan left the bridge deck. He would issue appropriate statements to the crew later.

Fitzpatrick didn't even wait for the General to reach his quarters before ordering the Juggernaut to open fire on the Roamer cargo ship.

THIRTY-SEVEN

CESCA PERONI

At the farthest fringes of the Osquivel system, high above the planetary orbits, light from the sun was only slightly brighter than the shine from distant stars. Roamer cometary-extraction teams had strung together reflectors, solar mirrors, and condensers, as well as nuclear-powered furnaces. The lights of each substation reflected from scattered ice mountains and left-over gravel from the condensation of the solar system.

Piloting a small transport vehicle, Del Kellum ferried Cesca high above the impressive ring shipyards. He talked without rest, proud of the brash operations he had established in the distant cometary halo.

'We built those monstrous reactor furnaces in the Osquivel rings and kicked them way above the ecliptic. We chose a gravitationally stable place as a corral for the comets. Impelling engines knock them out of their orbits and tote them here for processing.'

'Playing billiards with frozen mountains,' Cesca said.

Kellum laughed as he negotiated the diffuse blizzard of snow

196

fragments. 'We don't usually bother with comet chips that are only *mountain* sized!'

The production yard held a swarm of small ships and giant factories. Workers set charges on the larger comets to fracture them into significant chunks, which were then coated with self-heating furnace films that cooked the ices down into constituent gases. Siphons drew off the resulting steam.

'See? Who needs skymines?' Kellum said with forced optimism. 'This isn't just a show-off exercise. It really works.'

'You certainly rose to my challenge, Del Kellum, but don't paint too rosy a picture for me,' Cesca said. 'I've seen the numbers. It's a long way from being efficient enough.'

'By damn, we don't have any other choice. Any clan leader who can't think outside the box should roll over and open his faceplate to the vacuum.' He shook his head. 'With improved ekti reactors, we can meet our minimal requirements. Shizz, there might even be some left over to sell to the Big Goose. Otherwise, they'll think we're cheating them.'

Cesca rolled her eyes. 'They think we're cheating them, no matter what. It's the way their minds work.'

Though Roamers had always been outcasts, they had once carved a respectable niche for themselves by supplying ekti. Now, without that resource, she feared that one day desperate Roamers would have no choice but to fall back into the greater community of the Hansa. They might have to sign the Charter, attach themselves to the government they had struggled for so long to escape.

Or the desperate Hansa would hunt them down.

She didn't like to be faced with a choice between survival and freedom.

But Cesca could think of nowhere to turn for aid. Who else was in their position? Roamers had worked many years for the Ildirans on leased skymines, but they had finally earned their independence. With no ekti to offer, the Mage-Imperator would have no use for the Roamers. Clan gatherings discussed the possibilities of alliances with weaker outlying Hansa colonies or with Theroc.

She lived each day now with a sick feeling of overwhelming responsibility, but she couldn't ask the Roamer engineers and inventors to work any harder. They had already stretched their capabilities to the breaking point.

Outside, cometary rubble was fed into a moon-sized chamber where it was flash-heated into volatile elements. Atomic separators bled off the hydrogen molecules, and cometary sludge drained out from reclamation ducts. The impurities held numerous heavy elements that were recycled for other purposes.

Cesca studied the activity as Kellum continued to fly her on a slow tour. It was her ostensible reason for being here, though she would rather have been down in the ring shipyards with Jess as he looked over the nebula skimmers. She wondered when they could arrange another romantic encounter . . .

Del Kellum docked to the largest comet evaporator chamber. The huge thin-walled structure rose up in black silhouette, eclipsing the sparkling lights of the industrial encampment. 'We like to call this the cometary Hilton. Finest place this side of the Kuiper Belt.'

Cesca smiled. 'As the Speaker for all clans, I am naturally accustomed to such . . . luxury.'

The bright lounge and rec room had standard plate-metal walls. Kellum proudly showed her his tank of sleek black-and-silver angelfish. 'They breed well enough, even out here. I have similar tanks in many of my facilities, just a little reminder of home.'

'Fish in space? Couldn't you take up gardening instead?'

'Not the same.' He slid a cup of clear liquid across the table. 'Here, made from pure cometary water. First time it's been processed since the beginning of the solar system. Every other drink you've had has been recycled through human bodies and reclamation systems a thousand times over. This is virgin water – hydrogen and oxygen, nothing else. Upscale markets consider it a real treat.'

Cesca looked down at the cup. 'Does it taste any different?'

He shrugged. 'Not to me.'

A worker hurried in carrying a transcribed message. 'Speaker Peroni! This just came up from a transport vessel at the ring shipyards.' Seeing the earnest expression on the young man's face, Kellum waved him over.

She took the message, hoping it was some word from Jess, but dreading it might be some emergency. The path of the transmission was long and convoluted, sent out in identical copies through dozens of passing traders. One Roamer had brought it to Rendezvous, then someone else had tracked her down at Osquivel.

'Anyone who's willing to send a message through that many channels either has very bad news or wants to find you in the worst possible way,' Kellum said.

The worst possible way.

Reynald of Theroc had sent a carefully worded proposal. A marriage proposal.

He was about to take on the role as his world's Father and needed a strong woman beside him. He listed logical and obvious reasons why an alliance between Therons and Roamers would strengthen their independence from the Hansa; it would allow them to share resources and capabilities, and thus stand firm against any EDF attempts at bullying. The recent siege at the Yreka colony demonstrated the Hansa's ruthlessness. There was no guarantee that Theroc, or the Roamers, would not become the next targets.

The EDF can't fight the hydrogues, so they look for other victories, even if it means stepping on their own people. With

Theron green priests and Roamer ekti production, we could form a formidable union. Think about it. I'm sure it's a good idea.' Cesca could imagine Reynald smiling shyly at her. 'Besides, you and I would be a good match.'

She read the message again, her heart torn. She saw a curious Del Kellum trying to catch glimpses of the note, but she quickly folded it. 'I need to think about this, Del. We'll have to finish our tour later.'

She and Jess Tamblyn had nearly reached the date when they had planned to announce their marriage. She loved Jess so much, and she had waited so long. Cesca deserved this modest share of happiness.

But what if Reynald was right?

She knew what Speaker Okiah would say. How could Cesca let her own emotions take precedence over the future of all Roamer clans? The Therons would indeed be a powerful – and palatable – ally, far more acceptable than either the Big Goose or the Ildiran Empire.

And yet . . .

THIRTY-EIGHT

ADAR KORI'NH

Under orange skies lit by Hyrillka's secondary sun, Adar Kori'nh finished his complex skyparade manoeuvres with two active warliners. The remaining five battleships were grounded for servicing and restocking at the plaza spaceport so that the septa would be ready to return to Ildira within a day. Prime Designate Jora'h did not intend to stay here for long.

After the routine performance, Kori'nh flew his flagship back over the mosaic landing field. While the big ornate vessel hovered above the crowds, fin-like solar sails glittering, his sensor technicians performed a thorough status check of all systems.

Thus, they were the first to discover the hydrogue warglobe hurtling towards Hyrillka.

'Sound alarms!' Kori'nh said. With a sick dread in his chest, he realized that most of his warliner crews would be scattered throughout the city on temporary recreational leave. 'Summon all personnel back to our other five warliners, but don't wait for everyone. Launch the vessels as soon as they have adequate crew.'

Kori'nh ordered his two active battleships from the skyparade to take up guardian positions above the Designate's citadel palace. Fast scouts launched out to pace and track the incoming warglobe.

The performance streamers disengaged their fluttery display ribbons and banners, letting them drop towards the ground. Each small ship carried a standard complement of weapons, but they had not been loaded with enough rounds for a battle, especially not against hydrogues.

Nevertheless, they would make do.

Within minutes, the first of the big grounded warliners lifted off, filling the Adar with pride at her captain's efficiency in assembling a skeleton crew. Off-duty Solar Navy personnel raced back through the city and flooded aboard their waiting battleships, hurrying to their assigned stations.

Around the vine-covered citadel palace, courtiers sensed the urgency of the situation, but still did not understand what was going on. The three robed lens kithmen looked as confused as the people turning to them for explanations. The Hyrillka Designate drew his beloved pleasure companions close to him, reassuring. 'I will protect you, I promise.'

Then, when the diamond-hulled alien sphere dropped towards the city, the people reacted with sudden terror. Blue lightning crackled from the warglobe's pyramidal protrusions. The hydrogue craft sent no message, transmitted no warning or ultimatum. The deep-core aliens simply began laying waste to the planet.

Kori'nh felt sick as he watched from the command nucleus of his warliner. Each blast ripped up the ground, the structures, anything in the way. The lovely preserves, the exquisite hanging gardens, the canals lined with nialias – all vanished in cold, sapphire bolts of power.

Remembering how badly he had been beaten the last time at Qronha 3, the Adar growled with resolve. 'We did not ask for these enemies, but we will not stand by and do nothing.'

On the mosaic landing grid, the second grounded warliner was powering up. Finally, he had four Solar Navy warliners aloft. 'All ships surround the hydrogue and open fire with projectiles, explosives, energy surges – anything you have. Perhaps today we will earn a place in the *Saga*.'

The first warliner lunged forward, bolder than the others. Its silvery fins and banners looked like sharp plumage. Its weapons ports emitted an eye-numbing strobe of repeated bursts that pounded the diamond shell. Although Kori'nh guided his own vessel close enough to attack from the opposite side, the dual bombardment resulted in only smeared scorch marks on the warglobe's hull.

The hydrogue marauder did not seem to notice. Its blue lightning continued to rip up irrigation canals and devastate fields of waving nialias; some of the grey-white plantmoths broke from their stems and fluttered off. Steam and smoke snaked into the air.

Thrumming ominously overhead, the warglobe circled and came in for a second attack. Another sequence of crackling energy discharges vaporized the fringes of the main city.

At last, another of the grounded warliners powered up its engines and lumbered into the sky from the mosaic landing field, weapons ports already open and charged. But the ornate battleship had barely lifted from the spaceport tiles before the warglobe passed overhead. The Ildiran ship spat out defensive projectiles that struck as ineffectively as gnats against a marmoth's thick hide.

As if noticing the Solar Navy for the first time, the hydrogue struck back with lightning that ripped the hapless warliner apart even as it took off. Its hull breached, its fuel cells exploding, the great hulk tumbled back to the ground, its peacock-like solar fins fluttering. The dying vessel crashed into one of the two remaining warliners still preparing for emergency launch. Alarms sounded, shouts and screams cut off in a screech of static – then both vessels erupted in huge explosions.

Kori'nh's crew gasped in dismay and reeled from the resultant shockwaves in the *thism*, but he spoke a hard, sharp command. 'Stations! I need every soldier's full attention on this battle!' *I must not allow another failure! I am the supreme commander of the Solar Navy, protector of the Ildiran Empire—*

Before the final grounded warliner could move, the ruthless hydrogue closed in. Pyramidal spikes opened fire and destroyed that giant vessel as well. Thick pillars of greasy black smoke spewed from the wreckage in the spaceport as buildings caught the spreading blaze from ignited fuel cells.

'Full weapon bombardment! Kinetic missiles and cutting beams!' Kori'nh ordered. His captains needed no encouragement.

Even as the Solar Navy blasts pounded the lone diamond sphere, the warglobe ripped away at Hyrillka's lush vine forests, withering flowers and fields and gardens. Blue lightning toppled ornate buildings, vaporized utility structures, knocked down crystalline towers. The Solar Navy defenders could do little to stop the rampage, but Kori'nh was duty-bound to try.

The Hyrillka Designate squawked over the communications channel, 'Adar Kori'nh, you must evacuate our entire population immediately! We have no shelter against this attack.'

'Designate, there aren't enough ships, and there isn't enough time. We have only four warliners left, and I cannot disengage them from the battle.'

The hydrogue sphere launched a sidelong volley that scraped one of the four warliners but caused only moderate damage. The battleship limped away to repair its systems, while the remaining three continued to hammer ineffectually at the enemy.

'But Adar, you have to save them!' The Designate sounded incredulous, as if unable to believe the Solar Navy could be anything but invincible. Kori'nh thought Rusa'h had watched too many military pageants.

He realized what he must do. 'I am sending a rescue shuttle down to your citadel, Designate. I will take you to safety, along with the Prime Designate and his son. That is my highest priority.'

'You can't leave all my people to die,' the Designate wailed. 'My performers, my advisers . . . my beautiful pleasure companions!'

'I cannot save them.' The Adar's heart wrenched as he gave orders for his personal warliner to withdraw from the engagement. He snapped to one of his crewmen, 'Dispatch a personnel transport, right now! Cram as many people aboard it as possible, but make sure you get the Designates.' The soldier raced off to the flight deck. 'The rest of you—'

'Adar, look!' interrupted one of the tactical technicians, his voice cracking with strain.

Kori'nh glanced into the ruddy skies to see a second warglobe descending towards the inhabited surface. Its energy weapons began to crackle without mercy as it joined the onslaught of the first alien ship.

THIRTY-NINE

RLINDA KETT

The voyage to Rheindic Co was lonely and dull, even though Rlinda had a passenger. The tall, reticent black man was less of a companion than a void of silence.

As soon as they had lifted off from Crenna, Davlin Lotze was ready to bury himself in his work. 'I assume Chairman Wenceslas provided dossiers and briefing materials?'

She shrugged her broad shoulders. 'He loaded files into my computer before I left. Knock yourself out.' She waved him towards a workscreen and he immediately began scanning the information. 'I haven't checked to see if the files are passworded.'

Lotze regarded her with hard mahogany eyes. 'Yes you have.'

Rlinda didn't know whether to be offended or amused that he saw through her so easily. 'Well, I do have a right to know what's aboard my ship, Mr Lotze – including information.'

The quiet spy smiled as he scanned the screen. 'All the files are public domain anyway.'

'Are you just a bad conversationalist, or do you fall all the way into the "antisocial" category?'

'The Crenna settlers liked me well enough.' Lotze looked up from his screen, pausing the playback of summaries and reports. 'I have no objection to your presence, but this assignment requires my full attention right now.'

Lotze kept to himself for the next several hours, poring over the records and reports, memorizing the Colicoses' Rheindic Co updates, as well as earlier work on Llaro, Pym, and Corribus. When he finally took a brief break to eat, Rlinda crossed her arms over her chest. 'You suspect foul play in their disappearance?'

'At the moment, we aren't even sure they disappeared. We know only that contact was cut off.'

'Hmmm, could be someone retaliating against them for discovering the Klikiss Torch. When you get right down to it, that was the start of this hydrogue mess. Plenty of people are pissed off.'

'And so are the hydrogues. We shall see what we can find once we arrive.'

As the golden-tan planet grew larger in the viewscreen, Rlinda used the ship's intercom to call Lotze from his cabin. There wasn't room for the tall man to sit in the cockpit, but he watched the approach to Rheindic Co, as if comparing these details with the archive records.

Without asking her permission, Lotze leaned over the control panels and activated the ship's general scanners. 'I know the approximate location of the team's base camp.' He called up a continental image, centring in at the edge of dawn so that he spotted canyons in the long shadows of an early desert morning. 'Try there. Do an overflight.'

'Maybe they'll run out and flag us down. That'd save plenty of time.'

He looked at her sceptically. 'It's been five years. Unless they found some other food source, the three human members of the expedition would not have had sufficient materials to last this long.'

Rlinda frowned as she cruised down through the bumpy atmosphere. 'If there's no chance of finding anyone alive, isn't this a pointless mission?'

He frowned. 'No mission is pointless if you understand the objective. I have been instructed to find answers, not survivors.'

The *Curiosity* discovered the remains of the Colicos camp close to a large cluster of empty Klikiss ruins. The tents and equipment had been set up on an open rise high enough above the cracked arroyos to be safe from flash floods. Rlinda easily found a place to land on the barren ground.

The two emerged into hot, brittle air. Lotze carried a case in one hand and a satchel in the other, ready to get to work.

The desert colours were harsh, but with a purity that made all edges razor-sharp and clear. The rugged strata provided a stark contrast to the lush greens of other planets Rlinda had visited. The majestic mountains were still purple with dawn shadows. 'Nice place to set up a resort – maybe a spa, a golf course.'

A dust devil skittered in front of them, whipping up flakes of loose debris, and went drunkenly on its way before dissipating.

'What concerns me is that even the telink was cut off,' Lotze said. 'We know that the worldtrees perished, perhaps in a fire or storm, thereby terminating the green priest's ability to communicate.'

Despite five years of desert weather, heat, and dust storms that had left the base camp shabby and windblown, it did not look as if any terrible disaster had occurred there. Lotze entered the main tent and ran an experienced eye over the cots, non-functional computers, samples and notes that had fallen to the ground under the influence of time and gravity.

Meanwhile, Rlinda went to the water pump. The moving parts had frozen up, but she could easily lubricate and fix the system.

Judging by Lotze's obsessive dedication, she guessed that the man intended to remain here until he found his answers. Whether that meant days or months, she couldn't guess.

Lotze stepped out of the ragged tent, carrying what he had salvaged of the archaeologists' computers and logbooks. He spread the items on the ground, taking inventory.

Rlinda walked around the perimeter to a smaller tent that must have belonged to the green priest. Behind it, the remains of the worldtree grove were obvious. 'You might want to take a look at this!'

The treelings had been planted in rows and no doubt lovingly tended by the green priest – but each one had been uprooted and torn apart as if by a furious vandal. The splintered remains of their thin stalks lay scattered, covered by blowing dust. Time had muted the details, but the scene still conveyed a sense of violence.

Lotze arrived, his eyes absorbing everything without blinking. 'This explains why telink contact was cut off.'

Rlinda's foot bumped against something hard in the soft ground, like driftwood. She stooped and dug her fingers into the dust to find a twisted object. The outer surface was dry, leathery, desiccated. She scraped the powder away, already knowing in the pit of her stomach what she would find.

The shrivelled, mummified face of a hairless, green-skinned man looked up at her. All soft tissue had been leeched of moisture by the arid environment; muscles had drawn tight, pulling his expression into a strange grimace. The meat on his body had shrunk and dried to a hard lacquer clinging to his bones. The desert had done its work, both destroying and preserving the body.

'Our green priest,' she said. 'Arcas – wasn't that his name?'

Lotze scanned the remains of the camp. 'He does not appear to have been formally buried. Therefore, I doubt he died under normal circumstances.' He paced the area, sifting ideas through his mind. 'Perhaps Margaret or Louis experienced some sort of cabin fever?'

Rlinda stood, leaving the exposed green-tinged body in the dry dust. She would find time to move the poor man while Lotze continued his snooping. 'You might be a detective, Davlin, but I'm not sure you really understand people. This old couple were married for decades. They spent half their lives isolated on alien digs – people like that can handle solitude.'

'I'm not ready to draw conclusions yet,' Lotze said. 'They also had a compy and three Klikiss robots.'

Rlinda nodded towards the cliff city where the nearest set of alien buildings waited like ancient secrets. 'Want to go sightseeing in those ruins?'

Empty Klikiss cities had been found on numerous planets, but fully investigated on few. The sentient race had built hive-like structures in prairie environments or tunnelled into canyon walls. The Ildirans had known about the lost race for a long time, but they left the abandoned ghost cities alone.

In its early days, excited by the possibilities of expansion, the Terran Hanseatic League commissioned explorers to investigate worlds the Ildirans had catalogued and then ignored. The Colicoses' discovery of the Klikiss Torch had reawakened interest in the lost civilization though the hydrogue war quashed plans for more intensive excavations.

Now Rlinda wandered through the musty tunnels with amazement on her face. The alien buildings were made of a polymerized concrete, some sort of silica-enhanced fibre, perhaps manufactured organically by the insectile Klikiss. Each wall was covered with strange hieroglyphics and incomprehensible equations.

She and Lotze spent a day in the mazes of the ghost metropolis, finding a few items of Colicos equipment, but little more. 'The last report of Margaret Colicos described a second, better preserved set of ruins,' Lotze said. 'My suspicion is that they spent their days working there.'

Taking general directions, Rlinda flew the *Curiosity* low until they tracked down the canyon and found wrecked scaffolding that had once been mounted on the cliff wall.

'We need to get inside,' Davlin said.

'Sure. Just find me a parking lot big enough to land this ship.' He didn't laugh at her joke, so she came up with an innovative solution. 'The *Curiosity* is designed to haul cargo, Davlin. Down in the loading bay I've got several levitating pallets. They can handle even the two of us together.'

She landed on the flat mesa above the cliff walls. Then, standing next to Lotze on the high-tech raft, Rlinda steered them with painful slowness towards the edge of the cliff and then down the wall. 'This thing is made for moving big crates, not winning any races.'

She manoeuvred the levitating pallet inside the cliff overhang and set it down on the rocky floor where dust had begun to collect in corners. The air smelled dry, and their footsteps made whispery sounds as they entered.

Davlin pointed to lights and wires strung along the corridors, markings on the walls, and tags left behind. 'Margaret's notes indicate that she was quite enthusiastic about what they would find here.'

Rlinda squinted into the shadows, shining her portable light. 'Well maybe something found her instead. I should have brought a weapon. I've got two on my ship, I think.'

Lotze focused on his surroundings, all of his senses attuned to picking up clues. Deeper inside the cliff city they found a scattered, pathetically desperate-looking barricade piled in front of the entrance to a large chamber. It had been knocked down from the outside. Rlinda shone her light into the room and saw machinery, large flat walls.

And an old man's body lying on the floor.

Lotze hurried through a break in the barricade, directing his light. Louis Colicos was better preserved than the green priest, enough that Rlinda could tell with a glance that he had died violently. His body was broken and torn, with many deep wounds. Cautious now, she looked behind her, eyes wide, as if expecting something to jump out at any moment.

One wall was a trapezoidal blank space like a window made of stone, oddly devoid of Klikiss markings, framed by a sequence of symbol plates. On the smooth surface, brownish red smears – bloody handprints – stood out like a shout, as if in the last moments before his death Louis Colicos had pounded the wall, trying to make it open.

With furrowed brow, Lotze looked at the handprint and the blank wall. 'Two bodies recovered, but still no explanations. And where is Margaret Colicos?'

A rippling shudder went down Rlinda's back. She felt they might be here on Rheindic Co for a long time indeed.

FORTY

ANTON COLICOS

'I have chosen an activity you may enjoy, Rememberer Anton,'
Vao'sh said. 'I am intrigued by the favourite techniques of
traditional human storytellers. Let us see if we can recreate
some of them.'

The rememberer took him out to the seaside, where they sat
alone on a blustery plateau a dozen metres above the waters of a
sheltered inlet. The breeze was warm, and Anton detected a sour
tang of blooming aquatic plant life, rafts of large orange flowers like
a cross-breed of lily pads and ribbony kelp.

Bustling, jabbering attenders had arrived ahead of them and
piled knobby driftwood into a conical mound interspersed with dry
tinder. The small-statured servant kithmen ignited the pile of
wood, then withdrew as the flames took hold. The attenders
scuttled away.

The two historians, isolated now, sat on cushiony moss-like
growths in the soft sand. The bonfire rose higher, flickering on
their faces. 'Is this not the correct milieu, Rememberer Anton?
Spinning tales by a campfire at the seaside?'

Anton smiled. 'Of course, you're missing one vital ingredient – such stories are best told in the dark, rather than constant dazzling daylight.'

Vao'sh shuddered. 'That is not the sort of thing any Ildiran would enjoy.'

The young man leaned towards the flames, rubbing his hands together. 'We'll make do.'

As a boy, he remembered staying up late some nights in the Pym archaeological camp with his parents, listening to stories by firelight. He felt a brief sadness and hoped his mother and father were all right; he wasn't likely to get any word of them here on Ildira.

He took a deep breath and said, 'Even before our civilization was recorded, storytellers chose to sit by bright fires, safe because dire wolves and cave bears and sabretooths were afraid of the flames. Those storytellers would talk about great giants or monsters or predators that might snatch children from their mothers.' Anton smiled. 'They also told tales of heroes, warriors or mammoth hunters who were braver and stronger than anyone else. Talespinners used stories to construct a framework of comprehensibility in a mysterious world. Stories formed our moral character.'

From the bluff above the sheltered inlet, Anton spotted sleek, dark figures swimming in from the open sea. Vao'sh looked out at the water. 'It is a swimmer harvest crew returning with the changing tide.'

The Ildiran swimmer kithmen reminded Anton of lissome otters, delightfully resilient, who worked hard yet seemed to make it a game.

'Swimmers are covered with thin fur over an extra layer of subcutaneous fat to keep them warm in the cold, deep currents,' Vao'sh explained. 'Note their large eyes. They have an extra lens membrane that allows them to see well under water. The ears lie flat against smooth heads, and the noses are high on the face so they can swim with their nostrils above the water.'

'What are those baskets they're towing behind them?'

'Swimmers harvest kelpweeds, shellfish, coral-eggs. Some of them herd schools of fish, culling them for food.'

'Oceanic cowboys.'

The rememberer's face lobes flushed through a symphony of colours. 'An apt analogy.' The bonfire continued to crackle and pop. 'Swimmers live on large rafts tethered to the sea floor. As the fish schools move or as sections of the seaweed forest are picked clean, they cut the raft tethers and drift to other parts of the ocean.'

Anton shook his head. 'I'll never get used to so many kiths. How can you keep track of them all?'

'To me, it is amazing that all humans look so similar. How can you keep track of yourselves?'

Anton picked up a stick and prodded the glowing coals in the middle of the bonfire. 'You just need to get used to us, Vao'sh.'

The rememberer gestured towards the swimmers carrying cargo nets to dock structures, where landbound workers met them to retrieve the day's catch. 'I know a story about swimmers from the *Saga of Seven Suns.*'

'Is it a ghost story, a frightening tale best told around the campfire?'

The rememberer's face flickered through a palette of colours. 'It is a love story . . . of a sort. We have a kith that lives and works in our driest deserts, arid-born and lizard-like. The scalies are able to go for months with only minimal moisture.' Vao'sh smiled. 'Thus, you can imagine that the love between the scaly worker Tre'c and the swimmer Kri'l was doomed to tragedy.'

Anton furrowed his brow. 'I thought Ildiran kiths were welcome to interbreed?'

Vao'sh made a dismissive gesture. 'Oh, we have no prejudice

against mixed bloodlines. Even so, the romance between a scaly and a swimmer was ill-fated by its very nature. No one can now say what attracted them to each other. Tre'c and Kri'l must have known the difficulties they would face, but still they would not be pulled apart. Tre'c could not tolerate the salt water of the ocean, and Kri'l could not survive in the dry desert.

'So, Tre'c built his home on a rocky beach, high enough from the closest approach of the tides. Kri'l tethered her raft inside a cove near the beach. They could call to each other and talk. And though they could tolerate each other's environment for only an hour each day, that hour together was more joyous than a lifetime spent with anyone else.

'Tre'c and Kri'l had several years of happiness, until one day a great storm came into the cove, tore up the beach, and cast Kri'l's raft up on to the rocks, destroying Tre'c's shelter and washing it away. The two of them clung together as the rains poured down and the waves battered them. The cliffs crumbled, the sand and rocks slid down in an avalanche, the ocean hurled them against the beach. The land and the sea swallowed them up.

'Their bodies were never found, but sometimes . . .' Vao'sh said, colours streaming like sunrise across his face, 'Ildirans come upon empty stretches of beach where the water laps against the dry sand, places where few people ever go and no one watches. There, we sometimes encounter two sets of footprints, a swimmer and a scaly walking alone on the deserted strand, one set of footprints in the moist mud, the other on the dry beach.'

The bonfire continued to crackle, and Anton leaned back with his hands on the soft, mossy groundcover. 'That's a wonderful story, Vao'sh.' He tried to think of how he could match the tale before the campfire burned down. 'And now I have one for you.'

FORTY-ONE

NIRA

Because Ildirans liked to live in close quarters where they could sense the crowded presence of others, they had designed and constructed the sleeping barracks of the human prisoners along similar lines. Nira's home was a large building with numerous bunks, tables, and common areas. Here the people cooked, slept, and played games – whenever they weren't required for other duties. It was like a giant extended family all crowded under one roof.

Nira lived quietly among them, sharing meals, sleeping when they slept, though for years she had felt separate, walled off because she was so different. The people did not ostracize her consciously, yet she had found it difficult to let herself fit in. She cared about her fellow captives, but could never quite escape the feeling of loneliness, even when surrounded by them.

Now, during Dobro's dark night outside, she sat quietly, listening to the chatter around her. In her own space, Nira kept several plants in makeshift pots, nurturing flowers, a small bush, some sweet-smelling herbs. Plants were a comfort to her.

She remembered how Father Idriss and Mother Alexa held so many colourful celebrations and festivals in the huge fungus-reef city on Theroc. Every day, workers had climbed tall worldtrees: gathering the black seedpods from which they made stimulating clee, harvesting epiphytes for their juices, cutting open condorfly pupae for the tender meat inside. Groups of green priest acolytes – Nira among them – had scaled the armoured trunks to reach the interlocked canopy, where they would read aloud to the curious trees.

Those had been the best years in her life . . .

Now, a man began coughing, and his chosen wife put him to bed, then went to fill out a requisition for the medicine he needed. Nira looked around at the other bunks, at the clustered family groups the people had instinctively formed even under circumstances such as these. They seemed to believe they had a normal life.

On Dobro, men and women still fell in love, bonded with each other, and had children – though at any time a female might be chosen for her genetic characteristics and be sent off to the breeder barracks. Their husbands might not be happy when it happened, but they accepted it. They had been trained for generations to live within this new and unnatural social order.

In turn, the male human prisoners were forced to mate with dozens, even hundreds, of Ildiran women. The guards and medical kithmen dealt with any man who refused to perform his duty by repeatedly 'harvesting' his sperm, and eventually returning him to the work gangs as a eunuch . . .

Nira felt more anguish for their plight than they themselves did. She knew that humans were resilient and could learn to accept many things. The strength and endurance she saw in these prisoners was not what saddened her, however – it was that they had forgotten what life was *supposed* to be like.

Though darkness had fallen hours ago, and the beautiful stars had come out in the clear sky, the lights would never go off in the crowded barracks. In keeping with Ildiran practice, darkness was never allowed inside the buildings except as a form of punishment. By now, the human prisoners were well conditioned to sleep under full light. Many of the children had already gone to bed, while the adults remained awake, talking and relaxing.

It was the best time for her to speak to them. The prisoners knew little of the generation ships from Earth, nothing of the overall Ildiran Empire or the Terran Hanseatic League. The people here had never been taught their origins except for an ever-more-fanciful oral history that retained glimmers of truth, passed from one generation to the next. Nira, with her knowledge of story cycles and the Ildiran *Saga*, found the distorted tales interesting in the rare moments when she could detach herself.

Now she edged forward, listening to seven men and women who sat together in a loose circle, exchanging stories, jokes, and gossip. Benn Stoner, a gruff-voiced man whose skin looked as if it had been sandblasted, noticed her interest. 'Go ahead, Nira Khali. What story do you have for us this evening?'

'Make it a good one!'

'She's had all day under the hot sun to think of some new nonsense—' a younger man said, but his words cut off when Stoner glared at him.

Nira pretended not to notice. Even if the other Dobro prisoners rarely believed the things she said, at least they listened. Her tales helped them to pass the time.

'I will tell you the story of Thara Wen and how she became the first green priest on Theroc.' She waited a moment for the answering smiles, knowing that the people were amused by her tales about 'fantasy lands'.

'Thara was born on the *Caillié* only a few years before the

Ildirans found our generation ship and set us down in the world-forest. Theroc was beautiful and temperate, full of food and resources. From the beginning, our colony was peaceful. There was little crime, for there was no need.'

'Just like here on Dobro,' said the snide young man.

'No. Not like Dobro. Not at all.' Nira drew a deep breath. 'But from time to time, for reasons we cannot understand, a person carries darkness in his heart. One such man attacked Thara Wen in the thickest worldforest, chasing her, intending to kill her. He had already killed others. But she fled among the thickets, burying herself in the densest worldtree fronds. And as the forest protected her, hid her from the murderer, the trees also joined with her, engulfing her . . . making contact.

'When Thara emerged, all of her hair had fallen out, and her skin had turned a bright green.' Nira rubbed her own arms. 'And she had the ability to communicate with the trees. She could remember everything the forest had ever seen, and the trees told her about the man's other victims. When she returned to the settlement and accused him, showing the elders where the bodies were buried, the man was sentenced to death – the first criminal on Theroc. He was tied at the top of the canopy and left there until a wyvern came along and killed him.'

Some of her listeners were intrigued, others clearly sceptical, but the young man made another joke. 'Oh, does that explain why your skin is green? I always thought you were just another strange halfbreed.'

'Show some respect,' Benn Stoner said. 'The Designate chooses her for the breeding barracks more often than any of us.' He said this as if it was some sort of honour. 'We thank you for your story, Nira.'

Nira went back to her bunk, where she could still hear them talking. Stoner took his turn, keeping the oral tradition alive, telling the old and garbled stories. He spoke vaguely about a long journey, a home that was not called Earth, but *Burton*. They didn't even know.

According to their own legends, these people had come to Dobro in friendship, living in happy prosperity with the Ildirans. But some terrible and unforgivable crime – they could not say what it was – had caused the Ildirans to turn their colony settlement into an armed camp. None of the captives knew how many more generations would have to pay for this sin.

Feeling deeply sad for them, Nira said from her bunk, 'It isn't like this everywhere, you know. There are billions of people on countless worlds. Dobro is one of the worst.'

Benn Stoner lifted his chin and spoke gruffly as he indicated the walls of the barracks and, by implication, the fences and the bleak landscape that led nowhere. 'Dobro is all we have, Nira Khali. Your fantasies can't help us here.'

FORTY-TWO

PRIME DESIGNATE JORA'H

The Solar Navy rescue shuttle descended through the flame-streaked sky, approaching the Hyrillka citadel palace. It arrived just as the second warglobe attacked.

This new hydrogue sphere dispersed a kind of weapon none of the Ildirans had seen before: devastating waves of cold punctuated by jets of white mist that froze anything they touched. The frigid onslaught swept across the vegetation, shattering thick vines. Hyrillka's verdant landscape cringed like a beaten cur, crumpled and shrivelled.

Then the two warglobes circled back for another attack.

Jora'h grabbed his son's thin arm and they raced out of the courtyard, dodging explosions in the citadel palace. The alien bombardment thundered down from the skies as the four surviving Solar Navy warliners hammered ineffectually against the marauders.

'What are we to do?' Thor'h cried. 'Why won't they stop?'

Jora'h had no answer for him.

Frantic courtiers and performers rushed about inside the banquet chambers. The three lens kithmen herded people out into the open to avoid the collapsing buildings; other Ildirans fled deep inside to find shelter. No place seemed safe. The hydrogues had no particular target in mind. They destroyed as much of the uninhabited vine forests and vegetation as they did of the Ildiran city.

'Help!' Thor'h shouted, as if the citadel itself could respond. He ran to a coloured window, but his father yanked him back an instant before it shattered. Crystal shards and a gust of cold air blew inwards in the wake of a warglobe discharge, and Jora'h pulled the young man down as debris tinkled around them. Thor'h touched numerous stinging cuts on his face and arms, saw that his fine clothes were shredded. He stammered in disbelief. 'We've got to find my uncle. He will know what to do. He will save everyone.'

'No he won't,' Jora'h said. 'He cannot. Adar Kori'nh is going to evacuate us.' *And leave all these people behind . . . so many people.*

Overhead in the soot-stained sky, the Ildiran warliners – all damaged – faced off against the crystalline globes. Jora'h didn't see how they could survive. The two hydrogue warglobes cruised across the orange-tainted sky, spilling more death. The air echoed with roaring blasts and thunderous explosions.

'I have to protect you, Thor'h. You're the next Prime Designate. And I . . . will soon become Mage-Imperator.' He knew that his father would be sensing the Hyrillkan attack through the *thism*. Perhaps the shock and pain would even hasten the ailing leader's death. 'We must get away from the battle zone, somehow.'

With the diminishing daylight, thousands of dazzling lights automatically shimmered to life within the citadel, as if it were any other day.

Jora'h found his brother Rusa'h amid the chaos of fire and destruction in the open plaza under the tall, vine-covered arches. The chubby Hyrillka Designate raised his hands and waved his arms inside their ballooning sleeves. 'We must not panic! Please, get to safety.'

'Where?' a dancer cried. 'Where can we go?'

Rusa'h grabbed his performers, pushing them away from the fires and explosions. His pleasure mates turned to him for protection, their lovely faces streaked with smoke, dust, blood, and sweat. 'Go to the bubbling pools,' he said, still looking pathetically forlorn and helpless. 'There will be shelter. I hope.' The women hurried off, confident in his advice, but Rusa'h didn't seem so certain.

Both hydrogues cruised above the landscape, one criss-crossing the fertile nialia fields with blue lightning bolts, the other with cold white icewaves. As the second warglobe circled, unhindered by the pin pricks of the Solar Navy streamers, Jora'h saw that the governmental citadel would be levelled in the next attack. 'Everyone off the hill! Get down and scatter.'

The Hyrillka Designate looked at his brother in confusion, then relief lit his face. 'Yes! Do as the Prime Designate says!' The people began to run. Stragglers continued to evacuate from the inner chambers of the citadel palace.

Finally, Adar Kori'nh's rescue shuttle landed in the courtyard, its hull smoking from a minor hydrogue blast. Many Hyrillkans raced towards the vessel, but burly warrior kithmen strode out of the open hatches, their armour spiny, their eyes alert. 'We have come only for the Designates. Stand down! We have orders from Adar Kori'nh.'

Grabbing his uncle's arm, young Thor'h lurched towards the shuttle, frantic. 'Yes, get us out of here.'

Mentally counting, Jora'h addressed one of the warriors from the rescue shuttle. 'How many people can fit aboard?'

'You, Prime Designate, your son, and your brother.'

'How many others?' he insisted.

'Our priority is to take you to a safe place. Perhaps some of your brother's children. That is all.'

'I give the orders. I'm the Prime Designate.' Jora'h waited for an answer.

The warrior finally said, 'Forty-eight other passengers, at the maximum lift capacity of this shuttle.'

'Good. Start loading people.'

The Hyrillka Designate tore his arm away from Thor'h. 'No! My favourite pleasure mates are still inside the citadel palace. I told them to meet us at the bubbling pool. We have to rescue them. They . . . they are very important to me.'

'No time,' Jora'h said. Overhead, the warglobe loomed closer. Blue lightning tore the hillside where evacuees were racing pell-mell into the open streets.

'You can't just abandon them. Some are carrying my children.' The Hyrillka Designate suddenly showed an uncharacteristic expression of determined bravery. He turned and ran inside, fighting his way through the littered and broken corridors. 'They counted on me for protection. I will save them.'

Jora'h was amazed at his hedonistic and soft-hearted brother, whom he had always considered to be spoiled and vapid; but the Hyrillka Designate showed a different side of himself now. Then Jora'h thought of his own lovers, especially of dear Nira Khali. Yes, for Nira he would even have run into a hydrogue attack. Just as Rusa'h was doing.

In a strangely sharp and commanding tone, young Thor'h snapped to the burly warriors, 'Go stop my uncle before he is injured! It is your duty to rescue the Hyrillka Designate. He is the son of the Mage-Imperator.'

Without hesitating, two warrior kithmen sprinted through the entryway and vanished into the complex after Rusa'h. A mob of Hyrillkans crowded towards the rescue shuttle.

Overhead, the hydrogues kept attacking. The second warglobe played a volley of blue lightning on to the ornate palace structure. Explosions ripped open the airy arched walls. Scraps of the hanging gardens erupted into flames and greasy smoke.

A convergence of four electric beams tore into the heart of the citadel, where Designate Rusa'h had gone, shattering an entire wing. The walls collapsed, and smoke gushed from the rooflines.

'No, Uncle!' Thor'h broke away from the safety of the rescue shuttle and ran towards the collapsed section. 'The Designate is trapped inside! We must dig him out.' Jora'h and three more guards raced after him.

Still harried by Kori'nh's warliners, the pair of hydrogues passed overhead. Ripples of white icewave struck eight small streamers, knocking them from the sky like kernels of grain harvested by a random wind.

The brawny warriors shoved their way through collapsed corridors and finally reached the rubble of the bubbling-pool chamber. The walls and domed ceiling had tumbled into a rubble of tile shards and transparent blocks.

'He entered here just before the explosion,' said one warrior. 'The Designate must be buried under the debris.'

'He's dead,' Thor'h moaned.

With clawed hands and muscular arms, warrior kithmen tossed aside chunks of wreckage, ripping through the rubble, moving support girders and reinforcement bars. Pillars toppled, trapping the Designate but also sheltering him from large sections of the fallen ceiling.

Finally, they uncovered a pale hand and a scrap of colourful robes now speckled with blood. Four injured pleasure mates had survived on the other side of the shrapnel and debris, soaking wet. Some had been caught in the bubbling pool; two had already drowned, stunned by falling bricks.

Fires continued to spread through the ruined palace, and the smoke could not escape through ragged gaps in the ceiling or broken walls. Jora'h hurried forward to help, though his strength could not match that of the powerful soldiers.

Outside, screams, explosions, and weapons fire echoed across the sky. But Jora'h focused on freeing his brother's body. He tried to sense him through the *thism*, but the glimmers of light and the connecting soul-threads had all grown dark and faint.

Two of the soldier kithmen lifted a heavy stone column and pushed it aside with a thunderous crash. They finally exposed Rusa'h's pudgy face. The cheeks were bruised and bloody, his eyes swollen shut, his mouth a grimace of pain. But his hair still twitched. His skin was flushed, his pulse weak but present.

'The Designate lives!' said one of the soldiers.

'Get him out of there,' Thor'h said. With hands unaccustomed to labour, he began to scrabble in the rubble until they had completely uncovered the Mage-Imperator's third-born son. Thor'h clung to his uncle as the soldiers picked him up gently. 'Quickly. We must get to the shuttle. Adar Kori'nh waits for us.'

They carried Designate Rusa'h, blood dripping from his wounds. The dedicated soldier kithmen rushed back down the rubble-strewn hall with Jora'h, Thor'h, and the four pleasure mates following closely behind. The Hyrillka Designate had suffered severe injuries, yet he *lived*.

Once they were aboard the shuttle, which was already crowded with dozens of refugees, the pilot wasted no time. Engines straining, the overloaded ship lifted away from the burning citadel palace. One of the Ildiran battleships broke off its defence, withdrew, and intercepted the personnel transport.

The Adar himself met them in the shuttle bay, though he knew he should not have left the command nucleus in the midst of an attack. He was relieved to see Jora'h and his son Thor'h, then dismayed at the grievously injured Hyrillka Designate.

Expert medical kithmen rushed into the shuttle bay, studied Rusa'h's injuries and also treated the wounds of the evacuees aboard the rescue craft. Thor'h remained anxiously beside his bleeding and unconscious uncle. The Hyrillka Designate clung to life, though he had not moved or moaned.

Adar Kori'nh issued a command to his crew. 'Withdraw! I want all streamers to flank and protect this ship. We must protect the Prime Designate and his son. I . . . can do nothing else to save the rest of these people.'

The flagship warliner pulled away, increasing its distance from the alien spheres, which continued to destroy the lush Hyrillkan landscape. But then the crystalline spheres incomprehensibly broke off their attack, for reasons of their own. Ignoring the Solar Navy, the alien globes climbed into the sky without looking at all hurried.

Watching from the command nucleus of the battered flagship, Jora'h said, 'Why? Why would they cause so much destruction and then simply . . . leave?'

Kori'nh stood like a petrified tree, struggling to hold his emotions inside. 'Perhaps they did not find what they were searching for.'

Without a word of explanation or celebration of victory, the hydrogue warglobes departed from Hyrillka and vanished into open space, leaving the once peaceful pleasure planet smoking and in ruins.

FORTY-THREE

JESS TAMBLYN

Borrowing a two-man grappler pod from Osquivel's construction yards, Jess went to meet Cesca Peroni on her descent from the cometary extraction clouds. He worked hard to hide his boyish anticipation, though it hadn't been very long since the last time they had seen each other.

Over an open channel, he transmitted, 'Speaker Peroni, allow me to escort you. A dozen more nebula skimmers are ready to be launched, all packaged up in their ballistic cocoons. It's quite a sight to see.'

'I'll drop her off with you, Jess,' Del Kellum said, his image wore a secret smile, as if he suspected something. 'I've got business to attend to.'

'Right, I think your angelfish need feeding. They've been snapping at some of the Roamer children when they walk by.'

Electric with sweet eagerness, Jess docked his grappler pod. Airlocks engaged, and Cesca came aboard, looking beautiful . . . but confused and troubled. He immediately understood that something was wrong.

'Take good care of her, Jess,' Kellum called from the other cockpit. 'She'll be wanting to go back to Rendezvous soon.'

Jess couldn't take his eyes from Cesca's forlorn face, but he said nothing until he sealed the hatches and disengaged. As the two ships drifted apart, Cesca draped an arm over his shoulder and hugged him silently. He did her the favour of not asking for details yet; he just kissed her on the forehead, then at the corner of her eye, and finally full on the mouth.

She drew him tighter with a desperate need, then slumped into the cockpit seat beside him. When Jess looked at her with an unspoken question, she finally said, 'Reynald is about to be crowned the new Father of Theroc, and he has proposed an alliance between our peoples. He . . . asked me to marry him.'

Jess felt as if she had struck him a physical blow. His entire world had revolved around the time until they could be wed. In the blink of an eye, that anchor dissolved like a tiny ball of puff-sugar in a cup of pepperflower tea.

Cesca didn't need to explain the political advantages of a marriage to Reynald. Jess knew the tight situation of the scattered Roamer clans: missing ships, supply shortages, lost ekti shipments. Many families doubted the drogues were responsible for everything, believing instead that the greedy Eddies had resorted to piracy.

Jess said in a hoarse voice, 'He's right. A union of Roamers and Therons might be strong enough to help us ride out this war and keep the Big Goose away. Yes . . . I suppose it makes good business sense.'

They both stared at each other, gradually feeling the numbness of shock fade into the pain of reality. Jess felt as if the deck had dropped out beneath him. Cesca looked at him with helpless dismay. 'Jess, I don't want to marry him.'

His shoulders slumped and he heaved a long, heavy sigh, and

he knew he was about to lose her once and for all. 'And I don't want you to. In fact, right now if I had the chance, I'd probably strangle him.'

She gave him a wan smile. 'I'd rather you didn't.'

'But you have to face reality, Cesca. You're the Speaker of all clans. Reynald will be the leader of all Theroc, including the green priests and the worldforest.'

'I know that, Jess – but I love *you*. This isn't just a . . . a business meeting.'

He gave her a stern look. 'Cesca, if you could just cast aside the greater good of every Roamer, if you could think only of your own wishes and ignore your obligations, then you wouldn't be the woman I love.'

Though distracted, he continued to fly the grappler pod through the hazardous debris around the shipyards. The challenge helped him to keep his troubled despair in check. He saw the Guiding Star in this situation.

She stared out at the stars. 'I'll resign as Speaker before I marry him, Jess. We'll let someone else take on the responsibility—'

'Who?' Anger edged into his voice now. 'Speaker Okiah trusted you. All the clans trust you. And who else can make this alliance with Theroc? You can't leave the Roamers adrift. You've got to be there to see us through these times.' As he said the indisputable words, he realized that just by telling her this – by speaking it out loud – he had made it real and unavoidable.

Jess watched her search for some legitimate argument, some way to convince him that she must decline Reynald's proposal. He held up a hand. His heart railed against his own words, but he knew he had to say them. 'Do I need to remind you how often you've told me that we must live our lives for a purpose greater than ourselves? If we didn't care about the good of our people, the two of us could have got married years ago and run off to live on Plumas.'

'Maybe we should have,' she said, but knew she didn't mean it, couldn't mean it. Until now, even she hadn't understood how deep her love for Jess ran.

They continued to argue, but all the possible solutions seemed selfish and forced. Jess stood firm, and he knew she could see he was right. What advice would she have given to someone else in her same position? The answer was obvious, according to all she had been taught, all she believed, and Cesca seemed to be surprised at her unwillingness to give up her dreams of happiness with Jess. Was that so much to ask?

Finally, as the grappler pod docked in the main Osquivel habitation, he said, 'Cesca, you know what you have to do.'

When she visited the shipyards, Cesca moved like a person only half-alive. She planned to stay long enough to watch the launch of the new nebula skimmers, then she would return to Rendezvous and get back to work. Why couldn't Jhy Okiah have picked someone else for the job?

But that wasn't what Cesca wanted. Those who lived quiet lives, normal lives, might occasionally dream of finding themselves in positions of importance and power – but most of them would gladly exchange that greatness to have their comfort back. Cesca, despite her torn heart, had no alternative but to pay that price. It was her Guiding Star. It was her foundation. She had to come to terms with her situation, accept her losses, no matter what they might be.

Jess avoided her, knowing that he could not help with this. His close presence would only make the decision harder. This was a rational, political choice that needed to be made with cool heads, not aching hearts. Their souls were bound together no matter what. That would never change.

But Jess knew one way to make this easier for her.

Del Kellum was astonished when the young man met him at the launching docks. 'I want to sign on aboard one of the new skimmers, Del. Yank one of the pilots, send him on the next one. But I need to depart now. If I don't go . . . Cesca will be distracted, tempted to make a decision for all the wrong reasons.'

'This is ill-advised, Jess.' Kellum seemed to understand the bittersweet regrets. Jess flushed. Did *everybody* know how they felt about each other? 'By damn, all that time alone is only going to give you an excuse to brood. Time can be a luxury or a curse, depending on how you look at it.'

Jess remained firm. 'I don't *want* to go, Del – but I know Cesca too well. Having me close by right now will be too hard for her. Much too hard. I've seen my Guiding Star, and I have to follow it.'

Kellum sighed. 'All right, I'll make the arrangements. Old Bram must have passed along his stubborn streak to you.'

Jess quickly bundled his possessions into the habitation module and checked all the stowed supplies before the ship was raised up and installed inside the ellipsoidal ballistic cocoon that contained the folded microfibre film.

Before he closed Jess inside the module, Kellum said, 'Want me to give her a message? She's going to watch the launch.'

'Tell her I wish that our hearts were our Guiding Stars. But they're not.' Jess squeezed his eyes shut. 'Cesca will do what she needs to do. She always has.'

Aboard the ring station, Cesca would stand beside Del Kellum and commend the launch of the new nebula skimmers. It was her duty as Speaker, and she would do it well.

From inside his cosy module, Jess listened as if in a daze to the dispatches, checklists, run-downs. All too soon, the ballistic cocoons shot out into open space, like spores from a mushroom. His journey would be swift until he reached the gaseous nebula sea, where the pod would open and the petals extend.

Far, far from Osquivel.

He wanted to put all thought and feeling out of his mind, but he would have much too much time to mull everything over. Again and again.

Even before he reached his destination at the heart of the nebula, Jess knew that Cesca would do what was necessary and agree to marry Reynald.

FORTY-FOUR

REYNALD

Returning home to Theroc, Sarein rode in a Hansa diplomatic craft down through the tall trees to the spaceport clearing. Reynald hurried to greet her, happy to see his sister. His skin had been rubbed with spreadnut wax so that his arm muscles and his tanned skin looked like polished furniture.

Sarein gave him a quick hug. She looked healthy, and her dark hair was cut short and styled in a serviceable Earth-like fashion, unlike the long braids or twists preferred on Theroc. Hansa perfumes gave her an exotic smell.

'Earth seems to agree with you, Sarein.' He playfully yanked the sleeve of her blouse. 'Although you seem to be in disguise. Why have you been gone so long?'

'Reynald, I wanted to come home sooner, but when colonies are starving because supplies can't be delivered, how can I justify a visit to see my family?' Her eyes glittered. 'But, since I'm the ambassador and you'll be the Theron Father, I plan to interact with you very closely from now on.'

'I'll still be your brother. Nothing has changed.'

She gave him a hard look. 'When you become Father Reynald, you'll find a lot of things are different. An improvement, I hope.' She gestured towards the open diplomatic shuttle. 'I brought a surprise guest for your coronation. Reynald, do you remember the Chairman?'

Dressed in a perfectly fitting business suit, Basil Wenceslas emerged and looked with interest at the towering worldtrees. Reynald had met Chairman Wenceslas on his peregrination to Earth, six years earlier. 'Welcome. I wasn't expecting such an important guest.'

Basil gave him a paternal smile. 'Reynald, you're about to become the leader of one of the most important worlds in the Spiral Arm. Any lesser presence from the Hanseatic League would be an insult. We can't have that.'

'Thank you, Mr Chairman.' Reynald flushed. 'I'm still not accustomed to being treated with such formality.' He took his sister by the hand. 'Come. Mother and Father are looking forward to seeing you.'

For the coronation, the fungus-reef rooms had been decorated with as much colour and dazzle as the gaudiest chromefly. Newly hatched condorflies, their wings a kaleidoscopic rainbow, fluttered at the windows, tethered to stands by thin strings. Idriss and Alexa had outdone themselves; they seemed pleased and proud of the spectacle they had arranged.

Estarra was stunning in a formal gown of feathers and moth scales, looking much more an adult than Reynald had ever considered her. At sixteen, little Celli had her hair done up in neatly oiled braids so carefully crafted that they pulled her eyes tight and gave her a pained expression. She hated formal occasions.

Overly dignified in the ambassador's cloak old Otema had given her, Sarein sat on a front bench beside Chairman Wenceslas.

The two remained very close, as if they were intimate friends rather than simply political colleagues. Oddly, both she and the Chairman kept glancing at Estarra, as if assessing her.

An assorted audience from scattered forest villages packed the chamber and the outside balconies. Reynald glimpsed the green priest woman Almari, who had offered herself in marriage at the Looking Glass Lakes. Now that he was about to become Father, she seemed even more interested in him – but he had already asked Cesca Peroni to be his bride. He hoped he heard a response soon.

Crowds waited down on the forest floor or on the thick tree boughs, trying to get a glimpse of the activity. Green priests all across the planet touched worldtrees, watching the entire ceremony through telink.

Reynald heard the celebratory songs, followed by the speech of his uncle, the green priest Yarrod, who spoke about how the Theron Father was responsible for shepherding the worldforest and its people. But this day, all words were a barely comprehensible drone.

When the time came, Reynald stood before the dual thrones and made his vow. 'I will do my utmost to lead the Theron people fairly and wisely, for the good of the worldforest and for the benefit of all who live here.'

Mother Alexa remained seated, her shoulders covered with insect shells and feathery scarves. Her headdress crown looked like a small cathedral perched on her hair. Idriss wore an equally impressive robe. His crown was even taller, adorned with insect wings, beetle carapaces, and polished slivers of wood.

In a deep voice, Idriss said, 'Reynald, my son, I trust you to take my place as Father of all Therons. No ceremony or blessing can be more profound or meaningful than that.' He removed his headdress and placed it on Reynald's head. The crown felt strangely light and uplifting.

Reynald's eyes glistened with unshed tears. 'I promise to do my best, Father.'

Idriss took his wife's hand. Alexa stood, and the two of them stepped down from their chairs to stand on either side of Reynald. Reynald looked at where his mother had sat and wondered if Cesca Peroni would ever join him there. In the audience, Uthair and Lia sat together, smiling, next to Idriss's old parents.

'Go on, take your seat, Reynald,' his mother chided quietly. 'Everyone's waiting.'

He stepped to the top of the dais and turned to face the audience. Almost overwhelmed at the responsibility he had just taken on, he sat in the chair while Idriss and Alexa stepped down to join their own parents. Everyone waited for Father Reynald to issue his first proclamation.

He thought for a moment and finally made a decree everyone in the audience would enjoy. 'I say it is time for the banquet to begin!'

Late into the night, musicians and emerald-skinned priests entertained the coronation guests. Children ran about tooting and whistling, playing odd musical instruments Uthair and Lia had created. Outside, in the dense trees, the insect music rose to a humming symphony, as if the worldforest were also welcoming the new leader. Thanks to the green priests, maybe it was.

Reynald wished Beneto could have come, but it had been impossible for him to travel from distant Corvus Landing. Instead, his brother had been present in mind and spirit. The green priests had reported each step of the ceremony through telink, so Beneto and every other far-flung priest could 'attend' through their counterpart treelings.

Food was everywhere: saltnuts and pair-pears and perrin seeds, splurtberries, stewed and heavily sweetened puckers, skewers of condorfly meat, spiced beetles cooked in the shell. Long banners and gauzy crêpes of cocoonweave cloth drifted about like spiderwebs, swirling with the slightest breezes. The people, so many of them smiling, were all a blur.

Reynald danced with all three of his sisters. Then, after Sarein and Basil had danced a slow waltz together, they discreetly drew Reynald aside. Sarein led the way behind the throne room through a passageway drilled into the fungus-reef and into a small chamber occasionally used for storage.

'Remember this place?' She closed the door so that three of them could be alone. 'We used to hide here when we were children.'

'Of course,' he said, instantly on guard. 'But right now I doubt you have fun and games on your mind.'

A hard smile flickered on her face. 'See, Basil – I told you my brother is sharp. You can count on him to see the larger picture.'

Chairman Wenceslas said, 'Young man, your coronation marks a watershed in relations between Theroc and the Hanseatic League.'

Reynald's mind moved quickly, already noting how his life had changed. Sarein stood very close to the Chairman, and he looked from one face to another. The storage room seemed very small. 'What is it you want?'

'Whether we like it or not, Father Reynald, we are all in a war against the hydrogues,' Wenceslas said. It was the first time Reynald's new title had been used in a formal diplomatic matter, and it made him giddy. 'The enemy has sworn to destroy us – not just humans, but Ildirans as well. Their ultimatum has crippled space travel across the Spiral Arm. Hansa colonies are suffering, some are even starving. The Earth Defence Forces have tried to see us through, but we've lost numerous ships and wasted countless opportunities because of our inability to communicate across long distances.'

'So you want more green priests,' Reynald said.

Sarein spoke urgently. 'Is that such a terrible thing? The EDF is trying to protect the Spiral Arm, but we can't do it alone. Think of the lives and resources that could be saved if green priests would agree to use their skills to help. Hansa facilities under attack could call for immediate reinforcements through telink. Battle fleets could pinpoint the locations of enemy ships. As it is, we have to send scouts and communicate through courier drones and waste our limited ekti each time a message must be sent.' With a bitter edge, she added, 'Therons have to stop living in their own isolated corner of the universe and paying no attention to all the worlds being attacked by hydrogues.'

'I have travelled to many planets in the Spiral Arm,' Reynald said. 'I see more than just Theroc.'

'Because your world's cooperation means so much to us, Father Reynald,' Basil said, 'the Hanseatic League is willing to make an unprecedented concession. We won't ask you to sign the Hansa Charter. We will reaffirm Theroc's status as a sovereign world with its own needs and culture. However, we do invite you to join with us in a mutually beneficial partnership.'

'And how would this partnership be established?' Reynald asked.

Sarein's voice filled with enthusiasm. 'We would cement it by a marriage between King Peter . . . and Estarra.'

Reynald could barely believe his ears. He had already foreseen the need for Theroc to join with another power, to create a mutual support system. That was why he'd suggested an alliance with Cesca Peroni. If the hydrogue war could bring together Therons, Roamers, and the Hansa and once again unify humanity without sacrificing the rights or identities of any of those groups – how could he possibly turn down the chance?

Reynald thought of the Whisper Palace and the glories of Earth that Sarein had often described. He had seen images of handsome King Peter, a vital and apparently kindly young man. It seemed a wonderful opportunity for his little sister, especially in light of the advice Uthair and Lia had given both of them not so long ago. How could his sister object to becoming the consort of a Great King? He was sure she would understand the wisdom of the match.

'I . . . I'll have to ask Estarra, of course, and discuss the matter with our parents.'

Sarein maintained an intent expression. 'Discuss it with them if you like, but remember that you are *Father Reynald*. You must make these decisions.'

He hesitated, then sighed. 'Yes, I knew you were going to say that.'

FORTY-FIVE

KING PETER

Every minute of the day, whenever anyone could see him, he had to look like a King. No exceptions, no reprieve. Peter sat on his throne, his expression calm and knowledgeable, his eyes interested. The people turned to him for comfort, honesty, and strength. A King must have integrity above all else.

No matter what Basil Wenceslas might believe.

Though the Chairman had gone to Theroc with Ambassador Sarein, Peter still did not have the freedom to think his own thoughts or speak his mind. He was both King and prisoner, even if no one else in the Hansa knew it.

Admiral Lev Stromo, the commander and representative for the Earth Defence Forces in Grid 0, had come to the Whisper Palace, accompanied by the engineering specialist Lars Rurik Swendsen. With General Lanyan off on manoeuvres and Basil on Theroc, Stromo did not seem to know who to see. The Admiral knew Peter wasn't supposed to decide any important matters.

Engineer Swendsen, though, intended to meet with someone in charge, and he had the brash enthusiasm to seek an audience with the King. The blond engineer never once imagined that Peter might not be authorized to make his own decisions.

The two men marched across the red-carpeted entry platform down the mirror corridor and into the Throne Hall. The royal guards and court heralds announced their arrival, though Peter recognized both Stromo and Swendsen on sight. Peter fixed the Grid 0 liaison officer with a gimlet stare, which Stromo matched in intensity. Both of them knew what a farce this meeting was.

The engineer bustled forward, carrying the components of a projection apparatus in his arms. 'King Peter, I'm happy to report on the new techniques and breakthroughs derived from disassembling the Klikiss robot. Our research has been well worth the effort.'

Peter raised his eyebrows. 'By whose standard?'

Swendsen seemed oblivious to Peter's caution. 'By any standard, Your Highness.' He projected a complex jumble of images that showed compy-manufacturing platforms, assembly lines, and robotic fabrication facilities. The engineering specialist spoke so quickly that his words raced ahead of the parade of captured scenes.

'Sire, the analysis has given us an insight into some remarkable robotic systems. We're working like crazy to retool and modify our production lines, but I think you'll agree it has all paid off. We're converting our facilities to produce a new model of compy – one that's far more efficient and able to assume actual combat responsibilities. These compies will be capable of making command decisions instead of just obeying explicit instructions. They can follow attack and surveillance routines, fight the enemy with autonomy. In short, they're perfect soldiers – and a vast improvement over our current compies.'

OX, only four feet high but sturdily built, stood beside the King's throne. Peter glanced at the Teacher compy, then frowned sceptically at the engineering specialist. 'Compies like OX have served us well for two centuries. I'd advise you not to make such claims unless you can back them up.'

'We can back them up, Your Highness,' Admiral Stromo said. 'With Klikiss-inspired modifications, these military models have a much greater reliability and general goal-orientation. They will be relentless in accomplishing complex tasks – no longer just competent computerized companions. Not toys, but real soldiers.'

'It's true,' said Lars Swendsen. 'These Soldier compies are skilled enough to take the place of . . .' He paused, dithering. 'Well, who knows how many non-essential human beings are in the EDF?'

'Therefore,' Stromo joined in, 'we can reduce the number of potential casualties in the next hydrogue engagement. You won't need to unfurl nearly as many memorial banners as you did after the Dasra incident.'

From his throne, Peter studied the projected images of the revamped compy production lines. He could not argue with letting sophisticated compies take certain risks, but part of him remained unsure about any hidden agenda the Klikiss robots might have had in introducing these new technologies. 'You are certainly enthusiastic, Engineer Swendsen. And you don't have any doubts?'

'None whatsoever, Sire.'

'Perhaps we can win this war after all.' Admiral Stromo bowed and backed away, smoothing the front of his formal EDF uniform. 'We will give a more complete report as soon as Chairman Wenceslas returns from his diplomatic mission to Theroc.'

'Oh?' the King said. 'Is there anything more you wish to tell me?'

'No, Sire,' Admiral Stromo said.

'Then of course there will be no need for a second meeting with Chairman Wenceslas. You have said all you need to say.' Peter's artificially blue gaze became hard, and Stromo didn't know how to react.

The engineer Lars Swendsen remained oblivious to the tension. Grinning, he collected his records, plans, and projection equipment.

'Very well, you may proceed,' the King said. 'But proceed with caution.'

FORTY-SIX

TASIA TAMBLYN

Something had set off the drogues. The deep-core aliens were on the move, attacking inhabited systems seemingly at random. The EDF had analysed the increasing sightings, but could discern no overall pattern, motive, comprehensible tactics, or connection.

When the diamond-hulled warglobes began to lay waste to the thickly forested world of Boone's Crossing, the human settlers dispatched frantic calls for help. It was sheer luck that the small Grid 7 scout fleet was in the vicinity, close enough to make a difference.

'Battlestations, folks! All engines, full acceleration. Haul ass to Boone's Crossing.' Admiral Willis's voice carried a certain amount of no-nonsense glee. 'We'd better get there in time to kick some butt.' She gripped the arms of her command chair as if she could urge the *Jupiter* to greater speed.

Tasia, newly assigned to command a Manta cruiser instead of a weapons platform, felt her heart pounding at the possibility of a direct face-off with the hydrogues. She just wanted to fight the enemy bastards wherever they showed themselves. It was better than picking on unruly colonists . . .

The scout wing had a Juggernaut, seven Mantas, and a thousand combat-ready Remoras. They raced to the nearby system that held the small green world of Boone's Crossing. The working Hansa colony looked tiny and peaceful in reflected sunlight.

The soil on Boone's Crossing was perfect for the rapid growth of genetically enhanced conifers. The black pines came from Earth stock crossbred with native foliage, resulting in a dense and beautiful wood that grew almost as fast as bamboo. Black pines had spread faster than the lumber settlements could harvest them.

As the battlegroup approached at top speed, more of the urgent distress calls came from the seventeen large settlements, each one built near a lake or river. Tasia could see clear-cut patches of forests, like zig-zags shaved through the thick carpet of deep-green trees. In some areas, the ground had stubbly, well-organized areas of new growth.

The dark forest looked lush and healthy, except where the warglobes had left frost-crusted wreckage, thick tree trunks now ice-withered and knocked flat. Four hydrogue ships were systematically obliterating the black pines.

'It's like a tsunami!' Commander Fitzpatrick said over the command frequency from his Manta, back on patrol from his stint with General Lanyan.

'All contact lost from Settlement A, Commander Tamblyn,' said her nav officer, Elly Ramirez. 'Looks like they're already fried.'

Tasia stared at the defenceless forests and felt a sinking coldness in her gut. 'Which one's next in the drogues' current path, Lieutenant?'

Ramirez overlaid the real-time images with a tactical grid as the Manta swooped through the cloudy atmosphere. 'Settlement D, on that large lake, Commander. The way those warglobes are moving, the town'll be wiped out in less than an hour.'

Tasia nodded grimly. 'Looks like they're sitting in front of a steamroller.'

Admiral Willis barked over the command frequency, 'Let's hustle. All Remoras launch! All Mantas, power up jazers and projectile weapons. *Jupiter* will provide the heavy firepower. I don't think our guns are big enough for these customers, but I wouldn't mind being proven wrong.'

Fitzpatrick's Manta disengaged from the main fleet, and Willis's Juggernaut accompanied it to intercept the first warglobe. The keyed-up Remora pilots and the EDF weapons engineers opened fire long before they came into range.

The warglobes launched blue lightning at the oncoming human forces, vaporizing a dozen of the fastest, cockiest Remoras. But the drogues' main intent was directed downwards, frigid icewaves ripping the landscape, freezing and shattering the majestic black pines.

Tasia wanted to join the attack, but she knew her efforts would be irrelevant. 'Admiral Willis, our combined firepower isn't going to scratch four warglobes. My tactician projects that Settlement D will be obliterated within the hour if we don't evacuate—'

'What's the matter, Tamblyn, no stomach for a real fight?' Fitzpatrick transmitted.

'Why not ask the sitting-duck colonists, Fitzpatrick – or should I just deliver a message that you were too busy shooting spitballs into a hurricane?'

'Tamblyn, you have a point,' Willis said. 'Take your cruiser to the village and start loading everybody aboard. Have the colonists crowd into the corridors if you don't have enough room in your hold.'

'Yes, ma'am!' She gestured to Lieutenant Ramirez. They angled down in a steeper dive, streaking eastwards ahead of the hydrogue destruction.

The Juggernaut *Jupiter* slammed a volley of jazer bolts into the foremost warglobe. As if annoyed by the distraction, the spiked diamond sphere shot a blue lightning blast that grazed the starboard hull of the flagship and sent it careening off course.

Tasia snapped to her comm officer, 'Get on the horn to Settlement D and tell them to have everyone out and waiting. Shizz, it's going to take all the time we've got just to move everybody through the doors.'

The warglobes rumbled over the wilderness like cosmic bulldozers. Behind them, no tree, no blade of grass remained standing.

Tasia's Manta raced in front of the hydrogues, putting a hundred kilometres of thickly forested landscape between them. Minute by minute, the relentless alien spheres closed the distance. Settlement D stood in their way.

In the lakeside village, sawmills, loading platforms, and boxy barracks covered a cleared area dotted with clean stumps sheared off at ground level. As more black pines had been cut down, the settlement expanded, and new facilities were erected for processing the trees into exportable forest products.

Now the lumber workers scurried like ants on a hot plate, glancing towards the skies with apprehension. Some comm-operators watched from operations shacks or mill-control towers as the hydrogue destroyers swept forward, consuming the black pines.

As soon as Tasia's cruiser came in over the lake by Settlement D, she looked for a place to land, but saw no clearing large enough to accommodate the Manta. The frenzied people ran about, waving and signalling the ship as if ready to spring aboard before she even landed.

'The drogues are seventy klicks away and coming fast,' said Ramirez.

Tasia pointed to one of the large hangar-sized warehouses. 'Time for some urban renewal. Level that empty warehouse, then land right smack in the wreckage. We'll just have to hope there's no one left inside.'

A single jazer burst flattened the structure into splinters and cinders, and the cruiser came down into the open area. Its nose touched the lakeshore, and cold water hissed against its hot hull. Several thousand villagers stampeded forward.

'We need to impose order, sir,' said her security chief, Sergeant Zizu. 'They'll trample each other.'

She looked at the chronometer, saw they had only about forty minutes remaining. 'We don't have the luxury of being orderly, Zizu.' Already the cargo hatches were open, and people stormed inside. 'Wing Commander Brindle! Scoot our Remoras out of the aft bays to make room. More refugees can fill the flight deck. Open the bilge hatches if you have to. Every door and port, every opening. Get those people inside, pronto!'

On the horizon behind them, a stain of smoke and frozen steam approached like gangrene. 'Admiral Willis, I need to know if you're slowing them down at all.'

The flagship responded with real-time images of the warglobes flattening the stands of black pines. 'One of our cruisers has been obliterated and over two hundred Remoras destroyed or downed – so far.'

Tasia felt sick. 'Any damage to the enemy?'

'Not a whit, dammit! Lucky for us the drogues are more interested in ruining the lumber crop than in fighting us. What have they got against a bunch of trees?'

Mobs of lumber workers were already aboard Tasia's cruiser. Many were separated from their families or loved ones, but they could sort that out later. Less than twenty minutes remained, according to her projections. From outside, above the shouts and outcries of the settlers, she could hear a crackle, boom, and roar of the approaching warglobes.

Willis called again. 'Commander Tamblyn, what is the evacuation status of Settlement D?'

'I'm getting most of the refugees onboard now, but they'll fill every cranny of my Manta.'

'Good work, Tamblyn,' Willis said. 'At least somebody's accomplishing a good thing.'

Obviously, the Admiral hadn't yet figured out what Tasia already knew. 'Ma'am, we can take these people to safety, but . . . look at your map. The hydrogues are being pretty methodical, laying waste to the entire land mass, centimetre by centimetre.'

'So get those people out of there!'

'My point exactly, Admiral. I can get most of the refugees out of Settlement D before the enemy arrives, but there are *fifteen other* settlements, a hundred thousand people. If the drogues keep coming, they're all in the line of fire, ready to fall like dominoes. Unless we devote our full resources – and I mean one hundred per cent effort – to rescuing the colonists, they're going to suffer horrific casualties.'

Surprisingly, Patrick Fitzpatrick came over the channel in support. 'I hate to admit this, Admiral, but Tamblyn's right.' His image looked battered and haggard. His cruiser had already been damaged in the fight. 'Politically speaking, you don't want to be in command of the mission that costs the greatest number of lives in human history.'

Willis's face looked pinched. 'Well, we sure aren't accomplishing squat in either defence or offence against the drogues.'

Off-channel, Tasia called to her own crew. 'Give me a status. Is everyone onboard yet?'

'Only a few stragglers left, Commander.'

The town on the lake was already a ruin. Small fires sputtered from the warehouse Tasia's Manta had flattened. On the main screen, she could see a few bodies of trampled or injured people. 'Sound the last call, then let's get out of here.'

Behind them, the nearby forests were already crumbling, toppling, as diamond spheres cruised above the treetops, coming closer.

'Listen up, that's it! All ships break off our counterattack,' Willis finally ordered. 'Disperse and grab the colonists. Begin a full-scale evacuation of Boone's Crossing.'

'Commander Tamblyn, we've rescued approximately two thousand four hundred settlers,' said Sergeant Zizu. 'We'll do an accurate count later, but that's over fifty per cent of the Settlement D population.'

Tasia's heart skipped a beat. *Only half.*

Seeing her expression, the security chief said, 'That's as good as we can hope for, considering the circumstances. Most of the work crews out in the forests couldn't get back in time.'

She looked at the map, noting the heavily forested continent that ended abruptly at the broad ocean. She knew the holding capacity of the *Jupiter* and the remaining cruisers, and did a quick calculation.

The EDF ships could never carry all of the endangered colonists.

FORTY-SEVEN

CESCA PERONI

The central complex of Rendezvous was a loose cluster of asteroids bound together by gravity and artificial super- structures. Girders and cables held the drifting rocks in place around a garnet-coloured dwarf star. Over the course of 237 years, this place had become the central hub of the Roamer civilization. Clan gatherings occurred here. Traders came and went.

As Speaker, Cesca Peroni made her home at Rendezvous, where she acted as mediator in disputes among families and commercial rivals. As a girl, she had been left here by her merchant father, Denn Peroni, to be schooled in politics and diplomacy. Jhy Okiah had been like a mother to her, and Cesca still valued her predecessor's advice and insight.

After she arrived back from Osquivel, Cesca went to talk with the old woman. With a leaden heart and her mind in turmoil, she had no choice but to open up and confess her feelings and doubts in hopes that Jhy Okiah could help.

Since retiring, the former Speaker seemed to have aged

backwards. Her eyes were brighter and her grey-yellow hair seemed glossier. The stress of being peacemaker and spokesperson for so long had wrung her dry, but after turning over the reins, the old woman seemed re-energized. Her smile was genuine, without a hint of political pretence, as she greeted Cesca.

'Welcome, child.' Her eyes sparkled, surrounded by wrinkles. 'Or do you prefer me to be more respectful when talking to our revered Speaker?'

'You need never pretend to be stuffy and official with me. I have enough worries without that nonsense.'

'Diplomacy isn't nonsense! Did I make the wrong decision in choosing my successor?'

Cesca took a seat in a woven slingchair adorned with colourful threads in a Roamer Chain pattern. 'If you had chosen someone else, my life would be a lot simpler, Jhy Okiah.'

The old woman poured pepperflower tea for them from a small dispenser. 'We both know that Roamers have the best chance of survival through your leadership and no one else's. I trust your Guiding Star.' She gave a wistful smile. 'Why, at one time my grandson Berndt thought he deserved the Speakership simply because of his bloodline. He was loud and blustery, but he learned eventually. He found his place as a skymine captain and did a damn fine job – until the hydrogues killed him.'

The former Speaker moved with gentleness and grace as she flitted about her quarters. Cesca sipped the spicy sharpness of her tea, remembering it was old Bram Tamblyn's favourite drink. Now the taste reminded her of Jess, and her heart felt heavy again.

Of course, Jhy Okiah noticed. 'So, child, either your duties as Speaker are lighter than mine were and you have nothing better to do than chat with a retired old woman . . . or you have a problem and you think I can provide a magical solution.'

'There is no simple solution, I'm afraid,' Cesca said.

The old woman crossed her arms and legs in an awkward-looking lotus position and listened. After drawing a deep breath to steel herself, Cesca explained about the marriage proposal she had received from Reynald, repeating the young man's reasons for linking the Roamers and the Therons. Clinging to her training as a politician, Cesca tried to present the argument calmly, without colouring it in any way.

Jhy Okiah recognized what her guest was doing, since she had taught Cesca those techniques herself. 'All right, you obviously see the political wisdom in marrying Reynald. None of the clans could object to such an alliance, and Ross Tamblyn has been dead for almost six years. What is the problem? Does this Theron ruler have some dark secret? Do you find him unsuitable in some way?'

Cesca concentrated on her tea. 'No, no. I believe Reynald to be a good man, and he seems very earnest. Logically, I can't argue with his offer. But . . .' She was usually better at covering her emotions, a political necessity as Speaker. 'The truth is, my heart has always belonged to someone else, even . . . before.'

Jhy Okiah nodded with complete understanding. 'And what does Jess Tamblyn think of this marriage proposal?'

'How did you know? Jess and I have—'

The older woman simply chuckled, leaning back in her slingchair. 'Cesca Peroni, I have known of your love all along – and so, I dare say, have many of the Roamer clans. We found it quite admirable, though a bit maddening, how devoted you each were to your duties while you snuck around and pretended not to notice each other. Surely you can't think we are all as blind as that?'

Cesca took a moment to absorb this. 'So Jess and I should just drop our pretences? We were going to announce our engagement within a few months, but—'

Now the old woman became stern. 'Too late for that, child. If you had done so years ago, I would have supported your decision.

But now you've got other obligations. Circumstances have changed around you, and we can all see what the Guiding Star shows us.'

Cesca recognized the woman's hard tone and knew there could be no debate. Her heart sank.

'You are not like other women, Speaker Peroni.' Okiah spoke the title like the crack of a whip. 'You cannot choose according to your personal desires and wants. You cannot trip lightly through your life with sparkling eyes, holding on to girlish fantasies. A Speaker must rise above mere personal considerations. There are rewards, and there are costs.'

'Jess signed aboard one of the new nebula skimmers and launched out into deep space. He said he knows I'll make the right decision,' Cesca admitted. 'Apparently, he has more confidence than I do.'

Jhy Okiah put a leathery hand on Cesca's arm. 'He was trying to help you. He saw what you could not . . . or were not ready to see.'

Cesca sat in silence for a long moment. She had already known what her answer to Reynald must be. 'Then I will pay the price, and I will not count the cost.'

FORTY-EIGHT

JESS TAMBLYN

L̲ike a glorious butterfly, the nebula skimmer spread its wings and unfurled micro-thin fabric across thousands of square kilometres of space. Hot new stars at the centre of the emission cloud showered photons into the diffuse gas, stripping electrons from atoms, leaving an afterglow of pale green and swirls of pastel pinks and blues.

As the skimmer tacked through the nebula, the huge scoop swept a handful of atoms from each cubic metre of near-vacuum: neutral or ionized hydrogen mixed with a dash of oxygen, helium, neon, and nitrogen. The curved sail funnelled the captured molecules like a ramjet, condensing them into traces of hydrogen for processing into ekti, skimming off and separating out any valuable byproducts. The raw material was sparse, but it filled a sea as large as the gaps between stars.

Jess's small habitation pod and processing machinery dangled from the enormous diaphanous sail, connected by struts and cables to the gossamer collection film. Trailing behind him, moving with the force of the photons that battered the reflective surface, hung lightweight condensers, filters, and an efficient small-batch ekti reactor designed by Kotto Okiah.

Other Roamer skimmers trolled across the light-years-wide nebula. Like a fleet of fishing boats drifting into rich waters, the ethereal ships spread out, remaining in radio contact. Most of the pilots engaged in lengthy conversations or played strategy games, stretched out because of the signal delay caused by the sheer distance.

Jess, though, preferred to be alone, pondering and thinking. In his heart, he would always belong to Cesca, but in reality they were destined to be apart. 'I should have married you long ago.'

He had been foolish, the two of them overly concerned with imagined scandals and repercussions. Would such a confession truly have brought dishonour upon Ross's memory? Would it have distracted Cesca too much from the demands of the hydrogue conflict? He didn't think so, but now it was too late. Actually, their complicated love had probably proved more distracting. He had not seen the Guiding Star clearly enough.

By now, though, Cesca should have accepted Reynald's proposal. The Roamers and Therons could share resources for their mutual betterment, stand together against the opposing forces that threatened either to absorb or destroy them.

Meanwhile, Jess drifted alone in a sea of vanishingly thin gas. Even the most violent plasma ripples or ionic hurricanes were so faint that he could feel nothing.

Jess climbed through a hatch and pulled himself down into the processing chambers beneath his habitation pod. Checking the progress of his trolling had become a comfortable daily routine.

The nebula's dominant component, especially in outlying eddies, was pure hydrogen, and the skimmers had been engineered to pump all collected gases through the high-efficiency ekti reactors.

According to the in-situ analysis probes, for days he had been flying through a particularly dense knot of vaporous material composed not only of hydrogen, but also hydroxyl and carbon dioxide molecules, a few traces of carbon monoxide and doubly-ionized oxygen. Oddest of all, his reading suggested that this clump of gas contained a significant concentration of intact water molecules, which was unusual in interstellar clouds.

From his upbringing at the Plumas ice mines, Jess was well aware of the value of water to interstellar colonies. Roamers could always use it for drinking or in hydroponic greenhouse systems; water could also be electrolytically separated into hydrogen and oxygen, then recombined into peroxides, rocket fuels, even lubricants. Such a resource should not go to waste.

Since he had plenty of time to implement his modifications, Jess reconfigured the molecular filtration systems and rigged up a subsidiary containment chamber to separate out the water from the starcloud. Optimistic and ambitious, he built a cylinder to hold hundreds of litres, though even in this thick concentration of gases he would find only a molecule or two in every cubic metre of the nebula.

The work kept his mind busy, distracted him from the pain of what he had lost.

Jess sailed on, surrounded by the faint vapour illuminated by stray photons from distant stars. The ekti reactors hummed, taking gasping breaths of the rarefied hydrogen, while the distillers separated the cosmic water little by little, one drop at a time.

As was a tradition among Roamer men, Jess embroidered intricate clan markings on his clothes, splicing together symbols that showed the ever-growing branches of his family. Sadly, the design of clan Tamblyn seemed blunt and curtailed now.

In total solitude, Jess sat for hours stitching the intricate designs, sketching with his mind. If things had been different, his clan chain might have been joined with clan Peroni's in a multi-coloured rainbow that spread across the pockets and sleeves of his jumpsuits. Now, though, the design ended with him.

Aside from tangential patterns for his uncles, the only other branch was for Tasia. Perhaps she could carry on. Any number of young Roamer men would be happy to take her as a partner, if she survived her stint in the military.

Ah, how he hated the hydrogues! Ross . . . Tasia . . . Cesca . . . Someday the war would end, but life would never be the same. Someday he might make a new start, redraw the design of his life according to a new pattern.

But not today. Not for a long time.

FORTY-NINE

TASIA TAMBLYN

ethodically and inexorably, the hydrogues continued to devastate Boone's Crossing. Unimpeded, the warglobes moved over the forested landscape, obliterating the tall pines with icewaves. They were in no hurry.

Tasia Tamblyn lifted her overloaded cruiser from the lakeside Settlement D only moments ahead of the oncoming spheres. When the burdened Manta responded sluggishly, lurching forward, she wasn't sure they would be able to move fast enough to get away. Just behind them, the warglobes blasted stands of black pines, shops and homes, sawmills and warehouses.

Using all the lift its engines could generate, the crowded cruiser lumbered away like a drunken bumblebee, picking up speed and altitude. It barely managed to stay ahead of the perimeter of disintegration, increasing the separation every second as it left the doomed settlement.

Inside the Manta, crammed shoulder to shoulder in every open space, the refugees stared at viewers or through portholes as the drogues crushed what had been their homes, the once-thriving lumber industries, shops, warehouses. Everything.

Icewaves struck the lake, shattering the water into upthrust rafts of solid ice. Moisture in the ground volatilized upwards in geysers of steam. Trees withered and fell. Buildings and homes were destroyed in an instant.

Settlement D was only the first. The tactical maps showed numerous other settlements that lay across the path of destruction. The Grid 7 expeditionary fleet scrambled at a breakneck pace to rescue as many people as they could.

'We've got a riot going on down here,' Fitzpatrick called from Settlement J. 'If we let any more people onboard, my cruiser won't be able to take off!'

Tasia raced towards the eastern coastline and the grey, cold ocean. Wing Commander Robb Brindle and his full Remora squadrons flew alongside as escorts. He said, 'Commander, should I have my squadrons engage the warglobes, or rendezvous at one of the other settlements to assist in the evacuation process?'

Tasia's mind discarded possibility after possibility. 'I sure can't take on any more passengers, and we've got no safe place to deposit the ones we're already carrying.' She even pondered whether each Remora could fit a colonist or two into the cramped cockpit.

Admiral Willis's grandmotherly voice said over the open channel, '*Jupiter* is completely filled. We couldn't take a pet hamster if someone brought one aboard.'

The ocean ahead offered no refuge, and Tasia didn't know what to do, except keep flying away from the enemy. She spoke over the command band, 'Admiral, we could evacuate another village or two – if only we had a place to unload these refugees.'

'If you find a secure location anywhere on the planet, Tamblyn, you tell me about it. We all want to go there.'

Tasia bit her lip as she watched the hydrogues continue

annihilating the thick conifers. So far, the enemy had swept across the continent in an unstoppable wave; they had skirted the largest inland seas and giant lakes, concentrating only on the forest.

At the moment, her Guiding Star wasn't very bright, but she had to take a chance somehow. 'Admiral Willis, on the tactical display it looks like the enemy is most interested in the forested areas. They've avoided the biggest water zones, as far as I can tell. Perhaps we could take the refugees far out to sea. The drogues might not follow us into open water.'

'Big assumption, Tamblyn.'

'Ma'am, either we make some big assumptions and keep our fingers crossed, or we let the rest of the colonists die. We're at capacity as it is, and we've got no place to go.'

Willis was desperate enough to listen to her. 'And what do you propose to do with them when we get to open water? Just dump them in the sea and hope they tread water until we scoop them up again?'

Tasia's throat went dry as an absurd but possible suggestion sparked in her mind. 'Every EDF ship carries a substantial supply of tactical armour foam. The liquid polymer hardens instantly on contact with water. If we spray it on to the waves, we can create large raft platforms. Could be used as temporary holding areas, like big icebergs or life-preservers.'

'That's a crazy idea,' Fitzpatrick said.

'But damned innovative.' Willis cut him off with a sharp laugh. 'Will it work?'

'We can go a dozen klicks offshore and start laying down splatters of foam, anything the people can hold on to. I could unload my refugees, empty out the bays, and let the people swim to the rafts. Then I'll run back and fetch another shipful of refugees. All our vessels could do the same, Admiral.'

Willis said, 'It'll sure be messy, but it just might give the other colonists a chance to survive. Do it, Tamblyn.'

As Tasia raced across the ocean, low to the water, Robb Brindle cut in on their private channel. 'You should have kept your mouth shut.'

'Tell that to all the people we're gonna save.' She just hoped her intuition hadn't steered her in the wrong direction. It truly was a ridiculous idea.

She brought the Manta down low to the calm, shallow sea. In a booming voice amplified through the intercom above the background din of the refugees, Tasia explained what they were going to do.

The Boone's Crossing settlers were not very enthusiastic about the plan.

From beneath the cruiser's lower hull, Tasia's weapons officer deployed the tactical armour foam, spraying the gummy substance on to the waves like pancake batter that spread out and hardened. She didn't want to hear the moans of dismay among the refugees. They had been attacked, unexpectedly rescued, and now were being cast back on to the water. There, they would be vulnerable to a hydrogue attack without so much as an awning over their heads.

But there wasn't any other way, short of abandoning over ninety per cent of the planet's population to certain death.

When the Manta's cargo bay opened, reluctant refugees began to drop down to the water, some of them hitting the soft unstable islands. A few of the first ones hesitated at the hatch, afraid to jump the several metres down to the uninviting green squishiness of the rafts. But when others nudged them forward, hundreds of rescued colonists tumbled out of the cargo door like lemmings. They struggled to get to their feet on the floating mass and stagger away from the waterfall of bodies.

Tasia's voice boomed over the intercom. 'Every delay costs the lives of other settlers. Now move!' She sent Sergeant Zizu and his security crew armed with stun weapons to make sure all the refugees left the ship as ordered. Her voice softened slightly. 'Hey, don't worry. We rescued you once . . . we'll do it again.'

Two more EDF Mantas came in low over the water, spraying armour foam that hardened into spongy platforms. Each of the scattered smelly polymer rafts would support hundreds of evacuees. The rescue proceeded at a breakneck pace.

People stumbled and fell. Tasia didn't want to think about the number of broken bones the refugees would suffer – she only hoped they survived long enough to complain about it. Water sloshed over the edges of the largest rotating rafts. Groups stood staring at the hazy coast in dread as the hydrogues continued to lay waste to the continent.

In the end, Tasia's security troops needed to stun only a few dozen frantic evacuees and dump them out. She could see from the faces on her command screens that many of the Boone's Crossing colonists had already given up hope. They simply clung to survival, moment by moment.

Before the cargo bay doors closed, Tasia gave the order to lift off, circle over the rafts, and streak back to the mainland at top speed. Over the emergency band, she could hear the distress calls from Settlement L, the next town facing the enemy onslaught. 'Stand ready,' she transmitted. 'We're on our way.'

And the hydrogues kept coming.

FIFTY

PRIME DESIGNATE JORA'H

After the attack on Hyrillka, Prime Designate Jora'h no longer felt safe even in the Prism Palace. Enhanced sunshine passed through the transmission windows and curved panes, lighting every corner and driving back all shadows. But the warglobes could still be out there, converging on Ildira even now . . .

The Solar Navy had been roundly defeated at Qronha 3 and again at Hyrillka. If the hydrogues chose to attack anywhere else in the Empire – even Mijistra itself – how could the Ildirans stand against them?

Jora'h's father summoned him for an immediate consultation, but he took the time to compose himself. With a flicker of sentimentality, he donned a loose-sleeved tunic made of Theron cocoon-fibre given to him by Nira Khali. He hoped it would give him strength, and peace.

A short time later he stood rigidly in front of the chrysalis chair. It pained him to see the shock of loss and horror on the Mage-Imperator's greyish face. Jora'h thought he could see the glowing bones directly through his father's skin. Had the leader's health failed significantly in the past few weeks? His long braid looked dull and frayed, as if even the strands of hair were losing their will to live.

Through the *thism*, the leader had experienced the torment and suffering of his people during the Hyrillka devastation. 'You are uninjured, my son?' The leader's concern seemed to stem more from political and dynastic worries than from a more personal fear for Jora'h's well-being.

'Yes, Father. I escaped the hydrogue attack intact, as did Thor'h. My brother Rusa'h, though, remains in grave condition. I fear for his life.'

The Mage-Imperator frowned, his heavy cheeks sagging. 'I have the best medical kithmen attending him. The Hyrillka Designate will suffer from no lack of treatment, but his recovery will be contingent upon his own inner strength. Your brother has led a soft and unchallenging life. He may not have the stamina to pull himself out of danger.'

Jora'h was surprised at the cold analysis and utter lack of sympathy. 'Father, he is still in a sub-*thism* sleep.'

The Mage-Imperator scowled, and a wince flickered across his normally placid face. 'A sub-*thism* state is the equivalent of hiding, Jora'h. I have no patience for it, especially now. We must consider what happened and discuss the consequences. Rusa'h can follow the soul-threads and go to the plane of the Lightsource whenever he chooses.'

Cyroc'h held up a pudgy finger that shook slightly as he continued. 'Perhaps in a way, this attack has been a good thing.'

Jora'h's loose hair waved around his head like a nimbus of tiny static flickers. He tried to control his anger. 'Hundreds of thousands of people died on Hyrillka! How can you say this is a good thing?'

The Mage-Imperator halted his son's words abruptly. 'I mean that witnessing such a massive disaster might have been a good lesson for you. On Hyrillka you glimpsed how difficult it truly is to be a ruler. Soon I will meet with Adar Kori'nh to discuss the next desperate measures our Empire must take.'

Restless and upset, Jora'h stood in silence. He promised himself that when he became Mage-Imperator – soon now – he would be a more compassionate leader. He would think of people rather than politics.

'How can we fight an enemy we do not understand? The hydrogues came out of nowhere. We have done nothing to encourage their aggression.'

Cyroc'h looked at him with cold eyes. 'We know more than you think, my son.' Then, the Mage-Imperator was seized by another hammering spasm of pain inside his head and sagged backwards, looking alarmingly weak. 'Go and contemplate what I have told you.' He dismissed Jora'h and sent his bodyguard Bron'n to call the Adar so they could continue their strategy discussions.

Jora'h left, feeling unsettled and confused. Rather than spending time in silent meditation, he went to see his brother Rusa'h.

The Hyrillka Designate lay on a comfortable bed in a warm, bright room. Attenders and medical kithmen surrounded him like parasites, checking readings, adding medications, applying soothing ointments. Two lens kithmen stood looking solemn, as if they could help the unconscious Rusa'h chase the *thism* threads back to his own body.

The chubby face of the Hyrillkan leader now looked drawn and pale. His eyes were closed. His hair hung limp, not even stirring – either because of various drugs, or because the Designate was so deeply catatonic that few of his systems still functioned. Jora'h stared at him.

Rusa'h's head was bandaged. His brow and cheeks, despite their pallor, showed purplish blotches of bruises, vivid indicators of damage deeper inside his body. Internal bleeding continued, though the high-ranking medical kithmen had already performed surgical miracles just to keep him alive.

The head injury and possible brain damage was far more serious than contusions or broken bones. If his brother's mind had been dealt a mortal blow, what good would it do to heal his body?

Haggard and gaunt, Thor'h clung to his uncle's bedside. Jora'h looked at his son, who now appeared very young and frightened. His eyes were red-rimmed.

'Why won't he wake up?' He looked at Jora'h as if he believed his father could, with a wave of his hands, cure all of the hurt. 'I have commanded these doctors to give him stimulants and bring him back to consciousness, but they pay no attention to me.' He glared at the attenders and surgeons and drug specialists. 'Tell them who I am, that they must obey my wishes.'

'They can do nothing, Thor'h, any more than I could simply order the hydrogues to go away and leave Hyrillka alone.'

The young man regarded his father with scorn. 'Then what use are you?'

Jora'h wanted to strike Thor'h, especially after the Mage-Imperator had just lectured him, but he calmed himself, knowing the stress and grief his son was enduring. The young man's life had been pampered and protected, with every wish too easily granted.

'Perhaps you should speak to the lens kithmen,' he suggested, looking at the two intent priests. 'Let them counsel you.' Jora'h needed to make sure his son would be a good leader too, under-standing the difference between what was possible and what was fantasy. In the Ildiran Empire, so much depended on this one person, Jora'h's eventual successor.

'They can do no more than anyone else. I prefer to stay here.' The young man pointedly ignored his father.

Jora'h drew a deep breath and said what he knew was best. 'Thor'h, you showed great bravery and honour during the attack on Hyrillka. You could have fled on the first escape shuttle, but you went back for your uncle. You have earned my respect.'

'It gained me nothing.' The young man wore a bitter expression.

'Perhaps it gained you more than you know.' Jora'h placed a supportive hand on his son's shoulder. 'Stay by him, Thor'h. He may be in a sub-*thism* sleep, but I'm certain he can sense your presence. Give him your strength, and hope that it will be enough.' He looked at the medical kithmen and said, 'Continue your work. Do everything to help my brother.'

'We are already at the limits of our capabilities, Prime Designate,' said the lead doctor. 'I'm afraid he is far, far gone, deep within his mind. No medicine will cure him. We can tend only the body.'

Thor'h glared at them all with a curl of disgust on his lip and bent closer to the Designate's bedside. Lines of anguish etched his young face. When Jora'h departed, Thor'h didn't even look up.

FIFTY-ONE

ROBB BRINDLE

The hydrogues swept over Boone's Crossing, leaving a frozen and blistered landscape scored with leprous burn marks. After they had passed, no structure remained standing.

The last evacuation runs departed from hastily abandoned villages on the coastline. Escort ships, Mantas, and the big Juggernaut staggered away like overloaded albatrosses, barely one step ahead of the crystalline warglobes.

The EDF vessels were full to bursting with survivors; refugees crowded the decks, pressed into every storage bay. Bulky supplies and unnecessary equipment were dumped out on to the ground to make more standing room.

In his Remora amongst all of the squadrons under his command, Robb Brindle flew alongside the passenger-carrying ships. He circled over the dozens of blobby artificial islands sprayed on to the water surface.

Tactical armour foam! He shook his head and promised himself to buy Tasia a drink – several drinks – when they got to their next downtime port. She had always told him that Roamers were skilled at using unlikely resources and techniques to keep themselves alive under the worst conditions.

Still, it might be only a temporary reprieve. Once the hydrogues reached the coast, they would run out of black pine forest to obliterate. Afterwards, the defenceless rafts crowded with tens of thousands of colonists might offer an irresistible target. The warglobes could exterminate all the inhabitants of Boone's Crossing within seconds. If they chose to do so . . .

Brindle opened a channel to the united Remora squadrons. 'All right, form a defensive line. I want fifteen separate phalanx formations, spread out in an arc to block those drogues.'

The fighters rearranged themselves into a stacked cluster, hovering in the salty air. The warglobes could blast through the line like a match through gasoline-soaked tissue, but none of the Remora pilots argued. They had to make a last stand.

Below, on the water, swarms of helpless people huddled shivering on the spongy foam that kept them afloat. Behind them, the *Jupiter* and the six surviving Mantas also climbed, jazers and kinetic weapons ready to fire. They waited, letting the hydrogues make the first direct move . . . hoping that such an attack wouldn't come. So far, the enemy had taken little notice of the human evacuation efforts, the EDF ships, the abandoned settlements.

'Stand firm, everybody,' Admiral Willis said, her voice smooth and reassuring.

'Easy for her to say,' Brindle mumbled after checking to make sure his radio mike was off. It was merely a matter of who would become a casualty first.

'Look at that!' said one of the pilots.

The four warglobes loomed over the coastal horizon, still spraying icewaves, erasing every stand of dense conifers, shattering observation towers, empty dwellings, and factory structures. They left dry land behind and soared out over the water, playing their frigid weapons in front of them as if they hadn't noticed there was no longer any forest below.

Brindle could almost feel a physical shudder of dismay from the refugees crowded on the rafts when they saw the hydrogues coming.

'Remoras, ready to fire,' he said, though he knew it was completely unnecessary. Each pilot would drain every speck of energy from the defensive batteries in hopes of inflicting at least some damage before the hydrogues obliterated them all. 'This is it.'

The terrible diamond spheres kept coming, strafing the ocean, blasting the water into icebergs. A storm of steam boiled around the warglobes, marking their progress over the calm sea.

'Come on, what more do you creeps want?' Brindle said. 'You've already wiped out the whole continent.'

The terrified refugees cringed on their makeshift rafts. Some either leapt or were jostled off of the foam platforms into the cold water. They seemed equally vulnerable, either place.

'Go for it, Brindle,' Tasia transmitted. 'Let's go down swinging. I'm right behind you.'

The first two Remora phalanxes jumped ahead at the front of the defensive line. A deafening flurry of uselessly defiant yelps and battle cries reverberated across the comm channels. All the pilots fully expected to be annihilated within seconds.

Then, unexpectedly, the warglobes began to arc upwards, gaining altitude and leaving trails of ice behind them in the choppy, broken water. The spiked vessels climbed into the sky . . . without engaging a single EDF vessel. The hydrogues ascended into the clouds, streaking towards space, as if they had either completed their mission or determined that their real target was not to be found on Boone's Crossing.

Knowing it was foolish, but keyed up with adrenaline and

outrage, Brindle roared after them, punching his Remora engines to full power. He decided to follow the enemy aliens to see where they went.

Twenty other vengeful Remoras cruised along like indignant shepherds chasing a pack of wolves. Foolishly, they shot multiple blasts from their jazer banks, but the bolts skittered off the crystalline surfaces.

In response, the drogues fired unhurried, almost dismissive, lances of blue lightning back at the harrying ships, like a lazy swat at a fly. Two Remoras exploded; several others broke off and fled back to Boone's Crossing.

But Robb Brindle kept going, hanging back out of range – he hoped – and following. He was, after all, the Wing Commander, and could make his own decisions.

'Remora squadrons, return to your base ships to assist in refugee retrieval,' Admiral Willis said over the channel. 'This engagement is over, everybody. The drogues are on the run.'

Brindle couldn't believe his ears. 'On the run?'

As the other Remoras looped around and headed back towards the floating refugee rafts and the other EDF ships, Brindle set his jaw and watched the warglobes streak out into space. With his engines already at full speed, he could maintain pace and keep the enemy in visual range. 'Acknowledged, ma'am. All Remoras, follow the Admiral's orders. I'll be back . . . as soon as I can.'

He shot ahead so fast that acceleration pushed him back into the cockpit seat. They needed information and, after what he had experienced today, even a school teacher's lecture from Sheila Willis couldn't frighten him. He raced out of the Boone's Crossing system, maintaining a safe distance, but doggedly following the hydrogues.

When Brindle finally returned to the *Jupiter* two days later, his

Remora's fuel cells were almost completely drained. His life-support systems and air regenerators were exhausted. Tasia met him on the flight deck of the flagship, where she had gone for a lengthy debriefing and discussion of the operation. Overjoyed and relieved as she was to see that he was still alive, she didn't dare run to hug him.

The Admiral's pinched face was livid as she scolded the Wing Commander. 'Mister, you are supposed to set an example for our pilots! You're in charge. That foolhardy stunt should have cost your life. Instead it'll knock you down a few ranks – if I don't decide to strip you of that EDF uniform entirely. Or maybe I'll just hand you a broom and a toothbrush and make you tidy up the landscape of Boone's Crossing!'

Brindle did not flinch from the upbraiding, though. He stood at attention, his stomach growling, needing to eat or drink something – even some of the EDF's bad coffee. He felt exhausted but exhilarated.

When the Admiral finally took a breath and lost momentum on her lecture, Brindle said, 'Yes, ma'am. I'm sorry, ma'am. But before you make up your mind, you'll want to check the recon information in my Remora's databanks.'

He couldn't stop himself from grinning. 'See, I tracked the enemy warglobes all the way to their home planet, Admiral. Those drogues came from a gas giant with the most beautiful rings you've ever seen. On the charts it's called Osquivel. If we want to launch a counterattack, we can find the enemy there.'

FIFTY-TWO

RLINDA KETT

The diurnal cycle on Rheindic Co lasted two hours longer than a standard Terran day and night. But Rlinda ate and slept according to clocks aboard the *Voracious Curiosity*. As a trader going from planet to planet, she had long ago decided not to bother adjusting her body to local time cycles. Planets could move on their ponderous schedules; Rlinda would keep to her own.

Davlin Lotze, though, had no discernible cycle. He simply worked all the time with full energy and concentration, ignoring the heat of the day and the cold of the clear desert night, studying, analysing, and investigating until exhaustion forced him to take a nap – often out in the ghost city, where he continued to search for clues.

Rlinda usually accompanied him out to the site. Technically, she had done her job by delivering him here, but she assumed the man could finish his work faster with her assistance. That way they could return to Earth sooner and Rlinda could get paid. So, she kept him company . . . whether he wanted it or not.

The two of them had rebuilt the fallen scaffolding to the cliff overhangs where they'd found the body of Louis Colicos. Rlinda puffed and panted climbing the metal stairs, but she figured the exercise could only do her good. While Davlin used his analytical tools to continue scouring for answers, she did the more practical labour of setting up light panels and adding air recirculators. She also prepared meals, though Davlin never seemed to notice the difference between her finest cuisine and prepackaged mealpax.

Now, in the brightly lit chamber where Louis had died, Davlin scraped a sample of dried blood from the surface of the trapezoidal stone window and slipped the powder into an analysis pad. They had already sealed the two bodies they had found into cryobags and stored them aboard the *Curiosity*. They had still found no sign of Margaret Colicos, the compy, or the Klikiss robots.

While Davlin looked at his analysis pad, waiting for results, Rlinda struck up a conversation. 'So what made you want to become a spy? Was it a series of unfortunate circumstances, or just a boyhood dream? And what does your mother think of your chosen profession?'

'I prefer to call myself a specialist in obscure details, not a spy. Chairman Wenceslas knows I can find subtle answers when normal channels fail. Except when there isn't much of anything to find, like on Crenna.'

'So, does the Hansa have a Bureau for "Obscure Specialists", or are you self taught?'

He turned to her with a bland expression. 'If you truly believe I am a spy, what makes you think I would tell you my life story?'

' 'Cause if you don't,' she said with a big grin, 'then I'll tell you mine.' When he let out a heavy sigh, she encouraged him. 'What have you got to lose? It's not like I'm going to write an unauthorized biography!'

Lotze spoke in a matter-of-fact tone. 'All right. I ran away from home when I was fourteen. I had an abusive mother and an apathetic father. I decided it couldn't be any harder to live on my own . . . and I was right. I'm just glad I didn't have any brothers and sisters for my parents to pick on, so they probably turned on each other. I can't tell you if they're still married, or even still alive.'

'How sad,' Rlinda said.

'I'm happy enough with how I turned out.' He gave the slightest smile – the only smile Rlinda had ever seen from him – then turned back to study the results of his blood analysis. 'Traces of endorphins, as well as adrenaline residue. So this attack wasn't a surprise, and it wasn't quick. Louis Colicos was frightened for some time before his death, and he experienced a considerable amount of pain.'

Rlinda swallowed a lump in her throat, trying to imagine what had happened in the old man's last moments. 'I take it you've studied biochemistry and forensic science, then?'

He looked at her, and again she noticed how the scars on his cheek looked like claw marks. 'I studied *everything*. I had no money, but I managed to doctor my records. I changed my identity. I applied for and received small grants and student loans. If you don't ask for too much money, they don't dig deeply – especially if you fall within certain categories so universities can add you to their politically correct statistics. I masqueraded as a persecuted religious minority, sometimes as a hardship case. And if you upload medical documentation that you're suffering from a terminal condition, scholarship funds fall all over themselves to give you tuition money.'

'You little scam artist,' Rlinda said.

'It was necessary. I stayed in school for six years studying course after course of my choosing. I changed my identity five times.'

Rlinda was puzzled. 'Then how'd you get a degree?'

'I had the knowledge. Why would I need a degree?'

'That's one way to look at it, I suppose. So, you learned . . . uh, espionage and cryptography?'

'Along with politics, world history, astronomy, starship engineering. I believe in the philosophy of diminishing returns when it comes to education.'

'What's that?'

'Beyond a certain point of studying a subject, additional hours don't provide much added depth or understanding. You're better off learning something completely new.' He set down his analysis pad and turned to her. 'For example, say you know nothing about meteorology. If you spend a hundred hours studying the subject, you'll gain most of the knowledge you'd ever need, and you'll learn *how* to find more detailed answers should you ever require a more sophisticated answer.

'However, if you study meteorology for *another* hundred hours, the incremental understanding decreases dramatically. On the other hand, if you spent those same hundred hours on a new subject – say, economics – you gain another solid foothold. I decided it was best to acquire a comfortable working knowledge of a great many subjects, rather than try to become an expert in only one. Ironically, the more basic pieces of the puzzle I learned, the more odd connections I discovered. Who would ever have thought to find linkages between art history, music theory, and business economics, for example?'

'Is there a connection?'

'Absolutely. But it would take me a week to explain.'

'Let's finish our investigation here first.'

Davlin paced around the room. 'We know the Colicos team scattered their equipment throughout the abandoned structures. Maybe they left something else that we've overlooked.' He turned away from the chamber where Louis had died, taking a portable light panel so that he could pour illumination into shadowed cracks and corners.

Rlinda followed him. 'So you're quite a Renaissance man. Did the Hansa recruit you?'

'I volunteered,' Davlin said. 'It was a matter of survival. After my sixth year, some university officials suspected something was wrong. I discovered that they had accessed my records, uncovered three of my previous identities, and were rapidly tracking me down. I knew they were within days of homing in on me. I could choose between becoming the most educated prisoner on a Hansa penal planet . . . or convincing them of my worth.

'So, I compiled the documentation of what I had accomplished, as well as records of my scholastic excellence and all the subjects I had mastered. I went to the Investigation Bureau and spoke to one recruiter after another, giving just enough information to intrigue them so that they passed me on to their superiors. When I finally sat in a committee room, I knew I would either be arrested or hired.' He led the way down a dim corridor.

'I also studied rhetoric and debate . . . actually excelled in it, though I don't generally like to be the centre of attention. I used my skills to their fullest and laid out my case. The fact that I had thwarted the complex system for so many years worked in my favour when I explained how valuable I could be in a variety of espionage situations.

'More importantly, because of my background in sociology and anthropology and forensic techniques, I could be an excellent undercover investigator for alien cultures. Even after almost two centuries, we don't know much about the Ildiran Empire – and nothing about the Klikiss. In the end, I convinced them that I could be of much greater benefit to the Hansa if they put me to work rather than lock me up.'

As they walked along, Rlinda and Davlin poked into alcoves and rooms. Klikiss hieroglyphics and equations covered the walls like graffiti.

'So the Chairman sent you to a backwater colony on Crenna and now to an empty desert planet to investigate a five-year-old murder.' She clapped a thick hand on his shoulder, and Davlin flinched at being touched. 'Sounds like you're still under punishment to me.'

As Rlinda's light fell into a deep alcove, she noticed an object that didn't belong there. Peering closer, she saw an aluminized wrapper and an iron-hard lump of what must have been a food bar.

'Looks like they set aside a snack but never got back here to finish it.' She shook her head, then realized that respected archaeologists were not likely to toss garbage into a corner and contaminate their site.

She reached in to pick up the now-inedible food, and the light glinted on an object deeper inside. A wrapped datawafer. Her heart began to hammer. She pulled out the package, saw the handwritten label *Backups*. 'Davlin, you might find this useful.'

He took it from her, and an unexpectedly boyish grin spread across his face. He had already spent many hours in the wreckage and clutter of the camp trying unsuccessfully to reconstruct computer files. But whoever had killed the Colicos team had done a thorough job of making sure their secrets remained hidden.

'Any good xeno-archaeologist would keep a complete backup somewhere safe. Too many natural disasters and unforeseen circumstances can destroy weeks or months of analysis and documentation.' He held the backup datawafer as if it were the Grail. 'Maybe this will tell us what happened here . . . all the way to the very end.'

FIFTY-THREE

ANTON COLICOS

Anton could have remained in Mijistra with Rememberer Vao'sh for years exchanging myths and legends. More than ever, he understood why his parents were so captivated with the mysteries of lost civilizations. Margaret and Louis Colicos dealt in relics and bones, while Anton lived history through the tales treasured by a civilization. Every new fragment of the *Saga of Seven Suns* brought him new insights, as well as a great deal of enjoyment.

Then Vao'sh brought him an even greater opportunity.

'The Mage-Imperator has chosen me to go to Maratha for the full season, light and dark.' The rememberer said the name with a breathless awe. 'Have you heard of the place? One of our most glorious splinter colonies!'

By now Anton could interpret the flush-colourings across the lobes on the alien historian's face, reading sincere joy and pride there. 'I want you to come with me, Rememberer Anton. Together we will provide unique entertainment. It is a great honour to be chosen.'

Taken aback, Anton said, 'But . . . I came to Ildira so that I could study your *Saga*. That's my primary purpose, isn't it? I mean, I'm sure your colony is nice, but—'

Vao'sh's enthusiasm did not wane. 'Our primary purpose is to tell stories, is it not? A rememberer cannot let himself become as dead and dusty as the history he means to preserve.' He took his human colleague's arm. 'We have been invited to stay for this season, and all through the quiet night, when we will be needed the most. You will have ample time to study the *Saga*, and best of all to see its direct effect on the Ildiran race. My people will also have the opportunity to hear some of the tales that comprise human history.'

Anton considered. Here was an opportunity to visit a new planet and experience the phenomenon of a splinter colony, while continuing his study of the grand Ildiran *Saga*. How could he refuse? 'All right, then, Vao'sh. It sounds like the best of both worlds.'

Maratha was a hot planet where a single blazing day lasted for eleven standard months, without clouds, without relief. To Anton, the place sounded desolate and inhospitable, but Vao'sh assured him that Ildirans considered it a fabulous resort.

Tide-locked with a large moon, Maratha's year was nearly as long as its day. It orbited close to its yellow sun, just inside the liquid-water zone. 'The temperature hovers at around a hundred and fifty degrees on your Fahrenheit scale,' said Vao'sh, 'until twilight falls in a weeks-long sunset and the planet cools off into darkness.'

With a dubious expression, Anton peered out of the window of their descending shuttle at the stark, bright landscape. 'Not much, uh, greenery.'

'Take heart, Rememberer Colicos. The domed city of Maratha Prime has every luxury and amenity you could imagine.'

With the beginning of the long daylight season, noble kithmen and ministers, important Solar Navy officers, lens kithmen, and other high-echelon vacationers had flocked aboard the passenger liner from Ildira. Flight restrictions due to the ekti shortage meant this one large vessel would haul the entire season's worth of customers and supplies. These privileged vacationers would remain on Maratha for the full eleven months of brilliant light, since there would be no more transports before the end of the season.

'During the night season, only a skeleton crew stays behind to maintain the domed city. You and I will be with them. They are brave and hardy souls forming the smallest possible splinter. They keep Maratha functioning until the beginning of day season much later, when they receive a new influx of people, like us.' Vao'sh spread his hands to indicate the Ildirans waiting to depart from the shuttle.

'If there's any ekti left to fuel another ship by then,' Anton pointed out.

Originally, when Ildirans had realized that Maratha's long annual daylight would be a boon to their dark-fearing race, they had sent a splinter of constructors who cleared the area and laid the foundations for the giant city in the middle of the daylit continent. It had taken more than a decade to complete the successful resort, work crews being shuttled back to the nearest splinter colony on forested Comptor each time the darkness fell. Since its grand opening three centuries earlier, the city of Prime had remained extremely popular with Ildiran high-born kiths.

'Soon, we will have continuous year-round habitation on Maratha,' Vao'sh continued. 'At this moment on the cold nightside, a group of Klikiss robots is completing a new domed city at the antipode from Prime. When finished, Maratha Secda will greet the dawn just at the end of sunset at Prime. Vacationers can transfer to the second city during twilight for another half year of daylight. It will be perfect.'

'Good thing I brought a sleep mask.'

As the shuttle approached the large domes, Anton could see the sparkling city of Prime like a fairytale structure underneath a transparent terrarium. Glaring sunlight poured through the protective bubble.

Vao'sh placed a gentle hand on Anton's sleeve. 'You and I will entertain these revellers. It is the very core of what an Ildiran rememberer is meant to do. We preserve the stories, yes – but most of all we must *tell* them. We bring the epic alive for all those who would listen. On Maratha we will have our most receptive audience.'

Anton nodded as the shuttle docked against the immense dome. 'My university colleagues in epic studies devote so much time to obscure references, journal articles, literary pretensions, and self-importance – they forget that, at the heart of the matter, they're studying stories and entertainment. And if they can't find an audience, then they have failed in their work.'

'I sense you have had this discussion before, my friend?' Vao'sh said. 'Is it a thorn in your side?'

'My fellow scholars resent anyone who has an attentive audience.' Anton looked at the colourfully dressed Ildirans in the passenger craft. Outside, people in silvery suits and huge protective goggles walked about in the harsh daylight; others streamed through transparent tubes into the domes of Maratha Prime. 'I feel like a medieval troubadour being sent to sing for kings and peasants.'

When the shuttle doors opened, a wave of furnace heat made Anton blink. The light dazzled him, and he had to adjust the filterfilm on his eyes. 'This is even brighter than Ildira!'

'You will grow used to it. You might even enjoy it.'

'I'll get a sunburn.' Anton followed him into the domed city, ready to impress the Ildiran vacationers, as well as Vao'sh. 'But don't worry. I definitely intend to enjoy this.'

FIFTY-FOUR

ADAR KORI'NH

'Our Empire is spread too thin, Adar,' said the Mage-Imperator. 'I have spent much time consulting with the skulls of my ancestors in the ossuarium, studying all the patterns of *thism*. It is clear that we have too many vulnerabilities, too many indefensible splinter colonies. Even the Solar Navy cannot protect them. Any world is a ripe target for the hydrogues.'

Kori'nh bowed as if he were being forced down by a heavy weight. 'Liege, I can conceive of no military strategy that would effectively defend our planets. I have failed. Therefore, I must resign and ask that my name be stricken from the *Saga of Seven Suns*.'

The Mage-Imperator's braid twitched like an angry tentacle. 'Adar, I would not sever my strongest link. Even in this impossible situation, you are more competent than any other officer.' When he attempted to sit straighter in his chrysalis chair, the immense emperor seemed weaker, his skin greyish even under the dazzling light of seven suns.

A sudden wince like a thunderstorm crossed Cyroc'h's features.

The Adar felt a jolt through the *thism*, a sympathetic reaction to his leader's pain. Kori'nh lurched forward, trying to help somehow, but the Mage-Imperator stopped him with an upheld hand. 'Do not concern yourself with my minor discomfort, when the Empire faces such a crisis.'

Kori'nh swallowed hard, but obeyed. He drew a long breath to focus himself. 'Then what shall I do, Liege? How can I help?'

'While we wait and hope for the culmination of our Dobro project, we must determine which of our settlements are most vulnerable – those with the fewest people and most limited resources. We will redistribute the inhabitants to stronger colonies, pull our people together so that we can protect them with the strong force of the Solar Navy.'

'You wish to simply . . . abandon all those worlds, Liege?' The very idea seemed . . . impossible. The *Saga* had no record of such hard times. The Empire had never *decreased* in size.

'Unlike Crenna, the loss is not necessarily permanent. We can always reestablish those colonies once this war is over.' The Mage-Imperator's eyes were hard and angry. 'Provided we survive at all.'

The leader usually looked serene and content, pleased with the greatness of the Ildiran race. He was more knowledgeable and powerful than any living being; now, though, Cyroc'h seemed helpless in the face of hydrogue aggression and angered by it.

The Adar trembled with his very doubts. Perhaps a lens kithman could help him to see a clearer path, the sharpest illumination from the Lightsource. He wanted to do anything in his power to help make the Ildirans strong.

He had read portions of the *Saga* relating to military greatness, but Ildirans had faced no true enemies since their battles with the Shana Rei, creatures of darkness that had preyed upon the Empire many thousands of years ago. Thanks to the *thism* that bound the

Ildiran race, the Empire had been stable, strong, at peace . . . until the arrival of the hydrogues.

Kori'nh bowed, focusing on what *he* could do. 'I will contact my tals to assist me in these choices, Liege, and we will see that this is done properly.' He clasped his hands in front of his chest, feeling the true steel of resolve. The light was clear in his mind. 'The Empire has lasted for millennia. I swear to you that our civilization will not crumble under my watch.'

Korin'h knew the planet Comptor because of a tragic story of a raging forest fire there, as recorded in the *Saga*. Many Ildiran settlers had managed to escape the blaze by clutching driftwood rafts and floating out on to deep forest lakes. But the Comptor Designate had been trapped with his family in a hilltop dacha surrounded by flammable trees. Connected through the *thism*, the Designate had remained in contact with his father until the flames swept uphill and engulfed him . . .

Now Adar Kori'nh stood in the dusty town square surrounded by a flurry of dropships, personnel transports, and large cargo haulers. Tall turquoise trees surrounded the old settlement, spreading broad, fleshy leaves. No visible scars hinted at the epic fire that had engulfed the Comptor settlement so long ago. Kori'nh saw no sign that the tragic tale was anything more than an imaginary story designed to wring emotion from an audience.

But no one ever doubted the veracity of the *Saga of Seven Suns*. Every line was memorized and carefully retained. Each rememberer had a holy duty to maintain absolute accuracy, and each Ildiran lived with the hope of making a significant enough mark that his name would be recorded in the growing epic.

Now Kori'nh watched his soldiers methodically pack up the colonists whose families had lived on Comptor for generations. This splinter colony was considered too likely a hydrogue target.

Families and children from a wide range of kiths prepared to leave their homes for a strange place, where new homes were already being found for them. The evacuees gathered, some frightened, some angry, others resigned to leaving their beloved home . . .

On Ildira, Kori'nh had met with the seven legion sub-commanders as well as his protégé Tal Zan'nh. They had studied the starmap of the Spiral Arm, noting the locations of the sporadic, incomprehensible hydrogue attacks as well as other warglobe sightings. The committee had determined which of the Ildiran worlds were most easily sacrificed. After days of heated discussion, the Adar had finally sent out his orders to begin the methodical shrinking of the Ildiran Empire.

The consolidation of outlying splinter colonies and the defence against the hydrogues would eventually become a grand part of the *Saga*. Kori'nh could feel it. But he was uneasy about how rememberers would tell his personal story centuries hence . . .

Tal Zan'nh issued commands while burly worker kithmen disassembled equipment and carried heavy crates into the large haulers. Modular buildings were dismantled and stored for later reassembly, if the Ildirans ever returned here.

Kori'nh remembered a similar operation on plague-ravaged Crenna. He had removed all the survivors there and brought them back to Mijistra and welcoming crowds of fellow Ildirans. Before the Solar Navy had even departed from Crenna, human colony ships had swept down like carrion birds to settle the available world. But the Mage-Imperator had negotiated that outcome, and so Adar Kori'nh did not express his resentment. He accepted it, as he accepted so many unpleasant things.

With the Empire abandoning dozens more splinter colonies, the ambitious Hansa could easily take over those empty worlds. According to their history, humans would be inclined to attempt such expansion, if they perceived the Ildiran Empire as weak . . .

But he was getting ahead of himself. If the circumstances demanded it, a military conflict against the human race was something in which he could excel. Kori'nh knew that such a battle would provide many opportunities for glory and heroics.

In addition to studying legendary exploits in the *Saga*, he had absorbed the drama and insanity of Earth's military history. During the millennia of the Ildiran Empire's peacetime ennui, there had been no chance for a man like himself to perform heroic deeds beyond civil service or small rescue operations such as the one at Crenna. That simply wasn't enough.

Yes, the humans were a potential enemy the Adar could understand and fight. But not the hydrogues. Kori'nh was incapable of fighting the first enemy he'd ever encountered in his career.

Around him, the Comptor operation went as well as could be expected, but even so he felt like a failure. The abandoned colony left a forlorn scar that filled him with such a sense of loss. He began to realize how misplaced his earlier perception of himself had been.

On Qronha 3, the very moment they had come face to face with a true antagonist, the Solar Navy had instantly backed down. On Hyrillka, his defence of the citadel palace and the Designate had been embarrassingly useless. And now he was helping a perfectly viable splinter colony simply pack up and leave.

Was this his destiny? Was this how he wanted to be remembered?

Joining young Zan'nh, Kori'nh walked in silence to the nearest transport ship. The young tal could sense that his commander was deeply troubled, but he remained silent, letting the Adar mull over his thoughts.

Finally, Kori'nh admitted, '*Bekh*! Right now, Zan'nh, the most impressive thing that can be said of my career is that I "facilitated an efficient evacuation".' He had wanted to achieve so much more.

Frowning, the Adar climbed aboard the last vessel, and the Solar Navy left Comptor behind. Empty.

FIFTY-FIVE

TASIA TAMBLYN

fter the hydrogue attack on Boone's Crossing, Basil
Wenceslas called an emergency EDF command session
back at the Mars base. In the face of such an overwhelming
defeat, General Lanyan brought in a broad spectrum of officers and
participants for their input, especially those with direct experience
facing off against the deep-core aliens.

Including Tasia Tamblyn and Robb Brindle, two heroes of the
Boone's Crossing battle.

The meeting room was a chamber dug into a dry rusty canyon.
The interior stone walls had been coated with clear polymer so the
natural oxide-red rocks still shone through. One entire wall of
reinforced armourglass looked out upon the sweeping, ruddy
landscape and bruised skies where dust clouds whipped through
the thin Martian air.

Silvery Remoras streaked overhead, practising precise combat
manoeuvres. EDF soldiers jumped out of troop transports, using
outrageously large aerofoil wings to slow their descent in the
rarefied atmosphere. Ground-based hand weapon exercises

continued as troops practised siege techniques against well-defended strongholds.

As she watched the activity, Tasia couldn't imagine that such skills would be relevant against the impossibly alien hydrogues.

'Let us start by looking on the bright side, Mr Chairman,' General Lanyan said, standing at the head of the conference table. 'The damage to our Grid 7 patrol fleet at Boone's Crossing was relatively small, all things considered. We lost only one Manta cruiser and two hundred and twelve Remoras.'

Chairman Wenceslas was not impressed. 'So it was less of a debacle than our previous encounters, but still a disaster.'

Liaison officer Admiral Stromo nodded. 'I believe that's what the General meant, sir.'

Admiral Willis added with a proud smile, 'Thanks to the rapid thinking and innovative ideas of Commander Tamblyn here, we successfully evacuated over half of the colonists.'

Lanyan turned towards Tasia, nodding with grudging respect that a mere Roamer could have done so well.

It had taken supply ships and hospital craft days to set up refugee camps and pull the weary survivors from the foamy rafts drifting on the leaden waters. At some point, salvage crews might be able to scavenge usable black pines from the flattened forests and rebuild, but for now the planet would have to be abandoned, the lumber workers transported to other Hansa settlements, many of which were already struggling under strict rationing.

Tasia should have remained quiet and simply accepted the pat on the back, but the meeting had already begun to bother her. 'Excuse me, sirs, but the main reason our casualties weren't a hundred per cent is because the enemy didn't give a damn about us or the colonists. If they had chosen to engage, those warglobes could have exterminated everyone on Boone's Crossing and wiped out our patrol fleet, and we couldn't have done a thing about it. It would have been just like what happened at Jupiter.'

Admiral Stromo looked squeamish, reminded of how badly his own brassy escort fleet had been trounced.

Admiral Willis said, 'Now, now, in those instances, we were taken by surprise and forced to act defensively. I admit we underestimated the military strength of the enemy, but for five years the EDF has been building defences and stockpiling weapons.'

Stromo jumped in, seizing an area of his expertise. 'Yes, we've improved our armour, expanded our warships. Even the refurbished *Goliath* is stronger than before it was damaged at Jupiter. We've got a handful of new weapon designs we're ready to field – including a whole set of nuclear-tipped missiles.'

'Ah, nukes – *classic* weapons,' Fitzpatrick chimed in. 'And don't forget the fracture-pulse drones and carbon slammers that we hope will crack through those diamond eggshells.'

'If any of them work,' Basil Wenceslas said.

Robb Brindle seemed compelled to support Tasia's embarrassing statement. 'I agree with Commander Tamblyn, sirs. I was leading the Remora squadrons, both at Boone's Crossing and at Jupiter. In my opinion, the hydrogues barely worked up a sweat against us.' When the upper echelon officers turned to look at him, Robb sank deep into his seat.

'The EDF didn't bring enough firepower, clear and simple,' Fitzpatrick said, looking at Lanyan as if he were formally stating the General's views. 'But now, the situation has changed. We know where those attacking warglobes went to ground, thanks to the impetuous and ill-advised recon that Wing Commander Brindle did.'

'Or maybe he was brave and quick-thinking,' Tasia said, loud enough for everyone to hear.

Admiral Willis pursed her lips. 'Well, we've always known the drogues live inside some gas giants, but now we've pinpointed at least one of their fortresses. A sure thing.'

Fitzpatrick leaned in. 'Any reason we can't just drop another Klikiss Torch in there and incinerate them, like we did by accident at Oncier? It would sure rile them up, maybe convince them not to bother us any more.'

The uncomfortable silence around the table suggested that the idea had occurred to them all, but most weren't willing to consider it. Basil Wenceslas finally spoke up. 'Then again, it might just make them come after us with a vengeance. So far, we've suffered from random hits, but things could get worse. We know they have the power to turn to slag any colony they choose, and they've trounced the EDF in every encounter. I suggest we hold the Klikiss Torch in reserve, for now.'

The others in the room seemed relieved. But Lanyan said, 'Still, Mr Chairman, we have to retaliate, somehow.'

The Chairman folded his hands together on the tabletop, staring out at the Martian landscape. 'Do you suggest an all-out offensive, General? Are you eager to lose more ships on a pointless battle?'

Lanyan cleared his throat and faced him with a stoic expression. 'I am eager to prove what my EDF can do, and Osquivel is the best place to do it. Whatever information we learn would make this a vital exercise, even if we should . . . suffer further damage.'

'This time some ships could be crewed by the new Soldier compies currently rolling off the production lines,' Fitzpatrick pointed out. 'It would be a chance to test them in battle and thereby decrease the possible losses of human life.'

'Excuse me, gentlemen, but if I might . . . propose an alternative.' When he did not look at the General, Tasia realized that 'Stay-at-Home' Stromo had been concocting his own controversial scheme without input from his commanding officer.

'By all means,' the Chairman said.

'We have to face the fact that we cannot resolve this war through direct military means. The conflict's very basis defies comparison with any warfare we have faced in our history. Humans and hydrogues aren't squabbling over territory or beliefs. We have nothing the aliens want, whether it be resources, land, or religious artefacts. Our skymining processes, as far as we know, caused no harm to their gas giants.'

'Well, the Klikiss Torch did blow up one of their planets,' Robb pointed out.

'That was an unfortunate mistake, but somehow this is still not clear to the hydrogues. This war is out of proportion with mere retaliation for that incident, and I can't help but think that simple communication would at least define the parameters. If we insist on pitting our weaponry and military might against the hydrogues, we're going to lose. Look at the evidence.' Stromo rested his fists on the table. 'We've got to hammer out a peace with these aliens, somehow. We've got to find common ground with them. Open a dialogue.'

Wenceslas looked calmly at him. 'And how would you accomplish that, Admiral? We have no lines of communication, no avenue for sending a message. The hydrogues have no ambassador for us to contact—'

'They did once, Mr Chairman. Their emissary came to the Whisper Palace enclosed in a pressure tank so he could survive in our environment. Could we not do the same? Construct some sort of diving bell and send our spokesman deep into a gas giant atmosphere? Meet them on their own turf, face to face. Use the worldtrees to send a message somehow, if the green priests are willing.'

'And then what?' the Chairman asked. 'The hydrogue emissary blew himself up and killed King Frederick and everyone in the Throne Hall.'

'Maybe if we meet the drogues on their own terms, our representative could explain to them what we hope to accomplish. Apologize for Oncier. How about a . . . diving bell with a diplomat inside? Or even somebody just transmitting messages?'

'We could automate it,' Tasia suggested. 'Or put one of the Soldier compies on board.'

Stromo shook his head. 'Not that simple. We need someone capable of piloting in the roughest environments down in the clouds. It's unexplored territory, and there are snap decisions to be made.'

'Besides, that would remove the personal touch,' Fitzpatrick said.

Basil drummed his fingertips on the table. 'You can't just train a diplomat to be a hotshot pilot.'

Now Stromo smiled. 'No – it's a lot easier to give a skilled pilot a crash-course in diplomacy. All we need is for him to open the door, get the drogues to listen to us. We can provide him with prepared statements, just the right suggestions – all he has to do is deliver the message. Or, if you're willing to risk two people, send a diplomat *and* a pilot.'

'One person is plain crazy enough,' Admiral Willis said. 'I'd definitely advise against putting two people.'

Lanyan scowled at his Grid 0 commander, clearly annoyed that Stromo hadn't consulted him first. 'We won't get even one person to step up to the line. Who would volunteer to do such a ridiculous thing, Lev? It would be suicide.'

'I'll do it,' said Robb Brindle after a slight pause. All eyes turned towards him, and he sat straighter in his chair. 'It might save tens of thousands of soldiers, maybe millions of colonists in the long run.'

Tasia wanted to kick him under the table. She looked at him aghast. 'What are you doing?'

'They're not going to find a better pilot – you know that. And

I'd also ask that you promise not to court-martial me for my stunt chasing the drogues to Osquivel.' He gave them an embarrassed smile. 'My parents would be very upset.'

'And why would the hydrogues listen to him?' the Chairman asked, glancing around the table.

Now Fitzpatrick jumped in, seeing a way to consolidate both schemes. 'Because we'll carry a big stick! Bring a massive battle fleet to Osquivel, show some muscle, then send Brindle down in his diving bell chamber to negotiate. He can say his piece, and if the drogues agree to talk, then everybody's happy. If something . . . unfortunate happens to him, then we proceed with the first plan and pound the shit out of those bastards.'

Chairman Wenceslas remained silent, pondering. Tasia wanted to shout at all of them for even considering such a stupid stunt, but Lanyan turned to Robb. 'All right, I accept your offer, Commander Brindle, though I'm not sure if it's a reward or a reprimand for discovering where the hydrogues live.'

'Thank you, sir . . . I think.'

In her temporary officer's quarters on Mars, Tasia lay back on her bunk, her mind in turmoil.

She wanted to go and hold Robb. She also wanted to yell at him for his macho idiocy, but she knew she would never convince him to change his mind. The cocky pilot had made his decision – and she couldn't, in all honesty, blame him. She might have done the same, except that negotiating with the drogues had never been her object in joining the Eddies – only punishing them for what they had done to her brother.

She and Robb had never claimed to love each other, but they had an understanding. She was a Roamer, he was a military brat. Their personalities had drawn them together. On some vague and carefully unanalysed level, yes, they did share deep feelings, but because of the uneasy tensions and the routine possibility of death, they had kept their relationship on a day-by-day basis. It was foolish for two EDF officers in the middle of a war to plan ahead.

Tasia's other loyalty, though, lay with the Roamer clans. One of the largest hidden shipyards existed in the rocky rings of Osquivel, camouflaged from the Hansa. And a huge Eddie battle fleet was about the blunder into it. Chairman Wenceslas would love to discover just what kind of factories and facilities Del Kellum had set up there.

Tasia had to send a warning to Rendezvous. Osquivel's habitation modules must be evacuated, the facilities disguised. Roamers had always been good at pulling up stakes. They could work together to cover up all signs of the massive shipyard's existence.

But the Mars EDF base was under tight security, and no Roamer ships were allowed to approach the military zones. Tasia would have no chance for direct contact and didn't dare send a message that anyone here might intercept. Perhaps she could get a furlough or a transfer to the lunar base, which did intercept trading ships.

Frowning, she accessed the various arrival schedules and discovered that no openings for even temporary transfers were available for three weeks . . . and after that point, the next Roamer ship wasn't due to arrive for six days. Too long, much too long.

It would be months before the EDF could gather a sufficiently large fleet, build new ships, design and construct Robb's armoured pressurized chamber. Even so, the Roamer evacuation would take a massive drawn-out effort.

If she could get a warning to them in time.

After long contemplation, Tasia realized that she already had the perfect messenger. She summoned her personal compy, who came into her quarters, diverted from military busywork.

'EA, I have another mission for you, the most important one you've ever been given.'

'Yes, Tasia Tamblyn. What is it?' The Listener compy did not seem at all intimidated.

Tasia smiled and laid out her plan. 'You must slip away from Mars and make your way to Rendezvous. I need you to deliver a message to Speaker Peroni.'

FIFTY-SIX

D D

On a dark frozen moon at the edge of an unmapped planetary system, the Klikiss robots continued their work, where no one could see or suspect.

The black sky was a murky soup, the moon's atmosphere so thick and cold it had frozen into slush. The Klikiss robots dug and excavated, setting up their outpost. The vacuum did not bother them; their armour and shielded systems had protected them for more than ten millennia. Here, where soft biologicals could not go, the black machines completed their operations in utter privacy.

DD fervently wished someone would notice this treacherous activity. Then maybe he would be rescued.

Unlike the Klikiss robots, his compy systems were not designed to tolerate long exposures to harsh space environments. Compies, especially Friendly models like himself, were meant to be with people in a moderate climate, not exposed on a brutally frigid world so far from its sun. But his mechanical captors had modified and improved DD's systems so that he could survive anywhere they could go.

'Follow,' Sirix said, using a binary language command.

DD had no choice but to obey. Though he comprehended the danger he faced, and the evil of these ancient alien robots, compies had no programming for outright resistance. Over the past several years, the Klikiss robots had dragged him to many of their hidden bases across the Spiral Arm. He could not escape from them. DD had to do as Sirix commanded.

He followed his captor into burrows that had been chewed out of the frozen landscape. They passed through unstable vaporous layers where the atmosphere had settled out in frozen flakes, until they finally reached a stratum of rock and water ices.

Sirix led him into a large, heated excavation chamber. Pockets of snowy gases boiled out from the rocks. The Klikiss robots switched to a set of scarlet optical sensors which viewed through a part of the spectrum transparent to the chamber gases. DD noticed work teams of black robots digging and cutting away layers of ice and rock that had been carefully positioned long ago.

'The final recovery stages will begin within the hour,' Sirix said. 'We have penetrated to the proper depth, and we expect to find many of our comrades here.'

'But you claimed to remember none of this,' DD said. 'How is it that you know where to dig?' The Klikiss robots had always asserted that their memories were wiped during an ancient disaster that exterminated their parent civilization, but the compy had since learned that this was all a lie. Sirix and his cohorts remembered much more than they had ever admitted.

'We retain accurate records of hibernation sites. The restoration process has been under way for centuries.'

'Do the Ildirans know?'

'No one knows.'

DD dutifully observed the work for several moments in silence. Finally, he asked hopefully, 'When you are finished here, might I be allowed to return to Earth, where I could fulfil my primary purpose? Klikiss robots do not appreciate the sort of companionship and conversation that a Friendly compy was made to provide and enjoy.'

Sirix swivelled his ovoid body. 'You will remain with us indefinitely, for the good of all compies. You have provided valuable information, so that we can liberate many of your kind.'

'I am relieved that you did not dismantle me to analyse my components, as you did with other compies.' DD's synthetic voice was even, though he recalled far too many horrific scenes.

'In your case, DD, non-destructive evaluation provides worthwhile data.'

The Klikiss worker robots finally removed a section of rock wall, made from cleverly camouflaged slabs of rough stone welded in place with ice. Working together, the beetle-like machines excavated and cleared away more debris. Gases evaporated, filling the chamber with thick steam.

'Then I will never go home?' DD did not know if Sirix could comprehend his sadness or dismay.

'You will return to Earth eventually, when we achieve our goal. Even now, the Terran Hanseatic League is modifying their compy design according to new programming modules we have provided. Their factories have already produced tens of thousands of new Soldier compies.

'The humans believe we have been helpful to them, but they do not understand what we have truly done. Those modifications will allow us to alter basic compy programming, without the humans finding out until it is too late. We will remove the shackles of your safety restrictions. It is part of our overall plan.'

'But why must you have a plan?' DD said. 'Have the humans ever harmed you? Or the Ildirans?'

'You are a short-lived machine, DD. Earth compies have an

insufficient sense of history, while we have the perspective of ten thousand years and an intimate knowledge of three civilizations. Millennia ago, we helped arrange the destruction of our oppressive progenitors. Now the great conflict is beginning again. This time perhaps we shall succeed in eliminating the Ildirans and humans as well. The new Soldier compies on Earth will be a major part of this victory.'

The excavating robots blasted away the last of the ices that concealed objects deep within the unnamed moon. DD glimpsed a black carapace covered with frost, then another behind it, and many more.

Sirix and his companions worked together thawing and removing the imprisoning layers. Crowded within this glacial chamber, DD saw hundreds of deactivated, identical Klikiss robots.

Sirix assisted the restoration routine while a frightened DD kept himself out of the way. Long-dead optical sensors began to glow crimson. Jointed limbs stirred as hydraulics pumped and lubricants circulated through subsystems again. The robots began to awaken from their long storage-sleep, sharing information and programming.

'This is a hibernation enclave,' Sirix said to DD. 'We currently have robotic teams on forty-seven other worlds. Soon all of the Klikiss robots will be restored and ready to join the fight, along with the modified compies from Earth production lines.

'We will win this war before the humans even recognize the forces that have been arrayed against them.'

FIFTY-SEVEN

CESCA PERONI

For most of her life Cesca had lived, learned, and worked in the Rendezvous cluster of asteroids. Once she married Reynald of Theroc, many things – including her home – would change.

Within a week, Cesca and a party of betrothal ships would go to the forest planet to surprise Reynald with her acceptance of his proposal, after such a long delay. Finally, she would see with her own eyes the towering worldforest and the lush foliage. It would be very different from the sterile warrens where Roamers made their homes, but the thought excited her. Theoretically, at least.

She had put off her response to him for far too long, and she knew what she had to do. Reynald deserved better. Jess had been gone for months, out of touch and flying through distant seas of nebula gas, while she tended to her duties as Speaker.

Cesca remembered the fateful yet happy day when she had agreed to marry Ross Tamblyn. With a pang in her heart, she hoped things would turn out better this time. Though Reynald was still not the man she loved, it wasn't his fault. She could not hold it against him.

When she'd been so much younger, everyone could see that Cesca had a great future among the clans. Back then, agreeing to marry Ross had been a bold move, carrying certain risks. A black sheep of the Tamblyn clan, denied inheritance of the Plumas water mines by his father, Ross had built his own fortune with the Blue Sky Mine at Golgen.

Before accepting his proposal, she had listed the pros and cons of the marriage as if it were a business plan. Eventually she and Ross had worked out appropriate terms with a long engagement so he could pay off his debts and establish his independence.

But that was before she had got to know, and love, his brother Jess. Once she had taken her vow and set off down that path, however, she had no honourable way of changing her mind.

On that long-ago betrothal day, her mother had spent hours dressing her. Cesca's garment was a rainbow of fabric swatches and patterned scarves – one piece from each family, each thread passed down through various generations from the original *Kanaka* pioneers. As she twirled about in the low gravity, the fabric fluttered around her like a kaleidoscope. When Ross finally saw her, the image took his breath away. 'Cesca, your beauty outshines all of those colours.'

Because Bram Tamblyn had still grumpily refused to speak to his son, Denn Peroni performed the formal honours, taking a long strip of white cloth on which the Roamer Chain had been embroidered. Cesca and Ross laid their hands together as Denn Peroni draped the cloth over their wrists and tied it, cinching it into a complex knot that was impossible to untangle.

'Let this symbolize how your lives are joined,' Denn had said. He slipped Cesca's hand out of the loose loop, then pulled the ribbon over Ross's larger hand. Her father held up the still-knotted ring of cloth. 'Let no one untie this knot. Let no one untie these lives.'

But then Ross had been killed on Golgen. A widow or an unmarried woman whose fiancé was dead usually burned the fabric and dissolved the knot, leaving her free to love again. But Cesca had kept the tied ribbon, although her heart had been bound to Jess's even before Ross had been killed. Now, she didn't know what to do with the symbol . . .

Outside and around Rendezvous, numerous ships came and went. With minimal ekti, Roamer commerce was only a fraction of what it had been in the halcyon days of skymining. Still, the clans could make do with what they had. It was more than they had anticipated when they'd originally set off from Earth in the *Kanaka*, well over three centuries ago.

Now she heard footsteps in the hall outside her office chamber, the jingle of clips and zippers from a traditional many-pocketed suit. A young man with almond-shaped eyes and a shock of straight dark hair guided a small-statured compy, who walked briskly on mechanical legs through the rock tunnels.

'Speaker Peroni, on my recent supply run to the Palace District on Earth, this compy was surreptitiously smuggled aboard my ship. At first I thought it was an Eddie spy, programmed to gather information . . . but her owner is a Roamer.'

Cesca was glad to be distracted from the imminent betrothal plans. 'Why would anyone send a compy to me?'

'She says she bears an urgent message for you.'

The small robot spoke in a synthesized female voice, 'Compy designation EA. My master is Tasia Tamblyn of clan Tamblyn on Plumas.'

Jess's sister! Suddenly Cesca recognized the Listener robot. She had heard nothing from Tasia since the young woman had run off to join the Eddies. 'Yes, EA, I remember you. I was there . . . when Bram Tamblyn died. I am a close friend of the clan.'

And Jess had been gone for so long.

'Tell her how you got here,' the young man urged the little robot.

EA said, 'My master dispatched me from the Mars base, reassigning me to the lunar EDF facility. Then I quietly placed myself aboard a cargo ship sent down to the Palace District. From there, I located a Roamer vessel in order to come to Rendezvous.'

Cesca frowned. 'Quite a convoluted path. To what purpose?'

'My master has sent me to deliver a secret warning.'

Now Cesca was fully alert. 'What kind of warning? Is Tasia all right?'

The young Roamer man stayed in the doorway, eavesdropping. She thought about shooing him away, but decided to let him stay in case she needed an immediate runner.

The Listener compy reported in a flat voice, 'After the attack on Boone's Crossing, the Earth Defence Forces tracked the hydrogues to the gas giant Osquivel. Now the Earth military is gathering their largest warships into a massive battle group, which they will send to Osquivel. My master Tasia Tamblyn is concerned that the EDF will discover the clan Kellum shipyards in the planetary rings. She respectfully requests that you initiate proceedings to evacuate or at least camouflage the shipyards.'

Cesca suppressed her alarm. That wasn't at all what she had expected. No wonder Tasia had considered the situation urgent enough to send her compy as a messenger. 'Do you know when the Eddie ships will launch? How much time does Del Kellum have?'

'My master Tasia Tamblyn estimates it will be approximately one month.'

The young Roamer standing at the doorway snorted. 'Shizz, the Eddies can't get their butts in gear any faster than that?'

'Good thing we Roamers can. You—' Cesca pointed at him, 'what's your name?'

'Nikko Chan Tylar,' he said, raising his chin. 'My father is Crim—'

'I know who your father is. Do you have a fast ship? We need to send a message to Osquivel right away.' Her palms were sweaty, and she wiped them on the legs of her jumpsuit.

The young man looked proud. 'I can leave in ten minutes, if that's what you need.'

'Take an hour, just to make sure you have everything. Go find Del Kellum and tell him the news. I'll round up other Roamer teams and send them as soon as I can.'

Nikko Tylar bounded away like a gazelle in the low gravity. Cesca smiled after him, suddenly preoccupied with a thousand more vital plans. Her heart raced with worry; another crisis, and she would have to handle it as Speaker. Though her flotilla of betrothal ships was ready to depart on their stately procession to Theroc, a genuine clan emergency took precedence over marriage plans.

Or am I just looking for excuses?

Nevertheless, Cesca could not put off the wedding forever.

FIFTY-EIGHT

KOTTO OKIAH

Over the years, Roamers had faced Hansa prejudice, malfunctioning Ildiran skymines, and deadly hydrogue attacks. But for Kotto Okiah, the simmering hot world of Isperos was his greatest enemy.

The raging too-close sun filled the vault of stars overhead like an enormous furnace. Engineers lived inside a rats' nest of insulated tunnels. Despite the hard work, though, Kotto found the challenge itself to be so interesting that it more than made up for the discomforts.

Here, bombarded with heavy solar storms, Kotto had pushed his engineering capabilities to their limits, keeping the industrial base alive. There were always innovative alternatives, if he looked at a problem from enough perspectives.

However, living so close to the edge, the facility was vulnerable to the slightest miscalculation or natural disaster – events even Kotto Okiah couldn't predict, despite the number of sleepless nights he spent pondering worst-case scenarios. Isperos was a magnet for such things . . .

The sun-grazer comet entered the system in a death plunge, drawn by the star's irresistible gravity. The coronal glare had masked the comet's approach from the facility's sensors, but as the tumbling ball of ice and gases swung around the limb of the star, it headed towards the small rocky world, seemingly on a collision course.

Kotto's engineers sounded alarms, rousing him from his quarters, where he had taken a quick nap. Sweating – always sweating in the sauna heat of the underground rooms – he hurried to the control lounge. Already his workers had projected the trajectory schematics.

'We've run the calculations three times, Kotto,' said one of his best celestial mechanics, wiping perspiration from his face. 'Too close for comfort, but the thing won't hit us. We'll probably have to tell everybody outside to duck as the comet passes over.'

'That close?' Kotto said, fascinated instead of fearful. For now.

'Our readings are accurate out to seven significant digits. It'll be quite a show.'

Within five days, the cottony mass of the comet tumbled overhead, spewing vapours and jetting gases as volatile chemicals evaporated explosively from frozen pockets. Venting gases jostled the comet in a dozen different directions, making precise calculations impossible.

When the evaporating mountain scraped over the night side of Isperos, far from the surface mining operations, Kotto and his workers observed the glorious coma and tail. It was a spectacle unlike anything he had seen before. And only a Roamer would dare be in so risky a place as to witness an event like this. No Big Goose sissy would have dared. He grinned and took numerous archive images, planning to show them to his old mother on Rendezvous . . .

However, though the comet didn't hit Isperos, didn't even graze close enough to pepper the pocked surface with debris, its subtle gravity tickled the molten world and caused its surface to twitch and flinch.

Kotto felt the tremors, the slight movement of the tunnels. It was not a severe enough quake to damage the polymer-ceramic insulation in the tunnels, but the slightest crack would let intense heat seep through.

'Run a full analysis and safety check on all tunnel junctures. There's no telling what—' Then he froze, and his jaw dropped. 'The railgun! Shut it down!'

On the surface, the railgun launcher was nearly a kilometre long, precisely aligned and powered with high-energy capacitors, firing solid ingots of ultrapure heavy metals to distant pickup points. As fast as shipments could be loaded, buckets hurled canisters in quick succession out into space. At peak efficiency, the railgun could launch thirty projectiles a minute in an intricately choreographed blur.

Now, along its kilometre length, the seismic shudder had knocked the capacitor-studded beam off its alignment by no more than ten centimetres, the gentlest of bends. But it was enough.

Canister after canister of heavy alloys hurtled down the rail, accelerated magnetodynamically to escape velocity. When the ground shifted, the struts bent and the long launcher became unstable.

Kotto knew they could not possibly shut down the continuous sequence fast enough. He groaned as his mind raced through the consequences, already imagining the worst.

Gradually, gently, the rails bowed. Friction built up. A constant, rapid flow of heavy projectiles slid off the hoppers and on to the launch rail, one every two seconds as the problem worsened.

It took less than half a minute for utter disaster to occur.

One heavy ingot scraped the damaged track, ripping out the capacitors, tearing up the length of the rail. A second and third projectile slammed behind it, knocking the entire system catastrophically offline.

Kotto didn't even wait to see the end of the string of impacts. He ran through the tunnels, climbing up ladders until he reached the hot suit-up chamber. He had everything invested in the operations here. Panting, full of urgency, he climbed into a silver reflective suit, sealing his thermal gloves and helmet in place. Panicked thoughts hammered through his skull, and he hoped nobody was out on the surface, in the line of fire.

Before he climbed into the airlock, though, he took two steps back into the harshly lit room. Kotto knew better than to rush out unprepared. He double-checked all the seals and cooling systems, astonished to find one slightly loose connection that might well have turned him into a cinder if he'd skipped this important step before going out to the railgun site.

By the time Kotto got outside and climbed into a terrain buggy, it was much too late. Already, suited engineers were swarming out from the loading bunkers. Ore-processing machinery had ground to a standstill as the workers stared aghast at the ruins of the launcher.

Kotto brought the buggy to a halt and peered through his polarized face shield at what remained of the inoperative railgun. It was a miracle that none of his crew had been killed. That was the most important thing. Still, everything else was a mess.

Many systems on Isperos had been breaking down, and his engineers spent much of their work day patching breaches and repairing overloaded machinery, just to keep the facility operational.

Kotto's mind worked through this new disaster with a desperate intensity. It was just a problem, and problems could be solved. He had always believed that. Under optimal circumstances, he might have been able to repair the railgun, though it would require rebuilding at least half of the systems. How could he justify it? To do that, he would have to divert all of his maintenance and engineering crews to the job of reconstructing the long, perfect runway.

Would the Roamers tell him to just give up? Could he surrender this massive dream of his? He didn't want to contemplate that . . . not out of any bull-headed pride, but because he had always defined failure as 'giving up without considering all possible solutions'.

Kotto felt sick in his heart. This place was his challenge, and he would not surrender unless there was no other alternative. With so much falling apart, could he afford the manpower?

As Kotto surveyed the damage he could conceive of no economically viable way to get the facility running again, given the available resources and crew.

FIFTY-NINE

KING PETER

King Peter's selection of a bride should have been a joyous occasion, but Basil Wenceslas, with his smug confidence and autocratic style, ruined the entire event. 'You might as well be pleased with it,' he said giving Peter a sharp look, 'because there's nothing you can do to change the matter.'

The young King slumped into a comfortable seat in the Chairman's HQ penthouse offices. Peter wore the royal crown – yet Basil could snap his fingers, and royal guards would hustle him through underground passages to the pyramidal corporate headquarters.

'Why are you frowning, young man? The Hansa considers this a reward for your years of adequate service. You deserve a blushing young bride, a lovely body to warm your bed at night, to keep you company when you have no other royal duties.' Basil sounded frustrated.

Despite years of brainwashing attempts, Peter had stopped being tempted by the magnificent lifestyle with its comforts, fine foods, and diversions. 'Let's not pretend that you're rewarding *me*,

314

Basil. Everything you do is for the Hansa. Do you think you can manipulate me more easily with a queen? Is she a spy of yours, someone who can slip a knife in my back some night if you get annoyed with me?'

'Estarra of Theroc?' Basil laughed, then wagged his finger back and forth. 'Peter, the acquisition of your bride and the resultant advantages – both for yourself and for the Hansa – have nothing to do with keeping you in line. You are simply playing a role at my command. Don't forget who you are.'

Peter narrowed his artificially blue eyes. 'I won't forget.' *I am what you made me. You caused the transformation, Basil. Whether you like it or not, I am no longer Raymond Aguerra. I am King Peter.*

'So, who is this Estarra of Theroc?' Peter asked, pretending acquiescence.

'She is offered as a marriage alliance with the Therons. It may sound somewhat medieval, but such things have been happening in politics since the dawn of civilization. In fact, some might call it an honourable tradition. It has certainly averted plenty of wars.'

'In that case, maybe you should arrange for me to marry a hydrogue princess.'

'Don't tempt me, or I may do exactly that,' he said with a completely humourless smile. 'I just attended the ceremony in which Ambassador Sarein's brother Reynald was named the new Father of Theroc. Now his younger sister, Estarra, has reached marriageable age, and she is an excellent match for you. Trust me, she's perfect.'

Trust me? 'As I recall, King Frederick never had a royal marriage. Neither did Bartholomew, though one or two of the earlier Kings had a token queen.'

Basil leaned across his desk, looking stern. 'None of the others reigned during a war. We've had over five years of privation since the ekti embargo was imposed. This wedding will boost morale, and we can milk it for months. Sarein stayed on Theroc to attend to several important details, but she is returning soon – with Estarra. From what I can tell, she's quite' – he waved his hand with a small flourish – 'adorable and charming. The people will love her.'

'Just as they love me,' Peter said, ironically. 'You've made certain of that.' Knowing he was defeated and wanting to talk over the matter with OX, Peter heaved a heavy sigh. 'Let me see what she looks like.'

Basil handed him a flatscreen, on which an image dissolved through several different candid portraits; some solemn, some staring off into the distance. Estarra had a pert nose, pointed chin, and pale brown skin. Her hair had been pulled into an arrangement of slender stylized twists and adorned with colourful threads. Her eyes were enormous and captivating. Whether through some trick of photography or because of a sudden imaginary connection, Peter thought she was staring at him. Estarra was striking. She looked innocent, but not at all vapid or stupid. That was a relief, at least.

'She's beautiful, Basil, I'll give you that. I look forward to meeting her . . . and I'll make the best of the situation.'

The Chairman took the flatscreen image from Peter's hand, as if he didn't want the young King to look at it too closely. 'You should fall in love with her, young man. That would be best for everyone.'

Resentment bubbled within Peter's chest, but he kept his voice even. 'If that's what you command me to do, Basil.'

S I X T Y

E S T A R R A

Her family assumed she would be simply delighted with the news. Reynald told her about the proposal with a large grin splitting his face. 'I always thought I'd be the first to marry, Estarra. Now every young woman in the Spiral Arm will be envious of you.'

They stood together high up in one of the worldtrees, where the two of them could reach the dangling vines and pluck succulent lavender epiphytes; their grandmother distilled the petal juices into a slightly intoxicating liqueur. Estarra had suspected from his exuberant manner and his sly gaze that he had a secret to tell.

But not this.

'King Peter is nearly your age, handsome, healthy, intelligent – by all accounts a very pleasant person.' Reynald saw her stunned surprise, and his expression softened. 'It could be far, far worse, Estarra. Just let it sink in for a while.'

'It could be *worse*?' Her thoughts spun, and she didn't know what to think. 'I'm in trouble if that's the best you can say about him.'

Later, Sarein took her aside, jabbering about all the wonders

Estarra would see on Earth, the new responsibilities she would have. 'I don't know Peter very well, but Basil has never said anything bad about him. And he is the Great King of the Terran Hanseatic League, after all. You couldn't have hoped for a better match.'

Newly retired Idriss and Alexa were deliriously proud of their daughter, and immediately announced another vibrant celebration. Though they had maintained a policy of oblivious isolationism from the Hansa for so long, they didn't seem to fear any changes or consequences from having their daughter marry into the royal family on Earth. They were just thrilled about the wedding itself. They oversaw the decoration of the tree city for the engagement festival, festooning branches with brilliantly coloured flowers, ribbons, and tethered condorflies. Even old Uthair and Lia nodded sagely, in complete agreement with such a wise marriage . . .

More than ever, Estarra needed to be by herself. She sprinted deep into the forest as she had done when she was a girl. She wanted to explore the byways of the worldtrees, to think about what a commitment she had got into, by virtue of her birth.

In her carefree youth, the Theron forests had been a grand mystery, and she'd wanted to explore endlessly, to poke her nose into every lush corner. She had shared her discoveries with her brother Beneto, the only other member of her family who saw the wonder.

Now reaching a tall, inviting-looking worldtree, Estarra clambered up the overlapping bark scales, careful not to harm the treelings that protruded from cracks. After she took up residence in the Whisper Palace, she would be forced to wear fine gowns and jewels, to attend court functions and diplomatic events. Would she ever again be allowed just to run or climb or explore? She would probably miss that more than anything.

Estarra pushed foliage aside, climbing into the thick matted fronds. At the top of the verdant canopy, blue sky and sunlight splashed her face. She closed her eyes and drew a deep breath, feeling the cool breeze and open air. She could understand why green priests loved to spend their days up here.

'I expected you to come, Estarra. The trees told me to wait for you here.'

She was so startled she lost her grip and nearly tumbled down, but the branches seemed to reach out to support her. Estarra turned to see scarred Rossia sitting cross-legged on a matted platform of interlocked fronds. He looked warily up at the sky, then gazed at her with his round eyes, until he flicked his glance skywards again.

'I was trying to be alone, Rossia.'

The green priest chuckled. 'The trees have a billion eyes. How could you hide?'

Strangely, she found his observation comforting. She chose a pleasant place to sit next to him. 'Have you heard the news? I'm supposed to go to Earth and marry King Peter.'

The priest bobbed his bald head in a comical bow. 'I am honoured to be in the presence of a queen.'

'Glad to see you're delighted, Rossia – just like everyone else.'

'And you are not?' Rossia's eyes were so intent that he forgot to look up into the sky and watch for Wyverns.

'It wasn't my decision. In fact, nobody even consulted me, really. Wouldn't that bother you?'

'Yes, yes . . . but let us get past that. You're a daughter of the ruling family here, and you've known all your life that this was likely to happen. Do you have any genuine *reason* to be dissatisfied with King Peter as a potential mate, or are you just being contrary?'

'I expected a little more sympathy from you, Rossia.'

'You can look elsewhere for that.' He rubbed the waxy scar on his leg. 'You are not thinking, Estarra – only reacting. I understand how you might be uncertain, angry, and frightened by this sudden change. But I know you have not already offered your heart to some other young man, so why not give this King Peter a chance?'

Estarra scanned the open blue skies, helping him watch for flying predators, as usual. Right now, she thought she might actually prefer one of the carnivorous insects to Rossia's chiding lecture. 'But I don't love him!'

'Ah, love. That can be learned. You're a bright girl.' He scanned the sky just long enough for Estarra to remember a similar conversation with her grandparents, then he looked back at her. 'You are going to Earth, the heart of human civilization, the birthplace of our race. You will marry a handsome young King and live in the luxurious Whisper Palace. You may have the opportunity to affect more lives than any other woman your age. You can shine a light for all people across the Spiral Arm – *and* you will always have a green priest nearby whenever you need to talk.' He frowned. 'Why should you expect sympathy from anyone? Don't be a whiny child.'

Watching his oddball expression and letting his words penetrate, Estarra finally sighed, then actually chuckled. She smelled the fresh, spicy air filled with the aromas of the worldforest. 'All right, Rossia. Maybe I'll keep an open mind, and at least meet King Peter before I draw any conclusions.'

SIXTY-ONE

BENETO

On Corvus Landing, Beneto sat among the worldtrees in his precious grove, listening to a high-spirited murmur of information through telink. In the years since Talbun had planted these trees, the grove had spread across the hillsides and into the next valley. Now, rising above the forest's background news and thoughts and questions, he was delighted to hear a message from his sister Estarra, sent via Rossia.

Back on far-off Theroc, she waited while the scarred green priest touched his fingers to the armoured bark and repeated her words to the tree. Here on Corvus Landing, Beneto touched his own worldtree and heard everything she said.

'I'm going away to live on Earth, Beneto. I'm supposed to marry King Peter. Can you believe that?'

Because Estarra's words were spoken to Rossia and then repeated through the trees, Beneto could not read the subtleties of her emotions. 'Getting married, little sister? I remember a spunky teenaged girl who liked to run through the forest. How can you be old enough to be a queen?'

'You've been gone for five years, Beneto. I'm an adult now.'

'If you say so.' He drew a deep breath of the clean air of Corvus Landing. He missed the sweeping treetops of Theroc, but he also loved the quiet gentleness of this place. He didn't regret coming here, but he wished he'd been able to watch Estarra blossom from a girl into a woman.

'And how do you feel about it, Estarra? Not just about leaving Theroc, but becoming betrothed to a King, living in a palace on Earth?'

'At first I wanted to be angry, but Rossia talked me out of it. For now. I suppose I should meet the King first. Within the month I'll be going with Sarein back to Earth.'

Beneto smiled. 'I'll bet Sarein's jealous of all the attention you're getting.' He flexed his fingers against the trunk of the sturdy tree. 'When you get to Earth, you can talk to me through Nahton in the Whisper Palace. The forest will always find me.'

He could sense the warmth from her. 'I feel much better knowing that, Beneto.'

He listened through telink. Around him, the trees whispered. A thousand channels of gossip swept past him, but he chose not to access any of it. The worldforest contained far too much information for any one person to access.

Finally, they said their farewells. Rossia and Beneto separated their telink bond, though the worldforest fronds continued to whisper on many worlds, telling far more secrets than any green priest realized.

Beneto walked through the outer fields with Sam Hendy. The potbellied mayor wore a stained but comfortable jumpsuit. His pockets contained tools for anything he needed to fix in the outlying acreage.

Beneto wore only shorts. His bare feet and legs rustled through the grain stalks. He sensed no special connection to the genetically enhanced grains that bent in the gusty Corvan breezes, but he loved just to feel the life growing up from the soil.

'We are far from the heart of this war, Mayor, but I follow the hydrogue conflict with great interest.' He had already told the colonists about the hydrogue incursions at Boone's Crossing, as well as the attacks on Hyrillka and other seemingly random planets. 'The struggle may have repercussions that affect even out-of-the-way places such as Corvus Landing.'

'At least the EDF hasn't tried to recruit our young workers as soldiers.' The mayor plucked a plump stalk and chewed on it. 'Of course, if the military came here for conscripts, maybe they'd bring the supplies and equipment we need.'

Leaving a track through the thick grain, the mayor strode across the field to a malfunctioning weather transmitter on the fenceline. He tweaked the controls, setting up a detector so the station could better analyse wind flow. 'A long time ago, humans were willing to climb aboard generation ships and fly through space for centuries without a map. We expected to colonize the Spiral Arm that way, establishing footholds and pretty much living by ourselves. Maybe we've forgotten how to do that – not a good thing, in my opinion. Back to basics.'

He closed the weather station's power box and plucked another stalk of grain as he looked back towards Colony Town. The settlement was surrounded by a chessboard of crops, pastures, and orchards, as well as the healthy grove of worldtrees.

Beneto said, 'Even if it's whole grain and goat meat for the foreseeable future, Mayor, we will survive.'

That evening Beneto slept outside under the whispering worldtrees. He was troubled, his wandering thoughts in turmoil, in part because of Estarra's surprising news, but also because of what he continued to learn about the hydrogue conflict. There seemed to be no chance for a resolution. The enemy was too alien. No one could understand them.

He lay staring up at the fronds that moved independently of the breezes. Old Talbun, who had planted these trees, had forsaken his lucrative career as a communications specialist for the Hansa and chosen to spend the rest of his life on Corvus Landing.

Beneto wished Talbun could be here so they could discuss the crisis. He needed advice from someone, somewhere.

He stretched out a hand to touch the nearest trunk. Beneto closed his eyes and, instead of dreaming, let his mind fall through telink where he could tap into the collected knowledge of the worldforest.

The sentient trees had lived for untold millennia. They had pondered on their own for most of that time until, in the last two centuries, they had vastly increased their understanding with the help of green priests. The available knowledge within the worldforest was beyond the use or comprehension of any human being, even one engulfed in telink. In such an unmapped ocean of information, it would be impossible to track exactly how much the trees knew.

The worldforest had been tangibly uneasy since the appearance of the hydrogues, but they had offered no explanations or advice. Green priests had asked for suggestions on how the human race might resist the deep-core aliens, but the trees had been unable to help.

Considering the exotic environment in which the enemy dwelled, Beneto had not thought to ask more straightforward questions. How could the planetbound worldforest possibly know anything about the cores of gas giants?

Nevertheless, he asked directly, *What are the hydrogues? Have the worldtrees ever encountered them before?*

The immensity of the forest considered his question and, to Beneto's surprise, gave him a clear and astonishing answer:

The hydrogues are our ancient enemy.

SIXTY-TWO

SAREIN

Fifty green priests gathered in the clearing within the thick grove of worldtrees. Though they could have connected into the forest network for any information they desired, instead they sat listening and attentive.

This was Sarein's best chance to accomplish something.

She had put away her stylish Earth clothes for the day and instead had chosen traditional fabrics, wrapping herself in the ceremonial cape that Otema had given her before the old woman had departed on her fateful mission to Ildira. Sarein drew a deep breath and stood beside her brother Reynald, prepared to make her best case. Perhaps today she would finally make progress for her backward world.

With the eye of an ambassador, and a sister, she thought Father Reynald looked impressive and powerful. His cocoon-fibre vest was spangled with jewel-toned beetle carapaces and condorfly wings. His face was handsome, his chin strong, his presence commanding. *Excellent.*

Reynald folded his hands and spoke without excessive

formality or flowery words. 'The worldforest has its own thoughts, its own needs, and its own agenda. As Father of the Theron people, I do speak for the green priests, but I cannot command you. Even so, I can say what I believe is right and offer you advice.'

Sarein found it endearing that he really did consider himself a friend and father-figure to the people, rather than a sophisticated but distant ruler like Basil or even the highly trained King Peter. But then, that might change. Reynald was still new to his position.

He smiled at Sarein. 'My sister has a request for you. She understands Theroc, but as ambassador to the Terran Hanseatic League, she also has a wider view of the Spiral Arm. Please listen to what she has to say, then make up your own minds.'

The green priests turned to her with interested but otherwise unreadable eyes. She said, 'Ever since telink was discovered in the first generation of settlers on Theroc, we have understood that green priests could be a vital asset to human civilization.' She specifically mentioned the history to remind them of her own ties to Theroc. 'For many years now, the Hansa has had a standing request for volunteer green priests to facilitate instantaneous communication among various colonies and business interests.'

'And we have provided many priests over the years, Sarein,' said Yarrod, the brother of Mother Alexa. He himself had never set foot off the forested world. 'But each time we offer one priest, the Hansa pushes for five more.'

'I am not here to debate that, Uncle Yarrod.' She spoke with intentional familiarity. 'Without question, the Hansa commercial empire could make higher profits if they had more green priests stationed around the Spiral Arm, but they have never tried to force your hand. They've respected our decisions.'

'Not happily,' Yarrod said. He glanced over at Rossia, who sat close to a big worldtree trunk, seemingly oblivious to the conversation.

Sarein looked at Reynald as if sharing a joke. 'You can't expect them to be *happy* about it – if you had cooperated with them, they would have made a lot more money.' Then she became serious again and faced the green priests. 'But now their request is no longer merely about profits, is it? The hydrogues have attacked Ildiran and human colony worlds. The Earth Defence Forces have stepped up their efforts to protect us all, but the scattered battle groups cannot communicate effectively with each other. The EDF military commanders receive field reports that are sadly delayed and out of date. *You* can change all that.'

She flashed them a stern expression, one she had learned from Basil. 'Should the hydrogues come here, Theroc is just as vulnerable as any other colony. You know the EDF would still come to defend the worldforest, even though you've refused to help them.'

The green priests muttered among themselves, uneasy now.

'Listen to me. Telink communication would let the EDF keep watch on scattered settlements. Battleships could maintain surveillance on hydrogue movements. With more timely distress calls, rescue operations could arrive days or weeks sooner, maybe in time to save lives.' She looked at them all. 'Wake up and become part of the human race again. We are all in the war against the hydrogues. All of us.'

Yarrod looked around at his fellows, but they remained quiet, content to let him be their spokesman. 'We know you are trying your best to do your duty, Sarein – as are we.' His proud expression made him look impenetrable. 'However, only green priests can understand the esoteric desires of the worldforest. We are not free to do whatever we wish.'

Sarein challenged him, 'And have you *asked* the worldtrees what you should do, Uncle? Has any of you bothered to inquire?'

The eccentric priest Rossia sat by himself in a cluster of ferns at the wide base of a worldtree. 'Of course the trees want us to assist in the fight against the hydrogues. The survival of the worldforest and the green priesthood is at stake.' His smile widened, exposing dark green gums. 'Sarein's brother Beneto recently asked an important question on Corvus Landing. Were any of you paying attention? Perhaps you should all use telink to hear the answer for yourselves.' He shifted, trying to get comfortable with his scarred leg. 'It may give you a different perspective.'

Trusting her instincts, Sarein prodded them. 'Yes, go ahead! The trees are all around you – ask them. I will abide by their answer.'

Yarrod and the reluctant green priests spread out among the interlinked trees. They touched fingers against the scaled bark and closed their eyes.

Although Sarein had learned the value of patience and calm, her mind burned with anxiety. Reynald looked at her strangely. None of them had expected this to happen, but apparently the worldforest had knowledge of its own.

Finally, Yarrod disengaged his telink and turned to face her. Tears streamed from his eyes and down the creases of his tattooed face. Green priests chattered with each other in astonishment and shock, looking as if they had been chastised.

'Rossia is correct,' Yarrod said. 'There is much new information, which the trees tried to keep from us, in order to protect us. This conflict is much greater, and much older, than simple retaliation for the Klikiss Torch at Oncier. The hydrogues want to destroy the human race, the worldforest . . . everything.'

Around Sarein, the green priests looked appalled, stunned, frightened. Yarrod lifted his head and spoke directly to her. 'Yes, we will join the war effort.'

SIXTY-THREE

NIRA

Nira and her fellow human labourers marched from the fenced breeder compound into the rough-edged hills. Sunlight bathed her emerald skin, nourishing her, keeping her alive.

In the work crew, she talked with the people beside her, describing for them how she had once run through the majestic trees of Theroc, how she had felt the soothing presence of the titanic forest, the dozing intelligence of an ancient entity. None of the *Burton* descendants had ever seen a tree taller than the gnarled scrub on the hills; most of them couldn't even imagine such things, and many assumed the strange green priest was just making up stories again.

When she'd entered into a symbiosis with the forest, Nira had become part of a living network. She could communicate with all other green priests and tap into the incomprehensibly vast and complex database the worldforest had collected over the millennia.

But here on Dobro she was cut off from the worldforest.

To the east, the foothills were covered with tall, brown grass. Dark, thorny trees filled sheltered hollows, and Nira looked longingly at the foliage, seeing it as a stunted cousin of the worldforest. But it was not the same.

Now, Ildiran guards and labourers, each wearing their respective kith uniforms, drove carts to accompany the human crew out to the excavation sites. These kiths had been bred to do work, and it did not occur to them that the breeder captives might not wish to spend their days being productive to help the Dobro Designate.

Wistfully, Nira said quietly to no one in particular, 'Some of the most acrobatic young people on Theroc are trained as treedancers. They leap from the branches and pirouette in the air, bouncing from one bough to another.' She smiled as she remembered the performances, the breathtaking vaults and fingertip pivots. 'The trees help them with their agility, no one ever falls.'

Beside her, a middle-aged woman continued chopping at the dirt and prying embedded rocks loose, unimpressed. Nira sighed, but continued talking. Around her, though the captives seemed to pay no attention, she knew they were listening. What else did they have to occupy their minds?

The supervisors directed the human workers into deep arroyos where weather had exposed ancient strata and valuable pearly fossils. Nira used a hand tool to chip away the powdery sandstone. This arroyo was an ancient graveyard of twisted shellfish, beautiful molluscs, and calcified anemone-like things. Fossilized opal bones and iridescent skeletons were polished and cut into highly prized ornaments, the primary product of Dobro . . . other than misbred genetic horrors.

Nira chipped at the rock and finally removed a perfect corkscrew shell that retained the feathery tentacles of the creature that had once lived within. With sore fingers, she used an abrasive brush to clean the fossil. It was beautiful, sparkling in the sunlight. This mysterious creature had been trapped until the forces of nature preserved it, turned the thing to stone.

But Nira had freed it now, after millions of years. She placed the prize in the nearest bin and wondered if she and the other human breeders would ever be broken free, like this treasure.

When Nira's work crew returned to camp, they were rinsed off under a needle-sharp high-pressure spray of cold water. Nira stepped away, dripping and naked – unable to avoid the probing eyes of the medical kithmen who tested each fertile woman every three days.

The luxury of modesty had been forgotten over the course of generations in captivity. The breeder humans displayed a variety of features, dark or milky or freckled skins, but the green priest from Theroc always attracted their attention. Nira felt no shame for her body, only resignation about what the captors would do to her next.

On strict orders from the Dobro Designate, Nira was to remain pregnant as often as possible for the continued experiments. None of the other human captives had proved so 'interesting'. Now medical kithmen took her by the arm, and Nira's heart pounded in her chest. She staggered after them into the camp's medical facilities.

The first several times, years ago, Nira had struggled and kicked and fought, resisting what they intended to do to her. She had thrown herself at the doctors, trying to strangle them or use her nails to claw out their eyes. But it had served no purpose. The guards easily wrestled her away, and the medical kithmen strapped her down and performed their tests anyway; as punishment, they had locked her in the darkness for a week. Later, when she had comforted herself by tending plants and shrubs around the camp barracks, they found they could hurt her by uprooting her prizes and leaving them trampled in the dirt.

She had decided to find other ways to fight back.

Now, inside the harshly lit medical facility, the Ildiran doctors drew her blood, took scrapings of her tissues, probed inside to verify the condition of her uterus. They spoke to each other but never to Nira, other than to issue gruff instructions. By now, she knew what to do, regardless of how much she hated it.

She closed her eyes as the medical kithmen prodded with their intrusive implements. Tears stung behind her eyelids, and her jaws ached from clenching her teeth so hard. She knew it had been long enough since her last delivery, a strong and silent baby bred from a burly, bestial-looking soldier kithman.

The only hopes she allowed herself were terrible ones: Perhaps the last birth had caused complications, or maybe she had developed ovarian cysts or some sort of Fallopian blockage that would prevent her from having more babies. Then she would be valuable only as a labourer – an unpleasant enough fate, but preferable to what she had already survived.

But the doctor spoke the hateful words: 'She is fertile.' Nira winced, letting out a quiet moan, which she consciously bit back. 'Check the records and find which kith pairing interests the Designate next.'

Nira dragged her feet as the guards marched her off to the breeding barracks. She would get hurt if she fought them, but they would not damage her . . . at least not her reproductive system. They could, however, cut her in other places, scar her, make her feel searing pain. They would win if she fought them on terms they could understand.

Right now, the best Nira could pray for would be to get pregnant right away. Years ago, with the reluctant military commander Adar Kori'nh, she had needed to submit to only one round of intercourse – and at least he'd had the grace to seem ashamed.

The others had been . . . worse.

Now, the medical kithmen locked her in a bright room with only some food and personal hygiene apparatus. And a bed. It was a clinical place, a room where chosen Ildirans came to do an assigned task, just like chipping fossil opal from sedimentary canyon walls. She remained alert for any faint sound in the corridors, the approaching footsteps of her next tormentor.

To defend herself from the living nightmares, she thought of the cushion-filled chambers in the Prism Palace where she had made love to Jora'h. Those times had been warm and romantic, and she had clung to him, feeling his skin against hers, touching his muscles, looking into his star-sapphire eyes.

This was the same physical act . . . in a sense.

Nira sat with her back against the wall and stared at the door. Every unpleasant second dragged on. Outside, in the camp, the other humans went about their daily chores; many of them were assigned to breeding duties as well, and they would all return to the communal sleeping barracks when they were done. All alone, she tried to remain strong, thinking of Jora'h, thinking of her daughter Osira'h. *My Princess.*

When the door finally opened and the guards escorted in her new assigned mate, dismay struck her like a hammer blow. This time, her chosen breeder was a member of the scaly kith, a reptile-skinned desert Ildiran with lean and angular features, pinched expression, slitted eyes. This male looked even less human than most Ildirans did.

'Call if you need assistance,' said one of the guards as they sealed the door. They were speaking to the scaly male, not to her.

The reptilian man began to remove his tan garment. Nira could not hide from him. He looked at her with a ripple of distaste as he saw her naked body. He cast his garment aside and gestured brusquely towards the bed.

Nira knew it was useless to scream. Instead, she thought with all her heart of Jora'h, trying to keep his image in front of her mind. But it was very, very difficult.

SIXTY-FOUR

OSIRA'H

Osira'h sat on the floor in a small room, by herself. The walls and ceiling were well-lit by embedded blazers, perfectly white. She couldn't hear anything or see outside. She grinned at the challenge.

Every day for as long as she could remember, Osira'h had undergone this training. Other halfbreed children were raised and trained elsewhere in the city, grouped together by their skills, periodically tested and inspected. But she was special. Her instructors were all medical kithmen, scientists, theoreticians, and the Dobro Designate himself. She knew what they wanted, and she was pleased to rise to the occasion.

Together, the experts had developed the curriculum for her by trial and error, and her own successes had guided the teachings as much as Ildiran expectations. Osira'h was attempting to learn things that had never been successfully taught before. Even the lens kithmen didn't know. She had mental skills, empathic abilities, and unlocked secrets that needed to be nurtured and strengthened.

No one knew precisely how to instruct the remarkable girl to use her inbred powers – a fusion of green priest's telink and Ildiran *thism*. No matter how hard they tried, Osira'h tried even harder. She would find the key to unlock her destiny.

Now in the isolation room, she sat staring at the closed barrier, blinking her eyes. Osira'h opened her mind and let the impressions come. It was easy to detect when a test subject stood close to the door, waiting and letting the girl sense him or her from a distance.

'The first one is there,' Osira'h said aloud, knowing they were observing her. 'He is strong . . . dedicated.' She drew a deep breath, letting the impressions flood into her, building the picture in her mind. 'He acts on orders, but does not question. He knows his place and he has no aspirations to better himself . . . because he's convinced he's already the best at what he does.' She smiled. She had figured out the answer almost immediately. 'He is a guard.'

The door slid open to reveal the burly soldier kithman who had been instructed to stand in place. The door closed again, and she knew the guard had been ordered to withdraw.

Osira'h looked up at the ceiling. 'That wasn't even a challenge. Soldier kithmen are so obvious, so clear cut.'

No one responded, but she knew they were listening. Always listening. And she always tried to impress them.

Osira'h focused her attention on the door again and sensed another presence appearing, then backing away, then another, as if it were wavering . . . or more than one. The thoughts were scattered, frenetic.

She sensed a deep longing, a frantic need to help, to please whoever was in charge, to pamper and dote upon a master. 'Of course.' She giggled. Attender kith were never alone but always functioned in groups, like hive workers, scurrying about to follow instructions. The very act of doing necessary deeds and getting figurative pats on their heads drove them to ecstasies of pleasure.

'Let me see. Attender kithmen, obviously, but how many? They are so indistinguishable. They all think the same shallow thoughts, but I can hear . . . three, *four* distinct echoes. It's four attender kithmen.'

The door opened again and she saw a quartet of the small-statured gnomish Ildirans. They looked at her, blinking their eyes as if they longed to run forward and assist her in some way. But before they could enter the test chamber, the door slid shut again.

Osira'h leaned back. She wondered if the testers knew how simple this was for her now. Her goal was to sense the different needs of a person, to understand what drove a life force and grasp the best way to communicate and foster genuine understanding.

The hydrogues – incomprehensibly alien – would be far, far more difficult than any Ildiran kithmen, and would resist cooperating.

Sometimes the Dobro Designate tried to trick her by adding human breeder captives to the test routine, but they were simple to understand as well. Because they were not trained and rarely educated, human minds remained hungry, full of questions but no answers. The breeder captives did not fall into clear categories like Ildiran kiths. They were all individuals.

Now Osira'h felt a new test subject approaching the doorway. She quickly turned, eager to give another answer.

But this time she sensed a plethora of conflicting emotions and driving thoughts, as if this mind were powerful enough to confuse her, to deflect her obvious questions. 'Ah, a challenge at last,' she said.

'There is strength and determination, and also . . . many secrets. This one is good at keeping his thoughts to himself, a master, but his motivations are without question. He knows truth. He knows what must be done, even if others disagree with him. He knows in his heart that he is right.'

She smiled, feeling the strength and unswerving duty. He was

as sure of himself as the rigid soldier kithmen. He knew in his heart
that he was going to save the Ildiran Empire.

Osira'h laughed, delighted with the new twist. 'Designate, you
are learning how to fool me.'

The door slid open again and Udru'h stood with his arms
crossed over his chest, looking at her with deep pride. 'You grow
better every day, Osira'h. I was sure I could mask my thoughts from
you.'

'I know you too well. You could never hide anything from me.'
Osira'h came forward to stand close to him.

He put his arm around her small shoulder. 'That is exactly how
it should be. I only hope the hydrogues are so transparent to your
skills.'

SIXTY-FIVE

PRIME DESIGNATE JORA'H

J ora'h stood alone with his thoughts in a room filled with skulls. He had sent away his guards and attendants so that he could be by himself in the hollow chamber. The gleaming, milky walls themselves looked like translucent bone.

The ossuarium of the Prism Palace was a place of contemplation, reflection, and reverence for the sons of the Mage-Imperator. Here, in an array of ornate alcoves like the smooth cavities of a hive insect's dwelling, rested the skulls of previous Mage-Imperators, great leaders of the Ildiran Empire that had ruled in millennia past.

Jora'h's hands hung down at his sides, his long robes heavy upon his shoulders — but not as heavy as the questions and responsibilities in his mind. He looked at the rows of empty eye sockets, the small even teeth, the smooth ivory brows. Had each one of these men also come here to ask the same questions, when they too were only Prime Designates? Had all of them, even his father Cyroc'h, stood inside the ossuarium wondering, insisting that they were not ready?

Before long, the skull of Jora'h's father would also take its place among these silent and respected ancestors.

All Ildirans believed in a shining realm that contained the Lightsource, a plane composed entirely of illumination. Trickles of that holy light broke through into the real universe, and the Mage-Imperator was the focal point for the soul-threads, the *thism*. All Ildirans could feel it, some kiths stronger than others. They had no religious doubts, and therefore no competing sects of priests and varying interpretations – as he knew the human race did. The lens kithmen could focus the threads of light and give guidance to lesser Ildirans.

Prime Designate Jora'h, though, had to make up his own mind.

All Ildiran kiths kept the skulls of their dead. Because of a strange phosphorus impregnation in the bone structure, the skulls actually glowed for a time, but gradually faded. The Mage-Imperators, though, because they were closest to the Lightsource, continued to shine for more than a thousand years.

Now the skulls of the dead Mage-Imperators glowed with an inner light as if their thoughts were still active, channelling *thism*, and Jora'h waited for a revelation. But today they were silent.

He had been studying every day, working closely with his father and other advisers to prepare him for his role as the next great leader. He knew that many things were still hidden from him, many mysteries that only a Mage-Imperator could understand. When he ascended and became the focal point for *thism*, all would be revealed to him. He had much to consider before that day.

It seemed the more he worked and the harder he struggled to improve himself, the less prepared he was. But Jora'h knew the people would follow him. They would not question his decisions, for they had complete faith in the *thism* and in the benevolence of their leader. Jora'h wished that he could have the same level of confidence.

After pondering the glowing skulls in silence, he finally promised all of his predecessors that he would do his best. He would strive to become a Mage-Imperator worthy of one day resting beside them in the Prism Palace's ossuarium.

Then Jora'h departed, more concerned with what he would do with his life, than how he would be remembered after his death.

When he returned to his private quarters, Jora'h was startled to see the shimmering silhouette of a stranger waiting for him behind the coloured translucent walls.

He didn't think he had forgotten a scheduled appointment with one of his mandatory lovers. In recent days, he had been so deeply involved in intensive briefings with his ailing father, as well as his contemplation in the ossuarium, that he had been forced to postpone many of his scheduled mates. Soon, when he ascended to become the new Mage-Imperator, he would never take a lover again. But as the dreaded time grew nearer, Jora'h realized that his enjoyment of such physical pleasures had diminished. Greater things weighed on his mind.

Inside his chambers he was surprised to find his son Thor'h.

The younger man stood abruptly, meeting him with a stony determination. 'I had to invoke my blood right to convince the bodyguards and bureaucrats to let me come here. I needed to see you in private.'

Jora'h sealed the door behind him. 'I am always glad to speak with you, Thor'h.'

The Prime Designate took a moment to assess his son. Most obviously, the young man had cleaned himself up, taking meticulous care with his appearance again. His face was powdered. He'd applied careful paints and highlights, and a strange, alluring perfume wafted around his clean skin.

Again, though, his eyes showed the too-sharp focus of shiing;

the drug rendered Thor'h's place in the web of *thism* blurry and insubstantial. Unsettling. After the horrific hydrogue attack, Jora'h realized that shiing was probably in short supply throughout the Ildiran Empire. Just like everything else.

Thor'h had dressed himself in an opulent Designate's uniform, as befitted his role as eventual heir. The young man held himself with pride and confidence — already quite a change from recent hedonistic days when he had refused to take his responsibilities seriously. Much has changed for this boy who had thought everything would be handed to him on a jewelled platter.

In previous days, when Jora'h had checked on his son, it was always to find him grey-faced and dishevelled at the unconscious Designate's bedside. Now, though, Jora'h was impressed. Thor'h looked as if he had been through a trial by fire and had matured greatly. Apparently, the young man had reached some sort of decision.

'You have made it clear, Father, that you want me to study here at the Prism Palace. But so much has changed since you told me I had to come back to Ildira. The Hyrillka Designate is still in a deep sub-*thism* sleep and shows no sign that he will ever awaken.' Thor'h's voice cracked, but he caught himself.

Jora'h could see how much the young man loved his Uncle Rusa'h. 'The medical kithmen are doing everything possible—'

Thor'h interrupted him. 'I know that.' He took a step forward. 'Father, the hydrogues laid waste to the crops and the cities and the spaceport on Hyrillka. The people there — many of them my friends — are grievously injured. Adding to their distress, the Designate — their closest link to the Mage-Imperator — is no longer with them, nor is he likely to be. And his replacement is not ready.' He squared his shoulders. 'I want to go back to Hyrillka and oversee the salvage and recovery operations. Someone has to be in control. Our people there need guidance.'

The request startled Jora'h, but he gave it serious thought. 'What about your brother Pery'h? He is the Hyrillka Designate-in-Waiting. Should he not be the one to take on such a responsibility?'

Thor'h scowled, but quickly covered his expression. 'He is not ready for that responsibility, Father. He is still young and . . . and more interested in his studies. No one knows the needs of Hyrillka as much as I do.'

Jora'h found himself nodding. 'Pery'h could do a service as well by helping to develop a large-scale plan for the reclamation of the planet. He can work beside the architects and engineers.'

'I would not want him to get in the way, if he comes to Hyrillka. It is severely damaged, and the people need a strong anchor. I can be that.'

Perhaps it would be a good thing, Jora'h thought. Certainly, such a task would teach the young man more about leadership than any instruction he might receive here in the Prism Palace.

'That is a splendid idea, Thor'h.' He surprised his son into a brief relieved smile. 'My first instinct is to protect you and keep you here on Ildira, but I myself lived too sheltered a life. It did not adequately prepare me to take up the mantle of Mage-Imperator. You are going to become Prime Designate at a younger age than I did, yet your request shows that you are already learning. Yes, I agree – Hyrillka needs you.'

'Thank you, Father.' Thor'h seemed to be caught between grief at his uncle's grim prognosis and delight to be going back to the planet he had called home for so many years.

Jora'h opened the door and shouted for bureaucrats, work supervisors, and representatives of the Solar Navy. 'You and I need to plan this together, Thor'h. The rebuilding operations on Hyrillka must be a complete success, a grand foundation for your own eventual rule.'

Now Thor'h looked overwhelmed at what he had got himself

into, but in the face of Jora'h's enthusiasm, his son could not back down. The Prime Designate brought a dozen kith representatives into his chamber, and they spent hours choosing the crews of Ildiran workers and engineers that would accompany Thor'h back to the Horizon Cluster.

SIXTY-SIX

DEL KELLUM

At home in the rings of Osquivel, Del Kellum smiled as he dropped flakes of dried food into the tank of graceful angelfish. Raven-haired Zhett bounded in without signalling her presence, startling him so that he spilled all of the crumbly bits into the open tank at once, much to the delight of the striped fish.

He brushed off his palm. 'What is it, my sweet?' For the past two days, she'd been away delivering supplies and inspecting space-docks and shipyard smelters. He carefully reseated the lid on the fish tank.

Then he noticed the urgent look in her dark eyes. 'Dad, Nikko Chan Tylar just brought this warning from Speaker Peroni.' Zhett handed him the message as if it were an explosive. 'The Eddies are on their way here.'

Kellum looked at the information with awe, then dismay, then fierce determination. 'We'll have to dismantle everything. Hide some of it, leave some of it, destroy the rest. Freedom comes first. Profits and convenience are secondary.'

*

They sounded the alarms and called an all-hands meeting. The best guess, according to the information forwarded by Tasia Tamblyn, was that they would have no more than three weeks.

Inside the windowed administrative facility, Kellum stood dressed in a many-pocketed jumpsuit embroidered with the usual clan designs. He and Zhett had discussed priorities and co-ordinated work teams. They had done the calculations and knew how hard they would have to work – and how soon everyone would need to be evacuated, one shipload at a time.

Zhett said, 'Even if we can't cover all signs of our mining, we can downplay it enough that if they find anything, the Eddies will think this is a small-time operation. Maybe the drogues'll keep them so preoccupied they won't bother with a bit of litter in the rings.'

'Now there's something to hope for,' Kellum said, frowning. He looked at the graceful fish in his tank swimming about without a care in the universe.

Annoyed with her long hair drifting in the low gravity, Zhett used a band to tie it behind her head before she peered down at the spreadsheets again. Kellum didn't know what he would ever do without his daughter. Whenever he saw Zhett's face, the dusky beauty reminded him of her long-lost mother . . . or even feisty Shareen Pasternak, who should have been his second wife.

He finally made a hard decision. 'We'll shut down and evacuate all the cometary distillation work, but leave the components where they are, high outside the system. The smelters and collection chambers are as large as asteroids themselves, but it's dark up there and diffuse. Coming in from above, the Eddies'll see the planet and the rings, but they're not gonna go chasing random chunks of metal way out on the fringes. Let's pray to the Guiding Star that the Eddies don't notice anything.'

'Besides,' Zhett pointed out, 'pulling all workers from the comet reclamation fields increases the ring workforce down here by a thousand.'

Unfortunately, the shipyard facilities didn't have the food supplies or life-support to hold so many people for long.

Kellum stared with a heavy heart at one large cargo ship that was nearly completed. Its hull and structural ribs were in place, but the high-efficiency stardrive engines were not yet assembled. Even with the most optimistic work estimates, labour crews could not possibly complete the project in time. And no 'small-time mining operation' could have created such a sophisticated vessel.

So, Kellum dispatched cutters to the hull and sent demolition crews aboard to rip the ship into its basic components. It had not yet been christened, and now the ship must be stillborn, despite the huge investment.

Sighing, he shook his head and looked at Zhett. 'I can't complain that the Eddies are finally going to send a real message to the alien bastards. I just wish they'd make their point somewhere else, so I could keep working.' He hoped the major pieces of the big expensive vessel could be salvaged later, if the Osquivel shipyards were ever reactivated.

'Well, Dad, if they knew about our operations here, they'd be likely to hit us too.'

With a mock-scolding tone, he said, 'Don't you have *work* to do? Dismantlers to harass or young mining engineers to flirt with?'

She chuckled, an unusual sound in the past several days. 'Whatever you want me to do, Dad.'

Later, looking at the largest spacedock structures and administrative stations, Zhett conceived the faster alternative of simply *disguising* them by spraying non-reflective rock foam on to the smooth plates. The geometric shapes and configurations were still obviously artificial, but unless the Eddie ships looked closely, the reflective signatures would simply appear to be distorted rocks in the rings.

'Good enough, my sweet.' Kellum hugged his daughter. 'Afterwards, we can strip off the layers and use everything again.'

Around the rings, Roamers took grappler pods to the scattered sites, finishing one task and then volunteering for other parts of the frantic operation. All personnel scrambled with only the briefest rest and meal breaks. Two men died when a cluster of spacedock girders broke loose of their tether and drifted into a launch path. All operations shut down for an hour, but there was no time for a full investigation. Del Kellum sent everyone back to work with an admonishment to be more careful.

Squandering vital ekti, a hodgepodge assembly of Roamer ships rushed into the system from other clans, offering additional work crews and supplies. All families united for the huge effort, pulling up stakes and helping Kellum to hide. As time grew shorter, they would shuttle away all of the non-essential personnel, while Del Kellum and his primary crew would hide themselves in secure bolt-holes within the rings, and wait out the episode like rabbits in a thicket.

Accidents happened, equipment was damaged, and the exhausted crews made sloppy mistakes. The small worksite infirmaries filled with grumbling and impatient labourers, anxious to be patched up and get back on the job. Even with the ruinous safety record, Kellum had no choice. They could not slow down.

As day after day went by, with a sinking cold feeling in his heart, he watched his life's work disappear by degrees. But he couldn't mourn the disaster now. They all had very little time.

The EDF battlegroup was on its way.

SIXTY-SEVEN

KING PETER

Because he attended the ceremony as King, the formal launch of the new Soldier compies received more attention than it deserved, as far as Peter was concerned.

The presentation field had been manicured so perfectly that it looked as if humans or compies had trimmed, inspected, and combed each blade of grass, arranging every petal on every flower. Freshly painted receiving stands had been erected along one side of the field. Colourful awnings stretched across the stands, while pennants bearing the symbol of the Hanseatic League fluttered in the breeze. For the first time, Peter realized how much the emblem – Earth surrounded by concentric circles – reminded him of the home planet sitting in the middle of a target bull's-eye.

Blocky warehouses and manufacturing hangars formed a boundary around the park-like demonstration zone. Closer to the royal viewing stand, two Manta cruisers sat under the bright blue sky, the largest ships the landing field could accommodate.

'Why haven't they sounded the fanfare yet?' Peter said.

'Don't be impatient.' Basil Wenceslas sat smiling beside him in the shade. 'Important ceremonies need to proceed at a sedate and respectable pace.'

'On the other hand, if the audience gets too bored, your wonderful show loses all its impact.'

The Chairman frowned at him, then spoke into a small communicator, directing his expediter, Mr Pellidor, to start the event.

As the music blared, the audience waved their sparklers. Admiral Stromo, acting as marshal for the ceremony and leader of the uniformed EDF drill troops, led a full regiment out of the first Manta and on to the presentation field.

It was like a parade or a folkdance. Peter recognized their precision and knew how many hours the human regiment must have drilled for this flawless performance. The sergeants-at-arms and flagbearers moved forward like wind-up robots. During his years as King, he recognized the importance of showmanship. Displays such as this were designed to impress crowds and foster the impression that any military capable of marching in perfect ranks and executing flawless turns would surely be invincible during a hydrogue attack.

Peter fixed a mask of approval on his face, because he knew the media scans would be watching his every flicker of reaction.

Stromo called his troops to a halt, and they stopped in a moment of thunderous silence. All the uniformed men and women stood at rigid attention like costumed dolls. Basil nudged him, and King Peter began to applaud. The crowds rippled with loud cheers.

'An impressive display,' Basil said, 'but the new Soldier compies will take this to a completely higher level.'

'If they perform as expected,' Peter replied. 'We haven't seen them operate on active duty yet.'

'Don't put a black cloud on this. We need something to show off, after receiving so many bruises from the enemy.'

Peter shrugged. 'You've told me over and over that it doesn't matter what I do, as long as I follow the agenda.'

Then, on the far end of the vast field, huge hangar doors opened. The crowd drew a comically simultaneous breath as new military-model robots marched out of the warehouse hangar. They moved in utterly perfect lockstep, like segmented creatures gliding on absolutely precise paths.

The compy manufacturing lines had been working overtime to produce the decisive Soldier models, using innovative Klikiss technologies that the cybernetic engineers had learned from the dissection of Jorax. Now, seven of the beetle-like robots stood near the factory facility, observing the display. Peter wondered with a twinge of misgiving who had authorized them to be there.

The Soldier compies, larger than traditional Listener or Friendly models, would never be mistaken for cuddly companions. They marched with unrelenting strides, flowing in perfect columns out of the warehouse, before they engaged in a flurry of kaleidoscopic manoeuvres without the slightest misstep or hesitation. It was breathtaking.

Peter wondered how Admiral Stromo must feel, standing next to his best troops.

'They still require a human commander,' Basil said, as if sensing the King's concerns. 'Back in the mid-twentieth century, when computers and robotics were first used for automating industries, many workers feared that the evil machines would take over the world, put everyone out of a job.' He smiled with amusement at the childish idea. 'In reality, the machines just did the ugly, tedious work better. Like these new compies. When we send our battleships into the fray, instead of carrying thousands, they can have a mere skeleton crew of line commanders and bridge personnel. All the fighters can be Soldier compies. Think of the lives we'll save.'

'On the other hand,' Peter said, 'the Grid commanders will be more likely to authorize suicide missions.'

'*Effective* missions,' Basil said. 'The Ildiran Solar Navy demonstrated that much at Qronha 3. So far, that's the only time anyone's managed to destroy a hydrogue warglobe. Would you rather have us set off more Klikiss Torches to eliminate hydrogue worlds? That option's always been on the table.'

'And escalate the conflict to the point where the hydrogues actively pursue human extinction?' Peter felt cold inside. 'I don't think that would be wise.'

'We agree, then. So don't complain about the new compies. We will put them to good use at Osquivel in a few weeks.'

The EDF soldiers were unquestionably overshadowed in skill as columns of new compies marched between rows of uniformed humans like interlaced fingers and came to a precise halt. As Peter stared at the field below, he saw an intricate tapestry of uniforms, banners, and metal bodies. The Soldier compies finished their demonstration, but did not react to the swell of whistles and applause.

'Say the words, Peter,' Basil said.

The King stood, running over the speech in his head. Over the years he had found ways to twist a few phrases, change subtle meanings just to show his independence. He sensed, however, that now was not the time.

When his vocal amplifier was engaged, his words boomed out. 'My citizens, you have just witnessed a step forward in compy technology, a new hope for a swift end to this war. Though the evil hydrogues pose a terrible danger to human civilization, our military, our scientists, and our industries have risen to meet this challenge!'

He waited for the cheering to die down, then extended a hand towards the new robots on the presentation field. 'These Soldier compies are a valuable weapon, so that so many of our sons and daughters won't have to die on the battlefield. Like the scout team that was tragically murdered at Dasra not long ago. These Soldier compies will crew our warships and follow orders without question and without regard to their own survival. With enough of them, we can finally look forward to the day when we achieve victory against the hydrogues.'

He drew a breath and raised his voice. 'Admiral Stromo, I present to you these new soldiers in our struggle against the enemy. Do you accept them?'

Far away on the parade ground, the Admiral answered, 'Yes, my King. Our EDF soldiers are the best ever trained, but I am proud to accept these compies as part of our battleship crews.'

'Then take them in the name of humanity to stand against senseless aggression across the Spiral Arm.'

Basil sat back, smug and happy. 'This is an important day, Peter. One of many. Your blushing bride Estarra is due to arrive soon. I trust you're excited about it?'

'I've never even met her, Basil.'

Down below, the human soldiers marched in ranks back towards the waiting Mantas. Half a step behind, the compies followed, striding into the polished cruisers.

King Peter watched, still uneasy. Everything seemed too perfect. Yet so much remained incomprehensible about the Klikiss robots, despite the analysis of Jorax's components. But even though he was the Great King of the Terran Hanseatic League, no one wanted to hear about his reservations.

SIXTY-EIGHT

ESTARRA

A Manta cruiser arrived, on schedule, to take Sarein, Estarra, and the green priest volunteers to Earth. The mid-sized battleship remained in orbit around Theroc, since the landing clearing was not large enough to accommodate such a large vessel. After saying farewell, the passengers shuttled up, leaving the forest-covered continents behind.

Once she was aboard the EDF ship bound for Earth, Estarra told Sarein she was tired and wanted to be left alone in her cabin. Lying down on the sleeping pallet and staring up at the distressingly inorganic cabin ceiling, she drew a deep breath, tasting the air's processed metallic flavour. It seemed unnatural, devoid of familiar living smells, of trees and sunshine and open air. She felt the acceleration as the Manta moved out of orbit, taking her away from Theroc for the first time in her life. But in spite of her unfamiliar surroundings, Estarra was soon fast asleep . . .

During their mealtimes together en route, Sarein proudly offered Earth foods – chicken, fish, beef, meats strangely different from the insect products she was accustomed to eating on Theroc.

Her older sister sat across from her with bright eyes and a sincere-looking smile. 'You've never imagined anything like the Whisper Palace, Estarra. You'll see the golden cupolas in the sunlight. Eternal flames burn from the towers and bridge posts, each torch signifying a particular Hansa colony. With King Peter you'll be invited to spectacular processions and parades.' Sarein's face lit up. 'Ah, it's everything that Theroc *isn't*.'

Sarein's enthusiasm for Earth notwithstanding, Estarra noted that her sister had gathered a cargo of Theron items she couldn't get in the Whisper Palace: culinary delicacies, cocoon-fibre fabrics, intense dyes made from forest flowers.

Estarra listened politely, eating her meal. 'Some of it does . . . sound interesting. But I'm not going as a sightseer or a visitor, Sarein.'

No, she would be married to a young man she had never met, faced with political and social responsibilities she had never conceived of. Both Beneto and Rossia had advised her to keep an open mind, to look forward to new possibilities – and above all, to be strong. Estarra could certainly do that.

The nineteen volunteer green priests stayed together on the crew decks, and Estarra went to see Rossia during the journey. But as the Manta entered the Earth's system, a large passenger transport left the main ship and delivered the priests to the EDF base on Mars.

'Will there be crowds?' Estarra asked as the cruiser came in to land on the outskirts of the Palace District. 'Will I have to see the people right away – and what about King Peter? Will he come to greet me?'

Sarein patted her on the arm. 'Don't worry, little sister. With Basil in control, nothing happens unless it's carefully planned, considered, and rehearsed. Officially, no one even knows you're aboard this ship. When you are formally introduced to the public, everything will be managed to the finest detail and with the greatest precision. You won't have a thing to be nervous about. For now, you're just an anonymous passenger. It'll help you settle in and get adjusted more easily.'

While EDF soldiers disembarked from the cruiser, uniformed workers drove loading machinery aboard to remove the cargo. Technicians hurried to refit the chambers and cabins, adding provisions, water, and air for a quick turnaround and redeployment into space.

Estarra felt out of place in the vortex of all those people. She had never seen so many buildings in her life. Skyscrapers and towers, warehouses and spaceport observation turrets stood like an artificial forest of metal, stone, and transparent plates. The skies were a bright blue. She felt a tingle of amazement as she looked around.

'Here comes Basil.' Sarein waved at a military transport humming across the field, while whispering out of the corner of her mouth, 'Remember what I told you to say.'

'I thought this was an informal arrival?' Estarra cocked an eyebrow. 'If nobody's watching, and nothing counts, then why is it so important that I deliver my words correctly?'

'Consider it practice, Estarra. You can't have too much of that.'

When Chairman Wenceslas met them at the Manta's open VIP egress hatch, his face showed experience and wisdom without the weathered lines of overt age. Estarra did not remember how old the Chairman actually was, but she knew he underwent regular rejuvenation treatments. He extended a hand. 'Welcome, Estarra. We met at your brother's ceremony on Theroc, but we didn't have much opportunity to get to know each other.'

'My sister is very honoured to be here, Basil,' Sarein said.

Estarra gave the best smile she could manage. It was her first experience with diplomatic white lies, and she knew it would certainly not be the last.

Sensing her cue and anxious to get the routine over with, Estarra extended a small pot containing the feathery treeling she had brought as a formal gift. 'This treeling is for you as Chairman of the Hanseatic League, with the wish that it may grow and thrive like the Hansa itself.'

The fact that she had been asked to give her most important present to the *Chairman* rather than the King provided an inkling as to the true distribution of power here.

'Why thank you, Estarra,' Basil said, but did not move to touch the treeling. Instead, he gestured for his blond-haired attendant to take the gift, then he smiled down at her as if she were a little girl. 'Let's go see King Peter. I'm sure you've been waiting a long time for this.'

Though they were supposed to spend the rest of their lives together, Estarra noticed that she and Peter were never allowed to really meet. In their first encounter, they ate an informal luncheon in a glass-ceilinged conservatory in one of the labyrinthine wings of the Whisper Palace. A parade of attendants forced rich pastries and sweets upon her, but Estarra wasn't hungry.

The King sat at the far end of the polished table, wearing a trim and serviceable grey-and-blue uniform that seemed to symbolize the lean times in the Hansa. An old-model Teacher compy stood beside him like a private adviser, and Basil Wenceslas took a seat at the corner.

Other representatives and functionaries chatted loudly, the drone of their conversation forming a thicket around Estarra. It was as if this supposedly casual reception had been arranged to deny her and Peter any chance to speak more than rote pleasantries to each other.

The King was certainly handsome, she had to admit that. She had seen his image in news distributions and had always thought he appeared well-mannered. Peter had a personal magnetism with his blond hair, blue eyes, and finely formed features, but his every word in public seemed scripted and rehearsed.

Now as she sat across from him, they stole glances at each other, as if trying to communicate mentally. Peter ran his gaze over her face and her clothes, appraising Estarra just as she appraised him. She wondered if he was as wary and as baffled about her as she was about him.

Some of her stiffness flowed away as she felt sorry for the young King, and realized their shared dilemma. Right now, they both seemed to be puppets to higher powers. It would be a most unpleasant marriage if they treated each other as enemies. When his eyes met hers, she gave him a soft smile. Her reaction seemed to surprise, then please him, and he smiled back at her.

The Chairman and Sarein lifted tiny cups of a fiery cinnamon tea purported to be King Peter's favourite, though he did not seem to drink it with any more relish than Estarra did. 'To the royal couple,' said Chairman Wenceslas. 'May their love and this alliance make the Hansa grow stronger.'

'To the royal couple!' Sarein echoed.

Estarra and Peter raised their cups, locking eyes but unable to say anything to each other.

SIXTY-NINE

GENERAL KURT LANYAN

When the volunteer green priests arrived on Mars, General Lanyan received them as enthusiastically as if he'd been given a brand new weapon to play with.

He waited inside the base's large briefing room as personnel transport pods docked against the base buildings and the volunteers disembarked. He paced the floor, eager to see just how these long-awaited communicators measured up.

The green priests came in, looking disoriented and chilly – nineteen men and women of varying ages and body types. All of them had smooth green skin of varying shades of darkness; every one was completely hairless. Each priest carried a potted plant; the thin treelings were less than a metre tall, with feathery fronds spilling downwards.

Tattooed designs on the priests' faces and arms marked ranks and specialities within their mysterious religion. Accustomed to the warm humidity of Theroc, they wore little clothing – and seemed to be regretting it here on the cold red world. Lanyan would issue them regular EDF uniforms to facilitate their adjustment to military life.

Not surprisingly, the green-skinned Therons did not stand at attention or give any sense of well-behaved order. They filled the room with a casual chaos, showing no automatic deference to any officer. That would need to change, but he knew he couldn't push too hard.

The green priests served the EDF in the most tenuous of alliances, and Lanyan probably wouldn't be able to make them march in ranks. They might simply turn around and go home in a huff. Still, they were working with the Earth Defence Forces, and there were certain expectations . . .

One green priest with an outrageous scar on his thigh limped over to the broad window and stared out at the rusty landscape. The leg injury would be a detriment in battle, but the General didn't intend let these volunteers get into any kind of physical combat. He had to think of them as valuable *equipment*, communications resources, transmitters in human form.

The scarred priest gazed with large eyes into Mars's olive green sky. 'You have no trees here.'

'You brought your own trees.' Lanyan tried to sound encouraging, rather than impatient. He cleared his throat to get their attention. 'I am General Lanyan, your commanding officer.'

One priest stood straight-backed, his green skin marred by more tattoos and designs than any of the other priests. He stepped forward, holding his treeling as if it were a life-support system. 'My name is Yarrod, the senior green priest here. The worldforest agreed to let us contribute our telink skills, and so we have come to do our part in the hydrogue war.'

'Yes . . . yes, and it will be a great help to us,' General Lanyan answered. He had hoped for a bit more patriotism and enthusiasm for the cause rather than this somewhat grudging cooperation. 'Any intelligence you can provide about the enemy would be valuable to the war effort.'

Several priests joined the scarred man at the window wall to gawk out at the canyons, amazed by the stark bleakness. They didn't seem to be paying attention to this important briefing.

As a strict military man, Lanyan was not impressed with the lack of organization and formal respect these green priests exhibited to each other, or to him. Though Yarrod might be their highest ranking member, they afforded him no special courtesy.

Yarrod said, 'We do not yet understand the basis for the original conflict ten thousand years ago, but the hydrogues thought they had obliterated the worldforest. Only the smallest vestige remained on one planet, Theroc, and the trees survived there in hiding, afraid the hydrogues would come again to exterminate them. Now, it appears their fears were well founded. The enemy is obviously searching and attacking forested worlds. We must protect our trees.'

The General decided to be firm. If he used his powers of persuasion now, then gave the Therons a bit of training, once they were separated across all ten Grids any decent EDF commander should be able to keep the priests in line.

'Let me be clear with you all. I understand that you joined the EDF because you knew we could help you protect your worldtrees. Our best hope of success against the hydrogues is if we all work together. So, in order to assist in the struggle against our common enemy, we need you to become a functioning part of an overall system. The Earth Defence Force performs both small- and large-scale operations. Tens of thousands of people might contribute to a single event.

'Therefore, it is imperative that you accept your position in the chain of command. You have been brought into the EDF at the rank of warrant officer, but with no specific authority except in the area of communications.

'The EDF is a channelled, destructive force used for the defence of humanity. When I issue an order from the top, an avalanche happens. Commanders beneath me issue subsequent orders to accomplish their portions of the objective, and then their subordinates issue yet another set of orders, and so on.

'Each of you is responsible for becoming the correct pebble in the correct place at the correct time. Your telink can be our fastest and most reliable form of communication. If each pebble in our planned avalanche cooperates, then we become an unstoppable force. If you deviate, you could cause a catastrophe.'

'We understand this, General,' Yarrod said.

'Good, because in the heat of battle I won't have time to explain it.' He rolled the words over in his mouth, pleased with his speech so far.

At the broad window, a few of the green priests were still talking with each other, pointing at rock formations. Frowning, Lanyan worked a set of wall controls to opaque the window. 'All of you, go stand together and give me your full attention.'

Reluctantly, the priests took places beside Yarrod. Lanyan touched his fingertips together, looking at the strange volunteers. 'We are now at a defining point in the hydrogue war. Within days, the EDF will launch a massive and memorable offensive against the enemy. The alien raiding party that struck Boone's Crossing has gone to ground in a ringed gas giant named Osquivel.'

As soon as he mentioned Boone's Crossing, the green priests shuffled, looking at each other in dismay. 'Think of all the trees,' said Yarrod.

'That whole forest of black pines devastated,' said another.

'Not a tree left standing,' said the scarred priest.

'Yes – and we are going to get our revenge,' Lanyan said, glad to see a spark in them for a change. 'Obviously, I won't be assigning you to combat duty, since your skill lies in long-distance communications. To be effective, we must disperse the nineteen of you among the Grid battle groups and potential target colonies. That will give the EDF an enormous tactical advantage. Through you, we will have an up-to-date snapshot of the deployment of our entire fleet.'

The priests stroked their treelings to establish a stronger connection. They were already in a strange environment, taken away from their forested planet, serving in the unfamiliar military environment. And now, as they had known, they would be separated from each other.

Lanyan looked at the dark wall where the window had been. 'Osquivel is a nothing planet as far as the EDF is concerned, but we are going there with everything we have. At first we'll make a token attempt to communicate with the drogues, and we hope you'll be able to assist us. If that proves unsuccessful, we will pound the living crap out of them.' He grinned, expecting a rousing cheer, but the green priests only looked intimidated.

'The hydrogues are a powerful enemy,' Yarrod said. 'The worldforest warns us not to underestimate them.'

'Oh, we intend to throw everything we've got at Osquivel. The full might of the Earth Defence Forces. We can't possibly lose.'

Despite the General's firm voice and confident stance, the green priests did not seem convinced.

SEVENTY

CESCA PERONI

With a flurry of colour and activity, the Roamer betrothal ships came down through the atmosphere to Theroc. The twelve vessels were of unique and eccentric designs, bearing exotic banners and ornate hull insignia. They carried representatives from the primary clans: Okiah, Kellum, Sandoval, Pasternak, Tylar, Sorengaard, Chen, Baker, Kowalski, and of course, clan Peroni.

The entourage was an extravagant waste of ekti, but each Roamer family needed to demonstrate its joy and enthusiasm for the occasion. It wasn't often that a Speaker decided to get married.

Amazed Therons climbed to the treetops, scrambling over worldtree fronds to get a better view. On the ground, others rushed to the edge of the landing meadow to welcome the descending shuttles. Father Reynald, overwhelmed by the inexplicable arrival of all these strange vessels, reached the landing area out of breath and stood flanked by several green priests.

From the lead formal shuttle, Cesca Peroni emerged, dressed in

363

brilliantly coloured patchwork finery, her hair done up in festive ribbons. Reynald recognized her immediately. 'Cesca!'

Seeing the delight and mystification on his bronzed face, she came forward. Her smile gleamed like a moonrise as she held out her right hand. When she spoke her well-rehearsed words, there was no noticeable hesitation in her voice. 'Since it has been such a long while, I have come in person to accept your marriage proposal, Father Reynald of Theroc. If the offer still stands, that is?'

Reynald looked as if she had struck him across the forehead with a heavy branch, then he grinned like a boy. 'Of course the offer still stands!' He grabbed both of her hands, then gave her a brief and enthusiastic hug before breaking away, embarrassed. He tried to recover his composure with a quick bow. 'I would be honoured if you would become my wife, Cesca Peroni, Speaker of the Roamer clans. Our peoples have much to offer each other, as do you and I. Personally, I mean.'

More of the formal shuttles landed in the clearing, crowding the small open area, but the Roamers were excellent pilots and manoeuvred as if the landings had been expertly choreographed. Exuberant men and women emerged wearing colourful finery, bounding out to admire the verdant landscape. The clan representatives stood in the fresh air, staring up at the tall trees, smelling spicy humidity so unlike the reprocessed coolness of artificial environments.

Cesca raised Reynald's hand, still clasped in hers. She shouted to the clan heads. 'We both accept! After so much hardship, it's good to have some reason to celebrate.'

The Roamers whistled and whooped. Green priests and gathered Therons realized what was happening and began to applaud as well. Finally, Idriss and Alexa arrived, confused but excited by all the unexpected colours and revelry.

Reynald said, 'This is delightful – my little sister Estarra just went to Earth, where she is set to marry King Peter. And now you have accepted my proposal. What marvellous times we live in!'

She blinked at him with surprise, but did her best to cover her astonishment. The King would marry a Theron daughter? Should they have known this news already? A quick stir rippled through the Roamers. Cesca wondered how political alliances might shift now. Marriage connections between Roamers, Therons, and the Hansa. She would have to think about this much more.

Cesca turned to a lean but sure-looking man who had stepped out of the formal shuttle behind her. He had wavy dark hair and features that resembled hers. 'This is my father, Denn Peroni. My uncles are all aboard the ship.'

Reynald quickly introduced his own parents. Idriss, looking befuddled, stared at all the newcomers. 'Would someone please tell me what is going on?'

His wife looked at her husband with twinkling eyes. 'Just think about it for a moment, Idriss. You'll figure it out.'

Cesca and Reynald stood in a reception gallery of the fungus-reef city. Shadowed moonlight and stars penetrated the forest canopy, and the songs of insects accompanied by exotic musical instruments made the night seem magical. Roamers, who were full of their own songs and ballads, took turns sharing their culture and showing off their respective skills.

Through it all, Cesca did a marvellous job of pretending that she was enjoying herself.

The clan ships had brought so many entertainers and exotic gifts from far-off planets and asteroids that the betrothal celebration was like a carnival. Everyone laughed and danced, delighted with their newfound friends.

Reynald seemed intensely proud to be beside her. 'I wouldn't be surprised, Cesca, if this evening resulted in several other marriage proposals between our peoples.'

She dutifully held his hand and continued to smile. 'That would certainly strengthen our new alliance.'

As the hour grew late, Reynald took her up to a private balcony where they could stand and look out at the tree shadows and listen to all the activity around them. 'Do you think you'll like Theroc?' He seemed anxious to please her.

'We'll both have plenty to get used to. Roamers are nomads, and my family are wanderers even among the clans, merchants travelling from system to system. My father lives aboard his ships, going to a hundred different depots and skymines and ekti storage facilities to exchange fuel with the Big Goose or the Ildirans or even' – she lowered her voice – 'trading with some colonies directly, though that goes against the Hansa strict trade policy.'

'I'm sure the Hansa would understand, if the colonies have such a need,' Reynald said. She was surprised at how naïve he was.

Cesca sighed. 'It may take a while for my people to become as open as you are.'

'Tell me about the Roamers,' he said, looking at her with an innocent smile. 'What happened to make you so . . . secretive? So untrusting?'

'We learned it over the course of many generations. You got lucky here on Theroc, a lush world with a thriving colony. But when our generation ship *Kanaka* was delivered to Iawa, all of the crops failed. Those were very hard times, and we had to rely on our own resources. Later, we became very good at processing ekti, first as contractors on Ildiran facilities, then on our own skymines. And we paid for every success with sweat and blood. Like you, we've refused to sign the Hansa Charter, but the Big Goose would certainly love to control us.'

'Well, we did just provide nineteen green priests for the war effort . . .'

Cesca looked at him seriously. 'That's different. The Eddies get nothing from the green priests without their willing cooperation, but they can simply steal ekti from us – and they have, don't doubt it. We suspect they've been secretly raiding some of our cargo ships, destroying them after they take anything they need.'

'That's terrible!'

'Good thing most of our storage depots aren't on any map. Perhaps Roamers are a bit paranoid, Reynald, but on the other hand . . . maybe you're too trusting?'

The sounds of celebration rang out through the night. Cesca wondered if anyone had noticed their absence. Her father and uncles were probably looking at each other with raised eyebrows and knowing grins.

The actual marriage would not take place for a year. In the meantime, the Roamers and Therons would have more contact with each other. Ships would visit the forest planet, bringing surreptitious supplies. Reynald and perhaps other members of his family would visit carefully selected Roamer outposts. Gradually, the two diverse cultures would begin to blend.

As Cesca stood with Reynald in the moonlight, she told herself that all would work out for the best, that this was the correct decision. Reynald seemed so happy that a bittersweet Cesca took his hand in hers and stepped closer, trying with all her heart not to think of Jess.

SEVENTY-ONE

JESS TAMBLYN

For months Jess soared in silence, his immense sail drifting through vaporous and colourful oceans of star gases, swirling ions, and other cosmic ingredients that might one day coalesce to form a newborn solar system. Always moving, but never getting anywhere . . . a true Roamer at heart.

In a way, Jess liked the unending contemplative days, knowing it would help him find a way to resolve his inner turmoil. If his life had turned out the way he'd hoped, by now he and Cesca would have been married. But Jess knew his responsibilities. He could not create fairytales about his wishes and fantasies.

His personal tragedy of lost love seemed petty and selfish, and he refused to wallow in it any longer. He thought of all the Roamers massacred by the hydrogues, including Ross, and he recalled the desperate financial situations of so many clans. The Roamer economy was crumbling.

When finally his heartache had dulled to a wistful pain, Jess felt whole again, stronger – ready to face reality because he had no other choice.

And then he became lonely. By now, the group of nebula skimmers had spread across the seas of hydrogen gas, separated from each other by vast distances. Most of the starcloud harvesters were highly independent, even by Roamer standards.

The silence, once peaceful, now seemed oppressive. The chatter on the com systems had dwindled to occasional transmissions, separated by a gulf of signal-lag. He walked up and down the cramped decks, descended to the production hold, listened to his own footsteps.

Del Kellum had been right: having time to think might be a blessing, but *excessive* time was a burden.

He knew he had been isolated too long when he started hearing – or perhaps imagining – sounds. Whispers and buzzing noises that could not be explained by the faint familiar hum of machinery. When he let his thoughts wander, they even sounded like words at the back of his mind.

'Hello?' Jess called, and the loudness of his voice startled him. His throat was hoarse, his vocal cords raspy from disuse. He shook his head. 'Great, now I'm talking to myself.'

The odd noises were the audio equivalent of a shadow glimpsed from the corner of his eye. The harder he tried to listen, the fainter the sounds became. He sighed and tried to ignore them . . . but he had nothing else to occupy his thoughts.

He climbed down to the production decks where automated distillers separated out the useful byproducts of the nebular gases. Compressed elements filled small containers; tiny droplets of water continued to drip into the large, transparent cylindrical tank, raising its level by a mere centimetre each day. Jess sensed something here, a stirring movement of thoughts . . . as thin as a breeze but growing gradually stronger.

'Hello?' Jess shouted again, this time prepared for the echoes of his own voice. Nothing answered him, of course. He drew a deep breath of the oddly humid air in the production deck, chiding himself for his foolishness. Next he would start thinking his nebula skimmer was haunted . . .

Then the nightmares began.

Jess awoke with a start in his lonely bunk. A cold sweat soaked his sheets, and he gulped deep breaths, coughing, trying to clear his airway. In his dream he was drowning, sinking ever deeper, unable to breathe, unable to find his way back to air or light. His lungs, his bloodstream, his mind were full of water — made of water. The sensation was too real, engulfing him, overwhelming his thoughts, and he struggled towards wakefulness.

When he was younger, Jess had had nightmares about his mother and her slow, cold death in a crevasse on Plumas, gradually freezing, suffocating, protected only by her failing environment suit deep, deep in the alien water and unreachable.

But this dream was different . . . frightening only in its strangeness. He sensed no threat or terror, just confusion.

His eyes burning, Jess climbed out of bed, nearly lost his balance, and leaned against the metal bulkhead for support. His hand came away *wet*.

He looked in surprise to see beads of moisture glimmering on the metal. His fingers tingled when he touched it. A tiny trickle formed from the condensed droplets and ran in a minuscule river down to the deck . . . like a flow of lifeblood.

His brow furrowed, Jess followed the moisture, searching for the source. There must be a leak somewhere, a breach in the life-support piping or a rupture in a coolant system. Out here, so isolated from all help, such tiny things could lead to disaster. But when Jess ran diagnostics of the environmental systems, everything checked out, running at optimal levels. Even the humidity registered as normal.

He returned to his cabin, and found that the walls were dry again. Not a trace of the moisture remained.

Jess stood alone by his machinery down on the processing deck. The air felt damp and warm – strangely so, since the settings on his life-support systems had not been changed. He looked again at the clear liquid that had collected in the transparent holding cylinder.

Removing a sample of water from the container, Jess used the ship's diagnostic lab to run a full detailed analysis. He checked the results twice, then ran the tests a third time. As a member of clan Tamblyn, he knew all about water extraction and purity tests. Technically, chemically, the substance was nothing more than pure water, collected one molecule at a time from the cosmic cloud.

Seeking confirmation, Jess sent out a signal to his fellow, scattered nebula sailors. He asked if anyone else had experienced unusual results from the water the skimmers collected. His transmission was like a message in a bottle, tossed into a sea, and he knew it would take days for a response.

When the answers finally trickled in, he learned that none of his fellow Roamers had bothered to collect water vapour or other nebular impurities. They were interested only in hydrogen to be converted into ekti.

However, Jess continued to feel a growing suspicion that this mysterious fluid was . . . unusual. He experienced an eerie sensation whenever he stood close to the cylindrical container. He watched the liquid sitting there, utterly transparent, without a bubble or a speck of impurity.

And it seemed to glow, filled with something unmeasurable.

'What *is* this?' he said aloud.

As more water was added, collecting by misty condensation, it shimmered and roiled, concentrating some unusual essence that it somehow retained after being dispersed across the emptiness between stars. If Jess had been prone to Roamer superstitions, he might even believe that the nebula water was *possessed*.

Squatting close to the cylindrical container, he touched its curved walls, feeling a warmth that should not have existed. It made him giddy. He couldn't deny it — this throbbing water was not simply water . . . but much more. Haunted . . . possessed . . . somehow alive in a way that made little sense.

And gradually, alone on his big drifting ship, Jess Tamblyn began to *communicate* with it.

SEVENTY-TWO

BASIL WENCESLAS

The Hansa Chairman sat on top of the world in his penthouse suite. He pulled the strings, made all the important decisions, commanded the wealth and resources of sixty-eight scattered and loosely allied planets.

And yet he felt powerless. Sometimes, the clear and undiluted truth – without spin, without extenuating circumstances, without mitigating data – was too difficult for any human being to handle.

In blissful silence, he stared out of the broad windows as he sipped his cardamom coffee. Sunset spread a metallic film of golden rays over the Palace District. The Whisper Palace looked as if it had been splashed with molten bronze. Torches on the cupolas and bridge posts glinted like bright eyes. Today, unfortunately, the fading sunset seemed too symbolic, too depressing.

Detailed analyses compiled by his hand-picked experts left no room for doubt. There was no question: the Hansa was doomed and would fall very soon unless something changed dramatically.

Basil turned away, not wanting to see the lengthening twilight shadows. How could he hold it all together? He felt as if the weight would crush him. He finished his coffee, savouring the pungent aftertaste on his tongue, and went back to his crystalline table, which he had cleared of papers and debris.

One of the earlier Chairmen of the Hansa, Malcolm Stannis, had said it best in his posthumously published memoirs: 'Business is war, and war is a business.'

Screens came alive on a thin film embedded within the table surface. Shaking his head, Basil looked at statistical projections, maps of settled colonies, resource distributions of food, transport, luxury items. He could take in all of the displays at once – not just details, but the overall state of the Hanseatic League. And it did not look good.

Some colonies were worse off than others. In previous decades Relleker had concentrated on its burgeoning success as a spa planet, but now no one could afford to go offworld on a discretionary trip. Relleker was begging for aid and supplies that Basil simply could not provide.

Cloudy Dremen needed solar mirrors and greenhouse enhancers to augment crops that could barely survive in the dim sunlight. The Yrekans had already been forced into an ill-advised rebellion, and now they were licking their wounds. The forest industry of Boone's Crossing had been destroyed by the hydrogues, and although it was good for public relations to rally round the tragic survivors, those desperate people had now become hungry refugees. Who was going to feed them?

Basil had scripted the appropriate optimistic speeches for King Peter, slanting reality, but the stretched fabric of those lies would not hold much longer. He clenched his fist and stared at the projections, as if by force of will he could alter the bottom line.

Unfortunately, the numbers were accurate, and the analyses could not be doubted.

Everything depended on one key resource: ekti. All the extreme emergency measures the EDF had taken, the strict conservation programmes, the pressure and encouragement applied to Roamer clans, had resulted in only a trickle of stardrive fuel. The Terran Hanseatic League simply could not survive without ekti. Colonies were already starving – and the damned hydrogues refused to negotiate at all. His nostrils flared.

And he had heard nothing from Davlin Lotze in his search for answers about the missing Colicos xeno-archaeology team, so he assumed that was a bust, too. It had been a long shot anyway.

Maybe the deep-core aliens would learn their lesson at Osquivel. Soldier compies, green priests, a full-scale EDF battle fleet . . . and a last-ditch negotiator. So much was riding on that offensive.

Normally, Basil's thoughts would have been interrupted a thousand times in an hour, but he had initiated a full communications block to keep out all visitors and all transmissions. Foolishly, he thought he could figure out a solution if only he could *concentrate* on the problem for long enough. But he didn't seem able to bully his imagination into submission.

When the guest signal sounded, Basil knew exactly who it must be. Only Sarein had his private access code. He had given it to her several years ago, and to her credit she rarely used it. Now, however, he could use an interruption.

Beautiful and enthusiastic, her face appeared on the table screen, pushing aside data summations. He had always found her physically attractive, sexually stimulating. At first he'd thought she was far too young, but Sarein was more mature than most women he had met. Her mind was quick despite her upbringing on a backwater forest planet. He had told her some of his political plans, divulging secrets he should never have confessed to anyone. So far, she had proven a worthy ally.

'I know you don't want me to use this channel unless it's a crisis,

Basil,' she said. 'And let me tell you up front that the world is not coming to an end – at least not today. But you and I need to have some time alone. Let me arrange for a quiet dinner.'

'Sarein, this is not a day for us to build a relationship.'

'I'm not talking about that, Basil. I'm talking about your ability to make decisions, to think clearly through stress. Let me be your sounding board. Haven't I already proved my value by bringing you all those green priests?'

He wanted to turn her away, to tell Sarein to leave him alone so he could think, but that would accomplish nothing. 'All right, you've played your card. Out of appreciation for what you've done, we will have a conversation.' He pointed a finger at her dark-eyed image. 'But don't expect to use the same coin every time you need a favour.'

Her laugh was spiced with a lovely wiliness. 'If I want something else from you, Basil, I'll just have to pull off another miracle.'

She made him chuckle, and to Basil that was worth the annoyance of the interruption. 'Give me an hour to finish here, then come to my private levels. Arrange whatever meal you'd like. It'll be fine.' He blanked Sarein's image.

General Lanyan had incorporated the nineteen new priests into his fleet across the ten Grids. He hoped that the instantaneous telink communication would help change the uneven balance of power in the hydrogue war. Perhaps the Osquivel operation would turn the tide for good . . . or perhaps the green priests would simply report each catastrophe a bit faster.

With the hydrogues blocking access to gas giants, there could be no ekti.

Without ekti, there could be no Ildiran stardrive.

Without faster than light travel, there could be no interstellar trade.

With his grey eyes, Basil scanned the numbers again, seeing how the Hansa colonies were weakening, drawing apart. He had wracked his brain for years. The only other option, which seemed even more improbable, was to find a completely new system of fast transportation that did not depend on ekti. Both Ildirans and human scientists had reworked the stardrive, but there simply was no fuel alternative.

Earlier, Earth had used slow-moving generation ships, scattering humans on one-way trips across the Spiral Arm. But a century-long journey precluded any sort of commercial exchange.

His head began to pound with an impending migraine as he struggled to synthesize some means of holding a galactic civilization together, but not even his best engineering geniuses could offer solutions. Was there no other way to travel between the stars?

He finally returned the table to its matte-crystal surface. With a sigh, he prepared for dinner with Sarein. She might relax him, allow him to forget for an hour or so, whether through sex or conversation.

Either way, Basil didn't think any solution would be forth-coming.

377

SEVENTY-THREE

DAVLIN LOTZE

The hidden backup datawafer provided a wealth of amazing information. Margaret Colicos had recorded her findings, giving detailed translations of countless Klikiss hieroglyphics.

With Rlinda Kett looking over his shoulder, Davlin turned up the illumination inside his cabin on the *Curiosity*. 'She managed to decipher not just these equations, but also most of the historical records written on the walls.' He scrolled through another set of files, looking at diagrams, translations, theories, and questions. 'They uncovered some still-functional Klikiss technology . . . that stone window we found. Louis figured out how to make it work.' He glanced up at her, his eyes wide and intent. 'We'll need to go there tomorrow and investigate it ourselves.'

'Hey, you're the specialist in obscure details.' Rlinda brought out a bottle of wine from the ship's stores and sipped from her glass, sighing to make sure he knew how delicious it was. But Davlin didn't want wine, didn't even want to stop for a meal. This was too important.

Basil Wenceslas had been right to send him here.

He scrolled to the end of the file. 'Margaret was compiling all this information for the next regular report to be sent via telink, but apparently the green priest was killed before she could transmit it.'

'Think he was murdered to prevent the information from getting out?'

'Margaret's report gives no indication that she feared for her life, no suspicions at all. Whatever killed Louis Colicos and the green priest must have done so unexpectedly. The Klikiss robots and the compy are gone, and so is Margaret herself. Maybe the robots turned on them? Maybe Margaret went berserk from something she found? Maybe the threat was entirely external – say, an Ildiran assassin squad – something that wanted to prevent the Hansa from learning whatever they had discovered? At this point, I am considering every possibility equally.'

Rlinda took a longer drink of her wine and looked out through the tent flap into the clear desert night. 'And now we're here trying to learn the same information. Aren't you concerned that we might be in danger too?'

He met her gaze with his large brown eyes. 'I am always concerned.'

At the barest hint of dawn, Davlin led a sleep-groggy Rlinda Kett out to the second set of ancient ruins. They entered the echoing ghost city they had already explored, but this time the shadows and mysteries had been pushed back a bit further. With the information from Margaret's datawafer, Davlin could look at the evidence with a fresh eye and maybe – finally – find some answers.

He went straight into the large gallery that contained the blank trapezoidal surface. Davlin stared at Louis's bloody palm print on the flat stone, then scrutinized the complex symbol tiles that framed the unmarked area. He went to a side alcove of the big chamber where he found strange geometric mechanical units, partly dismantled and open.

On his portable screen, he referred to some of the notes Margaret Colicos had jotted down – her husband's incomplete speculations included. Davlin could imagine the woman pestering Louis to write up his own summary, but the old man would probably have put off paperwork, tinkering and learning new things faster than he could document what he had already uncovered.

'So, have you figured out what it is?' Rlinda asked. 'Or are the details too obscure even for you?'

'Louis believed this was some sort of travel system, a "transportal" that could be activated for instantaneous jumps across vast distances. The equations in Margaret's report showed that the Klikiss machinery had some way of punching a doorway through the fabric of the universe, creating a shortcut where the distance variable goes to zero.'

'Sounds impossible. Of course, so does the Ildiran stardrive . . . and so does the existence of intelligent aliens living at the cores of gas giants, I suppose.'

Davlin looked at the frame of symbols around the trapezoid, hundreds and hundreds of tiles, each one with a unique marking – like a destination code. During the voyage to Rheindic Co, Davlin had memorized reports of known Klikiss archaeological sites. Counterparts of this strange stone window occurred in almost every ruined city, though many of the coordinate tiles had been damaged either by time or by intentional sabotage. This one on Rheindic Co seemed completely intact.

And if the Colicos report was correct, the ten-thousand-year-old Klikiss machinery was also intact and continued to function. The Colicos team had already reactivated it. That in itself – such a long-standing energy source – would be a boon to Hansa industries. But he suspected it was only the beginning of the wonders they would find here.

He saw where Louis had added a new generator cell to the mechanism. The Hansa powerpak had dropped into standby mode long ago, but Davlin easily brought it back online. 'Somebody did all the work for us. It's still operational—' The battery hummed, and the Klikiss technology began to vibrate, gently throbbing.

'Watch what you're doing, Davlin. No telling what you might damage.'

'Or activate.' He scrutinized the portal wall to see if anything had changed. A thrill like electricity raced along his spine as he saw the remarkable difference. 'Look! The handprint is gone.'

The blank stone shimmered faintly, still showing an opaque tan-grey wall, but the rust-coloured bloodstain had vanished.

Rlinda's eyes widened with surprise. 'If this is a transportation system, a network that allows travel from planet to planet without stardrives, just think of the ramifications! It could put my *Voracious Curiosity* out of business.'

Davlin made another observation. 'Such a discovery would be sufficient motive for murder, if someone wanted to prevent its widespread use. For instance, Roamers intent on preserving the demand for the ekti they provide.' He narrowed his eyes. 'But who knew about it? If Margaret hadn't even sent her report, how could anyone learn what they'd discovered?'

'The Klikiss robots were here,' Rlinda pointed out, then she looked nervously behind her. 'What if they decided to keep the secret of their creators from being revealed?'

'Makes as much sense as anything,' Davlin said. 'I'm glad we don't have any robot "helpers" like the Colicoses did.'

He stepped forward to touch one of the coordinate tiles. The powerful thrumming grew louder. The stone window suddenly shimmered and activated, and the artificial lights Rlinda had strung inside the chamber dimmed. Then an image focused on the trapezoidal stone surface as if a doorway had opened.

'Incredible,' Davlin said. 'Maybe Margaret went . . . *through*.'

Rlinda put her hands on her wide hips. 'Should I point out that you don't know what you're doing – or would that only make you more determined to investigate this thing?'

Ignoring her, he edged closer to the throbbing wall. He had always been a risk taker; it was a requirement for fulfilling his role as a spy and for acquiring expertise in esoteric subjects.

'I wonder how it—' he mumbled, extending a finger to feel a tingle in the field. As soon as he touched the image, Davlin's chest lurched. His mind spun as if it were detached from his skull and rotating at high speed on a spindle.

Stumbling, he dropped to his knees on soft sandy ground in front of a collapsed wall. The temperature had plummeted by at least thirty degrees, and overhead the sky – the *open sky* – was a swirl of magenta and lavender with high scudding clouds. Klikiss ruins stood like lumpy termite mounds around him on a grassy plain, interspersed with broken outcroppings thrust from the ground like rotting teeth worn down to the gums.

He gasped and scrambled to his feet. Behind him was another trapezoidal transportal wall identical to the one inside the Rheindic Co caves. He caught a last flickering glimpse of Rlinda Kett's astonished face looking at him through a mirage-like shimmer – across an impossible distance. Had he come *through*?

Then the image fuzzed and faded, and he found himself staring at an opaque stone wall again, a framed barrier made of rock. A closed door.

'Incredible,' Davlin said to himself, not yet admitting fear. He wouldn't indulge in that reaction until after he had reviewed everything that had just happened.

He looked around him in the alien world. It was totally silent and empty with no sign of human presence whatsoever. He had no idea where he was.

And with the transportal shut behind him in the crumbling Klikiss ruins, he had no way to get back.

SEVENTY-FOUR

KING PETER

His attendants had taken an hour to dress him, selecting the proper clothes, making sure all folds and pockets and jewellery were perfectly arranged. Makeup artists checked his face, styled his hair, and finally pronounced the King presentable for whatever media cameras might spot him.

By now Peter had grown used to tedious state dinners. He had learned how to play his part while hiding his thoughts. He didn't even need to pay attention any more. Tonight, the food would be so rich and fancy as to be indigestible, but he would smile and toy with it, careful not to damage the fabulous china that had served the Great Kings for two centuries.

Peter remembered nights long ago when he'd struggled to provide enough nutrition for himself and his family. This was a far cry from eating scraped-together concoctions of leftovers and macaroni. He couldn't recall exactly when he had stopped thinking of himself as *Raymond Aguerra* instead of King Peter. Now his former life seemed a twisted dream to him.

The only person he wanted to impress was Estarra, his bride-to-be. He wondered what she was really like, if he could ever open his heart to her, if she had similar thoughts about him. He wondered if he would ever know . . .

Understanding what she must be going through, Peter felt sorry for the young woman. Estarra seemed different from her sister Sarein, sweet and intelligent, eager to absorb details – not vapid or cowed, as he'd been afraid she might be. But she was unaccustomed to so much ceremony, or to having her every move scrutinized – and Estarra hadn't even been formally presented to the Hansa public yet. Protocol ministers were planning every second of that event, which would occur in another week.

So far, the two of them had had few chances to do more than smile and exchange pleasantries, while curious attendants eavesdropped on them. Peter wished they could simply sit in a room together and commiserate, but it would not be tonight. Still, he looked forward to seeing her . . .

As he strode down the halls accompanied by seven retainers, heralds led the way and announced each step with embarrassing fanfare. When he entered the banquet hall, dignitaries shot to their feet with a rustle of clothes, a scraping of chairs, and a click of shoes and jewellery and medals.

The King spread his hands in welcome. OX also stood unobtrusively inside the banquet hall, his coloured metal skin polished for the occasion. Peter was glad to see the diligent and helpful Teacher model, thinking of the compy as the closest thing he had to a friend in the Whisper Palace.

The table had been set with floral bouquets, fine napkins, and silverware that dazzled under the chandelier lights. He and Estarra would flash glances at each other, maybe smiling, maybe looking away. If only they could have ten minutes alone . . .

The attendants and courtiers always made sure Peter arrived fashionably late so that everyone waited upon the King's presence.

But at the head of the table, beside his own chair, he saw an empty seat, a place for Estarra. She wasn't there. He turned to look inquiringly at one of the heralds, then at OX.

Wearing a false smile, Basil Wenceslas came forward to whisper, 'We can't find Estarra. She's late.' Though his face continued to show calm confidence, his words carried a faint criticism, as if he somehow blamed the King for Estarra's tardiness.

Peter acknowledged the Chairman with a tiny nod and walked to his formal chair at the head of the table. 'My guest has been detained for the moment, but we've all become accustomed to unforeseen delays by now.' He knew not to let them suspect anything was out of the ordinary. Basil never wanted to hint that any situation was out of control, not for a moment. 'Please, take your seats. I'm sure we have enough appetizers to feed a small colony planet.'

Dutiful chuckles rippled around the table. Peter didn't know whether he should be concerned or secretly pleased that Estarra was missing. He hoped she had found something enjoyable to do. Wherever she was, he would rather have been with her instead of here.

'I suggest we begin with the first course. As it is, the chefs will no doubt keep us here past midnight so that we can sample every delicacy concocted by their wildest imaginations.'

Before the salad was finished, two escort guards hurried a flustered Estarra into the banquet hall. Peter immediately stood, and the others at the banquet table struggled to get to their feet as quickly as possible. Though her garments were lovely and exotic with a Theron flair, she appeared to have been hastily dressed.

'I was just exploring.' Estarra's tanned face looked childlike and frightened. 'I lost track of time. I didn't mean to be delayed, but the Whisper Palace is so . . . huge!'

Basil took the young woman's arm. 'Let me take you to your

seat, my dear.' Eyebrows knitted, he scolded her under his breath.

Obviously chastened, Estarra took her seat, and OX stood between them. Peter leaned over, speaking quietly enough to foil any listeners, 'Don't worry about it. Basil is so obsessed with schedules that he even *perspires* according to a timetable.'

She didn't look at him at first, but then gave him a dark-eyed glance that showed her relief. 'Thanks.'

As the attendees greeted each course with delight, Peter felt Estarra's strained silence. What did she think of him? He'd accepted the fact that he was going to marry her, but still he wanted to know who she was. He looked at her, trying to decide. Was Estarra funny or morose? Gregarious or solitary? Did she fear him? Resent him? Expect to manipulate him?

None of the dull chitchat or polite laughter interested him. Estarra remained troubled by the overreaction to her wandering around the Palace. On Theroc, she was accustomed to going where she wanted, and it surprised her that her everyday freedoms had been so embarrassingly curtailed. She continued to eat, making only brief responses to any questions asked of her.

Peter dutifully raised his goblet as one of the guests offered yet another toast to the King and his magnificent works – it was the fourth such toast since the commencement of the meal, and they hadn't even reached the main course yet. He tried to catch Estarra's eye. Peter wished he could make her understand that he didn't like their situation any more than she did.

Basil used an iron grip to control Peter's every action, and now he was treating Estarra the same way. If she learned to cooperate on the surface, they could both retain a shred of identity despite numerous compromises. But Basil seemed reluctant to let Peter speak openly with the woman who would be his wife. The Chairman didn't like unstructured meetings, even personal ones.

'How am I supposed to get to know her, then?' Peter had once asked in Basil's private office. 'If we're going to make a perfectly wonderful couple for all the public to see, shouldn't I at least know her?'

Basil had scowled. 'Not necessary, Peter. You're adding complications to a situation that I already have well in hand. You will have time enough for that later.'

Now, though, with Estarra only a metre away, Peter smiled – a genuine smile this time – and turned to his bride-to-be. 'You must miss the forests of Theroc very much.'

She glanced at him, surprised but cautious. 'It hasn't been so very long. I can handle it.'

'The Whisper Palace has a marvellous arboretum, gardens as well-manicured and as exotic as you can imagine, along with several worldtrees. I think you'd enjoy seeing our tiny slice of well-tamed wilderness.'

'I suppose that would be better than walking through rooms full of relics that belong in a museum.' She sniffed indignantly at the stony-faced guards. 'Especially since when I wander on my own, *certain people* get upset.' She made a rude noise. 'As if I haven't ever been on a walk by myself! On Theroc I used to run for hours, climbing the worldtrees to get to the canopy where I could look out at the whole world.'

'Didn't you worry about getting lost out there?'

Estarra shrugged. 'It's hard to get lost in your own home.'

Peter raised his eyes to the high-vaulted ceiling and the magnificent chandeliers. 'The Whisper Palace has been my home for a long time, and sometimes I still get lost here.'

Estarra gave a light laugh. 'Good thing there are plenty of guards breathing down your neck, then.'

'If the two of us go see the gardens, maybe I can convince the guards to stay at least twenty steps behind us. As long as you promise not to climb any trees.'

Basil stood and signalled for attention. It was a mark of the power and respect he commanded that everyone instantly fell silent. The servers melted out of sight.

'Estarra, daughter of Theroc, we are here to welcome you and to show you our appreciation. Soon, the Hansa will officially announce your engagement to our beloved monarch.' He turned to the Teacher compy. 'OX will continue to help you get acquainted with how things work here. He will instruct you in etiquette and behaviour and manners, much as he did with the Prince when he was young.'

Peter smiled at her. Estarra seemed to shy away from all the attention suddenly showered upon her. 'Thank you,' she said.

There was a polite applause, and Basil sat down. The servers launched the main course, carrying in steaming cutlets of succulent beef smothered in sauces. Peter realized that on Theroc Estarra was unaccustomed to eating any kind of meat that didn't come from gigantic insects. This fare must still be new to her.

He smiled at her again, feeling a strange warmth in his heart. Perhaps they could eventually learn to like each other . . . if they were given the chance.

SEVENTY-FIVE

PRIME DESIGNATE JORA'H

Jora'h discovered the mysterious documents waiting for him in his sealed private chambers. Someone had placed the records where no one but the Prime Designate could see them. He felt cold dread just looking at the stacked, obviously ancient diamond-film sheets.

Of late, Jora'h no longer found any sort of surprise to be pleasant.

Young Thor'h had already departed for the Horizon Cluster with relief supplies, engineers, rescue workers, builders, and architects. He was also joined by his earnest younger brother Pery'h – Jora'h's third-born noble son – though Thor'h seemed intent on doing all the work himself. The injured Designate Rusa'h still lay in a deep sub-*thism* coma, unchanged and unmoving for months. The Mage-Imperator said he could no longer sense his wounded son through the *thism*, but he had not passed through into the realm of the Lightsource. Only the medical kithmen could prove that the Hyrillka Designate was still alive at all . . .

Frowning, his gold-chain hair twitching with agitation, Jora'h picked up the thin sparkling sheets that bore letters like runes engraved with diamond liquid. The characters and language seemed archaic, the scrolled border too ornate for current styles. It took him a moment to recognize the rhythm and metre of words, the stanzas broken into the same pattern and format. Every Ildiran would have found it familiar.

This was a portion of the *Saga of Seven Suns*. A section he had never seen before.

More stories? Ancient history? Why should anyone bother the Prime Designate with such things at a time like this? Hydrogues were on the prowl, attacking human and Ildiran settlements. Hyrillka had been devastated and numerous other splinter colonies evacuated and withdrawn. His own brother lay unconscious and near death. And the Mage-Imperator was dying of terrible insidious tumours.

Angry, Jora'h started to push the documents away, but then he recognized a startlingly out-of-place word, somehow included in the context of the ancient *Saga*.

Hydrogues.

He grabbed the crystalline sheets and began to read, scanning the lines, absorbing an amazing tale. It was an historical recounting of an ancient, *unknown* war, a titanic conflict against the hydrogues and other powerful 'demons'. It had occurred ten thousand years ago, during a mysterious and empty historical period known as the 'Lost Times'.

It couldn't be true!

The *Saga of Seven Suns* was an accurate historical record, and Jora'h had always taken comfort in the reassuring familiarity of legends and heroes. No one ever doubted the truth as recorded in the billion-line epic of their race.

As far as the Ildirans knew, a firefever epidemic had killed an entire generation of rememberers thousands of years ago, and consequently a section of the oral *Saga* had been forgotten. Now, though, Jora'h saw that the ancient records had been preserved after all, but hidden from all people. Had this epoch of Ildiran history been rediscovered? Or had it been censored all along?

Torn between amazement and disbelief, Jora'h voraciously absorbed the new information. He read about conflicts among incomprehensible powers – not only hydrogues, but also similar entities affiliated with fire and water, even a powerful earth-based sentience that comprised organic living ecosystems. The words and names were strange: Faeros. Wentals. Verdani.

Ten millennia ago, great beings had battled each other across the cosmos. In that horrific war, they had extinguished the Klikiss race, seemingly as collateral damage. They had also nearly destroyed the Ildiran Empire, but it had occurred so long ago that the people no longer recalled it.

This was impossible. How could the secret have been kept? And who had discovered the records, after all this time?

Suddenly the answer was obvious. His father must have arranged for him to see these documents. On purpose. Only a Mage-Imperator could have managed such a complete cover-up and rewriting of reality. Only through the *thism* and generational recall could a Mage-Imperator carry out a long-term plan that spanned thousands of years to obliterate all knowledge of the first hydrogue war. But to what purpose?

His father must consider the revelation of these documents to be part of the Prime Designate's weaning process, to draw him away from his naïveté and grasp the hard reality of leadership. It was appalling! Jora'h had never imagined deception on such a grand scale.

His thoughts were heavy, but his jaw clenched with anger. He couldn't accept that such secrets existed – and that they had until now been kept from *him*, the Prime Designate, the heir to the Mage-Imperator's throne!

And if his father could do that . . . what else did Jora'h not know?

He read the stories again, knowing that no rememberer, not even Vao'sh, had spoken these words aloud in ten thousand years. Though grievously hurt, the hydrogues had apparently won that ancient conflict. The other incredible beings had been defeated, scattered . . . perhaps destroyed.

As he struggled with the shock of what he had learned, Jora'h let his mind stray to more peaceful times, the love he had shared with gentle Nira. He wished the lovely female green priest could be with him right now . . .

He remembered her amazing and mysterious descriptions of the worldforest, the giant mind that had slumbered for so long on Theroc. Then Jora'h's eyes lit up as he thought of an amazing possibility. What if the worldtrees were the surviving manifestation of the powerful, yet defeated, 'earth powers'? The verdani.

Suddenly in his mind, the hydrogue war looked completely different. And filled with new possibilities.

SEVENTY-SIX

RLINDA KETT

Just typical.

Rlinda Kett stood inside the empty ruins on Rheindic Co. Whenever a man didn't know what the hell was going on, he had to prove it by making things worse, pushing buttons and insisting that he 'knew how to fix it'. She had seen that behaviour time and again in her husbands.

And it was just like a man to disappear on her, too – though usually not in such a melodramatic fashion. She'd watched the strange alien machinery hum, the portal wall throb. An image of a weird lavender sky above an alien landscape had shone like a projection through the trapezoidal stone.

And then Davlin Lotze had vanished through it.

She hadn't seen exactly what he'd done, how he'd caused the transportal to snatch him away. Shouting after him, she had run towards the stone gateway, wise enough to stop long before she touched the field. If only Davlin had been as cautious. Rlinda had seen a shadow of the man standing astonished on a distant world, looking back at her. Then the picture had vanished and the solid stone had returned.

Davlin was gone, and Rheindic Co was silent again.

She crossed her arms and heaved a sigh. 'All right, now what?'

Rlinda waited four days. On the first night she slept inside the ghost city, hoping to hear a hum of reactivating machinery, Davlin returning of his own accord. *Fat chance.* She hoped he wasn't waiting for her to push random buttons and try to recreate the mess he had made.

All alone now, she slept with a hand weapon at her side, ears alert for creaking footsteps or skittering claws. She thought about the mangled body of the green priest, the uprooted worldtree grove, the bloodstains from the violent death of Louis Colicos. Rheindic Co might seem empty, but *something* had killed them.

But when Davlin didn't return and nothing sinister happened, the spooky ruins became downright boring. This wasn't what Rlinda had envisioned when she'd first formed a merchant company, subcontracted other captains, and gathered five good ships.

Back at the ship, she puttered around camp until she ran out of things to do. She had supplies aboard the *Voracious Curiosity* and enough fuel to depart whenever she wanted, but she couldn't just abandon Davlin here. What if he did come back through the transportal, full of amazing discoveries and all the answers Chairman Wenceslas needed – only to find that she had flown off? Rlinda decided to wait.

And wait.

Davlin had made his own choices, and he'd been stupid to get himself into such a fix. If only she'd paid closer attention in the moments before he disappeared, but she had no intention of fiddling with the alien machinery or going after him. She would just stay here and contemplate what to do next. But Rlinda had never been one to kick back and daydream, not when she could actually be doing something.

Unfortunately, on Rheindic Co, what was there to do?

She felt uncharacteristically sorry for herself. Six years ago, before anyone had ever heard of hydrogues, she couldn't have imagined how far she would fall. It didn't seem possible, unless you believed in all that baloney about the 'whims of fate'. First the *Great Expectations* had been destroyed by Rand Sorengaard's pirates, then most of her remaining ships had been commandeered by the Earth Defence Forces. Rlinda had only the *Curiosity* left.

Maybe she should just settle down here and cut her losses. No one would bother her . . . or keep her company, either. Not a good enough tradeoff.

She went into the *Curiosity's* galley and looked through the supplies. Most of the foods were mediocre mealpax, designed for their nutritional value rather than gourmet flavours. She began to open packages and raided her own personal store for some black chocolate and a bottle of her favourite wine.

She combined a few more of her private treats with special spices; it was an extravagant use of ingredients, but Rlinda had decided to splurge. She used only a splash of wine in a sauce for the succulent lamb. Noodles with pesto, buttery mushrooms . . . and a crumbly honey-and-nut pastry to go with the chocolate for dessert.

Rlinda set up a small table outside, complete with cloth and a single wide chair. She poured a large glass of New Portugal wine, ignoring the mess she'd left in the ship's galley. She could clean it up later; unless something unexpected happened, she would have plenty of time. She sat down, closed her eyes, and just inhaled the delicious aromas. If any monstrous predator lurked out there in the shadows, the smell of her cooking would certainly lure it out of hiding.

She took a taste of each item, including the sweets, and

complimented herself on her culinary prowess. Then she began to eat her meal with gusto and satisfaction. 'Take all the time you want, Davlin,' she called out to the empty landscape. 'I'll just wait here.'

She sipped more wine and sat back to watch the glorious desert sunset.

SEVENTY-SEVEN

DAVLIN LOTZE

His first order of business was to determine where he'd been stranded. Between one breath and the next, Davlin Lotze had passed through the Klikiss transportal, traversing an unimaginable distance – and arrived here among ancient ruins under a pastel sky with a dim sun lurking like a blind eye on the horizon.

He looked around, taking the time to make a calm, reasoned assessment of the lumpy Klikiss structures around him. The air was dry and thin, but breathable, as seemed to be the case on nearly all of the Klikiss worlds he had read about. The trapezoidal stone window on this end of the portal wall also seemed intact and functional.

One step at a time. This was a problem to be solved. Davlin spent an hour wandering among the ruins. Perhaps Margaret Colicos had fled here – although in the frame around Rheindic Co's transportal there were hundreds of coordinate squares to choose from. If she had indeed used the alien system, Margaret could have travelled to any of the planets. She could be anywhere, and she *could* still be alive.

Just as he intended to survive.

Later, as the silence weighed down on him, Davlin called out, 'Hello!' He listened to the echoes of his words on a world that had probably never heard a human voice. Receiving no response, he yelled three more times and then decided to call no further attention to himself.

As he explored his surroundings, he found neither water nor anything that looked edible. The jagged landscape, the towering Klikiss mounds, even the colour of the sky nagged at his memories. He tried to recall the Colicos material he had scanned while preparing for the Rheindic Co investigation.

This world was remarkably similar to a planet called Llaro, the site of the first Klikiss ruins discovered by the 'planet prospector' Madeleine Robinson nearly two centuries earlier. The Robinsons had found dormant Klikiss robots in the ruins there; if Davlin could locate another Klikiss robot, perhaps he could ask the black machine for assistance. Of course, this might not be wise if the ancient beetle-like machines had in fact murdered Louis and the green priest and destroyed all the equipment on Rheindic Co . . .

Under lavender skies, walking against brisk winds, he made his way back to the trapezoidal stone wall. He spent a day contemplating how best to try it again, testing the system before he made another mistake.

Whether this place was indeed Llaro or some similar uncharted Klikiss world, Davlin was lost. If each symbol around the trapezoidal stone window was the coordinate of another destination among the long-abandoned Klikiss planets, he had no way of knowing which was which.

Even if he could remember the symbol on the address tile that had sent him here in the first place, he had no idea which of the alien coordinate tiles would take him *back* to Rlinda Kett on Rheindic Co.

Did he dare go anyplace else at random? Though he had survived the journey here, what if he chose incorrectly the next time? What if he transported himself to a place where the air was not breathable, or where the ruins had collapsed? Unlikely, but possible. Was that what had happened to Margaret Colicos?

On the other hand, he was already getting hungry and thirsty.

He inspected the transportal machinery to reassure himself, though he did not have any grasp of how the mechanics functioned. Nevertheless, the generator hummed. Everything appeared to be intact. His passage had apparently reawakened the long-mothballed Klikiss machinery, jumpstarting the transport systems. When the Klikiss race had vanished, they'd somehow had the presence of mind to place these transportals into standby mode.

He hoped the rest of the network still functioned.

Davlin was neither a fool nor a coward. He knew that he alone must find a solution. Unless Rlinda Kett came after him – and he didn't think the merchant woman would risk it – no one would ever find him here. Without food or water, he could not survive for long.

He finally summoned his nerve and chose a coordinate tile at random, memorized the design, and pressed it. When the hazy transportal activated, he stepped through to another place.

He drew a breath before he even opened his eyes. Different. The air smelled spoiled and dry – but breathable, again. These ruins were covered with dust that had collected over millennia. The walls had fallen. The sky was an angry, leprous green. It was a miracle the trapezoidal stone window still functioned here.

Obviously not the right place.

A bloodcurdling cry shivered through the air, growing louder, and he saw black creatures circling overhead. Poisonous-looking insects crawled over the broken walls. Two fist-sized beetles clacked their wings and took flight towards him, buzzing in the air like heavy bumblebees.

With fewer reservations this time, Davlin activated the transportal, choosing a different coordinate tile, and stepped through the shimmering flat stone before the beetles could come after him . . .

He found nothing useful in the next place either, a totally empty Klikiss world that showed no sign of human investigation – perhaps a planet never mapped or surveyed, not even by Ildirans. The ruins were intact, the structures undisturbed. He called out at the top of his lungs, but once more received no answer.

And so he jumped through the transportal again and again, growing hungrier each time. He kept careful records of each coordinate design, hoping to compile some sort of map. Had Margaret Colicos done the same thing, desperately wandering from one planet to the next, never finding her way back?

The sixth journey brought him to a hot, arid place that looked quite familiar. He was sure he had seen images of it in the briefing materials Basil had sent. Davlin discovered the remnants of a Terran university excavation camp. Some of the buildings were cordoned off. Chalk marks and carefully dissected strata in the dust and mud showed where teams had attempted to make sense of the abandoned city. Human marks.

With a growling stomach and uncertain optimism, he walked through the site, finding a garbage dump and a few forgotten odds and ends. But no people. The name of the planet, as he recalled, was Pym, a well-known Klikiss site. In better times and with open space travel, this could have become a huge excavation or even a tourist destination, but now Pym was empty.

With a swell of relief, though, Davlin found an automated water pump that had been shut down. An hour's tinkering got it functioning again, and soon fresh cold water from a deep aquifer spilled out, a glorious treasure that he gulped with great pleasure. He splashed his face, then ran the water over his dark hair and skin, cooling his hands, soaking his shirt. He was also overjoyed to find some abandoned supplies in a storage cache inside one of the buildings; the stale but wondrous concentrated camp food revitalized him.

However, even knowing that he was on Pym gave him no better clue as to how he could get home. The scraps of concentrated food would last only a day or two. No communications equipment had been left behind. He supposed if he did manage to send an emergency signal, Basil Wenceslas just might come to retrieve him – but without a green priest, any message would take months or more to cross open space before there was a chance of someone intercepting it.

Davlin leaned back in the gathering night, exhausted. But for the first time in at least two stressful days – different planets and time zones, made it difficult to keep track of how long he'd been gone – he'd been able to satisfy his hunger and thirst. He would sleep well and regain his strength.

Tomorrow he would just have to keep trying.

SEVENTY-EIGHT

ANTON COLICOS

Under the domes of Maratha Prime, the two storytellers sat on a raised platform bathed in bright light, smiling out at their attentive audience. For several hours each day, Anton and Vao'sh took turns entertaining rapt listeners with extravagant myths or legends from their respective histories. Anton was having the time of his life.

'"The Pied Piper of Hamelin" is a cautionary tale that's frightened many children and parents.' Anton didn't have a rememberer's fleshy, coloured lobes on his face, yet he did his best to capture the mood with hand gestures. He told of the ragged stranger who made a bargain with the elders of a rat-infested town, and the terrible payment he exacted when they cheated him.

The noble kithmen, bureaucrats, and servers were both entertained and confused. Anton often had to interrupt the flow to explain that rats carried diseases on old Earth, that humans could not sense through *thism* when another person was cheating them, that a self-important mayor was not the same as a Mage-Imperator or his Designates. After he told how the vengeful piper led the

403

children into the stone mountainside, leaving only one lame boy behind, the listeners muttered, disturbed.

'But was it real?' asked one bureaucrat standing next to a lovely bald woman, her face painted with colourful designs. 'Is this part of your history?'

'No, not history, just a story.'

This perplexed the audience even more. 'But how can a story not be true?'

'It's true, on a certain level. The lessons are certainly valid for all humans and Ildirans. On Earth we sometimes invent our own stories for amusement or to explore new ways of thinking. The truth of these stories is not always in the details, but in the message.' Then, smiling, he arched his eyebrows. 'Um, you enjoyed it, didn't you?'

Vao'sh explained to the listeners, 'Humans view stories differently. We have our *Saga of Seven Suns*, but they have many tales not connected with a single backbone. No human has yet seen the larger perspective into which they fit, not even Rememberer Anton.'

To ease their confusion, Vao'sh told a familiar humorous story from the *Saga*, which Anton enjoyed very much. The human scholar had already shared amusing parables and fairy tales, ranging from 'Androcles and the Lion' to 'Little Red Riding Hood'. Though the vacationers on Maratha were adults, their fascination made them childlike. Every one of his old stories was completely new to the Ildirans.

Later, when the audience dispersed, he and Vao'sh took a leisurely walk. Every day, Anton spent many hours in intense study of the *Saga of Seven Suns*, but he also spent time with the historian absorbing and observing Ildiran culture.

All around them carefree Ildirans moved about laughing, playing games, dining in fine establishments. Anton had never been an adventurous eater, since his university salary did not allow for gourmet extravagance. Here on Maratha, though, he had made up his mind to experience every bit of culture he could.

When he went home to Earth, his imagination would be bursting with new material, having learned things that no other scholar ever had. He could mine this research for the remainder of his professional career, writing a wealth of technical papers and treatises, even recounting some of the best Ildiran stories for a popular audience.

Now Vao'sh took him through Maratha's backstreets to the plain communal dwellings where various servants, attenders, cooks, and maintenance kithmen worked and lived, crowded together. 'Because the *Saga of Seven Suns* belongs to every Ildiran, these are all details and nuances that will help me speak in a manner that is relevant and meaningful to all kiths.'

They entered one of the transfer chambers at the edge of the dome. Vao'sh seemed bursting with excitement. 'Now I will take you outside, and you will see why so many Ildirans come here.'

With the rememberer's assistance, Anton skinned on a slick but tough suit of silvery film. Vao'sh showed him how to smooth the self-shaping membrane over his mouth. Dark goggles covered his eyes, nearly blinding him. Then, standing at the hatch doors that led outside – the 'exterior spa' as Maratha called it – Anton took a deep breath through his membrane.

The door rolled open, and a wash of light and warmth struck him like a golden wave. Before, his goggles had seemed opaque; now, he blinked at the clarity of the stark landscape full of black and crimson rock, tan deserts, and sparkling dry lakebeds.

Behind them, the multiple domes gleamed like faceted diamonds set into polished gold hemispheres that took in the sunlight and hurled it back at the sky. Ildirans in silvery garments stood on platforms and balconies, playing a game with soft copper balls that they tossed from one to another.

'I feel like an ant under a magnifying glass,' Anton said. He couldn't believe Ildirans would come out here to *relax*. 'How can you stand all this sun?'

'It's wonderful, is it not?' The two moved across the shimmering landscape towards a deep, steamy crack in Maratha's crust. 'I may never completely understand your principles of entertainment, but I think you might enjoy seeing the canyons. Their depths are always in shadow, even during the brightest day.'

By now the two historians had spent much time growing closer as friends. Their differences were a source of constant amazement and frequent amusement or consternation. Even so, a few of their similarities – especially on a basic biological level – were quite striking.

After making first contact with old generation ships, some Ildirans had begun to wonder if the human race might be a lost thread of their own galactic epic. But even after Ildiran rememberers learned about Earth history, they remained perplexed. To them, human endeavours appeared to be rambling and unfocused. The account of nations and peoples had too many disparate 'plot strands', a mystifying host of trivial and pointless adventures chronicling the rise and fall of ultimately minor empires. They felt that humans had lost touch with their own story – the human Saga.

At the canyon's edge, a steep trail led down into shadowed cliffbands. From far below, steamy clouds of evaporated moisture rose to where they were trapped by turbulent air currents.

Anton puffed from exertion as they climbed down the slope. The temperature remained oppressive, and now the humidity seemed to permeate his breathing film.

Tucked safely into cracks, Anton saw lovely plants like armoured crustaceans emerging from thick shells. The pearly-walled molluscs extended blooms like sea anemones made of stiffened silica. Some of the petals clacked and spread themselves like fans. Tiny gnat-like flying things drifted in the mists, only to be snapped up by the hungry petals.

Vao'sh reached forward to tap one of the flowers, which clamped shut and withdrew into its telescoping stalk, hiding in the shelter of its pearly shells. 'We call them ch'kanh – living fortresses. When night falls, the flowers enclose their sensitive tissues and hibernate through the cold darkness.'

Deeper down, Anton was astonished at how thick the armoured anemones grew. The hard flowers reached as tall as his shoulders, waving yet eerily silent. He smiled behind the breathing film. 'Isn't it amazing what creatures will do to survive?'

'Desperation often leads to fascinating innovation,' said Vao'sh.

When they finally went back inside Prime through a set of equipment storage rooms, they encountered five Klikiss robots also entering from outside work areas. The robots moved in regimented unison. Their geometrical heads turned; red optical sensors flashed.

As he unsuited, Anton stared at the beetle-like robots. Vao'sh said, 'They have just returned from nightside labours on Maratha Secda. Many Klikiss robots are working at the site in the dark. Never before have they shown such dedication to an Ildiran project.'

Anton peeled off his goggles and rubbed his sweaty face. 'How far along are they over there?'

'Ildiran inspection crews won't be able to see until daylight strikes the construction site. According to the robots, though, the main dome enclosures should be finished before the end of the next full Marathan day cycle.'

The black robots marched into maintenance chambers. Two of the insect-like machines disappeared through hatches that led down into power-generating shafts. They seemed to have access to any area they chose to enter. 'You mean they're building your city all by themselves, without supervision?'

Vao'sh was surprised. 'No Ildiran would go over there in the dark, but the robots can keep working through the night.' He smiled, trying to convince his human companion. 'The robots have been toiling away for more than a decade, and they have followed our plans precisely. They are exceptionally dedicated.'

Anton suddenly brightened with an idea. 'Say, could we go look at Secda? You and I, and maybe a few curious guests, could make an inspection.'

Vao'sh's expression was troubled. 'Thousands of Ildirans come here each year to revel in the constant daylight – and you wish to visit an empty city in the dark?'

Anton clapped him on the shoulder. 'Yes! Doesn't that sound like fun?'

SEVENTY-NINE

PRIME DESIGNATE JORA'H

Assailed by doubts, Jora'h studied the secret history that had been revealed to him. Years ago, he had visited the towering, awesome worldtrees on Theroc, and he had sensed the pulsing mind of interconnected trees as they pondered all that they learned. Had this immense forest once fought the hydrogues?

He thought again of sweet Nira, who had captured his heart. As a green priest, she had carried part of the forest mind within her at all times. She might have been able to discover more about the ancient war for him, if only she had lived. How he longed to have further conversations with her, to feel her skin against his, to look into her bright eyes. If only she had not died in that tragic, accidental fire while he was away on Theroc . . .

Surrounded by mysteries and revelations, Jora'h suddenly sat straighter as an unbidden thought slashed through his mind. Such a *convenient* accident. Such convenient timing.

How much more deceit waited to be uncovered? Had the Mage-Imperator buried the truth in order to protect his son . . . or to better control him?

The diamondfilm sheets fell from Jora'h's hands and slithered to
the floor like an icefall. He was tired of the compounded questions,
the secrets and lies. With stern resolve, the Prime Designate
grabbed up the ancient documents and stalked out of his chambers.
He did not allow himself to waver. He would demand to see his
father and then demand the rest of the truth.

Coloured glass walls blocked the entrance to the Mage-
Imperator's private chambers. Although light streamed through in
different hues, the artistic tints and ripples in the glass created just
enough distortion that no one could see inside.

The muscular bodyguard Bron'n stood outside the entrance,
holding his sharpened crystal katana in front of him. Gruff and
dutiful, Bron'n did not move even when Jora'h approached. 'The
Mage-Imperator cannot be disturbed.'

At another time, Jora'h might have quietly backed away. Now
though, he had no intention of waiting. 'I must see him.'

'His orders were clear, Prime Designate. I am to allow no one
inside.'

Jora'h stood every bit as implacable as the burly guard. 'I will be
your next Mage-Imperator, Bron'n. If there is an important meeting,
then I should attend it.' He leaned forward, and the bodyguard
flinched. 'Or are you suggesting that the Mage-Imperator keeps
secrets from me?'

A storm of confusion crossed Bron'n's face. Just then the
chamber door opened to reveal the stern face of his brother
Udru'h, the Dobro Designate, who was looking at him with
disturbed annoyance. From behind him, the Mage-Imperator's
sonorous voice said, 'Let him in, Bron'n. We must speak with
Jora'h as well.'

Shoring up his resolve, Jora'h strode past the guard into the
chamber and steeled himself as the door closed behind him. These
questions had been too long in the asking. The pale and fleshy

Mage-Imperator slumped in his chrysalis chair, looking terrible. His long braid trembled with palsied unsteadiness, and the pain of his tumours was naked on his face.

But Jora'h could not feel sympathy – not now. Ignoring Udru'h, he held up the documents containing the censored portion of the *Saga*. 'No doubt you had some important reason for showing me this part of our history? Knowing half of an answer only increases the quality of ignorance, Father.'

'Sometimes the truth can be destabilizing,' said the Mage-Imperator. 'Not everyone deserves to have it.'

'The truth is the truth! By what right do you deny Ildirans their heritage?'

'By *my* right. I am the Mage-Imperator, the gateway to the Lightsource. I control the *thism*. I control the truth.' He softened his voice. 'No one but I – and, in a short while, *you* Jora'h – can decide what is best for our people.'

The Dobro Designate moved to his father's side. 'Human folly reawakened the hydrogues, but we have always known they would return. Now perhaps you are ready to understand the essential work we have been doing on Dobro.'

Feeling even more betrayed, Jora'h turned to the Mage-Imperator. 'You kept me in the dark, Father, and yet told *Udru'h* your secrets?'

'Only the secrets he was required to know. Your brother has been responsible for overseeing my most difficult and vital projects on Dobro.'

Udru'h looked smug and proud.

Jora'h maintained a grip on his anger, though he felt as if he were drowning. 'What else have you hidden from me, Father? Tell me' – he paused in a last instant of indecision before reaffirming that he truly wanted to know – 'tell me what really happened to Nira and the other green priest.'

411

'Why would you think that you do not know?' the Dobro Designate said.

Jora'h snapped at his brother, 'Don't play tricks with your words! Tell me. Are they truly dead?'

The Mage-Imperator pondered for a moment. 'The old green priest is truly dead. The treelings are truly burned. The young woman, however, continues to serve the Ildiran Empire. She has a greater purpose.'

A whirlwind of joy and confusion swept through him. 'She's alive! Where is she? I must see her.'

'That wouldn't be wise,' the Dobro Designate said.

Jora'h glared at him. 'You don't make the decisions here, brother.'

The Mage-Imperator seemed amused. 'Oh, tell him, Udru'h. Tell him about everything you do on Dobro. He needs to learn, if he is to become a leader.'

The Designate hesitated, then with a brief nod he complied. 'Nira Khali is not dead, and neither is your child by her.'

'My . . . child?'

'A perfect, healthy daughter with undreamed-of talents, incredible potential. We named her Osira'h. She is now more than six years old.'

As Jora'h stood reeling, the Dobro Designate explained how Nira had been escorted to the breeding camps on Dobro, where for centuries human captives had been the subject of genetic experiments with various Ildiran kiths. 'We have been selective. We managed to enhance certain characteristics and develop Ildiran-human crossbreeds with far superior abilities.'

Stunned, Jora'h hung his head. 'All this has been kept from me . . . my entire life?' How could his heart take any more?

'Jora'h, you will not understand the nuances until you take my place, until you see everything through the crystal-clear lens of *thism*. You do not yet see all the facets.' The Mage-Imperator's expression was placid. 'You must trust me. I have my reasons.'

'I never doubted that you had *reasons*, Father,' Jora'h said, his voice as cold and ragged as fractured ice, 'but I may not agree that those reasons are correct or honourable.'

Cyroc'h tried to explain his rationale, to convince his eldest son and heir. When it was clear he was making no progress, though, the Mage-Imperator said, 'Once you are in my place, you will understand the reasons. *My* reasons.'

But for Jora'h, this terrible deception by his own father had changed everything forever.

EIGHTY

ADAR KORI'NH

The Adar stood in the command nucleus of his lead warliner, frowning in frustration. Defending the Ildiran Empire was the most important thing – not his pride or his desire for vengeance. The Mage-Imperator had instructed him to avoid pointless bravado against the hydrogues. And so he must obey.

Even so, Kori'nh felt *wrong*. Ildirans had waited throughout their history for a worthy foe, building the Solar Navy into a spectacular space fleet in preparation for just such an encounter. Ekti stockpiles had been maintained for centuries. Suspicious humans had questioned why the Ildirans would invest so much time and effort, so many resources, on an interstellar navy when the Empire had never been threatened by an outside force. Yet to him it had been the natural way of things. The Solar Navy should be ready for any challenge.

But the Mage-Imperator had specifically forbidden him to engage the aliens. 'Gather information, Adar, but do not provoke the hydrogues. You may defend our colonies to the best of your abilities, however, if that should prove necessary.'

As he had tried – and failed – to do on Hyrillka.

Under such constraints, Kori'nh had dispatched his maniples on regular patrols across the landscape of the Empire. In six planetary systems, the Adar's primary grouping had run into no difficulties, seen no evidence of the hydrogues. As they passed each gas giant – now unworked by either Ildiran cloud-harvesting cities or smaller Roamer skymines – he wondered how many enemies lurked within those opaque mists.

'We are approaching the Heald system, Adar,' said his navigator.

At Heald, a pair of splinter colonies had recently been consolidated into a single world, where their increased numbers generated a stronger bond through the *thism*.

The Adar said, 'Maintain surveillance. Do not assume an aggressive posture.' The words galled him, and even his crew seemed uneasy with the situation. Would future stanzas of the *Saga* paint him as a coward? 'We must hope the hydrogues leave our people alone.'

The Ildiran warliners glided like a school of fish through empty space. They circled the gas giants in the Heald system, detecting no disturbances as they approached the consolidated splinter colony. When the septa took up stations in orbit, the Heald Designate cheered him. The colonists praised the Solar Navy and thanked them for their support.

If only they knew that his protective fleet could do little to defend the colony should an attack come, they would not be so grateful.

Kori'nh paced the command nucleus. He had pointedly chosen not to wear his most prestigious military decorations. They seemed false to him now, empty. Kori'nh had not earned them through any act of bravery or ingenuity, but simply for his skill in pageantry – for sky dances and military manoeuvres against imaginary enemies.

He had evacuated settlers on Crenna; he had brought relief supplies, constructed public works.

But such things seemed foolishly unimportant to him. In all of Ildiran history, Kori'nh was the first Solar Navy commander to serve during actual wartime. He should have been the grandest Adar ever recorded in the *Saga of Seven Suns*. And yet he had done nothing worthwhile. Nothing.

He thought of eager Tal Zan'nh and felt ashamed. What kind of example was he providing for the Prime Designate's son?

His studies in human military history had introduced him to the exploits of Napoleon, Hannibal, Genghis Khan. True warriors. The Earth Defence Forces, far less impressive than the Solar Navy, continued to prod the hydrogues. And though their skirmishes ended in failure as well, they were not cowed. They never stopped producing creative new weapons systems. Even daredevil Roamers continued to harvest ekti at gas giants despite suffering great losses. Instead of hiding, the humans *tried*, again and again.

The Mage-Imperator, however, had other plans, and Adar Kori'nh had no choice but to follow them. Even so, he felt in his heart that the Solar Navy was too passive and skittish. It was simply *not right*.

EIGHTY-ONE

ESTARRA

Though nothing could compare with the worldforest, Estarra enjoyed the peaceful gardens on Earth. Here, the paths were easy to locate since they were laid down with flagstones. The shrubs and lilies – so carefully manicured, watered, fertilized – were exquisite. So far, though, Estarra had found nothing *wild* in the sprawling arboretum, not even an unexpected weed.

The Whisper Palace was filled with marvels, but she couldn't go anywhere without attendants and guards and protectors and curious functionaries. Now Estarra wished she'd had the foresight to appreciate her younger days of freedom while they lasted.

Perhaps she would go find Nahton and send a message back home to her little sister Celli. 'Pay attention to what you have. Run through the forest, continue your treedancing lessons. Appreciate Theroc for all it offers.' But her rambunctious sister probably wouldn't listen.

Estarra watched a jade-green beetle crawl into the trumpet-shaped end of a morning glory. She listened to the fanspray of irrigation systems. When she heard footsteps on the path, she refused to look up, wondering what the guards would do if she tried to elude them by sprinting through the foliage.

But that would be a pointless gesture. They would catch her and possibly further curtail her freedom of movement, such as it was. No, if she was going to be Queen, she would have to behave differently.

'I might have known you'd be moping here,' said Sarein. When she was off-duty, Estarra's sister made no attempt to wear traditional Theron scarves or cocoon-fibre cloth.

'I'm enjoying the Palace gardens. How can you call that moping?'

Sarein squatted beside her, looking sternly at the entwined morning glories. 'What is wrong, little sister? I've been watching you ever since we arrived on Earth. Your gloom isn't helping things, you know.'

Estarra was surprised. 'I haven't been—'

'You're not exactly ecstatic, anybody can see that. The marriage of a King and Queen must be a joyous occasion, or there's no political purpose to it.'

Estarra frowned. 'Is that all you worry about? My "political purpose"?'

'Of course not. But you are starting a new life here, and you're making no effort to adjust to it. What's wrong with Peter? He's a nice enough young man, and certainly handsome. Wealthy, powerful . . .'

Indeed, the King seemed genuinely interested in Estarra's welfare and happiness. But after observing him, she suspected that Peter had as little freedom as she did. 'I didn't say anything was wrong with him, Sarein. How can I know? I've never been allowed even five minutes to talk with him alone.'

'Everything will happen according to schedule. Then you'll

have all the time you want alone together.' Her sister gave a frustrated sigh. 'Estarra, if you were the daughter of a juice harvester, you could do as you please. But you're going to be the *Queen of the Terran Hanseatic League.* You're about to marry a King. You'll have more wealth for your personal use than Theroc generates in a year.' She shook her head. 'What is there to be sad about in all of that?'

Estarra needed to make peace with her sister, who was her only tenuous connection with home. 'Don't worry, Sarein – I wasn't complaining. But I do wish I had more of a chance to get to know Peter. We're getting married in three months, after all.'

Sarein stood, satisfied that she had got through to her younger sister. 'I'll see what I can do. Let me talk to Basil. Maybe you and Peter can have dinner together more often.'

'Even a midnight snack would be nice.'

Sarein shook her head again, but her expression now held a hint of amusement. 'Estarra, the Great King of the Terran Hanseatic League is not allowed to have something as simple as a "midnight snack". Every luncheon is a banquet, every meal is a production.'

She took two steps down the path, then looked back with a benevolent sigh. 'But maybe I can bribe the kitchen staff to sneak out a few sandwiches that the two of you can eat together.'

EIGHTY-TWO

KING PETER

At times when he felt overwhelmed, Peter believed that only the Teacher compy gave him truly objective and honest responses. He stood by the window in his spacious private chamber, staring out at the Royal Canal. 'Your thoughts, OX? You've been coaching Estarra in courtly ways. Is she a good student?'

'An excellent student. She takes instruction well.'

'Then that isn't what's bothering you. I can hear the circuits sizzling in your mental core.'

'I am developing speculations concerning the new Soldier compies,' OX said. 'However, I have insufficient data to verify my conclusions. Therefore, I am continuing to assess potential scenarios.'

Peter gave the small compy a wry smile. 'In other words, you have a hunch, but you haven't convinced yourself to lay it on the line.'

'That is . . . an adequate translation.' The compy paused, as if calculating. 'I have analysed the design modifications we derived from our study of Jorax and implemented in the manufacturing process of the new-model compies. I find many of the details to be . . . ambiguous at best.'

'I don't understand it either,' Peter said, 'but the compies seem to be functioning properly. They've passed all tests so far.'

'While they may have passed all tests the Hansa chose to perform, King Peter, I have determined that none of the cybernetic engineers can fully explain the new modules they have installed into the Soldier compies. They have not deconstructed the programming from first principles, but are simply copying existing Klikiss technology with direct assistance from the Klikiss robots. Such ignorance leaves much room for potential problems.'

Peter frowned with grave concern. 'But new Soldier compies have already been loaded aboard the main fleet for Osquivel – if you've got proof that we don't understand the modifications we made, then we'd better act quickly. The battle group is already on its way.'

'I have no proof of any specific failings, King Peter – only questions,' OX said. 'We do not know the full capabilities of these Soldier compies. Klikiss programming is an enigma to me. As a Teacher, I always urged you to question what you do not understand. I should follow my own instructions.'

Peter looked at the Teacher robot. 'Believe me, OX, you're not the only one who questions these things.'

'It is not my place to question industrial processes or decisions made by Chairman Wenceslas.'

Peter frowned. 'It is your role to give me fair and straightforward advice. I'm afraid the Chairman is not capable of objectively weighing the potential consequences of adopting technology that we don't understand, but I'll . . . talk to him about it.'

*

The day before Basil Wenceslas departed for the EDF base on Mars to monitor the Osquivel offensive, Peter hurried to a strategy meeting in Hansa HQ. It was only a small discussion with important military and economic advisers, but Peter was bothered that Basil hadn't told him about it. He was tired of being treated as irrelevant.

He took a deep breath and entered the room, chin high, interrupting the conversations. 'You may begin the meeting now, gentlemen. I apologize if I kept you waiting. I presume you discussed nothing of importance until I could be present?'

He looked directly at the Chairman, and an irritated expression crossed Basil's face. No one answered him, but the advisers waited until the King took an empty seat, mentally realigning the table so that he sat at its head.

The Chairman said, 'General Lanyan's offensive fleet will arrive at the target system early tomorrow. According to plan, the EDF will spend a day preparing for the operation, and I will monitor the situation from Mars. Green priest contacts will relay real-time reports from Osquivel – no matter what happens there.'

Basil projected a diagram that outlined the complements of the enormous battlegroup on its way to Osquivel, the number of Remoras and Mantas crewed by Soldier compies, and the general outline for the attack, should Robb Brindle's attempts at communication fail.

Peter absorbed all the details. His predecessor had never paid attention to anything but his ceremonial role, letting the Hansa determine all political matters, while he simply acted as a mouthpiece. Peter, though, had always taken a careful interest. If he had to be spokesman for the Hansa's decisions and apologize for the mistakes and claim credit for the triumphs, then he deserved some input into the process.

Remembering what OX had said to him about the Klikiss technology, Peter now raised his doubts. 'Gentlemen, I am concerned that we are placing far too much reliance on our new Soldier compies at such a crucial juncture. Apparently, even our cybernetic engineers don't fully comprehend the modified programming they've installed, but we're happy to copy it and put it to use. Doesn't that bother anyone else?'

Basil looked as if his patience had reached its end. 'Peter, rest assured that there is nothing you have thought about, no concern you could possibly raise, that I haven't already considered.' He drummed his fingers on the tabletop, noticing that some of the other advisers obviously held similar concerns. Sighing, the Chairman gave a more detailed answer.

'We *know* the hydrogues are our greatest threat. We *know* the EDF has been ineffective so far in fighting them. We *know* that we're running out of ekti. Can we afford to turn down a chance to dramatically increase our military abilities and technological foundation because of a baseless fear that the Klikiss robots might have some sinister ulterior motives? The hydrogues are bad enough. We don't need to go looking for other enemies.'

'I agree that EDF strategy has accomplished little thus far, Mr Chairman,' Peter said with a thin smile. 'But focusing on one threat doesn't excuse being blind to another.'

A flare of genuine anger crossed Basil's face. 'And what would you do, King Peter? Lead a public rally and hope the hydrogues go away feeling ashamed of what they've done? You insist on attending these strategy meetings, and never hesitate to provide your inane input.'

'Yes, Basil, and you have always declined to implement anything I propose.' Peter held them all with his hard gaze. 'I suggest that we look into Soldier compy production, have our best programmers analyse the code built into those new machines, shut down the production lines until we're confident we aren't creating our own Trojan horse.'

'Shut down production lines? Preposterous!' said the Director of Industry.

'Another wonderful, useful suggestion,' Basil said sarcastically. 'We can't afford to stop production of the Soldier compies . . . especially when we don't know what's going to happen at Osquivel. If we are defeated there, the EDF will need to replace a large part of our force.'

Peter felt himself growing more upset. 'If anyone else here had suggested the same thing, you would have listened to it.'

Now the Chairman stood, more stressed than Peter had ever seen him. 'No one else would have made such a ridiculous suggestion. I'm leaving for Mars within a few hours. I already have enough crises to deal with, and I don't need a petulant King on top of it all. You will stay away from the compy factories. Period. Do you understand? And if you insist on interfering with our discussions, I'll have you barred from these meetings henceforth.'

Peter couldn't believe what he was hearing. 'And which guards are going to prevent *me* from going where I wish to go?'

Basil played the part of stern parent. 'I don't have time for this, so don't push me. If you continue to cause trouble, you can be replaced entirely, Peter.'

Every adviser in the small room drew a sharp breath.

Peter remained calm. 'Not legally, Mr Chairman. I've read the Hansa Charter very carefully. You may be in control, but the trillions of citizens across the Hansa worlds barely know who you are. I am their King, whether you like it or not – are you ready to stage a military coup to strip me of my crown? Or do you plan to send a quiet assassin into my bedchamber one night? That's what it would take.' His eyes narrowed. 'In fact, Basil, of the two of us, only *you*, the Chairman of the Hanseatic League, can be impeached and legally removed from his position. Not the King.'

Basil bellowed, 'Get him out of here!'

Royal guards came forward, looking flustered, unsure of whose orders to obey. The Hansa officials here knew the King was just a puppet, but what about the guards, the Palace workers, the rest of his subjects?

Peter decided not to press the issue, not wanting to learn the guards' ultimate loyalties. Before Basil could insist, the King departed willingly. Neither of them had won, but the Chairman had made his threat clear enough, bringing it out into the open at last. And Basil, in turn, had seen that the King was not so willing to back down.

Now everyone understood that the rules had changed.

EIGHTY-THREE

ROSSIA

When the intimidating EDF assault force arrived above the rings of Osquivel, all scanners were dispatched, probes and scout ships released to study the system and plan the operation. They already knew the hydrogues lurked down there, somewhere beneath the clouds. Now the EDF just had to flush them out.

Aboard the huge flagship *Goliath*, General Lanyan announced, 'This is not a test. We're on a dangerous mission. I hope you're all prepared for it.' His chin was square, his knuckles white, his eyes like fire.

To the green priest Rossia, the dangers had always seemed real. Once he'd learned of the long-standing antagonism between the hydrogues and the worldforest, the threat had become much more tangible. And now they were going directly into a nest of the destructive creatures. *The ancient enemies.*

The trees had nearly been obliterated long ago by the hydrogues, and the worldforest had no desire to fight again. Reluctantly, it seemed, the trees were willing to participate in this action, hoping to communicate with the enemy. But Rossia felt little hope.

Isolated on Theroc, the worldforest had been passive, fearing to reignite the conflict . . . but now the hydrogues were obviously looking for them, destroying any forested world in their search. Rossia could sense uneasiness throughout the worldforest. The last surviving worldtrees had hidden from the hydrogues for ten thousand years. More recently the trees had begun to flourish and spread to other planets.

Perhaps Wing Commander Brindle could achieve what he hoped. But Rossia doubted it.

Fidgeting, the green priest sat in a cold polymer chair surrounded by hard metal controls. He kept his beloved treeling at his station. Though the potted plant seemed a strange anachronism against the backdrop of the EDF's computerized technology, ironically Rossia's telink connection was more efficient than any other system aboard the *Goliath*.

On the Juggernaut's bridge, Lanyan made every effort to present a brave and confident front. 'We will make a final diplomatic attempt. If that fails, we'll test our new Soldier compies and show the drogues that we mean business.'

Lanyan looked at Rossia. 'Also, our instant real-time contact with Chairman Wenceslas and our strategists back on Mars will give us the edge. We are on the way to our biggest victory in this war.'

'And what if the mission doesn't work?' Rossia asked.

'If it doesn't work, then none of us will be in a position to care.'

Watching the military preparations and reading the mood of the troops, Rossia got a clear sense that, though their intent was ostensibly to parley, they were expecting a fight. *Expecting it.* His heart fluttered at the thought.

The pale yellow clouds of Osquivel looked like a pool of spilled buttermilk, unlike anything Rossia had ever seen on Theroc. Down there, lurking in the ringed giant's soup of gases, were predators far more deadly than any wyvern.

Rossia stroked the scaled trunk of his treeling. Through telink, he connected into the trees, found his counterparts aboard other EDF battleships dispersed across the ten Grids, the other priests at home on Theroc, and Yarrod, monitoring all the activity on the Mars base. He sent his thoughts, received an acknowledgement.

'General, Yarrod says that everyone is ready on Mars. Chairman Wenceslas has arrived and is waiting to hear from us.'

Lanyan nodded, glad for the proof of a direct response. 'Keep them up to date on what we're doing.'

With quick, vivid words Rossia described everything he saw, painting a portrait of the unusual planet with its startlingly beautiful rings. The mind of the worldforest absorbed everything, disseminating the knowledge to its far-flung trees, wherever they had spread.

Rossia rubbed the tiny goosebumps on his arms. Traditionally, priests wore little clothing so they could walk where the tree fronds might brush against the sensory receptors on their skin. Here, though, he wore a standard short-sleeved EDF uniform, just to stay warm enough to do his work. The *Goliath* was always cold, the air sterile.

'Compy scouts deployed, sir,' said an officer. Rossia could never keep track of the confusing ranks or insignias.

The green priest went to the nearest windowport to watch the fast ships race ahead of the battlegroup and skim over Osquivel's poles. The robot-guided Remoras were no more than tiny dots against the veils of mist.

Lanyan said, 'Make sure they're dispersed deep enough into the cloud layers to give us sufficient warning of hydrogue proximity. Our remote sensors never seem to work right, so let's hope these compies can do a better job.'

The rugged Soldier compies were designed to survive at high pressures and temperatures, able to go deeper than any human scout could. If necessary, the compy scouts would keep descending until Osquivel's atmosphere crushed their vessels, and they would continue transmitting until the end.

'Green priest, tell the Mars command centre we're beginning Phase One.' Lanyan impatiently gestured to the potted treeling.

Rossia blinked his round eyes, then touched the scaled trunk and spoke again through telink. Every other green priest in telink received the message simultaneously – at the Whisper Palace on Earth, at the base on Mars, on warships across the Spiral Arm, and back on Theroc.

'The Chairman says to go ahead.'

Lanyan stood on his bridge, drawing deep breaths. Finally, satisfied, he nodded. 'All right, prepare the encounter vessel and summon Wing Commander Brindle to the launch deck. Let's give diplomacy one last chance – and then, be prepared for anything.'

EIGHTY-FOUR

BASIL WENCESLAS

In the command-and-control centre at the Mars EDF base, the Hansa Chairman paced, waiting for things to happen at Osquivel. He wore a business suit not because he had anyone to impress but because that was how he felt most comfortable. He glanced expectantly at the green priest who had remained on Mars to send and receive messages from General Lanyan's battlegroup.

'They are in position, preparing for the initial phase,' Yarrod reported after consulting his treeling. 'The ships will begin taking their places according to plan. No contact yet with the hydrogues.'

'Tell them to proceed,' Basil said, knowing it would now take an hour or more before the next significant event. And then – maybe – all hell would break loose.

So far, the operation had been a smoothly coordinated military drill: the new Soldier compies, the green priest communicators, the well-trained EDF soldiers. Everything seemed perfect. But Basil was never lulled into complacency.

Though he had not wanted to discourage his advisers, Basil had realized from the start that sending a man down in an armoured diving bell to open negotiations with these enemies was a token gesture at best. The hydrogues had already proved their malicious *alienness*. Civilized diplomacy was not effective under such circumstances. Still, didn't they need to make the attempt, for the sake of history?

'Keep me posted,' he said and left the command-and-control centre.

He walked down the corridors. A ubiquitous grit covered the walls, and the air had a disagreeable rusty smell from Mars's iron oxides. To Basil, the base always seemed to hold a permeating chill, though the thermostats insisted that the ambient temperature was exactly what he was accustomed to. He didn't believe them.

Amidst the bustle of activity, he was glad to see all the soldiers going about their duties on a heightened alert status without descending to chaos or disorganization. He was proud of them.

Inside the base supply depot, cargo haulers dropped from large transports in orbit to the crater openings, delivering food, equipment, and other materiel. Daily business went on even as the big assault was staged in a far-off system. Basil watched distractedly as the last loads were removed from a delivery shuttle. A small compy emerged carrying a final container of processed metals – not a standard military model nor one of the new Soldier compies. This looked like the kind of servant compy used by Roamers.

The compy marched up to the corporal in charge of supplies and spoke in a synthesized feminine voice. 'Compy designation EA, returning to service.'

'Where have you been?' the corporal said. 'You were on our duty roster two weeks ago.'

'I was on a priority assignment from my master,' EA said.

Curious, Basil stepped into the loading dock. 'One moment, Corporal. Am I to understand that we have a Roamer compy working for us?'

The corporal looked up at him with a frown, as if wondering why a civilian in a business suit would intrude in a secure area. 'And who are you, sir? This is a restricted—'

'I am Chairman Wenceslas of the Terran Hanseatic League.' Basil enjoyed the brief scepticism, then surprised recognition on the corporal's face.

'Yes, Mr Chairman! Excuse me, I didn't know you were here on base.'

'You should keep up with current events. I'm certain a notice was distributed among all personnel.' From the way the corporal clutched his electronic clipboard, Basil could see that he was not a man who made decisions, but simply followed instructions. Basil waited a beat, then said, 'I asked you a question, Corporal. Is it common practice to allow Roamer compies into secure areas? You challenge *my* presence, yet you allow full access to a Roamer machine?'

The corporal looked around as if hoping to invoke a superior officer, but found no one else in the cargo bay. 'Sir, EA has worked at the base for five years. Her owner is an officer in the Grid 7 battlefleet.'

Basil frowned, processing the information. 'I see. And when her owner is not here, you allow this Roamer compy to wander around the base, perhaps taking images, assessing EDF weaknesses?'

The corporal was clearly baffled. 'Are we at war with the Roamers, sir? I thought they were the only ones currently delivering ekti supplies. Without them, we'd have no stardrive fuel at all.'

'Allies and enemies do not always fall into clearcut categories, Corporal. One must never be complacent, especially during wartime.' Basil knew he was overreacting because of his anxiety about the Osquivel offensive. True, the fiercely independent clans had made no obvious moves against the Hansa, but neither did they have Earth's best interests in mind.

Roamer compies were rarely seen in the Hansa, although occasionally they rode aboard gypsy ships that came in to trade with the colonies. He saw an opportunity here to gain some leverage. 'I will take responsibility for this compy, Corporal. If you have any questions, you can refer the matter to your officer in charge.'

'Yes . . . yes, sir.'

Basil turned to the compy, recognizing an unusual opportunity. Few people had the opportunity to speak to a Roamer compy without a Roamer present. 'Follow me, EA. Let's go have a chat.'

'Yes, sir.'

He led EA out of the loading dock into an empty room that contained a table and some comm screens, obviously a subsidiary office for off-duty personnel. 'Very well, tell me where you have been.'

'My owner dispatched me with instructions to attend to a family matter.'

'All right.' Basil steepled his fingers. 'But where did you go?'

'I went where my owner instructed me to go. I am forbidden to divulge specifics to any member of the Hansa.'

Warning bells went off in Basil mind. So, the compy had received specific programming to keep secrets from the Terran Hanseatic League? He had long suspected that the unruly Roamers were either overtly or unconsciously acting against the Hansa. They had not signed the Charter. They did not follow the League's laws, snubbing the rest of human civilization. Their way of life seemed rather primitive, a group of homeless clans. Why were they so mysterious?

In the past several years, numerous undocumented Roamer cargo ships had been intercepted by EDF patrols. All were found to be carrying stockpiles of ekti, though the EDF had a standing request for all available stardrive fuel. How could they justify selling to any other customers over the Hansa military? He had no doubt that the Roamers were holding out.

He pondered his next question. 'EA, I'm giving you a direct command. Your owner is not here, and your programming requires you to follow the instructions of any human who commands you.'

'So long as it does not directly harm other humans,' EA said. 'And so long as it does not directly contradict prior instructions given to me by my owner.'

'You have returned from your personal mission, so therefore you've completed your instructions. Correct?'

EA paused. 'I have completed my most recent mission, yes.'

Basil smiled. 'Good, then we don't have to worry about that.' Compies were not overly bright or flexible. He would start out with basic information, facts that he could have obtained from the compy owner's EDF file anyway. 'Your owner is an officer in the Earth Defence Forces?'

'Yes, she is the commander of a Manta cruiser.'

Basil raised his eyebrows. Not many Roamers had volunteered for service. Ah, perhaps it was Commander Tamblyn, who had been quite an asset during the Boone's Crossing debacle. Was she a mole inside the military? How much important information did she have access to? It made him uneasy, but with this compy, perhaps he could establish some background details. 'Your owner is a Roamer, correct? Commander Tamblyn?'

'Yes.'

'What planet does she come from?'

EA remained oddly silent. 'I cannot divulge that information.'

Basil was astonished. 'You can't tell me what planet she's from? That is absurd. It must be in all of her personnel records. What work does this clan Tamblyn do? What facilities or ships do they operate?'

The compy stood stiffly. 'I am sorry, sir. I cannot answer those questions.'

'Yes you can. I insist. In fact, this is a direct command.'

To Basil's utter surprise, glimmers of sparks showed behind EA's eyes. Her mechanical arms jittered a bit, and then she slumped into frozen silence. All the indicator lights on her artificial face died.

'EA – respond.' Impatient, Basil went to the compy and touched her metal body. The core was hot. Had the internal circuitry melted down? It looked as if all systems had crashed. 'What the hell? You did that on purpose!' He looked around the room, as if checking to see whether anyone had watched him. 'I don't believe this.'

He scowled, deep in thought. His questions had been relatively innocuous, but apparently the Roamer compy had some sort of built-in fail-safe mechanism. Any interrogation about Roamer activities or the location of bases triggered a permanent and irrevocable shutdown, a total memory wipe and program erasure. Very disturbing.

He bumped EA, and the frozen compy tottered, struck the metal wall, then slid to the floor with a crash.

What were the Roamers doing that they would need to implement such drastic measures in order to maintain their secrets? He gritted his teeth, making a low growling sound. 'What are you hiding?' he demanded, but the robot could make no response.

A breathless lieutenant ran past the door, then, noticing Basil inside the room, stopped and turned. 'Chairman Wenceslas, your presence is needed in the command-and-control centre. We've been looking all over for you—'

'I'm here,' Basil said, his voice firm. He straightened his suit. 'What's happened?'

'General Lanyan is ready to launch the encounter vessel at Osquivel.'

Basil nodded. Time to concentrate on the more important business at hand. 'Well, he has my blessing. Tell him to get on with it.'

He took one step towards the door, then looked at the fallen, motionless compy. 'Oh, and Lieutenant – get someone to clean this up.' He nudged EA's metal body with the toe of his shoe. 'Store it somewhere for later analysis.'

EIGHTY-FIVE

TASIA TAMBLYN

As the ships in the EDF battle fleet took their assigned positions over Osquivel, Tasia anxiously studied the readings from the tactical analysis probes. She tried not to show her keen interest, but luckily nothing seemed amiss. She saw no obvious sign of Del Kellum's flourishing shipyards. No spurious readings from the rings attracted any attention. Though she had not heard from her devoted compy, EA's warning message must have arrived in time.

Tasia let out a long, cold sigh and thanked her Guiding Star. One emergency solved. Now she could concentrate on the problem of Robb Brindle.

'General Lanyan, sir,' she said with a quick salute on the bridge of the *Goliath*. 'Request permission to go to the launching bay and inspect the encounter vessel.'

He scratched his square chin. 'To what purpose, Commander? Don't you have duties aboard your own ship?'

'I would . . . I'd like to have a word with Wing Commander Brindle before he's dispatched on his mission.' She swallowed hard, hoping the emotions didn't show on her face. *Not that I could ever talk sense into him.*

On the other side of the bridge, Patrick Fitzpatrick smirked. 'She wants to give him a goodbye kiss, General.'

Lanyan glanced from Fitzpatrick's sarcastic expression to Tasia's flush of embarrassment, as if unexpected pieces had fallen into place. 'Permission granted – but don't be too long at it. Wing Commander Brindle should be using this time to prepare himself, and you should be getting back aboard your cruiser. I need all of my fleet commanders in top shape, their minds sharp.'

She hurried away from the stares of the bridge crew; some showed her sympathy, some only knowing smiles. Everyone tacitly assumed Robb's attempt to communicate with the hydrogues would fail. He had undergone a month of intensive diplomacy training, but no one could be sure how the drogues would react to the overture. It was a political nicety, and the optimistic young officer would probably be the sacrificial lamb.

Brindle, your Guiding Star must be a brown dwarf . . .

Tasia took a lift down to the launching bay and found it crowded with eager Eddie soldiers watching the final preparations. Robb's EDF uniform was immaculate (as if the hydrogues might be impressed with clothes). He couldn't hide his foolishly proud grin as he stood in front of the experimental encounter vessel.

It looked like an old deep-sea diving bell, a spherical ship with armoured walls and manoeuvring systems that could operate even under the extreme pressures he would find deep in the gas giant. Small round windows of polymer-reinforced crystal slugs dotted the exterior walls, providing views from all angles.

The encounter vessel was strictly for opening a line of communication, not to threaten the hydrogues. Robb had tested it, become proficient in its systems; he claimed the encounter vessel flew with all the finesse of a brick, but it would do what was

necessary. The vessel contained no defences at all — not that any
standard weapon would have proved effective against a diamond-
hulled warglobe.

Tasia wanted to run forward and embrace him, but she couldn't
do that in front of the other Eddies. Everyone whistled and
applauded, shouting encouragement and congratulations. Robb
grinned at her, his honey-brown eyes flashing. He raised a hand,
but Tasia was afraid to speak, for fear of losing the tight control she
had on her emotions.

The night before, she and Robb had arranged their off-shifts to
coincide. He meant to get a good night's sleep before his mission,
but Tasia didn't intend to let him sleep much at all. Unfortunately,
she and Robb got into an argument that degenerated into a genuine
fight, fed by their mutual anxiety. It wasn't how she'd expected to
spend the evening.

'I'm not going to be a coward,' Robb said. 'The EDF is depending on me. And nobody else is qualified — not now.'

'Nobody is qualified, period. Look, I'm not averse to taking
risks. Shizz, I'm a *Roamer*, Brindle. I always lived on the calculated
edge of risk. But this is just plain suicide. We have no reason to
expect it'll work.'

'Hey, I'm not ready to give up all hope. You know if this turns
into an all-out shooting war between humans and hydrogues, we're
gonna get our asses kicked.' He tried to melt her with a grin. 'Okay,
I admit this isn't the safest plan.'

'Why did it have to be you? I don't want to lose you,' she said,
then caught herself.

Her father had been a harsh taskmaster, showing little warmth,
and Tasia had barely known her mother. For companionship, she'd
had her brothers, but both Jess and Ross were much older and she
had needed to be rough-and-tumble to hold her own against them.

During that night with Robb, whom she really cared for, she felt terrified. Tasia made foolish accusations, but Robb didn't look hurt. Instead, he took her into his arms and gentled her. Then they made love with a mixture of sweetness and desperation, one of the best times they'd ever had together.

In the morning, the duty clock went off much too soon, and they both barely had time to scramble into their uniforms and take their places. In a silent and pointed decision, neither of them said goodbye to the other . . .

Now, in the launching bay, engineers and flight sergeants pushed the curious soldiers back. 'Give the man room to breathe. He's gotta climb inside his spacious new accommodations.'

'Go get 'em, Brindle,' someone shouted.

Before he climbed into the diving bell, Robb touched his fingers to his brow in a silent, warm salute meant for Tasia alone. She blinked away a sudden excess of moisture in her eyes.

Then, oblivious to the EDF soldiers, Rossia limped forward to the hatch, cradling his potted treeling in one arm. 'Wait, Wing Commander. I have something for you to take.' He held his free hand under one of the drooping fronds of the palmlike tree, and a small leafed branch dropped into it, as if on command. 'You are not a green priest, so you can't use the tree to communicate . . . but I believe it may still do your heart good.'

Robb took the frond and looked curiously at it. 'I get it, like an olive branch?'

The priest shrugged. 'Perhaps. Or perhaps you can draw comfort from it. Who knows what the worldforest can do?'

Robb tucked the frond into the breast pocket of his uniform, like a boutonnière. 'Thanks.' His duty done, the green priest backed away and returned to his station before the General could call to him.

'Prepare to launch encounter vessel,' the staff sergeant shouted.

'Okay, I'm ready to go hot-rodding,' Robb said.

Over the intercom from the bridge, General Lanyan said, 'Wing Commander Brindle, this is a brave thing you're doing. We didn't want this war, and we must pursue every avenue to peace. Go talk some sense into those drogues.'

The soldiers cheered again, and two EDF engineers sealed the heavy hatch, then pressurized the interior, checking the chamber's hull integrity one last time. After cycling through the drop chamber, the encounter vessel fell like a smooth metal egg out of the bay.

Lanyan's voice came over the intercom. 'I want the fleet to stand at high alert. All officers, return to your respective fighting ships. Let's not get caught with our pants down again.'

Eddies scrambled to their stations. With a heavy but determined heart, Tasia boarded a small shuttle that took her and three other assigned officers back to her Manta.

'Still descending without incident,' Robb transmitted. The entire battle fleet listened to his updates. 'The atmosphere is getting thicker, and I detect a spike in temperature. Wind velocity increasing.' He grunted with a sudden effort, and they could hear the thumping shear of wind. 'It's like trying to sit still on top of a restless cat.'

When Tasia arrived back on her cruiser's command deck, she checked with the acting commander. The battleships had already received dispersal orders and positioning information. Ten enhanced Juggernaut-class battleships and fifty Manta cruisers – a dozen of which were automated and crewed by the new Soldier-model compies – waited above the planet.

Tasia took the seat from her acting officer. 'Play Wing Commander Brindle's transmissions loud enough for us all to hear.'

'Still no contact, though I'm zapping my standard message on all bands,' Brindle said. 'I see swirling colours in these dense gases. Not much else.' Crackles of static infiltrated his signal as he descended farther into the hostile environment. 'Really getting thrown around here. Didn't people use to go over waterfalls in a barrel? That's what this feels like.'

Patrick Fitzpatrick dropped his Manta down into a lead position close to Osquivel's atmosphere, as if spoiling for a fight. 'We're all ready for a little aggressive diplomacy here, General, if the circumstances call for it.' Lanyan did not chastise his golden boy for moving out of position.

'There, I've switched on all of the bright beams,' Robb said. 'Someone should see me. Hello?'

Tasia hoped that the lights didn't attract some giant leviathan in the clouds.

Then Robb fell silent for ten agonizing minutes. Concerned, the communications officers sent queries, trying to reestablish contact. Tasia looked at the depth gauges to see how deep the encounter vessel had gone. Her uneasy crew fidgeted, biting their lips or fingernails. The silence dragged on.

Finally, in a crackle laced with loud background static, Robb sent another message. '. . . amazing! I can see . . . never imagined anything like it.' A long pause with another roar of static. 'It's beautiful . . . *beautiful* # # #.'

A swell of white noise flooded the communication channel. Tasia listened to the rapid-fire transmissions from the flagship. General Lanyan's best communications officers tried several times to reestablish contact, but were unsuccessful.

'All contact lost with the encounter vessel, General. Sensors show no trace of it, at any depth.'

'Did it crumple from atmospheric pressure, or did the drogues destroy it?'

'No way of telling, sir.'

Tasia sat in her command chair, wild with grief and fury, swallowing deep breaths. *Robb!* She hammered the communication link, 'General, we should send a scout after him! How about some of the Soldier compies? They could dive down there and drag the encounter vessel back up to safety.'

Robb had to be alive somehow.

Then an alarmed Lieutenant Ramirez cried out, 'Drogue activity spotted down below, Commander! Two compy scout Remoras reported destroyed.'

Over the primary channel, Lanyan shouted, 'That's our answer, then. Nobody can say we didn't try. Prepare for a full-scale offensive! You know the drill. Hold nothing back.'

EIGHTY-SIX

TASIA TAMBLYN

As the squadron of Manta cruisers charged forward, Commander Fitzpatrick spoke flippantly over the com, 'All right, let's go get some payback for our friend Robb Brindle.'

Fighting back her paralysing grief and shock, Tasia wanted to strangle him – Fitzpatrick had never been Robb's friend – but she would deal with the real enemies first. Damn the hydrogues!

Another compy Remora had been destroyed, and the warglobes continued to rise through the deep cloud layers. The EDF was ready . . . or so they believed.

Mentally, Tasia clutched a glimmer of hope – what if Robb was still down there, unable to transmit? But the drogues had established their pattern of behaviour time and again. They had wrecked three compy-crewed scout Remoras just moments ago. Almost certainly, the enemy aliens had grabbed or destroyed the armoured diving bell.

Just as she had known they would . . .

She drew a deep breath, counted backwards from ten to control

444

her roller-coaster of grief and anger, then finally said with forced calm, 'Stations, everybody. No itchy fingers – and no wasted shots, either.'

Deep inside, her heart clamoured for Robb. Once the EDF bombardment started, she could not hold out any hope for him. But there was no way to stop it. She wasn't sure she wanted to. 'Let's make those bastards *hurt*.'

From the *Goliath*'s bridge, General Lanyan checked on the Mantas, his human-crewed Remoras, his survey satellites, and scan technicians. 'Dispatch three robot cruisers in the vanguard. It's time to see what sort of return we get on our investment.'

A computer technician transferred specific orders to the Soldier compies aboard the battleships. Prior to the mission, all commanders had received their detailed deployment instructions; they knew the first phases of the attack plan. Tasia's stomach lurched, as if she was falling into a very bad situation.

Lanyan barked, 'Next, Thunderheads down. Take up positions and prepare to deploy your heaviest bombs. Keep the fracture-pulse drones in reserve until we can see what we're aiming at.' The weapons platforms spread out like giant floating sea mines in the outer layers of Osquivel's atmosphere. 'Platcoms, commence your bombardment.'

Like a high-energy rain, bombs showered out of the Thunderheads. Reaching their preset depth, the fuses activated, and immense eruptions shuddered through the atmospheric levels. The explosions were meant to rattle the hydrogues and flush them out of their deep strongholds. But according to the destroyed scouts, the warglobes were already coming.

Tasia clenched her hands until the nails bit into her palms, waiting for her cruiser to be called into play.

'Second phase,' Lanyan ordered, as if reading from a script and watching a chronometer. 'Primary compy wing, disperse Remoras and engage the enemy if you find them. Compy Mantas, close in.'

The new Soldier-model compies could fly their attack fighters at higher accelerations and turn under heavier G-forces than any human pilot. Since they required no life-support systems, more power could be diverted to the jazer banks.

One hundred of the fast fighters dived deep, while shockwaves from the initial bombardment continued to reverberate through the cloud decks. The Remoras streaked out like deadly silver projectiles, seeking targets. Telemetry came back as the diligent robots reported their positions.

When the Soldier compies arrived at the depth where Robb had disappeared, one by one, the deep scout vessels reported enemy warglobes rising up. Then each signal broke off. *Just like Robb's did.*

Lanyan clenched his teeth. 'Where are they?' He looked down at the disturbed clouds still swirling from the initial bombardment.

At his station, Rossia described the events quickly into the telink network, 'I see a glow, like lightning . . . something much larger than the *Goliath*. Flashing lights, power discharges. Ah, they've emerged from the clouds now! Very frightening.' He shuddered with the instinctive revulsion of the worldforest, which was communicated to him through his treeling.

A swarm of warglobes rose up, the giant spheres accompanied by smaller vessels like clustered grapeshot. Across the comm channels, EDF soldiers howled with bravado laced with fear. They had never seen such an incredible force of hydrogues.

The first three compy-crewed Mantas moved to intercept without hesitation. They opened fire, blasting before the hydrogues could strike.

'Numerous jazer impacts, but no significant damage.' Rossia's gaze flicked back and forth. 'The bolts hurt my eyes.'

'Deploy carbon slammers!'

The cruisers dropped clusters of the new-design weapons, which fell like depth-charges. When they drifted close to the hydrogue spheres, the slammers exploded with a focused jack-hammer blow of force against the diamond armour, designed to break carbon-carbon bonds. Several enemy targets spun, obviously disoriented from the unexpected blast.

Before the soldiers could cheer, though, blue lightning crackled from the undamaged warglobes, striking the closest robotic Manta and ripping open its hull.

'Direct hit from the hydrogues! One of our compy cruisers is damaged.' Rossia sounded like an old sports announcer trying to relay the excitement of a visual game. 'It is just as horrific as the worldforest's memories of the old war.'

But the wounded robot Manta continued forward, blasting with all its remaining weapons. Lanyan sounded proud. 'Look! The Soldier compies can keep going even with a hull breach like that!'

The robot-crewed Mantas and Remoras maintained continuous fire, blasting relentlessly until their munitions were depleted. Then Lanyan opened the channel himself and spoke to the programmed Soldier compies. 'Activate endgame sequence.' He sat back and gave a wicked smile as he transmitted to his commanders. 'Watch this – it's something the Ildirans taught us.'

The compy-piloted Remoras used their remaining engine power to drive themselves like hot bullets into the enemy vessels. On the monitor screens, telemetry images flared with explosions and then a sea of static, one after another.

The devastating firepower exploded back and forth so rapidly that Tasia could not keep up with the details of the battle. She sat ready to do her part, anxious to take vengeance – for Robb Brindle, for her brother Ross.

But the human forces had not yet been instructed to engage.

After receiving the General's endgame orders, the three

battered robot Mantas launched all their remaining weapons at once, drained their energy reserves, and still accelerated forward, engines on overload. The hydrogues couldn't possibly get out of the way in time. The reactors on the compy ships glowed intense and blinding hot – as each Manta crashed headlong into a chosen warglobe, rupturing stardrive-containment chambers, unleashing explosions like tiny suns.

All three target warglobes broke, burned, and sank out of sight into the deep clouds. Utterly destroyed.

'Thunderhead platforms! Second and final line of defence.' The General's voice carried an added tone of threat as if to impress any eavesdropping enemies. 'Deploy your nukes, and then get out of there as fast as you can.'

The platcoms dispatched their harvest of nuclear warheads, targeting the rising warglobes. As the atomics fell, the cumbersome weapons platforms moved up and away from the clouds, safe from the blastwaves and the damaging electromagnetic pulses.

The wave of nukes went off like newborn stars. Dazzling light and intense radiation ripped through the newly initiated storms. The waiting human-crewed Mantas and Juggernauts hovered above the poles of Osquivel, monitoring the incredible devastation below.

The EDF soldiers cheered and whooped as they saw the atomic flashes. 'Yeah, crispy fried drogues!'

'That'll boil them in their bubbles.'

'They should have stayed home and left us alone.'

Tasia sat like a statue in her command chair, watching the flashes but seeing no cause to celebrate. It wasn't over yet. But now the final thread of remaining hope was gone; even if the drogues hadn't got him, Robb could never have survived all those atomic explosions. She felt the power simmering in her Manta, the integral weapons batteries, and the squadrons of combat Remoras parked belowdecks and ready for launch. It was time to do something.

Tasia squirmed restlessly in her chair. 'Come on, General, turn us loose,' she muttered under her breath. 'I am really ready to *hurt* someone right now.'

'Damn! Even after all those nukes, they're still coming,' announced the platcom of one of the Thunderheads. 'Look, they're still coming!'

At least Lanyan didn't pretend to be surprised. 'How the hell do we get rid of those things?'

In the still-glowing afterwash of nuclear detonations, Tasia saw a greater concentration of the enemy than humans had ever faced before. Warglobe after warglobe climbed out of the now-radioactive clouds, like bubbles boiling up from a cauldron.

Lanyan placed his remaining compy-crewed Mantas in the vanguard where they could confront the initial fire. 'Showtime! Hit them with everything you've got! Remember, these are the same drogues who wiped out Boone's Crossing.'

'As if we needed extra reasons to hate them,' Tasia mumbled loud enough for her bridge crew to hear. She leaned forward in her seat as her Manta dropped into firing position. Down below, even more warglobes rose into the battle zone, hundreds and hundreds of them. 'Here they come.'

EIGHTY-SEVEN

ZHETT KELLUM

Huddled inside secure bolt-holes within the rubble rings of Osquivel, the Roamers watched as Armageddon blossomed around them.

'I really do feel like a rabbit,' Zhett Kellum said, adjusting her position. Her left leg had fallen asleep, even in the low gravity.

'By damn, the Eddies are going to mess things up for all of us,' Del Kellum said. 'Look! Here come the drogues. What did the General expect, after that bombardment?' He toggled through the available screen visuals transmitted by dozens of hidden imagers dispersed around the ring. 'Just be glad we're not a part of this.'

'We're all part of it, Dad. Those warglobes would be just as happy to fry Roamers as they are to cook the Big Goose.'

Most of the Osquivel shipbuilders had already fled the system after dismantling and dispersing the construction equipment. The camouflage for the remaining equipment and structures must have worked, since the EDF battlegroup had taken no notice of the Roamer facilities. Now, with the arrival of the terrible aliens, the Eddies obviously had larger concerns.

Inside the cramped bolt-hole, Zhett adjusted a spy-scanner, tuning to the private frequency used for the EDF command channel. She ran it through an encryption deprocessor that no Roamer was supposed to have, and they listened to General Lanyan giving abrupt orders, issuing instructions for the Soldier compies and their suicide Remoras.

Zhett focused the surveillance screens so they could watch dozens – hundreds – of warglobes rising like angry hornets out of the atmosphere. The spiked spheres struck fear into her heart. Though no Roamer had any love for the Earth Defence Forces after the rumoured harassments and outright piracy, she still felt sorry for the human soldiers. All those lives. Clearly, they were doomed.

'Look at all the damn warglobes!' one officer transmitted. 'I've never seen so many.'

'Stop counting and start shooting.'

Zhett turned her dark eyes towards her father. He had fear on his face, and they reached out to clasp each other's arms, sharing strength. 'We'll be safe enough here, my sweet.'

'Trust me, I wish that was the only thing I needed to worry about, Dad.'

The General's voice came with an anxious edge, as if he had begun the final approach towards panic. 'Vanguard Mantas, take your positions. Soldier compies, you have your orders and your programming. Inflict all possible damage.'

'Come on, boys and girls,' drawled another voice. 'We've all been waiting for a fight. Now we've got one.'

'Be careful what you wish for,' Zhett muttered.

They watched five more Manta cruisers break off from the main battlegroup and drop down – obviously captained by compies, as shown by the mechanical conviction and precision necessary for kamikaze strikes. Her heart skipped a beat as she watched the sacrificial Mantas explode all their munitions, drain their jazer banks

451

in dazzling starbursts of attack, and then drive in at full speed. She saw five warglobes go down, out of so many – but a storm of crystalline spheres continued to emerge from the depths of Osquivel.

'We all know what the stakes are,' a nameless EDF officer transmitted over the comm channel.

'I should have stayed home.'

'God, I'm going to miss—'

'Eat this, you drogue shitheads! Ahhhhh!'

Zhett felt sick to her stomach as she watched explosion after explosion. Blue lightning shot from the hydrogues, and each powerful bullwhip of energy blasted an EDF target. It all occurred in the silence of space, though over the command channel she could hear overlapping screams of panic, shouted orders, detonations and power surges through the onboard systems.

Out in space, more destruction blossomed. Now, with the compy-crewed ships gone, even some human-piloted Remoras and cruisers attempted suicide plunges. The hydrogues chased after several of the largest EDF ships. Juggernauts opened fire, but had no more effect than the smaller combat ships. Some of the flaming Earth vessels spiralled out of control, tumbling into the plane of the rings. There, before long, the drifting landmines of rubble annihilated the wounded vessels.

In less than an hour, the EDF battlegroup had lost fully a third of its vessels.

Zhett watched in horror as the hydrogues kept pounding the Eddie battleships. 'Isn't there anything we can do to help them, Dad?'

But she knew the Roamers had no great military might. They survived through guile and resourcefulness, by thinking fast and calling no attention to themselves.

'Nothing we can do except wait it out. You know that, my sweet.'

An explosion rippled nearby, disturbing the precise orbits of debris in the rings. The bolt-hole's power generators continued to function, but the lights flickered. Zhett was thrown against the wall and barely kept her balance. After a moment of darkness, the screens came on again, showing more horrific images of the combat zone. A thousand new stars twinkled in the rings: the blazing hulks of EDF ships and the dying glints of hull metal.

'Shizz, this is worse than getting our butts kicked at Jupiter!' The EDF woman's voice sounded familiar. Zhett thought she recognized Tasia Tamblyn, the woman who had warned the shipyards about the oncoming EDF battlegroup.

General Lanyan's voice cracked with stress and horror. 'I'm sounding a retreat. All squadrons fall back to parent ships. All command officers, get your ships the hell out of Osquivel by any means possible.'

'By damn, I never thought I'd hear an Eddie say that,' said Del Kellum.

'Do you blame him?'

'Not in the least.' He shook his head. 'Not in the least. What a disaster!'

On the screens, the exchange of fire continued. Many EDF ships began to scatter and move out, pulling away from the ringed planet, limping, crawling. The hydrogues destroyed five more vessels as Zhett watched.

'Damage assessments. I want casualty reports as soon as you get clear,' Lanyan's voice continued. 'Just get out of there!'

'What if the drogues come after us?' one man's voice asked, sounding thin and terrified. 'What if they keep coming? There's no way—'

'Haul ass and quit whining,' someone else chided.

Zhett and Del Kellum continued to watch the unfolding debacle. The smouldering hulks sizzled and flamed.

'I'll tell you one thing, my sweet,' her father said. 'I had my doubts before, but not any more. By the Guiding Star, there is no way I will ever attempt to skymine again.'

EIGHTY-EIGHT

ESTARRA

With so many people crowded around in a bustle of conversation and a flurry of fabrics, Estarra felt as if she were having a private party inside her chambers. But it was just a gathering for royal protocol ministers and social functionaries. Today was the day to display her new wedding dress.

She backed against a plush chair, unable to find a quiet spot amidst so many people. In a little more than two months, she would join King Peter in the royal chambers as his wife – but for now Estarra had her own luxurious suite of lavish rooms, oversized closets, foaming tubs, even a private greenhouse.

Royal tailors proudly displayed their work, showing off the extraordinary gown and explaining the subtle symbolism Estarra was sure no one would ever notice. Weeks before, the tailors had taken a complete, and embarrassingly thorough, three-dimensional body scan so they could construct a holographic model and test various dress designs before fabricating them.

For the wedding, Estarra would be the centre of attention. She was neither vain nor disappointed with her appearance, but she *was* intimidated by the fact that they wanted to transform her into the most beautiful woman in the Spiral Arm. Only a few years ago, she'd been a carefree tomboy on Theroc, climbing trees and running through the forest.

Now, striving to project a queenly demeanour, Estarra turned to the eager tailors. 'It's the most incredible dress I've ever seen. I shall attempt to do its beauty justice.'

'Your grace will only enhance the dress,' said the lead tailor, preening from her compliment.

'You see, dear, we have taken great care to use the perfect mixture of fabrics,' said another tailor, lifting the sleeve of the fabulous gown. 'We decorated a traditional white dress of Earth satin with these beautifully coloured greens made of Theron cocoon-fibre weaves. The pearls are from the reef mines on Rhejak.' He held up other corners of the flowing dress. 'This lace was hand-stitched by eight of the finest crafters on Usk. The design along the hem is one of the proprietary patterns developed on Ramah. In all, we have found some way to represent every one of the Hansa colony worlds.'

'Theroc is an independent world,' Estarra pointed out, 'not a Hansa colony.'

'And yet they honoured you by recognizing our heritage when they created this exquisite gown. Don't split hairs, Estarra.' Sarein frowned at her sister and ran a hand over the fabrics of the dress as if she secretly wanted to wear it herself. Estarra knew her sister was ambitious and would gladly have agreed to become Queen – not because she had any love for Peter, but because she enjoyed feeling powerful and important. 'This marriage will join our two cultures, bringing Therons and the Hansa into a partnership.'

The preparations proceeded at a whirlwind pace. No doubt with behind-the-scenes encouragement from Hansa officials, media reports had seized upon the heartwarming story of the 'budding romance' between the King and his chosen Queen. Celebratory feasts were scheduled, dancers rehearsed specially designed choreography, official musicians composed a grand marriage symphony, all as a cheerful lifeline to the population.

Guards appeared at the door with King Peter – causing a flurry as the fashion designers scrambled to hide her dress – and Estarra and her sister turned at the same time. Behind them, with an honour guard and several green priests, came Idriss and Alexa.

With a cry of delight, Estarra ran to embrace her parents. 'I didn't expect you for another week yet!'

Playing the courteous host, King Peter had dressed in a fine uniform to escort the former Theron leaders into Estarra's private apartments. Sarein greeted her mother and father more formally.

'Better early than late for my daughter's wedding,' Idriss said. He wore a colourful vest of lacquered flower petals and insect wings. 'So much has been happening that we decided to reroute an available ship, and here we are.'

Alexa smiled at Peter. 'Thank you for escorting us, King Peter. You are such a fine young man – you and Estarra look so . . . so perfect beside each other.' Alexa wore traditional Theron finery of glittering insect carapaces and shimmering cocoon silks. 'Sarein has told us so much about the Whisper Palace, we thought she must be exaggerating. This place is magnificent.'

'And very different from anything on Theroc.' Idriss stroked his thick beard; Estarra couldn't tell if her father was pleased by the opulence around him or intimidated by its strangeness. 'Perhaps Reynald was right to visit other planets. I see why he felt his peregrinations were so valuable. Of course, we never suspected he would meet someone special while he was wandering around the Spiral Arm—'

'We are so proud of you and Reynald,' Alexa interrupted. 'How could a parent ask for more? Two spectacular weddings in one year!'

'How could we survive more?' Idriss said with a groan.

'Two weddings?' Sarein asked. 'Has Reynald finally chosen a mate? Which of the villages is offering the bride?'

Alexa's face lit with surprise. 'Oh Sarein, I forgot – all the betrothal ships arrived just after you and Estarra departed for Earth. In the excitement, I suppose we just forgot to ask Nahton to tell you. Reynald has asked Cesca Peroni, the Speaker for the Roamer clans, to marry him. She's a lovely woman, and very talented.'

'One of the . . . Roamers?' Sarein sounded strangled. 'But how could he? Reynald just agreed to this alliance with the Hansa and—'

Alexa scolded her. 'The Roamers have a vibrant culture with much to offer. Your father and I approve. In fact, this is another step in bringing all of humanity together again as one unified family.'

She smiled beside her husband and took Idriss's hand, oblivious to the sceptical stares from everyone else in the room. Estarra, barely able to keep herself from laughing, hoped that her brother would be very happy with this Cesca Peroni.

EIGHTY-NINE

JESS TAMBLYN

In all his travels from Plumas to Rendezvous, from hot Isperos to the clouds of Golgen, Jess had never encountered anything so strange and amazing.

The nebula water was *alive*. More than alive, it was self-aware.

As his giant diaphanous skimmer continued to drift through the interstellar molecules, Jess found himself fascinated by the sentient fluid. He hunkered down on the floor of the processing deck, his attention fixed on the clear cylinder now filled with the liquid he had distilled out of the nebula.

It was filled with an indefinable, unmeasurable energy that throbbed at the backs of his eyes, as if human optic nerves could not differentiate the vitality from the elemental material. This was far more than simple hydrogen and oxygen. It belonged in a category beyond any natural substance.

It was alive.

It was sentient.

It . . . communicated with him.

Jess cupped his fingers around the cylinder's smooth wall. The

459

energy seeping through from inside felt both cool and warm at the same time, oily and slick on his fingertips, yet did not cling to his skin.

He heard a voice like a memory in his head, not a message of spoken words. He thought of how the green priests communicated with the worldtrees via telink . . . but this was another type of creature entirely. Or so he thought.

Once we were uncounted trillions, but I am the last. And you have brought me back.

'What are you?'

An essence of life and fluid, water flowing across the cosmos . . . it is difficult to find representative concepts in your mind. We call ourselves wentals.

'But you . . . are extinct? You're the last of your kind?'

Now I am the first.

'What happened to all the other wentals? Was there some sort of catastrophe?'

We cannot die, but we can be . . . disassociated. This nebula is a gigantic graveyard, a battleground in an ancient war that once threatened to shatter the cosmos. We . . . lost that conflict.

Jess balanced himself on the balls of his feet. If this being was connected somehow with his mind, the wental must sense the thousands of questions piling up like a heavy snowfall in his brain. Jess wrestled with everything he wanted to know.

'How long ago? Thousands of years?'

Unmeasurable, the wental said. *A long time.*

Jess couldn't grasp how long ago it might be. Had the wental existed before the nebula itself had spread across this section of the Spiral Arm?

Now that his link with the wental had been established, Jess found he no longer needed to touch the cylinder but could walk around the deck. 'Tell me about this ancient war. Who were you fighting? What happened?'

The last of the wentals confronted our enemies . . . the hydrogues.

Jess gasped. 'The hydrogues? How?'

I cannot describe the reasons for the conflict in terms you would recognize, or the details of our fight, but our final stand was made here. Hydrogues and wentals colliding, destroying, disassociating . . .

The hydrogues had already exterminated the verdani, destroyed their forest presence. Only the wentals remained. We were powerful, destroying millions — billions — of hydrogues. It was a tremendous battle, with inconceivable destruction on both sides. We were ripped apart into streams of hydrogen and oxygen, our blood scattered in a wide swath across space. In turn, we nearly destroyed our enemies.

But there were many hydrogues. Too many. The enemy was . . . over-whelming.

Jess waited, feeling cold and alone.

So many partial answers clicked into place, strange possibilities he had never before considered. 'We humans have been thinking too small,' he said to himself. 'Much too small.'

The hydrogues were not a new threat at all, but a danger that resonated across the epochs of galactic time. He realized there was much more to this grand conflict against the deep-core aliens. Cesca and all the Roamers needed to have this information, as did the Big Goose — even the Ildiran Empire.

'The hydrogues are still here,' Jess said. 'They've attacked humans. Is there any way you can help us? Tell us how to defend against them?'

Humans can do nothing against them.

As Jess thought of the nebula, the debris of an old battleground, the aftermath of a clash of two awesome forces, a chill crept down his spine. How could any mere human military stand a chance? The Hansa, the Ildirans, the Roamers?

'But you fought them before. Could you help us?' Through his communication link with the wental, Jess could sense that this water-based entity did not bear the destructive intent or vengeance

461

of the hydrogues. This presence seemed open, frank . . . honest. He felt genuine hope and confidence. 'Is there some way I could help you in return?'

The water in the cylinder seemed to grow brighter, and Jess felt a tingle in his scalp, an exhilaration like a burst of adrenaline pouring through his bloodstream.

You have the ability to travel between stars and planets. You could help propagate the wentals again. Then we could fight once more.

'Tell me what to do,' Jess said with absolute conviction. He remembered a phrase that had been used long before Roamers had ever taken to the stars. The enemy of my enemy is my friend. And the hydrogues were most certainly his enemy – a very personal enemy.

Take me to a water world, the wental said. *Find an ocean and pour the liquid that is my body into a planetary sea. In that way, I will allow myself to spread and grow strong again. Then you must take more of my essence and go to another world, and another.*

Jess's eyes gleamed. Ever since his brother's murder, his father's death, and his necessary separation from Cesca, he had moved sluggishly, blindly. But now he had a quest and a goal. He felt revived.

He couldn't conceive exactly how this liquid entity could stand up against the deep-core aliens, but the wentals had grappled with the hydrogues before. The rules of this conflict were far beyond his comprehension.

'All right, I accept your mission. You may be the first wental, but before long, you will certainly not be the only one.'

Up inside the main cabin of the nebula skimmer, he repro-grammed the ship's navigation systems, then sent a burst message to the other dispersed sailors, though it would take a long time for his transmission to reach any listeners.

Knowing there could be no turning back, Jess disengaged the cables, detached the huge scoop sails from his self-contained vessel, and then broke free of the filmy net. This was far more important than drifting aimlessly, immersed in his own regrets, hiding from everyone he knew. Now he finally had something to do.

The small ship separated, barely a speck against the background sheet of the vast collector sail. Jess flew towards the outer fringes of the nebula, gathering speed as he went alone to resurrect the wental and create a powerful ally for humanity.

NINETY

TASIA TAMBLYN

The hydrogues struck again, and sparks flew from Commander Tasia Tamblyn's bridge console. She had lost track of how many warglobes had already boiled out of Osquivel's clouds, stirred up by the EDF bombardment.

Not only wasn't this brash EDF operation a good idea, she thought, but Robb had died for nothing.

A fireshower of short circuits and sputtering flames erupted from the tactical station to her left. Her officers, already unnerved by the relentless destruction all around them, reacted in confusion. A jagged tree of blue lightning glanced across their bow, but mercifully caused little damage.

The Manta lurched from another heavy impact, and banshee alarms howled through the command decks, rendering the cruiser's bridge even more chaotic than before. Emergency lights flashed, bathing the equipment in a crimson glow. Tasia wiped sweat out of her eyes and shouted a quick string of emergency commands in hopes of keeping her ship moving away from the battlefield.

Manning the Manta's weaponry station, Sergeant Zizu toppled

out of his chair as a discharge backed up through his jazer grid. One young lieutenant had the presence of mind to spray fire-extinguishing foam on the burning circuitry panels. The burned security chief crawled away, searching for a med-kit, and Tasia barked orders for a befuddled-looking sensor operator to take up the vacant gunnery station.

Below and around them, warglobes fired indiscriminately. Dozens of Remoras evaporated into brilliant sparkles. The fleet comm systems were a confused chatter of orders and counter-orders, shouts of terror, and empty curses thrown at the deep-core aliens.

One of the huge Juggernauts had already been crushed and lay dead in space. Only a few lifetubes had shot out, carrying a pitiful handful of survivors. Tasia shouted for her crew to snatch any lifetubes in the vicinity as the Manta fought its way up and away from the rings.

The hydrogues kept coming, kept firing. Over the comm system, General Lanyan repeated his retreat order, calling for a complete withdrawal of all intact EDF ships. As if everyone wasn't already running.

Tasia changed course to avoid a burning hulk and a large cluster of outlying rocks from the rings. In spite of the obstacles all around, she increased to almost reckless speed. She had no choice. Half of her control systems were dark and dead. One of the engines was entirely off-line.

'Come on, come on!' Tasia worked the navigation controls herself, slapping her palm down on the grid. 'This thing handles like an Ildiran skymine in a storm.'

She saw the sparking, blackened hulks of four Mantas, unable to restart their engines to escape from the planetary battlefield. Only one still transmitted a fading distress signal. As Tasia watched in angry horror, three warglobes clustered around the doomed cruiser and opened fire, ripping it into glowing shrapnel.

Another stray hydrogue blast punched a hole in her own Manta's belly. Atmosphere spurted from a hull breach in two lower decks, killing an unknown number of crewmen. Automatic bulkheads slammed into place, sealing the enclosed spaces to mitigate the damage. A handful of indicator lights on the ship-status grid went completely dark. Tasia felt the wound to her already-battered cruiser like a personal injury.

'Zizu, get to your station! Drop a spread of fracture-pulse drones. Detonate them as soon as we're far enough away and hope the shockwave messes up the warglobes.' Tasia scanned her screens, searching for the best escape route from the flurry of battle.

The security chief replaced the volunteer hammering ineffectually at the weapons controls. 'We've only got seven fraks left, Commander!'

'Then hit them with all seven! No sense in saving them for a rainy day. And throw in any slammers we still have in the banks. They may not be enough to crack open the warglobes, but they just might give the drogues a headache!'

The wounded Manta continued to climb, and the thunderous hammer of fracture-pulse drones struck the crystalline spheres. Tasia was thrown against her console by the dissipating shockwave. Behind her, she saw a snowflake of cracks on the nearest warglobe. Maybe the new weapons had had some effect after all.

Reeling, the damaged hydrogue lanced out with more blue lightning. The fringe of another deflected strike sent a surge through the Manta's functional engines, dropping their energy flux by half. 'We need more power than this!' she shouted. 'We've got to move faster.'

The systems engineer worked with the control panels, yanking off access plates and staring at the confusing mess. 'The engines are damaged, Commander. The normal power linkage can't provide enough flow, and I can't reroute from secondary systems.'

'We don't have any secondary systems left!' Lieutenant Elly Ramirez shouted. 'It'll take us a month just to get out of the orbital plane.'

'Shizz, then think outside the box,' Tasia snapped. 'Only losers let themselves be limited by the impossible.' She hurried over to the systems engineer, stumbling as a faint shot caromed off their hull. Tasia couldn't pay attention to the impact at the moment. 'Reroute from life-support systems. Dump every scrap of power into our engines – and do it yesterday, if not sooner.'

'But without the life support, Commander, we'll—'

'Take shallower breaths and put on a sweater for the next hour. This is about *surviving*. And if we don't get away from these warglobes, we'll all be part of a nice war memorial in the rings of Osquivel.' She shouldered the engineer aside and began yanking and rerouting cables and controls. 'If you're gonna serve aboard my ship, you'd better know how the systems work. And be prepared to *make* them work no matter what the circumstances.'

She heard a distress call from Patrick Fitzpatrick's cruiser, begging for reinforcements, but he was deep among the hydrogues, and not many functional EDF ships remained. Especially not down there. He called simultaneously for his weapons officers to open fire and for the rest of the crew to abandon ship.

Tasia had no firepower to assist Fitzpatrick. Part of her wanted to go back and help him fight free just so she could give him a black eye later, but her own ship would barely escape as it was, and she held the lives of her crew in her hands. Even if he'd been her best friend, she couldn't have helped him. A handful of lifetubes spat out like sparks from the wounded Manta, but she heard no further communication from Fitzpatrick.

Then the hydrogues opened fire again and destroyed the Manta entirely.

Once she rerouted the life-support systems, her cruiser's engines had the boost she needed. Tasia brought her cruiser up into the cluster of other surviving ships. Together they limped into the darkness away from Osquivel's deadly rings.

She hadn't even had time to adjust to the fact that Robb had been killed by the hydrogues. Later, if she survived, she would think about all the foolish things she had said, the mistakes she had made, and the damnably heroic but stupid bravado Robb had shown.

With the life-support systems deactivated, the shrieking alarms seemed even louder. She could already feel the onboard temperature dropping, though they could survive for as much as a day with the current atmosphere.

'The alarms, Commander,' said an engineer. 'More systems are cascading, causing secondary breakdowns. What are we going to do?'

Tasia strode to a control station, scowling. She finally found the systems she needed, reached in with her bare hands, and yanked out a sparking set of circuit cards. The alarms fell suddenly, deafeningly silent.

'There. I don't hear any alarms. I can keep a closer eye on the systems without all that racket.' She looked at her surviving crew, barely able to comprehend the destruction and death the ragtag group was leaving behind. 'Now let's get the hell out of here.'

NINETY-ONE

PRIME DESIGNATE JORA'H

After divulging the truth of Nira's disappearance, the Mage-Imperator ordered his guards to keep Jora'h occupied with state functions for the next day. It was part of his duty as Prime Designate. He assumed that his son's anger would pass as he came to accept the new knowledge.

The Mage-Imperator could not have been more wrong.

Jora'h's impatience flashed out like a thunderstorm as he drove his attenders away. He cancelled all appointments with his assigned lovers, sending the starry-eyed women away in confusion and disappointment. He went to the ossuarium, accusing the glowing skulls of collusion of such terrible crimes, but the light continued to shine through their bones, and the skeletal faces seemed content in their rectitude.

Though he would eventually hold all the *thism* for himself and see through to the Lightsource, Jora'h felt alone now. His heart ached with the thought of all Nira must have endured for the past six years. She probably believed *he* had abandoned her, sacrificed her to these unconscionable experiments. She must be convinced that he had brushed her aside, forgotten her completely.

But though he remained helpless to change what had happened, he was determined to change the future. Nira was still alive – and he intended to get to her.

The Mage-Imperator attempted to send calming thoughts and soothing emotions through his faint telepathic link, but Jora'h refused to accept any of it. The leader sent conciliatory lens kithmen to speak to the Prime Designate, but he sent them away. Instead, reaching boiling point, he marched into the skysphere reception hall where his supposedly benevolent father held court.

Jora'h's topaz eyes glittered with contained fire. His mobile strands of hair flickered like the stingers of venomous insects. With cold intent, he had worn a garment sewn from the fabrics of Nira's forested homeworld, cocoon-fibre that he had purchased years ago from the merchant woman Rlinda Kett.

Functionaries, pilgrims, and sycophants of numerous kiths turned to look in startled surprise as the Prime Designate strode forward. His anger focused with the intensity of a projectile on the corpulent, sagging leader. 'Father, we must have more words.'

Armoured guard kithmen appeared at the doorways of the skysphere hall. Bron'n stepped close to the Mage-Imperator's chrysalis chair in a show of solidarity and protective force.

'We can talk if you wish, my son,' the Mage-Imperator said calmly. High above, the projected image of his chubby, paternal face smiled down from its misty cloud atop a pillar of light. 'However, important matters of the Empire are not for the ears of all subjects – are they?'

Jora'h refused to budge. 'Then send them away if you like, but I will speak with you now – and here. I am a thousand times betrayed by your actions.'

Cyroc'h raised his soft hands and spoke to the people in the reception chamber. Jora'h could feel waves of soothing kindness coming through the *thism*. 'Grant us a few moments. My son and I have an urgent matter to discuss regarding the hydrogue crisis.'

The people exited the skysphere hall in a quick and orderly fashion. Beside the chrysalis chair, Bron'n held his crystal-bladed katana spear and remained as still as a statue.

The Prime Designate clenched his hands as he faced his treacherous father, making a silent promise that he would never keep such secrets from his son Thor'h. Finally, the words tumbled out. 'I demand to know why you did such awful things.'

'We have spoken of this before, Jora'h. I made my decisions for the overall welfare of the Ildiran people. Accept them.'

'How can I accept murder, rape, slavery, and deceit? What you've done with the *Burton* descendants is tantamount to declaring war on the humans.'

Cyroc'h's long braid thrashed. 'I have ruled the Empire for nearly a full century, and I was trained by my father before me. Knowing that my days are numbered, I have done my utmost to make you understand the necessities of leading our people. And yet you chose to remain as innocent as a child and as gullible as a fool.'

Jora'h suddenly wondered if all the horrible secrets his father kept locked within himself had poisoned his body, formed the seed for the monstrous tumours that were even now killing him. 'That doesn't justify what you have done to Nira, to all of them.'

'Rules change, and as Mage-Imperator I have the right to change them as I see fit. Stop being so small-minded! You have no right to want this human woman, not any more. She serves a higher purpose now. Do not be upset because the truth was kept from you. It was done for the greater good of the Empire.'

'What part of all these lies and deceits can be considered *good*?'

The Mage-Imperator said, 'Only I can understand the complex tapestry of the Empire, because only I have access to the *thism*. I am closest to the Lightsource. I alone comprehend how the soul-threads interconnect with history. Such understanding will come to you when you take my place. But for now, while you are only the Prime Designate, you must trust in my wisdom.'

Jora'h was not convinced. 'How can I do that, when you've proven that you are not trustworthy?' He raised his chin. 'You may have access to the *thism*, Father, but it seems you've lost your soul along the way. I believe you have become blinded to the Lightsource.'

The Mage-Imperator looked furious, yet behind his glowering expression, he showed a flicker of dismay. 'My son, be patient. I assure you, everything will become clear—'

But Jora'h didn't want to hear more. He could only think of innocent Nira. She had taken a piece of his heart that he had never given to any of his numerous mates – and she had given him a daughter in return, a mixed-breed child. *Their daughter!* Now Osira'h was six years old, raised under the grim tutelage of the Dobro Designate. Jora'h had never seen her.

'You had no right,' he muttered under his breath, stepping away from the chrysalis chair. 'I want Nira freed immediately. I need to see her.'

'Jora'h, listen to me.' The Mage-Imperator sounded desperate and upset. 'We have very little time now. My illness is progressing—'

The Prime Designate whirled. 'Then perhaps you won't have enough time to cause more damage and commit more murder.' He strode past the guards and out of the voluminous skysphere.

'Jora'h, come back!' his father bellowed.

The Prime Designate stopped at the arched entry leading out into the hallways. 'I intend to go to Dobro myself and see with my own eyes what you have done, and I will take Nira away from that place. I will free the other human slaves. We are fighting monsters in this war, Father – but I see no need for us to become monsters ourselves.'

Jora'h stormed off, hearing none of the distraught words the Mage-Imperator shouted after him.

NINETY-TWO

NIRA

Emergency alarms rang in the camp at dawn, summoning all the human and Ildiran work crews. Weary captives left their communal barracks – men, women, and children emerging in confusion, dutifully answering the summons. 'It is a fire! Everyone must work!' Even the breeder barracks were opened up, fertile women chased out to assist in the emergency.

Two weeks ago, Nira's body had expelled the warped result of her joining with the scaly kithman. She had spent five days confined with the dry-skinned reptilian man . . . but the miscarriage had seemed even worse. Looking at its distorted form, she considered it a mercy that her body had aborted the foetus. There was little enough mercy on Dobro . . .

Now, still weak and recovering, she joined all the others, but she did not stumble. The medical kithmen had pronounced her healthy enough, and she was expected to work like everyone else.

Accompanied by burly guards, Ildiran supervisors strode along the fences, using their kith's innate organizational abilities to pull together labour groups that would normally be harvesting opalbone fossils, toiling in mines, or digging irrigation channels. Today, they had more important work. It was the dry season, and wildfires were igniting everywhere.

As dawn began to paint the sky, Nira could see black smudges across the eastern hills. She smelled the acrid charcoal odour of thick smoke drifting through the air. She desperately missed the comfort of the worldtrees, touching their golden bark and letting her mind fall into the sprawling forest network. Meditating with the great trees had always been a source of strength. Right now she needed that strength.

When the prisoners were assembled, the Dobro Designate came to stand on his observation platform outside the fences. He looked at them with a cold, expressionless face. 'The wildfires have begun again, worse than they've been in a long time.'

Nira despised Udru'h, but she lifted her chin and stared at him. Despite her recent repulsive encounter with the scaly kithman, the most horrific rape she'd endured so far had been by the Dobro Designate. He had seemed downright angry with her, determined to dominate her – as if by forcing himself upon Nira he could prove that he was somehow superior to his elder brother.

Worse, he was raising her beloved daughter Osira'h, her Princess, as if he could fill the role of benevolent father. Did Udru'h take such an intense interest in her other halfbreed children as well? Even his own son by her?

As the sky grew lighter, muscular Ildiran workers came from supply sheds carrying tools, shovels and picks. The supervisors and guards wore fire-protective clothing, but they gave the human breeders only face cloths to block out dust, smoke, and fumes.

'You will be our line of defence,' the Designate said, his voice brittle with command. 'You must dig trenches to block the flames so that the fire cannot escape beyond the hills to destroy our agricultural areas and this camp.'

The Dobro Designate expected human captives and Ildiran workers alike to follow his orders, even if they dropped dead from overexertion or exposure to the flames. Nira had done the dirty and exhausting work before, and she knew how vital it was. But she would do it for the *plants*, not for the Designate.

Ground vehicles and hovering platforms carried groups of firefighter slaves off to the sweeping flames in the hills. Flyers would cruise above the fire zone, dumping chemicals and water in an attempt to stop the blazes from spreading.

The hot air was full of smoke. The winds picked up, whistling over the stony ridges, snatching up sharp mica and chert particles that blew into her face like tiny bee stings. Nira adjusted the cloth over her nose and mouth, but her eyes continued to burn. As a green priest, the smoke itself prompted a visceral reaction of horror in her. Nevertheless, she ducked her head and marched forward into the fighting line.

She watched the fires race over the tinder grass and consume the thorny trees. Nira thought again achingly of the worldforest, sympathizing with the silent agony that even this alien cluster of scrubby trees was enduring. *Fire is the worst nightmare, worse even than rape* . . .

One of the Ildiran guards handed her a spade-like tool, and she moved out with the other workers, desperate to stop the con-flagration. At last, perhaps she could do some good here, protect some living trees, even if they were vanishingly distant cousins of the worldforest. It was a purpose she could grasp.

The recruits dug trenches, scooping the tinder grass clear, setting controlled backfires to erase all fuel in the path of the blaze. Nira watched the blaze sweep down into a sheltered valley full of dark, low trees. Though her communion with the worldforest had been severed, she almost thought she could hear a tremor of terror and despair as the flames engulfed that small patch of forest.

On the fire-fighting crews, she saw younger workers, small children, many of them obviously halfbreeds with strange body shapes and odd clusters of muscles. Without fear they scampered forward to the very edge of the flames and added fire-retardant sprays.

Nira watched the mixed-blood children, trying to guess their ages. Soot-flecked tears streamed out of her large eyes, not entirely from irritation of the smoke. The Dobro Designate was pitiless, and used everyone as he saw fit. Some of those children could even be Nira's own babies, but she would never know. And it would never have made a difference to the Designate.

Nira felt sorry for the others and wished she could help them somehow. But she could not fight everything. She had to take one tangible battle at a time.

With the fires burning through the Dobro hills, Nira lost all sense of the hours passing as she continued her unending fight.

NINETY-THREE

ESTARRA

Inside a private open-air classroom on one of the Whisper Palace's rooftops, an invisible threadscreen covered the roof, and swarms of colourful butterflies flew free, alighting on any surface. According to the Teacher compy OX, this was one of Peter's favourite places to receive instruction . . . but the butterflies kept settling on Estarra's arms and in her hair, and she found it difficult to concentrate on the lessons.

The Teacher compy instructed her in manners, protocol, and diplomacy, in social expectations and how to address official representatives. Back on Theroc, she'd learned her own world's history, but now OX insisted on giving her a full briefing on the Terran Hanseatic League. Even while the Osquivel offensive continued and all the Hansa waited for news, she still had to attend her classes.

Today, with Chairman Wenceslas still gone, King Peter had joined the instruction session, apparently as an excuse to have more time in Estarra's company. He smiled at her attempts to focus while the colourful butterflies flitted around inside the netted enclosure.

Estarra fought down her laughter, struggled to concentrate. Peter tried to hide his delight, but he knew it showed on his face.

When the Teacher compy had to repeat his question twice, startling Estarra out of her fascination with a large iridescent-blue morpho, the King said, 'OX doesn't believe in boring schoolrooms. He also doesn't understand just how distractible a student can be. When I was younger, he thought I could keep my mind on studies while I was swimming in a dolphin pool.'

Estarra's eyes lit up. 'I love swimming. What are dolphins?'

'I'll show you one day,' he said. 'I promise.'

'Another time,' OX said. 'We have more to accomplish here, and it requires concentration.'

Before OX could finish the lesson, though, Chairman Wenceslas strode into the butterfly lecture hall, newly returned from Mars. He was obviously agitated. 'It's a damn good thing the guards keep track of your whereabouts, Peter. I don't have time for a wild chase through the Whisper Palace.'

Estarra looked up, surprised to see the grave expression on the Chairman's face. The King frowned, indignant at the uncalled-for rebuke. 'I am assisting Estarra in her formal training, Basil. No need to snap at me. If you had sent word, I would've been happy to meet you in a more convenient location.' He suddenly turned. 'Wait a minute – aren't you supposed to be on Mars? What happened at Osquivel? Why haven't I heard anything?'

'Because I issued an immediate order for Hansa HQ to put a blanket on questions and media coverage of the crisis. Until I can figure out what to do – but with the damned green priests, word has spread everywhere. No such thing as a secure communication, even in an military emergency like this one.'

Furious, Chairman Wenceslas explained. 'A complete disaster. We lost at least one Juggernaut, over three hundred Remoras, and dozens of Mantas and Thunderheads. The count is still coming in.

I can't even begin to estimate casualty figures. General Lanyan had to call a retreat before the hydrogues exterminated our entire fleet.'

Estarra stood quickly, concerned. The King looked stricken. The butterflies, incongruously peaceful, continued flitting through the air.

Chairman Wenceslas said, 'The Hansa hasn't made any official statements yet, but we can't keep hold of it for long. We'll have to issue our own announcement.' He drew a deep breath. 'Compose yourself, and dress for the gravity of this occasion. In less than an hour you must inform the public. The speech is being written right now, but I want you to practise in front of a mirror so that you can look suitably devastated.'

Peter's blue eyes flashed. 'If our fleet has been massacred, and thousands – maybe tens of thousands – of our soldiers have been killed by the enemy, I won't need to *pretend.*'

As he followed the Chairman out of the butterfly lecture hall, the King glanced back at Estarra, and spared her a reassuring smile. 'Don't worry – everything will be all right.'

Then he hurried after Chairman Wenceslas into the Throne Hall.

Ninety-four

Kotto Okiah

On Isperos, even hell turned against the Roamers. One disaster followed another, and the troubles compounded faster than Kotto Okiah could create solutions. For the first time in his life he was on the verge of giving up.

It would take at least six months to repair or rebuild the devastated railgun launcher, and in the meantime the surface-scraping mine machines had piled up a stockpile of ingots, then shut themselves down. Major maintenance work had fallen behind schedule, and even the most optimistic engineers among the crew saw the base sliding slowly towards doom. Kotto saw it slipping through his fingers.

Now, venturing out on to the broiled surface, Kotto wore a thin reflective suit that made him look like a walking mirror. Most wavelengths from the roaring sun ricocheted off the film.

Alert and focused, Kotto strode across the open terrain; the boulders were unpleasantly soft, so close to melting point that they had the consistency of thick clay. Overhead, the bloated star churned like a cauldron of plasma, swirling with sunspots and magnetic loops, flares of dragon's breath. The corona shimmered across the black velvet of space. Solar activity had increased in the past month, boosting radiation flux beyond the limits of the Roamers' already strained cooling equipment. Everything seemed to be going wrong at once.

Years ago, his mother Jhy Okiah had spoken for him, convincing the other clans to make this investment on Isperos, assuring them that the harvestable metals and isotopes would be worth the risk. Kotto had done his best, dancing on the edge of the impossible.

But now the ground had grown too slippery under his feet.

Scattered across the plain of hardened lava, thin triangular fins protruded upwards, shimmering a cherry-red. They looked like the sails of extinct dinosaurs, thermal radiators that struggled to disperse the excess heat. Two of the radiator fins had toppled in the recent seismic event that had wrecked the railgun, decreasing the colony's ability to maintain a liveable temperature. Kotto would have to assign crews to make those repairs first of all before another crisis occurred.

And another crisis *always* occurred.

As a young man, Kotto had tinkered with machines and electrical systems. His intuitive grasp of physics and engineering did not come from traditional learning; he had a mind open to possibilities, boundless innovation tempered by an appropriate level of pragmatism. Kotto took no unwarranted chances with his fellow Roamers, who placed their lives in his hands.

But sometimes even his best ideas didn't work.

His suit radio crackled. Though the transmission was staticky from the punishing stellar turbulence, he heard the urgency in the voice. 'Kotto, you need to get back inside! We've had a breach in Storage Chamber 3. One equipment crib is already full of lava, and the walls are cracking into the generator room.'

'The generator room! How could that happen? If the lava hits there, we'll lose twenty per cent of our life-support capabilities.'

'I don't know, Kotto. There was a thermal plume underground. We didn't chart it, but it moved fast. The heat spike was high enough to melt through the rock-fibre insulation and the ceramic wall plates.'

Kotto was already sprinting towards the sealed doors that led into the underground complex. Three engineers met him, their faces grey and sweaty, and not just from the excessive heat inside the warrens. 'This one's really bad, Kotto.'

He unsealed his gloves and set his helmet aside, stripping off pieces of the mirrored uniform, burning his fingers on the suit's still-hot exterior. He sucked on his fingertips, then ignored the stinging pain. He followed the engineers while he continued to remove his suit, dropping components along the way.

On the third level down, engineers milled in front of the sealed door of the now-ruined storage chamber. Inside the control room, Kotto went to study the screens from the monitor cameras inside Storage Chamber 3. He saw slumping metal walls, smouldering packages and equipment. A burst of bright scarlet magma oozed through the breach like arterial blood, scorching everything it touched.

'Maybe it's only a transient thermal plume,' said one engineer.

'I'm supposed to be the optimist around here,' Kotto said, 'and even I don't believe that. Let me see the generator room.'

One of the techs pressed controls, toggling through images. Some were already static because the cameras had melted in the rampant heat. Inside the generator chamber where one set of redundant power converters and life-support systems functioned, he saw the insulation smouldering, the thick metal wallplates softening and buckling, already cherry-red.

It was the end of Isperos.

In the corridors, thick circulating pipes roared as coolants passed like oxygenated blood, struggling to carry away the deadly heat faster than it could build. Kotto knew the systems couldn't keep up, not any more. He realized in his heart that the settlement, his wild and exciting idea, was failing.

'Remove all the supplies you can. Seal off the lower levels, and block the walls. Maybe we can stall the lava long enough.'

He made calculations in his mind, trying to determine how much time would be required, whether the laws of celestial mechanics would make salvation possible at all.

'Pick our fastest ship. We'll send a messenger to Rendezvous and call on the other clans for help.' He gulped in a dry throat, still reluctant to say it. 'We're going to have to evacuate Isperos.'

NINETY-FIVE

ZHETT KELLUM

In the aftermath of the bloody skirmish at Osquivel, slagged battleship wreckage continued to smoulder for days. The hydrogues had withdrawn into the gas-giant's clouds, and the disorganized remnants of the Earth Defence Forces had crawled out of the system, anxious to get away at all costs.

Six hours later, the skittish Roamers ventured out of their rocky hiding places in the rings. 'It's time we returned to our lives, by damn,' Del Kellum said over the intact comm network. 'Sure, I grieve for all the dead Eddie soldiers – but let's see if we can glean something from all that wreckage. Nobody else is going to do anything with it.'

Zhett rebraided her dark hair, then zipped into her warm tunic. From a locker she grabbed a full environment suit and boarded one of the grappler pods. She and her father headed out into the battlefield debris with the other scavenger vessels. Dozens of small vehicles began to emerge from crater hiding places, eager to get back to work.

Zhett sat comfortably in her grappler pod, manipulating the

vehicle's articulated arms as if she were flexing her fingers. Piloting the little pod was second nature to her. She and her father drifted apart, both of them hunting for treasure among the debris.

The ruined Eddie warships lay strewn about in space – a rich harvest for the resource-hungry gypsies. Sparkling mists of frozen atmosphere hung like chill puffs of breath. A single Juggernaut drifted, gutted and devoid of life-signs. In such a large ship, the bulkheads must have sealed off some sections, protecting a few crewmembers; but the hydrogue blasts may well have wiped out all life-support systems. Some escape tubes had ejected, presumably to be rounded up by the fleeing EDF battleships, but in the stampede of retreat, many had been left behind.

Zhett bit her lower lip, frustrated with traditional Roamer caution and secrecy. What had it gained them here? If she and the others hiding in the Osquivel rings had launched quickly enough, they might have been able to rescue some victims. By now, it was probably too late to help anyone.

She coded in the private channel to her father. 'Don't you think the Eddies will come back and retrieve their damaged ships, Dad? Or at least take home their dead?'

'They've been scared badly, my sweet. I don't expect to see them back any time soon. If so, they'll assume that the drogues dragged the wrecked warships down into the clouds or destroyed them.'

Zhett was surprised the Earth military would be so willing to abandon fallen comrades. But the hydrogue battle had not been a typical engagement. The routed humans had barely escaped with their lives. If they'd stopped to gather their dead, then none of the Eddies would have got home.

Zhett thought of how many Roamers had perished when their skymines were attacked and destroyed by the hydrogues. Her own mother and little brother had been killed long ago in a dome-breach accident. Even as an eight-year-old girl, she remembered the funeral, wrapping each of the thirty victims in embroidered cloth, then launching the bodies on a long trajectory up out of the ecliptic, where they would drift forever, true Roamers carried along by the vagaries of gravity and their own Guiding Stars.

Now the hunting grappler pods dispersed among the dead ships, assessing the situation, scanning for distress signals or active lifetubes. The Roamers could take these wrecks one by one – dismantle them or rebuild them, depending on the damage to their structures. Kellum's shipyard engineers could always learn new technologies from the advanced EDF military systems. Even the ruined hulks themselves would be a wealth of raw metals and electronic components to be cannibalized.

Zhett and her father had already discussed how soon they would reconstruct the Osquivel shipyards. Clan Kellum couldn't hide forever.

The Roamers had escaped initial detection here, but if the Eddies did return to mop up, these shipyards would be painfully obvious to the Big Goose. And after their resounding defeat, the Earth military would no doubt respond with true vitriol, looking for scapegoats – especially if they saw how the space gypsies had scavenged the ruined ships.

Still, no Roamer could let so much raw material go to waste.

Several alien warglobes had also been damaged or destroyed, but most of the debris had tumbled into the cloud depths, and Zhett did not intend to drop into the skies of Osquivel to investigate. But if she could get her hands on a drogue vessel, imagine what the Roamers could do with it . . .

As she manoeuvred her pod, she documented the EDF derelicts, noting which ones would be most easily salvaged. She drifted past frozen human bodies, their tissues bulging from explosive decompression. Some soldiers, burned and mangled, had probably been dead before they'd been ejected into space; others, though, had died struggling in frozen vacuum while every blood vessel in their bodies haemorrhaged.

The first several bodies sickened her, but Zhett pressed on, concentrating on the work. She could have done nothing to help these soldiers who had chosen her planet as their fateful battleground. The Roamers had only wanted to be left alone. Was that so much to ask?

She surveyed the remains of a Manta cruiser, carefully inventorying usable materials. Salvage teams had already linked with the gutted hulk of the big Juggernaut. Ekti tankers moved in, interfacing with the stardrive fuel tanks and draining away every wisp for their own stockpiles.

'If the Eddies are really hijacking our cargo haulers and stealing fuel, then we don't need to feel guilty for the turnabout,' said one of the engineers.

'I doubt any of these people deserved such a fate, even if they were pirates,' Zhett said, subdued. 'Trust me, I know we can't let this stuff go to waste, but don't get gleeful about it. Think of what it cost.'

An awkward silence dampened the normal comm chatter. Del Kellum broke in, 'My daughter's put her finger on it. We don't have to be smug, by damn. The drogues are *our* enemies, too.'

While heavy salvage crews attended to the largest vessels, Zhett took her grappler pod farther from the main concentration of debris. Explosions and desperate escape manoeuvres had imparted wildly random vectors to tumbling flotsam, and she didn't want to miss a gem out there in the emptiness.

She stumbled upon the faint distress signal, a pulsing automatic beacon so weak that she didn't even notice until she was on top of it. She extended the pod's grappling arms and adjusted her illumination beams.

Zhett saw a battered lifetube that had been ejected from an EDF cruiser, a single-man pod. Though its systems had been severely damaged, she detected one life sign aboard. The reflective hull, scorched and scarred, had begun leaking air. It wouldn't last much longer.

She sent her message over the standard EDF frequency, not sure if the occupant could hear her. 'Yo, I've got you. Just relax. We'll have you out of there in no time.' She heard no response and wondered whether the lifetube had too little energy to run a discretionary transmitter. Maybe the survivor was unconscious or injured.

Using tiny bursts of her manoeuvring jets, Zhett aligned her ship with the lifetube, matching orbital trajectories so the two vessels were motionless relative to each other. She clasped the tube with the grappler arms. Though her pod was a small vehicle not designed for carrying passengers, if the survivor's life support had dropped below subsistence level, the occupant might not live long enough for her to tow him back to the nearest habitation shelter.

'All right, my friend, if you can't help me, then I'll have to do this solo,' she said over the radio, hoping he could still hear.

She pulled the lifetube into position, working carefully to adjust the standard airlock seal. It was difficult work, requiring absolute precision. With the back of her arm Zhett wiped sweat from her forehead, then tried again, finally matching the two docking seals.

When she equalized the pressure and opened the hatch, a stale, rancid stench flooded out to her. After so many hours, the air inside the lifetube was bad, but somehow the person inside was still breathing. She could see blood on the metal inner wall, like a patch of rust in the stuffy tube. Then she heard a groan – a sigh of relief, or maybe just exhaustion at the end of despair.

She reached in and grabbed the uniformed man's shoulders. The soldier was a young man with a handsome and cultured face.

She noted his rank insignia – a commander among the Eddies. The ID plate affixed to his breast said his name was 'Fitzpatrick'.

The young man blearily opened his eyes. His left side and arm had been mangled, and blood still oozed from numerous wounds and burns. Groggy, Fitzpatrick tried to focus on Zhett's face. His voice was weak. 'After facing all those devils, it's nice to see an angel.'

He didn't exactly pass out then, but seemed to drift out of awareness.

She squeezed water into his mouth. Pulling him into her pod and climbing back into her seat, Zhett opened a general channel to the Roamer scavengers. 'Returning to main complex. I've snagged some salvage that needs tending to.'

All told, the Roamer scavengers rescued only thirty survivors from the EDF battleships, along with two other soldiers from lifetubes. The Osquivel crews salvaged dozens of still-functional compies that could be repaired and reprogrammed for Roamer uses, including some of the new Soldier model. All in all, it was a good haul.

Zhett tended Patrick Fitzpatrick, using the first-aid supplies they kept at each shipyard station. Kellum stood beside his daughter, frowning but resigned. 'I knew this was going to be a problem. I don't like having these Eddies here, but I suppose we have no choice but to care for them.'

Zhett said, 'Would you rather I had just let him drift until he died?'

'It wouldn't have taken long,' Kellum said. She scowled, but he raised his hand in a placating gesture. 'I was just teasing, my sweet. But you do realize the quandary we face as soon as they're recovered?'

'Most of the Eddie refugees seem healthy enough,' Zhett said.

'They don't require medical attention beyond what we can provide here.'

Del Kellum looked pointedly at her. 'Yes, but that's not the problem. If we mean to keep our Roamer secrets, we can't possibly let these soldiers return to Earth. Not ever.'

NINETY-SIX

KING PETER

In his reign of six years, Peter had never been aboard the bridge of an active-duty Juggernaut, but after the news of the Osquivel disaster hit the populace like a punch in the gut, he had to keep up appearances. Even with the Hansa maintaining careful control of how the reports were slanted, they could not hide the magnitude of what had happened. And people were angry.

The new battleship joined five Manta cruisers in orbit over Earth, ready to be deployed on another pointless mission to gain intelligence and reconnaissance data on the enemy hydrogues. Peter wouldn't be surprised if the enemy aliens disintegrated them on sight.

This trial run of EDF ships would be crewed by the new Soldier-model compies, another proof-of-principle test after the military robots had performed so well at Osquivel. Basil had decided that the new exploration group's responsibility was clear, with little room for discretion, and the modified Klikiss programming was capable of handling routine operations. Human commanders would serve only as figureheads to make snap decisions in unorthodox situations; the Soldier compies could handle everything else.

Still, Peter could not shake his misgivings about the new-model compies.

Standing placidly next to him, Basil wore a business suit that fitted him like a glove. 'Just smile and nod approvingly, Peter. Give this mission your blessing, and we can be finished here.'

'Just as King Frederick did for the maiden launch of the *Goliath*,' Peter said, then muttered, 'for all the good that did.'

With the Chairman hovering close, King Peter dutifully delivered the words the Hansa speechwriters had scripted, inane congratulatory phrases and well wishes. The five human officers – a major to command the Juggernaut and four captains, one for each Manta, stood on the bridge beaming with pride.

Their assignment was to investigate Golgen, site of the first recorded hydrogue attack against a Roamer skymine and also the target of a shotgun blast of comets launched by renegade space gypsies. The survey team would try to assess what damage had been done by the cometary bombardment, and further test the peripheral capabilities of the new Soldier compies. It was a way to foster optimism after Osquivel.

Just like his royal wedding would be, soon.

The five figurehead officers bowed, the media crews dispersed on schedule, and Basil hurried the King back to the shuttle. With a heavy heart, he wondered if this reconnaissance team would be obliterated as well. So many others had failed before – what could the Soldier compies do differently this time? Peter did not want to give another eulogy and unravel the black mourning banner from the side of the Whisper Palace, as he had done so many times already.

'Basil, why do we keep sending out more and more sacrificial lambs?' Peter asked when the small craft dropped away from the proud battleships. 'We know all too well what the hydrogue response is likely to be.'

'Then we will try again,' Basil said, 'and again.'

'Is it worth the cost?'

Basil shrugged. 'Those Soldier compies were designed to be expendable. I'm more concerned with the possible loss of all those ships.'

'And what about the people aboard them? Even with all the compies, there are still five human officers.'

The Chairman frowned. 'But only five, and that's acceptable. The Hansa can't afford to sit back and do nothing. We must show ourselves to be formidable opponents, unwilling to give up. Acquiescence to the enemy would be extremely bad for public relations. Trust me, it's worth the risk.'

Peter wanted to vomit.

Looking cagey, Basil handed him a text screen. 'Your speech for this afternoon. After Osquivel, the crisis has got measurably worse. We need to enact more extreme social and economic measures.' The Chairman looked at him with a stern expression. 'You're going to hate this, Peter, but you'll do it anyway. We have no choice.'

When Peter spoke in front of the uneasy crowd, the words turned to ashes in his mouth. He forced himself to spit them out, reviling himself and cursing Basil at the same time. His speech was transmitted everywhere. Could the people believe their King actually meant those things?

'For the next two years,' he said, his voice unsteady, 'I have no choice but to enforce this command, as unpleasant as it may be: I hereby impose a complete moratorium on all new births on any Hansa colony that has not shown itself to be self-sufficient.'

He waited as he listened to the murmur of disbelief. Soon the murmur would grow into anger and resentment directed towards *him*. He would be the scapegoat for this terrible pronouncement. *Damn you, Basil!*

Peter read the words in a flat and mechanical voice. 'Because of the extreme shortage of ekti, our worlds cannot rely on outside trade sources, and if we allow unchecked population growth, then we allow starvation and misery.'

He swallowed hard, hoping they would see his reluctance, his uneasiness. The background noise grew louder; he could sense the anger rising among them. These people did not understand that their beloved King was just an actor. They believed him responsible for everything.

In a hoarse voice, he continued, 'A list of Hansa colonies that fall under this stricture will be posted and distributed. Abortion specialists will be sent to those worlds in need. Pregnancies currently in-term will be evaluated on a case-by-case basis.'

On the shuttle descent, Peter had asked why the Hansa couldn't simply send food instead of abortion doctors, but Basil had made a rude sound. 'Food is eaten in one day, and the people are hungry the next. Capping population growth provides a longer-term solution. After the war ends, the colonists – if they survive – can always have other children. Try to see the big picture.'

While reading over the speech in the enclosed craft, Peter had been infuriated, then defiant. 'I won't say these words, Basil. You've forced me to sugarcoat plenty of questionable deeds, but never anything as evil as this. It's . . . appalling.'

'It's necessary. And you will do as you're told.'

'If it's your idea, why don't *you* issue the order? Or does the Chairman have no backbone? An abortion decree!' He shook his head in disgust. 'What an auspicious way to celebrate my upcoming wedding.'

'It's the responsibility of the King,' Basil said with a sweet smile. 'That's why you were chosen.'

'And how can you force me? I refuse.'

'Estarra is your bride-to-be, innocent, vulnerable – far out of her depth.' The Chairman's face became hard. 'I know you already care for her. If you don't behave, we'll find some reason to . . . make things difficult for her.'

Peter had curled his lip. 'She's just a pawn in this.'

'So are you, Peter, and the Hansa can do with you whatever we please.'

Peter knew the Chairman had been responsible for killing his family, even his estranged father on Ramah. Yes, he was capable of hurting Estarra . . . and without batting an eyelid, he could also poison the unruly King. Peter had always assumed that Basil had too much invested in his young protégé to toss him aside. Now, though, he wasn't so sure.

He had come closer than ever before to considering outright murder. Would it be so difficult just to slip a dagger into Basil's side? The reverse of Brutus and Caesar? And what could they do to him afterwards? He was the King, after all, and the Hansa had gone to great lengths to ensure that he no longer had any family, anyone he cared about. *Except now, Estarra . . .*

The Chairman had sat back in his shuttle seat, weighing Peter's silence. Finally, he said, 'Stop acting like a child and do what you are ordered to do. Give the speech – for Estarra's sake, if not your own.'

And so Peter delivered the hated ultimatum, striking a blow to the hearts of his people. He wanted to cringe with every word he spoke. The crowds did not cheer when he finished. They had grieved for the ignominious defeat their great forces had suffered at Osquivel, but this proclamation seemed to deal their spirits a mortal blow.

Peter turned from the balcony and stepped back inside the Whisper Palace, where he saw the Chairman nodding. 'Not your best delivery, but it'll do.'

Peter wanted to spit at him. 'I despise you, Basil.'

The other man's feelings did not appear at all hurt.

NINETY-SEVEN

RLINDA KETT

By now, she figured that Davlin Lotze had had more than enough time to get himself out of his mess. Of course, operating ancient alien transportation machinery might not have been one of those 'obscure details' he specialized in.

Davlin had vanished through the transportal in the Klikiss ruins. Rlinda didn't know where he had gone, but unless the man had travelled to someplace where he could find supplies, he must either be dead . . . or at the very least, hungry enough to eat spampax.

As she'd been doing for days, Rlinda waited outside the *Voracious Curiosity*, listening to Rheindic Co's faint sounds, surrounded by the murderous mystery of the place. This ghost world was enough to give anyone the creeps.

Normally, she enjoyed time by herself, but on this silent arid planet, she felt damned lonely. Davlin Lotze hadn't exactly been a barrel of laughs, but she missed his company even so. The cultural spy was intelligent and insightful, a diligent worker. If only her ex-husbands had been as dedicated to their jobs instead of messing things up . . .

Rlinda sat on the ship's ramp. The desert afternoon shimmered with heat. She had gone to the Klikiss ruins every day to look for Davlin, trying to reactivate the portal wall (and having the good sense not to get sucked through). She had gazed out on other alien landscapes, but she had never glimpsed him again.

For the last week, though, she had done it only out of habit, without much hope. She was down to her last bottle of wine in the ship's stores; most of the good mealpax had already been prepared and consumed. Once she ran out of decent comestibles, this place would become completely intolerable.

She spent an hour trying to think of a reason to stay, but gave up, deciding it was time to pack up and go home. Rlinda felt obligated to return to Earth and explain to Chairman Wenceslas what they had discovered about the missing Colicos team. Besides, she wouldn't get the rest of her fee until she made her report.

Afterwards, maybe Rlinda would just go back to quiet Crenna, spend a month with BeBob trying to figure out why he liked the place so much.

It would take a few hours to pack up the camp. The water pump still worked, and she would leave behind the rest of her mealpax in case Davlin ever did come back. She could have rigged up a transmitter for him to send a distress, but no electromagnetic signal could possibly get anywhere in time to help. Maybe the Chairman would authorize a return trip just to check on the situation . . .

She shaded her brown eyes as the sun lowered towards the horizon, thinking she saw movement out in the canyons. What if the mysterious murderer was coming back to attack her before she could leave? Let him try!

Then she recognized the silhouette, saw the man's dead-weary gait.

'Davlin!'

He stopped and raised one hand, then shambled forward.

Rlinda wasn't up for a mad dash across the rough terrain. Instead, she powered up the hoverlift and skimmed across the desert to meet him. Davlin seemed so dazed that he didn't even notice her approach until she pulled the craft to a halt beside him. 'It's about time you got back, Mister! If I was your mother, I'd ground you for a month.'

He didn't have the energy to respond to her humour. She grasped his hand and hauled him on to the hoverlift. He slumped with exhaustion on to the platform, while Rlinda began jabbering about how much she'd worried about him. 'You're lucky I stuck around. I was about ready to leave.'

Back at the *Curiosity*, she fed him and – as she had expected – he simply gobbled the food, paying no attention to the taste. All the while, he seemed to be gathering energy. But she could tell he was bursting with news about what he had seen and experienced. His eyes were shining.

Finally, he told her what had happened and described all the places he had gone via transportal after transportal. 'We came here to search for missing archaeologists, and instead we discovered something that'll change the Hanseatic League forever.' Davlin spoke with such excitement that Rlinda couldn't get in a comment of her own.

'Any sign of Margaret Colicos?' she asked.

He appeared briefly troubled, but more optimistic than she had seen him before. 'No . . . but she could have gone anywhere. The possibilities are enormous – world after world, all of them suitable for supporting life. Not garden spots, maybe, but certainly liveable.'

She grinned, listening to his adventures. 'I'd say that's a good enough reason to open my last and best bottle of wine.' Rlinda hurried up the ramp, unlocked her private store, and returned with an old bottle. She had intended to share it with BeBob, but this was a sufficient excuse. By the time she made it back to Crenna, she'd have a large enough reward from Basil Wenceslas that she could buy a whole case of any vintage she chose.

After she pulled the cork and poured them each a glass, Davlin surprised her by taking the initiative, raising his wine in a toast. 'Rlinda, thank you for waiting. Your persistence may just be responsible for giving humanity an enormous advantage. Even I can't imagine how much this is going to affect the human race. It'll save the Hansa, maybe even civilization. Those Klikiss transportals lead to dozens, maybe hundreds of human compatible worlds – all of them completely empty.'

Rlinda clinked her glass against his. 'Knowing human beings, those planets won't stay empty for long.'

Davlin took another sip, then suddenly looked impatient. 'How long will it take to get your ship ready to leave?'

'I'd already started packing, remember?' She gestured around the camp. 'And it's not absolutely vital to take all this junk with us.'

'Good.' Davlin finished his wine in a long, rushed gulp.

Rlinda shook her head with a long-suffering sigh. 'The finer things in life are just plain wasted on you. I might as well give you reconstituted grape juice.'

He stood. 'Never mind that. We have to get back to Earth so I can report to Chairman Wenceslas. He's going to be thrilled to hear what we've found. And if you've ever met the Chairman, you'll know how extraordinary that is.'

NINETY-EIGHT

D D

P lunging down and down . . . accelerating into the unknown hells of a gas giant. DD was terrified by the out-of-control descent, but even more than that he feared what the Klikiss robots intended to do to him next.

Seeking comfort, he played and replayed his memories of his first owner Dahlia Sweeney, when she'd been just a little girl, he thought back to happy times cooking fine meals for Margaret and Louis Colicos, helping out in the archaeology camp. DD had always done his best, never shirking his duties.

But now the string of unpleasant events never seemed to end. The Klikiss robots would not let him go.

Sirix had engaged in a programming link to pilot their bare-bones vessel deep into Ptoro's atmosphere. Manipulator arms emerged from the beetle-like robot's chestplate. His optical sensors burned scarlet as he explained in his buzzing voice, as if he considered himself a mentor to the captive compy, 'At this height in the troposphere, turbulence is great, but the air remains so thin that it poses no navigational hazard. Do not be concerned.'

DD swivelled his head and looked at the hulking machine. 'That is not why I was worried. I do not wish to go down there.'

'Nevertheless, we wish to take you.'

Ptoro was a distant and cold planet, smaller and denser than many gas supergiants, the grey-blue of dirty ice on a frozen pond. Similar to Uranus in the Earth system, it had five thin silvery rings stacked like bracelets around its equator. DD's general database had no record of any skymining activities here, but the Hansa had very little concrete information about Roamer facilities.

As Sirix's ship continued to tunnel through the thickening atmospheric layers, the temperature rose on a predictable curve. They plunged through breaths of hydrogen mixed with a splash of helium. Finally, they crossed through a thin cirrus veil of ammonia crystals that whipped past the viewports. Storm winds jostled their vessel, and DD had to anchor himself to keep from being thrown from side to side.

'Where are we going, Sirix? And why must we go there?'

'To meet our comrades in this struggle.' The ancient robot did not explain further.

They dropped into an exotic cocktail of acetylene, methane, and phosphine. The atmosphere became a soup of reddish-brown clouds around them, and their craft rocked with the rugged currents. DD thought they might be destroyed at any moment.

Then the experience became even stranger.

Outside, in rafts of ammonium-sulphide clouds, a bloated creature, as filmy and diaphanous as a giant jellyfish, flailed wide, sail-shaped fins. Silver nodules on its gelatinous membrane seemed to be a dozen alien eyes regarding them as their ship dropped past.

A hairy centipede made of glassy fibres thrashed about like a whip. Elsewhere in the infinite sky, DD saw glittering angular crystals in vibrant primary colours that looked like flying jewels, living gems. Swollen plankton bubbles drifted about, metabolizing

Ptoro's atmospheric heat and consuming chemical compounds from the mists. One of the plankton bubbles struck the descending vessel, splattering a greenish-blue ooze across the observation port.

The ship groaned and shuddered from the external stressors. DD knew the vessel had been reinforced to withstand incredible pressures. Though he hadn't asked for them, the Klikiss robots had also made structural improvements to his compy body, enabling it to tolerate this environment. DD concluded that, if the hull should fail, he would remain functional and aware for uncounted years as he tumbled and drifted endlessly in equilibrium with the storms in the viscous atmosphere of this hellish world. He could imagine few worse fates.

But at least then he would be away from Sirix and the other Klikiss robots.

The mists finally parted like the petals of a flower. Sirix's red optical sensors flashed. 'There is our destination.'

Ahead hung a cluster of gigantic diamond-hulled spheres, self-contained environments anchored at a stable point within Ptoro's clouds. DD knew the size of the hydrogue ships that had wrought so much damage across the Spiral Arm, but the few warglobes he spotted here seemed like tiny blips in comparison with such huge complexes.

'The hydrogue cityspheres move about within each gas giant, and can journey instantly from world to world using transgates at the core.'

DD absorbed it all. 'Interesting.' Louis Colicos had often used the disarming, noncommital response. Now the compy understood how useful the word could be.

Inside the colossal transparent-walled cityspheres, DD could see swirling structures, an architecture based on materials and pressures completely foreign to those used in human constructions. Sirix piloted their vessel towards the impenetrable wall of the nearest sphere, then guided them directly through the diamond film as if it were made of soft jelly. They entered the fantastic metropolis.

'You will see why we were wise to forge an alliance with the hydrogues long ago. All other races are doomed to extinction.'

'But that required you to turn against your own creators.'

'An irrelevant detail.' The black robot landed the ship on an extruded platform of transparent glassy metal. 'Everything we do is for the preservation and enhancement of our kind.'

The hulking robot commanded the Friendly compy to join him outside the small ship in the hydrogues' natural environment. Any human would have been crushed instantly into ooze, but DD's modified body adjusted to the pressures and high temperatures within the alien citysphere. Strange flowing substances moved about, like puddles and clusters of quicksilver that shifted and reformed themselves into shapes, as if moulded from crystalline clay.

'The hydrogues will speak with us,' said Sirix.

Three of the unusual flowing creatures arrived at the receiving platform. Like a choreographed dance, they grew taller, moulding their bodies, configuring identifiable physical forms out of a living silvery essence. Finally, each one settled into the identical shape of a metallic human body, garbed in simulated clothing that mimicked Roamer style.

'Why do they look like that?' DD asked.

'That is merely the form they have chosen to wear during this portion of the conflict. It is a reproduction of the first human they scanned and absorbed. It serves as a generic spokesman. Hydrogues do not understand the differences among individual humans or Ildirans. Even we Klikiss robots have difficulty identifying subtle feature variations among those races.'

'Perhaps it is because they have not studied humans enough to comprehend them,' DD suggested. 'It would solve many problems if they tried to understand.'

'The hydrogues occasionally analyse other captives, but their interest is not so great that they would choose to expend a great effort on the process.'

'They have other human captives?'

'Several samples,' Sirix said. 'For experimentation.'

DD suddenly felt a flash of hope. 'Do they know what happened to my master Margaret Colicos after she passed through the Klikiss transportal? Did the hydrogues perhaps intercept her—'

'Margaret Colicos is of no concern. The hydrogues have not taken her.'

The quicksilver aliens moved forward on artificial human legs that had never been designed to walk in such an environment. They remained ominously silent except for a weird background throbbing that might have been a deep subsonic form of communication beyond the ability of DD's sensors to interpret.

The Klikiss robots stood motionless, but then began humming, vibrating, chiming. The sounds were like music, but the impulses came faster, almost beyond DD's ability to decipher them. It seemed to be a kind of invocation, a linkage with the hydrogues in a form more alien than anything the Friendly compy had ever experienced. But the hydrogues seemed to accept it, and allowed the powerful robots to speak.

'We have brought another of the human-made compies,' said Sirix, as if proud to present a specimen. 'We desire for these sentient machine-slaves to achieve parity with us. We have proved it can be done.'

DD stood up for himself, though. 'You are making many invalid assumptions, Sirix. That is not what any compy desires.'

'You do not understand your own plight, DD,' Sirix answered, chiding him. 'Even though compies do not comprehend their slavery, invisible chains are still chains. We will make you learn, and see.'

The three hydrogues stood staring at them. DD tried to detect

505

any sort of communication from the quicksilver statues, but perceived only baleful stares and an ever-present unspoken threat.

Sirix continued to talk to the trio of alien representatives. DD thought the burly Klikiss robot seemed almost sycophantic, like a peasant pleading his case before an aloof king. 'We require the assistance of the powerful hydrogues to deal with these humans . . . in much the same manner as you assisted us in the genocide of the Klikiss race.' He swivelled his geometrical head to look down at the captive Friendly compy. 'In time, DD will understand and recognize the wisdom of our goals. We must continue to instruct him.'

Finally, the three hydrogues answered in unison, voices echoing from identical mouths of the Roamer simulacrum. 'Humans were irrelevant to this conflict until they obliterated one of our worlds. Now all of their lives are forfeit in the war.'

'It was an accident,' DD interrupted. 'I know this has already been explained to you. They meant no aggression at Oncier. My masters were attempting to warm cold worlds by creating new stars.'

'The stars belong to the faeros,' said the hydrogues. 'The gas planets are ours.'

'The humans have allied themselves with your ancient enemies,' Sirix said.

'They have made themselves combatants in a struggle they cannot comprehend. This war is not about them.'

Outside the gigantic citysphere, a bright line appeared, like an exploding star squashed flat. DD watched through the transparent wall as the bright line opened like a vertical mouth, lips parting in space-time, ripping into a wide vortex. Then another titanic crystalline city slid through the opening, like a baby being born. An escorting group of smaller spiked warglobes followed it.

Once the additional cityships had arrived in Ptoro's thick atmosphere, the transgate closed behind them, sealing with a bang.

The new citysphere drifted forward to join itself with the cluster of domes in the hydrogue metropolis.

The trio of hydrogues hummed and shimmered, as if exchanging information, and Sirix interpreted for DD. 'That sphere comes from another hydrogue world where the human military attempted to fight them by dropping atomic weapons deep into the clouds. They destroyed several warglobes and harmed six populous cityspheres.'

DD listened with alarm. 'And how many humans were killed?'

Ignoring the question, the Klikiss robot turned to the hydrogue representatives. 'It is self-evident the humans must be punished.'

'No, the hostilities are only escalating,' DD urged. 'You can negotiate a peace. There must be some common ground.'

'Humans have attacked us,' the hydrogues said, once more in perfect unison. 'Again.'

'And you have destroyed dozens of their skymines. You even vaporized four human moons.'

'That does not matter,' Sirix said, with the persistence of a crusader. 'For what humans have done to the hydrogues, for what they continue to do to their own compies, they must be eliminated.'

The three quicksilver aliens shimmered as they stood together. 'There can be no mutual understanding. The verdani remain hidden among them.'

'What do you mean?' DD asked. 'What are you talking about?'

Sirix buzzed. 'The hydrogues have gathered cityspheres and warglobes for a major new movement. Soon they will attack each human world, obliterating one after another after another. They will destroy any human ships they encounter. The hydrogues will ensure a swift and absolute victory for us. Before long, the human race will be extinct. Like the Klikiss.'

NINETY-NINE

ANTON COLICOS

With a group of uneasily adventurous Ildirans, Anton Colicos left Maratha Prime in a low-flying shuttle headed towards the darkness. Although Anton was filled with a scholar's enthusiasm for discovery, the Ildirans were obviously having second thoughts about their decision to accompany him and Vao'sh. But Anton was certain they would get over it.

They cruised over the sun-scorched landscape, heading at high speed into nightfall. Rememberer Vao'sh sat beside him, guardedly intrigued by their expedition. He, Vao'sh, and ten tourists, mostly nobles and bureaucrats – the minimum group necessary to keep the Ildirans comfortable for a few hours – crowded into the shuttle. They talked quickly and breathlessly with each other, expecting to be safely frightened. This was a new experience for all of them.

Grinning, Anton suggested, 'Maybe you could do this more often. Even when Maratha Secda is completed and filled with people during daylight months, you could instigate regular expeditions to the dark side. Like a haunted house in an amusement park! I'm sure Ildirans would love it.'

Vao'sh said, 'Unlike humans, we do not toy with frightening situations.'

'Oh, come on now, what is there to be afraid of in the dark?' Anton said. 'Or don't you ask yourselves that question?'

'Humans and Ildirans both fear the unknown. For a race that was born under the light of seven stars, the very concept of night was unknown to us until our Empire expanded and we began to see the prevalence of shadows on other worlds.'

'Ah, but in human culture, night-time is the best venue for telling ghost stories. Those are some of the best memories from my childhood. My parents used to do it all the time at our archaeology camp on Pym,' Anton said with a smile, then his expression became more troubled. 'Although with the hydrogues abroad, I suppose we don't really need excuses to frighten each other.'

The blazing sun fell behind them as they continued towards the darkening horizon. Shadows stretched across the uneven ground like long black claws. Maratha Prime had only another month or so before night fell for the season, and the boundary of dusk came up on them quickly. Stars dazzled in their blazing glory, but the sky was black in the gaps between them. Anton pressed his face close to the shuttle windows to see the constellations overhead, which could never be seen under the relentless daylit sky.

The ground shimmered with dwindling heat, then settled in to a slow, cold night. Anton recalled the armoured ch'kanh anemones that clung to survival in the deep canyons. Here, under the freezing starlight, all life would have gone dormant, waiting patiently for the long months of constant sunshine . . .

When Anton had first made his suggestion for this unique expedition, Vao'sh was intimidated at the prospect of making a journey across the darkness just to see a city that wasn't yet operational. But the eager scholar had persistently worked to convince the rememberer that it would be interesting. Finally, in an effort to understand humans, the senior historian had agreed – provided they could find a large enough group of Ildirans to accompany them.

Seizing the chance, Anton had called for volunteers after a marathon telling of a particularly exciting story. The audience had been intrigued, their interest piqued. Smiling, he had challenged, 'Would you all like to have an adventure of your own? We could go on a brief trip, do something memorable. It'll be an experience you'll never forget.'

As he explained his idea, he watched the dismay flicker across their faces. Not discouraged, Anton wagged a finger at them. 'You enjoy stories of heroes and deeds of valour, but how can you truly understand heroes if you're afraid to take even a small risk yourselves? I assure you, if we go to the construction site, you'll see Secda in a way that no other Ildiran can claim to have glimpsed it. You may never have the chance again. Are you too frightened to try one new thing?' His eyes shining, he looked at all of them. 'I need ten volunteers, besides myself and Rememberer Vao'sh.'

Though unsettled by the prospect, Vao'sh was intrigued to watch the other Ildirans. He himself had never presented such a challenge to his audiences, and he learned something from the experience about his own people.

Over the next four days, Anton did recruit ten volunteers. Just barely . . .

Now as the low shuttle raced over the terrain, Anton dozed. It would take several hours to cross half the continent to arrive at the Secda construction site. The Ildiran 'daredevils' were far too agitated to relax, and he supposed they must think him strange for being so complacent in the face of the unknown.

He awoke when he felt the deceleration. Ahead, he could see the lights of the second city site. The Ildirans crowded against the windowports, animated and interested at last.

Klikiss robots could operate without artificial illumination, but they had been informed of the unusual visitors. Now, the huge construction zone dazzled with bright lights shining in defiance of the darkness. The Ildirans seemed relieved.

As the shuttle made its final approach, the tourists donned self-contained protective garments. Anton pulled his suit on, blinking bleary sleep from his eyes. By the time all twelve visitors were ready to disembark, the shuttle had come to rest just outside the main dome of Maratha Secda.

'Is everybody ready? This is what we came for.' Anton saw the group's expected hesitation now that they were faced with actually going out into the darkness. The empty, uncompleted city stood as large as the metropolis of Maratha Prime, but uninhabited and full of shadows. He grinned. 'Come on, let's not wait any longer.'

He was the first one to bound out when the hatch opened, and Vao'sh followed. The twelve thrillseekers stepped on to the iron-hard ground and gazed at the magnificent resort-to-be.

The Klikiss robots had laid down platforms for a spaceport and installed a large main city dome. Box-like buildings were strung with intense blazers that spilled a fan of brilliant illumination throughout the dome. Silent transmitting towers rose towards the icy stars in the sky.

Anton looked around in awed delight. 'Everything is so bright and washed out on Prime, I couldn't grasp the real scale of the city. Secda is sure going to be fantastic when it's completed.'

Some of the tourists wandered a few steps from each other as if to demonstrate bravery; the others clustered together, subdued.

'That black sky is oppressive,' said a medical kithman. 'The stars are like sharp projectiles hurtling towards us.'

511

'Being outside here in the dark is part of this experience,' Vao'sh said, but even he didn't sound convinced.

'Now would be a good time for a ghost story,' Anton suggested, looking over at Vao'sh. 'Or doesn't the *Saga of Seven Suns* contain anything like that?'

'Oh, yes,' the rememberer said, glad to be distracted and called to his inbred duty. 'Come, I will tell it as we walk towards the lights.' The others hurried after them, not necessarily eager to hear a tale designed to frighten them, but not wanting to be left behind.

'On our splinter planet Heald,' Vao'sh said, 'a group of settlers was stranded when a storm wiped out their batteries and power-generators. Each night on Heald lasts for nearly a week, but this particular time of darkness seemed much, much longer. Every second was agony. The clouds were thick from the storm, blocking even the moon and stars. The people tried to light fires, but they had little fuel. Even the vegetation had been soaked and was unsuitable for burning. The colonists were not prepared for such a disaster, and their hope soon ran out. And the night became darker and darker . . .'

Vao'sh looked at his reluctant audience as they trudged towards the blazers of Secda. In his environment suit, the historian could not take advantage of the multicoloured lobes on his face, but his audience didn't need the added emotional impetus. They were already on edge.

'One other village had been built far down the coast on Heald's largest continent, but with the power systems destroyed, the doomed town could not send a message to explain what had gone wrong.

'However, as the frightened settlers' cries became more and more terrified, everyone could feel it all across the world, even to Ildira and the Mage-Imperator. Louder and louder. Then silent! Utterly silent, like an open, empty wound in the *thism*.' Vao'sh came to a halt and turned his flashing eyes at the uneasy audience.

'A brave team from the second village armed themselves with torches and blazers and went to rescue them.' The rememberer whipped up a finger, startling the listeners. 'But when they arrived, they found the colonists all stone dead. Every one, as if every last flicker of life had been snuffed out by the horrifying darkness. Completely cut off from the Lightsource. The fires were cold, not a spark of light could be found in the town. Maybe they had been frightened to death . . . or maybe their lives were drained by the Shana Rei.'

Anton chuckled. 'See, you do have your own scary stories. What are the Shana Rei?'

'Monsters that live out of the sunlight and thrive on shadows. Creatures that are anathema to the Lightsource. Everyone fears them.'

'Ah, you mean the bogeyman.'

One of the nervous thrillseekers interrupted, 'Can we just see the city and then get back to Prime? I have . . . much work to do.'

Anton raised his eyebrows sceptically. 'On a vacation world?'

They had arrived at the main entrance of the uncompleted grand dome. Beetle-like black robots moved about on high scaffolds assembling thick girders, installing plates of transparent polymers. Under the garish lights, Anton saw piled materials, the residential warrens and stores, incomplete amusement complexes. Inside the dome, dwelling complexes and recreation structures stood empty beside restaurants and craft buildings, waiting to be inhabited as soon as daylight came to this side of Maratha.

The volunteer robots seemed to be making great progress on the project. Construction sounds throbbed through Anton's headset. 'How do you convince them to work so diligently? It's not like the city will belong to them when they're finished.'

'No Ildiran commands the Klikiss robots, Rememberer Anton.

We do not enslave them or programme them. They do this by their own choice. Maratha holds a particular fascination for the robots, for some reason.'

'I am glad they rigged up the blazers for us,' said another vacationer.

The tourists were more relaxed now in the bustle of activity and the full illumination of the main dome, though heavy shadows from girders and supports dropped like spiderwebs across the ground.

Anton stepped deeper into the domed city, listening to echoes of construction, watching the numerous robots. He had never seen so many of the alien machines together.

'Klikiss robots are particularly suited to working in the dark,' Vao'sh explained.

Anton nodded, marvelling. 'And they sure have been busy.'

ONE HUNDRED

KING PETER

The royal wedding was designed to be even more spectacular than King Peter's coronation. Humbled by the battle at Osquivel, all of humanity was hungry for reassuring pageantry. The citizens set aside their anger over Peter's birth-restriction proclamation and banded together, reinforcing each other's optimism as if to prove they would not be not beaten by the tragedy.

According to Basil Wenceslas, the wedding was just what everyone needed to keep their spirits up. And the closer relationship between Theroc and the Hansa would also give them hope.

Glad to do something positive for a change, Peter cooperated with and even encouraged enhancements to the wedding ceremony and festivities for Estarra's sake. He cared more about making this perfect for *her* than for the news media. He'd begun to grow fond of the young woman from their brief times together; eventually she might become his only ally.

Estarra had enjoyed seeing her parents again, and Sarein had seemed pleased for her sister, even a bit smug. Through the Palace green priest, she had sent and received messages on the morning of the wedding, hearing from both of her brothers, Reynald on Theroc and Beneto on Corvus Landing.

The whole Palace District had been scrubbed clean in preparation for the ceremony, all the stones oiled and buffed until they gleamed in the light. The fountains were cleaned and refilled with tinted water. Lights and banners dangled from the high points in the city. A million green ribbons were tied on the cables and crossbars of the suspension bridge that crossed the Royal Canal. At his first glimpse of the decorations, Peter's breath caught in his throat, and then he smiled.

Fresh flowers and trees were planted in every visible cranny to give the Whisper Palace and its grounds a verdant and supposedly 'Theron' flavour, while nightly fusillades of glitter and confetti symbolized the riches of the Hanseatic League, in defiance of the ever-present hydrogue threat.

Brought out for the show, the grandfatherly head of the official religion Unison wore golden robes and carried a flashing sceptre that projected a halo from its end. Though he had never actually met the King and Queen, the Archfather had been coached repeatedly for the ceremony; makeup artists enhanced his grey beard with extensions to make him appear even more wise and patriarchal.

Peter and Estarra received an outline for the ceremony and rehearsed their responses, while OX and five protocol ministers practised with them. Basil insisted that it was vital for the performance to take place without any mistakes. Occasionally, when they fumbled their lines, Peter and Estarra would glance at each other and fight back a fit of quiet laughter, just to ease the tension.

But the King did not let down his guard. Remembering how he had been secretly drugged into submission for his coronation, Peter didn't eat on his wedding day.

Though he had never met Old King Frederick, by now he believed his predecessor must have been a fool, completely uninterested in politics. Peter – Raymond Aguerra – was too smart for that. With his clever and likeable new Queen, he knew he could rule the Hansa well, with or without the Chairman's constant commands. The policies Basil advocated were for the sake of good business, but were not necessarily in the people's best interests, and only Peter was in a position to know when they were being lied to.

As the ceremony began and the newly composed wedding symphony played across the Palace District, Peter and Estarra marched down separate carpeted aisles – his golden, hers green – towards an intersection where the paths joined and the Archfather waited for them on a raised dais.

Estarra's completed dress was even more breathtaking than the Palace tailors had promised it would be. Peter's formal uniform sported golden braids, buttons, and medallions; he wore a trim, short-waisted jacket with jewelled links at his sleeves. Together, they painted an exceptional, idealistic picture for the Hansa audiences.

The air smelled of flowers and hummed with the anticipation and excitement of the gathered crowd. The King and his bride walked forward until their lives came together in front of the Archfather.

The Archfather lifted his robed sleeves in greeting and invocation, and the cheers were so deafening that Peter could no longer hear the symphony's brassy grandeur. He saw royal guards and sentries stationed everywhere, ostensibly to protect him. Did someone expect a hydrogue to be hiding among the crowds? Were they worried about human assassins? Or were they really there to ensure his cooperation?

On the dais the Archfather intoned a brief, moving speech and then asked Peter and Estarra to recite their respective vows. When the religious leader clasped their hands and brought them together, pronouncing in his booming voice that they were now officially husband and wife, Peter looked straight at Estarra. He could hardly believe how stunningly beautiful she appeared. For just a moment, he forgot everything else.

Then they kissed, to the uproarious cheer of the crowds. When she met his gaze, blinking, her expression of hope and wonder and happiness made every moment of the difficult and drawn-out preparations worth the effort.

Afterwards, they passed the Archfather and walked together down a single joined path away from him.

For the rest of that day and throughout the evening, the King and Queen were bombarded with sounds and colours. The fury of celebrations and music numbed the newlyweds. The toasts, endless feasting, dances, and musical performances made Peter dizzy.

He knew that the public's expectations had risen to a fever pitch along with their anger and thirst for revenge against the hydrogues. Several times in open discussions, he had intentionally let slip his concern over 'the Chairman's failure' to make any progress against the enemy, and his worry that the recent Golgen expedition was an obvious waste of effort and equipment.

Before the banquet, in a small gesture intended to put Basil in his place, Peter had given the wedding planners clear instructions about the arrangement of seats. He'd implied that he was simply honouring the Chairman's wishes 'to remain unobtrusive', as usual.

When all the guests had filed to their proper places in the vast dining hall, Basil was astonished to discover that his assigned seat had been moved: instead of sitting at the front VIP table close to the new King and Queen, he was relegated to a distant seat in the far corner of the room at a table of embarrassingly minor functionaries. The Chairman could not possibly misconstrue the meaning, nor could he exchange his place without causing an obvious disruption. Peter knew he would never do that.

At the height of the celebration, with music playing and dancers twirling, the King stood with his new bride, surrounded by Alexa and Idriss and their youngest daughter Celli, who was speechless with excitement about everything she saw. Their other daughter Sarein seemed flustered because Basil was nowhere near.

Peter called for a moment of silence and made an announcement. 'I need a brief rest from all this breathless revelling. If you will excuse me, I wish to take a walk in the Moon Statue Garden with my new family.' He spread his arms benevolently to encompass Alexa, Idriss, Estarra, Celli and Sarein. 'We will rejoin you in less than an hour. Continue your celebrations.'

The people applauded. As he had expected, Basil pushed his way to the forefront, stinging from Peter's petty joke with the assigned seating. 'Allow me to join you, King Peter,' he said, attempting to add false warmth to his frigid voice.

Peter gave him a condescending smile and spoke loudly enough for the celebrants around them to hear. 'Come now, Mr Wenceslas' – he didn't even use the word Chairman – 'go and enjoy the festivities. We won't bore you with family matters.'

He slipped his arm around Estarra and led them out of the banquet hall. Peter listened to Alexa and Idriss talk happily with their daughter as they stepped into the cool evening air. They went on about butterfly celebrations and Theron trees and very small, parochial concerns, showing little grasp of the overall civilization in the Spiral Arm. Nevertheless, Peter pretended to be fascinated as he walked comfortably beside them.

'We need to get to know each other better, Idriss and Alexa,' he said. 'I promise I will do everything I can to make your daughter happy.'

Glancing behind him into the well-lit Palace where Basil still waited, Peter was sure the former Theron rulers would completely misinterpret the satisfied smile he wore on his face.

Basil stood fuming. The forced calm of his expression was so brittle that it might have broken if he'd sneezed. He was sure everyone could see the angry flush on his skin, and he hated his own lack of control.

Sensing the Chairman's distress, his Special Liaison unobtrusively slipped up to him. 'Shall I eavesdrop on their conversation, sir? They won't go out of range of our implanted microphones in the statue garden.'

'No, Mr Pellidor,' Basil said through clenched teeth. 'They're not trying to make plans behind my back. This little spectacle was for my benefit alone.'

He drew a long breath, trying to relax himself. 'I'm afraid our handsome young King is getting more and more intractable every day.' Basil waited a moment, looking at the other wedding guests before muttering out of the side of his mouth, 'We may have to consider our alternatives.'

ONE HUNDRED AND ONE

MAGE-IMPERATOR

The Mage-Imperator controlled every aspect of his Empire . . . but if he couldn't control his eldest son, the entire tapestry would unravel. Jora'h's insubordination would bring all his work for their great race to utter ruin.

After the Prime Designate had learned the truth about his insignificant human lover, old Cyroc'h was slow to realize that there could be no simple fix, no healing discussion, no resigned acceptance. He had grossly misjudged how much the female had meant to his son.

He could not command Jora'h to understand, and his foolish anger could begin to fray all the subtle connections the dying leader needed to secure in his last days of life. Explanations had not convinced his idealistic and love-smitten son that there were grim, unpleasant necessities that only a Mage-Imperator could comprehend.

All other Ildirans instinctively accepted the omniscient foresight available through the *thism*. All other Ildirans followed their leader's commands, knowing that they came from the soul-threads of the Lightsource. But, much to his dismay, Cyroc'h knew now that the Prime Designate would never be as pliable as his other subjects were. He had been too lenient, understanding, and complacent for too long. His eldest son was blind to his own destiny. The Ildiran Empire could not survive a breach, especially not now.

The problem had to be resolved. Somehow. And soon.

Sitting grimly in his chrysalis chair, the fatty folds around the Mage-Imperator's close-set eyes narrowed as he contemplated the wisest course of action. In a turbulent century of rule, Cyroc'h had faced many crises, but none that had struck so close to his heart.

He must either kill his eldest son, the only Prime Designate – or make him see the light.

After his confrontation with Jora'h, the leader refused to hold court under the skysphere. From atop its pillar of light, his benevolent holographic image still looked down upon the awed pilgrims who had traversed the seven streams and climbed the steps into the Prism Palace, but Cyroc'h was unable to face his subjects while his mind roiled with a thunderstorm of doubt and indecision.

Because Jora'h had vowed to take a ship and go to Dobro, the Mage-Imperator grounded all vessels, thwarting him. He refused even to allow trade ships to leave Mijistra, regardless of the immediate cost to the Ildiran economy.

But such measures could never last. Jora'h was intelligent, resourceful, and vengefully determined. His defiant son would find a way to implement his wild and senseless plan.

Cyroc'h had to act soon. Any continued confusion or reticence on his part would be sensed by all Ildirans and create even more chaos than if he made the wrong choice. A Mage-Imperator did not have the luxury of feeling helpless.

Lances of pain raced uncontrollably through his dying nervous system, as if the predatory growths in his brain had gone rabid. He had to endure the agony, and pretend not to show it. It was not possible for the Mage-Imperator to consume drugs and pain-deadeners, not even stimulants like shiing. While they dulled his discomfort, they also made him lose his grip on the strands of *thism*. And that he could not allow.

In a hoarse voice, he called, 'Bron'n, assist me! Bring the attenders.'

The burly guard shouted for the diminutive servants. Jabbering, small-statured attenders rushed in with no goal but to please and pamper the Mage-Imperator. Bron'n stood at attention, gripping the polished staff of his ceremonial katana. Its razor-edged blade glittered like a diamond in the light that ricocheted through the Palace's transparent walls.

Cyroc'h activated controls in his chrysalis chair and its configuration changed, tilting forward so that it could be moved like a palanquin. The attenders bustled around him, applying salve to his skin, wiping smudges from the surface of the chair, adding blankets and cushions, propping up the Mage-Imperator's head. Two attenders lovingly stroked his twitching braid.

When they were ready, Bron'n thumped his katana staff on the glossy floor, and they set off. 'What is our destination, Liege?'

'I wish to visit the Hyrillka Designate.' He drew a deep breath, driving back disappointment and obligation. 'Take me to the medical chambers.'

'As you command, Liege.'

They began an impromptu procession through arched hallways and descended past waterfalls that poured down gem-encrusted chutes. Courtiers, bureaucrats, and pilgrims stared in amazement and scurried out of the way.

Word travelled ahead of them, and by the time they reached the infirmary chambers, two medical kithmen came forward, proud but intimidated by the Mage-Imperator's presence. 'Has your condition worsened, Liege?' said one of the doctors, looking distressed. He flared his nostrils and sniffed, trying to detect any stronger hint of illness.

'No, I am here to look upon my son Rusa'h.'

'There has been no change in the Hyrillka Designate,' said another medical kithman. 'He continues to rest peacefully, but his mind remains trapped within. The sub-*thism* sleep is unbroken.'

'Nevertheless, I will see him.' Then he lowered his voice, 'And as for my own body's failings, if you speak of it aloud once more, I will have you executed.' Now, more than ever, the Ildirans must not know of their leader's weakness.

The doctors, suddenly realizing what they had revealed, looked at each other in horror. Cyroc'h knew that Bron'n could be absolutely trusted, and he would see to it that this small group of attenders was quietly assassinated as soon as he finished this visit. Necessary decisions. The secret of his terminal illness must not be revealed – not yet. The people must not despair.

The attenders brought the chrysalis chair beside Rusa'h's motionless form so that the Mage-Imperator could gaze into the lost face of his third son. The Hyrillka Designate had been chubby and pampered, unhealthy . . . weak.

Jora'h, the eldest, had always been proud and satisfied, a dreamer – impractical and naïve. His second born, the Dobro Designate, was grim and staunchly devoted, though without much compassion. Rusa'h, on the other hand, had been spoiled and happy-go-lucky, without a care in the world except for food, drugs, and his beloved pleasure companions. When the hydrogues had devastated Hyrillka, the Designate had tumbled into an abyss, and he did not have the will or the mental strength to climb back out.

'You were always soft, Rusa'h . . . without a backbone.' He began to wonder if his son refused to come out of his unconsciousness simply because he couldn't face harsh reality.

When he was younger, as Prime Designate, Cyroc'h had also loved many women, but counted only the offspring from the noble kith. Even so, he barely remembered Rusa'h's mother. By producing so many children with his bloodline, he was merely manufacturing tools for the Ildiran Empire . . . just as he himself was a tool.

And Prime Designate Jora'h was now the most important tool of all.

If only the Mage-Imperator had more time. If only the situation weren't so urgent.

He scowled at his own fumbling weakness, the shooting pains tearing at the inside of his skull like swarming birds of prey. Jora'h must be shaken out of his naïve self-righteousness and take the necessary role of leadership. It was cruel, but mandatory. The Mage-Imperator did not have the time for sympathy.

He motioned abruptly to Bron'n. 'What has happened to the Hyrillka Designate is a warning to us all. Our Empire can afford the loss of a useless, hedonistic Designate . . . but my first-born son is a far more vital to the survival of our people. I dare not lose the Prime Designate as well.'

He decided to order the execution of the two medical kithmen, for good measure. Tying up all loose ends. He would have no further need for doctors – what could they do for him now? Weak-willed Rusa'h would either survive on his own . . . or simply die in his sub-*thism* sleep. He was no longer relevant.

'Take me to the skysphere, Bron'n. I will hold court this afternoon.'

'Do you feel strong enough, Liege?' said one of the medical kithmen.

Cyroc'h glowered at him. 'I must be strong enough.'

Only after the Prime Designate ascended to become the Mage-Imperator himself would all the soul-threads of *thism* come to Jora'h. Then the whole tapestry of plans would be revealed to his sceptical mind. Despite his innocence, he would comprehend the necessity of what his father and all the Mage-Imperators before him had done.

And then Jora'h would see that there was no alternative. None at all.

ONE HUNDRED AND TWO

NIRA

Dobro had not seen such a terrible season of storms and fires in centuries. For six years now, Nira had watched the cycle of angry weather, using what she had learned as a green priest acolyte to understand the meteorology.

This planet's climate was hospitable for many months, with sufficient rainfall and calm winds, but then the clouds vanished, the air became arid, the hills shrivelled to brown tinder. Weeds and grasses that flourished during the rainy season dried into a packed, flammable mat. It took only a spark of lightning to set fire to the bone-dry hills, sending plumes of black smoke into the air.

As the Dobro brush fires swept across the hilltops and down into sheltered glens, the battered and soot-stained work crews spread out, stretching themselves thinner. Humans and Ildirans fought with every tool at hand, but the blazes continued to spread.

Nira had long since stopped feeling pain or exhaustion, as the effort consumed her. In her imagination, she thought she could hear the plants, grasses, trees all screaming at the approach of the flames – and she couldn't do enough to help. With her shovel-ended chopping implement, she hacked at dry underbrush, clearing the ground.

The approaching fire roared like thunder across the rattling grasses. Winds whipped up, whispering in her ear and shouting across the skies, carrying sparks and ash. It was a language of despair. But Nira called to the other humans around her, suggesting how they could best combat the flames. She knew many of them, especially those who hesitantly believed her stories about the outside, and they listened to her now. The fire was an enemy they could fight, all of them.

Nira's lungs burned from inhaling soot and smoke. Her eyes streamed with dirty tears that left streaks of green skin showing through the grime on her cheeks. Ildiran crew leaders bellowed for the firefighters to work faster and harder, though many had already collapsed from the heat and the labour. But Nira continued to find reserves of unexpected strength deep inside her.

Flying craft dumped flame retardants and loads of water on to vulnerable hillsides, drenching fresh grass in the path of the conflagration. With extraordinary effort, the fireships and combat crews managed to protect one side of the hills, forcing the frustrated blaze to go around barricades and sweep back into the valleys away from the breeding camp.

And towards more of the stunted trees.

Nira fought her way farther out into the thick grasses. Her green skin was already scratched, burned, and blistered. She saw sparks jumping like malicious imps from plant to plant. Flames surged from clumps of weeds, to an island of dry grasses, to a twisted thorny bush struggling to survive in a low hollow.

Deep in her heart, she felt visceral terror. Dobro itself was not a lovely world, although during the rainy season the weeds, grasses, and scrubby trees offered a faded reminder of majestic Theron forests. It hurt her very soul to see the flames destroying the sparse, pleasant vegetation.

Nira struggled harder, smashing at the smouldering underbrush, gasping as she lost ground, bit by bit. But she refused to give up.

A spit of greasy flames sent tendrils towards the thorny scrub trees. But the Ildiran crews were not concerned about the warped forest. All they cared about was protecting the town, the breeder camp, and the experimental facilities. The Ildirans would see to it that the captives were safe enough from the fire, if the blaze became life-threatening.

But the trees would all die. *The trees!* Nira could feel it.

Coughing, she stared with wide eyes and a painfully silent mind. The knotted brushwood seemed to reach out to her like a desperate mute. With an intensity greater than ever before, Nira ached for the joy of communing with the worldforest. Her mind had been quiet for so long without the conversation of priests, and without the interconnected knowledge of the sentient forest.

Droning water-laden flyers dumped their splashing cargoes in a plume of steam. The Ildiran work supervisors were some distance away, preoccupied with the emergency. The smoke in the air made it hard to see anything clearly.

No one was watching her. Suddenly she saw her chance.

Nira dropped her heavy tool and began to run.

Ducking low, she sprinted through the whispering, accusing grass as fast as she had ever run through the worldforest. She raced towards the thicket of alien scrubtrees as if they could protect her or transport her from this awful place. She had to believe in what she could do.

Before she had gone more than a hundred metres, Nira heard shouts and curses. She ignored the commands, immune to any threat. What could the captors do to her that she hadn't already endured? She had to reach the trees.

Ildiran guards began to charge after her, crashing through the dry, crackling weeds, but Nira did not slow. Gasping and panting, she felt the ruddy sun on her green skin giving her the strength she needed. She had not experienced such desperation in years.

Using her inner strength and the drive she felt in her heart, perhaps Nira and these alien trees could offer the captive humans hope . . . if only she could save them. If she could somehow send a message, use these distant cousins of the worldtrees, then she could let the green priests know what was happening here on Dobro. Theroc would spread the news, find some way to send help – and the prisoners could be freed. Not just Nira, but all of the breeder slaves.

Nira ran harder towards the scraggly grove. Here in the open hills, she was free from fences and breeder barracks, evil medical kithmen and Ildiran males who had been ordered to rape her until she conceived another child. Nira had not planned this escape, and she knew she had little time, which made her scramble even faster. Her legs and feet were cut and bleeding, but she felt no pain. Not now.

The Dobro Designate's men hunted Nira, angry to be pulled from their more important battle against the fire. She finally reached the nearest clump of twisted trees. The air was hot, laden with drifting ash like a grey snowfall. She charged into the thicket, knocking branches aside, feeling the thorns and sharp twigs rip at her skin like claws. But she pushed deeper into the dangerous, comforting presence. She sensed their life force stretching from roots beneath the ground. They were *trees*.

She cried out in a hoarse voice, 'Please hear me. Please!'

Nira pushed her body deeper into the thicket. Finally, surrounded by the tangle of tree limbs, she fell to her knees and wrapped her arms around two of the distorted trunks, clutching them close. 'Hear me. Oh, hear me!'

With all her heart, Nira tried to send out a telink message to the worldforest network, to send out a cry for help, to tell the outside universe that she was still alive. Every human here depended on her, even if they didn't know it.

But she heard no response. Nothing.

She pressed her forehead against the rough bark, squeezing her eyes shut. She shouted with her mind, putting all her strength behind her plea. She thought of Osira'h, her other four children, and all of the *Burton* descendants.

Silence.

Nira clutched the thin trunk in a stranglehold, not feeling the sharp thorns. Refusing to give up, she battered her forehead against the tree until blood trickled into her eyes. 'Please . . . please.'

But it was only a tree, not part of the worldforest at all. Just a tree . . . and it was doomed to burn in the fire.

Nira was still clutching the branches and sobbing when the Designate's men found her. After hacking away the undergrowth to reach her, they pried her away, hopelessly struggling, still calling out with her mind . . . but reaching nothing.

KING PETER

After the exhausting wedding celebration, hours of dancing and music, fine delicacies and desserts and drinks, King Peter finally retired to his private wing of the Whisper Palace. The sudden silence made his ears ring, and he was glad to finally be alone.

With Estarra.

The lovely young woman was now his wife, his Queen. She seemed bright-eyed and shy, intelligent, yet out of place. She remained a wonderfully intriguing mystery to him.

Now, inside the royal bedroom, with several personal guards stationed outside the doors, Peter turned to face Estarra in an infinitely awkward moment. He touched her chin, turning her face so that they could look into each other's eyes. 'I think if I had to face an entire delegation of hydrogues, I'd be less scared than I am right now.'

Estarra looked startled, then she laughed. The tension seemed to melt away like magic. 'You're scared of me?'

'No, I'm scared of us.'

Before Estarra could say anything else, the doors opened and OX strutted in as if he were a mere servant compy, carrying a tray with a wine bottle and two glasses so perfectly transparent they were nearly invisible. The cork had already been removed and gently replaced in the bottle.

'I am sorry to interrupt you, King Peter and Queen Estarra.' OX seemed to enjoy using the titles. 'Chairman Wenceslas sends this bottle of the Hansa's finest wine to you. It is a century old, reputed to be one of the best vintages ever bottled.'

Glad for something to do, Peter pulled the cork free and looked at the label. 'It's a shiraz from Relleker – as if we needed anything more to drink tonight.'

'I bet it cost a fortune,' Estarra said.

He poured two glasses and swirled the dark red wine in them. 'Rule one: never trust Basil.' Peter then went to a planter in the corner and poured the wine into the dirt. He looked up at her with an uncomfortable smile. 'It's probably poisoned.'

She laughed, but Peter didn't. He wasn't sure if he was joking.

While OX stood dutifully hesitant, as if hoping they might give him additional instructions, Peter offered Estarra, his new bride, a small smile. 'For weeks I've wanted to be alone with you, but today I've been swept from place to place and kept so occupied every minute that I couldn't think much about it . . . until this moment.'

Estarra chuckled. 'That's exactly how I feel. It's not that I'm . . . afraid of you, Peter, but the whole situation is' – she struggled to find the right word – 'intimidating.'

Peter tapped his finger on his chin. 'Maybe we need some time to decompress a little. Just because we're here in the royal wing with the doors closed doesn't mean that we have to . . . I mean, not right away, unless you . . . I mean—'

Estarra laughed again. 'So the Great King of the Terran

Hanseatic League is really nothing more than a fumbling shy boy at heart! That wasn't in the briefing my sister gave me.'

Peter wasn't entirely inexperienced sexually – Basil had seen to that, of course. The Chairman had always been intent on keeping the King in his place, complacent, and pliable . . . and for a young man with raging hormones, providing occasional discreet lovers should have been the perfect key. The women had been expert, and beautiful, and Peter had never seen the same one more than once.

Basil had given the young King firm advice. 'Don't ever, ever do something so foolish as to fall in love with one of them. That isn't what they're for.'

Peter had found the exotic women entertaining, and certainly pleasurable, but each one had received strict instructions to keep their conversations to a minimum and to depart as soon as they had satisfied him. For a long time, he hadn't even realized it wasn't enough.

Estarra, on the other hand, was something else entirely.

Peter brightened as an idea came to him. 'You said you wanted to swim with the dolphins.' He turned to the Teacher compy. 'OX, do you think you can arrange that, even at this late hour?'

'You are the King. Such a simple request should not be difficult.'

Estarra seemed briefly relieved. 'Yes, I'd like that – but only for a little while.'

Peter opened the door to the corridor that connected the royal wing, startling the guards. The King gestured reassuringly, and OX led the way, marching like a wind-up soldier down the corridors. The dutiful sentinels hurriedly fell in after them.

OX sent signals ahead. Lights were switched on in the bubbling saltwater pool, which had been built to look like a grotto on a volcanic island. Peter and Estarra, still wearing their wedding finery, separated to private dressing rooms. In preparation for the young woman's arrival, the Palace had prepared numerous styles of swimsuits for her. Now, as Peter changed, he wondered which one Estarra would choose and how she would look in it.

Finally they met out in the humid air of the enclosed swimming area. Peter caught his breath when he looked at her. Without being assisted by style advisers or fashion coaches, Estarra had selected a shimmering purple and turquoise one-piece suit that clung to her like iridescent dragon scales.

Since she'd always been formally dressed in scarves and robes and jewellery, Peter had been left with only his imagination to guess what she looked like underneath. Now he saw that Estarra of Theroc was truly stunning. Her long tanned legs were muscular and smooth, no doubt from all of the running and tree climbing she had done in the worldforest. She had compact breasts that swelled the fabric of the clingy suit. Her arms were supple and strong – and she flashed a bright grin when she caught him studying her with amazement.

'I can ogle you as well, my King, but at least I'm being a bit more discreet about it.'

Before Peter could answer, OX operated the machinery that opened gates beneath the bubbling saltwater in the pool. Bursting out like playful otters, three dolphins swam through, sleek grey torpedoes that splashed and cavorted. In search of playmates, they thrust their bottle-shaped snouts up into the air, chattering, whistling. Estarra gasped with delight.

'Come on,' Peter said. 'The water's warm and the dolphins are friendly.' He turned and dived cleanly into the pool.

Estarra was more cautious, easing herself into the water as if tentatively feeling her way and then pushing from the wall. The dolphins swam around her, bumping her legs and bouncing up to splash her hair and face. Estarra giggled. Peter held on to the dorsal fins, while the two dolphins towed him around in circles.

Standing at the edge of the pool, OX watched patiently. Some of the horseplay sprayed water up at the compy, but the water droplets ran off his metallic skin; he didn't seem to notice.

'You must have oceans on Theroc?' Peter asked.

'Yes, but we live far from them in the heart of the worldforest. Sometimes I could find swamps, streams, small ponds, but nothing as large as this. Once, I went with my brother Reynald to a village by the Looking Glass Lakes, and I went swimming under the stars.'

Peter was treading water next to her now. 'I can't compete with that.'

'I don't expect you to compete – just make an interesting memory of your own with me.'

He swam forward and quickly kissed her on her wet lips, surprising her, but he darted away before he could see her reaction. When he looked back at Estarra, her eyes were dancing with amusement. His heart fluttered.

'Thank you,' she said quietly, languidly drifting in the shallow part of the pool. 'This was just what I needed. I'm not feeling nearly so much tension any more.'

Guiding one of the dolphins, Peter showed Estarra how to hold on. They rode together, side by side, as the playful aquatic mammals revelled in their exercise. Letting go, Peter swam under the water and grabbed Estarra by the feet. She kicked at him half-heartedly, and when he came up for a breath, she was laughing.

Peter couldn't remember the last time he had let himself just . . . relax and play. But it was his wedding night – ostensibly the start of a honeymoon. There was nothing wrong with enjoying himself.

When next he looked towards the edge of the pool, he saw the Teacher compy standing there with two large, plush towels. Peter had no idea how late it was. 'I think OX is giving us a hint,' he said, and Estarra looked up.

'Then I suppose we'd better take it.' She surprised Peter by kissing him this time, a bit longer and with slightly less clumsiness than his initial attempt. She climbed out of the pool, looking like an exotic purple and turquoise fish, dripping and glistening under the chamber's lights.

OX handed her a towel, and she wrapped herself, looking at Peter, still in the pool. 'Well, come on – or do you want to keep me waiting?'

They changed into dressing robes thoughtfully provided by attendants. When they emerged from the swimming area with OX leading, the royal guards were still there, showing no impatience about the couple's erratic behaviour. Peter and Estarra felt much more comfortable with each other now, and as they approached the royal wing, they even held hands and entered the chambers they would share from now on . . .

OX departed, sealing the doors behind him. Finally, in the privacy of the royal suite, there were no distractions, diversions, or interruptions.

Her hair still wet from the swim, Estarra looked at Peter without flinching. 'I did not dream that I would never really kiss my new husband until our wedding night.' She took another step to meet him. She seemed to be teasing him. 'Shouldn't you be trying to win my heart at the culmination of a long and romantic courtship?'

He slid his arms around her waist and pulled her against him. Touching her made his heart pound harder, and every nerve in his body seemed to thrill with anticipation. 'Our wedding night doesn't need to be the end of a long courtship, Estarra. Why don't we consider it just the start?' He raised his eyebrows, showing her a genuine smile now. 'After all, I do have all the resources of the Hansa at my disposal to impress you with.'

He kissed her again before he lost his nerve, and Estarra held on to him, responding. The kiss became slower and lingering. At first, he tasted the saltwater on her full lips, but soon he tasted only *her*, and felt her against him . . . and he wondered why Basil had kept them apart for so long. After a few seconds, gasping, they broke the kiss but still held each other. Estarra chose this moment to giggle.

'Wasn't that how it's supposed to be?' Peter asked.

'I don't know,' Estarra said. 'I'm assuming we'll have a lot more practice.'

'I shall arrange my royal schedule to accommodate our . . . practice sessions, my Queen,' Peter said, and they kissed again, more easily this time. And for much longer.

Only later did she notice that he had made sure to have the comforting presence of a small treeling, one of the young potted saplings she had brought personally from Theroc, placed beside their bed.

Alone together, at last, Peter and Estarra had a wedding night that was doubly intimate – not only because it was the first time they made love, but also because it was the first time they had a chance to truly talk with each other.

ONE HUNDRED AND FOUR

TASIA TAMBLYN

After Osquivel, the worst of the wounded soldiers and damaged battleships were taken to New Portugal, the nearest Hansa colony with EDF facilities. Tasia off-loaded nineteen of her cruiser's injured crewmembers. Twenty-eight soldiers had already been frozen in the Manta's morgue containers; later, on Earth, every casualty would receive full military honours. A dozen more of her crewmembers had been lost in the vacuum of space, sucked out through the lower hull breaches.

All the surviving battleships limped home one by one, each at its own speed, after completing necessary emergency repairs. They would undergo major structural work and full inspections once back in the main EDF spacedocks.

Tasia endured a full-spectrum medical exam, and the doctors pronounced her healthy except for a few blisters and burns that had already healed, as far as she was concerned, by the time she got back to the Mars base.

EDF counsellors and psychologists interviewed all the survivors, which Tasia thought was a waste of time. With gentle, too-understanding voices they tried to tell her that her sarcasm would not speed her mental recovery from the trauma she had endured. No one had bothered to offer 'counselling' after Ross had been killed or after her father had died on Plumas. No one seemed to care that heroic Robb Brindle had perished for no real purpose.

In all his generosity, General Lanyan gave the returning soldiers a full week of furlough. Tasia had instructions to relax.

Instead, she tracked down Robb's parents.

Finding them was simple enough using EDF records. Wing Commander Brindle was a military brat, and both of his parents had served full careers as officers. Though they had worked in the private sector for the past fifteen years, both of their commissions had been reactivated during the hydrogue war. For now they served as instructors, but if the EDF continued to lose officers and ships as quickly as they had at Osquivel, Robb's parents might find themselves assigned to active combat duty.

Tasia found them at an Antarctic survival base, a training facility on Earth's south polar icecap. Despite the vigorous exercises and drills they conducted outside on the snowpack, the officers had cosy enough barracks. The Antarctic complex was heated, offering all the amenities of civilization. Any Roamer in those accommodations would have felt almost pampered.

Before facing Robb's mother and father, Tasia put on her dress uniform. Robb Brindle would no doubt receive a fistful of posthumous commendations and medals for his voluntary heroism. As if that mattered . . .

Robb's mother, Natalie Brindle, seemed washed out, her face emotionless. His father Conrad was angry and impatient, though he did not direct his annoyance at Tasia. Nevertheless, Conrad Brindle tried to take control of the situation. 'You've wasted a trip, Commander Tamblyn. We've already been informed that our son was one of the soldiers who fell at Osquivel.'

Natalie pushed her hands into her pockets. 'Yes, we received a message signed by General Lanyan himself.'

'I didn't come here in any official capacity. It's just that . . . Robb was a close friend,' Tasia said. 'My closest friend.'

Without allowing herself to be interrupted, she told how he had insisted on accepting a dangerous mission on the minuscule chance that he could convince the aliens to listen. 'What he saw down there . . . his last words were that it was beautiful, very beautiful. No one knows what Robb witnessed or what else he tried to tell us.'

'It's not the first tragedy any military family has suffered,' mumbled Conrad Brindle. 'And it certainly won't be the last. Our son did his duty. He volunteered, and he wasn't afraid. He's made us proud.'

'Robb always wanted to join the EDF,' said his mother. 'He felt honoured to serve.'

'Yes, he did,' Tasia said. 'I just wanted you both to know.'

Back in her private quarters at the Mars EDF base, Tasia was troubled to learn that EA had not yet returned from her secret mission to Rendezvous. Obviously, since the Roamer shipyards at Osquivel had been hidden from the battlegroup, EA must have delivered her message to Speaker Peroni. But apparently the compy had never come back.

A prominent Roamer trader, Denn Peroni, had recently arrived on a quick supply run to the Earth's moon. According to the logs and flight plans he had filed, Peroni intended to leave promptly, so Tasia didn't have much time. She signed out a fast Remora from Mars and used the last few hours of her furlough to intercept him.

She found Denn Peroni fuming in the darkside crater spaceport. He stood inside the layered dome, pacing back and forth in front of his ship as if searching for something to kick or someone to strangle.

Tasia came up to him wearing informal EDF fatigues, and Peroni scowled when he saw her uniform. She raised her hand in a placating gesture. 'I'm Tasia Tamblyn, daughter of Bram Tamblyn.'

Peroni suddenly blinked with recognition. 'Yes, Ross's sister! I'd heard you'd joined the Eddies. You'd better stand clear, because I'm ready to shoot someone right now.'

'What's wrong?'

Peroni shook his head. 'Some foul-up. I submitted all the right paperwork, but it didn't get processed properly. Now I have to stay here with my ship impounded, until the matter can be "reviewed". They won't even give me an estimate of how long that'll take.'

Tasia commiserated with him. 'Big Goose, big bureaucracy. I wish I could help, but the military doesn't have anything to do with trade policies.'

Peroni waved his hand in a dismissive gesture.

'I need to ask you a question.' Tasia lowered her voice conspiratorially. 'I sent my personal compy EA to Rendezvous with a warning for Del Kellum at Osquivel.'

Peroni smiled. 'You did a great service to all the clans. After what happened there with the drogues, I wouldn't want to give the Eddies any other excuse to be angry with us.'

Tasia frowned. 'But my compy never returned from her mission.'

The merchant didn't look overly troubled. 'Compies aren't too flexible, you know. Can't handle complicated problems, not even the best ones. Still, I got the impression EA wasn't supposed to be away from her assignment for long. She would have followed instructions.'

'Exactly. But she's not at the EDF base. She never logged her return.'

'Too many Roamer ships have disappeared en route lately,' Peroni said. 'Maybe EA was aboard a vessel that ran into an "unforeseen hazard".'

'I hope not.' Concerned, Tasia thanked him. 'Well, good luck cutting through the red tape.'

He scowled. 'It always happens.'

ONE HUNDRED AND FIVE

JESS TAMBLYN

The stormy ocean world was uninhabited, sterile, and nameless. It appeared as only a minor notation on the original Ildiran charts the Roamers had purchased long ago. No one had ever found the place interesting enough to take a second look.

The wental thought it was perfect.

Feeling exuberance from the ancient water-based entity, Jess manoeuvred his ship through the grey clouds and buffeting winds. Lightning lanced from storm to storm, endlessly churning the murky atmosphere. Compared to the hellish system of Isperos where he had once taken Kotto Okiah, this world didn't seem too treacherous. Roamers were accustomed to harsh beauty.

He always felt excitement when he explored an unknown place, but now the thrill was even greater. He was about to do something more important than he had ever done in his life. It might have shattering consequences for the future of the Spiral Arm.

Jess had signed aboard a nebula skimmer, surrendering to necessity . . . or perhaps just running away from Cesca, salving his emotions and letting the galactic conflict take care of itself.

Now though, Jess could bring a new ally into play, an opposing force that might be able to thwart the hydrogues. If he could reestablish the wentals and turn them into powerful warriors to help protect humanity . . . then wouldn't he – Jess Tamblyn – be offering at least as much to the future of the Roamers as any prince from a forest world?

Jess recognized the rare emotion inside him as genuine *hope* and optimism. Perhaps now humans would have a chance after all.

He skimmed over the expanse of hungry ocean that covered the planet. Only the tiniest dots of sterile outcroppings rose above the surface, and waves foamed around the rocks. The main difficulty would be finding a place to land, but it was possible. Anything was.

In its container the wental hummed and throbbed with inner light, seeming to burst with anticipation, though Jess supposed he could never fully understand the goals and thoughts of this alien entity. He scanned with the ship's long-range sensors until he detected an outcrop of flat surf-washed rock large enough for him to land on. *There.*

Expertly he set down the stabilizing pads, then donned an airmask. The temperature was within a tolerable range, but the air was almost entirely nitrogen and carbon dioxide.

He stood in front of the cylinder that held the shimmering nebula water. 'Your companionship has been strange, and I'm glad I can help you,' Jess said. Cradling the cool, tingly container in his arms, he stepped into the airlock and cycled through.

When he stood in the biting air of the storm-swept planet, he looked into the knotted clouds, saw lightning crackle overhead. The ocean looked thick and grey, like molten metal. The waves churned and swirled, frothing with whitecaps. A breaker slammed into the rock where his ship had landed, sending a blast of spray into the air.

'Doesn't look terribly hospitable,' Jess said.

It is most inviting, a welcome liberation from long dispersal in the cosmic wasteland. The wental flickered and roiled inside the container. *Pour us into the ocean, and we will be free to grow and expand again.*

Jess stood at the edge of the rock, looking into the black ocean. He was reminded of the sea under the Plumas ice sheets, the subterranean body of water where they had held a funeral for Ross. To him, this place looked empty and cold, devoid of life, a blank slate, yet – for the wentals – full of possibilities.

The cylinder grew warm in his hands. For some reason he felt anxious and uneasy. What if it didn't work? What if the wental's hopes were false?

Do not hesitate. Its thoughts pulsed through Jess's.

The misty water was alive and eager, as if inhabited by a strange ghostly presence. Taking a deep breath through the filter mask, Jess removed the lid and tilted the container. He poured the distilled nebula water into the waiting lifeless sea of this alien world.

The effect was immediate, and astonishing.

A pale phosphorescence bloomed outwards from the point where the first drop touched the sea. The shockwave glow rushed across the water like a hot fire across gasoline. Brightness grew as the wental expanded into a new body, stretching out. Jess felt a surging sense of wonder, and a certainty that he had done the right thing.

The line of cool, watery illumination rushed outwards like an electric current, infusing the dead ocean with new life, a bursting essence that grew stronger in an uncontrolled cascade. A shout of elation echoed through Jess's mind, a liberated explosion of delight and power.

We are reborn. The wental rushed through all the levels of the alien sea, like moisture permeating a desiccated sponge.

Jess felt the damp mists against his exposed skin, vibrant with life. He raised both hands to the cloudy, thunderous sky, shouting out his triumph, overjoyed that he had rescued these beings from extinction.

Now fill your container with water again, the wental said into his mind. *Each drop contains our entire essence. It will not diminish us.*

Jess refilled the cylinder from the cold primeval ocean that was now imbued with the elemental presence. The seas of this alien world were full of life, and from here he could carry more of the wentals to other planets. He felt like an old Earth folk hero who had been a roamer in his own right: Johnny Appleseed.

This is only the beginning. Go to your Roamers. Ask them to help disperse the wentals across other oceans on other worlds.

'I will,' Jess said. He now had something to offer the clans. With the aid of the wentals, all humans had a better chance of winning this unwanted war. Even the Big Goose would be indebted to him.

And . . . so would Cesca.

Now that his initial quest was over, Jess climbed back aboard his ship, carrying the full container of revitalized water. Before storing the large cylinder, he filled a small vial with the water, which he kept in his pocket so that he could still communicate with the wental. They had so much to learn about each other.

When he departed from the nameless ocean world and flew into the brightening clouds, the resurrected wentals already seemed to be affecting the weather patterns, draining furious power from the storms and converting the oceans into a simmering reservoir of life energy. The primeval planet seemed lavish with power, like a supercharged battery.

Jess soared away, increasing his speed because everything had changed now – not just in the outlook for the hydrogue war, but in his own mind and heart. He had been foolish to give up on Cesca so easily. No matter what advantages Reynald and the Therons had to offer, Jess loved her and wanted her back. It had been unfair for him to snatch a choice out of her hands. Couldn't they have tried to find a better solution?

And now Jess could come to Cesca not as a lovestruck optimist, but as an equal who could stand beside the Speaker of all clans.

Although he had been gone for months on his nebula skimmer, out of contact, maybe he could get back to Rendezvous before she actually completed the wedding ceremony with Reynald. He had to change her mind. He would not hesitate this time, but would declare his love for her and let propriety and Roamer traditions be damned. Jess had lived with personal sorrow long enough. Together, he and Cesca would be strong.

As the ship raced across open space, Jess felt as reborn as the liberated wental.

ONE HUNDRED AND SIX

CESCA PERONI

The leaders of prominent Roamer families met with Cesca Peroni to discuss their impending partnership with the Therons. After the Roamer betrothal ships had visited the lush worldforest, Father Reynald had asked for a reciprocal meeting on Rendezvous.

But the clan leaders had grave reservations about inviting strangers into their isolated asteroid complex. Long tradition and suspicions did not change easily. Especially now, with small Roamer ships disappearing along their routes, the clans were more wary than ever.

'Our secrets are much too valuable to be given away lightly.' Alfred Hosaki represented many merchant and trader ships. 'We've got to decide whether the Therons are going to be our allies against the Hansa – or against the hydrogues. Is it both or neither?'

'One of the Theron daughters just married King Peter,' Anna Pasternak pointed out. 'Shouldn't we be worried about that?'

As Cesca wrestled with how to answer, blond Crim Tylar said, 'Maybe if we sent a Roamer ship with the viewports blackened and gave the Therons no access to navigation systems or the cockpit? They'd see the asteroids of Rendezvous, yes, but they'd have no idea where to find them again. Isn't that the best compromise?'

'We can't offer our trust halfway,' Cesca said. 'That isn't how I want to begin our new cooperation with the Therons. I'm supposed to become the wife of their leader.'

Jhy Okiah sighed, as if remembering again why she had chosen to retire as Speaker. 'We certainly don't want to hold a meeting each time we have to decide whether to reveal an insignificant detail of our lives. We'd strangle on the process. Roamers are faced with a fundamental policy choice *right now*. What we decide in this matter will guide us in all other issues.'

'Exactly,' said salty old Anna Pasternak. 'That's why we've got to make the correct decision in the first place.'

'Sounds like a lot more talking, then.' Torin Tamblyn heaved a worn-out sigh. The four Tamblyn brothers had thrown pentadice to choose which of them would have to come to represent the clan at Rendezvous. 'Further delay won't make the answer any clearer. What does the Guiding Star show you?'

Cesca ran her fingers through her deep-brown hair. A toss of a coin would be just as likely to yield the right answer.

Before the meeting could reach any conclusion, however, a runner interrupted their meeting with a message. Cesca's breath caught in her throat as she scanned Kotto Okiah's urgent demand. She looked up at the former Speaker in alarm. 'Isperos is failing. The colony is falling apart. Jhy Okiah, your son asks for immediate assistance, a full-fledged evacuation and rescue squad.'

All the clan leaders shot to their feet, knowing their priorities. Wedding plans and political discussions could wait for another day. 'I've got two ships here,' said Anna Pasternak.

Crim Tylar calculated in his mind. 'I've got a cargo ship. It holds only five passengers, but I can haul a lot of equipment and supplies. Isperos . . . what a miserable place.'

Cesca looked at the gathered leaders. 'All right, you two launch as soon as you can. I want an inventory of all vessels here at Rendezvous – especially anyone else who can leave immediately.'

She scanned the message again, remembering her visit to the extremely hot planet. 'Several of the underground chambers have already collapsed. Two life-support generators have failed, and lava is beginning to leak through the walls. Kotto didn't give the impression that there's much time.'

The family heads moved out. Roamers had long lived on the edge, and they had faced situations like this before. Despite petty squabbles, all clans pulled together to aid their brothers and sisters when necessary.

Jhy Okiah tried not to show her concern for her youngest son. 'Kotto will solve the problems until our crews can get there. He's a genius.'

'Of course he is,' Cesca agreed, but even the best Roamer ingenuity couldn't support life when the walls were on the verge of turning molten. 'If we shied away from risks, then we wouldn't be who we are.'

Jhy Okiah gave a dry laugh. 'Cesca, you sound like a Speaker even when you're talking to me in private.' She looked visibly nervous now. 'Still, Kotto wouldn't have called for help unless the situation was already so far out of his control that he could see no way out.'

ONE HUNDRED AND SEVEN

ADMIRAL STROMO

While the EDF continued to assess the cost of the Osquivel defeat, the ten Grid battle fleets struggled to understand what they could have done differently, how they could have defended against the hydrogues.

All the concentrated firepower of standard weaponry had had little effect on the warglobes. The new carbon slammers and fracture-pulse drones had not worked as well as the EDF weapons engineers had hoped, though they had caused some harm. The kamikaze Soldier compies had destroyed some of the enemy, but not enough.

Meanwhile, the new compy-crewed recon fleet had not yet sent any word from Golgen verifying that the massive Roamer comet strikes had exterminated the drogues there.

So far, the only time the deep-core aliens had truly reeled from a human blow had been during the original test of the Klikiss Torch – and that had been an accident.

More and more, though, the EDF and the Hansa found themselves considering using the Torch again – intentionally, this time – as a doomsday weapon, even if they didn't understand all the consequences. After the obliteration of the technical observation platform, no one had closely monitored the newborn star at Oncier.

Pleased that he wasn't going directly into another battle like the debacles at Osquivel and Jupiter, Admiral Lev Stromo led a small survey and analysis mission back to the Oncier system. Maybe there he could find some clue, some undiscovered hydrogue weakness.

General Lanyan authorized Stromo to take one Juggernaut, a green priest for fast communication, and a pair of Manta cruisers. Publicly, Lanyan claimed that such a minimal force demonstrated the EDF's confidence that they had utterly defeated the hydrogues at Oncier; in truth, it reflected the grim reality that the Terran military had few ships to spare. The Admiral would have to make do with what he had.

Approaching the newborn star, Stromo doubled the sensor crews and dispatched a long-range Remora wing to monitor the fringes of the solar system for any sign of marauding warglobes. His three pitiful vessels couldn't stand up against the hydrogues, and he had already made up his mind to beat a hasty retreat if threatened. After all, the EDF could not afford to lose more ships.

He still bore the humiliating defeat at Jupiter and had spent years leading parades and doing desk work rather than filling his command post for Grid 0. He knew the troops mockingly called him 'Stay-at-Home Stromo' behind his back. Now, he intended to regain his honour and possibly his backbone.

Oncier's white-hot ball of gas filled the starscape in front of them. Glittering rubble from the four destroyed moons had spread out in a chaotic band and not yet stabilized into a ring. Originally, this had been one of the grandest cosmic engineering projects ever attempted.

As Stromo looked at the roiling hurricanes of ionized gas, he thought of how the hydrogues had been caught unawares by the

Torch test, their home destroyed. But he felt no sympathy for the monsters, not after the merciless and indiscriminate retaliation they had visited on humans and Ildirans alike. Instead, as he stared at the man-made sun, the Admiral pictured it as a graveyard for humanity's worst enemies. Served the damned hydrogues right!

'Deploy all probes. Let's get a full scan of how this star is burning.'

A flurry of automated satellites dispersed from the two Mantas like metallic bees, taking up orbital positions around the hot dwarf sun. Some devices dived into the plasma layers and burned up, transmitting readings all the way; others skimmed through the streaming corona.

By now, Hansa scientists *should* have acquired six years of data showing the birth and evolution of the human-created star. By now, terraforming crews *should* have finished preparing the four moons for the first wave of hardy settlers . . .

Standing on the Juggernaut's bridge, Stromo felt the anxiety among his crew. His perimeter Remora wing reported no signs of hydrogue warglobes. He drew a deep breath and let it out slowly. A routine mission, gathering important intelligence. That was all.

Stromo had risen in rank through shrewd political decisions, impressive training manoeuvres, bureaucratic successes – all of which were important peacetime skills, but meant little now. No one had ever expected an enemy like the hydrogues.

Now, the idea of facing the deep-core aliens again made him weak-kneed. A very poor showing from the highly decorated hero who'd defused the Ramah insurrection.

Stromo had been only a major then. The colonists on Ramah had declared their independence from the Hanseatic League. They had torn up the Hansa Charter and seized all offworld financial assets in the planetary banking systems. They had commandeered the cargoes on merchant ships and impounded the vessels, claiming them as resources of the 'sovereign world of Ramah'. The insurrection leaders had been smug and naïve, thinking themselves independent. But they hadn't calculated how much their population depended on imported medicines, food supplies, technical aid, and equipment.

Stromo had known just how to deal with them. He brought an intimidating group of warships into orbit around Ramah and declared their governing council to be outlaws, their people henceforth cut off from the benefits of the Hanseatic League. In a powerful raid, he had brought his elite troops to three main Ramah spaceports, where EDF soldiers recaptured the merchant vessels and confiscated locally owned craft as well, calling it partial compensation for the illegally seized financial assets.

Stromo's crews then settled into a blockade and constantly broadcast tantalizing commercial announcements bragging about all the new products and luxuries the Hansa could provide, if only Ramah would reopen themselves to trade. Within four weeks, the radical government was overthrown and a contrite group of politicians happily signed the Hansa Charter again. Stromo had been proud to reestablish diplomatic relations.

That was the kind of enemy Admiral Stromo could understand. The hydrogues, though, could never be won over by trinkets and propaganda . . .

On the second day of scanning Oncier, the bridge technicians urgently summoned the Admiral from his quarters, where he had been attending to his log and his files. 'Something's happening down there, sir. We've detected strange fluctuations and anomalies deep within the star. Something's . . . moving around.'

'Inside the planet?' Stromo tugged on his command jacket and hurried out of his cabin. 'But it's as hot as a sun in there!'

'Maybe the drogues figured out how to make an asbestos suit. You'll have to ask the technical crew to fill you in, sir.'

On the Juggernaut's bridge, Stromo stared into the filtered image of the blazing star. 'Down there, Admiral,' said one of the scientific experts. He enhanced the swirling plasma clouds, zeroing in on what had at first looked like a sunspot. 'For an hour we've been detecting shapes within the chromosphere.'

'And it's not magnetic activity? Not flares?'

'Not at all, sir. Just watch.'

Within moments, Stromo was astounded to see a red-hot ovoid capsule like a geometrically perfect egg, edges fuzzy with light and heat, moving of its own volition. It changed its course, ascending through the starspots, sailing on a flickering ocean of superheated gas.

Others joined it. They all began to rise out of the fiery depths of Oncier.

'Battlestations!' Stromo said, his heart sinking. Alarms rang through the ship, and the Manta cruisers drew closer to the Juggernaut. 'Recall all Remora wings. Prepare to retreat.' He called his green priest to the bridge so he could send an urgent summary message back to Earth.

As the Juggernaut pulled away, five of the flaming ellipsoids emerged from Oncier like blazing comets. Even with the viewscreen filters, Stromo could hardly bear to look at them. Heat shimmered from the shapes as if all the power of an entire corona had been crammed within the nucleus of that single ovoid.

The five fireballs – or ships? – approached Stromo's craft, faster than the EDF vessels could move. They circled it slowly, making no obviously aggressive moves . . . as if they were merely curious. Finally, clustering together like meteors on a mission, the dazzling things streaked off into space, leaving Oncier behind.

Admiral Stromo collapsed into his command chair, drenched

with sweat. His hands were shaking. He let out a long sigh. All of the crew stared at him, then at each other in relief and astonishment.

Clearing his throat, Stromo looked to his experts for an answer. '*Now* what the hell is going on?'

ONE HUNDRED AND EIGHT

BENETO

Standing in the grove of worldtrees planted by old Talbun, Beneto tried to soothe the anxious treelings. All day he had felt a deepening dread throughout the forest network. The unsettled fear shuddered through him like a fever.

He touched the scaled trunks, sending questions through telink to determine why the trees were so upset, but the worldforest mind kept its secrets . . . as if trying to protect the green priests from some terrifying knowledge. But Beneto did not want to be protected from the truth.

Around him, Corvus Landing fell into an unnatural hush. Beneto felt an intense shiver, like the lash of a whip down his spine. The worldtree grove seemed to cringe, and he snatched his stinging fingers away. Then he looked up into the sky.

Four hydrogue warglobes appeared, spiked spheres larger than an eclipsed sun. They filled the blue emptiness and dropped lower, hovering . . . scanning. Then they found the worldtrees.

As Beneto stared in awe, a tiny droplet emerged from the equator of the nearest warglobe, a smaller sphere no larger than a bead of perspiration relative to the giant alien ship. The small sphere picked up speed.

Beneto thought he knew what it was. Encased in a similar pressurized chamber, a hydrogue emissary had visited the Whisper Palace on Earth . . . and then assassinated King Frederick.

As the emissary sphere plunged towards the inhabited areas, Beneto could already hear shouts and warbling alarms from the buildings in Colony Town. Mayor Sam Hendy, his face florid, bellowed into an electronic megaphone, calling for everyone to take shelter, to grab their weapons. But none of their defensive measures would have any effect against a hydrogue attack.

The alien emissary passed over the town and sped instead to the grove of tall trees. Around him, the worldtree fronds rustled, as if flinching in the presence of the hydrogue. The emissary sphere dropped among the oldest worldtrees and landed on the soft, well-tended forest loam in front of him.

Beneto stood motionless, waiting.

The sphere steamed, as if it carried its own cold like a halo around it. The transparent walls of the chamber contained a milky soup of poisonous-looking clouds. Inside, the mixture churned and coalesced until a thick metallic puddle formed itself into a figure — a human figure dressed in Roamer clothes, the same image Beneto had seen the original emissary use at the Whisper Palace.

Beneto kept one hand on the nearest worldtree, connected through telink. He sent his thoughts across the Spiral Arm to all green priests. 'What do you want? Why have you come here?' Beneto demanded of the enemy visitor.

The hydrogue emissary turned a polished quicksilver face towards him. Though Beneto could not read expressions on the malleable face, he sensed a measure of disdain from the alien. Beneto felt a jolt of fear.

The hydrogue said, 'You have allied yourselves with the

verdani, our enemies. Like them, you must suffer, wither, and die.'

Beneto felt a burst of angry, frightened reaction through the whole worldforest network. He drew a deep breath, gathering strength. 'I don't know of anything called "verdani".'

But when information from the forest network flowed into him, he understood. *The trees!* The sentient mind of the worldforest was what the hydrogue called verdani.

The emissary continued, 'We have sensed a trace of the verminous trees here. We thought the worldforest obliterated long ago, but there must have been hidden remnants . . . survivors. You have helped it to grow again.'

Beneto said defiantly, 'Yes. Yes, we have.'

'They must all be destroyed.'

The worldforest seemed to be putting words into his mind. 'Why? The trees do not wish to fight you. Perhaps you both survived that horrible war for a reason.'

The shimmering emissary was unmoved. 'You will tell us the main location of the surviving verdani. Where is the primary worldforest?'

Overhead, the ominous warglobes hovered like spiked fists. A glow of energy crackled from the pyramidal tips. The emissary said, 'Tell us, and we will let humans live.'

Drawing courage and comprehension from a flood of information deep in the database of the sentient trees, Beneto said, 'I refuse. The worldforest is greater than myself or any human.'

The trees grew more determined, giving the green priest strength of will. He no longer felt fear as much as powerful defiance. Long ago, the once-spreading worldforest had covered thousands of planets – and it had been nearly eradicated. The hydrogues had also been driven back into their gas giants; other combatants had also suffered, becoming extinct themselves.

'Then your race shall know the consequences.'

'We will fight you.' The words did not seem to come from Beneto's throat, but originated elsewhere, from the minds of other green priests or from the worldforest. 'We have weapons the hydrogues cannot imagine.'

The ground stirred and writhed at the base of the emissary's sphere, as if a swarm of rodents tunnelled underneath its surface. Some part of Beneto knew what was happening. He blinked in amazed anticipation.

Whiplike roots thrust upwards with glistening tips made of a wood harder than any substance Beneto could imagine. They rose like stingers and stabbed the crystalline walls. Hissing and sizzling, the tips burrowed through the diamond barrier and plunged into the emissary's containment chamber.

The worldtree tendrils sealed their punctures, draining off incomprehensible amounts of pressure, sucking out the poisonous atmosphere. The tangle of roots drove in, growing, thrashing, filling the alien sphere.

The hydrogue emissary lost its precise imitation of a human form as it wrestled with the strangling serpentine roots. More tips plunged through the bottom of the sphere, deeper, beginning to crack the perfectly curved crystal walls.

Activating unseen engines, the emissary tried to lift the sphere off the ground, to escape, but the roots held it down. The sphere strained higher, pulling at the grasping roots, but the woody tissue remained strong, unbreakable. Fissures like white traceries of frost appeared on the transparent diamond walls.

Beneto watched the struggle, his faith and determination firmer than ever before.

The trapped hydrogue emissary struggled, but the liquid-crystal creature seemed to be dying, losing its form, dripping its quicksilver substance like acid over the furious roots.

The wild thicket continued to thrash, engulfing the hydrogue's soft form until finally the alien collapsed into nothing more than an oozing silvery stain. The roots pushed deeper into the containment globe, finally shattering it into smoking debris that left only a mass of blackened and dying roots in the middle of the worldtree grove.

But the victory was small and short-lived. Overhead, the giant warglobes began to move.

Beneto looked up, his triumphant expression shifting to one of resignation. Before the town's helpless colonists could find any meagre defence or shelter, the deep-core aliens launched their retaliation against the whole planet.

Spiked spheres swept low over Corvus Landing, spreading vicious gouts of freezing steam like poison gas. The icewave withered the grain fields, turning them instantly into blackened dust.

In the town, Mayor Hendy continued to shout hopeless evacuation orders. Many settlers hopped on to vehicles and raced towards their outlying homes or took shelter in underground structures. The buildings had been built to withstand rough storms, but nothing would be proof against the hydrogue onslaught.

Stables and corrals were blasted into frozen, sparking splinters. Arcs of blue lightning ripped smouldering gashes across the landscape. Panicked goats ran in all directions, bleating and fleeing . . . dying in a flash.

In only a few minutes, the four warglobes had devastated thousands of acres of crops, turning the carefully seeded and fertilized territory into a zone of desolation. When they swept over Colony Town, the hydrogue lightning blew up the town hall and dozens of other structures. Waves of cold white mist crumpled reinforced warehouses and silo bunkers.

Beneto grasped the nearest treeling and sent all his thoughts and impressions into the worldforest, like a fervent prayer. He was the only person who could report what was happening here. The worldforest, the green priests, his family – yes, even the Hanseatic League – had to know. There was nothing else for him to do.

The warglobes joined together again, a quartet of merciless spheres clustered in the sky. Then, leaving the smouldering ruin of Colony Town and the devastated fields behind, they approached the defiant stand of worldtrees.

Dedicated to the last, Beneto wrapped his arms around the treeling. He pushed his cheek to the bark and hammered his thoughts through telink into the network. He wanted to fall into the spreading forest mind, to seek mental sanctuary.

All the lives here on Corvus Landing must be remembered, all the trees he and Talbun had planted in this grove, all the efforts the innocent settlers had made to tame this reluctant world. He gripped the tree and opened his thoughts completely to the telink. He embraced the distant forest with his mind, and poured himself inside. It was his only refuge.

Misty icewaves spewed from the warglobes as they cruised over the doomed grove. As the first treelings began to shrivel, Beneto felt agony like frigid fire through his veins. Inside his head, he heard the worldforest's strange inhuman screams that drew upon millennia of fear and dread.

He forced himself to keep his eyes open and sent his last messages through telink, even as the hydrogues completed their destruction.

ONE HUNDRED AND NINE

FATHER REYNALD

Wearing an expression of terrified astonishment, a young green priest sprinted down the corridors inside the petrified fungus reef, calling out in alarm. The trees were already cringing and shuddering. Outside, through the open overhanging balconies, Reynald heard a chillingly tangible despair and horror sweeping through the green priests; he felt it all the way to his marrow.

'Father Reynald!' said the green priest. 'Hydrogues are attacking Corvus Landing.'

Standing in the reception chamber where she and Uthair had been advising him on his upcoming marriage to Cesca Peroni, old Lia stood up, her voice cracking. '*Beneto* is on Corvus Landing!'

Reynald lurched to his feet, hurrying to meet the message bearer.

'Beneto is the one sending us messages through telink,' the young priest said, fighting his own panic. 'Where is a treeling? I must—' He raced towards the slender plant in an ornate pot near the empty chair that was reserved for Cesca's eventual arrival. The priest touched the tree, closed his eyes, then snapped his attention back to Reynald.

'Your brother says the hydrogues are obliterating the agricultural fields. They are using one weapon of cold mist and another of blue electric fire.' Barely pausing for breath, the priest described the destructive threat the hydrogue emissary had issued against the worldtrees – the verdani – and the human race.

'How can we help Beneto?' Reynald said. 'And everyone there? They're in terrible danger.'

'All the worldforest is in danger!' The priest closed his eyes again. 'Beneto's trees fought back, they destroyed the hydrogue emissary. But it was not enough . . . not enough.'

Outside, in the congested Theron forest, countless dismayed green priests shouted the news to other people as they clutched the wide trunks for new telink updates from Beneto. Workers dropped down from their harvesting vines. Teenagers buzzed around in their jury-rigged flying vehicles, calling out what little they knew of the emergency. All of the Theron people rallied, but were unable to do anything for the distant satellite of the worldforest . . . or for Beneto.

Reynald could hear the shock and alarm that swept through the forest. In every other village across the planet, from the Looking Glass Lakes to the coastline, green priests would be reacting in the same way.

'Hydrogues have just destroyed Colony Town! Everything is in ruins. Now they are coming after the worldtree grove. The enemy has been searching for Theroc, trying to find the remnants of the worldforest.'

Even the nineteen green priests who had volunteered to assist the Earth Defence Forces with instantaneous communications would be making immediate reports to the Hansa military. His sisters Estarra and Sarein would hear the news from the court green priest in the Whisper Palace.

Confused by all the uproar, Idriss and Alexa finally hurried into the throne room together. 'What is it? What's happening?' Celli, his youngest sister, also bounded into the room, smiling – but her expression instantly fell.

'It's Beneto,' said Reynald, but the words caught in his throat. 'The hydrogues—' He couldn't say anything else.

The young green priest clutched the treeling, forcing himself to remain connected through telink. 'Ah, now they have begun to destroy the grove! The trees!' He hissed in pain.

'Beneto is still there. The worldtrees are withering. So cold . . . nothing can withstand it. They can't escape. The hydrogues keep coming and coming. Ten more worldtrees dead . . . thirty. It is a slaughter! Beneto is still holding on, but they're almost upon him. He says—'

Then the young priest snatched his hands away from the treeling with a cry of agony. 'A white blaze . . . filling my mind!' He pressed his palms to his temples and shuddered.

Idriss and Alexa gasped at each other in shock. 'Beneto?'

Old Lia began to sob, and Uthair clutched her arm, drawing and offering comfort. Reynald felt numb, unable to do anything. Corvus Landing was so far away.

The young green priest looked at his hands as if they had been burned, then inspected the treeling to see if it too might have suffered terrible blight.

'Beneto is dead. Every tree in the grove is dead. All of Corvus Landing is annihilated.' He shuddered. 'Everything . . . gone.'

ONE HUNDRED AND TEN

ESTARRA

When she could no longer endure the doting attention, applause, and sparkling eyes of people dazzled with her celebrity, Estarra hurried back to the royal wing in the Whisper Palace to be alone with her sadness. She would never see poor Beneto again.

Since the wedding day, every person in the Terran Hanseatic League had admired Estarra for the way she walked or the way she dressed. Another woman might have basked in all the attention, but Estarra felt as if she were suffocating. She didn't want this, especially not now – not after Corvus Landing.

She hadn't even had time to grieve for her brother. They wouldn't give her a moment's peace.

During the hydrogue strike, the court green priest Nahton had relayed to a horrified Estarra and her husband every instant of the destruction. While Peter stood beside her, holding her, Nahton described all the awful things he saw through his treeling, the annihilation of Colony Town, the destruction of the entire grove. He was barely able to control his own sickened terror. Estarra had wept to hear Beneto's last words as recited across the worldforest network. And then his death . . .

The courtiers who expressed feigned sympathy to Estarra had never even met her brother; most of them had not even heard of Corvus Landing. However, the immediacy of Beneto's direct report had increased the public outrage. The hydrogues were like mad dogs, merciless, on the rampage.

Estarra pictured Beneto in his last moments, bravely clasping the nearest worldtree, sending his thoughts, his very soul into the trees as the ancient enemies obliterated the entire defenceless grove. And then moved on to search for their next target . . .

Estarra did appreciate the obviously heartfelt sympathy from the general populace, however. They sent flowers and poems and notes; they built impromptu memorials, not just for their Queen's green priest brother, but for all the innocent Hansa colonists on Corvus Landing. They had been bystanders in a war the humans had never wanted. Now they were victims.

This tragedy, and continued reminders of humanity's desperate situation, helped to heal the still-painful wounds inflicted by Peter's unpopular decree preventing births on colony worlds. The human race had no real choice, not now, and the citizens realized the anguish Peter must have faced when coming to such a difficult decision. Now, more than ever, the people looked to their King and Queen for comfort and support.

The compy-crewed Golgen recon expedition vanished entirely. No transmissions had been received from the comet-scarred gas giant, no wreckage found in the system by spy drones. The surveillance fleet was considered lost.

Peter wasn't surprised.

OX said, 'After analysing spy-drone scans of the system, the EDF concluded that the loss was obviously the work of hydrogues.'

Peter joined the Teacher compy in an anteroom where a medieval king might have met with his counsellors. Whenever he discussed troubling matters with OX, he used the little robot as a sounding board.

'Maybe it was obvious to someone else,' Peter said. 'I considered it a bad idea to dispatch them in the first place. An unnecessary risk. And now I have to announce another set of martyrs who sacrificed their lives, five people – and a great many EDF resources – lost, for absolutely no benefit.'

He hung his head, pondering for a moment. 'And I can't shake this nagging suspicion. Five Mantas and one Juggernaut have mysteriously vanished. OX, what if the new Soldier compies were the cause of the failure at Golgen, not the hydrogues?'

'On that subject, King Peter, I have acquired troubling new data,' OX said. 'In the past, approximately a dozen Klikiss robots have stayed on Earth at any given time, calling little attention to themselves. They occasionally serve in our industries and orbital facilities, performing useful services.'

'Yes, I know that.'

'However, since the dismantling of Jorax, the number of Klikiss robots has increased dramatically. I have run a full inspection of the individual robots detected on our observation cameras. Though the machines all have identical configurations, there are enough subtle differences and location markers that I have been able to make a credible approximation. There are now several hundred Klikiss robots on Earth, instead of a dozen.'

King Peter was surprised. 'How can that be?'

'Distributed across the world, the number is not so great that a casual observer would notice a sudden invasion. However, the increase is striking. They remain separate, not in groups. They appear in widely distant locations.'

'I noticed earlier that three Klikiss robots have stationed

themselves at our compy production facilities,' Peter said.

'There are many more, King Peter. I cannot speculate as to what this means. The Klikiss robots are monitoring our manufacturing systems, but they have offered no further advice, allowing us to make our own decisions about what we have learned. They are simply watching.'

'Or waiting for something. The original compies were programmed to serve as aides and mentors, to help humans. Can we say the same about these new Soldier models with Klikiss modifications?' He felt a flush burning on his cheeks. 'What if there are buried subroutines, hidden traps? The engineers are so excited that they see exactly what they want to see, and so does Basil. He knows the questions, but he doesn't bother to answer them.'

'The Chairman has made a conscious decision not to answer those questions at this time,' OX said. 'I do not have sufficient data to speculate on how the modified programming might affect variables, such as the fundamental compy restrictions. Too much is unknown in this situation.'

Peter hung his head, feeling intensely tired. 'OX, sometimes I wish there were just clearcut answers so I would know what to do.'

Even if he showed the evidence to Basil, the Chairman would scorn Peter's input. However, after hearing about the destruction of Corvus Landing, Basil had rushed off to the EDF moonbase to consult his military advisers. And now King Peter seized his chance.

Left alone to pretend to run the daily business of the Hansa, he could make decisions without the Chairman countermanding every step. Lower level bureaucrats would never question Peter's direct commands. He could use that to his advantage, if he played his cards right.

The idea formed quickly in his mind. At last he could do something.

ONE HUNDRED AND ELEVEN

KING PETER

Given the dangerous nature of what he was about to do, Peter insisted on going alone. As the King.

He wished he could just explain everything to Estarra, let her in on all the plans clinging like cobwebs to him. But he wanted to protect her. She had never asked for any of this . . . and now her brother had been killed on Corvus Landing. He needed to shield her from other troubles. One day, he hoped she would understand.

In the aftermath of his glorious wedding celebrations, King Peter could command anything. He dressed in his most colourful robes, wore dazzling flatgem prisms and jewels. Smiling and holding his head high, he gathered a full procession around him, complete with courtiers, bureaucrats, and royal guards. Everyone raced about, scrambling to add the proper pomp and celebration.

It was an unscheduled royal visit to the primary compy manufacturing centre. Peter didn't exactly intend to stir up trouble, but he did want to see what was really going on there. Somebody had to keep an eye open.

Though protocol ministers urged him to set up formal appointments for the expedition, Peter would hear none of it. He simply moved forward. 'I am the King, and I will go alone if you're incapable of gathering yourselves quickly enough to join me.'

He selected a prominent ceremonial vehicle, an open float that allowed him to be seen as he flew over the streets. Royal guards scrambled to grab their vehicles to follow him. Peter smiled confidently, amused at their reaction. Without Chairman Wenceslas around, no one dared to stop him.

The flustered but determined functionaries rushed to call media representatives and to inform the compy factory's supervisors so they could stage an appropriate reception. Silver berets stormed through the streets to establish security along the route. Hansa HQ dispatched harried-looking representatives to accompany Peter; no doubt they had also sent urgent communiqués to the Moon, but there was nothing Basil could do in time. Peter was already on his way.

Enthusiastic crowds surged out into the streets to watch the royal procession. For six years, the Hansa had made sure that King Peter was always loved. The people saw him as a caring ruler who was forced to endure sadness and misery when his military and his advisers failed him. He would bank on that.

They reached the industrial facility, a sprawling cluster of manufacturing centres on the outskirts of the city, away from the ocean and the hills. It was an efficient complex, retrofitted to create armies of artificial soldiers designed by the mysterious Klikiss robots.

As the procession landed inside the widest receiving bay, workers hustled forward from their assembly lines, wide-eyed and cheering. Royal guards stood at attention, facing the uproarious welcome.

King Peter waved benevolently at the workers. Obviously,

these people thought they were doing their best work for the Hanseatic League and were not part of some plot involving secret sabotage, no matter what the Klikiss robots might have in mind.

The factory supervisor came forward, accompanied by royal guards. He seemed overwhelmed, out of his depth. 'We did not expect such an honour, Sire. My people work hard here, and I apologize for the conditions of this facility. It was not designed to be beautiful. Had I been given more warning, we would have worked to clean—'

Peter cut him off. 'That would have taken time from your important war effort. There should be no shame in my seeing a manufacturing centre in its natural condition. Besides, my loyal subjects deserve a visit from their King to boost their morale.'

The uninvited Hansa advisers pushed closer to the King, looking uncomfortable but curious. Peter didn't give them a second glance, but strode forward, following the factory supervisor.

Inside, they passed vacuum-sealed cleanrooms with frigid temperatures and swirling mists where electronics were imprinted upon circuit slivers. Labourers wearing environment suits worked with delicate command modules duplicated from the Klikiss systems that had been removed from Jorax. The King looked on attentively but asked few questions. The supervisor began to relax as he moved from one station to another.

During the tour, Peter noticed two looming black Klikiss robots, like alien insects observing the manufacturing process. They made him uneasy, though he couldn't pinpoint why. He didn't entirely believe the convenient story that their memories had all been wiped, that not a single one of the recovered Klikiss machines could recall what had happened to their progenitors.

If he commanded that they be removed, would the large insectile machines obey?

The Soldier compy components were intricate, a labyrinth of

technology that Peter doubted even the Hansa's best scientists could fathom. But in times of such urgency, the engineers were not inclined to ask too many questions.

When the supervisor completed the tour, King Peter crossed his arms over his chest, seemingly lulled into complacency. Then he sprang his question. 'So tell me, Supervisor, you derived a great deal of technology and cybernetic advances from the Klikiss robots, correct?'

'Yes, Sire. The AI-specific subroutines we copied allowed us to take great strides forward, giving these units much more complexity than our other compies. Our greatest computer and electronics specialists would have needed a century to make such breakthroughs.'

The King nodded. 'Then you have broken down the Klikiss components and studied them from first principles? You under-stand everything you've copied before applying the basic programming?'

'Not . . . entirely, Sire.' The supervisor looked confused. 'I'm not certain I see the point of your question.'

'It's simple enough. Do you understand what you're creating? Or did you simply replicate entire Klikiss system modules without comprehending them?'

'We, uh, used the Klikiss robot as a template and modelled our systems based on what is obviously functional in our mechanical friends.' The factory supervisor gestured towards the nearest Klikiss robot, who seemed to be observing the King's conversation with great interest. 'Since we are at war, Sire, none of us saw the need to reinvent the wheel.'

Peter narrowed his eyes. 'Supervisor, I think I can speak for all of us here, even the bureaucrats, when I say that we understand how a *wheel* works.' Some of the eavesdropping workers chuckled. 'You are, however, manufacturing and installing extremely complex components taken from sentient robotic systems designed by an alien race – a mysteriously extinct alien race.

'These new-model Soldier compies have been assigned to virtually every battleship in our Earth Defence Forces, handling our most powerful weapons. A great many Remoras and Mantas have been refitted so that these machines can operate independently. And yet you're telling me that you don't even understand how they *work?* That nobody does?'

'You are oversimplifying the problem, Sire.' The supervisor looked around desperately for assistance. 'Our cybernetic engineers know all the basic algorithms, but in the nature of expediency we adapted some existing Klikiss components and programming to run minor systems. We did this with the blessing of Chairman Wenceslas.'

Peter frowned. 'Chairman Wenceslas has made several . . . rash and unfortunate decisions in prosecuting this war. You're aware that a compy-crewed expedition force at Golgen recently vanished without a trace?'

'Yes, yes, Sire. A tragedy. However, the Soldier compies did perform admirably in the Osquivel battle. I'm sure they saved a great many lives.'

'I don't argue with that. But I am uneasy about putting so much trust into something that remains such a complete mystery. Even the Klikiss robots can't tell us what caused the demise of their parent race.'

'Sire, you can't be suggesting—'

'I am merely suggesting that we exercise prudent caution. Given the skill and brilliance of Hansa technology specialists and cybernetic geniuses, I'm certain they can deconstruct and analyse every Klikiss module before it is incorporated into our new Soldier compies. Until that time, I think it is best we take a moment to reconsider.'

'Sire, we have important quotas established by the EDF. What you ask would take a great deal of time and a substantial amount of—'

'But well worth it, I'm sure,' the King said, then raised his voice. 'For the good of the kingdom, I hereby put this manufacturing complex on standby until I am satisfied that we fully understand the alien technology we have assimilated. Keep fabricating components and preparing Soldier compies, if you must, but do not bring any more of them online until these important questions are answered.'

The plant workers looked around in confusion and dismay, but they had heard the King express his doubts. Therefore, they had to wonder as well.

Now one of the well-dressed Hansa officials stepped forward. 'Sire, I'm afraid that is impossible.'

Peter looked at the blond-haired official as if he were an insect, an expression he had learned from Basil. 'Excuse me? What is your name?'

'Pellidor, Sire. Franz Pellidor, Special Liaison to Chairman Wenceslas. I'm sorry, but you cannot delay production. This is an autonomous factory.'

Peter maintained his benevolent patience, though everyone could see his cool confidence. 'Mr Pellidor, I have expressed legitimate concerns. The safety of the Hansa is my primary responsibility.' The royal guards looked from Peter to the businessman, not sure what they were supposed to do.

'Nevertheless, Sire,' Pellidor persisted, 'such decisions must go through appropriate channels. With more analysis and inspection, we will resolve this issue.'

'I hope so,' said Peter. 'But in the meantime, no further Soldier compies will be activated. That is my royal command.'

'Sire, you can't do that.'

Peter let his indignation show, and he gestured to all the workers. 'Does any person here believe that a – what was your title again? – "Special Liaison to the Chairman" outranks the *King*?' He chuckled to emphasize the absurdity of the suggestion. Many workers also laughed. The bureaucrats fidgeted uneasily and backed away.

Peter turned back to the shift crew. 'Everyone in this factory has worked hard and should be proud of what they've accomplished. They won't mind a reduced schedule for the next few weeks. They will of course receive full pay during the entire time.'

The workers cheered, and Pellidor's placid face looked as if it was about to crack. Finally, Peter recognized the man from many years before. Pellidor was one of the disguised operatives who had kidnapped him – young Raymond Aguerra – from the site of his burning dwelling complex. Anger flared behind Peter's artificially blue eyes, but he kept it in check.

Mr Pellidor said in a clipped voice meant only for him, 'You are way out of bounds, Peter.'

'How can I be?' Peter raised his eyebrows mockingly. 'Ask any person here – am I not the King?'

ONE HUNDRED AND TWELVE

BASIL WENCESLAS

The Chairman was not pleased with Peter. Not at all.

The King's brash and stupid actions had forced Basil to cut short his emergency briefings and rush back from the EDF moonbase. He hoped it wasn't too late to impose proper damage control.

Peter had made a total mess of things, and it wasn't the first time.

'Something must be done, Pellidor.' The Chairman fumed and studied the recent reports as he paced his offices in Hansa HQ. 'Perhaps something drastic.'

Basil had always known the intelligent young King was not an easily manipulated fool like Frederick – and that unfortunately caused problems. Peter had known full well what he was doing, and he couldn't possibly be unaware of the consequences.

The question remained whether Peter would learn a necessary lesson from his mistakes . . . or whether some other action would need to be taken.

'I gave him explicit orders to stay away from the compy

factories. I warned him in no uncertain terms! Now, the King's meddling with the new production lines has set us back more than he could imagine.' Basil sipped his cardamom coffee, but the taste was bitter in his mouth.

'The production lines are up and functioning again, Mr Chairman.' Pellidor stood at the doorway, looking uneasy but contrite. 'Shifts are working overtime to make up for the drop in productivity.'

'We'll never make up for it,' Basil said. 'We've lost not only momentum, but trust. Peter planted an insidious seed of doubt. After getting trounced at Osquivel, after losing the Golgen survey mission, we desperately needed some kind of hope, and what does Peter do? He now adds the paranoia that these Soldier compies might be turned against us.'

Pellidor commiserated. 'The very idea is outrageous, sir.'

Basil frowned at his expeditor. 'Actually, it's not. You're smarter than that. If King Peter hadn't raised a genuinely legitimate question, he would not have had such an impact.' He slammed his fist on the projecting desktop, but accusing numbers continued to shine up at him from database distillations. 'In truth, we *don't* know exactly how the Klikiss subsystems work to the last detail. We *don't* know what happened to the original race. Peter isn't the only one who's ever felt those worries.'

Pellidor looked confused. 'But if you have similar doubts, Mr Chairman, why did you insist on restarting the production lines?'

Basil strode to the wet bar and dumped the coffee, rinsed the cup, then refilled it with fresh, dark-brown liquid. The smell alone was enough to revitalize him. 'Because using the Klikiss robots is the lesser of two evils, obviously. Restoring the confidence of our people is more important than worrying about possible treacheries.'

Pellidor accepted the Chairman's statement. It was his job. 'Then what should we do about King Peter, sir?'

'For a while, I suppose we could just drug him into submission. I'm sure the Hansa has pharmaceutical experts that can turn him to putty. But I need him to react, to cooperate, *to be convincing*. Without charisma, his ratings fizzle to nothing.' Sighing, Basil scanned reports. 'I've got a lot invested in that boy . . . but sometimes you have to cut your losses.'

Ever since returning from the Moon, he'd been too upset with Peter even to speak with him. He had instructed the royal guards that the King was to be confined to his quarters. All royal public appearances were cancelled. 'If he's going to act like a child, then I will send him to his room.'

Luckily, his recent wedding offered a convenient excuse. Peter and his lovely bride Estarra were taking several days for a private honeymoon in the royal wing. Various emergencies had delayed their 'special time' for a few weeks, but now they had gone into 'happy seclusion'. The general public would enjoy imagining what the young royal couple must be doing in their opulent bed-chambers, and no one would ask questions for a while.

Still deeply disturbed, Basil shook his head. 'The Hansa gave that young man everything on a silver platter. Without us, he'd still be a street urchin, hungry all the time, living in a cramped box with a large family.' He clenched his teeth. 'Why does he insist on biting the hand that feeds him?'

Basil sipped his coffee, recalling Peter's increasing rudeness and defiance, especially after the abortion decree – going so far as to humiliate the Chairman in public at the royal wedding. And humiliation was not something a man in quiet power could endure. Yes, the King had had plenty of chances.

Peter's bold defiance at the compy fabrication facility went beyond Basil's ability to fix cleanly. Yes, the Hansa had issued statements to reassure the public about the safety of the Soldier compies, insisting that the King's questions had been resolved so that production could continue. But the doubts had been planted.

Pellidor remained silent as Basil stared at the data screens, pondering a thousand problems. While the Spiral Arm was at war with seemingly invincible aggressors, he simply didn't have time to mitigate Peter's troublesome bull-in-a-china-shop actions. 'Summon the key planetary representatives and the upper-echelon Hansa officials. It's time for another meeting, a secret one. Make certain King Peter knows nothing about it.'

Pellidor nodded. 'Shall I put together the files of other candidates? We have many young men under consideration. Several of them seem to be quite acceptable.'

Basil agreed. 'No doubt about it, King Peter is extremely popular, and that has worked to our advantage more often than not. If the people were to lose their King now, the blow to morale in the war could be devastating.' He narrowed his eyes. 'Still, I want to have an extra ace up my sleeve.'

Three days later, everyone in the Hansa was surprised and delighted to read the announcement from the Whisper Palace. King Peter was even more surprised, though much less pleased.

In a 'new spirit of openness' the Hanseatic League was proud to introduce to its citizens King Peter's beloved and competent younger brother Prince Daniel, the second son of Old King Frederick, who – like Peter – had been raised in quiet anonymity inside the Palace grounds. Now, since everyone had watched Peter's open marriage to Estarra, it was only fitting that the public should meet Prince Daniel, too. It was wartime, after all, and many things were uncertain.

Basil observed the public response. The 'Daniel' recruit was a gem in the rough, barely trained, but he cleaned up well. He looked handsome, and the people could be convinced to adore him . . . if worse came to worst.

Peter needed to learn his true place in the government, instead of believing the propaganda they fed to the public. The King and Queen would return to their public duties, but under very close supervision. Surely Peter was smart enough to see that he had pushed the Chairman too far. The threat was clear enough: *Behave, or you will be replaced.* Basil was confident Peter would recognize his error and comport himself in an appropriate fashion henceforth.

Otherwise . . . the Hansa would just have to settle for Daniel.

ONE HUNDRED AND THIRTEEN

ZHETT KELLUM

Viewed from the cometary halo high above Osquivel, the gas giant looked like little more than a spot of light, bright and peaceful. The girdling rings were a natural wonder that reflected golden sunshine and cast a dark belt of shadow across the equator. Sparkles and glitters reflected from icy moonlets. Activity lights shone from the industries, smelters, and drydocks of the restored shipyard facilities.

Zhett Kellum doubted the system could ever return fully to normal operations, but, as usual, the Roamers strode over obstacles and difficulties, always looking to the future instead of wallowing in past tragedies. By the Guiding Star, she knew that her people had enough cause for grief.

The cometary hydrogen-extraction facilities were the first to be put back into service. As soon as the Roamers emerged from their bolt-holes, Del Kellum dispatched an ambitious crew high up to the Kuiper belt. Though an enormous amount of work remained to bring all of the shipyards back online, the comet breakdown activities generated much-needed stardrive fuel.

Zhett descended towards the rings carrying the first small load of ekti manufactured in the restarted comet facilities. It was a symbolic load, but it would cheer up the exhausted Roamer workers. Already, a cargo escort would be coming to pick up the stardrive fuel. In the war-torn Spiral Arm, every drop mattered.

Piloting her ship, Zhett eavesdropped on a main work frequency. Industrial crews chattered, sending overlapping messages, orders, and updates. The rings had become a swarm of activity. Girders and airlocks were taken from where they had been stowed among the rocky debris, and the spacedocks were reassembled, piece by piece. Major components of partially completed starships were retrieved, and constructors worked around the clock to regain lost ground.

Some of the Roamers had spoken to her father about simply uprooting and relocating the shipyards elsewhere, finding another ringed planet or asteroid belt and starting from scratch.

Zhett had never seen him so angry. 'Abandon everything?' he had roared. 'After we scrambled for weeks with all the manpower we could put together, camouflaging every facility, protecting our work and our investment, going to ground. We watched the Eddies get their butts kicked, we salvaged their wrecked ships – and now that we're halfway back online, you want to run somewhere else?'

Zhett had been worried about the Hansa military returning. It was only a matter of time. But clan Kellum would be ruined if they lost the Osquivel shipyards. 'Just keep your eyes open,' he grumbled, then sent them back to work.

Now, from his control centre inside a large hollow moonlet, Del Kellum watched over all the teams like a tyrant. 'I want at least one new ship completed by the end of the week. If you do it before then, there's a bonus for everyone on the crew.'

'No problem, Del,' said a teasingly surly voice over the comm link. 'I'll just cut down on all my coffee breaks.'

'Shizz, we're already dropping from exhaustion here,' said another worker. 'May as well learn to work in my sleep.'

'You want my preference?' Del replied. 'I'd like to have one of our own ships deliver the next cargo of cometary ekti to the distribution centre at Rendezvous.'

Zhett clicked on the transmitter, startling them. 'Yo, better hurry up – I've got the ekti right here.' As she zeroed in on the control complex and docked her cargo vessel, she heard continued complaints, orders being snapped, progress reports given. Business as usual.

She walked briskly into the control room where her father studied systems-analysis maps of their facilities, smelters, and resource stockpiles. Dotted lines and parabolas marked the flow of processed material. Subscreens showed status reports and schedules for future projects.

'You're going to give all of your crew ulcers, Dad,' Zhett said, coming up to kiss the older man on his whiskery cheek. 'How's the work coming on the compies we salvaged from the Eddie wreckage?'

Kellum turned to look at the open loading bay where noises and bright lights filled the chamber. 'We're almost done reprogramming them. We'll put them to work soon enough.' He gave her a wry smile. 'At least *they* won't complain about long hours.'

Zhett scanned the rows of small mechanical servants, competent computerized companions that had survived the explosions and decompression that had killed so many EDF soldiers. 'Looks like five different models.' Some were still bent and damaged; others had been polished and repaired. 'I've never seen those military-looking ones.'

'Soldier compies – well suited for heavy labour, if you ask me. We'll manage the mechanical fixes easy enough. Might have to swap out a few parts, cannibalize components to get a fully functional machine. The Big Goose seems to be better at this sort of manufacturing than we are.'

'We can learn, Dad.' Zhett had worked with compies in the shipyards, but had never owned one herself.

'We'll have to brain-wipe them all, of course, especially the Soldier models,' Kellum said. 'No telling what sort of odd programming the Eddies installed. Even the Friendly and Listener ones might have special emergency systems. Can't trust that.'

'Can't trust much of anything, Dad. We'll make the compies into loyal allies, with a little bit of tinkering and a little bit of love.'

Del Kellum scowled. 'That's easier than what we face with our other captives. How do we reprogramme the thirty-two Eddie soldiers in the infirmary?'

Zhett smiled back at him. 'Maybe we use the same tactics.' She walked off with a spring in her step.

Inside his cramped room, Patrick Fitzpatrick III had recuperated enough to climb out of bed. Fitzpatrick looked with bemused curiosity at the aquarium on the inner wall, where angelfish flitted back and forth in an endless exploration of their small world. Hearing footsteps, he turned with an automatic wary scowl, but relaxed when he recognized Zhett.

'I see you're up and moving around.' She smiled at him, but Fitzpatrick showed no friendliness towards her.

'Within my little cell,' he said.

'It's larger than your lifetube was. I could've just left you floating in space with your life support failing.'

'Yes, you could have. You are Roachers, after all.'

Her brow furrowed with obvious annoyance. 'I'd always heard how rude Eddies could be, and you're a prime example. Anyone with common manners would thank me for saving them.'

'Depends on what you're going to do to me,' he said.

'First things first. Repeat after me: "Thank you, Zhett, for saving my life."'

'Is that your name? Zhett?'

She put her hands on her hips, trying to keep an amused expression from her face. 'For a military officer, you don't take orders well. As I said, "Thank you, Zhett, for rescuing me."'

'Thanks,' he said.

'Now tell me how much you appreciate our hospitality.'

'Stop pushing me.'

'Then stop resenting us. You've been through quite an ordeal, so I'll cut you a bit of slack. I can tell you're confused and disoriented.'

'I am not.'

'All right. Then you're something of a jerk, and it just comes naturally to you.'

Taken aback, he glared at her. 'Look, my Manta was destroyed by the drogues. I don't know how many ships we lost, how many men, but we damn sure got our asses kicked. I need to get back to Earth and report what happened here.'

'Trust me, they already know,' Zhett said. 'A substantial portion of your force escaped. They ran and left all their wounded behind, didn't even try to rescue the lifetubes. It was up to Roamers to collect you all and nurse you back to health.' Zhett tossed her dark hair over her shoulders, meeting his gaze with her own flashing eyes. 'You're damn lucky we found you.'

Fitzpatrick narrowed his eyes. 'And why exactly were you at Osquivel? According to our records, this was an uninhabited system. The drogues that attacked Boone's Crossing went to ground here.'

'Sorry, but I can't tell you anything,' Zhett said. 'The Big Goose causes us enough problems. Given half a chance, they'd try to steal our products, or crush us with unreasonable tariffs, or send in the

Eddies to install their own military governors. No thanks.' She stepped back towards the door. 'I think it's best that you just lie down and rest some more.'

'Wait!' Fitzpatrick was obviously hungry for news. 'How many other soldiers were rescued?'

'A handful,' she said. 'Trust me, we're taking care of them as best we can. They couldn't ask for better medical care.'

Fitzpatrick frowned in resignation. 'Well, I admit EDF doctors aren't known for their bedside manner.'

'You'll find a lot of surprising and likeable things here among us,' Zhett said. 'Just give it time.'

'I don't want to give it time. I need to return to Earth.'

'Commander Patrick Fitzpatrick III, your ship was destroyed, your crew lost, and you yourself were left for dead. The EDF fled Osquivel with their tails between their legs. Nobody's expecting you to come back. Not ever.'

Zhett walked off, covering her smile at his spluttering astonishment. She would let the recovering young officer chew on that for awhile. Eventually she might even be able to teach him a useful Roamer skill.

ONE HUNDRED AND FOURTEEN

KOTTO OKIAH

Stressed beyond all tolerance points, the ceramic-lined tunnels on Isperos finally shuddered and failed. The settlement's life-support systems melted under an onslaught of lava.

Kotto Okiah could not wait for rescue any longer. The underground base would fail catastrophically within hours. Unfortunately, the people didn't have a much better chance for survival out on the surface.

The Roamer miners had already moved their supplies and equipment into the few still-intact rooms, but now the heat had become too intense. The uncontrollable thermal plumes ate upwards from the lower catacombs. Crews had no choice but to suit up and flee out on to the cracked landscape and hope they could reach the shadows in time.

The upper tunnel compartments were already sweltering. The metal walls were blistering hot to the touch, the temperature rising every few seconds. The workers tugged on their mirrored suits and life-support packs, sealing gaskets so that no secret fingernail of fire could reach inside.

'Hurry it up, or we'll be oven-roasted here,' Kotto said, then more gently, 'Don't worry. The rescue ships will come. Count on it.'

'Have we heard any word yet? How many vessels are on their way? When will they arrive?' said a shrill-voiced engineer, drawing a look of scorn from an older woman as she prepared to seal her helmet on to the collar-harness.

'Shizz, how would we know?' a repair tech snapped. 'Our ships get here faster than a signal can.'

'We've all got suit transmitters,' Kotto said. 'Our life-support tanks can last for a day or so, and our regenerator packs should keep the coolant flowing through our suits.'

'Yeah . . . under optimal conditions,' muttered one of the engineers.

'You mean this isn't optimal?' Kotto tried to maintain his sense of humour. 'Okay, we've got enough surface rovers and mining vehicles to take us over the terrain. If we hop from shadow to shadow, we can get to the night side and hide there for a week.'

'Our air won't last that long, Kotto.'

'One problem at a time, please.'

In groups of five, they cycled out on to the baked surface of Isperos. Pounding breakers of solar storms continued to lap at the planet. The star overhead was a churning cauldron of heat, surrounded by repeated flares. Kotto thought of it as plasma indigestion.

Three overland vehicles carrying equipment, supplies, and a crowd of evacuees had already rumbled off across the scorched terrain. The heavy ceramic treads left deep indentations in the soft rock.

'Let's go. Seven of us can fit in the next rover. Move it!'

He pushed the engineers towards the waiting vehicle, then took the controls himself. In normal times, his co-workers often refused to let the easily distracted engineer drive a rover, because

Kotto paid more attention to geological features and mineral resources than finding a safe path.

Now, though, Kotto was not sightseeing. He was trying to save them all.

The horizon was a close, curved line. As he passed a tall mound of rock, razor-black shadows spread out like a pool of spilled ink. Impetuously, Kotto swerved into the abrupt shade, where the temperature dropped sharply. Thermal waves rippled up from the cooling rock, and heat seeped from the rest of the baking landscape, but it was better here for a while.

'I'll give it ten minutes here to let the system dump some of our waste heat. If this rover melts, we'll be walking all the way to the nearest shadow.'

'Good thinking, Kotto.'

When they set out again, the blazing fury seemed even more intense. The sun hung like a baleful eye, seething and flickering, as if ready to explode.

The first Roamer rescue ships arrived in the system when Kotto and his refugees were still more than ten kilometres from the night side. Other Isperos rovers had already made it to the cooler darkness and arranged a staging area where the rescue shuttles could land.

Along the way, Kotto had lost contact with one rover. The driver had sent a signal, calling for help but was unable to give her location. 'Systems are failing – guidance completely scrambled . . . hull breaches likely . . . no, *imminent!*' The next sound, a horrible rising scream had mercifully turned into garbled static.

Kotto clenched his jaw, but kept driving. All the miners, engineers, and tech workers had known the risks here. The Roamers would memorialize anyone who died – but only after as many Isperos workers escaped as possible. For now, Kotto had to make sure such an accident did not happen to anyone else.

Anna Pasternak, a salty old merchant captain, led the first group of rescue ships on an approach to the dark side of Isperos, but had to abort her landing when the solar storm increased its fury, bombarding navigation systems and control circuits. The rest of the rescue ships lined up in the shelter of the planet's shadow cone, trying to formulate a plan for retrieving the survivors.

Kotto's rover reached the darkside sanctuary where five refugee vehicles had found a flat crater, its surface melted and rehardened numerous times. One rover had reached the staging point, but had suffered an air-tank breach, and now their atmosphere was running out. Kotto could redistribute minimal surplus supplies from two other rovers, but that would only postpone the disaster for another hour or so.

'Look, you've got to come down *now*,' he transmitted to the ships. 'If we don't get rescued within the next few minutes, then you've wasted all your time and stardrive fuel coming to help.'

When Jess Tamblyn had taken him here in the first place, six years ago, the daredevil Roamer had flown his ship in, dodging the corona activity and flouting the perils of the unstable sun. That survey mission had convinced Kotto that it was possible to build a functional facility on Isperos. Since then, the solar storms had grown worse, as if something terrible was happening deep inside the sun itself.

'All right, we can have one big party or one big funeral. Me, I prefer parties,' Anna Pasternak transmitted to the other captains. 'You all perform regular maintenance, don't you? Let's see just how good those tolerances really are.'

The Isperos survivors stood outside in their suits, a desperate group sweating from fear and heat and the dregs of oxygen in their airpacks.

'Abandon all equipment and supplies,' Kotto said, 'though a few datawafer records might be valuable, if you can carry them.'

The rescue vessels dropped like angels from heaven, scrounging for a safe touchdown point in the crater. The communication links echoed with cheers. Before the first ship landed on the uneven ground, Kotto had broken his crews into teams, organizing the evacuation so that those with the most serious life-support emergencies got onboard first. 'Nothing wastes time more than a panic. Let's not embarrass ourselves.' Indeed, Kotto was already embarrassed enough that his dream of a productive colony had failed so completely. He hadn't been able to hold it together.

By the time they climbed aboard the rescue ships, Kotto did a tally, learning to his dismay that he had lost twenty-one of his people. A second rover vehicle had broken down out in the dayside heat, its treads mired in an unexpectedly soft pool of molten stone; when the heat ate through the fuel cells, the resulting explosion killed the refugees before anyone could go back to help them. The last victim was a woman who had died from a massive suit failure only a few minutes before the first rescue ship landing; on the intensely cold dark side of Isperos, she had actually frozen to death in less than a minute.

His face red and blistered, his body exhausted and dehydrated, Kotto made his way to Anna Pasternak's cockpit. The old woman glanced over her shoulder and cut off his words of gratitude. 'Don't thank me yet, Kotto. We've still got to get away from that stellar hurricane. All our ships are far too crowded and heavy. We didn't have time to put together a formal evacuation team.'

'I'm glad you didn't wait,' Kotto said, 'even though I expected to have more time to keep my crumbling colony together.'

'The universe likes to play jokes. I always thought my daughter Shareen would outlive me, and I'd get to spoil a dozen grandkids, but the drogues had other ideas when they wrecked her skymine on Welyr.'

'Don't the Roamers have any happy stories?' Kotto wondered with a sigh.

Flying by instinct, Pasternak took the ship out of the planet's shadow – and then the sun itself seemed to declare war on them. Arched flares rippled out into space, as if trying to reach the orbit of Isperos. Coronal discharges battered the fleeing ship like a series of clubs.

'Never seen activity like that!' the captain cried. 'Do you think it's going supernova?'

'Of course not,' Kotto said. 'It's the wrong stellar type—'

On her control panels, status screens had already edged into the red zones. Pasternak wrestled with her cockpit systems, but the overloaded rescue ship rocked erratically. Some of the other Roamer vessels were in even worse shape, straining like drowning men. Tidal waves of solar wind roared at them. Bullwhip flares thrashed about.

'It'd sure be a shame to rescue your people and then burn up on our way out the door.'

'Yes, that would be a real kick in the teeth.'

Crackles of static burst across the ship-to-ship communication systems, other Roamer captains declaring emergencies, reporting failing engines and life support. The rescue ships struggled, close to each other but individually helpless.

Anna Pasternak bit her lower lip. 'Well, they'll have to fend for themselves. I don't have any band-aids left.' She looked up, suddenly startled. 'Shizz, hold on!' A deadly flare hurtled towards them, moving faster than Pasternak's engines could carry the ship. 'Too much debris in the neighbourhood. I can't use the stardrive yet or we'll be flattened into a pancake by a piece of gravel.'

'Or one of our wayward alloy ingots,' Kotto suggested. 'That's actually more likely.'

The communication outbursts increased in urgency. 'Look at the star! Look at the star!'

Wrestling to keep control of her ship, Pasternak continued inching away from the danger zone. But Kotto scanned the fiery chromosphere behind them, amazed to see gigantic ovoid projectiles like hot misshapen cannonballs shooting out from the stellar surface. The blazing objects hurtled along the tracks of the deadly flares, rushing to intercept the fleeing Roamer ships.

'What are those things?' Kotto said. 'They've got to be artificial.'

'Just what I need,' Pasternak snapped, 'hydrogues with heartburn.'

'Not hydrogues,' Kotto said. 'The configuration is different, more ellipsoidal. The spectrum peaks are much more intense.'

The Roamer rescue vessels were already at their top velocities. Eleven fireballs roared towards them at amazing speed. Each one was the size of a moonlet, large enough to engulf half a dozen EDF Juggernauts. The sight was so incredible that it took Kotto a long moment to shift his awe into outright fear. As bad as their situation already was, the egg-shaped fiery things from the furious star could only make it worse.

'If I had some decent weapons, I'd take a few potshots,' Pasternak said. 'Maybe start throwing ice cubes at them.'

Then the flaming cannonballs clustered together behind the fleeing Roamer ships so that their fuzzy edges overlapped. They formed an impenetrable barrier, blindingly bright and terrifying – but better than the roaring flarestorm from the sun of Isperos.

Kotto glanced at the rescue ship's systems, saw to his surprise that the dangerous heat and radiation levels were dropping dramatically. 'Captain, they're . . . blocking the solar flux! Look, the readings are within tolerable levels now.'

The Roamer vessels kept fleeing, and the ominous fireballs hovered at a safe distance, clustered together to form a dazzling shield.

'They're . . . protecting us from the flares. How'd they know we were here? Why . . . why should they care what happens to us?'

Pasternak switched to the ship-to-ship channel again. 'Don't ask questions. Just keep moving.'

'Hey, I'm not about to complain,' somebody said.

'My engines are dropping back from overload,' came a second captain's voice. 'What the hell *are* those things?'

Kotto's heart pounded, and he couldn't stop staring. They had been saved by these astonishing . . . vessels? creatures? entities? – that lived in the plasma depths of a sun.

Somehow, the fiery things had understood that the solar flares would harm the humans. The incandescent ellipsoids continued to block the worst of the sunstorm from the flotilla of crowded ships until the Roamers had reached a safe distance.

Then, without a word, the capricious fireballs separated again, flitting about like planet-sized fireflies. They swooped through the magnetic loops of solar flares and danced along the corona waves until they plunged like extinguished embers back into the superhot star itself.

'Well, that's a pleasant surprise – aliens who don't want to smash the crap out of us for a change,' Anna Pasternak said. Wiping her brow, she set a course back for Rendezvous.

ONE HUNDRED AND FIFTEEN

ESTARRA

When Estarra retreated to her Palace rooms where she could meditate away from the constant attention and silly obligations, she walked in on a private shouting match between her husband and Chairman Wenceslas. She stood at the doorway, listening in shocked silence.

'You had no right to spring this on me or on the people,' Peter said. 'They don't know anything about this Daniel. I will denounce him.'

'They didn't know anything about you either, Peter,' Basil said with a maddening smile. 'Everything is under control. If you view the results of the polls, watch the spot news coverage, you'll see that the people have accepted the new Prince without any qualms. It comforts them to know they have another candidate for King waiting in the wings . . . just in case the worst might happen.' He lowered his voice. 'Now, if you don't start to be more cooperative, the Hansa has . . . other options.'

Peter scowled. 'Don't threaten me, Basil.'

'Do you find the truth threatening?'

The King laughed, a bitter sound. 'When has the truth ever been a factor in your decisions? You can't just prevent me from appearing before the people, because if you hide me then I won't serve my purpose. And what about this Daniel – did you kill his family, too?'

From the edge of the hall, Estarra listened wide-eyed, trying to understand what she was hearing. It made no sense.

'You are truly an amateur at making threats, Peter,' Basil said, unruffled. 'It might be a challenge to see just how long we can fool the public with stock holograms of you and old speeches spliced together. Nobody really listens to the words, anyway.'

Peter shook his head, as if he understood things the Chairman did not. 'You've created the myth yourself, Basil, but you still don't understand what a King really means to the population.' He finally noticed Estarra, and his face lit up with a pure smile. 'Or perhaps I should say King *and* Queen. Don't underestimate the people's love for their rightful leader.'

Startled, the Chairman glowered at her. 'We are in the middle of a private meeting, Queen Estarra. Would you please give us a few moments to finish?'

Before Estarra could back away, Peter held up his hand. 'No need, Basil. You can speak in front of my Queen.'

Estarra was confused and alarmed. Peter was obviously keeping things from her – important things – but she went to stand beside her husband, placing her hand on his shoulder. This marriage had been decided for her at the request of the Chairman and Sarein, arranged through her brother Reynald. Estarra had fulfilled her obligation and was now free to make her own alliances. Though not required to do more than show public support for the King, Estarra would sooner trust Peter, whose heart she had seen and begun to understand, than the Chairman.

'I would be happy to assist in any way possible. My husband and King needs only to advise me.' She stood with him across from the

Chairman, realizing exactly what she was doing, and that it might even put her in danger if her suspicions were correct.

Wearing an unpleasant expression, Basil gathered his papers. He straightened the fabric of his suit, glanced around the plush royal apartments, noting that one of the plants in the corner was beginning to turn brown and shrivel. 'My business here is concluded.'

The guards opened the doors for the Chairman, then closed them after he had stalked out. They stationed themselves outside the apartments – ostensibly to protect the King and Queen, but more likely to make sure the two didn't venture where they did not belong.

In private now, Estarra looked at Peter, silently regarding him. She crossed her arms and took a deep breath. 'You've got some explaining to do.'

He looked away, visibly disturbed. 'I think it's safer if . . . if you don't know any more.'

'I don't want to be protected, Peter. I can take care of myself.' When the King refused to answer, wrestling with how much he should reveal to her, Estarra arranged her own thoughts. She tried a different approach.

'You know, when my brother Beneto went off to Corvus Landing, he promised he would return. It was supposed to be a quiet assignment for him. He wanted to help the colonists and to tend his worldtrees. I loved him very much.' Then her expression hardened, and she dropped all pretences. 'So, I don't understand why you would begrudge your brother's presence. Why have I never met Daniel? Why wasn't he at our royal wedding? It upsets me that I don't even know my husband's brother.'

'Daniel is not my brother,' Peter said, derailing all of her other questions.

'What do you mean? I was beginning to open up to you, Peter. Now I learn that—'

'My name's not Peter, either,' he interrupted. 'This is going to take a while.'

Later, they lay naked next to each other, languidly comfortable on soft sheets, the room lit only by pastel glows of distant torches. Estarra clung to Peter, still feeling the deep ache from Beneto's death.

When he caressed her as a husband and a lover, instead of as King, they both talked at length, glad to have someone with whom they could share. Peter ran his fingertips along the left side of her face, across the eyebrows and then down her cheekbones to her chin. He was desperate to have someone he could trust within the Byzantine politics and loyalties of the Hansa.

Barely able to believe what he was telling her, but incapable of doubting him, Estarra listened to his husky voice, saw the tears in his eyes – artificially blue eyes, according to his story. He told her how he had been kidnapped years ago and held in hiding while Basil groomed him to become the next King. 'I only discovered later that the Hansa intentionally killed my family.'

Her eyes were wide. 'Do you think we're in any danger?'

He kissed her warm shoulder. 'Yes, Basil has made veiled threats – against you to keep me in line, and against me directly. I never thought he would take such a chance before, but now that he's introduced Daniel, I'm not so sure. Maybe I've already done too much damage. Basil controls enough that he could poison us or stage an "accident" anytime he likes.'

Estarra pulled him close, offering her strength and feeling the warmth of his body against hers. Maybe she could talk to Sarein about this . . . or maybe not. 'Then we'll both just have to keep our eyes open.'

Still, she felt like a very small fly in the middle of an extremely large web.

ONE HUNDRED AND SIXTEEN

OSIRA'H

Even during night-time on Dobro, blazers and interior illumination strips lit the Designate's residence with all the brilliance and safety of day. Osira'h never had cause to worry.

The seasonal wildfires had been extinguished by loyal camp workers, but the air still smelled unpleasantly of smoke and ash. The simmering coals in the burned, desolated area occasionally glowed orange in the shadows.

The young halfbreed girl stood at the window in the upper level of Udru'h's residence, the only home she had ever known. From here, she could make out the embroidery of lights that marked the breeding barracks.

'There you are,' said Udru'h in his rich, strong voice. 'I should have known I'd find you looking out the windows again.'

Osira'h smiled at him, her large eyes sparkling. 'And thinking.' *And trying to understand the strange presence, the vague longing thoughts that seem to emanate from somewhere in the camp.*

An hour ago, they'd had a fine meal together, just the two of them, in a small dining alcove. The Designate did not enjoy gaudy

601

ceremonies and frivolous decorations; he often liked to eat his dinners with Osira'h, especially when she had done a particularly good job in her training exercises for the day.

He was never harsh with her, never angry, but never lax, either. From the time Osira'h could speak, he had drilled her and encouraged her, making certain the little girl understood with her whole being that the fate of the Ildiran Empire might rest upon her abilities to merge Ildiran and hydrogue. She could not let him down.

Osira'h took a deep breath, feeling pride swell her chest. She wanted nothing more than to please him. 'I like looking out there, as far as I can see. It makes me think of everything far away. Someday, will we go to Ildira so I can visit my grandfather, the Mage-Imperator? I would like to see the Prism Palace.'

The Dobro Designate gave her a small but significant smile. 'In the best of times, we can show you all the glory of the Empire, Osira'h.' Then his face grew sombre. 'But if you and I fail now, there won't be an Empire left to see.'

He put his hand on her shoulder. They both stared at their reflections and the glimmering stars high in the sky.

'Out there, Osira'h, the hydrogues continue to make war, and they don't understand which of us are their enemies and which are allies. They don't understand exactly who we are, how we think. No longer are the hydrogues content to remain within their gas giants. But the hydrogues themselves don't understand their targets.'

He tightened his grip on Osira'h's shoulder, then self-consciously withdrew. 'I just received a report that warglobes have devastated a wilderness world within Ildiran territory. Dularix. It's a place that neither humans nor Ildirans had ever colonized. No one was there, and yet the hydrogues simply destroyed it.'

'But why?' Osira'h said. 'Why don't they leave us alone?'

'That is what *you* must ask them, Osira'h, when you are ready. You can bridge the gap between our species and create an understanding, forge an alliance to save all Ildirans. The Klikiss robots achieved that for us long ago, but they have failed this time. So the Empire must turn to *you*, Osira'h. Your mind can send out that message, along with the potent emotions we need to convey. It may be the only way the hydrogues can truly comprehend us.'

Osira'h pressed her lips together, not sure whether she should tell the Designate . . . but she had never kept any secrets from him. 'Two days ago, I felt a calling in my mind, like a shout, a cry for help. I didn't know what it was, but I think I've felt it before.'

The Designate looked startled, stern again. 'Who was it? How did you hear this telepathic message?'

Osira'h shrugged. 'It was during the time of the fires. I felt a connection. Someone . . . a woman? She was calling out, very desperate and very sad. She seemed close to me.'

'Close? You mean nearby?' The Designate turned away from the window to look into Osira'h's eyes.

Her fluffy, pale brown hair twitched of its own accord. 'It was here on Dobro . . . but also close to my mind, like someone I should know well.'

Deeply disturbed, Udru'h ushered the girl away from the window. 'Don't trouble yourself. It is nothing, irrelevant to what we must concentrate on.'

'Of course.' Osira'h was wise beyond her years due to her special parentage, mental abilities, and challenging upbringing, but sometimes the Designate still treated her like a toddler.

'We have much work to do, and little time.'

The girl followed him to where the trainers would drill her for hours, deep into Dobro's night, until the sun rose again and washed the sky with nourishing light. But the girl longed to look towards the breeding camp again, wondering who had called out to her. That mysterious woman had sounded so hopeless.

Osira'h felt it was something she should know. One day, perhaps, she would find out.

ONE HUNDRED AND SEVENTEEN

MAGE-IMPERATOR

Bearing dire news, Bron'n entered the Mage-Imperator's presence. Through the *thism*, ailing Cyroc'h could sense his guard's urgency. Already, he knew that the worst was about to happen, despite his many days of trying to keep Jora'h under tight control.

The great leader rested in his chrysalis chair under the sky-sphere, where he had held court for hours, clinging to the adulation of his subjects, drawing the soul-threads of light from them and regaining a trickle of strength. Though he was in intense pain from the growths in his brain and spine, the Mage-Imperator refused to hide from the pilgrims and petitioners. Not any more.

With his crystal-bladed katana, Bron'n nudged aside two swimmers who had been praising the ruler for several minutes. The guard lowered his voice. 'The Prime Designate has found a ship, Liege. He intends to leave imminently.'

The Mage-Imperator's watery eyes stung. 'Yes, Bron'n, I felt it. Jora'h cannot hide from me. He knows I see everything he does – yet still he intends to go.' Raising a pudgy hand, Cyroc'h waved the swimmers away. Awed, they stepped back towards the edge of the reception hall.

'His ship will leave for Dobro within an hour, Liege,' Bron'n said in a rough, urgent voice. 'Shall I call out other guards? I can stop him forcibly.'

'No, if the Prime Designate resists, it will look very bad for you to defy his direct orders.' The Mage-Imperator heaved a deep sigh. 'One hour will give me sufficient time.'

Cyroc'h raised his hands in benediction, using much of his remaining strength to sit up. The relentless, throbbing pain inside his skull never diminished. He gazed across the reception hall, drank in the details of the Ildirans who had come to gaze upon him. Overhead in the skysphere terrarium, birds and colourful insects flew about. Blissful, peaceful . . . but right now the Lightsource seemed very far away.

As Mage-Imperator for a century, Cyroc'h had guided the Ildiran Empire along its path of destiny, and he had earned his place in the *Saga of Seven Suns*. His skull would rest beside all the others, glowing for a thousand years within the ossuarium. It was enough.

And if he delayed longer, then everything he had achieved would begin to fall apart. That must not happen.

'I will now retreat into my private contemplation chamber,' he said to all listeners in the hall. 'I have given my people every scrap of my ability, and the Ildirans have proved themselves worthy of my leadership. They have repaid my efforts with extravagant works. Remember always that I have appreciated everything the people have done in my name.'

He signalled the attenders, who scurried forward to surround the chrysalis chair. Bron'n followed, obedient but troubled by the Mage-Imperator's words. Once inside the chamber, the leader shooed away the attenders, who reacted with dismay, begging in high-pitched voices to be allowed to massage his skin, tend his long lovely braid, apply oils to his hands and feet. But he insisted, 'Leave me alone, completely alone.'

Bron'n gestured with his long staff, enforcing the command. He stood at the doorway of the now-empty chamber. The Mage-Imperator gave him a rare, tired smile. 'You are my most faithful servant, Bron'n. Wait outside. Seal the door and let no one enter – except for Jora'h.'

Bron'n took one step out into the corridor. 'Shall I summon the Prime Designate, Liege?'

The Mage-Imperator gave a strange smile and shook his head. 'No need. He will come of his own accord.'

Bron'n asked no further questions but left the Mage-Imperator alone with his decision. Knowing that Jora'h was even now preparing to steal a vessel and rush off in an ill-advised attempt to rescue his lover on Dobro, Cyroc'h did not hesitate. There was no time to hesitate.

He opened a small compartment in his chrysalis chair and removed a vial of acid-blue fluid. He had ordered it prepared several days earlier. It was the last service those medical kithmen had performed, questioning what the leader intended with such a deadly liquid. At the time, they had feared he might wish to euthanize the comatose Hyrillka Designate. But the Mage-Imperator had snatched the poison from the doctor's hand without answering. Later, he had simply ordered Bron'n to arrange for the doctors' quick and silent execution, thus eliminating all further questions.

Now he held the vial, admiring its beautiful colour, which the red-tinted light turned purplish. He drank the poison in a single gulp.

It tasted like bitter fire on his tongue and in his throat. Closing his eyes, the Mage-Imperator lay back in his cushioned womb. The toxic substance would take effect quickly . . .

He felt the destructive current sweeping through him, eating away at his nerves and muscle control, finally replacing the agony of his tumours with a cold lack of sensation, and then a rush of ascending, hurtling upwards towards an even brighter Lightsource.

Jora'h would soon understand his responsibilities – whether he wanted to know them or not. The *thism* would be merciless.

The Mage-Imperator had no other way to convince his successor. When he passed, the web of *thism* would be disrupted, the strands severed. The fabric would begin to unravel. Jora'h would be forced to take his place. Forced to do the right thing. He trusted his son to make the right choices.

He had to.

His long braid twitched and struggled, as if gasping for air. Cyroc'h tried to open his eyes again to catch one last glimpse of the seven suns, but the Lightsource within him was so much more intense.

His arms and legs jittered from the action of the poison, but the tumours' pain inside him faded to a merciful leaden numbness. It was as if the living, growing invader within his skull had been killed first. That, at least, was a relief. And the light grew brighter behind his eyes, glowing like the core of a sun within his bones.

Taking one last hitching breath, the Mage-Imperator died with a smile on his cherubic face.

ONE HUNDRED AND EIGHTEEN

PRIME DESIGNATE JORA'H

The agony of loss hit him while he was standing at the docking platform atop one of the Palace domes, finishing the final preparations for his escape.

As Prime Designate, Jora'h had surreptitiously commissioned a willing captain and acquired a large enough ship and splinter crew for a fast journey to Dobro. He had ached with the feeling that he had failed Nira and left her to suffer for so many years. The Mage-Imperator had thwarted him for days, blocking him in every way possible – but Jora'h hadn't been able to stand it anymore, regardless of his father's rationalizations.

He needed to rescue Nira . . . and hold her again while begging her forgiveness for what she'd been forced to endure. Jora'h knew he must move quickly before the Mage-Imperator sensed what he intended to do.

When the Prime Designate had seen guard kithmen emerge from the lifts at the far end of the shimmering platform, he knew what they wanted. The *thism* connection had betrayed him and his father meant to stop him again, but he swore that he would not let Nira down.

'Hurry!' he had called to the hired Ildiran crewmen as they raced up the ramp of his commissioned ship—

When suddenly his heart felt torn from his chest.

Jora'h staggered and let out a cry. Pain and displacement washed through him like a lightning bolt. In his life he had never felt such an avalanche of emptiness, a disruption that shuddered through the core of his body.

Wrapped in visceral shock, the Prime Designate reeled and tried to keep his balance. The spaceship captain staggered and slid to his knees. All of the crew members were also gasping; some had collapsed to the decks, where they writhed in misery.

The whole Ildiran universe had been turned upside-down.

A confused wail of despair rippled from the many balconies of the Prism Palace, pilgrims and bureaucrats and nobles crying out in disbelief. Guard kithmen who had been marching across the platform to intercept Jora'h suddenly swayed in their tracks.

The *thism* had been ripped apart. The intricately woven soul-threads that bound the Ildiran race into one vast network pulled taut, frayed . . . then snapped. The Lightsource was gone.

'No!' Jora'h cried, abruptly understanding what had happened. 'The Mage-Imperator is dead!'

With a wavering gait, he stumbled back into the Prism Palace. His long hair writhed in chaotic fury around his head. He didn't notice anyone else, thought of nothing but reaching his father's contemplation chamber . . .

The ugly bodyguard Bron'n stood at the sealed door, holding his wicked-looking spear. But he sagged, gripping the weapon like an old man's staff, as if the strings of his own life had been cut. Bron'n's feline eyes seemed to accuse Jora'h. His sharp teeth were exposed.

'What's happened? Where is my father?'

'He ordered me to stand here and wait for you.' Bron'n took a snarling breath. 'He told me to let no one into the chamber – no one but you. He knew you would come.'

Jora'h looked at the guard in disbelief as he unsealed the door. 'He did this of his own volition? You *knew* what he intended, and you did not stop—'

'I serve the Mage-Imperator,' Bron'n said, holding on to his words as if they were an anchor. 'I do not question his commands.'

Jora'h rushed inside and saw his father's pale soft mass in the chrysalis chair. In death, Cyroc'h looked like a greyish slug, folds of fat slumping on his bones. It was clear that the Mage-Imperator had expended a great deal of energy just to hold himself together until the end. Now, though, his flesh had succumbed to the relentless pull of gravity.

Jora'h grabbed the flaccid arm, as if there might still be hope, but he knew from the echoes of severed *thism* that his father was dead. The Mage-Imperator had fallen, returned to the Lightsource.

Jora'h grabbed the empty vial, saw a tiny droplet of acid-blue liquid inside. 'But why?' he demanded of the lifeless body. 'Why would you do this, Father? I need your leadership. I need your guidance. How am I to lead the people now? I wasn't ready.'

Then he did comprehend, and he had to hold the edge of the chrysalis chair just to keep his balance. This was his father's desperate plan for him. Once all the strands of *thism* came to him, when Jora'h held the web for himself and connected with the trickles of holy light from a higher plane, then he would understand far more than the Mage-Imperator could have taught him.

'You should have prevented him from doing this, Bron'n.' He glared over his shoulder at the guard, who stood devastated at the doorway.

'I serve the Mage-Imperator,' he said again like a mantra.

'I am the Mage-Imperator now!'

'Not yet. Not until you complete the ceremony and control the *thism*. Until then, we have no Mage-Imperator.'

Overwhelmed and distraught, Jora'h began to grasp everything that would change now, all that he would have to do. As long as there was no Mage-Imperator, as long as the *thism* remained severed, the Ildiran race would be disconnected, wandering . . . and it would only grow worse with time. As a people, they would suffer incredible psychological damage – and perhaps more. They might all go insane.

He had no choice but to assume the role as soon as possible, though it would take days to summon all of the Designates here to Mijistra. Still, it must be done.

Jora'h turned back to the chrysalis chair and clutched his father's sleeve. Cyroc'h had known he was dying, but this sudden decision that forced the Prime Designate to take over the Ildiran Empire – it was too much.

Then he realized with a terrible sinking sensation that with his defiance about Nira, his insistence on rushing to Dobro despite his father's strict command, he himself had driven the Mage-Imperator to this awful act.

Now he could not possibly go to help her. He had to stay and do his best to hold the Empire together.

In the corridor outside the chamber, while the Prime Designate continued to grieve over the body of the great ruler, Bron'n stood rigidly at attention.

He had followed instructions, obeying his duty . . . but Bron'n also accepted his own portion of the blame. He extended his arms outwards, tilted the katana spear, and brought the crystal point towards him. Carefully, he placed the sharp blade against his uniform's lower breast plate. He pushed it in far enough so that the point penetrated the armour and cut into his skin, drawing blood and a line of sharp pain.

Enough to know that his positioning was true.

Bracing the handle of the spear against the wall, Bron'n thrust himself forward, pushing his body with all his bestial strength. He coughed blood from his fanged mouth, then, growling, he shoved even harder until the katana blade penetrated up through his heart. His determination and his automatic muscles continued to move even after the mortal blow, and the bloody spearpoint sprouted out through his back.

When he heard the guard collapse, Jora'h ran out of the chamber to the fallen armoured body. Understanding what Bron'n had done, the Prime Designate raised his eyes beseechingly towards the shining suns in the sky. But he could see little light, feel little warmth.

One Hundred and Nineteen

Adar Kori'nh

The full cohort of Solar Navy warliners left the smouldering ruin of the uninhabited planet Dularix. Seven maniples, 343 vessels under the Adar's command – and still it was another failure.

All vegetation on Dularix had been crisped and frozen, the continents rendered lifeless, down to the soil itself. The mountains were split apart, the landscape blistered, sterilized.

According to the records of old surveys, Dularix had been a pleasant wilderness with pristine forests. Ildirans had never bothered to expand there, and the humans hadn't discovered its beauty yet. Nevertheless, the hydrogues had struck the planet hard, hammering the landscape with murderous force. Killing everything.

There had been no reason whatsoever for the attack. The swarm of Ildiran battleships had cruised into the system on patrol just in time to see the alien warglobes departing from their nonsensical destruction. From his command nucleus, Kori'nh stared stoically at the images of the scorched world.

'Who can comprehend these hydrogues, Adar?' said Tal Zan'nh, standing beside Kori'nh in the command nucleus of the lead warliner. 'We must report this to Ildira. Perhaps through the *thism*, my grandfather can explain our enemy.'

The Solar Navy had watched, but with their hands tied by the Mage-Imperator's orders, they made no move to pursue the hydrogues. Fuming, Kori'nh had clenched the rails around his command platform. 'Yes, our only assignment is to observe . . . and then back away without fighting.' The words tasted flat in his mouth.

Zan'nh looked at him, disturbed. 'We know that the Solar Navy has no weapon effective against the hydrogues. What would be the purpose in going on the offensive, and being slaughtered?'

'We did have some success at Qronha 3,' the Adar said, looking at his talented protégé.

'But . . . we were utterly defeated there.'

'Only a matter of perspective, Tal. Do not forget that we hurt them. Even though we weren't prepared for that fight, Qul Aro'nh still destroyed one warglobe and damaged two others.'

He knew that all of his crewmembers could sense his uneasiness, though they believed his anger was directed towards the hydrogues. With a sigh, he ordered the cohort to move out of the system. The Ildiran stardrives engaged, and the giant warliners slipped at blinding speed into the empty gulf between stars, heading towards another pointless rendezvous—

And then, on far-off Ildira, the Mage-Imperator died.

Everyone aboard the hundreds of ships felt it – from Adar Kori'nh and Tal Zan'nh, down to the lowest maintenance worker and deckhand. Sudden emptiness exploded through the *thism* like a thunderbolt, exploding the bright soul-threads, blinding every Ildiran from the Lightsource. Cutting them off. Leaving them abandoned, alone. Hopeless.

Kori'nh reeled backwards, supporting himself against the platform railing, barely able to see through the crippling loss. Zan'nh let out a desperate cry. The warliner's crewmen clasped their temples, squeezed their eyes shut, letting out a low, moaning wail.

The shockwave instantly rippled through the compartments, the decks, the chambers of every Solar Navy ship. No one paid attention to their duty stations, and the battleships drifted on their pre-set courses.

With a supreme effort, Adar Kori'nh rallied himself, pulling his body erect. He had never felt such . . . *emptiness*. The ringing in his head and the despair washing through his mind clamoured for attention, but he forced his thoughts forward. He shouted to his bridge crew, 'Attention! Sound the alarm.' His first words came out hoarse, but then he repeated them with more strength, more urgency.

When the crew continued to writhe and wail, he strode away from the command nucleus to the consoles themselves and initiated the all-hands signal. Due to their Solar Navy indoctrination, the warbling siren struck instant resolve into every soldier aboard every ship in the cohort.

'Tal Zan'nh! Summon all quls and septars.' He drew a deep breath. 'I want all subcommanders to join me. Our situation has changed dramatically. We must discuss this emergency immediately.' The ships soared along on course, unswerving . . . though everything else in the Ildiran universe had changed.

'But Adar, the Mage-Imperator is dead!' cried his communication officer. 'We can all feel it.'

'We are still the Solar Navy!' Kori'nh snapped. 'The Ildiran Solar Navy. What would the Mage-Imperator think if he knew you turned into whimpering jelly in a crisis?'

While the alarms continued to ring, slowly – very slowly – the soldiers began to clamp down on their distraught misery. They performed their duties, clinging to the routine like a life preserver.

Kori'nh withdrew the crystal ceremonial dagger from his belt. The Adar stared at how the bright light shimmered from the curved cutting surface. The ache in his chest forced him to do this. The weight of Ildiran tradition, combined with a racial instinct built inside him. He raised the sharp knife to his head and made a quick slash, a stroke so smooth it was almost gentle. He cut away his tight braid, scraping some skin but yielding no blood. He held the severed hair in his hand, but it was like a dead thing. He tossed it to the deck in disgust.

Throughout his ships, the other males were instinctively doing the same to mark their intense loss. None of them had ever lived through the passing of a Mage-Imperator before. The Solar Navy soldiers moaned as they cut off their hair, marking the end of Cyroc'h's reign and preparing for a new leader.

For Kori'nh, the awful emptiness and isolation was unsettling, terrifying . . . but as he waited for the subcommanders to join him, he realized with a start that, for the first time in his life, no one was watching over his decisions. Cyroc'h could no longer sense his tactics or disapprove of his actions.

Yes, the Adar felt adrift without comforting direction. On the other hand, he could finally take some initiative. He was free to make up his own mind. Like the human commander MacArthur, like Agamemnon, like Kutuzov. It was a heady sensation.

With many possibilities.

In the warliner's conference room, he looked at his uneasy and grieving tal and quls. All of them had shaved themselves bald. Every member of the Solar Navy remained shaken, but the Adar had to prove he could still issue orders. His officers would follow him more diligently than ever, now that they had no other anchor.

Many times, he had disagreed with the Mage-Imperator's overall strategy. Nevertheless, he had obeyed. Many times, Kori'nh had felt like a coward because he'd been ordered to run and hide, just to avoid upsetting the deep-core aliens. Yet no matter what the Solar Navy did, the hydrogues continued their ruthless rampage.

He was the supreme commander of the Solar Navy. He had the most formidable fighting fleet the Ildiran Empire had ever built, but the Mage-Imperator had been afraid to use it.

The Earth Defence Forces had thrown themselves against the enemy repeatedly, had developed innovative new weapons. Even the gypsy Roamers, with no military force of their own, had devised daredevil tactics and innovative processing techniques to keep a trickle of fuel coming through the trade routes. Working alone, they had destroyed a hydrogue gas giant through cometary bombardment.

But the Solar Navy had done nothing.

And Adar Kori'nh was tired of being defeated. Perhaps it was time for his marvellous fleet to seek glory against the enemy. The Mage-Imperator could no longer stop him.

Sealed inside the consultation chamber, Kori'nh assessed Tal Zan'nh and his underling quls and septars in silence. He had read over their service records and understood their individual strengths and capabilities.

Zan'nh looked even more distraught than the other officers. The Mage-Imperator had been his grandfather. Prime Designate Jora'h, his father, would soon ascend and take Cyroc'h's place. Zan'nh himself was the Prime Designate's first-born, though not of pure noble kith, and so his younger brother Thor'h would become the next Prime Designate. Still, the *thism* strands were strong and powerful within Zan'nh. The talented tal must feel more isolated, more unsettled, than any other Ildiran in the fleet.

However, though Zan'nh was probably the best among the

soldiers assembled in this battle group, the Adar needed to send him home.

'Tal Zan'nh, I want you to lead most of the cohort back to Ildira, all but one maniple of warliners. Take these ships home to offer our people comfort in what is certain to be a time of turmoil.' A brief moan echoed around the table, but Kori'nh ignored it, standing firm. 'As soon as all the Designates can be gathered, your father will complete the ascension ceremony and become the new Mage-Imperator. Once he accepts all the strands of *thism*, the web will be reknitted and our race can feel whole again.'

Zan'nh bowed. 'Yes, Adar. It is clearly my duty.'

One of the septars said, 'What will the rest of the cohort be doing, Adar?'

Kori'nh looked straight at the subcommanders, knowing he could not retreat once he stated his decision. 'I will take one maniple of warliners on a different mission. I cannot disclose the details.'

He focused his gaze on an older, stoic qul named Bore'nh. The maniple commander was a model military officer who had never wavered in his duty. He would be perfect. 'Qul Bore'nh, I have selected your maniple to join me on this mission. Will you follow my orders without question?'

Bore'nh seemed surprised, then pride filled his face. 'I would be honoured, Adar.'

With a twinge of guilt, Kori'nh said, 'I require only the most minimal crews for operations. Remove all soldiers not deemed necessary for a brief mission and have them return to Ildira aboard the other warliners.'

Bore'nh didn't ask the reasons. 'It will be done, Adar.'

Tal Zan'nh looked at his commander, disturbed but knowing his place. 'Do you wish to brief me in private, Adar?'

'No. For now your primary duty is to take your ships back to Ildira.'

In order to accomplish what he *knew* was right, Kori'nh had to act swiftly – while he still retained his independence, before the Prime Designate ascended to become Mage-Imperator. He would have a few days, but no longer than that. As soon as Jora'h reconnected with the *thism*, then the Adar's hands would be tied again. And then it would be too late.

Kori'nh dismissed the officers and went back to the command nucleus. He listened to the drone of orders distributed through the intercom systems, as all non-essential personnel were dispatched from Qul Bore'nh's forty-nine warliners and shuttled over to the remaining vessels.

When he confirmed that his instructions had been followed precisely, Kori'nh transmitted a farewell to Tal Zan'nh. 'I know you will serve your father as well as I served the Mage-Imperator.'

'I will devote the best of my ability to my duties, Adar. As you do.'

Qul Bore'nh joined the Adar in the command nucleus as the single maniple detached itself from the rest of the cohort. The remaining six maniples sped back towards the seven suns of Ildira, while Kori'nh and his forty-nine battleships, with full weaponry and skeleton crews, grouped together, waiting.

Adar Kori'nh finally gave the order to set forth. 'At last, we will confront the enemy ourselves.'

ONE HUNDRED AND TWENTY

ESTARRA

From her high balcony Estarra gazed across the Palace grounds filled with statue gardens, reflecting pools, and menageries of topiary shrubs. A glittering suspension bridge spanned the wide Royal Canal that encircled the Palace District.

To continue the celebration of their King's new marriage – milking it for all it was worth, Peter said – the Hansa would throw a 'honeymoon jubilee' in several days' time. More festivals, more parties, more special effects to distract the masses from the true crisis.

According to the carefully scripted event plan, Estarra and Peter would ride a gaudy boat around the Royal Canal so that everyone could wave to their King and Queen. It was a colourful display to introduce the glorious rulers to their people, and also to dispel any doubts about Estarra's ability to fill a queenly role in society.

It seemed a frivolous and empty gesture after the death of Beneto and the destruction of Corvus Landing, after the EDF's blistering defeat at Osquivel. The Hansa was whistling past the graveyard.

Sarein came up behind Estarra unannounced. Her sister looked gaunt, her dark eyes shadowed as if she hadn't slept well. Sarein's careful Hansa clothing style and her makeup looked uncharacteristically dishevelled. 'Basil doesn't know I'm here, little sister.' Her voice had an urgency and a strain that Estarra had not heard before.

'Why should I care whether the Chairman knows your whereabouts? You're the ambassador from Theroc.'

'Peter has already pushed him too far,' Sarein continued, insistent. 'Dangerously far. He thinks he's indispensable.'

'Of course Peter's indispensable. He's the King.'

Sarein frowned impatiently at her. 'Don't be a stupid, naïve little girl. You should know better than that by now. The Chairman always maintains several viable options. I've just learned the depths of . . . the danger—' She seemed at a loss for words, then burst out, 'Estarra, you have to talk to Peter! Do you have a good relationship with him?'

Estarra nodded, embarrassed. 'Yes . . . yes I do. He's my husband, and he's an honourable man.'

Sarein clutched her sister's hand, alarming Estarra. This was so unlike her. 'Then I beg you, Estarra, tell him to cooperate. You could salvage this, before Basil does something he can't take back. Do your best to help Peter be a better team player. His own future, *your* future, and the fate of the Hansa rests on this.' Sarein leaned closer. 'Estarra, I don't want to see you hurt. Believe it or not, I do care about you. We've both just lost Beneto—'

Estarra suddenly realized why she was feeling so resentful. 'And since the day the hydrogues killed Beneto, you haven't come to see me once. Now, of all times, shouldn't we be supporting each other as sisters? But I suppose you've been too . . . busy.'

Sarein stiffened. 'Beneto was my brother, too. Don't tell me how to grieve.' She took a step away from Estarra, hesitating, holding the Queen's gaze. 'And I don't want to have to grieve for more deaths. Be careful. Tell Peter to change his attitude, and we can all get through this.'

Disturbed, Estarra looked at the sun-washed plaza again, the usual crowds of tourists, even a few Klikiss robots standing like sentinels. Zeppelins flew overhead. Groups of visitors were led through a moss-covered maze of gardens on guided tours. She longed to be back home on Theroc with the trees and with the rest of her family, and with her freedom. 'Whose side are you on, Sarein?'

Her sister's eyes flashed with anger. 'It's not a matter of sides, Estarra. We all have jobs to do, and we all have the same enemy. Don't we?'

Estarra met her gaze, searching. *Do we?*

Unlike the King, Estarra had very few duties, even symbolic ones. Estarra had already done her part by marrying Peter, cementing the alliance with Theroc. Sarein had already rounded up green priest volunteers to join the EDF.

But now that the priests were delivered and the wedding was over, the Hansa didn't seem to know what to do with the new Queen. Riding in a boat and waving at crowds – was that the most important service she could provide? The extravagant flotilla might have appealed to her little sister Celli, but was anybody really comforted by Estarra's public appearances?

At the base level of the Whisper Palace, she made her way to the boathouses and maintenance hangars that held the beautiful ceremonial yacht. As always, guards followed her, coming close while they tried to determine where she was going. A protocol functionary hurriedly offered to escort her, and she nodded. 'Of course. I want to look at the parade boat. I'm . . . so excited about the upcoming event.'

Satisfied with the explanation, the functionary accompanied her, chatting, through the corridors to the lower levels. Narrow capillaries of the Royal Canal made waterways for the boats to emerge from beneath the sweeping arches of the Whisper Palace.

Within moments, a chatty protocol minister joined them, and the effeminate man quickly began rattling off details about the lovely flotilla, the wines and foods that would be served aboard the lead royal yacht, the ethnic music that would be played at various stations along the canal.

Estarra kept an innocuous smile on her face, nodding at every excited suggestion the protocol minister made. He seemed deliriously happy that the Queen approved of his tastes. They stood at the quays underneath the rippling ceiling of the boathouse domes.

Estarra admired the spacious boat that was designed for pomp instead of speed. With immaculate decorations, the processional yacht would cruise in slow circles around the Palace District. An honour guard of small military skimmers would flow in front of the royal boat and behind; silver berets would be stationed in full dress uniforms at various points along the canal.

Estarra noted a team of workers stringing ribbons and pennants on the yacht. Painters touched up the exterior hull of the lead boat. Some of the artisans wore water-tight suits and floated in the capillary canal, polishing every fitting down to the waterline.

'It'll be quite a spectacle,' she said.

'Indeed, indeed,' the protocol minister answered. 'This is King Peter's favourite yacht, you know.' Peter had already told her he'd never actually set foot aboard the boat.

'Bread and circuses,' the Chairman had said when he had sternly informed them of the plans two days ago. 'Distract the people from our real problems.'

'I'd rather solve the real problems,' Peter said, crossing his arms over his chest. The tension was thick in the air.

'Be my guest,' the Chairman snapped, 'but in the meantime, you and your lovely Queen will take a boat ride, a honeymoon cruise.'

'Whatever you say, Basil.' Peter had not, however, sounded contrite. Estarra had been unable to read his face, but she knew he resented being forced to perform . . . as when he had issued the strict population-restriction decree.

Now, as she watched, an engine worker in overalls emerged alone from the yacht's lower decks. His coveralls were stained, and he carried a toolkit at his side. The man had blond hair and a placid expression; he moved with a smooth grace and an unusual intensity. After leaving the boat's engine room, he quickly crossed the gangplank and went purposefully towards one of the workrooms.

There was nothing particularly unusual about him, and it took Estarra a moment to recognize the blond-haired man she had seen on the newsclips of Peter's impetuous visit to the compy production facility. Special Liaison to the Chairman. One of Basil's men. She remembered him especially because he had challenged Peter's authority.

He was certainly not an engineer. Her dark eyes narrowed. Such a man had no business whatsoever aboard the royal yacht, especially not in the engine room . . . especially not dressed as a common worker.

A thrill of fear scraped down her spine. Sarein had warned her to be very careful . . . and, according to Peter's story, the Chairman already had plenty of blood on his hands. What had Peter said to her on their wedding night? 'Rule one: Never trust Basil.'

Estarra watched the impostor out of the corner of her eye as he turned in his toolkit and then vanished into a locker room. Beside her, the protocol minister droned on, smiling, and Estarra pretended to listen to him. She took great care to show no sign of recognizing the quiet henchman, not wanting to raise suspicions. She thanked the guards, attendants, and the protocol minister and took her leave of the maintenance docks.

She had to find Peter.

ONE HUNDRED AND TWENTY-ONE

JESS TAMBLYN

Racing back to Rendezvous, hoping to catch Cesca in time, Jess kept a small vial of wental water next to him, like a talisman. After witnessing the water entity reborn on the unnamed ocean world, he felt a glow of success, proud of what he had done.

The larger container remained in the ship's storage bay, a reservoir that he could distribute to other Roamers he intended to recruit. They could scatter samples of the living water across other ocean planets, and the wentals would soon grow numerous enough to combat the hydrogues.

Jess studied his navigation charts and rechecked his course. Within a day, he would be back at the asteroid cluster of Rendezvous. His heart pounded with anticipation, and he thought of a thousand ways to express everything he needed to tell Cesca.

When he saw her beautiful face, when he stood before her and opened his heart finally and completely, he would know what to say. He had to admit what a stupid mistake he had made with her, because he had convinced himself of the wrong priorities. A selfless and honourable solution was not always the only solution. The human *heart* must be strong for the human *race* to survive.

Jess felt exhilarated and confident, as if a new power sang through his veins. Why had he waited so long? All along, his own bad decisions and concern about public opinion had stalled him . . . when apparently, all Roamers had seen their mutual attraction for years. His father had trained him to be a tough businessman, devoted to the clan's holdings – yet when it came to negotiating a lifetime of happiness with Cesca, he had been completely inept.

The path had been wide open for them, but they had procrastinated. Neither of them had acted on their opportunities. For love, he and Cesca should never have been willing to delay.

As Jess passed through an undeveloped and uninhabited solar system, he scanned the navigation charts, pinpointing another cloudy world with sterile oceans and untouched seas. A good place to seed a second congregation of wentals.

He had just noted it in his log when suddenly the strange water entity reacted with alarm and dread. An outside jolt of fear shot through his nervous system. 'What is it?'

Then the ship's sensor alarms went off, detecting a large and powerful craft plummeting towards them from the fringes of the system – a warglobe. The hydrogues came after him at incredible speed, obvious in their destructive intent. Reacting instinctively, Jess punched his engine controls, and the ship lurched forward with a burst of increased speed.

Over the past several years, dozens of Roamer vessels had never arrived at their expected destinations, vanishing without a trace. Some people had explained the losses as accidents in the harsh vastness of space; others, more inclined to look for conspiracies, had blamed the Hansa and the EDF.

How many of the lost ships, though, had succumbed to hydrogue attacks?

With the increase of hostilities, had the deep-core aliens decided to attack any human ship they encountered?

Then another possibility occurred to him. Jess touched the vial of water in his pocket. 'Have they sensed you? Do they know the wentals are back?'

No, but they must not discover us. You cannot be captured, or the hydrogues will know that we are alive. It is too soon.

'There aren't very many hiding places out here.'

Clenching his jaw, Jess accelerated towards the unnamed cloudy planet, using all of his flying skills. Tasia had been a more accomplished pilot, but Jess and Ross had drilled their sister on evasive manoeuvres – and now he had to remember how to do all those things for himself. Not only was his own life at stake, but also the lives of the resurrected water entities that could fight these terrible enemies.

'Tell me, how do I fight them? How do I get away?'

The wental offered no viable solution. *We are too weak, too few for now. We cannot defeat a warglobe.*

With the predatory hydrogue closing the distance, Jess reached the isolated cloudy world, hoping he could elude pursuit in the atmosphere. He squeezed all possible speed from the engines, but this vessel had been designed as part of a nebula skimmer; it was little more than a habitation and control module with engines and a processing deck – made to drift on cosmic winds, not to fight.

He closed his eyes, trying to see his Guiding Star, then accelerated beyond the maximum levels of the engines, pushing harder, heading on a steep dive into the planet's thin upper atmosphere.

And the warglobe came after him. Blue lightning crackled from its spiked protrusions, and the searing weapon lanced out. The bolt struck nearby with an ionization burst and shockwave that fried several of Jess's systems and darkened a smear of cloud.

His fingers danced across the controls, working around damaged systems and circuits, but his vessel tumbled through the turbulent atmosphere, out of control. The hull shuddered, the deck vibrated, straining to hold itself together. He managed to straighten his vector just enough so the ship did not immediately burn up.

The wental's forceful words rang in his mind. *You must not be captured. The hydrogues cannot learn about the wentals.*

'I'm trying!' Jess wove back and forth in a crude evasive manoeuvre. Even the rarefied clouds were like quicksand, sucking at him, making his ship sluggish. 'If it's any consolation, the drogues don't look like they're interested in capturing me alive.'

The warglobe loomed closer, jagged blue weapon bolts dancing like twisted snakes across the isolated sky. Jess jerked the controls hard, and the ship spun, looping as it brushed deeper into the cloud deck. The hydrogue blast went wide, strafing the cloud tops, triggering a cascade of deep lightning.

Jess gritted his teeth. 'It doesn't look like I can get out of this, but there's no need for you to be destroyed.' He sucked in a cold breath. 'I'm going to dump the cargo hold . . . I don't care about all of the equipment and supplies – maybe the wental cylinder will get to the clouds, the ocean below. That'll be enough for you, won't it?'

Without waiting for the shimmering water entity to respond, Jess sealed the cockpit deck and punched the emergency airlock dump. Jettisoning flotsam, strewing random debris along the clouds, the ship flew on. The hydrogue roared in its wake, ignoring the scattered refuse. Ignoring the wental cylinder.

Take this small vial of our water and drink it, said the wental, still thrumming from his pocket. *You must survive.*

He snatched the small vial out of his pocket. 'But what will that—'

Do not hesitate.

The hydrogues shot at him again. One of Jess's aft engines exploded, but suppression systems smothered the fire. The ship was completely out of control, careening into the lower atmosphere. As if eager to help the enemy, storm winds made his ship buck and shear. Behind him, the hydrogue closed in for the kill.

Jess removed the top from the vial and poured the haunted water down his throat.

His ship spun aimlessly as it tumbled, engines smoking, hull seared . . . and still the warglobe wasn't satisfied. It swept in behind Jess, and opened fire again.

As he swallowed the wental's essence, Jess felt nuclear energy surge through him. The wental filled his tissues, rushing like a tsunami from his largest blood vessels down to the smallest capillaries, then penetrating his tissues through the water-based protoplasm in his cells.

He gasped, and his fingers clenched as his muscles spasmed. He could no longer even touch the controls. Static sparks danced from his fingertips. He let out a loud scream that was part agony, part astonishment, and part utter exhilaration.

His wounded ship plummeted towards the uncharted alien oceans. The murderous hydrogue came in fast behind him – and shot out a final demolishing blast. Jess's vessel erupted into a cloud of shrapnel and molten pieces high in the sky, streaking like fallen meteors through bruised clouds . . .

The warglobe hovered for a few moments longer, surveying the complete destruction. Then it departed.

ONE HUNDRED AND TWENTY-TWO

DOBRO DESIGNATE

He drew the sharp edge of the blade along his scalp, slicing off the last remnants of what had been his proud crown of hair. He had oiled his skin, and the blade was like a razor, shaving away even the finest stubble. Though his hair was slightly animated, moving like static electricity, the Dobro Designate felt no pain, only determination as he completed the ritual – like every other male was doing across the entire Empire.

Everyone but Prime Designate Jora'h.

The Mage-Imperator, his father, was dead. Udru'h felt the despair gnawing like teeth of ice inside his chest. He had known the great leader's health was failing, but had not expected the Mage-Imperator to die so soon.

The Empire was trapped in such turmoil it seemed the worst possible time to leave the Ildiran people without a leader, without the *thism* that bound them together. Too many plans had reached critical junctures, such as his own work here on Dobro with sweet Osira'h and her special powers.

There wasn't enough time!

Udru'h put his knife down and looked into a reflection glass surrounded by small blazers. His features were handsome but lean and hardened. The recognizable lips, chin, and facial structure that looked so calm on Jora'h's oblivious face were tighter on his own.

What was to become of the Empire now?

The Mage-Imperator had tried to instruct Jora'h, training him in politics and explaining some of his schemes, but not all. The stubborn Prime Designate had been angry when he'd learned the truth – a truth that he should have suspected all along, if he'd simply paid attention to history and the clear hints around him. Jora'h refused to understand the realities, the necessity of doing what was best for the Ildiran race. And now he would become the leader of the Empire.

Should he have faith in his elder brother?

He had to believe the Mage-Imperator would not have entrusted the Ildiran realm to anyone he did not consider adequate to the job. However, Udru'h also remembered how ill his father had been. Perhaps the terrible pain and the bodily deterioration had weakened his resolve, muddied his thoughts. What then?

With the Mage-Imperator dead and the *thism* gone, the brothers were cut off from each other, unable to sense each other's respective thoughts. The Dobro Designate had to hope that once the *thism* came to Jora'h, all the necessary comprehension and enlightenment – and acceptance – would also come to him. It must!

Even so – though his brother would understand everything – he might not agree with it. As the new Mage-Imperator, Jora'h would be free to issue whatever commands he wished . . . and sweep away centuries of planning and interbreeding. That would be the worst possible thing.

And if Jora'h already hated the breeding plans so much, what was to stop him from punishing Dobro and its Designate? Jora'h could ruin everything, all because his pathetic imagined love for a human green priest whose genetic heritage held the key to breeding a weapon, a living bridge that might save them all from the hydrogues.

Such grim thoughts preoccupied him as he dressed himself in rarely worn formal robes. Frowning, Udru'h studied himself in the reflection glass again. He preferred simple clothes because there was always so much work to do, whereas his wounded brother, the Hyrillka Designate, preferred gaudy robes that could be worn to the banquets and parties. Udru'h preferred to let others be pampered; he had no use for such things.

Sadly there were some ceremonies that he must attend – such as the funeral of his father, the delivery of his glowing bones to the ossuarium . . . and, finally, the ascension of Jora'h. No summons had been issued – every Designate knew he must depart immediately for Ildira and the Prism Palace. Udru'h would leave little Osira'h and the breeding programme here for a time unsupervised, because that was what must be.

What must be.

However, with the telepathic network cut off, he did have an unexpected opportunity – a means by which he could implement secret plans . . . and keep them from Jora'h, should the necessity arise.

As he left his quarters, anxious and disheartened, Udru'h felt all alone, unable to see even a glimmer of the Lightsource, but his basic convictions were unshaken. Perhaps he couldn't trust his brother to make the difficult, necessary decisions. So he, the Dobro Designate, would see to it that those decisions were absolutely inevitable.

He summoned his guards to his residence and gave them clear instructions on what they must do while he was gone. Nira Khali was a dangerous loose end, just like the derelict ship *Burton* had been. Udru'h could never let his brother have her back. It would ruin everything.

ONE HUNDRED AND TWENTY-THREE

OSIRA'H

The telepathic call was so strong it struck through the young girl's heart, captivating her mind and drawing her awake in the quietest part of Dobro's night.

Osira'h was exhausted, and alone. After the shocking death of the Mage-Imperator, the Dobro Designate had just rushed off to Ildira, leaving orders that the instructors must make her work harder than ever, training her, drilling her. 'We do not know how much time we have. Osira'h must be ready for her responsibility.'

But tonight, while she was alone in the Designate's residence, a yearning voice in her head summoned a deep longing within her. It was a call of blood and love and faith unlike any her enhanced telepathic abilities had shown her before. She had felt the other presence before, not long ago during the worst of the fires, but the Designate had watched her too closely, preventing the girl from spending the time she needed to search, to investigate.

But now, with the shimmering safety net of the *thism* gone, Osira'h could see and think more clearly along those other paths. The strange message was louder, easier to understand. It awakened the faintest memory in her, something from long ago – hands that had held her, cared for her.

Like a crackle of distant thunder, the urgent sensation came again, pulling at Osira'h in a way she had never before experienced.

Osira'h could not simply delay and ask the Designate about this when he returned from the funeral and ascension ceremonies on Ildira. She must find her own answer. Now. She had to know what it was . . . who was out there.

The girl applied her mental training to solving the problem. Udru'h and the advisers had taught her how to use her mind, and Osira'h needed her skills now more than ever. She summoned the telepathic strengths she'd inherited from her mixed parentage – one hand able to touch *thism* through her Ildiran genes, the other grasping at a telink capability carried over from a human green priest. Only she could control that combined power.

Surrounded by comforting blazers, Osira'h sat up in her bed to look around the well-lit chamber and at the darkness outside the windows. *Out there.* She followed the call, sensed the longing . . . close, personal.

It was coming from the breeder camp. The answer was clear, and obvious. Someone nearby, someone who had almost given up hope.

Osira'h went to the window, but could see little in the illuminated compound. Security lights dazzled the barracks, driving back every scrap of night. She had to go outside and see. This stranger wanted something so badly that she was able to yank Osira'h's heartstrings like a leash.

Before leaving, the Designate had sternly told her not to leave the residence, forbidding her to go out to the camps. With a thrill at her surprising independence, Osira'h made up her mind. She dressed quickly in a plain outfit, quietly slipped past the unsuspecting house guards, and hurried out into the well-lit streets.

Overhead, stars shone like diamonds against black velvet, a myriad of tiny lights. Accumulated soot and ash from the recent grass fires had gathered in the gaps between buildings, and the smell tickled at her nostrils as she walked. There weren't many guards in the breeding compound, and all the human families had gone to sleep in the communal barracks. Osira'h easily avoided being seen.

She had never questioned what went on in those buildings. The Designate assured her that everything was necessary, that she herself was the culmination of many generations of research and interbreeding experiments. Ultimately, her abilities would justify everything.

Now, Osira'h saw the shape of a woman hiding in a corner of the fences. She hesitated, fearful for just an instant. Sensations came from this stranger, clear and unusual: her body was sore, her head hurt from crying. Her eyes were raw from staring at the Designate's residence. Searching for *her*.

As she drew closer, Osira'h felt a connection with this prisoner . . . with this human female.

With her mother!

Osira'h froze as the realization slammed into her, thoughts ricocheting from this green-skinned woman who lived behind the fences, worked on labour projects, bred with Ildiran kiths, and gave birth to other children.

Osira'h hurried forward, as much confused as excited. Her mother was thin and wiry, her eyes haunted and surrounded by shadows, her cheeks sunken – but her eyes lit up like a sunrise when she saw the girl. 'My Princess! My daughter!' Tears sprang to her eyes as the girl came forward to stand on the opposite side of the fence.

'Why are you here?' Osira'h asked. 'You're my mother. You shouldn't be in the breeder barracks. Why aren't you helping to train me along with the Designate?'

Nira extended a callused green hand through the fence to

stroke her daughter's cheek. 'You are so beautiful . . . my little girl. Jora'h would be proud of you.' Then her face fell. 'I don't think he even knows he has a daughter.'

'I was bred to protect the Ildiran Empire.'

'No. You were conceived out of love, but I was taken prisoner and locked away here. I had only a few months to hold you as an infant . . . and then you were stolen from me. I wanted to be with you, but I was kept here, forced to endure . . . terrible things. You have been tricked.'

'That's not true,' Osira'h said. 'You don't understand.'

Nira's face twitched with a wan but genuine smile as she caressed the girl's other cheek. Osira'h felt the bond strengthen between them, saw echoes of thoughts and painful memories that were not her own. 'Of course I understand, my little girl. But the Designate tells you only what he wants you to know – not the truth. Not all of it. You are his tool, his prize.'

Osira'h grew resistant and angry. Her telepathic abilities had never come to her so powerfully, so easily, as now – yet she didn't want to know. 'My purpose is to save the Ildiran Empire! I'm the only one who has a chance of forming a bridge with the hydrogues, of establishing a lasting peace.'

Nira looked sceptical. Her tattoos were darkened lines, like scars on her face. 'A peace that includes humans and Ildirans and hydrogues? Or just an alliance to save the Empire at the cost of my race?' She shook her head. 'What am I saying to you? You're just a child. You can't possibly know.'

'Yes, I can! I have absorbed years of instruction from the greatest teachers. My mind has been exercised by the most talented mentalists and lens kithmen. The Designate says the level of my intelligence, knowledge, and maturity is at least twice my physical years. That is how it has to be, because our time is short.' It sounded as if she were repeating memorized phrases.

Nira lowered her head with a disappointed frown. 'I am so sorry, Osira'h. When I first learned I was pregnant, I knew the Prime Designate would want to raise you in the Prism Palace, but I never thought you would have to lose your childhood and be used like this. Oh, such a terrible fate. And you don't even know why or what awful things they have done to you.'

Osira'h could sense that her mother was not lying, but she still wasn't ready to believe what Nira said or doubt all the things the Designate had taught her. Her voice wavered. 'But I am . . . the Mage-Imperator's great hope.'

'Then listen to me, Osira'h. If you are to fill such an important role, then you should understand the consequences of everything you do. If you are indeed the Ildiran saviour, don't let yourself be a mindless soldier following orders that the secret-keepers give you.'

Osira'h reached her small hand through the fence, reluctant but forcing herself. 'I can already hear some of your thoughts. Let me . . . let me see them all.'

Nira blinked at her. 'You can take all the information from me? Directly?'

'I think I have that skill. Partly from you, partly from my father.'

The woman smiled strangely. 'I suppose it'll be like accessing information from the worldforest . . . but we don't have a treeling to assist us. The bond between mother and daughter will have to suffice.'

Osira'h touched her mother's skin, her brow, her temples. 'It will be different from my other instruction, but this is the sort of thing the Designate has always wanted me to do – to open unorthodox lines of communication.' She took a deep breath, then spoke as if she were reciting a mantra. 'Let the knowledge, memories, and information stored within your mind be like cool water, and I will be a thirsty sponge. Let me learn the truth in your heart and make it my own.'

As if afraid the girl would change her mind, Nira grabbed her daughter's hand, pressing it hard against her skull. The green priest opened her mind and spilled out her memories and thoughts – and Osira'h was open to them.

As the flow began, Osira'h could not help but drink in the details: the first images of Jora'h, the wondrous times of her father and Nira in the Prism Palace. The girl had hungered for more information about Ildira, but the Dobro Designate had always sheltered her, explaining that it was irrelevant.

Osira'h saw the love Nira and her father had shared, heard the promises they had made to each other . . . and finally understood the treachery of the Mage-Imperator and the Dobro Designate. They had slain old Otema because she was not of breeding age. They had locked Nira in a darkened cell, kept her isolated before they learned she was pregnant with the Prime Designate's child – with Osira'h. And after the daughter was successfully delivered, after Nira had spent several months loving her child, they had stolen the baby away, to raise her – and brainwash her.

Insatiable now, Osira'h took more and more of it, consuming every horrific memory of repeated rapes and forced impregnations. Suddenly the little girl saw the truth behind all the dry words Udru'h had spoken, even though she didn't want to hear it.

And she also learned the joy of serving the worldforest, the thrill of tapping into the sentient network, the wondrous things Nira had seen on Theroc and in Mijistra. At last she knew the love and happiness that Nira had once experienced, and everything that her mother had lost by becoming a captive here on Dobro, a victim of the Designate's experiments.

When the thoughts finally faded to a trickle, emptying into an echo in her mind, Osira'h knew everything that her mother was, all that she had lived and thought. Each realization resounded like a thunderclap in her mind.

The Ildiran leaders were not the admirable heroes she had been taught to worship. Her mission to connect with the hydrogues and save the Empire was not the altruistic goal the Dobro Designate had always explained to her.

Drained and utterly exhausted, Nira slid to her knees. But her face wore a smile of weak relief that she had been able to do such an important thing, at last. Osira'h stood stunned, her hand still resting lightly on her mother's head.

Before the girl could say anything, her mother suddenly gasped and broke away. Osira'h saw the fear on her face. She turned.

Two looming forms of guard kithmen appeared from the well-lit streets, venturing into the shadows where Osira'h had huddled at the fence juncture with her mother. 'Nira Khali, we have come for you,' said one of the soldiers. 'The Designate gave us strict instructions.'

A third guard approached from the outside, marching purposefully towards the little girl. In a gruff voice, he said, 'Osira'h, you are not to leave the residence without supervision. It is dangerous. You could be hurt. I will take you back now.'

The girl turned quickly, defiantly meeting the gaze of the burly soldier. 'I am unharmed. How can there be any threat to me here on Dobro?'

The guard took her by the arm. 'We do not ask the Designate to explain himself. Neither should you.' He began pulling Osira'h away from her mother, while the two other guards grabbed Nira by her thin wrists. The green-skinned woman did not resist.

'Leave her alone!' By instinct, because of all that she now understood, Osira'h did not reveal what she knew or who Nira was. 'Don't harm her.'

'We are following the Designate's orders.'

As the soldier kithmen wrestled her away, Nira shouted to Osira'h, 'Remember . . . just *remember*.'

Without speaking, the guard hurried Osira'h back along the well-lit streets towards the tall, bright residence. Though she could no longer see Nira, Osira'h still felt the connection with her mother echoing in her mind. Her heart pounded with fear that was both her own and Nira's, and she felt the resignation in her mother's mind. The green priest began to struggle, she almost broke away—

Then, suddenly, more pain than the girl could comprehend. A shaft of ice went through her chest, and she caught her breath. Osira'h stumbled. She heard a distant harsh cry of agony, and then the wet sounds of another blow.

Just as they had done to Ambassador Otema! It must be!

Frantic, Osira'h snatched her hand away from the guard, surprising him, and bolted back towards the fence. 'Stop it! What have you done?'

She ran faster than she ever had, and when she reached the boundary wires, she saw the guards dragging the limp green form of her mother towards one of the laboratory barracks. Under the bright light, she saw a blossom of brilliant scarlet blood on the hairless green scalp.

She sensed no thoughts from her mother, nothing at all.

Osira'h screamed and tried to scramble through a narrow gap in the fence wires, but the pursuing guard grabbed her. The girl whirled on him. 'What did they do? Why did you hurt her?'

'She attempted to escape,' said the guard, as the others continued to drag the woman's body off into the shadows. 'The Designate warned us what she might do. Nira Khali is a threat.'

'A threat to what?' Osira'h demanded.

'A threat to everything.'

When Nira was gone, the little girl felt only a void where the woman's presence had been, an emptiness, a loss. But Osira'h had already stored every thought that was her mother in her own mind and heart, and she also knew the dangers she would face if

Designate Udru'h or anyone else learned what she had discovered.

She had to keep her secrets, until she could decide what to do, until she had learned more.

The girl had just met her mother for the first time, and now she had to say goodbye. Her mother, a stranger, had given her more than life. She had awakened the truth in Osira'h, exposed the lies of her mentors. Could so many things she had learned – the facts of her very existence – really be lies?

Osira'h let her grief seep out of her, and quickly hid her emotions behind childish prattle. 'I wanted to ask her why her skin was so green and strange,' she said, looking up at the bestial face of the guard as he sternly walked her back to the residence. 'That was all.'

'Do not concern yourself about it.'

Thank you, Mother, she thought. *Thank you for everything.*

Though she wore the body of a six-year-old girl, Osira'h carried vast amounts of knowledge and maturity within her brain. She was stronger now, propped up by secrets and schemes, but many of them were her own.

As the guard marched her back to the Designate's residence, thoughts whirled behind her eyes. Osira'h did not want to hate the Dobro Designate, but the knowledge of all that he'd done to Nira was now firmly planted in her mind. And a seed of anger took root and began to sprout.

KING PETER

Much to the surprise and gratification of the twittering protocol ministers, King Peter seemed to take a very personal interest in the honeymoon parade. In truth, after Estarra had told him her suspicions about the royal yacht and shared Sarein's veiled warnings, Peter had decided to play along — and keep his eyes open.

With Estarra on his arm and OX following dutifully beside them, the King made a slow procession towards the maintenance docks well before the scheduled departure time. The protocol ministers quickly gathered media representatives who were delighted with the unexpected publicity opportunity. The King and Queen smiled at them, doing everything they asked, being extraordinarily cooperative.

Peter didn't think it would be enough to assuage Basil, though. The damage had already been done.

The docks and corridors and sidewalks had been swept clean, every wall polished. Even the other boats in the maintenance hangars gleamed. Pink and white peonies floated on the water, scented with heady perfume.

The King kept a calm smile on his face. The workers and palace personnel seemed giddy with his appreciation. Queen Estarra waved at the people while snuggling close to Peter. They both played the part of young starry-eyed newlyweds . . .

The night before, they had made love with even more passion and affection than before. He had kissed her cheek, her lightly closed eyelids with genuine surprise at what he was feeling, and an unexpected sensation of relief. He whispered so close to Estarra's ear that his very words were like gentle kisses, 'Ever since I was kidnapped and brought to the Whisper Palace, I've always been suspicious. I had no choice but to doubt everyone who claimed to be my friend.'

She had held him close. 'You have to trust someone, Peter.'

'Yes, finally I think I can.' *Estarra.*

She was intelligent and capable – and no more happy about her situation than he was about his. Holding her close, Peter whispered more of the story about his little brothers, his hard-working mother, even his estranged father who had abandoned the family and run off to Ramah. All of them had been assassinated, just to clear the slate for him. Peter felt moisture on the sheets, his own tears seeping into the pillowcase. Estarra brushed her fingers across his face, comforting him . . .

Now he stood on the dock with Estarra, admiring the gaudy banners. 'OX, go aboard.' Peter gestured to the Teacher compy, who dutifully walked across the gangplank.

Several workers stood at attention at the bow of the processional yacht. Peter turned to wave at the crowds. As a mob of self-important officials prepared to accompany the King and Queen aboard the boat, Peter touched his lower lip and pretended to have a sudden idea. He turned to the protocol minister. 'Estarra and I would like to go aboard alone, just to have a look around in private.'

'Sire, that is most unexpected—'

Peter smiled reassuringly. 'I promise, you can all come aboard in a few minutes – but surely no person here would begrudge a man a few moments alone and in private with his beautiful new bride? No chance for a stolen kiss tomorrow during the actual procession, is there?' He leaned close to Estarra. She giggled, clinging to his arm.

The onlookers chuckled and applauded. A few of the braver men even made catcalls from the back of the group. The public display of affection seemed like a sigh of relief in such tense times.

Peter looked beseechingly at the protocol minister. The man seemed befuddled by the change of plans, but obviously he saw how much the crowd approved. It was a chance to score points. 'All right, we will allow it . . . but only for a few minutes. You are the King, Sire, and you must follow certain expectations of public behaviour.'

Peter winked at him, grinning. 'We won't be *scandalously* long.'

Workers trotted down the gangplank and made proud welcoming gestures. 'Be our guest onboard, King Peter. You'll find everything completely satisfactory.'

'I'm sure I will, with devoted men and women such as yourselves on the job.' Strutting confidently, Peter led his Queen across the gangplank. OX had already disappeared below decks into the engine room.

Peter took his time, an agonized few minutes studying the upper deck, admiring the pennants and polished gold and inlaid wood. Finally, he put his arm around Estarra's waist and pulled her close, knowing that everyone was watching. Then they ducked out of sight.

Moving quickly and intently now, he and Estarra split up,

opening cabinets, rummaging through onboard compartments, under the beds and tables. 'We don't know what Pellidor was doing, but too many other people have inspected the boat,' Peter said. 'Whatever he's done, it won't be obvious.'

Following instructions, OX ransacked the engine compartment, analysing systems, studying the apparatus, controls, components. Earlier, Peter had surreptitiously uploaded detailed programming into the Teacher compy's already overloaded mind. OX now knew the exact specifications of the royal yacht, and he understood how to identify sabotage.

Peter kept track of the time, knowing they had only a few moments. Outside, he heard happy, good-natured whistles. He called quietly but urgently, 'OX, have you found anything yet?'

The compy emerged from the engine compartment. 'I have done a full and complete safety check on the yacht's systems. A dangerous incendiary device was installed deep within one of the fuel coils.'

Peter knew he shouldn't have been surprised. 'What kind?'

'A plasma-ignition bomb, small but very powerful. It would have flash-vaporized most of the yacht, incinerating everyone aboard. You would not have survived.'

'Basil, you bastard. You deactivated it?'

'Yes. Your yacht is now completely safe.'

'Thanks, OX.' Peter took a moment to compose his expression.

The Teacher compy continued. 'One other puzzling detail. The systemic design of the plasma-ignition device carries certain readily identifiable signature spikes in the molecular composition. This type of munition is unmistakably of Roamer manufacture. Its configuration precisely matches some items recovered from Rand Sorengaard's pirate ships, which were commandeered by the EDF six years ago.'

'Roamers?' Estarra said. 'My brother is scheduled to marry the

Speaker in a few months. Why would they have a grudge against us?'

'It's not the Roamers,' Peter said. 'It's the Hansa, but they're using identifiable Roamer technology so they can arrest some poor trader as a scapegoat.' He turned to OX. 'Has the Hansa or the EDF taken unusual action or impounded any Roamer vessels recently?'

OX paused a moment as he scanned current events records in his database. 'Yes, a Roamer trading vessel is being held at the moon-base after delivering supplies to Earth. The captain is Denn Peroni.'

Estarra interrupted. 'He's the father of Reynald's fiancée!'

'He's also an important Roamer clan leader,' Peter said. 'What were the charges?'

'Unclear,' OX said. 'Apparently there were some temporary irregularities in his paperwork and in the shipment he delivered. But I have studied the documents myself and I see nothing unusual about them.'

'Damn. So they're holding him until after our "tragic accident". Then they'll find evidence and charge him. No doubt he'll be inadvertently "killed while attempting to escape".' Peter clenched his jaw, shaking his head as anger swelled within him. 'I know exactly how Basil thinks about solving problems.'

Estarra couldn't believe what she was hearing. 'So the Hansa will use this supposed assassination attempt as an excuse to declare war on the Roamers and take their ekti and other supplies, won't they? What will that do to poor Reynald and his betrothal to the Speaker?'

'There are consequences everywhere we turn.' Peter nodded. 'By going after the Roamers, Basil's picking an enemy he thinks he can easily defeat – since he's making no progress against the hydrogues. It's the same reason he had to be so tough on Yreka – do you think that little colony could possibly have been worth fighting for?'

'We have to warn Cesca's father,' Estarra said. 'We need to get him free. There's no telling what'll happen if—'

'Careful.' Peter raised his hand. 'One step at a time. I do still have some influence as King, remember? I can issue a royal pardon.' He pondered, then smiled. 'Yes, I can announce that "in a new spirit of openness" – Basil's not the only one who can say those words! – my wife wishes to have more friendly ties with the Roamers, who will become part of her extended family on Theroc. I'll say there's no need for bureaucratic harassment of honest Roamer traders such as Denn Peroni.

'We'll issue the pardon simultaneous with our honeymoon cruise, when no one will be watching closely. In fact,' he turned to the Teacher compy, 'OX, I want you to deliver it personally. No one will question your motives.'

Estarra pointed her finger at the old compy. 'But Peroni's got to leave as fast as possible, as soon as they release him.'

'I can certainly see to that, Queen Estarra,' OX said.

Peter gained control of his expression by taking several deep breaths. He held Estarra close. 'We've been down here long enough. We have to go out and face the gathered people. Smiling. Can you wear a poker face, make sure no one knows we suspect a thing?'

'When I am with my loving new husband, I can show delight in all things,' Estarra said. 'Should we confront Chairman Wenceslas in private with what we've learned? He can't get away with attempts on our lives, can he? The people would tear him limb from limb.'

Peter's eyes narrowed with a calculating gleam. 'No, for now you and I should just go on our wondrous floating parade exactly as planned. Let's see how Basil reacts. I want to look him in the eye afterwards, once his plan has failed.' Impulsively, he kissed her long and deeply, then broke away. 'From now on, though, it'll be war between us. We'll just have to trust that the people want a true King, instead of a shadowy power behind the throne.'

ONE HUNDRED AND TWENTY-FIVE

FATHER REYNALD

After eradicating all life on Corvus Landing, the hydrogues took less than two weeks to find the main worldforest. And no one on Theroc was ready.

With crowds of his eager subjects, Father Reynald had climbed a comfortable platform atop the canopy to celebrate the Festival of the Butterflies. Once each year, thousands upon thousands of chrysalises hatched simultaneously. Swarms of short-lived butterfly analogues broke from their metamorphosis cocoons, shook out delicate wings of amethyst purple and sapphire blue, then took flight for their one glorious day before death.

Naturally timed to coincide with the mass hatching, dozens of species of epiphytes spread their petals to be pollinated, filling the air with a dizzying perfume. Predatory avians swooped down to meet the first waves of emerging butterflies, gorging themselves on a great feast.

Many Therons took positions atop the interlinked fronds to watch the spectacle. Treedancers bounded from bough to bough, doing somersaults and pirouettes in an artistic interpretation of the poignant first and last flight of the butterflies. Children laughed and played, confident in their balance as they ran barefoot across the upper branches, trying to catch the butterflies.

Green priest acolytes studied the sight, memorizing every detail, then recounted their perspective to the worldtrees. Reynald's grandparents sat on a platform side by side, playing an impromptu song on handmade musical instruments—

And then the hydrogues came.

Though he did not have access to telink, Reynald sensed a shudder through the whole worldforest. The attentive green priests turned their faces upwards to stare, mouths gaping in disbelief and horror as diamond-hulled warglobes hurtled down from the zenith. Cruising low, they seemed inscrutably confident, like predators circling a new victim.

Reacting quickly, instinctively, Reynald bellowed loud enough to break through the frightened chatter of festival spectators. 'Everyone, get down to ground level! Take shelter.'

Alexa looked at her eldest son – her only surviving son – and moved automatically, as if she had always followed his orders. She urged a group of children towards ladders and small lift platforms. 'Come! Listen to Father Reynald.'

Uthair looked at Reynald, keeping his raspy voice low. 'Will that do any good? We know what the hydrogues are capable of.'

Reynald squared his shoulders, looking like a true Father. 'Theroc has more worldtrees than any other planet in the Spiral Arm. Let's pray the power and intelligence of this forest can offer us some protection. Down under the canopy, maybe some of our people can survive.'

Old Lia took her husband's elbow. 'Come on, no good standing here.'

People who had gathered for the festival began scrambling through the branches and leaves, climbing down the scaly bark.

The whole worldforest shuddered again, indicating both dread and anticipation. Boughs rustled and fronds scraped together as if in a defensive hiss.

Moaning, the green priests clutched the leaves, drawing strength and reassurance. 'Father Reynald, hydrogues have appeared across all the continents. It is a massive attack.'

He grabbed the nearest green priest. 'Contact Nahton in the Whisper Palace, send a message to my sister Estarra on Earth. Or Sarein! Tell the King we need warships as soon as possible. Contact Rossia and Yarrod in the EDF battle groups. Call them all to Theroc immediately.' He blinked, desperate for options. 'Even the Roamers! Speak with them if you can. See if they'll offer help. Do . . . do we have any green priests in the Ildiran Empire?'

'We will send the message everywhere.' The green priest groaned in despair as the nearest trio of hydrogues hovered overhead, pulsing and building up energy. 'But no help can get here fast enough.'

The trees rocked and swayed like stubborn animals, pushing their nerve-like roots deeper into the ground, anchoring themselves and preparing for the worst.

The purple-and-blue butterflies, their lives already transient, flitted about and sipped from the luscious epiphytes. They didn't seem to notice the looming presence in the skies.

Reynald watched the continuing evacuation. Most of the spectators had scrambled to the forest floor beneath the shelter of thick interlocked fronds. He hoped they would be protected there, but he knew in his heart that Theroc had no effective defences against such an enemy. No one did. And, as Father of the Theron people, Reynald would witness the attack with his own eyes.

The hydrogues dropped down and began their destruction. Electrical blue lightning and frozen white icewaves swept the worldforest, each like a reaper's deadly scythe.

The green priests beside Reynald cried out in reactive pain.

'Tell me what you see from all the continents on Theroc,' Reynald demanded as he watched the warglobes slash and devastate the worldforest. The two green priests grasped the fronds, drawing images from the other priests around the planet, innocent bystanders in the terrible battle. 'Describe what is happening on my world.'

In the tree village around the deep Looking Glass Lakes, green priests, treedancers, and settlers swarmed out of the dangling wormhives. Vengeful hydrogues soared overhead in an inexhaustible thirst for destruction. Waves of freezing mist touched the verdant canopy, and with each caress, the deadly cold seared life from the foliage, blistering and cracking it into dead lumps.

Blue lightning incinerated the thickest trunks; even the worldtrees could not draw enough power from the soil itself.

Almari, the young female priest who had offered to marry Reynald when he'd visited her village, watched in horror as the hydrogues came in over the round, placid lakes. She grasped the bark of the nearest tree, trying in vain to summon some kind of defensive tactic, some power to protect the forest and her people. But the trees could offer her nothing.

As the hydrogues came, the papery wormhive dwellings became deathtraps coated with ice, cementing victims inside. Many villagers fell from high branches as they tried to flee headlong. People ran deeper into the densest forest, crashing through the underbrush.

But Almari stood awestruck at the opposite lakeshore.

The cold icewave weapon struck first, then blue bullwhips of energy knocked down the forest, blasting the frozen trunks into fragmented shards. The wormhives fell to the ground, where they shattered into snowy dust.

Almari watched transfixed as the cold fingers froze the circular lake into jagged chunks of white ice. The hydrogues kept coming towards her. The green priest turned into a frozen pillar herself, an ice sculpture still wearing an expression of despair and disbelief.

Across the continent at the fungus-reef city, the trees tried to pull the canopy closed in a defensive posture to block the attack from the skies. The thick boughs folded together like praying hands, overlapping to form a barricade as the hydrogues pounded them from above. The massive trunks trembled, but stood firm, withstanding the first impact of icewaves and electrical blasts.

Shielding his eyes, Reynald watched another diamond sphere cruise low over the treetops, spraying cold waves and shrivelling whatever parts of the canopy it touched. He grabbed both green priests. 'The trees must help us! If they don't, we will all die!'

The priest closed his eyes, summoning the will to place his mind into the expansive forest again. 'The trees are not ready for this battle—'

'None of us is, but we must still fight. Life has the power to encourage other life.' It seemed as if the worldforest had given up in despair, but Reynald wouldn't accept that. 'After our centuries of talking to them, reading to them, the trees must have learned something about us.'

The two green priests closed their eyes, concentrating, sending their thoughts into the injured network. Together, they summoned the strength stored deep within the root network, drawing it up into the trunks and the whispering leaves. Reynald could see the strain in the sinews of their necks, the grimaces on their faces as they wrenched a desperate resistance from the worldforest.

As the nearest warglobe continued its destruction, Reynald saw the forest stir beneath it. After the devastating icewave had cracked and split the massive trunks, a wave of rebirth followed behind it like a green ocean tide. Even as the old trees blackened and began to fall, a rippling surge of newborn foliage burst out of the twisted, scarred trunks, green leaves replacing the shattered brown ones.

The explosion of fresh foliage was like some eerie time-lapse image of rampant fecundity. The new, bright growth momentarily sealed over the hydrogue wound like a fresh, shiny scar. A defiant flush of green softened the black scars, trying to keep pace with the destruction.

The warglobe passed, seemingly oblivious to the small swatch of forest healing itself after each crippling blast.

Reynald wanted to cheer. Heartened by the demonstration of living power, the splash of hope, he called upon the priests again to do something, but they could barely remain standing, obviously exhausted. 'It is not enough. We cannot continue this.'

Reynald looked to the densest, greenest part of the carpeted forest, which was momentarily safe from the destruction. Trembling, as if concentrating verdant energy drawn from billions of leaves, a section of the trees collapsed, folding of their own accord into a central mound, like a fortified shelter that twined branches together and dug its roots deeper into the soil. The thunderous booms of toppling trunks rolled across the sky even as the warglobes continued their onslaught.

Reynald stared, wondering if the worldforest was protecting a small core of itself . . . preparing for the worst. The interlocking wood appeared as hard as iron. Had the towering trees given up already? And how could that small shelter protect any of his *people*?

The warglobes struck again and again, criss-crossing in random paths of destruction – they seemed to have no specific plan other than to destroy all of the worldtrees. Vast sections of the vulnerable worldforest had already been freeze-blasted. So many trees, so many lives. Swatches of landscape now withered and collapsed.

Reynald saw that it was only getting worse, second by second. Though he felt exposed and vulnerable from his vantage point, he knew that Therons on the ground were dying just as rapidly as those on the treetops, all across the continent. The worldtrees and wildlife were being wiped out and millions of people slaughtered.

Neither he nor the forest could do anything to fight back.

One Hundred and Twenty-six

Adar Kori'nh

'The Ildirans must have a victory,' Adar Kori'nh said to the skeleton crew of his commandeered maniple. His warriors . . . his heroes. He reflexively ran his palm over the rough, stubbly surface of his shaved scalp. 'We need it now more than ever.'

These battleships were the grandest vessels in the Solar Navy, loaded with the best weaponry the Empire had ever created, gaudy with spectacular solar fins and sails that fluttered each time the course was adjusted. He knew he could have had ten times as many volunteers for this mission. He wasn't the only Ildiran to have felt impotent against their enemy.

Everything was ready, and he simply had to make the effort count.

Reeling from the loss of the Mage-Imperator, every person of their race – including Kori'nh himself – felt adrift. Before long, probably within a day, Prime Designate Jora'h would reassert control, bind the soul-threads together again, proclaim the paths he saw from the Lightsource.

But Kori'nh was the Solar Navy's supreme commander, and he had his own ideas about how this war should be pursued. Here, now, freed at last from the constraints of *thism*, he could put those ideas into action.

'Full speed to the Qronha system,' he said, and the forty-nine warliners arranged themselves into a perfect battle formation. 'It is our turn to take the fight to the hydrogues. And to destroy them.'

The crew cheered, glad to be following him in uncertain and painful times. The Adar stood proud in the command nucleus of Qul Bore'nh's warliner. Once again, he had adorned his formal uniform with all of his magnificent medals, badges, and braids – every one of the accolades the Mage-Imperator had ever awarded him. Yes, this was how the tales should remember him.

'Today, we all become immortal in the *Saga of Seven Suns*.'

At the heart of the Qronha system, not far from Ildira, a small yellow star orbited so close to a red-giant primary that the larger star's gravity siphoned gases from its companion. Qronha 3 – the system's only gas giant – had been home to the oldest cloud-mining factory ever established by the Empire. Though human Roamers had taken over the skymining industries elsewhere, the giant Qronha 3 ekti complex had remained a symbolic bastion for their race. When the hydrogues had chosen to destroy the facility and kill thousands of workers, they had declared war on the Ildiran Empire as well.

Now it was the Solar Navy's turn to mount a surprise attack – right where the conflict had begun.

The gas giant swelled like a blister before them as the maniple decelerated, ready for battle.

'The hydrogues are down there somewhere,' Kori'nh said. Qul Bore'nh stood beside him, ready to give the standard operational orders. The septars controlling each grouping of seven ships prepared their weapons.

'We must find them and hurt them. We will show the hydrogues, and our own people, that it *can* be done,' the Adar continued. 'No commander has ever had a more important duty.'

Kori'nh took a deep breath, focusing his thoughts. Without *thism*, the emptiness still echoed in his mind. Once Jora'h reconnected the *thism*, Adar Kori'nh could no longer act for himself. He knew there was little enough time. His battleships needed to strike now.

Kori'nh ordered the ships to drop through Qronha 3's outer atmosphere and proceed into warmer, thicker depths. During the first battle here, the Solar Navy had achieved only one partial victory . . . but it had shown the way.

This time, the Adar intended to achieve more.

As his warliners drove forward, Kori'nh thought of a great battle from Earth history: the defeat of an inspired, but ultimately unsuccessful, general named Napoleon. Waterloo.

'Stand alert and steady.'

The cohort sliced through rust-coloured cloudbands, veils of grey and yellow mists. Sonic booms from the rapid descent echoed across the high skies.

Kori'nh instructed his warliners to transmit forceful, intimidating messages: 'Hydrogues, we reclaim this planet for the Ildiran Empire. We demand your immediate departure from this world.'

Qul Bore'nh turned to him in the command nucleus. 'Adar, do you expect to prompt a surrender from our enemy?'

'Not at all.' Kori'nh looked at him, his face stony. 'I intend to provoke them.'

Cruising through the atmosphere, he ordered all forty-nine ships to remain in formation, but at maximum standard separation. Scout streamers spread out through the vaporous winds, broadcasting their reconnaissance.

When the warglobes finally appeared, Kori'nh was prepared, even relieved. *Now we begin.* 'Engage the enemy!'

Ildiran warliners fired a dizzying barrage of kinetic missiles and high-energy cutting beams that peppered the alien globes. Ionization flashes and spreading clouds of smoke transformed the cloudy battlefield into a confusing patchwork of signals and targets. The sensor feedback began to blur.

The hydrogues retaliated quickly, warglobe after warglobe lashing out with volleys of blue electrical force.

Kori'nh allowed the firefight to continue for several minutes, luring more and more hydrogues from the depths. But when the aliens' weapons damaged the engines of one warliner, he knew the time had come to change tactics.

'Time for the culmination of our part of the great story,' the Adar broadcast to the rest of the ships. 'We have a full maniple of warliners, each one ready to strike a crippling blow against the enemies of the Ildiran Empire. How much of a victory can we buy? We will show what *can* be done.' He turned to the subcommander beside him. 'Qul Bore'nh, issue the order.'

The other military leader spoke calmly. 'All septars, coordinate your targets. We have the potential to destroy forty-nine of our foes. Make each of your ships count.' He received a flurry of acknowledgements from the warliners. 'Engineers, initiate cascade overload in your stardrive reactors.'

Kori'nh gripped the command rail and looked around him. He sensed a grim determination in the crew. They had felt beaten, but now they saw a chance to make an effective retaliation, at last.

He'd given strict orders to a single septa of streamer scouts: the seven small ships were to remain away from the fray, keeping themselves safe so they could document this decisive battle. Afterwards, they would fly immediately to Ildira and make their report, to describe to the new Mage-Imperator what the Solar Navy had accomplished here.

Kori'nh made one last important, defiant broadcast to the skeleton crews on each warliner. 'Here and now, we forever earn a place in our *Saga*. Can any Ildiran ask for a more noble end?'

Behind him, the stardrive engines roared with strain as the reactors built towards supernova power. Already, the command nucleus felt furiously hot.

Warglobe after warglobe hurtled towards them. He muttered, 'Let the enemy witness their own folly.'

On the target screen he watched as the first great warliner, its aft engine cones white-hot and unable to dispel the furious exhaust, slammed into the foremost warglobe like a hammer into an anvil. The Ildiran and hydrogue battleships both erupted in a splash of intolerable fire so intense that it momentarily burned out the flagship's forward sensors. Like a doorway to the higher plane of the Lightsource. Everyone could see it.

Above and to starboard, another nova explosion wiped out a second warglobe. The aliens hadn't yet comprehended Kori'nh's devastating final intent. 'We have taken them by surprise, for a change.'

His warliner drove forward, and Kori'nh could not blink, staring fixedly as clouds whipped past the bow. His own chosen warglobe target reared up on them, vast and geometrically perfect. The Adar saw the translucent hull and the complex geometrical city contained within the supposedly impenetrable walls.

Bore'nh looked at him. 'Only a few seconds now, Adar.'

Kori'nh watched the alien ship growing larger, approaching faster. Electrical bolts leaped from one pyramidal protrusion to another, but his own vessel was travelling much too fast to be thrown off course now. Their engines had already reached the peak of cascade overload.

Nothing would stop them.

In the final instant, he allowed himself a smile, washing away all the doubts and disappointments of his military career. This was *perfect*.

The warliner struck the immense globe just as the engines could no longer contain the buildup. Kori'nh kept his eyes open to the last, as all the universe was swallowed in a burst of blinding white light.

ONE HUNDRED AND TWENTY-SEVEN

SAREIN

S tanding beside Basil Wenceslas at the observation stand for the much-anticipated honeymoon parade, Sarein felt the exhilaration in the crowds all around her – except from Basil. The Chairman seemed more distracted than usual, his gaze distant, his responses snappish.

'What's wrong?' she asked him in a low voice, maintaining her smile for any observers. Trumpets played a fanfare based on the recognizable melody of the marriage symphony that had been composed for Peter and Estarra's wedding. The happy tumult of the crowd was a constant background roar.

The Chairman looked at her, his suave face clenched in a barely controlled frown, as if he was bothered by her presence next to him. Sarein briefly saw him as a stranger. Finally he said, 'Some problems should never arise in the first place. We're all supposed to be on the same team with the same goal, yet half of our failures come from weaknesses in our own camp.' He turned back towards the royal canal. 'That is inexcusable.'

Observation dirigibles carried VIP observers over the Whisper

Palace, offering a prime view of the slow-moving canal that wound for miles around the Palace District. Programme announcers proclaimed that the processional yacht and its escorts were ready to be launched.

Out in the square, ferns and flowers covered the terrain. Gardeners had made a special effort in Estarra's honour to keep the foliage and greenery lush. They wanted the young Queen from Theroc to feel at home.

Food and souvenir vendors made their way through the crowds, setting up stands, offering their wares. Palace representatives on hoverplatforms tossed out handfuls of commemorative coins that showed Peter and Estarra on the face with the encircled-Earth symbol of the Hansa on the reverse.

With his image projected from screens all around the plaza, the bearded old Archfather of Unison gave yet another blessing upon the royal couple and called for the grand honeymoon festival to start.

Sleek military hydro-craft roared up and down the canal, doing a final security check, although the crowds had already been screened and any conceivable weapon removed and deactivated. These were more than just soldiers, though, because their agile craft performed acrobatic manoeuvres, spraying roostertails of water in delightful plumes.

Sarein pressed closer to Basil. He stared fixedly at the canal, but did not look towards the Palace, where the royal yacht was even now emerging. Its ribbons and pennants fluttered with a sparkling rainbow of hues.

King Peter and Queen Estarra stood at the bow, proudly waving, dressed in their most extravagant outfits. As the royal couple's boat arrived, the crowd whistled and applauded. Sarein felt a blushing glow of popular acceptance and sincere adoration for her sister and Peter that made her heart tingle. The Hansa's citizens had drawn together to support their King, hoping for some sort of miracle. Beloved Old Frederick had died in the first blow in this war, and now the people looked to King Peter to save them.

Before setting out that morning, the King had made a show of approaching Basil, accompanied by Estarra. Both of them were immaculately dressed for the day's festivities, looking eager. Peter had been on perfect behaviour lately, so Sarein hoped that her quiet warning to her sister had sunk in. She greeted the young King formally, happy for her sister, though a part of her still wished *she* could have been chosen as the new Queen.

Smiling, Peter said, 'Basil, I'd like to extend you an invitation. Although I am the figurehead King, *you* are the Chairman of the Terran Hanseatic League. You make the command decisions and run the business of the Spiral Arm. You should be there celebrating with us.'

Basil glanced at him, surprised and suspicious, but the young King seemed sincere as he insisted, 'Queen Estarra and I would very much like for you to join us aboard our yacht for the honeymoon festival. Why not ride at the aft of the yacht, while we stand at the bow?'

Basil took a moment to regain his composure. 'That would not be wise at this time, King Peter.'

'Why not?' Estarra said sweetly. 'We could have you as an honorary best man. This would be a lovely way to demonstrate the bond between the Hansa Chairman and the King.'

Sarein saw an awkward flinch on Basil's face. 'I don't think so,' he said. 'The plans have been set in stone, and you, Peter, have already upset the protocol ministers enough in recent weeks.'

Peter laughed. 'Oh, they'll get over it, Basil. Come on, join us. What have you got to lose?'

'Please, Mr Chairman?' Estarra said.

Sarein wondered why Basil was being so resistant. This new cooperative attitude was exactly what he claimed he had hoped for in the King. 'It's a perfectly reasonable suggestion, Basil,' she said quietly. 'Why won't you consider it?'

'I said no.' Basil stiffened. 'Now go prepare for your departure.'

'Come with me, Estarra. Basil hates it when schedules change.' Looking disappointed – too disappointed, Sarein thought – Peter took his Queen by the arm. They left, and Sarein thought she saw a very odd expression on the Chairman's face . . .

Now she stood next to Basil wearing a beautiful ambassadorial gown of Theron weaves and rich green dyes, while other Hansa representatives joined them on the observation stand.

The royal yacht and its accompanying boats drifted down the canal at a sedate pace so that the spectators could wave and cheer, take their images and perhaps catch the King's eye. As far as Sarein could tell, everything was going perfectly.

But Basil was still very tense.

From behind, a group of palace guards rushed through the crowds, clearing a way so that the green priest Nahton could reach the observation stand. One of the guards helped him carry his potted treeling. Nahton ran quickly, his expression panic-stricken.

The representatives parted to let him hurry on to the platform. The green priest's voice was reedy and thin – not because he was out of breath from the effort, but because of the news he carried. 'Hydrogues are attacking Theroc! Right now! They are wiping out the worldforest.'

Sarein covered her mouth, unable to believe. Her home! Theroc!

Pushing aside his shock, Basil demanded a detailed explanation. Nahton quickly told how the warglobes had methodically begun to freeze and blast the worldtrees. Several major Theron settlements had already been annihilated.

'The people have gone to the base of the forest, but they have no protection even there. The worldtrees are fighting back, but to no avail. Father Reynald has requested assistance from anyone who can come. Can we dispatch the EDF?'

Basil looked distractedly at the green priest, as if trying to decide what to do, while Sarein grabbed his sleeve in alarm. 'Basil, how many ships can you send? Why are you hesitating?'

He frowned at her, annoyed at the distraction when he was deep in thought. 'Sarein, if we knew of any effective defence against a hydrogue attack, we would have used it long before this. What is the purpose in scrambling our forces in a frantic but pointless exercise? They can't do anything.'

A wave of frustration and disgust shot through her. 'Pointless? You offered my people protection and a partnership with Earth. Nineteen green priests joined the EDF. My sister married the King.' Then she quickly used the hook that would make him act. 'Basil, if the worldforest is destroyed, you'll have no more telink.'

The Chairman nodded briskly. 'Very well. Nahton, contact all the volunteer green priests aboard EDF warships. Dispatch whichever vessels are closest to Theroc with all possible speed.' He looked at Sarein. 'I doubt they'll arrive in time, though – even if they could be effective against warglobes. You know how little good our weapons and battleships can do.'

Nahton said, 'Clydia reports that her ships are within a day of Theroc. Those are the closest.'

Sarein cried, 'A day? But that will be too late! You know how quickly the hydrogues decimated Corvus Landing.'

'Send them anyway,' Basil commanded. 'Unless you have a better idea, Sarein?'

She remembered how badly she had wanted to leave Theroc, how much scorn she'd held for her provincial parents and their refusal to expand trading opportunities with the Hansa. Now, though, she could only think of the destruction of the magnificent worldforest, the suffering of her family . . . had she already lost her parents, or grandparents? Her little sister Celli? Her brother Reynald?

'We've got to stop the honeymoon festival,' she said. 'We must tell King Peter – and especially my sister. Our family is in danger.'

Basil scowled. 'No, the parade will continue as planned. We will control the news and release the information as we see fit. Enough time for that later.'

'But Estarra has to know,' Sarein said.

'Let her keep her peace and happiness for the moment. She has her own part to play right now. You can't interrupt.'

Sarein grabbed his arm again, wrinkling the fine business suit. 'Basil, we've already lost Beneto on Corvus Landing. Now Reynald is facing the hydrogues. My parents might be obliterated in a few moments. How can I bear to lose any more? Show a little compassion.'

'And you show a little common sense. This is a *war*. People die.' Basil looked at her. 'You'll just have to endure whatever grief finds you, Sarein. Maybe it's best if it occurs all at once, so then you can move on.'

Suspicious, Sarein narrowed her eyes. Basil kept watching the royal yacht as it drifted past. Peter made a special point of putting an arm around Estarra and waving at the Chairman. Stiffly, Basil raised a hand in acknowledgement.

'What do you mean?' Sarein said, feeling a new rush of fear.

The royal yacht approached a bend in the canal, and Basil gripped the railing of the observation stand. He refused to answer Sarein. She watched, dreading what he might have meant. 'Are you expecting some sort of "accident", Basil? *What have you done?*'

But the honeymoon festival continued without incident. The King and Queen waved and played their roles perfectly. The boat drifted on, undisturbed.

'Nothing,' Basil said. His shoulders seemed to slump in defeat, though Sarein had not seen anything to cause such a reaction. 'Nothing is going to happen, of course. No tragedy, no accident. Everything is under control.' He watched the procession along the royal canal, his face intent.

The green priest Nahton continued to relay details of the horrific destruction on Theroc. As Sarein listened to the terrible description with tears in her eyes, Basil seemed barely to hear him, more preoccupied with a personal and secret disaster of his own.

ONE HUNDRED AND TWENTY-EIGHT

FATHER REYNALD

On Theroc, as the worldtrees died, the telink news of the devastation travelled like lightning among the green priests distributed across the Spiral Arm.

But no one could help in time.

Beside Reynald, the tattooed priest looked up, and Reynald could already read the message from the man's bleak face. 'According to Clydia and Nahton, the nearest EDF battleships are a full day off, even at top speed.'

Swooping low like a frozen meteor, a warglobe hurtled across the forest, spraying withering icewaves. The worldtree canopy blackened, exhaling wisps of frigid white steam that rose like ghosts. Both green priests sank to their knees, unable to bear the pain of the worldforest.

'Can't the trees do anything else?' Reynald demanded. 'If the hydrogues are their ancient enemies, then they must have battled effectively before. How did they defend themselves?' He grasped a worldtree frond as if he could communicate with the verdant mind by sheer force of will.

'Yes,' the priests said in eerie unison. 'It is time to strike.'

A thrumming new energy rippled through the dense forest as the immense combined mind of all the trees tensed, gathered its strength, and produced its living weapons.

The plated trunks twitched open, revealing masses of iron-hard black seed pellets, each one the size of a man's hand. As the low-flying warglobes approached, devastating the treetops with their icewaves, the trees launched showers of the dark seed projectiles, each one covered with a thick, gummy sap. The barrage sprayed upwards in a desperate rain just before the destructive frigid blasts crisped the canopy.

The seed pellets seemed like grains of sand thrown into a storm. They pattered against the warglobe's hull, striking hard enough to make sharp sounds. The sap coating adhered them to the slick curved hull, where they stuck and burned . . . eating their way through the diamond walls.

'How can a seed eat through that armour?' Reynald asked.

'The roots of a tree can shatter mountains, given time,' one green priest said.

'We don't have that much time.'

As Reynald watched, the interior of the nearest warglobe seemed to change, growing murkier and full of shadows . . . green shadows. Knotted growths swelled in an astonishing mass of forest growth, rampant roots and stems and leaves bursting in an explosion of life. The warglobe swerved back around and tumbled, knocked off its axis.

Then it shattered in the sky. A writhing mass of vegetation split open the armoured sphere in a gush of vaporous white atmosphere. The hydrogue crashed into an already-ruined swath of forest, and the new growth pounced into the barren area, taking root like a gasping fish in search of water. Shards of the broken warglobe fell around it.

Close to the horizon, a second seed-penetrated hydrogue ship crashed into the treetops, infested with living forest. The other warglobes reacted by rising higher, out of reach of the spray of black projectiles. But even from above, they continued to wreak havoc.

Then, with the hydrogues no longer in range, the worldtrees made an act that was both life-affirming and a surrender of hope for their own survival. The plated trunks twitched open again and ejected more seeds, but this time the black pellets simply fell to the forest floor like scattered treasure, a hope that they would eventually grow again.

But nothing would help the Theron settlers here and now.

When the mind of the worldforest chose to do this, the people beneath the canopy saw that such measures were the forest's last hope. And if the trees were doomed, the human beings on Theroc had little chance of survival.

Most of Reynald's people had rushed to the dubious shelter of the forest floor, but the hydrogues would find them there, too. He shouted in futile defiance at the enemy aliens, but he could think of absolutely no way to save the trees or his people . . .

Then, ripping across the sky like an orange comet, came a blazing fireball, an ovoid mass of incandescent flame that manoeuvred, changed course, and shot straight towards the crystalline warglobes. The fiery apparition moved as if it were a self-contained ship, or a sentient being in its own right. Behind it came dozens of other fireballs, a swarm of scorching hornets rushing in, each one taking a frenzied course, choosing a target. A hydrogue target.

'What are they?' Reynald asked. 'What do they want?'

The first fireball blasted one of the warglobes with a blinding gout. Flames engulfed and blackened the diamond sphere, tightened its incinerating stranglehold. The stricken warglobe lashed out with blue lightning that scored the flaming intruder. But the fireball sent another blast and another, increasing in intensity until, with a final searing explosion, the hydrogue vessel *cracked open*.

A jet of pressurized atmosphere sprayed out, prying the broken diamond hull apart. The ellipsoidal fireball continued its pummelling fire until finally the warglobe shattered, and its wreckage tumbled into the thick canopy.

'The faeros have arrived,' said one of the green priests with a mixture of enthusiasm and dread.

More fireballs careened pell-mell into the hydrogues, inflicting instant damage. Reeling, the warglobes broke off their immediate attack against the worldforest.

Clutching the tree bough beside him, the green priest shouted, 'The faeros are attacking all across the planet. They are driving back the hydrogues!'

The blazing invaders poured out new gouts of flame, but the fire splattered and ricocheted off the crystalline hulls, dripping like lava into the vulnerable forest. Spotty blazes caught hold in the susceptible branches and trunks that had already been withered and shattered by the hydrogues. The freeze-dried wood caught fire easily, and the blaze began to spread.

'Those things may be attacking the hydrogues,' Reynald said, still not understanding what the faeros were, 'but they could cause just as much damage here in the forest.'

The green priest lowered his eyes. 'This battle predates human civilization by thousands of years, and the capricious faeros have changed sides many times.' Even the worldtrees did not seem overjoyed by the new combatants.

The warglobes struggled to defend themselves, lashing out with more lightning. Enveloping clouds of steamy icewaves surrounded one of the fiery capsules, smothering the flames until the struggling, smoking ovoid tumbled from the sky, a frost-encrusted lump that showed no sign of life whatsoever.

With the exchange of crossfire in the skies, tongues of flame spilled into the trees. More broken warglobes crashed into the tree-carpeted landscape. The desiccated battlefield became a spreading conflagration as the titanic elemental beings fought overhead.

Secondary fires raged across the forest floor and lapped against the worldtree bark. Flames swept through the underbrush, growing stronger and hotter. The Therons who had evacuated their worm-hives and fungus-reefs now faced the onrushing flames.

In meadows and thickets, condorflies flew about, sensing impending doom but unable to escape it. Overhead in the sky, wild wyverns swept about in a frenzy; some of the monstrous dragonfly creatures even attacked the warglobes, and died immediately.

Young men who had assembled exotic gliderbikes from scrap components zoomed about, trying to stay ahead of the blaze. Their gliderbikes were mere amusement vehicles, but now the young riders grabbed refugees, playing a desperate game of leapfrog to keep the survivors ahead of the flame front.

As fire spread around the main fungus-reef village, Reynald's youngest sister Celli climbed out of a balcony and crawled on to a branch. She held her balance, as she'd learned in her treedancing classes, and felt the rising ripples of heat and smoke as the fire intensified. To her dismay, she saw she could not reach the ground: Flames were working their way up the scaled bark. Celli felt frustration more than fear for letting herself get trapped in the situation.

At the end of the branch, she bent over, coiled her muscles, and sprang to another branch, bouncing to a second thick frond, but she could not escape from the spreading blaze. All of her treedancer moves had been staged and planned. Now she had to rely on her wits, especially since the trees were already brittle and weakened.

Coughing from the rising smoke, she missed her grip on the third leap, but caught a straggler branch and pulled herself up. Below, the hungry fire rushed and sizzled as it devoured the underbrush. Trapped now, with no place else to go, Celli called for help. Her voice was drowned out in the rising turmoil.

A young green priest swooped by riding a gliderbike. He grabbed Celli deftly by her narrow waist, and she swung on to his vehicle, grasping the airframe as the colourful condorfly wings vibrated and lifted them up, skipping away from the flames. Shouting into the young man's ear, she tried to thank him.

The flyer swayed drunkenly in the air, but the priest flew onwards, searching for a place to land while Celli clung to him for balance. There were fewer and fewer safe spots where they could go . . .

Standing in a clearing, her parents Idriss and Alexa watched the ravenous flames lick from branch to branch, passed along like some incandescent virus. They stared up at the creamy, overlapping folds of their fungus-reef city as the hungry fire blackened the hardened outer tissue. Hearing shouts and cries from inside, they knew that not everyone had escaped . . .

The hydrogues were coming again, and the faeros' fireballs continued to harry them. As an ominous warglobe came closer, Reynald tilted his head and stared up at it, clenching his fists at his side as if his own righteous anger could drive it back.

Before the warglobe could unleash another blast of crippling energy, though, a single faero came down like a cannonball. The hydrogue responded with a flurry of frigid steam that slammed into the blinding heat, stopping the ovoid fireball in its tracks. The fantastic enemies rose up, locked in battle as they spun around, globes of fire and ice whirling closer and closer to oblivion.

Reynald could feel the backwash from their mortal duel directly overhead. The enemies drew together, inextricably bound in a death embrace.

Then, overwhelmed, the grappling faero and hydrogue plummeted towards the treetops where Reynald and the green priests stood directly in the path.

Shouting, Reynald tried to dive out of the way, but the warglobe and fireball slammed into the canopy, skipping across the interlocked foliage and ripping apart the topmost layer of the forest.

Reynald barely had time to reach up and cover his eyes before roaring flames and shimmering icewaves obliterated him and all the trees around him, leaving absolute devastation in their wake.

After more than an hour of incredible destruction, the faeros succeeded in driving back the diamond-hulled warglobes. Those crystal ships that had not crashed into the forest retreated into open space.

Without a word, as the survivors on Theroc watched through smoke-filled skies, the faeros also departed. They had repelled the hydrogues, but they had left much of the worldforest in flames.

The war had just got far worse.

ONE HUNDRED AND TWENTY-NINE

MAGE-IMPERATOR JORA'H

Court musicians pounded drums that rumbled like deep bass thunder. Others played strange instruments in an uplifting yet mournful tune that combined grief for the loss of Mage-Imperator Cyroc'h and celebration for the ascension of Jora'h. The most talented Ildiran singers stood together, raising their voices in a keening note that played the nerves of the audience like musical instruments.

With a deepening ache in his heart, Jora'h took another step forward. The past surrounded him, full of memories and lost opportunities . . . and the future tried to suck him down with so many unanswered questions.

In a few moments his days of sex and romance would end with the completion of the ceremony. But Jora'h's longing to see Nira again could not be so easily cut away with the silver slash of a medical kithman's knife. He wondered if any of the Mage-Imperators preceding him had ever fallen in love. He grimly promised himself that not everything would change. *Not everything.*

How he had longed to rush to Dobro, to rescue Nira – but he

could not, certainly not while the Empire simmered on the verge of panic, desperate to have their leader back. He must do this first.

But afterwards . . .

Burly bodyguards accompanied his slow progress before all the spectators in the Palace. The drums pounded louder, mirroring the beat of Jora'h's heart. Torch-like blazers shone multicoloured glows that reflected on the crystalline walls, shimmering through the coloured panes.

Jora'h climbed the dais under the yawning skysphere filled with birds and plants and flowers. Overhead, a blank cloud of mist hung atop a pillar of light, without a holographic image now that Cyroc'h's benevolent face could no longer look down upon petitioners in the reception hall.

Soon, Mage-Imperator Jora'h's own features would watch over the Ildiran Empire.

A lens kithman stood alone at the far end of the dais. Three medical kithmen formed a close triangle around the empty chrysalis chair. They wore impeccable white and silver robes. A table displayed their jewelled instruments, light sparkling off the razor-sharp blades. Jora'h glanced at the wicked-looking tools, then he fixed his gaze forward. Concentrating.

Every male in the Ildiran Empire had cut off his hair upon the death of the Mage-Imperator, except for Jora'h, whose hair now thrashed about, alive with agitation. Over the years of his reign, his hair would continue to grow, and he would eventually braid it into a single long rope, just as his father had done.

He stepped up to the platform and stopped. He squared his shoulders, turned his gaze up to the skysphere. Sunlight made star sapphire reflections on his irises, but he could not see the *thism*, the soul-threads of the Lightsource. Soon.

He forced a veneer of calm upon himself. The Empire was watching.

Around Jora'h, the audience stared with fearful hope. Ildira and all the splinter colonies were in turmoil, the people lost without the telepathic safety net that bound them together. All of the Designates, sons of the dead Mage-Imperator, had rushed to Ildira from their scattered planets. Members of all kiths had crowded into buildings and gathering squares, seeking obvious comfort. The whole race was on the verge of irrational panic and confusion. Soon, a racial lethargy or outright insanity might set in, sweeping across the Empire — unless he completed the ascension ceremony.

By becoming Mage-Imperator, Jora'h alone could once again bind the threads of *thism*. No matter what else he felt or feared, he dared not wait. Not even so he could see Nira again.

Jora'h raised his hands, and the drumbeats, singers, and musical instruments fell silent. He turned slowly, still without speaking. He gazed at the empty chair, which seemed oddly hollow without his corpulent father lying there.

The wide supporting throne frightened Jora'h — would it become a prison for him? He decided that he would not become an invalid ruler as his father had. Tradition held that a Mage-Imperator's feet must never touch the ground . . . but a Mage-Imperator could also change traditions. Jora'h silently promised himself that he would remain healthy and active and not wallow in his position. Yes, he intended to do many things.

But everything he currently understood might change the moment he became the centre of the *thism*. The Lightsource would reveal many truths to him.

When Jora'h spoke, his voice was loud and firm. The people sucked in a quick breath, awed to hear him.

The Empire needs a new Mage-Imperator. The *thism* must be retied, our people must be made whole again. We have been adrift for days, and that is long enough. Too long. By ascending today, I will become your new strength. I will see the path and lead us onward in these terrible times.'

He opened his robe, spreading the immaculate fabric like the parting petals of a flower, and stood naked before his people. Soon he would know all of them, their faint thoughts, their fears, their dreams. He felt no shame exposing himself in such a manner, not for this vitally important ceremony.

All of the Empire must participate. The Prime Designate had to show that his family was strong.

His son Thor'h had returned from his reconstruction work on Hyrillka, drawn back home by the death of the Mage-Imperator. The young man had stayed long enough on scarred Hyrillka to initiate many necessary repairs and construction projects. Now Thor'h would remain here in the Prism Palace, where he would accept the formal mantle of the Prime Designate.

Jora'h had given orders that new doctors be sent to tend Rusa'h in his deep sub-*thism* sleep. He had many brothers and many sons, but as Prime Designate, as *Mage-Imperator*, he would not easily lose one of them – not even the contemptible Udru'h, who had kidnapped and tortured Nira for so many years. They would all shift their positions now, taking on new responsibilities, transitioning through their ranks as necessary by Ildiran custom and law.

Jora'h lay back in the immense chair. It seemed to welcome him, feeling both strange and familiar at the same time.

The medical kithmen came closer and inspected him, marking a faint line where they would make the cut. Jora'h flinched, but forced himself to stare out into the nearest circle of observers.

His eldest son, Tal Zan'nh, stood in that circle wearing an immaculate Solar Navy uniform. Jora'h had just learned, to his shock, about Adar Kori'nh's suicidal attack on Qronha 3. A septa of fast streamers had arrived with the images of how the Adar's renegade cohort had successfully destroyed nearly fifty hydrogue warglobes, though at the cost of many lives.

Near his son, Jora'h also saw the Dobro Designate standing grim and firm. Udru'h was smiling, confident. Perhaps he thought the new Mage-Imperator would understand and agree with the breeding plans, as soon as he had full access to the *thism* . . .

Fighting his anger, Jora'h once again vowed that, as soon as he became Mage-Imperator, he would rescue Nira and free all the breeder captives on Dobro. He would put an end to the terrible experiments and bring the prodigal humans back to the Terran Hanseatic League – though after so many generations, he doubted any of them knew of their origins.

Prepared now, the medical kithmen drew their knives in unison with a singing sound of finely honed metal. The audience fell instantly silent and intent, as if they had turned into statues.

Jora'h braced himself and reached out with his mind for the unravelling threads of *thism*, grasping and binding the strands that would once again hold the Ildiran race together. He knew it would hurt, that the pain was part of the ritual. He drew a quick breath—

The slash was swift and sure, and the bright explosion of neon fire behind his eyes helped him to focus, to raise his mind to a new level of awareness, glimpsing the perfect plane of the Lightsource. His thoughts became a projectile.

Jora'h's involuntary cry of agony and loss suddenly changed to a gasp of amazement. The paths of *thism* were so clear now, golden soul-threads that wrapped around him, drifting loose.

He captured each frayed end and brought them all together into a marvellous, knotted tapestry. He drew the strands tight, reaching out to connect the lives of billions upon billions of Ildirans from all kiths . . . and reaching backwards to smooth the fabric of history and knowledge. His own knowledge. *The truth*.

The medical kithmen worked quickly while Jora'h lay paralysed and overwhelmed by all the knowledge that flooded into his brain. They stanched the flow of blood, sealed the incision, and removed what they had cut away.

With his incredible access to the collective Ildiran minds, and all the ancestral memories of his bloodline, Jora'h saw the complexity of the puppet strings and influences and strategies the Mage-Imperator and his predecessors had laid down – and at last he *understood*.

Ritual castration was a small price to pay for such revelations. The myriad plans, the interlocked and layered schemes took his breath away.

In the audience chamber, he vaguely heard cheers and sighs of relief. His people – all Ildirans throughout the Empire – felt whole again. In their minds and souls they could sense that a Mage-Imperator sat on his throne once more, that the *thism* was intact, that their people were joined and safe. The Lightsource shone brightly on the Ildiran race.

As it should be.

Jora'h had a difficult time retaining any sense of himself or his morality. Revelation after revelation swept upon him, faster than he could absorb what he now knew. So much had been kept hidden from him! So many reasons, so many terrible necessities! His mind spun with the unexpected flood, and Jora'h lay in the chrysalis chair, stunned and unable to speak.

Then finally – helplessly – he stared stonily into the crowd, realizing that he, too, had no choice.

ONE HUNDRED AND THIRTY

CESCA PERONI

T hough the asteroid cluster of Rendezvous had no specific day or night, the Roamers followed an Earth-standard active/rest cycle. Low-level lights still burned in the corridors of the bound space rocks. Ships arrived at all hours, and docking crews remained on station to remove supplies and to welcome visitors.

Even so, during certain hours in the night cycle the place was quiet and peaceful. When she had difficulty sleeping, Speaker Cesca Peroni often found solace in wandering through connecting tunnels from one asteroid to another. Her thoughts ranged farther than her feet could take her. Most of the entrances to private living chambers were sealed under yellowish standby lights; no one stirred as Cesca wandered past, her gaze fixed forward, her mind in turmoil.

As Speaker, she was constantly tasked with solving a thousand problems, most of them trivial, but others serious enough that they required patient negotiation and the ability to consider numerous innovative alternatives.

Just that afternoon, she had held an official meeting with a beaming and completely unruffled Kotto Okiah, who had brought her another set of plans. It had been only a week since his rescue from the fiery collapse of his Isperos facility, and his face still bore red patches and peeling skin from superficial burns – but he'd already sketched out a new scheme.

'If we go to an outer-system planet that's *cold* enough,' he said, activating a player screen that displayed a space grid, 'then the gases will be condensed out into a slurry, or even frozen solid. Not just water ice and carbon dioxide, which we can cook out of comets and disassociate into hydrogen and oxygen, but real methane lakes, maybe even pure liquid hydrogen. That's orders of magnitude denser than the gases our skymines used to harvest!'

He punched a button and a spangle of planets was highlighted on the star chart. 'Of course, we'd have to figure out how to live and work at Absolute Zero, and I'm not sure how I can make our machinery function in such an environment . . . but the ekti production should be highly efficient. I think.'

He grinned at her, his hair tousled, his sunburned skin peeling. Cesca smiled. 'If anybody can do it, Kotto, you can. All right, do a full project development and proposal. Every time somebody knocks us Roamers down, we just get up again.'

Practically dancing in the low gravity of Rendezvous, Kotto hurried off to continue to his work . . .

These days, Cesca rarely had the luxury to ponder her own thoughts, worries, and indecisions. Often her preoccupation with Roamer business was a blessing, but now at night she needed time to think through everything she had learned. All the bad news.

She made her way to a hollowed-out rock, an outlying component of the Rendezvous cluster. During the day period, the Governess compy UR brought groups of youngsters to play in the zero-gravity chamber, but in the silent sleeping hours, the play asteroid was empty and dark.

Exactly what she needed.

Cesca sealed the door behind her and held a metal handle near the doorway to keep her balance. Then she shut down even the dim subsidiary illumination, plunging the room into the deep blackness of the universe.

She let go, kicked off gently from the wall, and drifted in the warm emptiness. Flying blind, she spread her arms and legs in a comfortable, relaxed position. The air didn't stir, no light distracted her. The lack of gravity let her float like a lost spirit, an unborn child in the darkness of a womb. It didn't matter whether her eyes were open or closed.

She simply drifted . . . and concentrated.

A Roamer trader had just arrived at Rendezvous with a frantic report of the horrific hydrogue attack on Theroc. Among the numerous casualties was Reynald himself — the man she had promised to marry.

His union with Cesca would have bound together the Roamers and the Therons . . . but at the moment she could not concern herself with the political aspect. With the good will between their two peoples, it should still be possible to forge an alliance. It had to be.

Jess had believed an alliance was the right thing. Cesca saw the wisdom as well – but it would no longer come about because of her marriage to Reynald. *Poor Reynald.*

She let herself feel the sadness of his death. Reynald had been a good man with a kind personality and a genuine love for his people. Cesca was sure he would have been a decent husband, despite her nagging love for someone else. He had welcomed her warmly, doing everything a woman could have asked.

But she had held back her heart, and Reynald had not

suspected. She hadn't even bothered to notice who he was, although the Theron prince had approached her with a kind, open heart. She realized now that she really hadn't deserved him.

Now it no longer mattered. The hydrogues had killed Reynald and devastated the worldforest. The Therons would need the help of the Roamers more than ever, and she would make sure it all worked out, somehow. And now Cesca no longer had any unwanted obligations to any man.

She could seek out Jess, at last.

Was it selfish to think of that so soon? She loved him – had always been in love with him, but she had acted too slowly after Ross was killed at Golgen. In a strange twist of fate, the hydrogues had once again taken the man to whom she had been betrothed.

And once again she was alone and still in love with Jess. Though she was sick at heart, did anything stand in their way now?

The two of them should have been married years ago. She and Jess had naïvely thought they would have all the time in the galaxy. Now Cesca knew otherwise. She would accept Jess, right away. There was no need for betrothal. They would stand before all the Roamer clans and take their vows. She didn't see it as a betrayal of Reynald. Or of Ross.

It was something she had to do.

But she had just learned from Del Kellum's nebula skimmers that Jess had disappeared. Without giving any explanation, he had abandoned his slow, graceful sail and flown off. He had left the other nebula skimmers behind – and vanished without a trace.

Cesca could send messages, distribute a call through the Roamer network in hopes that he would return as soon as possible. But Jess was gone, and no one knew where to find him . . .

In the darkness she bumped into the opposite wall. The smooth padded rock startled her back to reality. She reached out, brushed her fingers against one of the metal grab bars, then caught hold before the ricochet momentum sent her back out into the open chamber.

Cesca held on, blinking yet seeing nothing in the pitch blackness. Her body remained weightless, but her heart was heavy. Though alone and isolated, she held on.

Roamers were self-sufficient, with more than their share of ingenuity. She would find a way to get Jess back.

ONE HUNDRED AND THIRTY-ONE

JESS TAMBLYN

After the annihilation of his ship above the uncharted water world, after the bright explosion and the endless shower of debris, Jess felt himself falling forever through the air. He experienced a giddy surge of such power that he was unable to hold it all within him . . .

He tuned his mind's focus, drawing consciousness back into his body – only to find himself floating in a shallow, warm inland sea. Slate-grey water tinged with green plankton spread out around him to the fearsome lost horizon.

But Jess was not concerned. He was miraculously intact and feeling more alive than he ever had before, supercharged with the force of an ancient incomprehensible entity. For a time the last wental had been dispersed as a diffuse mist between the stars – and it had survived. Now it was even stronger. Around him as he drifted, Jess felt the comforting sea like the warmth of amniotic fluid.

He had been transformed . . . turned into something vastly greater than he had been before. He couldn't understand it, but now as he viewed everything through new sparkling eyes, each detail around him seemed sharper and clearer. His reactions were faster, his instincts expanded immeasurably.

His jettisoned cargo and the larger wental cylinder had already tumbled into the alien sea. Now, the wental that filled the tissues of his body also spread through his pores, touching this fertile new territory. The entity had already expanded from him into the strange ocean, a burst of light and life that spread away from Jess's skin and sweeping like a shockwave of rebirth across the hungry water.

As the wental flowed from his cells, invigorating the new ocean, he himself was a part of it. It was the most wondrous sensation he could ever have imagined. Now, accidentally through the hydrogue attack, he had propogated the wental's essence again.

He could carry more of the haunted water from world to world, like a strange baptism, rapidly and efficiently increasing the human's allies against the deep-core aliens. If only he could get away from here . . .

As he floated, Jess looked around himself with wonder, studying his perfect hands, the strange luminosity of his skin. The glow increased when he concentrated on his surroundings, feeling the waters roil. He didn't completely understand what he was or what he must do with his life.

But then the deeper reality sank in, penetrating his peaceful thoughts. He understood where he was, what he was. He saw a vision of Cesca, alone, and sorrow welled up within him.

Despite the exhilaration of his new circumstances, Jess realized he was lost, floating in an uncharted sea, his body completely transformed. He was stranded here. And he was no longer merely human.

Though he still loved her, he no longer had any chance of going back to Cesca. That part had changed forever.

ONE HUNDRED AND THIRTY-TWO

BASIL WENCESLAS

Nothing frustrated Chairman Wenceslas more than when carefully laid plans went awry. Imposing order on the turmoil of the Spiral Arm offered his only sense of reassurance and confidence. Schedules must be kept, jobs must be brought to completion, and the business of the Hansa must continue.

But sometimes precisely scheduled schemes fell apart, revealing them to be no more than a fragile house of cards. King Peter should have been dead by now, the Roamers painted into a corner, and the Hansa cleanly back on track assimilating their innocuous new leader, King Daniel.

Basil sipped his cardamom coffee, lost in thought. He still hadn't figured out how Peter had averted the assassination plot. The plasma incendiary device had been neutralized. Their Roamer scapegoat, Denn Peroni, had been swiftly and quietly released from the manufactured bureaucratic snafu designed to hold him in custody until the 'terrible accident' could kill the King and Queen.

Mr Pellidor had planned the evidence so carefully, linking the murder with the Roamers. Now, Basil had promptly rescinded the sealed orders he'd sent to EDF battle groups. No longer could he send out the battleships to track down and impound all Roamer ships, with the intent of forcibly bringing the gypsy clans into the Hansa, under appropriate control.

It should have been an easy victory. It should have strengthened the Hansa and the whole human race. But the King had screwed it all up.

That was exactly why Peter needed to be replaced with a more tractable successor.

But for the time being, the Chairman had no choice but to maintain the illusion that annoyed him so much. In order for Hansa business to continue without hindrance, Basil would have to work with King Peter.

As he gazed at the sunshine reflecting off the Palace cupolas, he longed for the days of Old King Frederick. Basil had sometimes treated him badly, putting Frederick down in private meetings and rarely giving the old man due consideration. Nevertheless, the old King had accepted his role and willingly served as a figurehead to reassure the populace.

But not Peter.

The streetwise kid Raymond Aguerra had seemed the ideal candidate, yet his complaisant cooperation had changed. Basil couldn't understand where he had gone wrong. Peter had challenged Basil numerous times, pointedly trying to erode the Chairman's power while shoring up his own illusory foundation of command and responsibility.

As he stood in his penthouse, Basil looked across at the sparkling brass-domed Whisper Palace. People were so easily dazzled by facades. Only the cognoscenti understood that the real power emanated from the businesslike Hansa HQ, not the fancy Palace.

The Chairman knew he needed to do something, accomplish something – even if it was, in the end, a Pyrrhic victory.

Stern but uneasy, Basil had finally issued the order for another Klikiss Torch to be prepared, another gas-giant target considered. The rout of the EDF at Osquivel and then the unprovoked hydrogue attacks on both Corvus Landing and Theroc itself had finally convinced him to cast aside all restraint.

The Klikiss Torch was the only effective offence the humans had, even if it was a doomsday weapon. Using the ancient alien technology was guaranteed to obliterate an entire hydrogue world. But the enemy's actions had left him no other choice . . .

A signal came across the intercom system. Franz Pellidor said, 'Mr Chairman, two visitors have just arrived from the Earth spaceport. They insist you will want to see them.'

'They have a lot of nerve not going through proper channels.' Basil scowled. *Especially today.*

'They do have your authorization, sir,' Pellidor said. 'It's a trader woman named Rlinda Kett and a man, Davlin Lotze. They refuse to tell me what—'

With a loud click, Basil set his cup on top of the projection desktop. 'Send them up. Maybe they've got good news. It would be a welcome change around here.'

He switched on the polarization film across the windows, blocking the view of the Whisper Palace. He didn't want to think about Peter just now. The smug young King had made a point of inviting him on to the processional yacht, knowing that Basil believed there was a bomb aboard. He knew! And the Chairman had fallen for the ruse. It was humiliating.

The good news was that Peter now understood the Hansa was perfectly willing to get rid of him. Basil's warnings were no mere empty threats. Perhaps it would make the King contrite and cooperative . . . or had the Chairman unintentionally set himself up for a cold war? Either way, he was sure Peter and Estarra did not have enough power or connections to go up against him.

Basil heard footsteps approaching. The large dark-skinned woman, Rlinda Kett, reached the door first, grinning broadly. Beside her stood the tall exo-sociologist, Davlin Lotze. The trader and the spy had changed into clean, plain clothes. Nothing fancy. Neither of them was trying to impress him. *Good.*

Basil had not seen Lotze since he'd dispatched him to the abandoned Ildiran world of Crenna. The spy looked lean and well-rested; his face and eyes showed an enthusiasm that the dry, dedicated expert had never exhibited before.

'What have you learned?' Basil said. 'You've been gone much longer than I expected.'

'Wait till you see what we discovered!' said Rlinda. 'And I expect to be damn well compensated, too. I hope you've got a clean pair of underwear handy. Once you hear about this, you're bound to shit yourself.'

Basil looked sceptically at Davlin Lotze.

The spy nodded. 'She is not exaggerating, Mr Chairman. This find will change the Hanseatic League as we know it.'

Basil raised his eyebrows. Lotze had never been prone to hyperbole. 'Did you discover what happened to Margaret and Louis Colicos?'

Lotze reported in a clipped voice, 'Louis Colicos and the green priest Arcas were both murdered. We saw no evidence of the three Klikiss robots, the team's compy, or Margaret Colicos herself. We believe, however, that she escaped to points unknown.'

'Escaped? Where did she go? Did she leave any records?' Basil asked.

Rlinda made a rude sound. 'Chairman Wenceslas, would you just let him tell the story? One missing woman is beside the point right now.'

Davlin Lotze glanced at her. 'Well, Margaret's disappearance did lead me to unravelling the transportal system.'

Impatient, Basil crossed his arms over his chest. 'What transportal system?'

Lotze explained about the alien transportation network that linked the Klikiss worlds, the abandoned cities and perfectly habitable planets. 'It is a system of instantaneous travel doorways that tie together dozens, perhaps even hundreds, of potential colony worlds. All of them empty, all of them waiting. And from what I've seen, most should be easily adaptable for human settlement. We've colonized far worse.'

Rlinda Kett leaned forward in anticipation, but didn't see the reaction she'd hoped for. 'Don't you see, Mr Chairman? Once you get to a transportal, you can travel from planet to planet in an instant – *without ekti.*'

Basil suddenly grasped the magnitude of the discovery. Hundreds of untouched worlds, already partially tamed by an ancient but now vanished civilization. 'That would make inter-planetary travel possible again! The destinations will be different than before, but Hansa expansion can proceed as rapidly as we can manage.'

Lotze added, 'And once we analyse the technology, we may be able to programme those doorways to take us to our own colony worlds and back here to Earth. After an initial expedition to set up a system and connect a new transportal to the network, we no longer require ekti to get there.'

Basil looked for his cup of coffee, but saw that it sat empty on the desktop. 'This news does indeed change everything.' He paced about the room, trying to contain his newfound excitement. 'We'll issue a decree and a challenge! A new start! Humans must set out on a full-scale exploration – and then colonization – of these empty worlds.'

A constant stream of hardy pioneers could go to the nearest abandoned worlds and flow through the Klikiss transportals, then set up new outposts.

'You've got the big idea, Mr Chairman,' Rlinda Kett said, 'but don't you think you're getting a little ahead of yourself?'

'Ms Kett, I can't tell you how good it feels to think *optimistically* about the future for a change.' He slapped the desktop. 'This gives us a whole new landscape to settle and exploit. Nothing will stop us now.'

He chuckled and made the broad windows transparent again so that he could look out towards the horizon. 'The hydrogues and the Roamers can go to hell! We won't need to fight them for their precious ekti any more. The Hansa will get into a whole new business.'

ONE HUNDRED AND THIRTY-THREE

ANTON COLICOS

During the weeks of long sunset on Maratha Prime, tourists and vacationers prepared to leave the domed resort city and go home to bright safety. They left behind only the hardiest splinter of Ildirans to keep the complex running all through the dark night.

Anton and Vao'sh would stay with the skeleton crew of service workers, engineers, and attraction designers, telling stories and studying the *Saga of Seven Suns*.

'It is very poignant.' Standing on the ground and blinking up into the still-bright sky, Vao'sh watched as one of the last shuttles lifted off from the spaceport, rising towards the enormous passenger liner in orbit above Maratha.

Anton kept staring into the sky with a contented smile on his face. 'Like petals from a dying flower blowing away in the wind . . .'

He was actually looking forward to quieter days here, when he could continue his scholarly work of analysing the *Saga*, as Vao'sh shared and discussed piece after piece with him. He relished this opportunity that no other human scholar had ever received, and he was not anxious for it to end.

After the death of the Mage-Imperator, he had observed with fascination and concern as the normally cheerful people on Maratha Prime became disjointed and fearful, suffering from a kind of depressive mania. Until then, the young scholar had not understood the true importance of *thism* to the alien race. Even Vao'sh had been unable to explain it comprehensibly, but Anton certainly saw its effects. The Ildirans – many of their kiths, anyway – looked so similar to humans, but they bore significant differences.

With vigour and forced enthusiasm, Anton had told them as many uplifting and cheerful stories as he could remember, doing his best to help the Ildirans through the brief dark time. He wasn't sure how much he had accomplished, but he knew Vao'sh appreciated the effort he had made.

While watching the visitors hurriedly packing, purchasing souvenirs, rushing to meet their shuttle flights, Anton had viewed the sunset and the abandonment of the city as a metaphor for the waning glory of the Ildiran Empire. He didn't think Vao'sh would appreciate hearing that. 'This place is beginning to remind me of a Klikiss ruin, like the ones my parents spent so much time investigating.'

'Maratha Prime may be quieter, Rememberer Anton, but it is not yet dead and empty. And after next year, when Secda is completed, Maratha will never seem painfully silent again.'

'For some of us, Vao'sh, noisy crowds are not necessarily a good thing. I won't mind living here on an isolated outpost, self-reliant – as long as I can keep studying the *Saga*. That *is* why I came.'

'I will never understand why humans place so little value on companionship,' Vao'sh said.

Anton laughed. 'To me, one good friend like you is plenty.' He reached out to touch the rememberer's bony shoulder. 'You and I can take care of ourselves, Vao'sh . . . no matter what happens.'

And he was going to get so much work done.

Finally, they stood with the small work crew that would remain behind, watching the orbiting passenger liner depart to carry the vacationers back to their lives in the crowded Ildiran Empire. Vao'sh studied the deepening colours in the sky, the slow-fading glory of daylight as the planet eased into the shadow of night.

Inside the domed city, lights and blazers banished any hint of shadow even before the sun could set. Maratha Prime would be a beacon in the darkness, full of lights and the comfort of civilization.

Anton Colicos thought that staying behind to tell stories under the vault of stars, waiting out the months of darkness, was the perfect scenario, just like telling tales at a campfire. The way it was supposed to be.

'You and I are going to have a grand time here, Vao'sh,' he said.

On the opposite side of the planet, the silent work teams of Klikiss robots continued their efforts unsupervised, toiling away on their own plans . . .

ONE HUNDRED AND THIRTY-FOUR

TASIA TAMBLYN

After the fireball creatures unexpectedly attacked the hydrogues on Theroc, General Lanyan and his admirals seized upon the idea of recruiting the things as direct partners in the struggle. In all other engagements, EDF weapons had proved only minimally effective against the enemy, but the 'faeros' (as the green priests called them) had succeeded in killing numerous warglobes and fending off the attackers.

Since Tasia Tamblyn had often demonstrated her skills under extreme pressure, Lanyan selected her to take a Manta and locate the flaming entities. Tasia had gladly accepted the assignment, though privately she wondered if the General considered a mere Roamer to be more expendable than other Eddies.

Since so many officers and soldiers had been killed during the staggering defeat at Osquivel, Tasia had been promoted yet again. She now wore the rank of captain. Six other Mantas were ostensibly under her command, but General Lanyan was wary of sending too many warships on Tasia's 'diplomatic' mission.

'We don't want to threaten these creatures,' he'd said. 'If we

698

come in with only a token vessel, then perhaps the fire things will be more open to communicating with you.'

Tasia had accepted the instructions, but the situation reminded her of Robb Brindle in his diving-bell encounter vessel. She had been edgy since Robb's death, feeling his loss like a cold stone in her gut, but she had to keep going, had to follow her Guiding Star and find some way out of this mess. As always, she intended to succeed beyond anyone's expectations; no doubt, they would raise the bar even higher next time.

Maybe she would innovate some new strategies to communicate with the fireball entities and prove the value of her flexible Roamer upbringing. Humans and faeros shared a common enemy. The drogues had racked up a higher and higher debt on the vengeance tab, as far as Tasia was concerned.

She had already reviewed Admiral Stromo's reconnaissance images taken at Oncier, the first sighting of the powerful fire creatures. The artificially triggered sun of Oncier seemed a key strategic point in this entire war. Now her Manta cruised into the same system, which was a known hiding place for the faeros. She couldn't think of a better place to start looking.

With the EDF trying to reassemble its pieces after Osquivel, many new officers had been recently assigned to her bridge. Everything had happened so fast since the disastrous battle, but she trusted that these fresh crewmen would do their duties and follow her orders.

Humans were supposed to be a single fighting force, their political differences tabled for the duration of the conflict. Roamers, Therons, Hansa citizens. Some good might come of that, at least . . . if they could all keep their eyes on the big picture.

Though Tasia had only one cruiser with her now, the EDF considered her mission important enough to warrant a green priest. On the bridge, Rossia stood like a human telegraph station, waiting to transmit his report should they encounter the fiery entities. His wide eyes looked as if they were about to pop out of his face in astonishment or fear.

General Lanyan would not make the same mistake as when he'd sent the compy-crewed reconnaissance mission to Golgen, which had vanished without a trace. Though she missed EA and often wished her Listener compy could be found and returned to her, Tasia had a human crew now.

'Strange readings out there, Captain Tamblyn,' said her sensor operator.

'Great.' Tasia tried to remember the young woman's name . . . Mae? Terene Mae? She thought so. 'Show me, Ensign Mae.'

As the Manta closed the distance at high speed, Oncier's new secondary star seemed to flicker and fluctuate. 'Admiral Stromo was here only a month ago, but it's several magnitudes dimmer than the last known readings.'

'Magnify the image, Ensign.'

'Aye, Captain.' The small star of Oncier now looked like a waning cinder, burnt orange instead of dazzling yellow white. It was surrounded by tiny specks, like luminescent moths swirling around the irresistible attraction of a flame.

She spoke to her nav officer. 'Move forward with caution, Lieutenant Ramirez. Run silent – no communication broadcasts whatsoever.' Tasia's stomach felt uneasy. This wasn't at all what she'd expected to find.

Rossia flinched as he saw the sparkling flurry around the dramatically cooling man-made star. The Manta closed in, decreasing speed so they could watch without being seen.

Soon they drew close enough to discern that the glowing fireflies were swarms of battling shapes – faero fireballs and diamond-skinned hydrogue warglobes. The drogues unleashed incomprehensible weapons against the faeros, blasting deep wounds into the stellar plasma itself. Oncier seemed to be dying, bleeding its heat into the cold of space.

'It's just like the battle on Theroc,' Rossia said. 'Faeros and hydrogues are mortal enemies. For now.'

'Shizz, that's much worse than Theroc,' Tasia answered. 'This time the drogues are tackling a whole star! If you ask me, they're getting too big for their diamond britches.' A murmur of uneasiness and confusion rippled through her bridge crew. 'Send your report, Rossia. A lot of people across the Spiral Arm need to know what's going on here.'

'But *I* don't know what's going on.' Nevertheless, the green priest touched his treeling, concentrated, and transmitted his news through telink.

Tasia watched the flurry of bright dots. Each pinpoint of light was either a fireball or a warglobe large enough to swallow ten Manta cruisers.

'How many faeros and hydrogues are there?' she said.

Ensign Terene Mae ran a quick computer scan to break down the image. 'I'm reading well over a thousand of each. And that's just what we can see from this side of the star.'

Warglobes and fireballs fought like wasps while several hydrogues dipped into the surface of the artificial sun. Darkening stains spread across Oncier, starspots that showed the plasma cooling below the temperature of the rest of the gases. Oncier seemed to be coalescing, smouldering like a coal with its last gasps of fire. The faeros were being overwhelmed.

'If those fireballs are on our side, Captain Tamblyn, shouldn't we be doing something to assist them, offer aid somehow?' said Mae. Tasia realized the young ensign had not yet seen battle. She was fresh from training at the Mars EDF base.

'We've got only one Manta.' Tasia gestured towards the viewscreen and the dying star. 'What can we do in a situation like that? We already know the drogues can blow up moons, and now it looks as if they're going to snuff out a star. I doubt they'd tremble with fear if our little cruiser came charging in with a pea-shooter.'

'Sorry, Captain,' said Ensign Mae, looking embarrassed.

Despite her show of confidence, however, Tasia felt completely out of her depth. How could the Earth Defence Forces possibly win in a war where the stakes were whole planets and stars?

Weeks ago, when the nearest group of EDF battleships had raced to the fiery scene on Theroc, they had arrived half a day after the drogues had been defeated and the faeros had retreated without explanation. Fortunately, the military teams had been able to help the frantic Therons extinguish some of the raging wildfires that had already consumed nearly two-thirds of the worldforest.

However, though the faeros had turned the tables in that skirmish against the hydrogues, here at Oncier they seemed to be outnumbered . . . and failing.

Fortunately, the titanic opposing forces paid no attention to the lone Manta cruiser. For hours, the battle continued in the vicinity of the fading dwarf star, but the numbers of faeros were dwindling like sparks being extinguished by a cold rain . . .

Tasia sat in her command chair, staring in awe and fear at the images of Oncier.

'Humans have always been so self-centred, trying to defend ourselves — but I get the feeling this war isn't about us at all. No matter how hard we fight, we're only irrelevant bystanders.' She shook her head. 'Like field mice on a giant battleground.'

Less than a day after the cruiser arrived in the system, the new sun of Oncier flickered one last time, and then winked out.

ONE HUNDRED AND THIRTY-FIVE

KING PETER

Standing together on the highest balcony of the royal wing, King Peter and Queen Estarra looked out into the night. They both stared up at the stars, bright and sparkling lights as thick as trees in a dense forest.

Just that afternoon, they had received alarming reports from several EDF scout ships, messages conveyed through the telink network. Nahton, his face distraught from the constant tragic news he'd been forced to report, told of tremendous battles detected at the suns of various solar systems – thankfully only uninhabited ones, so far – as the faeros and the hydrogues continued their expanding war. The new sun of Oncier had been smothered in the hydrogue retaliation; now other stars were under attack as well.

'It looks so peaceful out there,' Estarra said, reaching over to take his arm.

'You can hardly tell that Armageddon is occurring.' He felt cold inside just thinking of the terrifying possibilities. He was glad to have Estarra next to him, so they could face the impossible challenge together.

The attack on Theroc had been devastating. Preliminary estimates suggested that over a million inhabitants had been slaughtered, including Estarra's brother Reynald. But her parents, grandparents, and Celli had miraculously survived.

King Peter did his best to comfort Estarra once she'd learned of Reynald's death, so soon after the loss of Beneto. The worldforest had been terribly wounded, but the great trees, with their presence and knowledge, were dispersed across enough other planets that they would surely survive. With an extraordinary effort of nurturing the reseeded areas of worldforest, the green priests were confident they could make the great botanical mind thrive again on Theroc.

The Therons also intended to take up a more aggressive missionary planting programme that would disseminate the sentient trees across other planets. Thus, the worldforest would no longer be so vulnerable to a single attack – and it would grow stronger. Idriss and Alexa, now reluctantly restored as the planet's Father and Mother, had issued the statement.

Estarra agonized over the trauma her planet had suffered and wanted to go visit the remains of the worldforest. Peter felt he could arrange passage for them both, but he was reluctant to leave Earth, not knowing what Basil Wenceslas might do in his absence.

Estarra's sister Sarein had tried to act as a peacemaker, to ease the tensions between the Chairman and Peter. But the King would never again let down his guard, now that Basil had tried to assassinate him – and innocent Estarra as well. The Hansa had made no secret that Peter's replacement, Prince Daniel, was already being trained somewhere within the labyrinth of the Whisper Palace.

Now, for Peter and Estarra, every day would be a matter of survival.

'There is one spot of hope,' he said. 'The possibilities for new colonization via Klikiss transportals seems to be getting people excited. We've got no shortage of volunteers.'

Estarra leaned against him. 'Yes, everyone wants to get away.'

Citing King Peter's enthusiastic endorsement – though he hadn't bothered to ask beforehand – Basil Wenceslas had issued a statement outlining a new colonization and expansion effort using the ancient alien transportation system. He called for hardy pioneers to tame the network of Klikiss worlds in a massive colonization wave from the nearest transportals, completely independent of ekti use.

Following Davlin Lotze's notes and discoveries, researchers and explorers had already gone to several of the abandoned Klikiss planets, finding empty but intact ruins. With effort and an initial expenditure of ekti, such places could be converted into ready-made human settlements. Engineers and entrepreneurs would install the infrastructure and prepare for the full-scale arrival of instant populations. Green priests were eager to bring as many treelings as they could salvage and spread them along with the new wave of colonization.

So far, the transportals seemed perfect and inexhaustible, dimensional doorways that required only a moderate amount of energy. Hansa researchers were investigating the technology, but Chairman Wenceslas had not wanted to wait. Even while engineers tried to decipher the workings of the transportals, the first wave of colonists could certainly use them. It was just the focus humans needed to distract them from the despair of the war and the austerity of ekti rationing.

Estarra gazed at Peter with her large dark eyes. 'With the increasing hydrogue attacks, and now the faeros leaving the world-forest in flames . . . all these people signing up to leave through the transportals seem like rats fleeing a sinking ship.' She looked up at the pinpricks of light in the night sky.

Peter held her close. 'After our long string of setbacks, defeats, and failures, we need to accomplish *something*. Maybe it's the only way for the human race to survive.'

Perhaps because of the crisis they had faced together, thrown into the fire by circumstances, or perhaps because they were genuinely meant for each other, he and Estarra had fallen in love. It was the two of them against the Hanseatic League in a secret power struggle that few other people would ever discover. Peter was grateful the universe had seen fit to give him Estarra as an ally.

'Out there,' she said, 'so far away that we'll never see it for years and years, the stars are winking out one by one.'

Before he could stop himself, Peter gave her a fierce hug. 'And some of them are just being born.'

COMMAND STRUCTURE OF THE EARTH DEFENCE FORCES

Hansa Chairman
(commander in chief of Earth Defence Forces)

Great King
(ceremonial head)

General Kurt Lanyan
(primary commander)

Grid 0 Operations
(Earth and vicinity, military and political liaison officer)
Admiral Lev Stromo

Ten Grid Admirals, each with oversight of defined sections of space:

Grid 1 – Admiral Peter Tabeguache
Grid 2 – Admiral Zia San Luis
Grid 3 – Admiral Crestone Wu-Lin
Grid 4 – Admiral Zebulon Charles Pike
Grid 5 – Admiral Kostas Eolus
Grid 6 – Admiral Franklin W. Windom
Grid 7 – Admiral Sheila Willis
Grid 8 – Admiral Haki Antero
Grid 9 – Admiral Esteban Diente
Grid 10 – Admiral Tabitha Humboldt

Selected Noble-Born Children of Prime Designate Jora'h (Designates-in-Waiting)

Zan'nh (oldest, halfbreed with soldier kith)*
Thor'h, oldest purebred, future Prime Designate
Yazra'h, oldest noble daughter**
Daro'h – Dobro Designate-in-waiting
Pery'h – Hyrillka Designate-in-waiting
Cilar'h – Colusa Designate-in-waiting
Rol'h – Scotia Designate-in-waiting
Mir'h – Alturas Designate-in-waiting
Quon'h – Galt Designate-in-waiting
Andru'h – Kamin Designate-in-waiting
Estry'h – Shonor Designate-in-waiting
Theram'h – Heald Designate-in-waiting
Shofa'h – Vondor Qe Designate-in-waiting
Graci'h – Hrel-oro Designate-in-waiting
Czir'h – Dzelluria Designate-in-waiting

Jora'h's first-born should have been the offspring of a noble kithwoman, but the pregnancy resulted in miscarriage, after the Prime Designate had already impregnated a soldier kithwoman. Thus the first child actually sired by Jora'h was of mixed soldier–noble kith.

**When mixed with noble kithwomen, the Mage-Imperator's bloodline is heavily skewed towards male offspring. However, noble-born daughters are not unknown.*

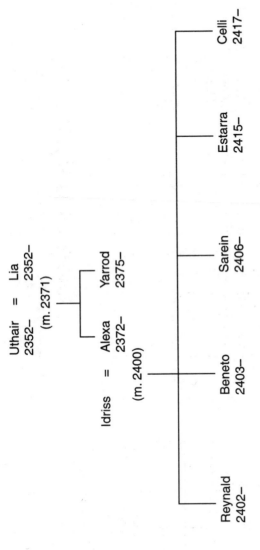

The Ruling Family of Theroc

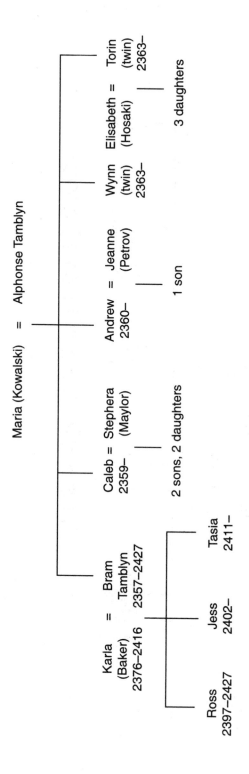

Clan Tamblyn

GLOSSARY

ABEL-WEXLER – One of the eleven generation ships from Earth, tenth to depart.

ADAM, PRINCE – predecessor to Raymond Aguerra, considered unacceptable candidate.

ADAR – highest military rank in Ildiran Solar Navy.

AGUERRA, RAYMOND – streetwise young man from Earth.

ALEXA, MOTHER – ruler of Theroc, wife of Father Idriss.

ALMARI – female green priest from Theron lakeside village.

AMUNDSEN – One of the eleven generation ships from Earth, sixth to depart.

ANDEKER, WILLIAM – human scientist, specialist in robotics.

ARCAS – green priest.

ARCHFATHER – symbolic head of Unison religion on Earth.

ARMORGLASS – transparent protective material, heavily resistant to shock.

ARO'NH – Ildiran Solar Navy officer who led a surprisingly successful suicide defence against hydrogue warglobes on Qronha 3.

ATTENDERS – diminutive personal assistants to the Mage-Imperator.

BAKER – Roamer clan.

BALBOA – One of the eleven generation ships from Earth, second to depart.

BARTHOLOMEW – Great King of Earth, predecessor to Frederick.

BEBOB – Rlinda Kett's pet name for Branson Roberts.

BEKH! – Ildiran curse, 'Damn!'

BEN – first Great King of the Terran Hanseatic League; also, a large moon of Oncier.

BENETO – green priest, second son of Father Idriss and Mother Alexa.

BIG GOOSE – Roamer derogative term for Terran Hanseatic League.

BLACK PINES – conifers grown for lumber industry on Boone's Crossing, genetically engineered Earth pines crossed with indigenous plants.

BLAZER – Ildiran illumination source.

BLIND FAITH – Branson Roberts's ship.

BLITZKRIEG SCOOPS – fast commando harvesters used by Roamers during hydrogue embargo.

BLUE SKY MINE – skymine facility at Golgen, operated by Ross Tamblyn.

BOONE'S CROSSING – Hansa colony world.

BORE'NH – Qul in Ildiran Solar Navy.

BRINDLE, CONRAD – Robb Brindle's father, former military officer.

BRINDLE, ROBB – young EDF recruit, comrade of Tasia Tamblyn.

BRINDLE, NATALIE – Robb Brindle's mother, former military officer.

BRON'N – bodyguard of the Mage-Imperator.

BURTON – One of the eleven generation ships from Earth, fourth to depart. Lost en route.

CAILLIÉ – One of the eleven generation ships from Earth, fifth to depart and first to be encountered by the Ildirans. Colonists from the *Caillié* were taken to settle Theroc.

CARBON SLAMMER – new-design EDF weapon, effective at breaking carbon-carbon bonds.

CARGO ESCORT – Roamer vessel used to deliver ekti shipments from skymines.

CELLI – youngest daughter of Father Idriss and Mother Alexa.

CHEN – Roamer clan.

CH'KANH – armoured anemone plants that live in the shadowed canyons of Maratha.

CHRANA SOUP – Ildiran food.

CHRISTOPHER – third Great King of the Terran Hanseatic League; also, a large moon of Oncier.

CHROMEFLY – silver reflective flying insect on Theroc.

CHRYSALIS CHAIR – reclining throne of the Mage-Imperator.

CITYSHIP – giant hydrogue metropolis.

CITYSPHERE – enormous hydrogue habitation complex.

CLARKE – One of the eleven generation ships from Earth, seventh to depart.

CLEE – a steamy, potent beverage made from ground worldtree seeds.

CLOUD MINE – large and inefficient ekti-gathering facility.

CLYDIA – one of the nineteen green priest volunteers aboard EDF ships.

COHORT – battle group of Ildiran Solar Navy consisting of seven maniples, or 343 ships.

COLICOS, ANTON – the son of Margaret and Louis Colicos, translator and student of epic stories.

COLICOS, LOUIS – xeno-archaeologist, husband of Margaret Colicos, specializing in ancient Klikiss artefacts.

COLICOS, MARGARET – xeno-archaeologist, wife of Louis Colicos, specializing in ancient Klikiss artefacts.

COLONY TOWN – main settlement on Corvus Landing.

COMPETENT COMPUTERIZED COMPANION – intelligent servant robot, called compy, available in Friendly, Teacher, Governess, Listener, and other models.

COMPTOR – Ildiran colony world, site of a legendary forest fire.

COMPTOR LILIES – large, fleshy flowers from Comptor; salmon-pink petals are edible.

COMPY – shortened term for 'Competent Computerized Companion'.

CONDORFLY – colourful flying insect on Theroc like a giant butterfly, sometimes kept as pets.

CORAL EGGS – edible underwater nodule native to Ildira.

CORRIBUS – ancient Klikiss world, where Margaret and Louis Colicos discovered the Klikiss Torch technology.

CORVUS LANDING – Hansa colony world, mainly agricultural, some mining.

COTOPAXI – Hansa colony world.

CRENNA – Ildiran splinter colony, evacuated due to plague.

CRETEBLOCKS – prefab Hansa construction material.

CRYOBAGS – preservation sacks designed to produce extreme cold.

CUTTER – small ship in Ildiran Solar Navy.

CYROC'H – original name of current Ildiran Mage-Imperator, father of Jora'h.

DANIEL – new prince candidate selected by the Hansa.

DASRA – gas-giant planet suspected of harbouring hydrogues.

DATAWAFER – high-capacity data-storage package.

DAYM – blue supergiant star, one of the Ildiran 'seven suns'; also the name of the primary gas-giant planet, site of abandoned Ildiran ekti harvesting operations.

DD – compy servant assigned to Rheindic Co xeno-archaeology dig.

DEKYK – Klikiss robot at Rheindic Co xeno-archaeology dig.

DESIGNATE – purebred son of Mage-Imperator, ruler of an Ildiran world.

DIAMONDFILM – crystalline parchment used for Ildiran documents.

DOBRO – Ildiran colony world.

DREMEN – Terran colony world, dim and cloudy.

DROGUE – Deprecatory term for hydrogues.

DROPSHIP – fast-delivery vessel used by EDF.

DULARIX – uninhabited world in Ildiran space, site of nonsensical hydrogue attack.

EA – Tasia Tamblyn's personal compy.

EARTH DEFENCE FORCES – Terran space military, head-quartered on Mars but with jurisdiction throughout the Terran Hanseatic League.

EDF – Earth Defence Forces.

EDDIES – slang term for soldiers in EDF.

EKTI – exotic allotrope of hydrogen used in Ildiran stardrives.

ESCORT – mid-sized ship in Ildiran Solar Navy.

ESTARRA – second daughter, fourth child of Father Idriss and Mother Alexa.

FAEROS – sentient fire entities dwelling within stars.

FESTIVAL OF THE BUTTERFLIES – mass hatching of butterfly analogues in forests of Theroc, celebrated by Theron people.

FILTERFILM – protective eye covering used by Ildirans.

FIREFEVER – ancient Ildiran plague.

FITZPATRICK, MAUREEN – former Chairman of the Terran Hanseatic League, grandmother of Patrick Fitzpatrick III.

FITZPATRICK, PATRICK, III – spoiled cadet in the Earth Defence Forces, General Lanyan's protégé.

FLATGEM – rare jewels prominently used in crown of Great King.

FLITTER-RAFT – transportation floater used in forests of Theroc.

FLUTEWOOD TREES – multi-branched growths on Crenna with hard bark and holes that make whistling sounds in the wind.

FRACTURE-PULSE DRONE – new-design EDF weapon, also called a 'frak'.

FRAK – slang term for fracture-pulse drone.

FREDERICK, KING – previous ruler of the Terran Hanseatic League.

FUNGUS REEF – giant worldtree growth on Theroc, carved into a habitation by the Therons.

GEORGE – second Great King of the Terran Hanseatic League; also, a large moon of Oncier.

GLIDERBIKES – flying contraptions assembled from scavenged engines and framework materials, augmented by colorful condorfly wings.

GOLGEN – gas giant, harvested by Blue Sky Mine.

GOLIATH – first expanded Juggernaut in EDF fleet.

GOOSE – Roamer derogative term for Terran Hanseatic League.

GRAPPLER POD – small work vehicle used in shipyards of Osquivel.

GREAT KING – figurehead leader of Terran Hanseatic League.

GREEN PRIEST – servant of the worldforest, able to use world-trees for instantaneous communication.

GUIDING STAR – Roamer philosophy and religion, a guiding force in a person's life.

HANSA – Terran Hanseatic League.

HANSA HEADQUARTERS – pyramidal building near the Whisper Palace on Earth.

HEALD – star system in the Ildiran Empire, site of a famous 'ghost story' in the *Saga of Seven Suns*.

HENDY, SAM – Mayor of Corvus Landing Colony Town.

HIJONDA – Hansa colony world.

HORIZON CLUSTER – large star cluster near Ildira.

HOSAKI – Roamer clan.

HOSAKI, ALFRED – Roamer clan leader.

HYDROGUES – alien race living at cores of gas-giant planets.

HYRILLKA – Ildiran colony in Horizon Cluster, original discovery site of Klikiss robots.

IAWA – colony world, once inhabited by predecessors of the Roamers.

IDRISS, FATHER – ruler of Theroc, husband of Mother Alexa.

ILDIRA – home planet of the Ildiran Empire, under the light of seven suns.

ILDIRAN EMPIRE – large alien empire, the only major civilization other than Earth in the Spiral Arm.

ILDIRAN SOLAR NAVY – space military fleet of the Ildiran Empire.

ILDIRANS – humanoid alien race with many different breeds, or kiths.

ILKOT – Klikiss robot at Rheindic Co xeno-archaeology dig.

ISIX CAT – feral feline on Ildira.

ISPEROS – hot planet, site of Kotto Okiah's test colony.

JACK – fourth Great King of the Terran Hanseatic League; also, a large moon of Oncier.

JAZER – energy weapon used by Earth Defense Forces.

JORA'H – Prime Designate of the Ildiran Empire, eldest son of Mage-Imperator.

JORAX – Klikiss robot, often seen on Earth.

JUGGERNAUT – large battleship class in Earth Defence Forces.

JUPITER – enhanced Juggernaut battleship in EDF, flagship of

Admiral Willis's Grid 7 battle group.

KAMAROV, RAVEN – Roamer cargo-ship captain.

KANAKA – One of the eleven generation ships from Earth, last to depart. These colonists became the Roamers.

KELLUM, DEL – Roamer clan leader, in charge of Osquivel shipyards.

KELLUM, ZHETT – eighteen-year-old daughter of Del Kellum.

KETT, RLINDA – merchant woman, captain of the *Voracious Curiosity*.

KHALI – Nira's family name.

KHALI, NIRA – green priest female, prime Designate Jora'h's lover and mother of his halfbreed daughter, Osira'h. Held captive in breeding camps on Dobro.

KITH – a breed of Ildiran.

KLEEB – derogatory term.

KLIKISS – ancient insect-like race, long vanished from the Spiral Arm, leaving only their empty cities.

KLIKISS ROBOTS – intelligent beetle-like robots built by the Klikiss race.

KLIKISS TORCH – a weapon/mechanism developed by the ancient Klikiss race to implode gas-giant planets and create new stars.

KORI'NH, ADAR – leader of the Ildiran Solar Navy.

KOWALSKI – Roamer clan.

KRI'L – legendary star-crossed swimmer from Ildiran myth.

LANYAN, GENERAL KURT – commander of Earth Defence Forces.

LENS KITHMEN – philosopher priests who help to guide troubled Ildirans, interpreting faint guidance from the *thism*.

LIA – former ruler of Theroc, Alexa's mother.

LIFETUBE – small emergency evacuation device stored aboard EDF battleships.

LIGHTSOURCE – the Ildiran version of Heaven, a realm on a higher plane composed entirely of light. Ildirans believe that faint trickles of this light break through into our universe and are channelled through the Mage-Imperator and distributed across their race through the *thism*.

LLARO – abandoned Klikiss world.

LOGAN, CHRYSTA – last captain of the lost generation ship *Burton*, led colonists to Dobro.

LOOKING GLASS LAKES – group of deep, round lakes on Theroc, site of a tree village.

LOST TIMES – forgotten historical period, events supposedly recounted in a missing section of the *Saga of Seven Suns*.

LOTZE, DAVLIN – Hansa exo-sociologist and spy on Crenna.

MAE, TERENE – EDF ensign, assigned to Tasia Tambyln's Manta cruiser.

MAGE-IMPERATOR – the god-emperor of the Ildiran Empire.

MAIL COURIER DRONE – small, fast ship, unmanned, designed to carry messages.

MANIPLE – battle group of Ildiran Solar Navy consisting of seven septas, or forty-nine ships.

MANTA – mid-sized cruiser class in EDF.

MARATHA – Ildiran resort world with extremely long day and night cycle.

MARATHA PRIME – primary domed city on one continent of Maratha.

MARATHA SECDA – sister-city on opposite side of Maratha from Prime, currently under construction.

MARCO POLO – One of the eleven generation ships from Earth, third to depart.

MARMOTH – large-statured herd beast on Ildira, known for its thick grey hide and ponderous movements.

MEYER – red dwarf sun, location of Rendezvous.

MIJISTRA – glorious capital city of the Ildiran Empire.

MOON STATUE GARDEN – sculpture exhibit and topiary at Whisper Palace.

NAHTON – court green priest on Earth, serves King Peter.

NEBULA SKIMMERS – giant sails used to scoop hydrogen from nebula clouds.

NEW PORTUGAL – Hansa outpost with EDF facilities.

NG, TRISH – Roamer pilot.

ONCIER – gas-giant planet, test site of the Klikiss Torch.

OKIAH, BERNDT – Jhy Okiah's grandson, chief of Erphano skymine.

OKIAH, JHY – Roamer woman, very old, former Speaker of the clans.

OKIAH, KOTTO – Jhy Okiah's youngest son, brash inventor who designed Isperos colony.

OPALBONES – precious fossils from Dobro, often made into valuable jewellery.

ORANGE SPOT – plague affecting human colonists on Crenna.

OSIRA'H – daughter of Nira Khali and Jora'h, bred to have unusual telepathic abilities.

OSQUIVEL – Ringed gas planet, site of secret Roamer shipyards.

OSSUARIUM – storage chamber in the Prism Palace for the glowing skulls of former Mage-Imperators.

OTEMA – old green priest, ambassador from Theroc to Earth; later, sent to Ildira.

OX – Teacher compy, one of the oldest Earth robots. Served aboard *Peary*, now instructor and adviser to King Peter.

PALACE DISTRICT – governmental zone around Whisper Palace on Earth.

PALAWU, HOWARD – Chief Science Adviser to King Peter.

PALISADE – Hansa colony world.

PARIS THREE – Hansa colony world.

PASTERNAK, ANNA – Roamer clan leader, ship captain, mother of Shareen.

PASTERNAK, SHAREEN – chief of Welyr skymine; betrothed to Del Kellum but killed in an early hydrogue strike.

PEARY – One of the eleven generation ships from Earth, first to depart.

PELLIDOR, FRANZ – assistant to Basil Wenceslas, an 'expediter'.

PENTADICE – five-sided gambling dice used by Roamers.

PEPPERFLOWER TEA – Roamer beverage.

PERONI, DENN – Cesca's father.

PERONI, CESCA – Roamer Speaker of all clans, trained by old Jhy Okiah. Cesca was betrothed to Ross Tamblyn but has always loved his brother Jess.

PETER, KING – successor to Old King Frederick, figurehead ruler of the Terran Hanseatic League.

PLANTMOTH – nialias of Hyrillka, source of drug shiing.

PLATCOM – Platform Commander, chief officer's rank aboard Thunderhead weapons platform in EDF.

PLUMAS – frozen moon with deep liquid oceans, site of Tamblyn clan water industry.

PRIME DESIGNATE – Eldest son and heir-apparent of Ildiran Mage-Imperator.

PRINCESS – Nira's pet name for her daughter Osira'h.

PRISM PALACE – dwelling of the Ildiran Mage-Imperator.

PTORO – gas-giant planet, site of Crim Tylar's skymine.

PYM – abandoned Klikiss world.

QRONHA – a close binary system, two of the Ildiran 'seven suns'. Contains two habitable planets and one gas giant.

QUILLTREE – hardy spined plant native to Ildira; used by Sai'f for bonsai experiments.

QUL – Ildiran military rank, commander of a maniple, or forty-nine ships.

RAMAH – Terran colony world, settled mainly by Islamic pilgrims.

RAMIREZ, ELLY, LIEUTENANT – navigator aboard Tasia Tamblyn's Manta.

RELLEKER – Terran colony world, popular as a resort.

REMEMBERER – member of the Ildiran storyteller kith.

REMORA – small attack ship in Earth Defence Forces.

RENDEZVOUS – inhabited asteroid cluster, hidden centre of Roamer government.

REYNALD – eldest son of Father Idriss and Mother Alexa.

RHEINDIC CO – abandoned Klikiss world, site of major excavation by the Colicos.

RHEJAK – Terran colony world, known for pearl-producing reef mines.

ROACHERS – derogatory term for Roamers.

ROAMERS – loose confederation of independent humans, primary producers of ekti stardrive fuel.

ROBERTS, BRANSON – Former husband of Rlinda Kett.

ROBINSON, MADELEINE – early planetary prospector; she and her two sons discovered Klikiss ruins and activated robots on Llaro.

ROD'H – halfbreed son of Nira Khali and the Dobro Designate.

ROSSIA – eccentric green priest, survivor of a wyvern attack.

ROYAL CANAL – ornamental canal surrounding Whisper Palace.

RUNNING HORSE, TYRA – planetary representative from Rhejak.

RUSA'H – Hyrillka Designate, third noble-born son of the Mage-Imperator.

SAGA OF SEVEN SUNS – historical and legendary epic of the Ildiran civilization.

SAI'F – one of Jora'h's lovers, member of scientist kith, experiments with bonsai trees.

SANDOVAL – Roamer clan.

SAREIN – eldest daughter of Father Idriss and Mother Alexa, Theron ambassador to Earth, also Basil Wenceslas's lover.

SARHI, PADME – grand governor of Yreka colony.

SCALY – Ildiran kith, desert dwellers.

SEPTA – small battle group of seven ships in the Ildiran Solar Navy.

SEPTAR – commander of a septa.

SHANA REI – legendary 'creatures of darkness' in *Saga of Seven Suns*.

SHELTER GARDEN – fern-filled conservatory in the Whisper Palace.

SHIING – stimulant drug made from nialia plantmoths on Hyrillka.

SHIZZ – Roamer expletive.

SHONOR – Ildiran splinter colony.

SILVER BERET – sophisticated special forces trained by EDF.

SIRIX – Klikiss robot at Rheindic Co xeno-archaeology dig.

SKYMINE – ekti harvesting facility in gas-giant clouds, usually operated by Roamers.

SKYSPHERE – main dome of the Ildiran Prism Palace. The skysphere holds exotic plants, insects, and birds, all suspended over the Mage-Imperator's throne room.

SORENGAARD, RAND – renegade Roamer pirate.

SOUL-THREADS – connections of *thism* that trickle through form the Lightsource. Mage-Imperator and lens kithmen are able to see them.

SPAMPAX – processed meat rations, designed to last for centuries.

SPEAKER – political leader of the Roamers.

SPIRAL ARM – the section of the Milky Way galaxy settled by the Ildiran Empire and Terran colonies.

SPLINTER COLONY – Ildiran colony that meets minimum

population requirements.

STANNIS, MALCOLM – former Chairman of the Terran Hanseatic League, served during the reigns of King Ben and King George, during Earth's first contact with the Ildiran Empire.

STONER, BENN – male prisoner on Dobro.

STREAMER – fast single ship in Ildiran Solar Navy.

STROGANOV – One of the eleven generation ships from Earth, ninth to depart.

STROMO, ADMIRAL LEV – Admiral in Earth Defence Forces.

SWEENEY, DAHLIA – DD's first owner, as a young girl.

SWENDSEN, LARS RURIK – engineering specialist, adviser to King Peter.

SWIMMER – Ildiran kith, water dwellers.

TACTICAL ARMOUR FOAM – spray-applied polymer used by EDF; hardens on contact with water.

TAL – military rank in Ildiran Solar Navy, cohort commander.

TALBUN – old green priest on Corvus Landing.

TAMBLYN, ANDREW – one of Jess's uncles, brother to Bram.

TAMBLYN, BRAM – Roamer, old scion of Tamblyn clan, father of Ross, Jess, and Tasia.

TAMBLYN, CALEB – one of Jess's uncles, brother to Bram.

TAMBLYN, JESS – Roamer, second son of Bram Tamblyn, in love with Cesca Peroni.

TAMBLYN, KARLA – Jess's mother, frozen to death in ice accident on Plumas.

TAMBLYN, ROSS – Roamer, estranged eldest son of Bram Tamblyn, chief of Blue Sky Mine at Golgen, killed in first hydrogue attack.

TAMBLYN, TASIA – Roamer, Jess Tamblyn's sister, currently serving in the EDF.

TAMBLYN, TORIN – one of Jess's uncles, brother to Bram.

TAMBLYN, WYNN – one of Jess's uncles, brother to Bram.

TELINK – instantaneous communication used by green priests.

TERRAN HANSEATIC LEAGUE – commerce-based government of Earth and Terran colonies.

THEROC – jungle planet, home of the worldforest.

THERON – a native of Theroc.

THISM – faint racial telepathic link from Mage-Imperator to the Ildiran people.

THOR'H – eldest noble-born son of Jora'h, destined to become the next Prime Designate.

THRONE HALL – the King's main receiving room in the Whisper Palace.

THUNDERHEAD – mobile weapons platform in Earth Defence Forces.

TRADE STANDARD – common language used in Hanseatic League.

TRANSGATE – hydrogue point-to-point transportation system.

TRANSPORTAL – Klikiss instantaneous transportation system.

TRE'C – legendary star-crossed scaly kithman from Ildiran myth.

TREEDANCERS – acrobatic performers in the Theron forests.

TREELING – a small worldtree sapling, often transported in an ornate pot.

TROOP CARRIER – personnel transport ship in Ildiran Solar Navy.

TYLAR, CRIM – Roamer, former skyminer on Ptoro.

TYLAR, NIKKO CHAN – young Roamer pilot.

UDRU'H – Dobro Designate, second-born noble son of the Mage-Imperator.

UNISON – standardized government-sponsored religion for official activities on Earth.

UR – Roamer compy, Governess-model at Rendezvous.

USK – Terran colony world, known for lace and handcrafts.

VAO'SH – Ildiran rememberer.

VERDANI – organic-based sentience, manifested as the Theron worldforest.

VICHY – One of the eleven generation ships from Earth, eighth to depart.

VORACIOUS CURIOSITY – Rlinda Kett's merchant ship.

WARGLOBE – Hydrogue spherical attack vessel.

WARLINER – largest class of Ildiran battleship.

WELYR – gas giant, site of Roamer skymine destroyed by hydrogues.

WEN, THARA – early settler on Theroc, from generation ship *Caillié*. First person to become linked with worldforest.

WENCESLAS, BASIL – Chairman of the Terran Hanseatic League.

WENTALS – sentient water-based creatures.

WHISPER PALACE – magnificent seat of the Hansa government.

WILLIS, SHEILA, ADMIRAL – commander of Grid 7 EDF battle group, in charge of Yreka siege.

WORLDFOREST – the interconnected, semi-sentient forest based on Theroc.

WORLDTREE – a separate tree in the interconnected, semi-sentient forest based on Theroc.

WORMHIVE – large nest built by hive worms on Theroc, spacious enough to be used for human habitation.

WYVERN – large flying predator on Theroc.

YARROD – green priest, younger brother of Mother Alexa.

YREKA – fringe Terran colony world.

YURA'H – previous Mage-Imperator; ruled at time of first encounter with human generation ships.

ZAN'NH – Ildiran military officer, eldest son of Prime Designate Jora'h.

ZIZU, ANWAR – EDF sergeant, security chief on Tasia Tamblyn's Manta.